Historians, dramatists, novelists
have told my story by
their own lights, now . . .

I, CLEOPATRA

with the intimacy of a woman
who must, at last, reveal what
is in her heart, tell it as it was.

I hide nothing. I speak, without mortal modesty, of my own virtues—my beauty, my wit, my political skill. I tell you openly of the men I loved—and the women. Of my triumphant night with Caesar, when I gave him my body to gain the world, and of my passion for Antony. You bear with me the weight of the double crown; the pain at the birth of Caesarion, Caesar's only son; the anguish of a bloody battle lost.

And, if you tremble with me at the discovery of treachery in my family, in my lovers and in those who sign with me treaties of peace, you share something of the burden of greatness. You know what it was to have lived and loved as a queen and a goddess, to be

I, CLEOPATRA

ABOUT THE AUTHOR

WILLIAM BOSTOCK was born in Johnstown, Pennsylvania, a second-generation American of English-Scots-Welsh descent. Since the age of eighteen he has lived in New York City. He has worked in publishing and film, and has previously published three novels of the contemporary scene. *I, Cleopatra* is his first work of historical fiction.

William Bostock

WARNER BOOKS

A Warner Communications Company

WARNER BOOKS EDITION

Copyright © 1977 by William Bostock
All rights reserved

ISBN 0-446-81379-6

Cover art by Elaine Duilla

Warner Books, Inc., 75 Rockefeller Plaza, New York, N.Y. 10019

 A Warner Communications Company

Printed in the United States of America

Not associated with Warner Press, Inc. of Anderson, Indiana

First Printing: December, 1977

10   9   8   7   6   5   4   3   2   1

For
JULIAN BACH

BOOK I

BOOK I

CHAPTER I

I, CLEOPATRA, Queen of Egypt and Queen of Kings, Daughter of the Sun and Sister of the Moon, the Chosen of Ptah, Living Image of the God Amon, whose divine spirit is the spirit of the Everliving Goddess Isis, and whose mortal blood is the blood of a millennium of kings, will cast a long shadow over the world, and my words and deeds will echo down through the halls of history. From my earliest memories as a Ptolemaic princess, I knew that mine would be an intricate fate, and that I would in time be not only Queen of Upper and Lower Egypt, but Mistress of the Mediterranean and Empress of the East, with the whole civilized world as my domain. This is my glorious destiny, which the high immortal gods have mapped out before me, and I have no choice but to embrace it.

Today there is no Homer, that sublime practitioner of the muse Calliope, to write of my life, a regret I share with Alexander the Great of three centuries ago from whose royal line I come. Alexander had only Callisthenes to write of his exploits. Callisthenes recorded all the facts, but his style left much to be desired. My venerable forefather Ptolemy the First, who founded our dynasty, was not only a great soldier and king, but an excellent writer, and his biography of his half-brother Alexander and his own memoirs are works of literary merit. In this tradition I, Cleopatra, will dictate the events of my life to my scribes, searching out the secrets of my soul, recording my dreams and achievements, and even my failures and follies, although with the help of the gods I hope the latter will be few. I will have the scrolls copied and preserved in the royal archives and the great library, and centuries from now my writings can be mused upon by savants and deciphered for the world when I am but ash in my tomb.

I was born under the sign of Capricorn, with Moon in Leo and a Scorpio ascendant, in the eleventh year* of the reign of my father King Ptolemy the Twelfth in the great palace in Alexandria. My father, who ascended the throne of the pharaohs at the age of twenty, had dutifully married his sister, Cleopatra Selene. They had been blessed with two princesses before I was born, so they were naturally hoping for a prince.

The details of my birth I got from my beloved aunt, the Princess Aliki, the sister of my sibling parents.

My father the king came into the birthchamber, after my delivery, followed by his entourage of courtiers and priests. Also in attendance were my sisters, Princess Cleopatra Tryphaina, who was ten years old, and the Princess Berenice Barsine, who was seven. My sisters stood by our mother's bed with their nurses and governesses.

Propped upon pillows, my mother tried not to show her disappointment in failing to give my father a prince. My mother was a great royal lady who put a graceful countenance on any situation, even if her heart was breaking. I was screeching with bursting lungs, fresh from the womb and dripping with birthing grime. A cloth of gold was wrapped around me, and Aunt Aliki picked me up in her arms.

My father inspected me, and in spite of his chagrin, in front of the court he spoke noble words. "You have given me another fair and healthy princess, Sister Queen, and you shall yet give me fine princes!"

Aunt Aliki held me out toward him. "Take the princess in your arms, O Brother King."

After a moment's hesitation, my father gingerly took me and cradled me in his arms.

*Cleopatra was born at the end of 70 B.C. or early 69 B.C.— WB

10

"What shall we call her?" Aunt Aliki inquired.

"Cleopatra," my father said.

In Greek my name means *Glory to her Father*, and I have always endeavored to deserve my name.

I was squalling wildly, and my Egyptian wet nurse, Tamaratet, came forth so that I might suckle at her bosom. My father handed me to Tamaratet, who bared her full ripe breasts. I began to suck contentedly at a teat, taking my first drink, as my parents and the courtiers looked on.

Although our Ptolemaic dynasty is of Macedonian descent, no monarch in our line in three centuries had taken the trouble to learn Egyptian, and many had never bothered to lose their Macedonian dialect when speaking Greek. I am the first Ptolemy to speak Egyptian as a native, and I owe this to my father's foresight in decreeing that an Egyptian should nurse me so that I might learn her tongue as I learned my Greek from infancy.

All the Alexandrians outside the palace rejoiced at my birth. They too would have preferred a prince, yet I gave them an excuse to celebrate around bonfires in all the public squares. My father distributed free grain and wine in bountiful amounts to the populace, and the festivities lasted several days.

When I was a week old I was formally presented to the court. Dressed in cloth-of-gold, I was carried in the arms of my father beneath a Canopy of Royal State borne by four Kinsmen of the King. In the Great Hall, a congregation of chamberlains and courtiers, priests and illustrious foreign envoys gathered to do me homage. To the blare of trumpets my titles of royal princess and high liege lady of the land were solemnly announced to the assemblage.

After spending six months in the royal nursery, I was moved to my own establishment in a wing of the palace, as befitting a princess. I had my own platoon of household guards, chamberlains, eunuchs, priests, serving girls, and slaves.

From babyhood I grew up amid the splendor of the most luxurious palace in the world, which has as many rooms as the year has days, in a court of complex ceremonies and filled with people garbed in colorful dress according to their station and rank. Even as a small child I understood the greatness of my birth, my position and my destiny.

As a child, the palace and the city was my world, with its many beautiful buildings, all made of white marble that gleamed brilliantly in the Egyptian sun: the greatest library known to man, the largest museum, the big stadium, the universities, the theaters and temples built to honor the gods. The palace is built on the harbor, and I loved to look out of the windows of my apartments at the busiest seaport and trading center since time out of mind, watching the ships sailing to and from the four corners of the world.

The Ptolemies have always been celebrated for their love of luxury, beautiful clothes, precious jewels, and fine rich foods. I took these things for granted, and they have meant little. The most important things have always been knowledge and feeding the insatiable appetite of my mind. I was a precocious princess, and learning became more important than games or frolic. Alexandria has a polyglot population of Egyptians, Greeks, Persians, and Romans, who speak many languages, and I quickly learned all these tongues as a child.

From my earliest days I was cognizant that I was a Ptolemy and a Princess of Egypt. I listened to bedtime stories from my Aunt Aliki and my royal nurse Tamaratet. They told me of my divine descent and of our royal line. My priests gave me religious instruction and explained that I was a divinity, a goddess as well as a princess.

I grew up in a cultivated court filled with music and dancing, for my parents like all the Ptolemies patronized the arts, loving literature, the theater, music, and dance. Whether I was in my father's apartments or my mother's or in the Great Hall, there was always a band of musicians playing the lute and the harp. My father always had a troupe of dancers who practiced the art of Terpsichore, and I have inherited this troupe from him. In all these things I am the true daughter of my parents, for I have a passion for dancing and music which is in my blood.

Like any child, even a princess, my first memories were of my parents, but especially my father. Although my mother, being a Ptolemy, had a passionate heart, her innate dignity constrained her outward feelings for her children, and we too were reserved with her. For my father I had an affectionate disposition which he unabashedly returned. "My little crocodile," he always called me. Only for me, of all his six children, did he feel this great affinity and love.

I truly loved my father and was his most dutiful daughter. I had deep pride and affection for this strange, sad, maligned and misunderstood monarch. There were pathetic qualities about him, to be sure, yet still he was proud and had about him a kingly majesty. He was conscientious and kind, and unless he was unforgivably betrayed, as he was many times, he was not vicious as many of our predecessors were. He was not the most handsome man in his kingdom, being short and overweight, and if some of his nose had been where his chin was not, he would have had a better profile to grace his coins. His eyes, however, were most beautiful, a Macedonian blue like the sky, kind eyes although they could on occasion flare with majesty affronted. Even in his last years, when he was obese and disease-ridden, he walked in his royal robes and carried with him an aura of divine authority, and all knew that he was indeed the god-King of Egypt.

My father was a great flutist. The Alexandrians, who have a penchant for nicknaming their kings, early on dubbed my father Ptolemy Auletes, the Flutist. It has often been said that my father's gifts on the instrument beloved of Pan were inferior, but I am an excellent judge of music and wish to record without filial prejudice that my father was indeed superior to most in his musical gifts. There are those who deprecate his qualities as king, and although I do not agree with this I will not dispute the point, but I take umbrage at any suggestion that he was not a master musician.

13

From babyhood I loved to sit on pillows on the floor near my father as he played the flute, while his boy attendants would dance around us, some of them dressed in female attire. His haunting, melancholy music would fill the rooms of the palace, the gardens, and the courtyards beyond. His songs were always lachrymose and plaintive, emanating from his tortured soul.

When I was three I began lessons with the Chief Musician on the harp and the sistrum, the instrument sacred to Isis. Sometimes my father and I would play duets to entertain the court, and our mingled efforts always elicited acclamation.

My beloved mother Queen Cleopatra had an ethereal, haunting beauty and a luminous radiance. She was humble and virtuous, unlikely qualities in the women of our line. A reclusive spirit, she stayed much in her apartments with her ladies, and although she carried herself with innate dignity and performed her public functions impeccably, she did not delight in them. Although she did not approve of my father's licentious habits, she honored him with all devotion due a king. She did not crave power as many of her female ancestresses had, but wished only to be a dutiful wife and mother and to give my father sons.

After me, however, my mother unhappily did not conceive again. Whether this was her fault or my father's, I know not, but after my birth I am led to believe he rarely did his conjugal duty.

Soon after I was born, my father took his distant cousin, the Lady Arsinoë, as his favorite. From my Aunt Aliki I heard that while my mother was recovering from my birth, my father attended the theater with Arsinoë clinging to his arm. This was unusual, since my father was seen in public either with my mother or with his male favorites.

The Theater of Dionysus that night gave a performance of *Oedipus Rex* by Sophocles. This great play with its condemnation of incest had a disturbing effect on my father.

It has been the custom of our dynasty for brothers and

sisters to marry and jointly share the throne, in the tradition of the ancient pharaohs, and this policy has preserved the bloodlines and kept our royal line pure.

That night while watching *Oedipus Rex* at the theater not far from the palace, attendants overheard the Lady Arsinoë whisper into my father's ear that we must learn from the ancient Greeks who warned against the sin of incest, suggesting that my father was being punished by the gods, who gave him only daughters.

Certainly the history of our dynasty has been a bloody one, rent asunder as it was with stark murders that easily could have been woven into a colossal tragedy by Sophocles. *Oedipus Rex*, in fact, could have been written about the house of Ptolemy as well as the house of Atreus. My father, sensitive and superstitious, was disturbed by Arsinoë's words, reflecting that perhaps he was cursed by the gods and the displeasure of Aphrodite.

The Lady Arsinoë herself, although not fully royal like my mother, did have some Ptolemaic blood, being descended from Ptolemy the Fourth. This king, one of the least virtuous of our line, murdered his father, brother, and uncle to gain the throne, and then poisoned his mother as well. Although Arsinoë herself was related to my father, she maintained that it was so distant a relationship that she could supplant my beloved mother as queen without the taint of incest.

"I will give you fine princes!" was her tantalizing cry to my father. "A Syrian soothsayer has assured me that I will bear only sons."

Arsinoë was bewitchingly beautiful in a blatant, stark way, her mouth always painted blood red. Her face had coarse, heavy features and an expression of great determination, a face totally different from my mother's refined, delicate features. Arsinoë was clever at cosmetics, unlike my mother, who had a natural simple beauty, and had to be prodded by her ladies to let them kohl her eyes and apply carmine on her lips.

Perhaps it appealed to my father's vanity to be seen with the glamorous, wicked Arsinoë. In the Greek fashion, he considered it the norm to love both sexes, while to prefer only one sex is frowned upon. It is a man's duty to society to marry and have children, and particularly to have sons to be soldiers, or if one is a king, princes to be heirs to the throne.

I was about three years old when I became aware of the importance of sons to the royal line.

"Oh, Mother, forgive me!" I cried beseechingly.

"For what, my child?" Mother asked gently.

"For not having been born a prince," I declared.

"That is not your fault, dear daughter," she consoled me. "You are my pride and joy, a pearl of Egypt, and a daughter worth a dozen sons!"

"If the gods had made me a prince, I would grow up to be king and marry one of my sisters, and then all would be well."

"Don't condemn yourself for what you cannot help," Mother said. "The gods will yet give me a prince, so have no fear."

I cursed myself for not having been born a man. Indeed, if I had been, the whole course of the world would be different.

Gossip from the grapevine of any palace is always rife, and even a small child princess can lap up as much as she wishes. I always knew what was happening in every corner of the court.

"I don't like Lady Arsinoë!" I announced to my mother with asperity when I was all of three or four years old.

"She is our noble kinswoman," Mother said. "She has come from a thin branch of our royal family tree, but you must show her all respect."

My mother was congenitally unable to utter an unkind word against anyone, even a mortal enemy.

"I detest her!" I cried vehemently. "She is a harlot and a bitch and I hate her!"

"Who has taught you such evil words?" Mother asked, shocked. "Remember, a princess never sullies her lips with vile words."

Everywhere my father was, there also was the Lady

16

Arsinoë, urging him to cast my mother aside; but he was reluctant to do so. At first he tried to put a law into effect that would permit the king to have two wives. The powerful ministers, however, headed by the Prime Minister, Pothinos, a eunuch who was kinsman to Arsinoë, opposed the legalization of royal polygamy. Pothinos, of course, wanted Arsinoë to supplant my mother as sole queen and not just to be another wife.

Finally after five years of Arsinoë's insidious inveigling, my father decided to accede to the judgment of the council and to discard my mother.

At the time my father came to the throne, his younger brother, my Uncle Ptolemy, went off to be King of Cyprus. My father decided to divorce my mother by royal decree and banish her, along with their sister Princess Aliki, to their brother's Cypriot court.

My father had not visited my mother for several months when he went to her one morning, commanding that Aunt Aliki witness the meeting. He explained gently that since my mother had not provided Egypt with a male heir, it was his dynastic duty to seek a new wife. My mother had no need to ask who the new wife would be.

"I will abide by the wishes of my husband, the King," my mother said. She had long anticipated and morally prepared herself for this moment.

My father was relieved that my mother was taking the situation with such good grace. The interview ended amicably with their tender embrace.

"We must make preparation to go to Cyprus," Mother told Aunt Aliki.

"Yes, we should begin at once," Aunt Aliki said.

"Tomorrow is time enough," Mother remarked calmly.

Aunt Aliki began to cry, and it was Mother who soothed and quieted her down.

That evening my mother commanded her three daughters to be brought to dine with her. We sat on divans before a golden table. Her favorite musicians were playing on a terraced balcony. Rich incenses were burning. My

17

mother, who was then thirty-three years old, appeared serene in the gentle flickering lights from the lamps. She had never looked lovelier to my eyes.

My sisters and I were totally unaware of what had transpired that morning between our parents.

"Always obey your father the king in all things," Mother admonished while we ate. "Obey your tutors and become learned princesses so that you will bring glory to Egypt, and above all, love one another."

At the time my sisters were fifteen and twelve and I was five. I dearly loved my eldest sister Cleopatra, who was so much like our mother, but Berenice and I shared a mutual loathing that even our mother's command could not alter.

"Always conduct yourselves virtuously," Mother counseled us in her sweet, soft voice. "Remember your duty and dignity, and never disgrace your heritage."

Our mother frequently spoke to us in this manner, and we did not think it unusual. At length she bade us good night. As she embraced us, her arms did not encircle us nor did her lips linger on our lips a fraction longer than on any other evening; and so we took leave of her and retired to our own apartments.

The next morning when her ladies went to awaken my beloved Mother, they found her dead.

I was finishing my prayers in my private temple when my beloved tutor, Protarchus of Pontus, came in with my Aunt Aliki. My aunt's face was twisted in anguish. She took me into her arms and told me the terrible news. A paroxysm of grief overcame me, and I burst into hysterical sobbing. Protarchus called for a potion to be administered to numb my despair.

Later that evening my father had his three daughters brought to our mother's bedchamber. She lay on her bed, stiff as the marble effigy that would later adorn her crypt in the royal mausoleum.

"As all the gods are my witnesses," Father cried with tears falling down his cheeks, "I had no hand in the death of my beloved wife. May the gods condemn me to Hades if I did."

One by one, we kissed our mother's cold still cheek, and were led sobbing away.

The Egyptian embalmers took my mother, soaked her in niter, and worked their wonders upon her. She was dressed in a robe of gold, a jewelled diadem was placed upon her brow, and she was laid upon an ornate catafalque in the square in front of the palace, hung with mourning wreaths. A squadron of guards surrounded the catafalque, and for three days people came and filed by their dead queen to pay their final homage. There was much sobbing, and not only from the professional mourners but from the people who had deeply loved their queen and now lamented her passing.

On the day of the funeral, the populace lined the avenues of the city to view the royal cortege. The catafalque was pulled by eight white geldings, led by priests and flanked by soldiers. The king and my sisters and I and the royal household followed in litters as my mother was delivered to the Sema and consigned to her marble sarcophagus.

It has been said that the Lady Arsinoë, not content with my mother's expulsion to Cyprus, had a hand in her death. Arsinoë was certainly capable of murder, but it is my belief that my mother effected her own end. She had been reared to be queen to her eldest brother, and it was beneath her royal dignity to be cast aside and to spend the rest of her days in exile. So she probably drank a poisoned draught which put her to sleep forever.

If she could not live a queen, she would die one.

At the age of five, as I gazed upon her face so serene in death, I decided that if the fates ever dealt me a similar cruel hand, I too would choose such an honorable exit. I am my mother's royal daughter with all her pride and dignity, and I believe there can be no better shroud than the royal purple.

With my mother's death there was nothing to impede the ascendency of Arsinoë. She and her kinsman, Pothinos, were responsible for my mother's end and earned my unmitigated hatred. I was five years old, yet the emotions of love and hate were known to me in all their great force.

My father, out of deference to the people, who from great to low lamented the untimely passing of their Queen, waited for two months of mourning before he took on his new wife. The upstart harlot, Lady Arsinoë, succeeded in all her designs. This unscrupulous usurper of my mother's place became Queen and was duly consecrated with the sacred oils and crowned. My father treated his people to a festival of games and feasting to mark the occasion.

It was none too soon, since six months later Queen Arsinoë gave birth to my half-sister, Princess Arsinoë. In the streets the people said, "It takes ordinary folk like ourselves nine months to make a baby, but a queen, being of better stuff, can do it in six!"

I was jubilant that my mother's foe delivered a daughter. I wanted brother princes, but I could not help being pleased that Arsinoë did not give at her first try what my mother failed to give in three attempts. And I was happy that Arsinoë proved her Syrian soothsayer to be not very sooth.

Queen Arsinoë—I am loath to honor her with this title but bear the title she did—was, in the three years that followed, to give my father two princes, Ptolemy Magus and Ptolemy Philippos. The people at first called her "The Piper's Harlot," but because she secured the succession with two princes, the resentment against her abated and she became popular. I despised her, yet because she was my father's wife, I always showed her a cool but civil courtesy. In turn, my stepmother could never forgive me for the special place I had in my father's heart.

As a child I was my father's especial pride and joy. I was vivacious and pretty, celebrated for my charm and winning ways. I was a princess of Egypt, yet still at the same time I was a true child of Macedonia, with flaxen curls and blue eyes, just like Alexander the Great.

I take deep pride in the Macedonians of the north

being the most ancient and purest of the Greeks. Unlike the Hellenes of Greece, we have not had our bloodlines polluted by the Doric invaders. We remain tall, blond and blue-eyed, true descendants of Argos.

For public and ceremonial occasions, even as a child, I have always worn straight black wigs modeled after those worn by ancient Egyptian royalty. It was the custom for the Egyptian queens to shave their heads to make it easier to apply wigs, but I prize my thick rich hair, a characteristic of all Hellenes, and so I have my hair pulled back and bound before the wig is put on. Since childhood my blond hair has darkened slightly to a golden bronze.

Even as a curly-haired, tow-headed child I knew how to win everyone's heart if I so desired, although I never tried it with my stepmother, sister Berenice, or the eunuch Pothinos. My eldest sister Cleopatra I deeply loved, but I never got on with Berenice, seven years my senior. Berenice was beautiful, but she lacked charm and always wore a hard, surly expression. The warm light of love from my father did not shine upon her, and she hated me for being his favorite.

I followed my father everywhere, even into the council chamber, and would climb onto his lap. Pothinos, with his dour disposition, would frown with disapproval, but there was nothing he could do since my presence pleased my father. Even as a small princess the affairs of the kingdom interested me more than playing with dolls. My father doted on me and would carry me in his arms around the palace and in the street, for all the court and the people to see.

I was a precocious princess, and my father liked to show me off. I vividly recall one incident that occurred when I was about six years old and has since become a legend. There was a banquet with the whole court and many distinguished foreign ambassadors in attendance. There must have been at least a hundred couches spread in the Great Hall. My father asked me to approach the royal dais.

21

"We're an ignorant lot with faulty memories, Princess Cleopatra," he said. "Would you be so kind as to tell us who were the parents of the nine muses?"

"Yes, O Father King," I said brightly. "Zeus and Mnemosyne."

"Ah, yes, but the names of their nine daughters escape me! Could you refresh my memory?"

"There was Clio, the Muse of History—" I began.

"Did you hear that, noble guests?" Father interrupted excitedly. "She starts off with Clio!"

The congregation laughed in appreciation and some wonderment.

"All the Muses are important!" I said solemnly. "I meant no preference by naming Clio first."

My father smiled. "And who are the sisters of Clio?"

I faced the assemblage with perfect poise and in a clear voice cried, "There is Calliope the Muse of heroic poetry, Erato the Muse of love poetry, Euterpe the Muse of music and lyric poetry, Melpomene the Muse of tragedy, Polyhymnia the Muse of sublime hymns and serious sacred songs, Terpsichore the Muse of dancing, Thalia the Muse of comedy and idyllic poetry, and Urania the Muse of astronomy—not to be confused, of course, with Urania who is Aphrodite representing spiritual love."

The gathering burst into cheers, and many goblets of wine were drunk to me.

My father beamed with pride. Queen Arsinoë, sitting beside him, forced a false smile.

When the cheering and drinking died down, my father wrinkled his brow in perplexity and said, "There's a statue out in the corridor of some big sinister giant with a beard. Who is that man?"

"Oh, that's King Philip the Second of Macedonia," I replied, "my great-great-great-great-great-great-great-great grandfather!"

Again all the guests burst into a chorus of cheers and laughter.

"I wondered who he was!" my father cried. "You may return to your couch now, Cleopatra."

22

I bent one knee to my father, and resumed my seat on the couch I shared with my Aunt Aliki and my tutor Protarchus.

Yes, I was my father's favorite, and may no one mistake it!

From the cradle I loved to hear stories about the long line of kings of our dynasty and of the pharaohs who ruled before, and I needed only to examine the busts and statues in the palace to connect them with tales I heard. Alexander the Great and Thutmose the Third and Queen Hatshepsüt were as familiar to me as my mother and father. At an early age, as soon as I began reading, I devoured books to learn all I could about my heritage.

Ptolemy the First, the founder of our line, was the natural son of King Philip of Macedonia and half-brother to Alexander. Philip, as I proudly declared to the guests as the banquet, was indeed my great-grandfather eight times over. As I dictate these words, Philip stares at me from a marble bust on my table. I feel I know him with his strong wide mouth, the drive apparent in the high cheekbones, the imperious gaze, the cryptic expression, all evident in the bust of this glorious general-king.

This mighty Macedonian monarch was a lusty, hard-drinking, and rough-hewn king who went on to become overlord of all Greece, conquering Thessaly and Thrace and all the Greek cities that had fallen to the Persians.

Philip had a personal favorite, the Lady Arsinoë, a woman of great beauty and noble Macedonian lineage. When he got her with child, being already married to Queen Olympias, he arranged that she marry a noble of his court, Lord Lagos. A short time after the marriage, Ptolemy was born, and it is from Ptolemy that I am directly descended in eleven generations. Ptolemy was called the son of Lagos, which is the name of our dynasty, but it has never been a secret from whose royal seed we have sprung.

Ptolemy grew up alongside his half-brother Alexander, and the two boys were devotedly attached. Ptolemy's position in the royal Macedonian court at Pella was as honorable as if he had been Philip's legitimate prince.

23

As he grew to manhood, he attained official stations of power.

When King Philip was assassinated, Alexander succeeded his father at the age of twenty-one, and Ptolemy became one of his brother's principal councillors.

Alexander, with Ptolemy at his side, marched his army out of Greece and crossed the Hellespont into Persia. He dealt Darius two great defeats at Issus and Granikkos, although the Persian host greatly outnumbered them both times. Alexander then conquered Phoenicia, and the cities of Sidon, Jerusalem, and Tyre.

It was at Tyre that an Egyptian, Tefnakht, went to meet Alexander and begged him to help his wretched country, so it was decided to go there. The Persian governor of Egypt, the satrap Mazakes, surrendered at Pelusium, and Alexander and Ptolemy entered Egypt with their army, liberating the country from the Persian yoke which had clutched Egypt in a stranglehold nine years before when the last pharaoh had been deposed.

Egypt received Alexander with jubilation. Alexander followed a policy of tolerance, differing from that of the hated Persian domination. He visited temples and sacrificed to the sacred bull Apis, which overjoyed the priesthood and the populace. Under the Persians, the temples had been looted, so it is no wonder that the Egyptians welcomed Alexander with great honor. At the Oasis of Siwa, the high priest greeted Alexander as Son of Amon Ra, and the priests and nobles of the two lands made him, at the age of twenty-four, pharaoh.

Impelled by destiny and favored by fortune, Alexander, with Ptolemy at his side, left Egypt and battered a passage eastward through Asia. Darius was decisively defeated at Arbela, fleeing and later being killed by a kinsman. Alexander became Emporer of Persia, and the great cities and treasures and palaces of Persopolis, Babylon, Susa, Ecbatana and Baghdad became his personal property. The Persians, who for centuries had been the scourge of Greece and Egypt in countless invasions, now paid the price for the horrors that they had inflicted. Alexander's office of King of Macedonia, a distant corner of his vast empire, became a minor adjunct to his great position as Emperor of Asia.

Ptolemy distinguished himself in all these campaigns, commanding one of the three divisions of the army, and rendered the greatest service to the cause of his brother. He conquered armies, reduced fortresses, and negotiated treaties. At great victory festivities at Susa, he was honored with a golden crown given by Alexander.

In conquered Babylon, Alexander suddenly died at the age of thirty-three. What caused his death—a swamp fever, poison, the pox of Aphrodite—only the high gods know. No man ever conquered as much as he, and perhaps none ever shall. He was the greatest maker of history the world will ever know.

With Alexander gone, it became apparent that the empire he had created could not hold together. The great Hellenistic civilization, however, which he formed by blending Greek and Persian cultures, has survived. After his death, his chief commanders carved the empire up between them. Pithon became King of Media, Lysimachus King of Thrace, Niarchos King of Lycia, Eumenes King of Cappadocia, Antigonus King of Syria, Alexander's half-witted half-brother Philip, King of Macedonia, and Ptolemy bargained for the biggest plum of all, Egypt.

Ptolemy set out with his army and a great number of Greek followers, taking Alexander's embalmed body to Egypt, to the raw city of Alexandria, which Ptolemy decided would be the seat of his capital.

A monumental marble mausoleum, done in the Macedonian style, was built in the center of the city to house the sacred remains of Alexander. The body, in a golden sarcophagus, is perfectly preserved to this day. There, too, in the Sema rest all the bodies of my forebears.

The Egyptian priests and nobles declared Ptolemy to be the legal successor to his brother, and made him King and Pharaoh. During Ptolemy's long reign, Alexandria rose to become the metropolis of the Mediterranean, surpassing Athens and Carthage. As for Rome, in those days it was just a small rustic village of little consequence.

Ptolemy married his half-sister, Berenice, a daughter

of Lagos. She was a woman of remarkable beauty and character. As for Ptolemy, his coins bear witness that he was incredibly handsome, with a sharp, hawk-nosed profile, and a virile, magnetic look that was godlike. The story of the love and devotion of these two, the founders of my dynasty, has come down through the centuries.

During a reign that lasted forty years, Ptolemy brought splendor to Egypt. He set the pattern for Ptolemaic patronage of the arts and sciences. A keen politician, he founded a sound policy based upon the experiences and capital of Greek financiers and opened Egypt up to trade with the rest of the world. He built Pharos, one of the seven wonders of the world, the lighthouse four hundred feet tall, its illumination provided by tall flaming wicks of oil lamps magnified and beamed far out to sea by reflecting mirrors. He built the royal palace, the university, and the great library. Greek scholars and philosophers, poets, and artists all flocked to Alexandria, which soon became the capital of the world.

In my childhood, as I assessed the family history, I realized it was under the first three Ptolemies that our house grew in splendor and revitalized Egypt as a great empire. These kings created the most glorious royal court in the world where artistic and intellectual life flourished.

Beginning with Ptolemy the Fourth, decline began as the honorable example of the first three Ptolemies was lost in a succession of terrible tyrants. I dislike dwelling on the complicated couplings of these bad Ptolemies, who lived only for lust and luxury, and whose reigns were marked by treacherous intrigues and cruelties. All the while, these kings took solemn and noble surnames, styling themselves Ptolemy Soter, the Savior; Ptolemy Philadelphus, the Brother Loving; Ptolemy Philopator, the Father Loving; Ptolemy Philomator, the Mother Loving. Yet at the same time they were murdering their fathers and mothers and brothers, and were deplorable despots who frittered away their great legacy.

As our dynasty declined, power diminished and possessions slipped away, but the Ptolemies were still great patrons, and art and science made enormous strides.

While Ptolemaic Egypt became weaker and Carthage fell, Rome was on the rise. As a child I soon became aware that there was another world outside Egypt. The world of Rome. The specter of Rome. The shadow of Rome lengthening over the rest of the world, and darkening sunny Egypt.

My childhood was filled with the dread of the Romans. I saw all the kingdoms of Asia Minor, enfeebled by internal squabbling, pounced on by the eagles of Rome. The commonwealth became a great power by exploiting the weakness of others as they marched from country to country, conquest to conquest. By the time I was ten, only Egypt remained independent, although in a weakened condition. I was haunted by the fear that Egypt would be next, following in the footsteps of Bithynia, Thrace, Pergamum, Syria, and Pontus, kingdoms which had become provinces of Rome.

"The covetous eyes of Rome are gazing upon us," Father would often say. "Our trade and wealth, our grain, and our treasures are tempting prizes!"

The thought struck terror in my little heart.

My beloved father wanted all his children, especially those of us who came to the throne after him, to realize the might and the danger of Rome, so that we would better be able to deal with this power. Of all his children I was the only one who learned the lesson well. I hated the barbarian Romans, but from childhood I realized Rome was a fact of life that had to be dealt with.

When I was ten years old, Pompey, Caesar, and Crassus formed the First Triumvirate and made a mockery of all republican institutions. Egypt was restless with an uneasy political situation and excessive taxation. My father had two sons and four daughters, but he realized that to secure his dynasty and to keep Egypt independent, he would have to travel to Rome and come to an understanding with the great men of the Triumvirate, and obtain official recognition and a treaty of alliance, cost whatever it may.

I loved my father with a fierce devotion, and I was filled with anguish at his departure.

"You will have Protarchus and Aunt Aliki and Tamaratet to look after you," Father said to comfort me. He did not mention my stepmother, since he knew I would get no solace from her.

As my father went off in a ship, the whole court waved farewell. I stood on the marble dockside, crying bitter tears in public, forgetting all royal dignity.

"Remember that you are a princess!" Queen Arsinoë snapped.

Arsinoë usually ignored me, much to my relief, concentrating on her own three children, but with my father gone I realized she would find fault with me at the slightest justification.

With my Aunt Aliki and Tamaratet holding my hands, I walked up the pink marble steps from the dockside to the palace. With a heavy heart, I went to my apartments and sat by the window, gazing sadly as my father's ship sailed out to sea.

I offered sacrifices of ointments and flowers to the god Poseidon, so that the seas would be calm during my father's voyage to Naples. I also made sacrifice and said prayers to the Greek God Hermes, the god of travellers, to his Roman counterpart, Mercury, and to the old Egyptian god of voyagers, Thoth, overlooking none of these great gods, seeking their combined divine assistance in watching over my father in his Roman mission and his return to Egypt.

From the moment of my father's departure, I was filled with a sense of foreboding, anticipating a dreadful happening. One night, after my father had been gone about a month, an incident occurred which proved that my fears and feelings had not been without foundation.

Tamaratet saw me to my bed each night. She would linger beside me, and sing Egyptian songs or tell stories, or I would confess my little-girl secrets that I never dared tell another soul.

I had a deep love for my eldest sister Cleopatra, Aunt Aliki, and my tutor Protarchus, but they were all reserved by nature and not overly affectionate with me.

Tamaratet, like my father, was free with warm embraces that I needed as a little girl. Tamaratet was a true daughter of Egypt, but do not think that she was a peasant whose forebears only the gods can trace, for she came from a distinguished line and had an uncle who was High Priest of Karnak. She had dark eyes and brown skin and a heart that overflowed with love and devotion for me.

After Tamaratet put me to bed, she would retire to her own chamber adjacent to mine. On this ominous night, the moon shone brightly into my bedchamber from the doors that opened onto the terraced balcony that faced the sea.

It was her habit never to leave me until I had fallen asleep. On this night I sensed she was extremely tired, so I pretended to sleep so that she would go off to her own bed, and she did.

I lay there awake and restless. I rarely fell asleep easily, for my mind was always alive, churning with the facts I had learned at my studies that day, or with worries about my father being away. My childhood was filled with uncertainties, and anxiety generally preyed on my mind during the dead of night.

On this particular night I was much at the mercy of my forebodings, but finally drifted off to sleep. I had not been asleep long, however, when I heard a moan or a sigh which awoke me. I opened my eyes to see Tamaratet standing beside my bed.

"Cleopatra!" Tamaratet cried. "Don't move, be still!"

I could see her clearly in the moonlight, her face struck with horror.

"Don't move!" she commanded again, her voice soft yet urgent.

I lay perfectly still. "Tamaratet," I whispered weakly, obeying her yet not understanding.

With a sudden spring, she threw her body across the bottom of my bed. I jerked upright, and saw her hands clutching a snake coiled near my feet, its head swaying in the air, poised to strike at me, hissing sounds coming from its mouth.

Tamaratet frantically clutched the writhing snake against her bosom, rolled off the bed and pulled the snake with her onto the floor.

I stood on the bed and screamed with fright.

Tamaratet moaned as the serpent, in predatory, pitiless pursuit, flicked its fangs at her throat, and her body went slack.

The serpent raised its head and looked at me for a moment, its tiny eyes blazing with an icy glitter in the moonlight. My screams shattered the silence of the night. The serpent unwound its thick girth from Tamaratet's body and slid onto the floor, its muscles moving beneath the sheen of the skin and its rippling mottled hide.

Again my screams echoed in the night as I watched the sinuous snake, which was more than a foot long, slither across the shiny marble floor in swift smooth movements, with a rustling of its scales, toward the opened doors leading out onto the balcony.

The door to the corridor burst open and a guard rushed in, his sword flashing.

"O Princess, what is it?" the young guard cried.

"A serpent has bitten my nurse," I cried, pointing to the retreating snake. "It goes there!"

The guard ran onto the balcony in hot pursuit. His blade crashed down on the snake several times, slicing it to pieces, and I saw all the pieces writhing separately.

I jumped onto the floor and knelt beside my fallen nurse. "Tamaratet!" I cried sobbingly. "Tamaratet!"

Other guards rushed into the chamber, some holding torches. The guard who had gone after the serpent returned and squatted at my feet.

"O Princess, I smote the serpent!" he cried triumphantly. "It lies in a dozen pieces."

I looked at his handsome face shining in the torchlight. "Thank you, noble guardsman," I murmured.

I looked back at Tamaratet, seeing at her throat a tiny crimson mark that the serpent's fangs had left.

"Call the physicians!" I cried. "Call the snake charmers, quickly!"

There was consternation in my chamber as several

soldiers rushed off to do my bidding, while others came in, all crowding around me.

"Stand back!" ordered the guard who had killed the snake, flashing his sword about. "Give the princess and her nurse room to breathe!"

"Oh, Tamaratet," I wept, wiping with my hand the moisture on her brow.

Tamaratet's bright eyes, filled with love, looked up at me. "I am dying, O Princess," she said calmly.

"No, you won't die!" I protested frenziedly. "The physicians are coming and they will save you."

"No, the snake was an asp and its venom works quickly." Already her lids were heavy and half-closed.

"Tamaratet, are you in pain?" I asked desperately.

"No, I am just going to sleep, forever," Tamaratet replied faintly. Her eyes struggled to focus on mine. "Promise me, Cleopatra, as you promised your mother, that you will harness your spirit and serve Egypt well."

"I promise, Tamaratet," I avowed earnestly.

"I saved my princess," Tamaratet said exultantly. "I heard men on the balcony moving past my window. At first I thought I was hearing things and almost went back to sleep, but then I came in to see that you were well. I saw the serpent crawling on your bed, and I intercepted it, saving you, saving my princess for Egypt!"

"Oh, Tamaratet!" I cried, breaking into sobs.

"Do not cry, Cleopatra," Tamaratet said, her voice stern. "A princess never shows her emotions."

Again I wiped her brow and smoothed the thick hair from her forehead. "I love you, Tamaratet!"

"I die happily," Tamaratet whispered, her eyes glittering in the torchlight, full of love and pain and acceptance. "My fate is to die, having saved my princess for her glorious destiny!"

I held her hands in mine. Soon her eyes closed. She breathed yet, but her lips stilled. I felt her pulse, the rhythm growing fainter with each beat.

"Where are the physicians?" I cried out.

"They are coming, O Princess," a guard assured me.

I looked at Tamaratet, at the face I loved, and I saw

31

her jaw had gone slack and her skin was covered with a slight moisture. She was dying and there was nothing that I could do about it.

I felt her pulse, and the beat was no more. I burst into great sobbing and placed my head on her breasts, the same breasts which had given me my first nourishment.

Finally Queen Arsinoë rushed in, with a cloak thrown over her bedgown. My eldest sister Princess Cleopatra, then aged twenty, came in behind her with a stricken look.

I was sobbing, and they had to pull me away by force from Tamaratet's body.

"Take her to the laboratory!" I cried hysterically. "Have the snake charmers suck out the poison!"

Cleopatra Tryphaina put her arms around me consolingly.

"The snake must have found its way up from the gardens," Queen Arsinoë cried. "How dreadful!"

I looked at her, and she looked at me. I knew from the look in her eyes that the doings of the night were of her instigation.

"Come, come to my chamber and sleep with me," Cleopatra Tryphaina said.

She went to lead me off, but I stopped short, searching for the young guard who had killed the serpent. I saw him standing not far away. He was tall, with a beautiful face, brown eyes, fair skin, and thick black hair. I walked over and stood before him, gazing up at his face.

"This guard smote the serpent!" I cried.

"I am honored to have served my princess," he said, sinking to one knee.

"What is your name?" I asked.

"Apollodorus, O Princess," he replied. "May I live to use my sword to smite all your enemies."

"Come, dear sister," Cleopatra Tryphaina said.

"I want Apollodorus to come," I cried. "Wherever I go, I want him at my side always."

Queen Arsinoë glared at Apollodorus. "Why, this guard is so young. How old are you?"

"Fifteen, My Lady Queen," Apollodorus replied.

"How long have you been attached to the Household Regiment?" Queen Arsinoë demanded.

"I finished my training and joined the Household Regiment two weeks ago and was assigned to night duty," Apollodorus explained.

"For your personal guard, Cleopatra," Queen Arsinoë said, "you should have a more seasoned soldier."

"I want Apollodorus!" I announced with authority.

She decided not to argue the point and swept out of the chamber, her cloak trailing behind her.

"Come, dear sister," Cleopatra Tryphaina said, reaching for my hand.

"I am coming," I said, but it was Apollodorus to whom I gave my hand. He smiled and as his large hand took my little one, I felt safe.

A cordon of guards accompanied us as we walked along the huge corridors, and at last we reached Cleopatra Tryphaina's apartments. Warm pomegranate juice was served, sampled first by her Numidian taster. Neither of us slept more that night.

From that night, until my father returned a month later from Rome, I slept in the same bed with Cleopatra Tryphaina, and Apollodorus was always on guard outside the door.

I knew that the serpent had not found its way to my bedchamber on its own, and that Queen Arsinoë was behind this attempt on my life. She wanted me, my father's favorite, out of the way, just as she had wanted my mother out of the way, and she had thought it best to act now during my father's absence.

For appearance's sake, Queen Arsinoë made much of ordering an investigation among the platoon of palace guards and sentries, to see if anyone had heard or seen anyone stealing about that fateful night. Nothing came of this, of course, since there had been much gold dispensed to silence tongues.

I had lost my devoted, beloved Tamaratet, but that same night I had found my valiant Apollodorus.

"If you permit me," Apollodorus gallantly told me,

"I will serve you all the days of my life and be your champion."

"I will permit you, Apollodorus," I said.

I was only ten years old, but as I look back I realize that from the night when the venom of an asp meant for me killed my beloved Tamaratet, I was never quite a child again.

CHAPTER II

A GOLDEN PRINCESS and a pearl of Egypt I might have been as a child, decked out in royal raiment and with a gold coronet circling my head to signify my rank, yet I trod a perilous path in the palace. Each morsel of food I swallowed, even after my taster had sampled it, made me shiver with apprehension. My father was out of the country and my hated stepmother and Pothinos ruled, and I was afraid that there would be another attempt on my life. After Tamaratet's death, every night I had nightmares about the serpent coiled in her arms, its fangs at her throat.

That summer of my tenth earthly year, with Tamaratet dead and my father in Rome, I turned toward my beloved tutor, Protarchus, with an increase of need and dependence. Alexander had Aristotle for a tutor, but I had Protarchus, who gave me a first-rate education and as much loyalty and devotion as any princess could ask for.

Protarchus was an austere and distinguished eunuch. Most eunuchs are gross and have waspish dispositions, but not so Protarchus, who was tall and elegant. He was a kind and gentle person of prudent temper and unimpeachable worth. He had an ascetic, narrow face, with deep hollows in the cheeks. His hair, laced with silver, fringed a wrinkled high forehead. His nose was long and sharp, and he had sparkling blue eyes which mirrored deep intelligence.

It has long been Ptolemaic custom to employ eunuchs for top official positions and as tutors, and most of our prime ministers have been eunuchs. Eunuchs were first appointed to oversee the women in the palace, for they would certainly never get a royal wife or princess with child. Later they assumed higher duties as court chamberlains, and often gained immense power. Having no families, ties, or children of their own, they are extremely faithful.

While my father was in Rome, I spent a lot of time playing chess with my Aunt Aliki. Even as a child I had a genius for this game, but I permitted Aunt Aliki to win every other match.

"When you grow up," Protarchus often said, "I hope you have as much dexterity in moving the pawns on the chessboard of the world."

At Rome my father was a guest at Pompey's villa, and he became acquainted with Julius Caesar, who was facing bankruptcy. Caesar, who was consul, consented to pass a resolution in the Senate called the "Julian Law Concerning the King of Egypt," confirming my father's right to the throne and giving him the title of "Friend and Ally of the Roman People." My father paid Caesar six thousand talents for this service, the equivalent of the entire revenue of the royal monopolies for one year.

Caesar and Pompey required the money immediately. My father was anxious that the embarrassing task of raising it from his subjects be postponed, so he borrowed half the whole sum from a Roman speculator and financier, Gaius Rabirius Postumus.

It was a glorious day when my father's ship returned to Alexandria, sailing into the harbor all decked out with garlands. The whole court welcomed him at dockside, and vast crowds of citizens had to be held back by soldiers. The King was coming home victoriously with a treaty, and the people greeted him with enthusiasm.

My father was happy to be back in Alexandria after the long hot summer in Rome. He celebrated his return by granting a general amnesty, cancelling all impending prosecutions, actions he hoped would soften the people before he imposed the stiff taxes necessary to pay off his Roman debts.

It was the time of the autumnal equinox. Life was

suddenly serene and certain. My father had returned, his dynasty was secure, and I was the happiest princess in the world.

"I have written your Uncle Ptolemy, the King of Cyprus," Father told me one day, "and he is going to pay us an official state visit."

A week later I was on the dockside welcoming Uncle Ptolemy as he disembarked with a retinue of male favorites.

The Alexandrians cheered him wildly. It had been twenty years since he had gone off to be King of Cyprus, but the people remembered him fondly and gave him a rousing reception.

Uncle Ptolemy was presented first to my two elder sisters according to rank, and then to me. I took his hand and sank to one knee. We looked at one another, and at a glance a deep bond was established.

Although my uncle was a year younger than my father, it seemed there were twenty years between them. The affairs of Egypt weighed heavily on my poor father, while time and events had dealt kindly with his brother. Uncle Ptolemy had a kingly bearing and was most vain about his appearance. He was blond in the Ptolemy way and wore his hair long and carefully combed. He had dignity, graceful manners, effortless charm, and the gift of laughter.

Uncle Ptolemy brought many presents for his two nephews and four nieces. He liked us all, but I was his special favorite, and I reciprocated the feeling. As soon as we arrived at my father's apartments, I climbed onto his lap.

The state visit lasted a month, and during all his tours of the city I was always at his side. We fed the sacred crocodiles as the cheering people looked on. We rode in a chariot or were carried in the same sedan through the streets. At the theater the audience applauded him with more fervor than the actors.

One night at a banquet in the Great Hall, Uncle Ptolemy said, "I have never married, Cleopatra, because

37

I have been waiting all these years for the right princess to come along."

Several of his male favorites tittered at this remark, but my uncle pretended not to hear them.

"Cleopatra," Uncle Ptolemy cried, plucking me under my chin, "I am going to ask your father if he will give his consent for you to be my queen."

I was ten years old, and I trembled with excitement.

"Would you like to be Queen of Cyprus?" he asked.

I reflected that I would rather be Queen of Egypt, but since I had two older sisters it was a remote possibility that I would ever wear the double crown of Egypt. There could be worse destinies, I thought, than being Queen of Cyprus and wife to my charming uncle.

"Do you think I would be worthy, Uncle Ptolemy?"

"You would grace Cyprus like a jewel," he replied.

"Being Queen of Cyprus would be an honorable fate for you, my daughter," Father said. "It would be a tranquil life, for in Cyprus the people are never violent and rebellious like the Alexandrians."

"My people are gentle and never give me trouble," Uncle Ptolemy said. "And the island is a paradise."

I looked around and caught the eye of my sister, Princess Arsinoë, who was five years old, sitting beside her mother Queen Arsinoë. My sister was looking at me with ill-disguised jealousy, resenting that I would be Queen of Cyprus, for, as the fourth princess in line, it was unlikely that she would ever come to any throne.

"Yes, I would be deeply proud to be Queen of Cyprus," I said clearly. "But, Uncle Ptolemy, you must ask my father for a big dowry."

"I will take you naked, without a garment on your back or a gold piece in your pocket," Uncle Ptolemy proclaimed grandly.

"Oh, don't do that, Uncle Ptolemy!" I cried.

There was laughter among the guests at this exchange.

After the banquet when I went to bed, I could not sleep for being so feverish with excitement. I no longer had nightmares about poisonous serpents. I was going to be Queen of Cyprus and live happily ever after.

The next day I could not concentrate on my studies.

"Will you come with me to Cyprus, Protarchus?"

"Wherever my princess goes, I will go," he said.

"When I am Queen of Cyprus, you will be the prime minister, and Apollodorus will be a general in the army."

"Apollodorus is but a young common soldier."

"I am a princess but I will be queen," I reasoned. "Why cannot a soldier become a general?"

"If the fates will it, but that is in the future," Protarchus said. "Today I am not a prime minister but a humble tutor, and it is my duty to pose problems for my princess to ponder."

"Yes, Protarchus," I said obediently.

I knew that Alexander the Great had a sister, Princess Cleopatra, who at fourteen had married her uncle, the King of Epirus. I, her namesake, would follow a similar destiny and marry my uncle and become Queen of Cyprus. It would be sad to leave Egypt and my father, but if it was my duty to go to Cyprus I would do so willingly. I would have many children, and I would make myself worthy of my Cypriot people.

The night before my Uncle Ptolemy left Egypt, a banquet was held in his honor at the palace, and my father formally announced our betrothal, the marriage to take place in four years. Uncle Ptolemy presented me with a golden necklace studded with rich gems. After the banquet, he walked me to my chambers.

"Why can't I go with you tomorrow, Uncle Ptolemy?"

"A princess must be at least fourteen before she marries," Uncle Ptolemy told me.

"Four more years!" I fretted with impatience.

"If you study hard, the years will fly quickly," Uncle Ptolemy said.

The sun god Ra shone in benediction the next day when my Uncle Ptolemy left Alexandria. In a solemn procession, my father, my uncle, all the royal family and royal kinsmen, priests in their white linen robes, and nobles and officials in ceremonial dress, all moved down to the dockside where my uncle and his retinue boarded their galley.

As Uncle Ptolemy embraced me, a great cheer rose up from the crowd, for word had spread that I would in due course become Queen of Cyprus.

With deep emotion I watched the ship sail away with my betrothed uncle. Each week afterward I wrote him, describing my studies and events. He sent me a casket filled with amethysts, stones that are found in large deposits on Cyprus. I was not quite eleven years old, and I dreamed of the day when I would be queen of my own island kingdom and life would be exciting and beautiful. For love of me, Uncle Ptolemy would banish all his male favorites. My father had not loved either of his two wives, but between Uncle Ptolemy and me there would be the undying love which the poets write about.

About a month after my uncle's departure, Roman ships anchored in the harbor, bringing a delegation to bestow upon my father the title of "Friend and Ally of the Roman People." There were many welcoming ceremonies in which I had to take part. I met all the Roman envoys and studied them. The Romans were arrogant and crude, and did not possess the cultured elegance of the Greeks, Persians, and Egyptians. I did not like them, but as Queen of Cyprus I would have to deal with the Romans in time, and I knew I would have to get to know and get along with them.

The Romans came to bestow the title on my father, ostensibly, but they actually wanted to bleed him for the money he owed them for that title.

A few days after their arrival, an incident occurred which left a profound impression upon me. One of the Roman soldiers killed a cat in the street and was immediately set upon by the people and torn to pieces.

The cat is one of our sacred animals. The Egyptians have always venerated the bull, the cat, the crocodile. It is a custom that is deeply implanted in the hearts of the people, who cherish the belief that these animals are sacred and all honors are due them, and our dynasty has always respected these beliefs.

My father was courting the Roman delegates with all possible zeal, wanting no pretext for complaint, so the cat episode struck dread in theirs hearts. However, since it had only been a common soldier who had been killed, it was decided by the Roman delegates that the event should not color the important issues at stake.

At a lavish banquet in the Great Hall, my father was officially presented with the document titling him "Friend and Ally of the Roman People," and various copies of the treaty were signed.

I was much impressed by the cat affair. I understood the potential fury and the power of the populace, and the delicate balance of relations between Egypt and Rome. I comprehended, as young as I was, international politics, and the brutality and corruption of the Romans.

The Roman delegation left, after emptying the royal treasury of all gold to take with them.

It seemed that some of my father's problems were solved, for the dynasty was recognized by Rome. Taxes had to be increased at an exorbitant rate, however, and my father hoped the people would not protest with violence. He prayed for a respite from troubles in the years ahead so he could get down to the business of putting the kingdom in order. There was a program of temple restoration he wanted to complete, and several reforms in the court system he wanted to establish.

One mid-afternoon, a few weeks after my eleventh birthday, while I was engrossed in my studies with Protarchus, Apollodorus was announced by the majordomo.

"A message, O Princess, from the King requesting your presence," Apollodorus cried.

A chill crept through me. My father knew I studied hard in the afternoons, and to command my presence indicated a matter of gravity, not a whim. With Apollodorus and a cordon of guards escorting me, I quickly traversed the long marble corridors to my father's wing. I found him sitting morosely on a couch, a goblet of wine in a trembling hand.

"My darling daughter," Father cried as I entered.

I went to his couch and knelt on one knee, even though he waved for me to dispense with this etiquette, but I persisted since I wanted to do him homage. I sat beside him and kissed his cheek. A heavy weariness hung over his features. I had thought that since his recognition by Rome his cares would be lessened, but he seemed more than ever depressed.

"Beloved daughter, I have melancholy news," Father said at last.

"Yes?" I whispered, tension gripping me.

"It is Rome!" Father cried out in anguish. "Rome!"

I threw my arms around his neck. "What is it, Father?" I asked.

Tears filled his eyes and his lips struggled to form the words. "They have annexed . . . Cyprus!"

"Cyprus?" I asked, stunned. "Annexed Cyprus?"

"Yes!" Father cried, struggling off the couch and restlessly moving back and forth. "Cato, that troublesome fellow, did it. He went to Cyprus and annexed the island on some flimsy excuse."

"And Uncle Ptolemy?" I asked with alarm. "What have they done to Uncle Ptolemy?" My heart stopped, waiting for the answer.

"They offered him the post of High Priest at Aphrodite's Temple at Paphos," Father explained.

"You mean they want Uncle Ptolemy to be a king no longer but merely a High Priest?" I asked.

"Yes," my father breathed.

"And Cyprus belongs to Rome?" I cried incredulously.

My father nodded, unable to meet my eyes.

"Will Uncle Ptolemy go to Paphos?"

"No, he refused the post of High Priest."

"Oh, I'm glad he refused," I cried.

My father sat beside me and took my hands in his. I searched his face, knowing he had more to tell me, and I tensed with apprehension.

"My daughter," Father said in a wavering voice, "your beloved uncle, my dear brother, took hemlock and died."

Assaulted by pain and shock, I sobbed heartbrokenly, and my father's arms encircled me and held me close.

"He died a king!" Father cried with pride. "A proud

Ptolemy could not allow himself to become a High Priest in a temple."

"You must avenge his death," I cried. "You must send ships and soldiers to Cyprus and kill Cato!"

"You know I cannot do such a thing," Father said with a sigh. "My hands are tied."

For a long while I cried out my distress. My father gave me a sip of wine to calm me. At last his chamberlain announced Queen Arsinoë, and I struggled to control my emotions in her presence.

"What a pity, Cleopatra," Queen Arsinoë cried airily as she saw me, "that you won't grow up to be Queen of Cyprus. Oh, well, perhaps we can arrange for you to become Queen of Mesopotamia."

Mesopotamia was far from Egypt. She would like to get me as far from Egypt as possible, I thought, if she could not kill me first.

"Thank you for your sympathy, Stepmother," I said.

Father held out his goblet for a servant to refill. "Cyprus gone!" he cried in a broken voice. "The last cornerstone of our empire gone, and now only Egypt proper remains."

"And for how long?" Queen Arsinoë demanded sharply.

My father ignored her, taking deep draughts from his goblet. "Cyprus, with her forests that made our ships, gone," he cried, stumbling around the chamber in a daze. "Cyprus, with her fine young men who became our sailors, and her rich copper mines that went into the minting of our coins, all gone!"

"Why did Rome do this?" I cried out in despair.

"They had no legitimate reason other than the motivation of greed," Arsinoë said. "Six thousand talents for that treaty, and it is worthless." She gave my father a reproachful look. "They will annex Egypt next!"

"Don't speak like that in front of Cleopatra," Father implored.

"She's old enough to understand," Arsinoë said harshly, circling my father like a tigress. "Something will have to be done, Ptolemy!"

43

"Father, you must arrange to have Uncle Ptolemy's body brought back and buried in the Sema," I said tearfully.

"Yes, perhaps the Romans will let me do that," Father said uncertainly.

"If you crawl on your hands and knees and beg them, perhaps they will," Arsinoë said with mockery and reproach. "But then, you do that so well, crawling to the Romans. You've had so much practice."

I trembled, outraged that she spoke to her husband and King in such a fashion. I wanted to lash out at her, but with an effort kept my tongue still.

Queen Arsinoë stood there, giving my father a withering look, and then she swept from the room.

My father, a goblet in his hand, sank wearily onto the couch beside me. He slipped an arm around my shoulders as I cried bitter tears for the handsome, charming uncle who was to have been my husband.

"So you will not be Queen of Cyprus after all," Father said. "The gods in their infinite wisdom are planning a more glorious fate for you than being queen of a mere island."

I vowed, sitting there sobbing, that whatever my destiny, I would use all my ingenuity, whether I would be close to the throne or sitting on it, so that the day would come when Cyprus belonged again to Egypt and my Uncle Ptolemy's death would be avenged.

A ship was sent to Cyprus for the body of Uncle Ptolemy. Cato, who had taken possession of all my uncle's possessions and fortune, released the corpse, and the ship returned with it to Alexandria. My father planned an elaborate funeral with full royal honors.

As my Uncle Ptolemy lay in state, riots broke out in the city. Notices were posted on the public buildings accusing my father of failing his brother in his hour of need. The point that the annexation of Cyprus and my uncle's death were accomplished facts by the time my father found out about them was not mentioned.

On the day of the funeral, a cortege along the boulevards was planned, but a rioting mob congregated in the

44

square in front of the palace. The Macedonian Household Guards broke up the mob, the coffin was taken directly down the Canopic Way to the Sema, and there was no procession.

I remember that night after the funeral sitting with my father in his apartments, listening to the rumbling noise of discontent that came from the crowds that gathered outside the palace.

"The mob is a savage beast," Father declared. "Never underestimate the power of the populace or of Rome. I think if not one, then the other will be the undoing of our house."

The following day the palace soldiers dispersed the mob, but only temporarily. In the days that followed, the soldiers no sooner broke up the crowd in one city square, than it reformed at another section of the city, successively growing more uncontrollable. These demonstrations appeared to be organized and not spontaneous. It became apparent to my father, confronted by this continued unrest in the capital, that he could not hold out against such anarchy.

About two weeks after my Uncle Ptolemy's burial, matters came to an abrupt and decisive head.

My father discovered that rumors were being spread in the city, whipping the people into a frenzy of revolt. Rabble-rousers were saying my father was not fit to reign and that Egypt needed a new government free of the Romans. The instigators were Queen Arsinoë in association with her lover, Theophrastus, a handsome, ambitious young captain in the army. Arsinoë and Theophrastus were hoping to murder my father and raise four-year-old Prince Ptolemy Magus to the throne, with themselves as his regents. Father was informed of the plot by one of his male lovers, who got it from a high-ranking army officer who was close to Theophrastus. My father had never loved Arsinoë, but he was still shocked and hurt by this turn of events. He responded, however, with deadly calm and swift action.

With a strong select band of guards, Father went to

the Queen's apartments, catching her unaware. He confronted her with the plot. Arsinoë vehemently denied the charges, but my father knew she was lying, and without further ado, he ordered one of his big Germans to run her through. The queen ran hysterically from the German, who backed her into a corner and with his flashing sword hacked her to pieces.

I was in my apartments at my studies when this momentous, grisly event occurred.

Apollodorus suddenly rushed in without even being announced.

"Queen Arsinoë is dead!" he cried, his face flushed.

"The gods have avenged my mother!" I cried ecstatically. After five years, a twist of fate had aborted my stepmother's career as Queen.

I immediately took a purse of rich incense to the small temple in my apartments and threw handfuls of it on the altar fire. I watched the incense burn, and the pungent fumes filled my nostrils. I prostrated myself on the floor and said a prayer of gratitude. When I was finished, I returned to my reception room.

"How did this come about, Apollodorus?" I cried.

Protarchus and I listened raptly as Apollodorus gave us the details, right down to the macabre finish.

Within the hour I was called to my father's chamber, and I went there with Protarchus and Apollodorus. I found Father in a state of agitation. Pandemonium reigned as servants rushed about, packing trunks in preparation for my father to leave the country. His train of male favorites were hysterical. From outside we could hear the ominous roar of the rioting mob.

To my chagrin, I also found Pothinos the Prime Minister hovering anxiously about my father. Somehow Pothinos had saved himself. He had my father wrapped around his fat little finger. I will never believe that Pothinos did not have a hand in my stepmother's schemes, if indeed he had not been the master mind behind them; but somehow he had escaped all implication. A kinsman of Queen Arsinoë, he had been the architect of her advancement, but in her downfall he emerged unscathed. My father had always trusted him, for reasons which I could never fathom.

"O Sacred Radiance, rest assured that Theophrastus will be arrested and executed!" Pothinos cried.

I made my way toward my father, who was sitting on a couch with a goblet in his hand.

"O Father my King!" I cried, bending a knee to him, and then throwing myself into his arms.

"Cleopatra, my darling daughter!" Father cried.

"Where are you going?" I asked anxiously.

"To Rome," Father replied. "I must, my child."

"But why must you go?" I implored.

"If I stay, I will be murdered," Father said with a grimace. "I am being deposed by rebellion that Arsinoë stirred up. There is a fever running high against me among the scurvy mob that will prove fatal if I linger. Only half the debt to Pompey and Caesar has been paid, so they are bound to intervene with force on my behalf if they want to collect the debit. I'll return with Roman legions to maintain order, and in the meantime my two eldest daughters will be my regents."

My oldest sister, Princess Cleopatra Tryphaina, who was then twenty-one, came forward. "Rest assured, beloved Father, that Berenice and I will hold the throne secure for you during your absence."

"Yes, Father, we will," Princess Berenice Barsine said staunchly.

My eyes darted to Berenice, standing not far away beside Diomedes, her crafty foster father and tutor. I did not trust either of these two.

I turned back to my father, embracing him. "Oh, Father, please take me with you," I pleaded.

"No, you must stay and continue your studies with Protarchus," he said.

Servants brought forth trays of food, but none of us could do more than nibble at a few bites.

"See to it that the late Queen is quietly yet honorably buried in the Sema," Father told his two eldest daughters. "After all, she was of Ptolemy descent and a consecrated queen, and the mother of three of my children."

47

A report was circulated among the mob that my father had been killed in a palace revolt. This was a ruse to conceal his flight. He disguised himself as a Persian merchant, wearing a robe of many colors, as did the dozen of his male favorites who were going into exile with him.

At midnight my father took leave of us.

"Father, I wish I could go with you!" I cried.

"I will be back in two months," he assured me.

I burst into tears, embracing my father with desperation.

My father left the palace with his friends by a secret passageway that took them out onto the harbor, and there under heavy guard he made his way to the ship that would sail to Rome.

An hour later I stood on the terraced balcony with my sisters and our attendants, and we watched the ship sail away. My heart was heavy with foreboding and I sobbed quietly.

My beloved sister, Cleopatra Tryphaina, came up to me. "Don't cry, Cleopatra," she said soothingly, putting her arms around me. "Our father will return soon, and in the meantime, we will take care of you. Won't we, dear Berenice?"

Berenice was standing some distance away beside Diomedes. Their heads were bent close together in urgent whisperings, and Berenice did not hear her older sister's entreaty.

I stopped crying, staring at Berenice, sensing some of the thoughts that were spinning through her head. I was just a child, but I already possessed a divine ability to perceive the thoughts of others.

A multitude of stars glittered in the sky. The night wind had a searing edge as it blew sharply in from the sea. The gulls overhead with their raucous screeching grated on my nerves. I could barely hear the whispering tides on which seaweed rocked against the palace walls below, which at night generally was pleasant music to my ears. On this night, however, the roar of the mob came from the square in front of the palace, drowning out the sound of the sea, although not the thumping beat of my own wretched heart.

Once again my father was leaving me, and I was in a state of shock and savage distress. I looked out at the ship, vaguely outlined under the pale radiance of the moon, as it carried my father away. The future loomed ahead, dangerous and uncertain. Although I was only eleven years old, I knew I would have to put aside all my childish tears and meet the future with all the wits and composure of an adult.

CHAPTER III

THE INSURRECTION IN ALEXANDRIA ceased as soon as my father, King Ptolemy, left the country. A rumor he had put forth that he had been murdered in a palace revolt concealed his flight to Rome, but within a few days the truth leaked out. Although the citizens were no longer rioting, they were still restless, and the palace was a confused court divided by conflicting cabals, factions, and intrigues. I thought it best to stay out of the current of affairs, and so I kept in my apartments with Protarchus and immersed myself in my studies.

About a week after my father's flight, my beloved sister, the Princess Cleopatra Tryphaina, came to my chambers.

"I wish to have a privy talk with you, dear sister," she said.

I left Protarchus and took my sister into my bed-chamber, closing the doors after us. We sat on the bed and clasped hands. I was eleven and she was twenty-one; yet as we sat there, it was as if I were the adult and she the child. I was calm while she was distraught, her hands twisting in mine and tears spilling over her eyes.

"Oh, Cleopatra, I am so unhappy," she cried. "Diomedes has seized control of the regency council. Pothinos is out of power and has fled the palace in fear of death."

"I thank the gods," I cried ecstatically. "I hate Pothinos, for he was responsible for the fate of our mother."

"Diomedes and the other councillors and the city fathers say that to bring stability to the kingdom a new course of action must be adopted," she cried nervously, "and they urge Berenice and me to take the crown."

I was speechless, yet not surprised, for I had discussed such a possible turn of events with Protarchus.

"I argued that we should be our father's regents," my sister went on, her words rushed and frantic. "They insist that Father be formally deposed and that Berenice and I commence a joint reign. This will be a betrayal of our father! I told them if they are bent on deposing Father, they should crown Ptolemy Magus, but Berenice insists that he is too young to rule and the state of emergency demands mature sovereigns. Even though you are so young, Cleopatra, you are well beyond your years in wisdom. What should I do?"

"Take the crown, dear sister," I said calmly.

She gasped, her eyes enlarging with shock.

"If you don't, Berenice will take the throne on her own. When Father returns, you need only to abdicate and turn the crown back to him. You will be taking it under duress now, and Father will understand."

"I can't betray Father like this!" she protested.

"It is the only way to preserve the crown for our father," I cried. "Berenice has no qualms, does she?"

"No, she is eagerly accepting the crown."

"And so must you, so don't efface yourself with such timidity, Cleopatra Tryphaina," I said urgently. "Assert yourself. You have no other choice."

After some time I convinced her of the wisdom of accepting the crown under the prevailing conditions, and she left me somewhat composed and reluctantly resolved to accept her fate.

The very next day there was a ceremony in the Great Hall to declare my father's dethronement and the succession of his two eldest daughters. I decided to feign sickness and stay abed that day.

By midmorning a courtier came from Berenice to convey the message that I was to take part in the proceedings. Protarchus explained I was too ill, and the courtier went back to inform Berenice of this.

I lay abed, closing my eyes, willing the hateful day to be done with.

I was soon alarmed at the stamping of soldiers' feet

in the corridor leading to my apartments. Diomedes, with the soldiers to reinforce his order, came into my reception room and encountered Protarchus. Diomedes brushed him aside and marched into my bedchamber, advancing to my bed and glaring down at me.

"Princess Cleopatra, you are to appear in the Great Hall to take your part in the ceremony which will proclaim your sisters as Queens of Egypt and pay them obeisance." His thin lips curled with diabolical satisfaction. "Either that, or you shall be escorted into a new chamber in the dungeons." He gave a slight bow toward me. "The choice is yours, O Princess."

With that he turned and abruptly left my apartments.

Protarchus rushed into my bedchamber, his hands twisting frantically. "Please, O Princess, do as your sister commands. Your father will know that your heart was not in today's doings."

With reluctance, I got out of bed, took some nourishment, and allowed my ladies to robe me in rich royal raiment and to adorn my head with the gold coronet which signified my rank.

The whole court was assembled in the Great Hall. When I arrived, a herald proclaimed my entrance, and I was the last to appear. As I walked down the center of the Great Hall, my head held high, all the courtiers and soldiers bowed.

My two sisters sat on the two golden thrones under the canopy of state, with royal fan-bearers and high officials grouped at their sides. I approached the thrones and sank to one knee. I saw Berenice give me a gelid glare for my tardiness.

"Pray rise, Sister Princess," Cleopatra Tryphaina said in the sweet, soft voice that recalled our mother's.

I rose and went to stand beside Aunt Aliki.

Trumpets blasted, and then Diomedes, who was now Prime Minister, stepped in front of my sisters, facing the assemblage.

"Nobles, soldiers, citizens!" Diomedes declaimed sonorously. "Egypt has endured twenty-one years of the crimes and misrule of Ptolemy the Twelfth, during which our affairs have deteriorated. Under his reign we have seen the collapse of our empire and our government replaced by anarchy. The people have revolted under these wretched conditions and are clamoring for a new government. The King has abandoned his throne, his country, and his people. The Egyptian people now formally depose King Ptolemy, and on this day a new era begins with the joint reign of Queen Berenice the Fourth and Queen Cleopatra the Sixth!"

The High Priest of Karnak came forward in his colorful robes. He faced my sisters, shaking on his old, frail legs. "Do you, Cleopatra Tryphaina and Berenice Barsine, accept the sacred crowns of Upper and Lower Egypt?" he asked in a croaking voice.

"I do!" Berenice cried affirmatively.

There was a silence while all eyes focused on Cleopatra Tryphaina.

"I do," she whispered faintly, staring at the floor.

"Long live Queen Berenice! Long live Queen Cleopatra!"

The whole assemblage echoed the words in one great voice as trumpets blared and cymbals clashed.

I was the first, as the highest ranking princess of the realm, to be led to the thrones and to sink to my knees and pledge an oath of fealty. After me came my little half-sister, Arsinoë, and then Aunt Aliki. My two half-brothers, Ptolemy Magus, who was five, and Ptolemy Philippos, who was four, had been kept in the apartments they shared. Diomedes had thought it best to keep these two princes out of sight and not on display while their rights were being usurped, for under Ptolemaic law a queen could only rule with a male co-sovereign.

Berenice, not quite eighteen, accepted the honors and powers of a monarch with overweening arrogance. She established herself in our father's apartments and enjoyed laying down the laws of the two lands. She was surrounded by her cabal led by Diomedes. She made certain that the least homage due the sovereign was punctiliously paid her. On the other hand, Cleopatra Tryphaina, being meek and mild, was pushed aside and stayed in her own apartments and took little part in the administrations of government.

"If my father does not return soon," I said to Protarchus, "how many months do you give Cleopatra?"

Protarchus thought a moment. "Six," he replied.

I shuddered, my heart rebelling at the thought, but I knew Protarchus was probably right.

"Yes, Cleopatra will never be able to match wits with Berenice," I said sadly. "Poor Cleopatra is a sweet little mouse."

"And Berenice?" Protarchus asked.

"Berenice is a rat," I replied.

I could only pray for my father's speedy return.

My father had been gone about two months and I had received no news of him, and then one day I was commanded into the presence of Queen Berenice. Apollodorus and a dozen soldiers escorted me along the corridors to Berenice's apartments. I found her at my father's large ivory and ebony desk, with several scrolls and state papers laid out in confusion before her.

As protocol demanded, I knelt at the entrance and then walked up to her and knelt again.

"Dearest Sister Queen!" I said, kissing the outstretched hand bearing the ring of state.

"Greetings, dear sister," Berenice said in a cold, haughty voice. She motioned for me to take a chair near her. "How are you faring with your studies?"

"I try to do all that my tutors demand of me."

"Oh, yes, we all know what a little scholar you are," she said with a tinge of jealousy since she herself had never been scholastically gifted and rarely unrolled a scroll.

"How is our sister, Queen Cleopatra?" I asked.

"She is in her apartments with her ladies and gives me no help!" Berenice cried with feigned irritation. "We are supposed to be joint monarchs, yet I do all the work while she does her looming. All by myself I am carrying out the sacred duties that our father shamelessly abandoned."

I could not find words to vouchsafe that.

"Some pomegranate juice, Cleopatra?" Berenice asked.

"Oh, yes, I am thirsty, Sister," I said.

Queen Berenice poured the juice into two goblets and handed me one. As we sipped, I noticed a satisfied smile playing about the corners of her mouth, so I knew she had news to tell me which would be good for her but bad for me.

"I have tidings of our father!" Berenice cried.

The goblet trembled in my hands, but with a great effort I showed no expression on my face.

"I am so ashamed of our father, Cleopatra," she cried with relish. "On leaving Alexandria, Father put his ship in at Rhodes harbor and discovered that Cato was lodged there. Cato, by the way, had all Uncle Ptolemy's treasure of seven thousand talents in gold, his gold plate and collection of jewels, all carted onto Roman ships and sent back to Rome. Our beloved father, finding Cato in Rhodes, decided to curry favor with him." She glanced sharply at me. "Drink your pomegranate juice, Cleopatra, it's good for you."

"Oh, yes," I said, obediently taking a sip.

"Where was I?" Berenice asked absently.

"Our father was at Rhodes."

"Yes, well, Father sent Cato a message to inform him of his arrival, supposing that Cato would hasten to such a great personage as the King of Egypt. Cato, however, was not impressed and sent a messenger saying he had no business with Egypt's King." Berenice gave a short, bitter laugh. "Cato added that if the King had business with him, he could come and see him. Father was obliged to repress his resentment, and he went to the fortress palace overlooking Rhodes harbor. Cato did not rise when our father entered his chamber, but remained seated on his toilet, explaining that he had just taken a laxative."

My innards gnarled to think that my father could be so badly treated. After all, although suffering a temporary reversal of fortune, he was still king in the eyes of the gods. My sister closely watched the emotions that played on my face, which I could not conceal.

56

"Our father," Berenice resumed drawlingly, "then made some silly statement of his case, hoping to obtain Cato's influence with the Roman Senate to interpose in his behalf. Cato, far from displaying any such disposition, censured him for having abandoned his kingdom and told Father he could do nothing in Rome but by the influence of bribes. Cato advised Father to return to Alexandria and rely on his hopes of extricating himself from his problems by the exercise of his own wits."

Berenice smiled triumphantly while I digested this information.

"Is Father coming back?" I asked.

"Don't be ridiculous, Cleopatra!" Berenice snapped. "Father was abashed at Cato's rebuff, but he knows if he returns to Egypt he will be torn to pieces by the people, so he and his party went on to Naples. They will soon arrive in Rome, but I don't think it will do any good. I've sent an ambassador to inform the Senate that he has been deposed and that new monarchs reign. I doubt if Father will get any help, for Caesar is busy conquering Gaul and Pompey is exhausted after his campaigns in Asia Minor. Don't you feel shame for our father, Cleopatra? How could he debase himself to Cato, the conqueror of Cyprus, the man who was responsible for the death of his brother and your future husband?"

She glared at me, waiting for a response.

"Aren't you ashamed of our father?" she insisted.

"A king must do what he must do," I replied.

"He is no longer a king!" Berenice rejoined sharply. "By the will of the people he has been deposed."

With great effort I stilled my tongue. I itched to utter the words that only the gods and death could alter the sacred state of a king.

Berenice sighed impatiently. "I know that you love him, but you must accept the facts, Cleopatra. Why, I've been going through the state papers and if the gods give me fifty years to reign I will not be able to correct all the follies he committed. He is an object of universal scorn because of his crimes, which forced his ignoble flight. As King for twenty-one years he was never concerned with the welfare of his kingdom, but only with his degenerate habits and playing the flute. You're young, but you're old enough to know about the vices of our father that brought scorn to our royal house."

"I know nothing about these things," I said obstinately. "I know only about my studies and books."

Berenice realized she could not undermine my love for my father nor break my will, and she gave a sigh. "There is an old Macedonian saying, Cleopatra," she said in a smug, reflective voice. " 'A man must drink the bitter brew he concocts.' That is what our father is doing now, and he has no one to blame but himself."

"By your royal leave," I begged, "I wish to go back to my studies now, dearest sister."

"You may go," Berenice said briskly.

"Give my love to my sister, Queen Cleopatra," I said, to remind her that she was not the only queen around. I sank to one knee and kissed her hand.

"Oh, by the way," Berenice said brightly, "do you have your dress ready for the coronation?"

"Yes," I replied.

"Oh, what a glorious coronation it will be!" Berenice said radiantly. "The people are happy at the prospect of my reign, a new era for Egypt!"

The coronation the following week, officiated by the High Priest of Karnak, was a splendid affair, even though it had been hastily arranged to firmly establish the reign of my sisters. I revel in pomp, yet it was with misgivings that I lent myself to the proceedings. After the coronation in the Great Hall, we were all carried in our litters through the streets of Alexandria in stately splendor. The populace screamed in wild acclamation, intoxicated by the pageantry.

Berenice and Diomedes were hoping that the coronation would be the final definition of my father's downfall, and when the news reached Rome it would impede his hopes for a restoration.

In the months that followed I rarely saw either of my sister sovereigns.

It was through Protarchus that I learned that my father arrived safely in Rome. Caesar was in Gaul, so Pompey was the great leader in the capitol. My father was on friendly terms with Pompey, having sent him a squadron of cavalry to Syria four years before. Pompey had also received a generous portion of the bribe which my father paid Caesar for the Roman alliance, and would receive the remainder in case my father was restored. Pompey received my father as a royal fugitive with respectful honors, and took immediate measures to urge the Senate to effect my father's restoration as an ally whom they were honor bound to protect against his rebellious daughters and subjects.

I prayed fervently to the gods that my father would have a swift return, but I soon realized that his restoration would not be effected overnight.

My sister Berenice, meanwhile, with her arrogant assumption of authority, had firm control of the government with Diomedes at her side.

I kept to my apartments during this time with my foster father, Protarchus. My household was quite large and took up one great wing of the palace, and consisted of a whole staff of tutors, eunuchs, and slaves, and my Macedonian Household Guards under Apollodorus. I devoted my days to studies of the arts and sciences, and pondered the why and wherefore of things. I was also learning about the grim realities of being a princess, with the insidious turnings of royal statecraft and the shiftings of power. The harrowing experiences and events of my childhood had given me a stern, harsh education.

At least once a week I visited my Aunt Aliki in her apartments and we would play chess. I could have won every time, but I was careful to allow her to win every other game. As we played, she would stuff herself with dates and sweetmeats and drink wine and whisper advice.

"Stay out of palace politics," she would say softly so her ladies in the far corners could not hear. "Keep away from a cabal. Protarchus is wise, but don't let him organize a cabal in your behalf, for while a cabal can conspire to raise you up, it can also smash you down."

"Protarchus has no such ambitions, Aunt Aliki."

"Keep it that way. Curb your spirit and insolence. Exercise your impertinence with impunity in the long time ahead while your father will be away."

"How long will he be gone, do you think?" I asked.

"Only the gods know, but meanwhile, keep your nose in books," Aunt Aliki advised. "Wait and watch and see."

Many courtiers thought Aunt Aliki was simple and stupid, that she cared only for sweets and wine and poppy juice. Like my father and many Ptolemies, she had a dependency on the Dionysian grape, but she only pretended to be a dense dullard, for she was actually astute. I strongly suspect that it was her pretense of puerility which had been her life-saver.

I loved my visits with her. We would sit for hours, playing chess and chatting. In many ways she was like my mother, and this was one of the reasons why I felt deep affection for her. On the other hand, Protarchus represented a father figure for me, while Apollodorus was an older brother every girl should have.

I wrote letters to my father, and in pursuance of my father's policy of cultivating friendly relations with Pompey, I did my part by writing a letter to him. I wanted Pompey to know that not all members of the house of Lagos were pleased with the new royal regime in Alexandria.

"Salutations, dearest Uncle Gnaeus," I wrote Pompey, adopting him there and then as my honorary uncle. "I am pleased to know that my beloved father the King of Egypt and his friends are with you. I had wanted to accompany Father on his visit to Rome, but he told me I had to stay in Alexandria so that my studies would not be interrupted.

"I send a gold medallion that belonged to my mother, Queen Cleopatra Selene, for your wife, the Lady Cornelia, whose great beauty and wisdom are universally praised.

"The world knows, dearest uncle, that you are a great gentleman with a princely heart, and I am hoping that you will come to Egypt soon so that I may take you with me when I perform my royal duties like feeding the sacred crocodiles, and so that my people may make your august acquaintanceship.

"A daughter of the Lagidae sends an expression of tender love to you and your wife.

"Farewell in affection from Cleopatra, Princess of Egypt."

This letter and the gold medallion were sealed in a scroll and sent in utmost secrecy to Rome, arranged by Protarchus. Later I learned that Pompey took this ingenuous letter about showing it to members of the Senate, reading it at will to one and all. Some thought it charming, while others said it was a sample of shameless servility.

Six months went by before Protarchus gave me a letter from my father, who wrote that he hoped the letter would reach me by my twelfth birthday, but it arrived a few weeks late. I was not to despair, wrote Father, for prospects in Rome looked good and he would soon return to his rightful place in Egypt.

The people of the kingdom, I learned from what my eager ears could pick up, were divided in their allegiance. The priests in Apollionopolis Magna in Upper Egypt refused to accept the fact that my father was no longer king, since he had never abdicated. He had favored them with large funds for the reconstruction of their temple, and they remained loyal to him. Try as Berenice might to denigrate my father's performance as king, she could not deny that it was to his credit that he had restored many of the ancient temples, and these temples in their gratitude still acknowledged him as king. Other parts of the country did favor Berenice, who was indeed queen, holding sway with the government absolutely in her hands.

Until my father had fled, I had always taken part in the court and public ceremonies. I was a pretty and spirited princess, and with my charismatic presence I drew all eyes to me. I reveled in pageantry and carried myself with grace and dignity, behaving with preternatural aplomb. After my father's flight, however, my duties were severely curtailed. Berenice was jealous of me and now had the chance to vent her spleen. Except for ceremonies where protocol demanded that I play my part, I was kept out of the way. No longer was I permitted to feed the crocodiles for the people to see and cheer me. For a princess who had from the cradle loved being in the public eye, this was a bitter deprivation. To compensate, I buried myself in my studies and lessons on the harp and dancing.

As a child I was never fond of other children, and I ignored the children about the palace. Being precocious, I could not endure their immature prattle. I did have spirit and could be full of childish pranks, but only to delight my father. I did not waste my spirits on other children. With those my own age I was apt to be superior and disapproving of their silly games and giggles. I never played in the palace gardens with them, and I preferred the company of adults and books.

Reports from Rome came that under Pompey's blandishments, and my father's promises of bribes, the Senate was determining to restore my father to his throne by force. It was decided the Roman forces stationed in Syria would be used to furnish the troops to effect my father's restoration. When Queen Berenice received these tidings, it sent her into a furor of activity.

One afternoon she summoned me to her presence.

"I have decided, Cleopatra," she explained, "that Rome should have the opportunity of hearing our side of the story and to know that the Egyptian people were justified in dethroning this perfidious king. I'm sending a deputation of one hundred people, some of the highest of the land, to lay our case before the Senate. This distinguished delegation will be led by the great philosopher, Dion."

Dion was merely a tenth-rate philosopher, but I did not argue the point. "Oh, how wonderful!"

"I am also sending Protarchus with this delegation," she added with a malicious smile.

My heart stopped at the thought of Protarchus being

taken away from me, leaving me defenseless. Apollodorus had vowed to commit daring feats in my defense, but he was only seventeen. I was afraid that Berenice would effect my death if Protarchus was no longer at my side.

In the fury of my fright, I threw myself at her feet, clutching her ankles. "Please, Berenice, don't take Protarchus away from me," I sobbed. "He is all I have now that Mother is dead and Father gone."

"You have me!" Berenice cried viciously.

"But you have Egypt and can spare so little time for me."

"You have Aunt Aliki."

"But Protarchus is my tutor—"

"You have an army of tutors!"

"But Protarchus is my wisest of tutors, and you know how much my studies mean to me. Without Protarchus my learning would suffer. Please, dearest sister, don't take Protarchus away from me!"

"Get up and regain your dignity!" Berenice cried.

I picked myself off the marble floor and resumed my chair, sobbing. Tears never came easily to me, but they flowed that day.

"I cannot stand tears, Cleopatra, stop it!"

Mustering all my control, I stopped crying. "Besides, dearest sister," I said in a quavering voice, thinking fast, "although Protarchus has sworn fealty to you, you know how fond he is of Father, and I do not think his heart would be in this mission." I saw her turning this thought over in her head, that she did not want Protarchus in the delegation if he were to sow seeds to undermine it. "That is why," I resumed, "you must be certain that all the delegates are your loyal subjects, so not one of them will defect to our father when they arrive in Rome."

"You give me sage counsel, Cleopatra, you clever little bitch!" Berenice said grudgingly. "All right, Protarchus can stay."

My heart lightened. "Thank you, dearest sister!"

In Rome my father had taken a villa on the Tiber and he and his entourage lived lavishly, accumulating a host

63

of debts. A syndicate was formed, composed of a group of financiers who pledged to put my father back on the throne, so that they might have their monies returned at interest.

At last the assemblage of one hundred persons left Alexandria, taking with them a long list of crimes my father had supposedly committed. My father hired ruffians to waylay the deputation when they debarked at the Bay of Naples. More than half of the delegates were slain. Those who survived were bought off by bribes when they reached Rome. The remaining envoys were so intimidated by the dangers which surrounded them that they did not dare take any public action to accomplish the business which Berenice had committed to their charge. I was happy to learn that my father had circumvented Berenice in all her efforts, and I was also overjoyed that Protarchus had not been included in the delegation, for he might have been among those murdered.

The assassinations of the envoys created a scandal in Rome. The Senate discussed the matter and wanted to question the leading delegate, Dion, but then Dion was murdered in the street the night before he was to appear.

My father, afraid of repercussions, and assured by Pompey and his syndicate that his affairs would be dealt with favorably, quit Rome and with his small retinue took ship and sailed east to Ephesus. He took up residence in a small villa in the sacred groves of Artemis and settled down to await the outcome of his affairs in Rome.

Queen Berenice called me to her apartments one day soon after news of all these events had reached our ears. She was now nineteen and I was twelve. A year had passed since her illegal assumption of the crown, and she was becoming increasingly arrogant with her growing powers.

"What are you studying now, Cleopatra?" she asked.

"Aristotle," I replied. "I'm reading the lectures he gave at the Lyceum on ethics, epistemology, aesthetics, and history."

"How interesting," she said, slightly bored. "Didn't Plato teach Alexander?"

"No, Plato taught Aristotle, and then Aristotle taught Alexander."

"Oh, yes, I get all of that mixed up," she cried.

"It was Alexander who told Aristotle that he would rather excel in learning than in riches or power."

"But then Alexander went on to conquer the world," Berenice cried. "That much history I know."

"Yes, he was forced to obey the call of destiny."

Berenice gave me a penetrating look with her blue eyes. "What do you want out of life, Cleopatra?"

"To live for the pursuit of intellectual investigation," I said.

"Indeed!" Berenice cried, giving me a skeptical look. She tapped the Great Seal possessively on top of the desk. "I suppose you know the latest news of our father."

I sat looking blank under her scrutinizing stare.

"Father realized that in Rome he could do nothing," she continued. "His creditors ran him out of town, and he went off to Ephesus. You can write him there. I know that you send him letters. I am Queen, and it is my business to know everything that goes on in Egypt! I have no objections to your writing him. You were always his favorite, and if a few lines from you can cheer his wretched heart, I certainly would not mind."

"That is very kind of you, dearest sister."

"Our banished father, I'm sure, will be happy in the lovely old city of Ephesus. As long as he has wine to drink, a flute to play, and a bevy of beautiful boys, he will be content. I am even considering, over the heated objections of my councillors, in sending him a pension."

"That would be most generous of you, sister."

"But I will only send the pension if he signs a deed of abdication which my ministers have drawn up."

I knew my father would never do that, even at the point of a sword, but remained silent.

"Our poor father is such a pathetic creature," Berenice resumed gloatingly. "Let us pray he will find peace in his last days at Ephesus. He is forty-three but old

65

beyond his years, and the way he drinks he surely is in the final stage of his life. Egypt is better off without him. I am bringing order to Egypt. You do think I'm doing an admirable job of being Queen, don't you, Cleopatra?"

"Yes, admirable," I said faintly. "The gods are pleased."

"All Egypt is pleased!" Berenice gave me a look of unmitigated hatred. "Well, back to your studies, Cleopatra, and I must return to my royal duties."

I knelt at her feet and kissed her ring. "Dear Sister Queen, how is our beloved sister, Queen Cleopatra? I have not seen her these last months."

"I rarely see her myself, I'm so busy with affairs of state," Berenice answered vaguely. "I trust she fares well with her spinning."

"I should like permission to visit her," I said.

"Send a message begging audience," Berenice said. "I am sure she will give you leave."

I did send a message to my sister Cleopatra Tryphaina requesting an audience, but I was not to receive a reply. Instead, a few days afterward I was informed that she was dead.

Protarchus had predicted at the beginning of the reigns of my sisters that Cleopatra would last only six months, but she survived a whole year before death struck. Berenice then, full of hubris in her sovereignty, did away with her sibling and joint monarch. I have never known by what means Cleopatra's death was accomplished. That last year of her life I saw her only a few times at ceremonial or religious rituals, where stiff protocol permitted only the briefest exchanges. I had sensed her doom was imminent, since Berenice in her ascendency would not tolerate her. Out of love for her I had wanted to do something to prevent her death, but I was just a child and quite powerless. When Protarchus informed me of her death, great was my grief but not my astonishment. I prayed to the high gods that she would have a peaceful life in the Infernal Kingdom, that she had joined our mother, and that she had not known pain at the moment of death.

Berenice issued a proclamation saying that Cleopatra had died suddenly from a feverish pox.

The corpse wore a serene smile, the same smile that our mother had worn seven years before in death.

I wept at the bier, but Berenice outdid me in her show of grief. Indeed, she outdid the professional mourners in her hysterical wailings. The people believed these demonstrations of lament were genuine and did not suspect that she had any responsibility in the demise of her sister Queen.

There was a procession of the royal cortege along the boulevards of Alexandria. A platoon of marching soldiers led the way, followed by a group of priests, and then the litter, draped in black and mourning wreaths, which bore the corpse. Berenice was carried in a litter directly behind the one bearing the coffin. My litter, which I shared with Aunt Aliki, followed after, with my brothers and then the nobles of the court bringing up the rear. Great crowds held back by soldiers lined the sidewalks, and shouts of sorrow punctuated the sad, sunny day.

Suddenly a strong male voice cried out, as my litter passed him, "There goes the golden hope of Egypt!"

I knew that he did not mean my lovely simpleton of an aunt, the Princess Aliki. No, he meant me! My heart was warmed, but only for an instant before cold terror struck, almost paralyzing me, for Queen Berenice, being carried just in front of me, surely heard those words.

The procession wound itself at last into the Sema, and I watched the coffin consigned into the crypt alongside our mother's.

Cleopatra Selene had lived to be twenty-two. I had just turned twelve. I wondered if I would live to be thirteen.

According to the matriarchal system of Egyptian royalty, I had become the all-important heiress to the throne. If my father should come back and be reinstated, he would surely do away with Berenice, and then my young brothers and I would be the heirs. There were two things I had to hope and pray for, that my father would be restored, and that until that time arrived I would somehow miraculously survive. The mortality rate among the Lagidae was increasing. I had robust health, yet that was no guarantee that I would live.

With a mere nod, Queen Berenice could seal the doom of the "golden hope of Egypt." It was a sobering thought for a twelve-year-old princess to entertain.

CHAPTER IV

AS TIME WENT BY Queen Berenice thought that her position would be strengthened by a marriage and her successorship settled with a son, so she sought a royal prince from a neighboring realm for a husband. At first she set her sights on a Syrian prince. Although the Seleucid dynasty had been deposed by Pompey some six years before, there were still several princes in Syria, sons of the late Antiochus the Great. These princes were the grandsons of Queen Cleopatra of Syria, who had been born a Ptolemaic princess, and so they were our cousins.

Berenice sent ambassadors to the eldest, Prince Philippos, making proposals of marriage. Philippos was about to accept, but was warned off by the Roman general, Gabinius, Proconsul of Syria. Gabinius pointed out to Philippos that plans were being hatched in Rome to restore my father, and once that happened, it would be the end of Berenice, so these negotiations fell through. I thought it a point well taken by Philippos.

"No honorable prince will have her," Aunt Aliki told me over the chessboard. "She has usurped the throne. She may end up an old maid like me!" She giggled wickedly at this thought.

My sister persevered and finally contracted a marriage with Prince Seleukos, a nephew of King Antiochus. It was said that this prince's mother had been a concubine. The envoys pointed out to my sister that Seleukos was not handsome, was feeble in intellect, and was considered a fool in Syria.

"I will do it for Egypt!" Berenice told Diomedes.

Berenice was frantic to have a husband, and Seleukos was a Seleucidae and partially royal, if not the son of a king. She wanted a royal stud, and his lack of looks and wit was an asset, since she fancied the idea of a husband who would be pliable to her will. Diomedes also wanted her to have a husband without character so that his influence over her would not be diluted.

It was during the summer equinox of my twelfth year when Prince Seleukos came to Alexandria to marry my sister. Berenice had prepared herself that he would not be a prince among princes, yet once he came into court and she met him face to face, she could not camouflage her chagrin. I was there and witnessed the encounter.

The bridegroom, about twenty-five years old, was short with thin, spindly legs, and his stomach protruded against his chiton like that of a pregnant woman. As for his face, Praxiteles would never have been inspired to sculpt it, for the gods had not chiseled the features with classical harmony. He had the constant grin of an idiot, which revealed rotten teeth. The Alexandrians, up to their old tricks, immediately dubbed him Seleukos the Saltfishmonger, and it was true, any fish vendor in the harbor market was more prepossessing in personality and looks than Seleukos.

Mustering her courage, Berenice married Seleukos, making him King of Egypt. Egypt had an idiot for a king.

At the wedding banquet in the Great Hall, the table manners of the King proved to be as atrocious as his looks. The bride and bridegroom, sitting on the royal dais, ignored one another as they broke the loaf of wedding bread and satiated themselves with food and wine. Seleukos made more noise while masticating than the sacred crocodiles at their time of feeding. The courtiers could barely conceal their amusement at the turn of events, and my sister could not disguise her disgust.

Diomedes at length whispered into Berenice's ear.

"The things I must do for Egypt!" she cried.

Gathering her strength, the Queen led her husband to her bedchamber, which was strewn with roses.

All the guests stayed at their couches in the Great Hall, gorging themselves and waiting until, as was the custom, the blood-spattered bridal sheets would be displayed at dawn. In the meantime, dancers and acrobats performed, Nubian slaves served golden plates heaped with delicacies, and the best wines flowed. There was much tittering among the guests about the spectacle that surely must be going on in the bridal bedchamber.

"Let us pray to the gods that tonight a future king of Egypt is being conceived!" Diomedes cried, raising his wine goblet.

Everyone at the banquet had to dutifully drink to that, even I.

Suddenly, an officer of the Queen's Guards rushed frantically into the hall and ran up and whispered to Diomedes, who blanched at whatever tidings he was given and ran with the officer out of the hall in the direction of the queen's chambers. Several of the courtiers followed in hot, curious pursuit. At the portal of the queen's chamber, only Diomedes was admitted, while guards barred the way against the others.

There was pandemonium in the palace. Protarchus suspected that grave circumstances were afoot, and with Apollodorus we hurried to my apartments to stay under heavy guard until the cause of the consternation surfaced.

Later I was to learn, as was all of Alexandria, then Egypt, and finally the world, what occurred that fateful night in my sister's bedchamber.

Berenice had taken her husband into her bed, and he became outraged to discover there was no royal maidenhead to break, that indeed another man had been given this precious prize which he considered his right. Seleukos called his bride vile names in a drunken fury, and savagely struck her. Berenice screamed and called out for Aristonicus to enter.

Aristonicus, the captain of the Queen's Household Guards, stood sentry outside her door. He was a young and handsome Greek who performed the same duties for Berenice as Apollodorus did for me. Well, perhaps not precisely, since it was whispered that he was overzealous in his duties and performed some that were not prescribed by his position. Moreover, it was rumored that it was probably Aristonicus who had broken the sacred hymen whose loss so infuriated Seleukos. All this could be mere court gossip, however, and I cannot vouch for its veracity.

On entering the bedchamber on the command of his Queen, Aristonicus found Seleukos naked and storming around the bed and breaking precious objects.

"Strike him through!" Berenice commanded.

Aristonicus drew out his sword. Seleukos, horrified as Aristonicus approached, jumped onto the bed and threw himself into the arms of his bride. Aristonicus jumped onto the bed in deadly pursuit. Seleukos, clutching Berenice, screamed for mercy. Aristonicus, careful not to harm his Queen, relentlessly bore down and pointed the edge of the sword on the protuberant bare belly of the bridegroom. There was an anguished scream that echoed through the palace as the blade was driven home into the bowels. The sword was withdrawn. Seleukos screamed, his hands clutching his raw, gaping wound. The half foot of steel was then plunged with a definitive thrust into the victim's heart, there was one final death cry, and then silence. King Seleukos was dead.

On her wedding night, the Queen's bed was covered with blood. It was the custom for a virgin queen to display her bloody bedclothes after her nuptial night, some witty courtier observed, but Queen Berenice was carrying things too far.

I was twelve years old, but this scandalous incident did not shock me, for I had already been exposed to some appalling events.

"I had to have him killed," Berenice told me after the funeral. "He struck me several times and wanted me to perform the most unspeakable acts of perversion, things that you are too young to understand."

"I understand, dear sister," I said consolingly.

"Now I must find a new king," she said fretfully.

"Why don't you marry the elder of our brothers,

72

Prince Ptolemy Magus?" I suggested, trying to be helpful.

"He is only ten years old. Would you have me wither on the vine until the marriage could be consummated?" Her mouth pouted petulantly. "I need a husband now, for Egypt's sake!"

The court took the fatal incident of Seleukos in stride, and many nobles were relieved after the initial shock that Berenice had gotten rid so quickly of one who would have proved to be definitely intolerable.

My sister was undaunted and began searching for a new husband. All Syrian connections were closed to her now, so she sent her ambassadors into Pontus to negotiate a marriage with Prince Mithridates, son of Mithridates the Great.

"If I had two lives to live, I would gladly lay down one for the Queen of Egypt," Prince Mithridates told the Egyptian envoys.

May it duly be noted that this Pontian prince had a ready wit.

Berenice's ambassadors then turned their attentions to Archaelous, a bastard son to Mithridates, born to one of his concubines. There had been several Ptolemaic princesses of Egypt who had married kings of Pontus, so Archaelous claimed a royal connection with our house, and even though he was a bastard, he was still a king's son.

Archaelous had gone over to the Romans before the decisive war, and Pompey took a fancy to him. After Pontus became a province of Rome, Pompey installed Archaelous as the High Priest at the Temple of Komona in Cappadocia. Archaelous, an ambitious man, was willing to give up his religious vocation to be King of Egypt. Berenice thought it was to her advantage to have a husband who was Pompey's protégé. She bade her envoys to instruct Archaelous that she had been married before, and so he was not to expect to find her a maiden lady.

Basically Berenice was a grim and humorless creature, with a surly disposition, but on occasion she could display a dash of drollery.

"I'm going to have a new husband!" she cried.

"Oh, Berenice, I'm so jubilant, for I shall have a new brother," I said.

Archaelous came to Alexandria and married my sister and became King of Egypt. It had been a year since Cleopatra Tryphaina's death, and since then Berenice had been occupied with matrimonial negotiations and that one fatal blunder. Now it appeared all her efforts were crowned with glory. Her second husband was in the acme of manhood, celebrated for his charm of manners, the beauty of his physique, and the eloquence of his words. Berenice was ecstatic with relief and rapture. Even I, fast approaching my thirteenth birthday, and showing my first signs of girlhood, became infatuated with my new brother-in-law.

Everyone at court rejoiced at Berenice's good fortune, with the possible exception of Aristonicus, who took an instant dislike to Archaelous. Not wanting Aristonicus to commit the same deed on her second husband as he had on her first, Bernice had him transferred to the garrison at the city of Crocodilepolis in Upper Egypt.

When Archaelous and I were first presented to one another, he flashed a brilliant smile of pure pleasure. Berenice noticed we liked one another, and this aroused her jealousy. Even though she was a beautiful woman and I a mere child, she was insecure and had always felt threatened by me.

The wedding was performed in the Great Throne Room before a distinguished assemblage of chamberlains, nobles, foreign ambassadors, and brightly garbed attendants. After the ceremony, the bride and bridegroom appeared on the Balcony of Appearances. The great square in front of the palace was filled with Alexandrians anxious to catch a glimpse of their queen and new king.

When I appeared on the balcony, I heard, amid all the shouting, cries of "Cleopatra! Cleopatra!" I had rarely been seen in public of late, and my appearance touched off cheers which displeased Berenice.

That evening at the wedding banquet, I was escorted by a majordomo to a table with Aunt Aliki which was at a great distance from the royal dais. My little sister, Arsinoë, who was seven years old, was seated at a couch adjacent to Berenice's. This was a marked slight to me, a definite sign that I was out of favor.

A sumptuous spread was laid on all the tables before the couches for the guests. Gymnasts and contortionists displayed the wonderful agility and magic of their bodies. Clowns roved about inducing one and all to laughter. A chorus of eunuchs sang songs of gods and heroes, of love and war, and merriment ensued all around.

All through the banquet, Berenice kept sending food from her own plate over to Princess Arsinoë, and also to the couch where my two little half-brothers sat with their tutor, Theodotus of Chios. No special delicacies from the queen's table were sent to me. I do not deny that it was pleasant to be honored for my rank, and distasteful to be slighted. All the eyes of the court were glancing at me. I ate, my face betraying no emotion, but the insult rankled. Berenice made me pay for the cheers I had received that afternoon.

I continued to show Berenice every mark of respect due her rank, usurped though it was, despising her though I did. After all, she had killed our eldest sister and her first husband, so what might she do to me? She had the crown and the authority firmly in her grasp. One word to any guard and it would be the end of me, like poor Seleukos. Berenice had a furious temper, she was neurotic and unpredictable, and sometimes she committed irrational acts. Power had gone to her head. I did not want her impulsively to put an end to her irksome sister.

Berenice definitely wanted me out of the way, yet she hedged on the point. I do not know what saved me in those precarious years, although my prayers and votive offerings surely helped. In my favor was the fact that it dawned on the people that Cleopatra Tryphaina had not died of the pox, but had been murdered, and Berenice was afraid of outraging public opinion by doing away with a second sister. Not only had I been the favorite of my father, for which Berenice had never forgiven me, but as a child I had indisputably been the most popular princess of the royal family. Berenice was forced to let me appear in public on occasion just to let the people know I was alive; and at those events, I was always wildly cheered. She could barely contain her hatred and jealousy of me, but contain it she did, for she never gave the fatal order for my demise; and I have lived to write about it all.

I was aware from the onset that Archaelous was favorably disposed toward me, and this created a complex situation. Since he liked me, he could always intercede on my behalf; but, on the other hand, his liking me could outrage Berenice to the point of murder.

Apollodorus was the captain of my Macedonian Household Guard, which numbered some two hundred soldiers. They all adored me and would lay down their lives for me, and I felt safe under their protection. Apollodorus personally selected these soldiers. They were all young and sturdy and not only excelled in swordsmanship and physical prowess, but were all paragons of masculine beauty. Berenice resented this tiny army I had under my wing, but there was nothing she could do about it since it was my right as a princess. Cleopatra Tryphaina's guards had been lax and cared only for dice, wine, and carnal pleasures. I would not be so easily eliminated as she had been, and with Protarchus and Apollodorus as my adherents, Berenice was wary about bringing me down.

Berenice was happy with Archaelous, and began to feel securely settled on the throne. They began enlarging the fleet and recruited soldiers, preparing to offer resistance to our father in case he attempted to return.

"Pompey has to choose between Ptolemy and Archaelous," Protarchus pointed out to me.

I shrewdly assessed the situation, and did my little bit by smuggling out another fulsome letter to Pompey, with a rich ruby ring as a gift for his wife. As young as I was, I was taking my part in intrigues for position and power.

My sister's marriage did not seemingly daunt my

father's friends at Rome who espoused his cause. His greatest asset became the vast debts he had run up in Rome. The syndicate of Roman businessmen were pledged to get him back on the throne so they might be repaid, and they demanded action.

Pompey was jealous of Caesar's conquests in Gaul, so he decided to lead his armies into Egypt to restore my father himself. He pleaded in the Senate for permission to do this, but he was met with opposition from gangs hired by Caesar, who heaped abuse on him during his speech. Pompey was forbidden to intervene on my father's behalf by a resolution of the Senate. Meanwhile, my father waited at Ephesus.

One day a few months after Berenice's marriage, I was commanded to her presence for a noontime meal. I was hoping to find Archaelous there, but Berenice sat alone surrounded by her ladies. I bent my knee and kissed her hand, and she bade me sit beside her on the couch. Food was already spread on the table before us, and we commenced to eat.

"What have you been doing this morning?" she asked.

"Playing with my dolls," I said brightly. "I have some wonderful new dolls made like Egyptian ladies of long ago."

Berenice threw me a skeptical sidelong glance. "Oh, come now, Cleopatra, you have long given up playing with dolls!"

I said nothing, concentrating on the food before me.

"Oh, Cleopatra, I'm so happy with Archaelous," she said radiantly.

"I'm glad, Berenice," I said sincerely. "I know that Archaelous will be a good husband and King."

"Together we will bring greatness to Egypt," she said with sunny optimism.

"Our blood has grown thin with centuries of inbreeding," I said, "and we need Archaelous to mix his strong new blood with our line."

"This marriage is not a mistake like the last one."

"I had hoped Archaelous would be eating with us."

"Yes, I'm sure you did, you little tart," she said in a

77

voice mixed with indulgence and reproach. "It's the scandal of the court that you are infatuated with him. Your animated conversation with him the other night at the banquet attracted attention."

I blushed. "Berenice, I only wanted him to feel accepted by all members of the royal family."

"Yes, but to do so must you flirt with him like a waterfront harlot in front of the whole court?" She forced a tolerant smile. "You're just a child and the court is amused by your infatuation, but such behavior is not seemly in a thirteen-year-old princess."

"Yes, O Sister," I said meekly, chastised.

"You're fast becoming a young woman, but you must preserve your virginity," Berenice pursued. "I'll try to promote a great marriage for you, and in a few years you might become Queen of Mesopotamia or Bactria, but in the meantime if you become a scandal of the court, no prince or king will have you."

"I assure you, Berenice, my virtue is impregnable!"

"Just see to it that your maidenhead remains impregnable, too!" Berenice rejoined.

For some time we were silent as we ate and drank and listened to the lovely music of harps.

"Our poor father," Berenice broke the silence with a sigh. "I guess you've heard about the latest reports of his dire situation."

I glanced at her with alarm, swallowing heavily.

"Well, the atrocious treachery of his crimes in Rome last year against our delegation has awakened a universal indignation," Berenice explained pleasantly. "It's a good thing he's in Ephesus, or the Romans would lynch him. The senators who oppose our father's cause have renewed their opposition and are gaining strength from the odium which Father's crimes have inspired. Father does have a few backers in Rome, of course, his creditors, but they're finding it difficult to sustain his cause any further. Even Pompey is losing heart in espousing Father, for Archaelous is his friend." She gave me a smile of triumph and a sharp look to assess the damage on my face.

I tried desperately to make my face appear like a marble bust.

"You are no longer hungry?" Berenice inquired.

"Oh, yes," I said, forcing myself to eat.

"There have been evil happenings in Rome that are bad for Father," Berenice went on serenely. "For instance, the statue of Jupiter on Pompey's estate was hit by a thunderbolt and the head was knocked off. What do you think of that, Cleopatra?"

I stared into my goblet, shrugging. "Since Jupiter is the god of the heavens, that is a portentous event by any reckoning."

"Exactly!" Berenice cried with delight. "And so thought the Senate, who decided to consult the Sibylline Books kept by the Vestal Virgins. In these sacred oracles containing prophecies of public affairs, they found the following passage." Berenice put down her goblet and reached for a scroll on a table, unrolled it, and holding it close to her eyes, since she was short-sighted, began reading slowly, " 'If a King of Egypt applies to Rome for aid, treat him in a friendly manner, but do not furnish him with troops, for if Rome does, Rome will incur tragic troubles.' "

Berenice looked at me with a smile of satisfaction. "Well, what do you make of this, Cleopatra?"

It took all my effort to contain my emotions at such blatant, mendacious propaganda from my father's opposition, but I merely replied, "The Sibylline Oracles are known for their sagacity and accurate prognostications."

"Yes, indeed. Well, this has taken the wind out of our father's sails. The Romans won't help him, and my councillors refuse to allow me to send him a pension. If worse comes to worst, he can always earn his bread by playing the flute in the streets of Ephesus. His cause appears to be hopeless, wouldn't you say, Cleopatra?"

I met her eyes, seeing she expected a response from me. "None of us can fight against our destiny," I remarked with airy obliqueness.

Berenice's expression hardened as she mulled over

79

this platitude, not quite knowing how to take it, but finally she shrugged and let the matter drop. Now that she had said what she had wanted to say, she commenced to eat with gusto. Her revelations had upset me, and as soon as I could I made my bid to depart.

"By your royal leave, Sister Queen, I beg to return to my apartments, for my tutor of trigonometry is expected."

"By all means," Berenice said, "go back to your studies, Cleopatra, and to your dolls!"

Back in my apartments, I closeted myself with Protarchus to discuss this latest news.

"The Sibylline Books, indeed!" I cried agitatedly. "It's an invention of my father's enemies."

"But of course," Protarchus said calmly. "It's all too conveniently contrived. Pompey's political opposition bribed the Vestal Virgins and fabricated this oracle as a warning to his ambitions."

"This will mean a setback for Father's plans."

"I'm sure Pompey and your father's friends in Rome will circumvent this little ruse," Protarchus assured me. "This won't dishearten Pompey, and it shouldn't dishearten you, O Princess. King Ptolemy's predicament is complicated, granted, but not hopeless."

Later I was to learn that the fraudulent oracle with the Senate's consent was posted all over the walls of the Forum. Pompey's attempts to evade the direction of the oracle created ad infinitum debates between my father's enemies and his friends. The Senate feared placing the task of my father's restoration in the hands of any one man. Months went by, and no decisive course of action could be agreed upon.

At last Pompey sailed to Ephesus to stay at my father's villa. He decided that he would make every effort to aid my father's cause without the Senate's approval. The idea of restoring my father appealed to his imagination, and he hoped to obtain for his favors the freedom to make use of the wealth of Egypt. Indeed, my father offered the bribe of ten thousand talents in a last desperate bid for the repurchase of his throne.

Pompey, not wanting to lead the army that would effect the restoration, went to Aulus Gabinius, the proconsul of Syria, to induce him to undertake the enterprise. Gabinius agreed to go against the Sibylline warnings and march from Syria with his legions along the Mediterranean, cross the desert, fight through the fortress at Pelusium, and traverse the Delta to Alexandria. He pushed forward the arrangements with all despatch, but then when everything was all set, he grew apprehensive about the possibility of disaster and wanted to renege on the deal.

Once again my father's destiny was held in the balance, and his restoration seemed to be a dimming dream. I was now fourteen; three years had passed since my father had gone into exile, and I began to despair that he would ever return to his rightful place.

Fate intervened in the form of a young man second in command to Gabinius, who came forward zealously and boldly marshalled the forces to proceed without delay.

A young man by the name of Mark Antony.

As reports of this Mark Antony and his inspiriting effect on the enterprise reached me, I was filled with hope that soon my father would be back in Egypt and on the throne that would be his until death, and after his death, would be mine.

One evening Berenice paid a surprise visit to my apartments. I had been playing chess with Apollodorus. As my majordomo announced her, I went and met her at the doors and knelt.

"Oh, please, Cleopatra," she cried, "we can dispense with such obeisance in private!"

It flashed through my mind that this was the first time since she had been queen that she had requested the slightest protocol due her rank be dispensed with.

Berenice smiled at Apollodorus, accepting his obeisance with a nod.

"O Sacred Radiance," Apollodorus muttered on his knee.

"Apollodorus, I wish to be alone with the princess," Berenice said.

Apollodorus gave a salute and was gone.

Berenice smiled at me, reached for my hand, and led me to a couch. She was dressed in a Grecian gown and wore a rich ring on every finger. As we sat on a divan, I studied her face, seeing that she seemed older than her twenty-one years. The affairs of the kingdom and the uncertainty of her future had left its toll on her.

She glanced at the chess table. "Who is winning?"

"I seem to be winning," I replied, "although the next few moves I make will predict the end."

"Good luck," Berenice said good-naturedly.

I poured wine into two goblets and handed her one.

She scrutinized my bosom. "Your breasts are becoming larger. Have you begun the monthly rite of flowers yet?"

"Oh, yes, for six months now, dear sister."

"Peasant girls your age are sometimes married and with their first child," Berenice said. "Archaelous and I will find a husband for you soon. A nicer husband than Uncle Ptolemy would have been."

"I trust my fate in your hands, Berenice."

Berenice gestured toward a table heaped with scrolls. "Do you actually read all these books?"

"I have a great passion for literature, sister."

"I wish I had time to read books, but I'm always inundated by state papers." At random she picked up a scroll, unrolled it, and read. "*The Memoirs of Ptolemy the First.* I suppose we have to be grateful to him, since he founded our dynasty. Someday I must read this book, but unlike you, I have no interest in history. I'm too busy making history to read about it. Of course, since you have nothing more to do with your time!" Her be-ringed hand found another scroll, which she unrolled. "*Love Poems by Sappho,*" she cried, turning flashing eyes on me. "Why do you read this trash?"

"Sappho is a great poet, Berenice," I said defensively. "Her lyrical lamentations of life and of love—"

"What would our beloved mother think if she were

alive and knew you wasted your time on such verses?"
Berenice demanded hotly. "You're a true daughter of
Sappho and of your father! Cleopatra, you're a young
woman now and you have certain feelings, but suppress
them. You know little of life, and I suppose it's only
natural for you to seek vicarious pleasure in literature.
I only hope these poems do not inspire you to take
lovers. I want to marry you off, and if it gets out that
you read Sappho and have lovers, it will be damaging to
negotiations. The foreign ambassadors at court pick up
every morsel of gossip. Don't let anyone know you read
Sappho's trivia. And as for Apollodorus—"

"He is my friend!" I cried intensely. "He is like a
brother to me!"

Berenice smiled indulgently. "I've no worries where
Apollodorus is concerned. I wouldn't trust him for a
moment in the company of our younger brothers, but
your maidenhead is perfectly safe with Apollodorus."

"You're lying!" I cried, tears flooding my eyes.

"You mean your maidenhead is not safe with Apollodorus?"

"I mean," I stammered, "what you say is not true!"

Her eyes enlarged with incredulity. "Cleopatra, you
don't know what the whole court knows?" She laughed
in cruel mockery. "Why, I had him followed, I have reports on him. At night when he's off duty he searches
the waterfront for companions, and he never ends up
with daughters of Venus, but always with sailors or
soldiers." Her eyes glowed with evil satisfaction.

"You're a liar!" I screamed furiously.

Her eyes flashed fire. "How dare you speak to me like
that! Do you happen to know who I am, or have you
forgotten that I am your Queen?"

I quickly decided that my only defense would be to
resort to tears, and I covered my face with my hands
and began trembling with sobs.

"Cleopatra, stop those tears, you know I can't stand
them!" she cried impatiently. "Now, I'm your sister as
well as your Queen, and I forgive your impudence. I
forget how young you are sometimes. Apollodorus is a

paragon of manly beauty and you have a childish infatuation for him, and there's no harm in that, but be careful this flirtation never goes further. Some of the ambassadors who don't know his reputation might suspect that he is more than the captain of your guards. It is all right to be precocious in your studies, but not in other matters."

"I have always been a proper princess and will continue to be," I said with dignity, controlling my sobs.

"Yes, with the help of the gods and a little restraint, I'm sure you will not prove powerless against the passions of your heart," Berenice said. "I must go now."

I walked with her to the door. "I'm sorry, Sister Queen, that I was remiss in respect to you."

"You are forgiven, little sister," Berenice said. "Tomorrow there will be a banquet in the Great Hall, and you must be there." At the door she paused to touch my face with both her hands. "You are becoming very beautiful, Cleopatra. I think we must set our sights on marrying you to the crown prince of Mesopotamia."

"I'm overjoyed that you have such grand designs for me," I said. "Farewell, O Sister Queen!"

"Farewell, O the future Queen of Mesopotamia!" she cried, going off.

Queen of Mesopotamia indeed, I thought. Yes, I wanted to be queen, but not in far-off barbaric Mesopotamia. Destiny had other plans for me. I sensed it in my bones. Surely my sister and her husband knew their days were numbered.

Apollodorus returned, and we resumed our game of chess. I sat there, looking at his handsome face, wondering if my sister's remarks about him were true. He had always said his favorite Euripides play was not the famous *Electra*, *Orestes*, or *Medea*, but *Aspasia*, one of the most obscure dramas by the master, concerning a soldier in love with Aspasia, the Princess of Simi. The King her father arranges for her to marry the King of Sparta, but Aspasia refuses, vowing her love for her soldier. The King has the soldier murdered, and the princess drinks hemlock.

Several times Apollodorus and I had seen *Aspasia* at the Theater of Dionysus, and we were always enthralled by it. I had taken his admiration and affinity for this play to signify that he felt a personal identification with the ill-fated soldier. I concluded that, if it was true what Berenice said, then Apollodorus had resolved that, if he could not have me, the princess he loved, then he would have no other woman.

The banquet Berenice invited me to the following evening had a surprise in store for me, for the major-domo escorted me to a couch that I shared with Princess Arsinoë next to the royal dais. This was the first time in two years that I had not been directed to a couch far back at the end of the hall. I could only surmise that I was once again back in favor.

Princess Arsinoë, under the influence of her tutor Ganymedes, had always been disrespectful to me. Now that I was to share her couch, she was perplexed and did not know how to take it at first. She was nine years old at this time. Her character had formed and she was a shrewd little creature. During the course of the banquet she turned false smiles on me and made polite conversation. She realized our father could be back on the throne within weeks, and it might be to her advantage to be sweet to me now.

My two little brothers sat at another couch close by with their eunuch, Theodotus of Chios. Theodotus likewise had always encouraged his charges to be defiantly disagreeable to me, but times were changing, Theodotus took note of it, and had the princes smiling and blowing me kisses.

The banquet was rather dull, not like the sumptuous, entertaining affairs for which my father was famous. Berenice had imposed a restricting sense of sobriety on her court. Many of the courtiers, especially the older, more degenerate ones who were set in their ways, nostalgically remembered the days of my father when the wildest behavior had been permitted. Berenice was a true hypocrite, for before Archaelous married her, she had conducted herself in an outrageous fashion in the privacy of her chambers, yet all the while showing a shocked face at the slightest breach of morals or manners among her nobles at court.

Suddenly the banquet was disrupted by sounds of violent retching. All eyes turned on Scopas, a trusted old palace retainer. Scopas had been one of my father's favorite friends and drinking companions. He was a charming old man, and I was fond of him.

"Remove that man!" Berenice cried furiously. "And may I never see his drunken face again!"

Guardsmen quickly made their way to the couch where the pathetic old offender sat, and Scopas was dragged out of the hall. In the days of my father, such an incident would have been overlooked or greeted with an indulgent eye. Times had changed. But then, I thought, perhaps they would change again.

"To think such behavior used to be the fashion at court!" Diomedes cried with contempt, sitting on the right side of the queen. "Surely the great gods who watch over Egypt are pleased with the strides our Queen has made to lift Egypt out of the wretchedness into which it had sunk under the unfortunate rule of the perfidious Ptolemy the Piper."

Nikostratos, a supercilious courtier, stood and raised his goblet. "With the gracious permission of our sacred sovereigns, I raise a toast to the gods in the hopes that they will see to the misfortune of that degenerate king who once ruled feebly over us and his associates Gabinius and Antony."

All the guests quickly raised their goblets to these sentiments. I was a bit tardy in lifting my goblet, which Berenice noticed.

"They say Gabinius was losing heart in the plans to invade Egypt," Nikostratos said, "and it was this Mark Antony who persuaded him with all eagerness to proceed."

"Antony is a friend of mine," Archaelous announced.

"An erstwhile friend," Berenice snapped.

"What can you tell us about this Antony?" Nikostratos asked curiously.

I sat up on my couch, stiffening with ears all alert.

"Like me, he has twenty-seven years," Archaelous explained. "I knew him well two years ago in Cappadocia. Born of a distinguished, patrician Roman family, his father died when he was young. His mother, the Lady Julia who is Caesar's first cousin, spoiled him shamelessly, and he became a wild and dissolute young man. He wasted in vice and folly the property which his father had left him and incurred enormous debts. From the age of fifteen he associated with some of the most depraved, lecherous old senators in Rome, and in the ancient Greek fashion, became their darling."

"You mean he was a whore boy?" Berenice asked.

"Antony admits it candidly," Archaelous said. "At length he involved himself in inextricable difficulties, and his patrons grew tired of his debts and refused to pay them. Harassed by creditors, he absconded to Greece. There he joined up for military training, lost his effeminacy, became a man, grew a beard, and learned all the soldierly skills of swordsmanship and riding."

"It takes more than a beard to make a man," Berenice said disdainfully. "Inside there must remain much of the former whore boy."

"Gabinius found Antony in Greece," Archaelous went on, "and invited him to join his army in Syria. Antony, being proud and lofty in spirit, demanded a command, so Gabinius gave him the charge of his cavalry. In Syria the last two years he has distinguished himself greatly in fighting against pockets of insurrection."

The Lady Lydia, Berenice's dearest friend and Mistress of the Royal Vestiture, asked, "Tell me, O King, what is this Antony like to look upon?"

"Oh, like a glorious gladiator!" Archaelous replied with frank admiration. "One would never imagine that he was once effeminate, although that is a phase many highborn Roman lads go through. Now he is rugged and handsome, of tall and manly form, with curly hair and beard, and looks like Hercules. He has a great excellence of character and a generous spirit. He is a favorite among men and women. He assumes an air of familiarity and freedom with his soldiers, and they would die for him. He joins in their sports, their carousing, jokes with them, and good-naturedly receives their jokes in return."

"It sounds like he takes it all as a game," Berenice said, smirking.

"Oh, to Antony, all of life is a game!" Archaelous cried. "He came to Cappadocia a few months before I left for Egypt, and we spent many days and nights in friendship, going to the baths and the taverns together, drinking and frolicking. He enjoys life with immense satisfaction."

Berenice, sitting beside Archaelous, bristled with jealousy at these remembrances.

"It appears then that Antony has charm and reckless energy," Diomedes cried, "and you say, O King, that he has been successful in stamping out pockets of insurrection, but the plans he is now embarking upon will not be a minor skirmish."

"Hear, hear," several voices eagerly cried out.

"You say he has the capacity to enjoy life," Berenice said, "but does he have it in him to become a great commander, another Pompey or Caesar?"

"Her Divine Majesty poses an interesting question," Diomedes said. "In truth, can Antony fight through the fortress at the frontier?"

"Pelusium will never fall!" a noble cried frenziedly from among the couches. "Our army at Pelusium will stand like a giant rock!"

The guests gave great shouts at this sentiment.

When the cries had died down, a certain courtier, in a timid voice, said, "They say the Roman legions are encamped at Gaza in the south of Judaea, ready to march to Pelusium."

"Yes, and in the heat of summer they must be roasting!" another voice cried out with a booming laugh.

Queen Berenice arrowed her bright blue eyes at me. "Our little historian, Princess Cleopatra, I'm sure can tell us that in history crossing the desert from Gaza is a desperate undertaking."

All eyes at the banquet suddenly turned to me.

"Oh, yes, Sister Queen," I cried, responding in a voice bright and eager. "As Herodotus tells us, the great protection of Egypt has always been her isolation. Those desolate sands which surround our kingdom can be traversed only with difficulty by caravans. In history there have been numerous instances when enemy troops, in attempting to march over the desert, were destroyed by famine, thirst, bands of bandits, or buried by storms of sand!"

"May such a fate await Ptolemy the Piper and this Gabinius and this degenerate fop, Mark Antony!" Diomedes cried with demented fervor.

Tremendous shouts echoed this proposition.

"Even if they do get across the desert," I continued when the shouting had died down, "our enemies will be exhausted by the heat and the hardships along the way, and will encounter at Pelusium our Egyptian army, which will be fresh and vigorous!"

"Our enemies will be slaughtered," Diomedes cried heatedly. "When our soldiers get through with them at Pelusium, the enemy will wish that they had perished in the desert!" He raised his goblet and drained it.

Every guest in the Great Hall did likewise, although as I drank my spiced coconut juice, I resolved to give prayers to the gods beseeching them to still the sands of the desert and make the way safe for my father and his legions.

Later as I made to leave the banquet to get to my prayers, I went to the royal dais and knelt.

"Like our father," Berenice cried out, "our royal sister the Princess Cleopatra has always been interested in these barbarian Romans, favoring them highly. She is, you might say, a Roman-lover!"

The whole court, taking their cue from their queen, laughed derisively, and with a great effort I lifted my chin defiantly as I knelt there.

"Here I have my ambassadors negotiating to marry her off to the crown prince of Mesopotamia," Berenice said scoffingly, "but perhaps I should find her some

Roman, one of Pompey's sons, or perhaps this whore boy, Mark Antony."

"But I believe," Diomedes cried, "it is against Roman law for their citizens to marry a foreigner."

"Perhaps they would give dispensation to a Roman to marry a princess of the royal house of Egypt," Berenice said. "Well, Cleopatra, would you like to marry one of these Romans?"

Again every eye was focused on me, and silence reigned in the hall.

"The day when I marry, O Sister Queen," I said with grave dignity, "I hope to marry, not only as a princess, but also as a woman."

There was a great silence while all the guests again waited to take their cue from their Queen.

"Only fourteen years old," Berenice cried in mockery, "and already she dreams of mixing politics and love!"

The guests picked up their cue and laughed loudly.

King Archaelous looked kindly at me. "Never fear, Cleopatra," he said tenderly, silencing the laughter, "Berenice and I will see that you end up with a good match, not only suited to your station and rank, but to your heart."

I smiled in gratitude at Archaelous, ignoring Berenice's look of displeasure. "Thank you, O Brother King!"

"You have our royal leave to go!" Berenice snapped.

Only a few days later as I sat on a bench in the palace gardens with my ladies in the afternoon sunshine, Apollodorus rushed breathlessly up to me bringing momentous tidings.

"Pelusium has fallen!" he cried, gasping for air.

"Eureka!" I cried softly, my heart fluttering at the mighty news, yet outwardly calm, wary of watchful eyes from palace windows. I slowly got up and passed fountains and sentries stationed every thirty feet, and made my leisurely way back to my apartments.

Protarchus was awaiting me, aquiver with excitement. "Fortune has turned her wheel in your favor, O Princess," he cried. "An hour ago a courier rode in on an exhausted horse and tumbled out of the saddle as the horse fell dead. The courier was taken to Queen Berenice, and he told her that Pelusium had been taken by your father's forces."

"I must give thanks to the gods," I said. I took a small gold casket of rich incense to my private temple, where I threw handfuls of the incense on the altar fire. As perfumed clouds rose in the air, I prostrated myself in thankful prayers.

Mark Antony, I learned later, had placed himself at the head of his cavalry, and accompanied by my father, crossed the desert in a safe and speedy fashion. Gabinius and his legions were left behind in Gaza to follow later. Antony and my father and the troop of horse arrived at Pelusium in the middle of the night. The fortress, caught unawares by the surprise attack, surrendered after a brief resistance. Gabinius was expected to arrive shortly with his legions, which constituted an overwhelming force, and in conjunction with Antony's cavalry would march to Alexandria.

I was told that Berenice, learning that Pelusium was in enemy hands, became hysterical.

"The people hate my father," she moaned. "They will fight, every Alexandrian and every Egyptian, to the death before they allow him back on the throne. The people love me! We will be victorious, won't we, Archaelous? We will have all their heads—Father, Gabinius, and this Mark Antony—all their heads will be stuck up on the city gates!"

King Archaelous remained calm and quickly mobilized his forces some miles outside the city.

The next day a courier brought news that the Roman army was marching toward the capital. Archaelous left the palace to join his army encampment. I went to the palace courtyard to bid him farewell.

"Archaelous, you go to fight your friend, Mark Antony," I said. "How sad this must be for you."

"Yes, Cleopatra, Antony and I were friends, but now duty demands that we fight each other," Archaelous said.

"Antony is a degenerate fop!" Berenice cried in a

91

voice verging on hysteria. "We will have his head for a trophy, won't we, Archaelous?"

"May the gods go with you, Archaelous," I said warmly.

"Farewell, fair princess," Archaelous said, kissing my cheek.

Berenice threw her arms around her husband. "My darling, I will join you in a few days."

"You must look after Egypt with your seal, and I will look after her with my sword," Archaelous said.

There was a tender, touching farewell between them. I gazed with misty eyes on Archaelous, who had never been more strikingly handsome in full military dress, gold armor, plumed helmet, a shining sword buckled at his side, and a purple gold-trimmed cloak tied with a gold lion-head clasp. Even though circumstances had made him my enemy, I still felt an affectionate regard for Archaelous.

At last he rode off on his beautiful red-gold Arabian stallion; and even though there were tears in my eyes, I had to hope that I would never see him again.

Two days later Queen Berenice commanded me to her apartments, and I found her dressed and ready to leave the palace.

"Come, sit beside me," she said with a wan smile.

I sat beside her, and her jittery hands clasped mine.

"I have a report that tomorrow the Romans will reach our encampment outside the city and there will be a battle," she explained. "I go to join my husband. By tomorrow's sunset all might be over, one way or another. It is all up to the gods now."

"Yes," I whispered solemnly.

Berenice turned moist eyes on me and gave a shaky smile. "I am with child, Cleopatra!" she said exultantly. "I take this as a good omen."

"I am happy for you, dear Berenice," I said.

"If I am victorious, my firstborn may be the next king of Egypt. I pray to the gods destiny will be on my side. And you will go off to be Queen of Mesopotamia. However, if fortune goes against me, you will have to stay here and take the throne when father dies. I'm sure you would rather be Queen of Mesopotamia, wouldn't you?"

I thought it best not to argue. "Oh, yes, Berenice!"

"Being Queen of Mesopotamia will be a more pleasant fate than being Queen of Egypt," Berenice said. "Mesopotamia is a poor country, and the Romans do not prize it. Sitting on the unsteady throne of the pharaohs is a perilous life, but of course we must all follow our star."

"Yes, we are merely toys of the fates, playthings for their amusement," I said philosophically.

"If I lose, Cleopatra, it will be the end of Archaelous and me," Berenice said soberly. "Promise me that you will intercede with Father, not to spare my life, for I know he thirsts for vengeance, but that Archaelous and I will have funeral honors worthy of our rank and will be buried in the Sema. I do not want us to be food for the vultures and ravens."

"I solemnly make that promise, Berenice," I said.

"You always had a way with Father and I never forgave you for that, but this is one time I may be grateful to you for it." She gave a deep sigh and rose. "I must go join Archaelous now."

Berenice and I kissed each other tenderly.

"Farewell, dearest sister," I murmured.

I stood on a balcony overlooking the courtyard and watched Berenice ride out of the palace gates in a chariot drawn by two white Arabian mares.

Later that afternoon, unable to concentrate on my studies, I dismissed my tutors and went with Apollodorus into the palace gardens. I sat in a small latticed arbor facing a large fountain in the Greek style. I had with me a scroll of Callimachus. Sitting on a marble bench inside the arbor, I read while Apollodorus patrolled the grounds before me.

The sun was shining serenely and it was pleasant in the gardens. The streams of water, gushing out of mouths of great bronze gods and falling into fountain basins, made soothing music and calmed my strained nerves.

After a while I looked up from my poetry and saw

not far off Princess Arsinoë with her eunuch Ganymedes and her ladies. Ganymedes whispered into her ear, and then she approached me alone.

"Good afternoon, dearest sister!" Arsinoë cried, sinking to her knee in deep reverence.

"Greetings, Arsinoë," I said, touching her cheek.

"May I sit with you, Cleopatra?" she asked.

"Please do, sweet sister," I said.

Arsinoë sat beside me, primly arranging the folds of her dress.

I could tell from her delicately chiseled nine-year-old face that when she grew into womanhood she would have a fair share of the beauty with which our line is blessed, and one could tell from her strong jaw that she had spirit and determination. She was a clever little thing as the fact that she was obsequiously sidling up to me indicated.

"Sister Cleopatra," she said in a troubled voice, turning a pensive face toward me, "I envy you because you are so much older, and I am only a child."

"Time goes quickly and you will soon be a woman."

In silence we watched a peacock with ornate plumage wander proudly by.

"What will happen if Father comes back and regains the throne?" she asked with an anxious look.

"Life will go on," I said with a shrug.

"But will it go on for Berenice?" she asked.

"Father has a merciful heart," I lied. "After all, Berenice is his own flesh and blood." I knew my father would forgive the betrayal of his meanest subject, but not the betrayal of his own child.

"What will Father do with me?" Arsinoë asked. "I paid Berenice homage all these years."

"You were only six when Berenice seized the crown, so Father will not hold it against you."

"Father did not show a merciful heart toward my mother, Queen Arsinoë," she said fretfully. "The last thing he did before going into exile was to have her murdered."

"No one knows what really happened that night," I said, again lying. "That may have been the work of

Diomedes, who was angling for power for himself and Berenice."

"That's not what I've been led to believe," Arsinoë said grimly. She paused, nervously biting her lower lip. "I haven't been clever like you, Cleopatra. I'm told you smuggled out secret letters to Father."

"Not so secret. Berenice knew about them."

"That kept you in Father's good graces," Arsinoë said. "I should have sent him letters as you did."

"The battle isn't over yet," I said, which gave her a measure of hope.

At last I stood and said I wished to return to my chambers, and she sank to one knee and kissed my hand. With some pleasure I permitted her to perform this obeisance. For three years Arsinoë had been in favor and I out of favor, and during that time she had shown me scant courtesy. Now things were different. If Father came back, I would be the heiress apparent. She was thinking of her future as she knelt at my feet and smiled tentatively, fearfully up at me.

"Farewell, dear Arsinoë," I said, turning away.

The fiery orange disk of Ra was at its zenith in the heavens, and as I walked along the garden paths I closed my eyes against the blaze of intense power from the supreme deity. The golden sun poured its sunbeams in profligate splendor, radiating its benediction all over me. I felt my star rising, to shine brightly in the firmament, controlled by the sun god. Destiny held my future, and fortune and all the gods were in my favor.

CHAPTER V

IN THE HEART OF THE DELTA my father and his Roman legions encountered a detachment of my sister's advance guard, and a pitched battle ensued. The Romans could make no headway until Mark Antony, revealing his contempt for personal danger, outflanked the enemy with his cavalry, attacking them from the rear, and brought about their complete defeat. Antony single-handedly carried the day. The Romans then continued on the road to Alexandria and soon came upon the main Egyptian army on the banks of one of the branches of the Nile not far from the sea.

A great battle was fought. The Egyptian soldiers were discontented and mutinous, perhaps because they considered my sister's government a usurpation. To his honor, King Archaelous fought bravely despite these mutinous troops and was slain upon the field in the thick of the fray.

When the battle was over, Berenice was apprehended in the royal pavilion. Antony's mind was troubled by the tidings that his friend Archaelous had been killed. My father rejoiced at the capture of his daughter, and Antony mourned the loss of a friend. Burial squads gathered up the dead for honorable interment, and Antony personally sought the body of Archaelous amid the fallen soldiers, and when he found it gave it noble treatment.

The army marched to Alexandria with Berenice in chains.

The news of the outcome of the battle reached the palace. Many of the nobles who had sat on my sister's council fled in haste. While the battle raged, I was sequestered in my chambers with Protarchus and Apollodorus, while Arsinoë and my two little brothers waited in their apartments with their guardians. We four children of our father were quiet spectators of the revolution, but were deeply excited by the events that were convulsing the country and which would decide our fates.

The Alexandrians gave my father and the Roman troops a rousing welcome as they entered the gates of the city. Musicians appeared out of nowhere and struck up a lively march of triumph, escorting my father through the streets to the palace.

I went to the central palace courtyard to meet my father, dressed in royal raiment and wearing my coronet, flanked by Protarchus, Apollodorus, and a cordon of personal guards. At last my father drove through the palace portal in a chariot driven by a tall handsome Roman. As my father stepped off the chariot, I ran toward him.

The crowd fell silent, for it was a pregnant moment as my father and I approached one another. Tears sprang to my eyes at the sight of him. There were no longer any traces of blond in his hair, for it had all turned white. He was only forty-six, but he looked as if he had threescore years. The three years of his exile had taken a great toll on him.

I began to sob, forgetting all royal dignity. "Father!" I cried out as I rushed into his arms. He held me tight against him as my body shook spasmodically. The crowds all around broke into wild cheering at this reunion.

"Cleopatra, my daughter," Father said, his voice choking, "you are no longer a child, but a young woman."

I smiled tearfully. "I have prayed to the gods every day since you left for your safe return to your kingdom."

Father touched my cheek. "Your prayers have been answered, beloved daughter."

Theodotus of Chios came forward, leading the two little princes by the hand. "O Sacred Majestic King!" he cried. "Your two princes rejoice at your triumphant return!"

"My sons, my two fine sons!" Father cried.

The two princes looked suspiciously at our father, for they could barely remember him.

"They are handsome and healthy," Father cried joyously, leaning down and kissing them each on a cheek.

Amid great rejoicing, I took my father's hand, and we walked up the great marble staircase and into the main corridor of the palace, followed by a crowd of nobles and attendants.

Theodotus approached and bowed. "Your Divine Majesty will surely want to rest in your old chambers now and take sustenance," he said unctuously.

"No," I retorted, with a glance at my father, "the King wishes to go to his throne room."

My father nodded and smiled fondly at me. "Yes, the Princess Cleopatra is right."

I took my father's hand and we walked side by side down the long corridor, and at last reached the Great Throne Room. The giant doors were opened before us, and we entered the immense chamber. When we had traversed half the length of the long room, my father was breathless and had to stop.

"Your Sacred Radiance," Theodotus cried anxiously, coming up to us, "do you wish to rest?"

My father looked down at the throne in the distance. "I will rest on my throne," he said firmly.

Taking a deep breath and holding my hand, he started to walk slowly. My father was a head taller than I, and it took a great effort to support him, but at last we reached the foot of the throne. I helped my father up the six steps to the two thrones of gold inset with a thousand jewels. As my father settled wearily onto his throne, I stood at his right side, holding his hand.

The huge chamber before us was quickly being filled with people, and within minutes the hall was thronged. People fought to get nearer the throne, then all sank to their knees in obeisance, crying out in acclamation.

"O hail to the King!"

"May the gods save King Ptolemy!"

"May King Ptolemy live forever!"

My father held up his hand for silence. When quiet came, he cried, "No, I do not want to live forever!" He gestured toward me. "Princess Cleopatra, sit on the throne where once sat your beloved mother."

"But Father, I have not been consecrated," I whispered.

"It is my command," he said with firm gentleness. "You are the heiress apparent."

I obeyed and sat on the throne next to his, and the throng broke into shouts and cheers.

My father held a hand up for silence. "As I said, I do not wish to live forever. Just a few more years, and then my beloved daughter, Cleopatra, will take over my burden. From childhood she has shown herself to be a princess of great promise, both in mental endowments and in beauty and personal charm. In time she will make a great queen for Egypt, greater than Queen Hatshepsüt!"

Again the assemblage broke into wild cheering, which warmed my trembling heart, and I held my head proudly as the cheers washed over me.

It was then that a tall Roman, whom I recognized as the driver of my father's chariot, broke through the crowd and stood on the first step of the stairs to the throne.

"Mark Antony!" my father cried out in greeting.

So this was the Mark Antony I had been hearing so much about. He was the most gloriously good-looking man I had ever seen, even handsomer than Apollodorus. As Archaelous had said, he was built like a gladiator, and had a strikingly noble carriage, tall and rugged, with an exceptionally well-developed and powerful physique. He had a great head with a high noble forehead, thick curly hair and a brown beard, an expressive face, brown eyes full of sparkle, and a high hawk-hooked nose. His body was a fit model for the Hermes of Praxiteles, I thought as I felt my blood racing.

"O King, may I speak?" Antony asked in a deep, beautiful voice.

"But of course, Antony, my dear friend," Father said with affection, "but first let me present the Princess Cleopatra. My daughter, it was Mark Antony who saved us. His dashing leadership and reckless bravery compelled all the fainthearts to follow him into battle."

Mark Antony quickly took the steps to the foot of the thrones, and bowed low to me. "O Sacred Princess, I am honored. King Ptolemy spoke so often of a child, but I meet a young woman who is as exquisite as a flower which has just burst into bloom."

"Mark Antony has a way with words," my father laughed, "and with women."

"Welcome, noble Roman, to Egypt," I said gravely.

Antony smiled at me and then turned seriously to my father. "Divine Majesty," he said briskly, "the false traitor, Diomedes, tried to escape in the guise of a merchant, but was caught. We have him in chains. Would you like to see him?"

"Bring him forward!" Father said sternly.

Diomedes, in chains, was led in by soldiers. He no longer had the robes and the golden chain of office of Prime Minister, but wore the multicolored robe of a merchant. He appeared distraught and beaten.

"Diomedes!" my father cried hoarsely. "My faithless protégé! You were a humble scribe at the library when I first became king, and I made you one of my secretaries. Through the years I bestowed great honors on you. I appointed you the foster father to my daughter Berenice and gave you a seat on my council. Then when unhappy circumstances forced me to leave the country, you made Berenice Queen and yourself Prime Minister. This, then, was your gratitude to me!"

Falling to his knees, Diomedes cried, "Mercy, Great King, Son of the Sun, mercy!"

"Take him to the dungeons and cut him to pieces!" Father cried, shaking with rage, "and throw the pieces as a feast for the crocodiles."

"No, mercy, Great King, mercy!" Diomedes screamed hysterically, falling forward in full prostration.

Soldiers came forward and dragged the kicking, screaming Diomedes from the Great Hall.

Archimedes, the Keeper of the Crowns, approached the throne with the double red and white crown on a purple pillow.

"O Sacred Radiance and Divine King," Archimedes cried, "your crown!"

"Antony, since you helped me win back my crown, I give you the honor of placing it on my head!" my father said.

Antony bowed and ceremoniously placed the crown on my father's head. Shouts and acclamations rang through the great room. My father smiled into my eyes.

"Make way for the General Gabinius!" a Roman soldier cried out in Latin.

The press of people parted, and Gabinius, a grizzled old Roman commander, came to the steps to the throne.

"King Ptolemy," Gabinius said in a deep, croaking voice, "Berenice begs to pay homage to you."

"Bring her forward," my father said painfully.

Berenice, her hands chained, came forward. It was to her royal credit that she held herself proudly. With grace she sank to her knees. "Beloved Father and Majestic King!"

A silence came over the room as my father glowered at her. This was the long-wished-for moment when he could satisfy the vengeance which had long slumbered in his breast and triumph finally over his hated daughter.

"I, King Ptolemy, decree that the head that wore my crown be cut off!" Father cried.

Astonished murmurs rippled through the hall. Berenice did not disgrace the royal house by resorting to hysterical tricks like Diomedes, but held her head even higher as she accepted her fate.

"Get her out of my sight!" Father began trembling and covered his face with a hand.

Soldiers helped Berenice to her feet, and with as much dignity as she could muster, she let herself be led from the Great Throne Room where a few days before she had sat in sovereignty.

A goblet was brought for my father and he sipped the wine.

"Great King, I beg leave to approach your throne!"

I looked at the man who had spoken. Some feet away stood Pothinos, who had been my father's Prime Minister before his exile. He had disappeared when my sister seized the throne, and he had, I thought, or rather hoped, been murdered by Diomedes at the time. He had kept himself in seclusion the last three years, and now he surfaced out of nowhere.

"It is your loyal servant and friend Pothinos," he cried, smiling fawningly.

"Pothinos, my dear old friend!" Father answered in delight. "Come greet your old King!"

Pothinos lifted the hem of his gown and quickly ran up the stairs and fell on his knees, clasping my father's hands. "Great King, the gods rejoice with us at your return to your rightful seat."

"Pothinos, how have you fared these last years?" Father asked.

"Like you, Sacred King, I have been in retirement, for it was my wish to serve no other king but you. Now that you have been restored, I offer my humble services in whatever capacity you so desire, no matter how humble the station."

"I desire you, Pothinos, to be not my humblest, but my most exalted servant," Father cried expansively. "My Prime Minister!"

My heart stopped. I despised Pothinos, who had caused my mother's downfall. I wanted to cry out to protest this spontaneous decision of my father's, but I could not, for to do so in front of the court would be disrespectful.

"I am deeply honored," Pothinos responded in his oily voice. "With the help of the gods, O King, I hope to serve you and Egypt to my dying breath. Together we will lead Egypt to peace and splendor."

"With the help of the gods, so we shall," Father replied fervently.

The golden collar which is the emblem of the Prime Minister was brought forth; and as Pothinos sank to both knees, my father placed it around his neck. The people shouted approval, but I merely sat there, closing my eyes against the hideous sight, impotent with despair.

"I wish to retire to my chambers," Father said.

The heavy crowns were lifted from my father's head and given to Archimedes for safekeeping. A fanfare of trumpets parted the mass of people, who sank to their knees as my father and I slowly passed out from the Great Throne Room.

We went to his apartments, which Berenice and Archaelous had occupied.

"Bring me wine," Father ordered, settling onto a couch.

"And some food," I added.

I sat on a stool beside my father's couch, taking his hand and kissing it. "Oh, beloved Father, this is the happiest day of my life!"

"It wasn't for myself that I came back, Cleopatra," Father said. "I am old beyond my years and would have been content to spend the rest of my days in tranquil retirement in Ephesus. I came back to overthrow Berenice so that you will be queen after me. Berenice is vain and stupid and does not possess your remarkable qualities. You are the best of my children, and it is you who will bring Egypt to glory and greatness again."

"Dear Father, I hope I shall justify your belief in me," I said, touched by his words.

I wanted to spend the evening alone with my father, but people kept coming and going. Mark Antony came in and out with instructions and orders, and also the despicable Pothinos.

"O King, the fate of Berenice must be sealed as quickly as possible," Pothinos said with relish.

"In the morning," Father said evasively, uneasily.

I begged my father that Berenice be permitted to kill herself by a painless poison and not have to go through the shame of a public execution. I whispered in his ear, so that none other could hear, that Berenice was with child.

"I want no grandchild from her womb," he cried. "Her head wore the crown. Now the crown has been removed, and so must the head. Pharaoh has spoken."

After I pleaded with him, however, my father did relent, and a chamberlain was sent to her to say that she had the choice of ending her life by poison. She vehemently rejected this proposal.

"If my father the King wants my life, then he must take it publicly and bear the responsibility," Berenice cried with spirit.

When this news was brought to my father, he became enraged. "What arrogance! Cut off her head as I have decreed."

At high noon the following day the deed was done. I watched the gory proceedings, which were performed in the courtyard, from a balcony with Mark Antony and my sobbing Aunt Aliki. My father closeted himself in his chambers.

Berenice was led forward. She would meet death with pride and dignity as befitting her royal blood. She wore her long golden hair flowing to her shoulders, and as she knelt at the block she lifted her hair over her head and carefully laid her long, swanlike neck on the block. The black-clad executioner cut the head off with one swift, sure stroke. My sister Berenice Barsine was executed for her unfilial usurpation, having lived twenty-two years and almost four of them as Queen.

I begged my father that she be given honorable burial in the royal crypt, and Mark Antony interceded with the same request on behalf of his friend, Archaelous. My father relented, but ordered that the bodies not be embalmed, that the burial take place in the dead of night, and that the bodies be placed in a dark corner of the Sema.

The funeral took place as my father ordained. He did not attend the service. Just a few witnesses, officiating priests, a sobbing Aunt Aliki, a handful of servants, and

Mark Antony, who seemed to lament the death of his former comrade with unaffected grief, stood there with me.

Excitement reigned in Alexandria at my father's restoration. The populace, who had deposed him with rebellion, had discovered no superiority in my sister's government and were now pleased to have him back. One and all eagerly welcomed him, except those who had been active in Berenice's government, who fled, committed suicide, or were summarily executed.

A festival of thanksgiving was held in the capital. The restoration was celebrated with games and spectacles, and programs of dance, drama, and sports. My father gave public sacrifices to the gods. The discus was thrown far, the torch race run in superb style in the early twilight, and equestrianship brilliantly displayed.

My father appeared years younger, and he gloried in the public rejoicing. Much interest was focused on me, always at my father's side, along with the distinguished Roman general, Gabinius, and his handsome commander, Mark Antony.

During all these festivities I was able closely to observe Antony. We were attracted and charmed by one another. I adored his boyish expression, his kind humor, his thoughtful and frank eyes, his broad and intelligent forehead. His mouth was a good deal more sensitive than his rather heavy chin would lead one to expect. His aristocratically hooked nose, rugged features, and thick eyebrows added aquiline strength to his otherwise jovial and good-natured face.

As my father had remarked, I had become a woman during the three years of his exile. I was not quite fifteen, but I had reached my physical maturity and my full height of five feet and three inches, which I am told is a perfect size for a woman. I have since filled out a little; but during that restoration summer, I was extremely thin, elegantly proportioned and moved with regal grace. With my enormous blue eyes, my high cheekbones, curved lips and aquiline profile, I was considered to be a great beauty. Like most Macedonians, my skin is an opalescent white with a tinge of blue like the finest marble. My hair had darkened to a light golden bronze and was thick but soft to the touch and slightly wavy. My voice is said to be most alluring, with a wondrous timbre that the listener finds compelling. I speak in modulated tones and rarely raise my voice, even when I am angry. Of all the gifts the gods have given me, the one I prize the most is my gift of laughter. I laugh easily and often, but always softly.

It was our shared sense of humor as well as physical attraction that brought Antony and me together that summer to an understanding and mutual affinity.

The restoration festivities went on for ten days and were climaxed by a sumptuous banquet held in the Great Hall. A fabulous feast was spread on the low tables before two hundred golden couches, and guests came in their richest raiment. A thousand oil lamps and torches blazed brightly. The flutists and harpists played marvelous melodies. Various Grecian compositions suitable to the occasion were presented by distinguished actors. Diodorus, my father's favorite dancer, danced his dance of *Dionysus*. Diodorus had not danced in the palace for three years, and at the end of the dance my father placed a costly necklace around his neck.

As I sat beside my father on the dais, I watched Antony moving about the hall from one couch to another, laughing and drinking. Men and women threw their arms around him, and he bestowed kisses on them all. I do not deny that I felt a pang of jealousy.

At last Antony came to our royal couch.

"Antony, my champion, my friend!" Father cried heartily.

"King Ptolemy!" Antony cried, taking my father's hand and bowing low toward me. "O Princess!"

"Greetings, my Lord Antony," I smiled, pouring him a goblet of wine and handing it to him as he took a chair facing us.

"What I love about this young man," Father said to me, "is his ease in any company. Look at him sitting comfortably here with us, King and Princess, yet he is just as relaxed with soldiers and common folk. He enjoys the refinements of life, but like Caesar he can endure hardships without complaint. You should have seen him, Cleopatra, with his men attacking the fortress at Pelusium. In adversity he is nearest to perfection."

Antony gave out with a booming laugh. "King Ptolemy, I love you too!" he cried with boyish frankness. He caught my eye, smiling fondly. "Your daughter is most beautiful."

"Cleopatra is my pride and joy," Father said affectionately. "And her beauty reflects her inner worth."

"My noble Roman," I said, assuming a serious tone, "I am grateful to you for all that you've done in my father's behalf, and on mine. I'm told Gabinius wanted no part of the Egyptian invasion, but you forced it through to a successful conclusion."

"O Princess, I met your father several years ago in Rome and was drawn to him," Antony said. "Do you remember all the times when we drank together, King Ptolemy?"

"I remember them fondly," Father said smiling.

"I'm always anxious to aid a friend," Antony said. "Besides, Caesar too is your father's friend, and I am quick to follow where my cousin Caesar leads. But most of all, there was the challenge of this Egyptian campaign which appealed to me."

"You were not afraid of the dangers of the desert crossing?" I asked.

"On the contrary, the anticipated glory of surmounting the perils of the desert induced me to embark on the expedition in the first place," Antony explained.

I reflected silently that one of the major inducements of the prospect was his share of the ten-thousand-talent bribe my father offered.

Antony took a draught of wine, and then gave me his dazzling smile. "Besides, O Princess, when the job was done, there was the tantalizing prospect of a holiday in Alexandria. Since boyhood I've dreamed of visiting this city which is great in glory and famous the world over."

My father gave a chuckle. "Surely, Antony, there must have been an easier way of visiting Alexandria."

"But not as exciting," Antony said. "I knew, of course, that Alexandria was more Greek than Athens, and so it is. I enjoyed my stay in Athens a few years ago, but I'm enjoying Alexandria more. Like many Romans, I revere works of Greek art, and I consider the finest example of it, in beauty, symmetry, and form, to be the Princess Cleopatra."

I blushed at this outrageous compliment, given in such a serious voice, but my father laughed delightedly.

"Now, now, Antony," Father cried, "don't flirt with my daughter as you would with the eager wives of my profligate nobles."

"O King, I meant no disrespect for the Princess," Antony avowed.

"Of course you didn't," my father said. "Cleopatra, pour our honored Roman guest more wine."

As I picked up the crystal amphora and poured wine into Antony's goblet, I asked, "What did you do in Athens, my noble lord?"

"I studied the art of oratory at the lyceum," Antony replied, "but only briefly, since fortunately I have inherited some gift for speech from my grandfather and namesake the famous orator and senator. Old folks in Rome still talk about my grandfather, who was unequalled in the art of addressing a crowd."

"They say Cicero is a great speaker," I said. "Do you speak as he does?"

"No, mine is the Asiatic style, rather poetic, careless and full of heroic words," Antony explained. "Cicero's speech is sonorous, pompous, and carefully worded."

"Cicero speaks from the head, but Antony speaks from the heart," Father cried. "Cicero speaks in pure concise Latin, but Antony just pours out his words with native eloquence."

"How does Alexandria compare with Athens?" I asked.

"Alexandria is more gay and beautiful," Antony said.

"And how does Alexandria compare with Rome?"

"In Rome we consider Alexandria to be the second city of the world," Antony remarked with a mischievous grin.

"Well, we in Alexandria," I retorted in pique, "consider Rome to be the third city of the world, after Alexandria and Athens!"

My father laughed heartily at this exchange.

"Alexandria is the cultural and commercial center of the civilized world," I resumed with spirit. "We have surpassed old Athens. Rome, that barbarian village of seven hills, cannot compare in beauty, riches, or grandeur to Alexandria. I will personally conduct you around our city and show you our sights and marvels, Antony."

"To be guided by the ranking princess of the realm would be an honor," Antony said, smiling.

"My Lord," I went on, "is it true that you Romans have just discovered the delight of a daily bath? It may be a novelty to the Romans but we Greeks have known for centuries that a bath is not a luxury but a hygienic necessity."

"Yes, the daily bath has become the fashion in Rome," Antony admitted.

"The Greeks have taught you that there are pleasures in the art of the bath with its refinements of oils, perfumes, and massages," I cried. "It is but one of many things the Romans have still yet to learn from the Greeks, if they are only willing to be our pupils."

"The Greeks and Romans need one another and can exchange ideas," Father put in diplomatically.

Fondness grew between Antony and me in our verbal sparring. He stayed on at our couch for some time, and I felt a certain regret when he left us and returned to circulate among the couches.

A little later I saw him leave the hall with one of the dancing girls who had danced one of the bacchantes. This particular dancer had been carried away into an impassioned frenzy as she danced, and Antony was obviously carried away by her. As I saw them leave with their arms around one another, I felt jealous, envious, and sad, and I tried to conceal my emotions behind an expressionless face.

My father gazed after Antony's departing figure. "A few years ago in Rome he was a beautiful youth loved by many older senators. He was said to be the cause of Scribonius Curio's attempted suicides. And now Antony is a giant gladiator of a man adored by women. A remarkable transformation, yet he gloried in his effeminacy just as much as he now glories in his powerful masculinity."

I refilled my father's goblet. "Does he have a great future, Father?"

"It is difficult to predict," Father said, and then took a reflective sip of wine. "I love the boy, but I think he is too tender-hearted and sentimental to reach truly great heights. He loves pleasure too much, though he is not afraid of enormous challenges. He lacks a hard core like Caesar, but then he does have a certain genius for military strategy and intellectual power, and he is ambitious." He paused and gave a deep sigh. "Only the gods can say who the great men of the future will be, Cleopatra."

Mark Antony stayed on in Alexandria for two months, and during that time he became the object of public regard and favor. He was conspicuous and charming with his easy and eccentric manners, and his frank and familiar ways. He wore his tunic girt low about his hips, a heavy sword at his side, and a cloak tossed nonchalantly over his great shoulders. He was as handsome as Hercules.

During these days, Antony made much of me, realizing that according to the matriarchal system of Egypt, I was now the heiress apparent to the kingdom and a daughter of destiny.

I took Antony all over Alexandria to places of general interest. Wherever we appeared, accompanied by his lieutenants and my entourage of eunuchs and ladies, at the theater, at religious ceremonies, or in the streets, we were always greeted with applause. I conducted him through the hallowed halls of the libraries and laboratories and the university and the museum.

"It was here in the museum, Lord Antony," I commented, "that Aristarchus of Samos submitted to Ptolemy the Second his dissertation revealing that the earth revolves around the sun."

"Do you really think the world is round?" Antony asked skeptically.

"Of course it's round!" I cried impatiently. "Are you Romans still bound by the belief that it's flat? Ptolemy the First long ago composed an atlas, the world's first comprehensive geography, with maps of the countries and seas of the world. During the reign of Ptolemy the Second, the great Eratosthenes calculated the circumference of the earth at twenty-five thousand miles around and seven thousand eight hundred and fifty miles in diameter."*

"Can this be fact?" Antony said with doubt in his voice.

I looked at Antony in amazement. "Have you not studied Euclid's works, which he did in this very building? Euclid's elements, the study of terrestrial conditions and speeds, and his great astronomical treatise demonstrating the movements of all the planets?"

"No, O Princess, but surely I must," Antony said.

"In this great museum, the birthplace of all the sciences, of anatomy, geometry, conic sections, hydrostatics, geography, astronomy, you can begin to widen your understanding," I cried.

One luminous, sun-splashed afternoon we were being carried in a sedan down the grand boulevard of the Canopic Way, with the glorious white marble buildings shimmering on all sides.

"My forefathers spent vast fortunes embellishing this city to make it the most splendid in the world," I explained proudly. "Only three hundred years ago this was a poor fishing village, Rhakotis, where Memelaus of the *Iliad* once touched upon. And then Ptolemy the First

---

*Seventy-five miles off modern figure.—WB

transformed the little port into a great metropolis." I pointed to the well-dressed people on the sidewalks. "As you can see, there are no beggars in Alexandria, for here everyone works industriously, Egyptians, Greeks, Jews, Syrians, foreigners from the four corners of the world, all of whose tongues I speak."

"Yes, I've noticed, O Princess, that you are an accomplished linguist," Antony said. "Your Greek is not the Macedonian dialect like your father's, but the purest Athenian Attic."

"Oh, I can speak the dialect of my father and my guards," I said, "and the Egyptian patois of the street-cleaners and market vendors, too!"

The sedan passed the Sema and began moving down the boulevard leading to the palace.

"Notice, Lord Antony, how grandly our streets are laid out," I continued. "In Rome my father tells me the streets are crooked and small, and except for the Senate buildings, there is nothing that is impressive. I'm told the tenements there are unbelievably wretched. Well, you will find no tenements in Alexandria."

"Much of Rome needs to be torn down and rebuilt," Antony said. "The day will come when great marble buildings will rise to replace the tenements, and then Rome will equal Alexandria. Until that day, Alexandria is the most beautiful city in the world. I half believe I am captive of an exquisite dream here."

"Perhaps you are, my Lord Antony," I said with a special smile.

I must confess that I was slightly overbearing toward Antony about the superiority of my culture and city, but he was not offended but indeed seemed charmed and captivated. We spent many days together, and in the evenings we would meet at the theater or banquets or at small parties in my father's apartments.

My nights were not shared with him, however, for I slept alone as befitting a virgin princess who was concerned with her honor. Although I must admit with all honesty that my thoughts were not always so pure, for Anthony had stirred my senses and emotions.

113

Needless to say, Antony never slept alone. Everywhere we went, young maidens and pretty bawds were constantly besieging him and hanging wreaths about his neck. He enjoyed the enchantments of the most beautiful ladies and courtesans of the city. I have never been interested in the gossip of my girls, but I strained my ears to hear them say that Antony's good looks were equalled only by his bad reputation, that he had no resistance where women were concerned, nor could they reject him. They said that he was an insatiable lover in the tradition of his ancestor, Hercules, and that in addition to all the experienced women he enjoyed, he had breached many a maiden. But the one maiden he wanted he dared not approach. I always suspected in my heart he longed for me, the ranking Princess of Lower and Upper Egypt.

About a month after my father's restoration, there was an outbreak of a revolt in Palestine, and Gabinius was called back to his Syria province to restore order there. Antony also began making preparations to leave for Rome, but first these Romans had to be paid for services rendered. Since my father must meet his obligations to his restorers, he condemned to death all those who had served in Berenice's government, her ministers and chamberlains, and confiscated their estates. Out of the monies, he paid Gabinius a large portion of the promised ten thousand talents and Antony a generous share for his efforts. Both Gabinius and Antony had come to Egypt poor but were leaving rich. Antony was also given a great sum to take back to Pompey.

"Never again will Antony have to market his body to old, depraved senators," Apollodorus remarked, jealous of my regard for Antony.

It was arranged that, when Gabinius and Antony departed, a portion of their Roman soldiers would stay behind, under my father's command, to aid him in keeping possession of his throne. These soldiers had fallen under the spell of Alexandria and were quite willing to settle down.

The night before Antony's departure, my father gave a banquet in his honor for the whole court. Dancers

114

danced, acrobats tumbled, and the repast was delectable. Antony sat on my father's couch, and I took a chair beside them.

"It is with deep sadness that I leave on the morrow," Antony said. "I have grown to love Alexandria, and I have become exceedingly fond of your Princess, O King."

My father smiled warmly. "My heart rejoices to see that you two appreciate each other."

"Yes, King Ptolemy, I admire your Princess, her blooming beauty, her wit, and her accomplishments."

"In a few years she will be Queen of Egypt," Father said soberly.

"Oh, no, Father, not so soon!" I protested fiercely.

"Death comes, even to god-Kings, and I do not enjoy the most excellent health," Father said. "In a few years I will be dead, Caesar will be dead, Pompey will be dead, and you, Mark Antony, will be one of the great leaders of the world. As Pompey was my patron and friend, I hope you shall be the patron friend of my daughter when she wears the crown."

"As I am your champion, O King," Antony said earnestly, "so I swear an oath to the gods to champion Queen Cleopatra."

"I will hold you to that promise, my Lord Antony," I said tenderly. "How many years has it been since you left Rome?"

"Seven years," Antony replied. "I left in debt and disgrace and went to Greece a fugitive."

"Now you return to Rome to be one of the most powerful personages in the Republic," I said.

"So it seems," Antony murmured.

"Father, you say soon Pompey and Caesar will be dead," I said, "but before they go, they will have time enough to bring much mischief on the world."

"Yes, a civil war is brewing inevitably between them," Father said.

I looked at Antony. "Whose cause shall you espouse, my lord?"

"Caesar is my mother's first cousin, so I will naturally

115

espouse the cause of my kinsman," Antony explained. "And rest assured that I will always intervene to see that Caesar espouses the cause of Egypt."

"In the past, Caesar wasn't always Egypt's friend," I reminded him. "Ten years ago he had a plan with Crassus, which Cicero foiled, to annex Egypt."

"That was ten years ago," Father said quickly. "Caesar has since been our friend, and four years ago he put the Julian Law through the Senate, recognizing us as Friend and Ally of the Roman People."

"You made it well worth his while," I remarked.

"That is what friendship and love is," Father said philosophically. "People who need and help one another."

I turned to gaze on Antony. "Have you seen Alexander's tomb during your stay, my lord?"

"No, my Princess," Antony replied.

"You cannot leave Alexandria until you do," I said.

"I sail in the morning," Antony said.

"I will take you there before you leave," I said.

"As you wish, O Princess," Antony replied.

I left the banquet early, for I disliked seeing Antony become deep in his cups. He would then carouse with the ladies of the court. It was his custom to take two or three of them back to the luxurious apartment which my father had assigned him, and I did not enjoy witnessing such a show of licentious behavior.

The following morning we met with my father for breakfast. Afterward Antony and I, accompanied by a few attendants, rode in litters to the Sema. We entered the massive marble mausoleum where more than two hundred crypts are arranged in neat rows, bearing the sculptured likenesses of the eleven Ptolemaic Kings and their various Queens and offspring sealed beneath.

I bade all our attendants to stay behind, for I wanted only Antony to pay respect with me to Alexander in his tomb in the underground chamber.

The massive doors were opened by guards, and Antony held a torch aloft to give us light. I led the way down the marble staircase into the large chamber, through a long corridor to the end where Alexander's body, enclosed in a crystal sarcophagus, lay on a marble catafalque. Eternal flames dimly lit the tomb.

In reverent silence I approached the sacred remains. I stopped and gazed in wonder at the beautiful corpse which was encased in gold armor, the hand clasping a sword. The skin-thin mask of gold was molded to the handsome face. A dreamy expression marked the features, the strong chin, the thick voluptuous lips, and the nose of classic mold like that of Hermes in the wondrous image wrought by Praxiteles. The blond-gold hair was still perfect, curling over his forehead like the mane of a lion. The power of his magnetic beauty still radiated from his face, although it had been stilled for two hundred and sixty-eight years. I stood, feeling dizzy, mesmerized by the golden form.

I emerged from my trance, suddenly aware that Antony had hung back in the distance. I turned to see him shifting uneasily from one foot to the other.

"Place the torch in the hook on the wall there, my Lord Antony, and come stand beside me," I urged softly.

Antony did as I requested. After a long scrutiny of the body, he observed, "The embalmers with their ancient craft did their work well." After a moment he put a hand on the crystal sarcophagus. "I read that this was once made of gold."

"Yes, but Ptolemy the Fourth had it melted down to pay for Syrian mercenaries to quell a rebellion in Upper Egypt," I told him. "The best crystal in the world is made in Alexandria. Someday when I am Queen I will have the sarcophagus fashioned again in gold." I paused in reflection. "But then again, perhaps I won't. I might reduce the body to ashes and scatter them to the four winds. Alexander wanted his ashes to be mingled with those of his great love, Hephaistrian, and dispersed together, but instead his brother Ptolemy brought his body to Egypt. In a way, it is sad to think that in all these years we Ptolemies have used his corpse as a political symbol. Alexander would have hated that."

"But this way we see him just as he appeared in life," Antony said.

"The statues and busts and coins are likenesses enough." I gave a sigh of exaltation. "In my veins flows the blood of Alexander, for his brother Ptolemy is my grandfather seven times over."

"I'm aware of your genealogy, O Princess."

"How old is Caesar now?" I asked.

"Forty-six," Antony answered.

"As old as my father," I said. "And when Caesar was thirty he wept bitter tears to think that he had accomplished nothing by then, as well he might, for at thirty Alexander had the world. All men forevermore will have to live in the shadow of Alexander and weep."

"You are in love with a man who has been dead for almost three centuries," Antony said with a bitter smile.

"Yes," I said simply. "But I hope that somewhere there is another Alexander walking the earth. A man can be sparked by Alexander's genius by sharing his dream, and in that way Alexander will be born again."

"His dream?" Antony inquired.

"The dream of Alexander, the dream of world unity and the brotherhood of man," I cried passionately. "He conquered Persia, but he mingled their blood and culture with the Greek, and Hellenism was born and has come down to us. That is where you Romans err, for you conquer the world and care nothing for the gods and customs of the people you conquer. You make slaves instead of brothers of the conquered. What Alexander did can be done again with the Romans and the Greeks and the Egyptians merging, one borrowing from the other in peace and harmony without wars. One world and one people."

"Alexander's dream," Antony said. "Cleopatra's dream."

"Yes," I sighed. "If only I were a man!"

"If you were a man you would not have brought me here," Antony said.

I looked him frankly in the eye. "No."

118

"Do you come here often, Cleopatra?" Antony asked.

"Whenever I need spiritual sustenance," I replied.

Antony gazed silently at Alexander, then shivered. "It is cold down here, so let us begone from this house of death."

"As you wish, my Lord Antony," I agreed.

In a public ceremony Antony made sacrifices to the gods at the altar in the square between the palace and the sea. Then in our litters, surrounded by soldiers and priests, we were taken in stately procession to the dockside to Antony's flagship. Thousands of Alexandrians, held back by soldiers, were cheering with wild enthusiasm.

"Your name will be remembered with respect among my people, Antony," Father remarked.

Antony, in full view of everyone, kissed my father on both cheeks and embraced him heartily, and then did the same to me. His mouth came precariously close to my lips, and with an effort I kept my regal composure in public.

To the blast of trumpets, Antony went on board the ship, and the gangplank was taken up. As the ship moved away under the power of the rowers, Antony stood on deck waving farewell.

In silence and sadness, my father and I returned to his apartments. He took wine and I drank some pomegranate juice.

After a while I moved to a seat at the window to watch the ship sailing by Pharos and out into the sea. My father came and stood near me. I closed my eyes and felt the tears, against my will, sliding down my cheeks. My father's hand gently wiped the tears away.

"My beloved daughter," Father said huskily.

I turned and buried my face against his chest, crying quietly.

"You are becoming a woman with a woman's emotions," Father said, gently caressing my hair. "I am deeply moved by this affection you feel."

I composed myself and looked up at my father with

a shaky smile. "But it is merely an infatuation, beloved Father," I assured him. "My great love will always be Egypt."

"Good girl," Father said with a smile of pride.

"And since I'm the heiress apparent now," I said, "I have chosen a motto for the time when I am queen."

"What is it, my daughter?" Father asked anxiously.

"*Everything for Egypt*," I said with fervor.

Tears came to my father's eyes, and he drew me against him, embracing me in eloquent silence as the cooling kiss of sea breezes came in the windows.

CHAPTER VI

I STOOD IN SPLENDOR AND GLORY next to my father now that he was again King in Egypt. For three years I had been neglected and in a precarious position, but now I emerged from Berenice's shadow to my father's side with all dignity and honor. All the nobles addressed me on their knees, and tongues could not sufficiently praise my virtues, my beauty and accomplishments. I was acquiring more every day a stronger sense of myself. I was fourteen and had quickened to womanhood, maturing early in both mind and body. I was proud of my slim, elegant figure and vowed I would preserve the body the gods had blessed me with, and that the house of clay my spirit inhabited would never be abused.

My doting father lavished much attention on me, and I loved him more than anyone in the world. The things he loved I loved, the things he despised I despised. I was his true daughter in all things. He was deeply dedicated to the attainment of his rights, to the sanctity of his kingship, and to the preservation of Ptolemaic power, and these same ideals he pressed into my soul as a part of me.

"We must be honest, we princes with one another," Father told me solemnly. "I am a sick man and I pray the gods give me another four or five years until you obtain your majority, and then I'll be content to go to my eternal rest and leave Egypt in your capable hands. Of the six children from my seed you are the best, so it is only right that you will inherit the throne. In all probability, when you become Queen your brother and co-

121

ruler will be young, and you will have to be the stronger and wiser. You will have to hold court and administer justice and see to the judgment of Egypt. All the nobles admire already your impressive intellectual gifts, but there is still more for you to learn."

From my father's side I had lessons in statecraft, preparing myself rigorously for the day I would come to the crown. I took my position with grave seriousness. I had few pleasurable pursuits. I continued my studies under Protarchus, rigidly following a faithful regimen. Protarchus was an unrelenting taskmaster and gave me a wide curriculum, and my scholarship increased. I spoke and wrote fluent Greek, Latin, and Egyptian, and was well on my way to mastering Ethiopian, Trygodyte, Hebrew, Aramaic, Syriac, Median, and Parthian. It was my father's wish that I would be able to dispense with interpreters, for his reliance on interpreters had always put him at a disadvantage.

I also had lessons on the lute and the harp, although my musicianship was not on my father's level. I am gifted in the dance, however, with an innate sense of physical grace and movement, and took pride in my dancing lessons. At small private banquets in my father's chambers I would sometimes dance while my father accompanied me on the flute. It was often remarked that if we had not been born royal, we could have found fame as dancer and flutist. At banquets I also gave readings of my favorite poems or passages from Homer that I had memorized, and I was praised for my dramatic delivery.

The mood of the court had changed with my father's restoration. Everyone sighed with relief after the three years of living under the restrictive rule of Berenice, and every night there was much drinking and carousing. Surrounded by corrupt influences and exposed to all exhibitions of vice, I remained pure, and in my position I was sacred and aloof, set apart from all others. The court was a hotbed of gossip, but I gave no opportunity for tongues to wag about me and did nothing to besmirch my honor.

Since the days when our dynasty had been established, all the foreign influence which had been exercised in Egypt, whether civil or military, had been Greek, but now with the coming of the Romans, a new element was added to the variety of excitement which animated Alexandria.

The Roman creditors pressed my father for repayment of monies they had lent for the tremendous bribes that he had promised.

"I am going to do something very clever," Father told me with a twinkle in his eye. "Rabirius Postumus is the Roman financier who represents the interests of Caesar and all my other Roman creditors, and I have offered him the key post of Minister of Finance!"

"Only Egyptians or Greeks have held this post before," I said, stunned. "And you give it to a Roman?"

"Yes, and that alone will make him unpopular. There is a method to my madness. Rabirius has jumped at the offer, and why not? He thinks that by holding such a position he will be better able to facilitate the looting of the land. As taxes are increased, however, the people will grow angry, and who will be blamed? The Minister of Finance, the Roman Rabirius!"

"Father, you are so shrewd!" I cried.

"A king must be shrewd. Kingship is a craft that must be mastered."

I met Rabirius many times at court functions and came to know him. I had always been curious about Romans. Rabirius seemed to typify the species—brash, vulgar, crude, confident, and overbearing beyond endurance. I thoroughly despised him. He never knew my feelings, of course, since I was always polite. Rabirius was ill-mannered and gross and not used to the ways of a civilized court. As Minister of Finance, he had virtual control of the currency; taxes passed through his hands, he obtained the monopoly of the crystal and glass works and took a large percentage of all revenues. From my chamber windows I saw ships sailing off from the harbor toward Naples, laden with grain, gold, gems, crystal, silver and copper, linen and papyrus. I watched with impotent fury while my hapless country was being pillaged.

In consequence of increased taxes, the people became restless and resentful. There was a worsening of the national economy, and waves of little insurrections washed over the kingdom. As my father predicted, the people centered their hostility on the Minister of Finance, Rabirius. At last the resentment erupted, and a mob of insurgents stormed the palace.

"Death to the Roman!" they cried. "Death to Rabirius!"

My father arranged that Rabirius could make his escape and take ship back to Rome. Needless to say, I was happy to see the Roman bloodsucker go, and the people quieted down with his departure.

Back in Rome, Rabirius and Gabinius were both brought to trial, Gabinius for having acted against the decree of the Senate and taking part in an unauthorized invasion of Egypt, and Rabirius for having held an administrative post under a foreign king.

"Such hypocrites, these Romans!" Father cried contemptuously. "Cicero is defending Rabirius by saying his client acted out of magnanimity of spirit in lending me money, and that I forced him to become finance minister. Cicero said even Plato had been associated with a tyrant, so this should not be scored too heavily against the kindly Rabirius. It's all such a comedy!"

Despite Cicero's advocacy and the distribution of bribes, Rabirius and Gabinius were found guilty, stripped of rank, and retired to the country.

"I'm thankful," Father said, "that our friend and patron, Pompey, has somehow kept his hands clean and there were no charges brought against him. Politics is a dirty business in Rome."

My father was not in the best of health, and the affairs of the kingdom were staggering for him. His hands shook with an occasional palsy, and the lassitude of sickness pulled at his limbs. In the evenings we always dined together, then he would play his flute a little, and we would sit until the late hours.

"I must find a new Minister of Finance," Father fretted one night. "Who, who, who?" He drank a deep draught of unmixed wine as if he would find the answer with it.

"Kallimachos!" I cried with sudden inspiration.

"But of course, Kallimachos!" Father cried.

Kallimachos was from one of the leading Macedonian ruling families, who had served our house for generations in positions of honor. Under my father he had been a viceroy and then Commander of the Red Sea, and had controlled the trade with India. When Berenice took the power, Kallimachos had refused to serve under a false monarch and had left court, retiring to his estate outside Canopus with his family. His son, the junior Kallimachos, who had been one of my father's secretaries, had also left court at the same time.

"Yes, Kallimachos!" Father cried. "He must be nearing sixty now. Do you think he would take the position?"

"Invite him to court to discuss it," I suggested.

Within a week Kallimachos, his son and granddaughter came to court. I was in the Great Throne Room, sitting in a chair of state beside my father's throne, when Kallimachos and his family came in for a formal audience. The senior Kallimachos was an elegant, silver-haired man well on in his years but tall and unbent. His son, who was about forty, was also a man of distinguished countenance. They knelt with graceful obeisance.

"It is a great honor for my son and me to pay homage to our beloved King!" the elder Kallimachos cried.

"Rise, my honored friends," Father said warmly.

"Majestic King," said Kallimachos, "I beg leave to present my granddaughter."

"Bring her forward, Lord Kallimachos," Father said with a nod.

A young girl came out of the crowd of courtiers and advanced toward the throne, and I was instantly struck by her true beauty of mien. She had a voluptuous figure, a skin of white and rose, flashing green eyes, and ringlets of reddish hair.

"Could this be the spirited little girl you used to bring to the palace, Lord Kallimachos?" Father asked.

"The last few years have transformed her into a young woman, O King."

"And a lovely one," Father cried, "but I do not recall her name."

"Charmion," the elder Kallimachos said with pride.

"Ah, yes, and a most apt name," my father remarked, "since it means the charming one."

"Divine King and sacred Princess!" Charmion sank gracefully to one knee and inclined her head.

"The noble house of Kallimachos has been honored friends of the Lagidae these many generations," Father said. "It is with pleasure that my daughter the Princess Cleopatra and I welcome you to our court."

After the formal audience in the Great Throne Room, I went with Father to his apartments where he divested himself of his robes and regalia. Kallimachos, father and son, were to join my father for the midday repast, and Father suggested that I entertain Charmion in my own apartments. For some obscure reason I was filled with wild anticipation as I hurried back to my chambers. Usually at my noonday meal I ate sparingly, having little interest in food, but I gave instructions to my chamberlains that since we were having an honored guest, a daughter of a house who had served us loyally, special delicacies were to be prepared. I went to my robing chamber and selected one of my most beautiful dresses to wear.

At last the Lady Charmion was admitted into my reception room.

"Welcome, Lady Charmion," I said, smiling.

"It is my great honor, O Princess," Charmion replied, sinking to one knee.

"Come share my couch," I said.

Charmion sat beside me and gazed at me with eyes that were like two flashing emeralds.

"Please join me in some wine," I said. The wine was watered, but I was dizzy in the presence of Charmion even before I took one sip.

126

"It is a pleasure to find you have become even more beautiful than you were as a child," Charmion said in her mellifluous voice. "Of course you don't remember me, O Princess, since you never left your studies to play with the children of the court."

"Please forgive me," I responded, "but, in truth, I knew few of the children then and can recall almost no one."

"You were such a serious princess," Charmion went on with a smile. "You could never tolerate me, for I was a frivolous little idiot. However, in the four years that I have been at our house in Canopus, I have applied myself diligently to my studies. I am no match for you in intellect, but I am hoping that now we will be able to discuss such things as literature and poetry."

"Forgive me, Charmion, if in our childhood I rebuffed you," I cried, taking her hand and squeezing it.

Charmion laughed, showing magnificent teeth. "Oh, yes, many times you refused to play hide-and-seek in the palace gardens with me and my friends."

"I must have been an impossible little girl," I said.

Charmion gave a devastating smile. "No, O Princess, you just had more important matters to attend to."

With reluctance I released her hand.

My serving girls brought oysters and quails, sesame cakes and wild honey, and a variety of rare fruit for us to eat. Charmion ate with gusto and delight. It was obvious from her rounded figure that she loved food. I was nervous and had no appetite, but watched with pleasure while she enjoyed the food with such abandon. At this time Charmion was sixteen years old, a year my senior.

At length Polydemus, the chamberlain of my household, appeared.

"O Princess, your Latin tutor is waiting," he said.

"Cancel all my lessons for the afternoon, my Lord Polydemus."

"Yes, Divine Princess," he cried, leaving.

"Princess Cleopatra," Charmion said, placing her hand over mine, "I don't want to interfere with your studies."

I drew her hands into mine. "Never mind, Charmion,"

I said in a tremulous voice, for I was stirred by new emotions. "The afternoon is not being wasted. I hope to elicit your aid in behalf of Egypt, to persuade you to influence your grandfather to sit on my father's council as Minister of Finance."

"We of the house of Kallimachos have always obeyed our King's wishes," Charmion said with intensity. "My grandfather has been in peaceful retirement at Canopus, but if his King needs his services, I know he will comply to his dying breath. And so would I, O Princess."

I was touched by her sincerity. For a long moment we sat there staring into each other's eyes.

"Please call me Cleopatra," I finally found my voice to say.

"Cleopatra," Charmion said slowly, exultantly.

"I hope, Charmion, that we will be friends," I cried, clasping her hands in mine. "I want to make amends for having slighted you in our bygone childhood days."

"I ask only to serve you, Cleopatra," she said earnestly, devotion sparkling in her bright green irises.

"You will serve me by being my friend, Charmion."

"I vow to be your friend to the end of my days," she cried.

I fell in love with Charmion that afternoon. Her very presence had made me feel radiant and happy. Her gaiety, grace, and beauty were a balm to me.

It was an unusually warm afternoon and no breeze came in from the sea. Charmion was overcome by lassitude from the warmth, food, and wine. We lounged on divans while a lute and a harp played soothing melodies in the corner.

"I am so hot," Charmion declared indolently. "I would like to relax in a cool bath, Cleopatra."

"We shall bathe together, Charmion," I said.

Charmion's lips curled tenderly and I quivered.

In my bathing chamber Charmion admired the murals of gods and goddesses on the walls and the mosaic floor. My ladies disrobed us with adroit fingers. I could not bring myself to look upon her nakedness, but slipped into the pool sunken beneath the floor. Only after Charmion had submerged with head and shoulders above the water did I permit myself to look into her eyes. We rested on opposite sides of the pool, gazing across the water, lapis lazuli inlays turned azure blue. Serving girls poured flagons of warm rose-scented water over our heads. Charmion squealed with delight, closing her eyes as the water fell over her.

I could see the huge nipples of her lush breasts breaking the surface of the water, and I felt weak and trembly. Her great globes of breasts were huge but beautifully formed, and I felt a pang of inadequacy at my own small bosom.

We dallied long in the pool. My ladies toweled us dry, and then Charmion and I found ourselves standing and staring at each other.

"Your face and form have great beauty, Cleopatra," Charmion said candidly, her green eyes inspecting me slowly from head to toe. "Your face is like a fine, exquisite cameo carved in ivory."

As a princess I had been complimented from childhood, often shamelessly and without subtlety, but I knew that Charmion spoke sincerely from her heart.

"Thank you, Charmion," I whispered. "And you are indeed as beautiful as Aphrodite."

Charmion responded with a musical, full-throated laugh. "Am I really, Cleopatra?" she asked eagerly.

"Yes," I said, moving my eyes over her body, savoring the sight of her naked beauty. I saw that her ivory skin was faintly tinted by nature. The pink nipples cresting her large blue-veined breasts, under my gaze, enlarged and took on a purplish tinge. "Your body is in perfect symmetry," I cried, "and has the sculptured beauty of the glorious Aphrodite of Praxiteles at Cnidus."

Charmion stepped toward me until our faces were inches apart, and her hot breath blew against me. "I marvel, O Princess, that the gods could fashion such beauty as yours out of human clay."

I smiled shakily and took her hand. "Come, let us have a massage."

We stretched our bodies on couches. The Nubian eunuchs, well schooled in body massage, poured precious oil of myrrh into their expert hands and stroked almost every inch of our bodies. We lay in silence, our bodies glowing. The wine, the bath, the massage, all conspired to render us in an indolent, sensuous, sensitized state.

After the massage I ordered one goblet of pomegranate juice for us to share, passing the cup back and forth as we more boldly appraised each other's bodies.

"Yes, we are both beautiful," Charmion stated simply. "We women have weak bodies, but when we are beautiful, we can use our bodies as weapons. We cannot fight with swords like men, but we can fight with our bodies with the bedchamber as our battlefield."

This was a revelation which had never occurred to me before. Perhaps Charmion could teach me things, I reflected silently.

The nakedness of Charmion was like a heady draught weakening my body, making me drunk, and finally I could stand it no more. I rose and signalled for my serving girls to dress us.

Late in the afternoon Charmion and I went to my father's apartments to learn that her grandfather had accepted the post of finance minister, and her father was assigned to be one of my father's secretaries. I requested that Charmion become my Lady of the Royal Vestiture, and she accepted with delight.

Charmion was assigned her own chambers near my apartments in my wing of the palace. She became my confidante and favorite. Apollodorus, who had previously held the position as my foremost favorite, could barely disguise his jealousy of her. My father greatly approved of my new friend, and he was pleased that I had at last found devotion in one my own age and sex. Charmion was in many ways my opposite, and we complemented each other. Under her influence, I was gay, laughing and giggling like a child, a luxury I never had permitted myself to enjoy in childhood.

One night in midsummer, about a month after Charmion had come to court, we went to the Theater of Dionysus with my father and his entourage.

I was flushed with excitement as our litters were carried the short distance from the palace to the theater. An escort of soldiers marched in a cordon of honor, clearing the thronging evening streets before our way. At last the great theater loomed in front of us. My blood raced as we alighted, passed through the long marble archway, and entered the massive theater built by Ptolemy the Second. Modeled on the amphitheater at Epidaurus, it is my favorite place in all the world since childhood. The people cheered rousingly as we entered the royal enclosure, with its golden canopy, at the right side of the stage. My father and I stood beside the marble balustrade, which was emblazoned with a Ptolemaic eagle fashioned in gold. We looked out at the vast semicircular rows of marble seats built in tiers, all packed with their full capacity of twenty thousand pleasure-loving Alexandrians. Father and I acknowledged the spirited ovations from our people with smiles and waves. It was a glorious spectacle that greeted my eyes as everyone was dressed in vivid tunics, lovely gowns, and flashing jewels.

At length I sat on a couch beside Charmion, and my father took a seat beside his favorite, Cleombrotus. Hawkers strolled the aisles selling wineskins, sweetmeats, and candies. On stage, jugglers performed their amazing exploits, and then Diodorus and his dancers came on. As music poured out of the pit, the stage became an orgy of physical movement in celebration of Dionysia.

When the dance was finished, the audience settled down and their babble of conversation ceased. All the torches were put out by the theater attendants, except for those surrounding the stage to light the actors. Trumpets blasted, a hushed silence fell, and the play was about to begin.

"Oh, I'm so excited!" Charmion cried.

"What greater pleasures are there in life than the dance and the drama?" I asked.

"Oh, there are others, my dear girls!" King Ptolemy cried with a laugh.

The company of actors took the stage and the play began. That night it was *Iphigenia in Taurus* by Sophocles. This tragedy definitely takes its place as one of the major masterpieces of the old Greeks, and the players did it full justice, bringing it vibratingly to life with all its pulse, poetry, and passion. The plight of Orestes has always appealed to my imagination, for I realize more than most that, as it did in his case, destiny can defeat and destroy dreams.

Sitting beside Charmion, I was deeply touched by the beautiful friendship between Orestes and his beloved friend, Pylades. There was one line in particular which struck me with its poignancy of feeling, when Orestes says, "We are not brothers in blood, but we are brothers in love!"

When this line was spoken with passionate intensity by the actor who played Orestes, I reached for Charmion's hand in the dark and squeezed it.

After the performance, we went to the chambers beneath the stage to pay our respects to the actors. I was thrilled to see that the two young actors who played Orestes and Pylades, now that their masks were removed, were both incredibly handsome. They stood close, and it was obvious that they shared a certain affinity of spirit offstage as well as on.

My father chatted a long while with the great actor Lysandridas, who had given a heartbreaking performance as Iphigenia. Lysandridas had been one of my father's boy friends a decade earlier, and they still felt a fondness for one another. What a tragedy and loss to the stage that Lysandridas no longer acts, for just about a year after this he lost all his teeth from a virulent gum disease, which garbled his speech, and he was forced to retire. My father settled a huge sum on him, and he now spends his days teaching young boys the thespian art, although of course elocution and declamation are no longer his strong points.

Charmion and I made our farewells to the actors, and

we walked down the marble steps to the square in front of the theater to our waiting litters. Soldiers held back the populace who were eagerly waiting to see their King and Princess come out. As I appeared, great shouting erupted.

Apollodorus helped Charmion and me into our litter. The people jostled for a sight of me, straining against the interlocked soldiers. Charmion and I, sitting opposite one another, chatted amiably, but I kept turning my head to smile at the cheering, waving people.

Suddenly, drawn by the screeching of cats, I looked to see two cats beside the litter on the pavement engaging in the act of copulation.

"By holy Eros, look!" Charmion cried excitedly.

Spellbound, we watched with mesmerized eyes as the two cats pursued their pleasure. The tom achieved gratification with a shrilling shriek, abruptly disengaged and scurried away, lost among the crowd. The she cat, left behind and obviously not having been gratified, frantically sprinted after the tom.

The crowd let out a rousing cry, for the cat is a sacred animal, and to have observed the cats in coitus was an honored thing, and even I, a princess, did not feel embarrassed to have witnessed the rite.

King Ptolemy was hailed with warm cries by his people, as he climbed into his litter with his favorite, Cleombrotus. Cleombrotus was a beautiful boy who had been my father's favorite and had gone into exile with him. Even now, though he had started to shave and sprout hair on his chest, my father continued to hold him in the highest affection.

The Nubian litter-bearers picked up the litters and we began the journey back to the palace. Apollodorus on his Arabian stallion led the way with an escort of soldiers, and torchbearers ran alongside the litters.

"May I draw the curtains against the chill of the night air?" Charmion asked.

There was no chill, and I usually rode in an open litter so that my people could see me, yet I nodded consent. Charmion deftly pulled the purple and gold curtains against the prying eyes of passersby, and we were suddenly enclosed in a private little world all of our own.

The excitement of the theater that night, the incident of the cats in coitus, the rhythm of the litter, and the proximity of Charmion's presence, all conspired to make me quiver with feverish intoxication.

Suddenly, as the litter turned a sharp corner, Charmion was thrown off her seat against me and our arms encircled each other. We did not utter a word, and could not disengage ourselves. I could hear the furious pounding of our hearts beating in unison.

"Charmion?" I whispered at last.

"Yes, Cleopatra?" Her breath caressed my cheek.

"Do you remember that beautiful line in the play tonight, when Orestes says, 'Pylades and I are not brothers in blood, but we are brothers in love.' "

"Yes, Cleopatra," Charmion breathed, "I remember."

I paused, for there was a catch in my throat. "That is how I feel about us, Charmion," I said in a voice husky with emotion. "We are sisters, not in blood, but in love."

"Oh, my beloved Cleopatra!" Charmion cried.

Charmion pressed her lips against my cheek. She had often kissed my cheeks before, but then she moved her mouth and found my lips. Only my father and my Uncle Ptolemy had ever kissed me on the mouth. Charmion then did something which was a wondrously new experience for me. Her tongue went between my lips and penetrated my mouth, setting my senses ablaze. I was fifteen and had never experienced this kind of kiss. The kiss was eternal, her tongue probing my mouth endlessly. I was in a delirium, and I thought I would die in the frenzy of the kiss, but I wanted it to go on forever.

Suddenly the litter was put down with a thud. We broke apart, and with an effort I composed myself.

Charmion pulled the curtains apart. Apollodorus helped us from the litter. We all went into the great corridor of the palace, kissed my father, and then Apollodorus and a few guards escorted Charmion and me to my wing of the palace.

At last we reached the doors of my chambers. I

sometimes invited both Apollodorus and Charmion into my reception room for a little repast before I retired, but this night I wanted to be alone with just Charmion.

"Good night, Apollodorus," I said, dismissing him.

An expression of pain crossed his face and glittered in his brown eyes.

I held out my hand and gave him a kind smile. "I will see you in the morning, Apollodorus."

Apollodorus kissed my hand and turned to Charmion. "Shall I escort you to your quarters, Charmion?"

"There are a few duties I wish Charmion to perform for me before she retires," I broke in.

Apollodorus gave a curt salute and went off with his soldiers. I could not understand why he should feel conspired against and pained, since after all he too had his friends.

I took Charmion into my reception room and dismissed all my servants. We were alone. I saw that her jade eyes were unnaturally bright, and I wondered if my eyes had the same feverish luster. She gave me a smile of peerless pleasure, and I felt myself tremble and seethe with emotions.

Silently I walked into my bedchamber, and she followed me. The only light came from a lone burning taper and the silver illumination from the moon that came in from the open windows facing the sea.

We turned to each other and gazed deeply. With trembling hands we each disrobed the other. I fell across my bed, and Charmion hovered solicitously over me. I inhaled the heady sweetness of her body and my senses spiraled. My heart raced as her hands slid over my burning breasts, my thighs, and I yielded to the tide of flame that engulfed me, crying aloud with the exquisite pain of her touch. Her tender fingertips and mouth explored my body in areas which had been touched only by the Chief Physician, but with a different purpose and result.

The silence and mystery of the night enveloped us as we clung to each other. We were two maidens in vital search beneath the shining moon. We were cast in a spell, and my bedchamber became a place of enchantment. We kissed, our mouths met and clung, and our bodies entwined in erotic loveplay, in love's complete embrace.

It was my first taste of the beatitude of love that the poets and philosophers have immortalized. I had never experienced these intimacies before and learned that night that the poets have never truly captured in words the deep-rooted, primal feelings that shake mere mortals to their souls, when all the elemental forces are set loose and we are swept out of ourselves. The nature of love was no longer a secret to me.

I marveled at the miracle of lovemaking as all night long we made love, exchanging kisses in lovely leisure, with long, languorous sighs. Sensation was a vortex whirling through the funnel of my being, and time and again I found myself brought to a pinnacle of passion that was almost unendurable.

"With us, it is not like the cats," Charmion whispered in my ear. "Nor is it the same as a man with a woman, or a man with a man. With them it is quick and sometimes brutal, but with us, like this, it is a sweet ecstasy as timeless as eternity."

That first night of love we exhausted each other with the excesses of ecstasy. At last the pale blue dawn began to light up the sky outside and seep into the bedchamber. Charmion arose from bed and pulled the curtains against the coming day, in a vain attempt to prolong the night. She returned to my arms, and pulled a satin coverlet over our bodies.

"Cleopatra, my love!"

"Charmion, my love!"

With this exchange of avowals, our bodies entangled and we finally allowed sleep to claim our wearied bodies.

As I look back, I realize that I was then emotionally and physically ripe for the relationship that blossomed with Charmion.

"When we were children you refused to play with me in the palace gardens," Charmion teased, "but you play with me now."

"Yes," I said with a delighted laugh, "times have changed."

Charmion became like a sister to me, and I found it more meaningful to have chosen a spiritual sister than to have sisters from the arbitrary lottery of birth. A young girl needs love and laughter. It was through Charmion's love and devotion that I touched reality and embraced my innermost being.

As the chosen of Cleopatra, Charmion did provoke some jealousy among my ladies who had never held my affection to the degree that Charmion now did. Charmion held an exalted place as my favorite and perhaps at times conducted herself with a certain arrogance. Apollodorus was extremely jealous of her at first, but it is to his credit and nobility of spirit that he overcame this attitude. Eventually the two of them formed a sincere friendship based on their mutual devotion to me.

For the most part, however, no fault could be found with my arrangement with Charmion and with our private moments of happiness. My father and the courtiers were content that I did not have a relationship with a man who might impregnate me. I would still go virginal to my marriage bed.

In the midst of my emotional involvement with Charmion, I still applied myself with great rigor to my studies. Charmion to my regret did not share my lessons with me, since she was not interested in intellectual pursuits. I studied alone with my grim-faced and solemn tutors. Charmion did share the hour of my daily dance lesson with me, although the effort was often too much for her. Charmion, with her indolent nature, did not like to overly exert herself. Only in loveplay was she inexhaustible.

At the time that I first became attached to Charmion and conceived a great love for her, I was immersed in Homer's moving account of the profound love and soldierly comradeship between Achilles and Patroclos. I am positive that their love took on physical dimensions, although Homer gives no indication that their love was such, unless one reads between the lines. Greek history and literature, of course, is full of passion between men.

In Athenian history, I recall the declared love between the handsome youths Harmodius and Aristogiton. They were lovers and were honored as heroes for having struck down Hipparchus, Tyrant of Athens. There is also the great god Zeus, the father of all gods, who craved both sexes. He seduced the beautiful Prince Ganymedes of Troy, and begot a large family of gods and demigods by various women.

On the other hand, there is little mention of love between women in our literature and history, but then all the writings have been by men, except for our one great immortal poet, Sappho. Women have not been encouraged to write. I am positive, however, that there have been great loves between women that have gone unrecorded and unsung in the tide of time.

My feelings for Charmion were manifold and I could not unravel them all, a tangle as complex as the Gordian knot. My private relationship with her gave me great happiness. In the midst of all the complex impulses and the ardent tenderness I entertained for her, I became conscious of a singular feeling, a feeling for which love would be hardly too strong a name.

If Achilles could have his Patroclos, if Orestes could have his Pylades, if Theseus could have his Pirithoüs, and if Alexander could have his Haphaistrian, why then could not Cleopatra have her Charmion?

CHAPTER VII

AS TWILIGHT FELL OVER THE CITY each evening it was my father's wont, after the long arduous day of state affairs, to relax by playing his flute. I would join him in his chambers, and we would dine with his favorite Cleombrotus and my Charmion and a few friends in attendance. As the night wore on, the others would be dismissed, and at midnight, my favorite time of the day, we were usually alone, just the two of us. He would sometimes play his flute again before retiring, and I enjoyed listening to the sorrowful music he made, a reflection of the sad state of his soul.

"I do not have the wind I once had," Father said regretfully one night, laying his flute aside.

I poured him more wine, and he lifted the gem-encrusted golden goblet to his lips to drink.

"Death comes to us all," he reflected, "from the humblest to the highest, and will soon come to me."

"Father, it is the wine talking," I chaffed him with a nervous laugh, although my heart chilled at the truth of this statement.

"No, death is coming to get me to take me on that journey from which there is no return," Father said. "My days are limited on earth. Death is a condition of living and I accept it calmly." He smiled stoically. "Today after the morning sacrifice, my soothsayer said I would live another ten years, that he read it in the entrails of a dove!" The corners of his mouth lifted ironically. "The pain in my own entrails, however, tells me this will not be so. I don't know how many months the gods will give me, but I am sure they will be few. There's an old Macedonian saying. 'Live for a century, learn for a century, and you'll die a fool anyway.' "

My father wheezed between sips of wine, and grimaced from the pain in his badly swollen legs. With the encroachment of age, he was much afflicted with an ache in his belly and with insomnia. His eyes were yellowed and bloodshot, lost between folds of puffy flesh, and purple veins spread out from his nose. I had been so gay and carefree in my happiness with Charmion that I had barely noticed my father's worsening health.

And then that night he made me face up to it.

"I am only seventeen," I heard myself say in an awed whisper.

"Yes, so young," Father said sympathetically. "I was twenty when I became King. I have done my best, but you will have to do better. When my time is up and I put down my burden, you will have to assume that burden. It will be up to you since your little brother is too young and not overblessed with wisdom, learning, or wit."

There was a contemplative silence while my father sipped wine. Then suddenly an expression of pain crossed his face and he clutched a hand at his belly.

"Are you all right, Father?" I implored, alarmed.

"Yes, my child," he said, his voice pinched with pain. The seizure seemed to pass, and he breathed easier.

"I will not have time to do all the things I want to do," he went on, gasping a little. "I am beset by unhappy subjects. I have been kept in power by the Romans. I am King of a decaying, corrupt, threatened kingdom. I've spent all these years plotting and scheming and bribing to hold my throne. Now it will be your turn, and I command you to be a better and greater monarch than I have been. You must exercise all your considerable abilities to revive the greatness that our dynasty knew in its first century, Cleopatra."

"With the help of the gods, Father, I will try."

"I am leaving you a perilously weakened throne," Father went on. "The temptation for Rome to annex Egypt for its own enrichment is just too irresistible. Only

140

by having an agreement with the most powerful Romans can you hope to save and stabilize your throne. Go after Pompey when the time comes, or Caesar, whoever is at the top. Remember that, Cleopatra."

"I will remember, Father."

"I know that you will always be willing to sacrifice your happiness for the sake of your kingdom," Father said with pride. "Your destiny is more important to you than your self. This is where you differ from my other children, for they would abjure all discipline and seek only pleasure." He gave a rueful sigh. "It is my misfortune to leave two strong daughters. Little Arsinoë is a pretty thing, although your beauty outshines hers as the sun outshines the moon. She is a sharp little bitch at twelve, so what will she be like at twenty? She is willful and headstrong, but without your sterling qualities. Of my four daughters, only poor Cleopatra Tryphaina was too sweet to live. The people do not like strong women, for they have had their fill of strong queens in bygone days."

I knew my father spoke the truth. In the Greek ruling class of Alexandria, women have always been barely tolerated. I was known for my strength of character and intellect. It was said I could be domineering, if given the chance. The people did not revere these characteristics in me. If my brother had possessed my exceptional traits, then all would have been fine, but I was merely a woman.

"It is not my fault that I am what I am," I said resentfully, "and that my brothers are what they are."

"No, not your fault," Father sighed. "The two boys leave much to be desired as princes; the elder is stupid and stubborn, the younger not so stupid but timid and weak. At eleven and ten their characters are formed, although we must pray they will improve. As for Ptolemy Magus, I'm sorry he is rather ill-disposed toward you, but he is only eleven. You are quite beautiful, and in a few years when he is fifteen he will be a man with a man's desires and might prove to be more susceptible to your charms."

"I've always tried to show him the greatest consideration," I said.

"Yes, I know you have, Cleopatra. Well, when I am dead, the claim of a son will be stronger than that of a daughter, but your outstanding talents cannot be ignored. I will settle the question as such difficulties have always been surmounted in Egyptian royalty. As Osiris married his sister Isis thousands of years ago, as I married my sister your mother, so you shall marry the elder of your brothers, and by the will of the gods, beget children to continue the dynasty."

"With the help of the gods, and the Romans."

"Yes, never forget the Romans. In all probability, when I die, Ptolemy and you will be too young to govern, and the affairs of state will be conducted by the men whom I designate. I have chosen a council, well-balanced in policies, to hold the ship steady. Pothinos is a good prime minister, and he will serve Ptolemy and you with wisdom. And Achillas can be relied upon to be a great commander in chief of the armies."

"You know that I have never liked either of them," I said.

"Yes, but as Queen there will often be times when you will have to subjugate your personal feelings for the sake of expediency."

"You know that I hold Protarchus in utmost esteem."

"So do I," Father said quickly. "Your wishes carry great weight with me, Cleopatra. Protarchus is a man of intellect, and he will have a place on the council, but he does not have the character to hold an important post. He is too cerebral, kind and gentle to wield power."

"I know that a gentle nature is a disadvantage in those who must command, yet his remarkable abilities must be utilized to benefit the kingdom."

"Protarchus is a noble but flawed figure," Father pronounced. "He is flawed by weakness."

"Pothinos is flawed by mendacity and greed," I stated.

"Pothinos is wise in administration, and after I am gone Egypt will have need of his abilities."

142

Because I did not want to argue with or agitate my father, I acceded to his wishes. "I shall in all things be obedient to your will, beloved Father. If you insist that Pothinos continue as prime minister after you, I accept him without question."

"We must make careful arrangements to prevent Egypt from being thrown into chaos at the moment of my death," Father went on slowly, measuring his words. "I don't want a change in rulers to stir up agitation about Egypt in Rome. In the Roman Senate there will be a party clamoring for annexation, of course, but to prevent this I'm going to draw up a will stating that I'm to be succeeded by my eldest daughter and son, and commit the execution of this will and the guardianship of my heirs to the Senate. At my death Rome will have a sacred honor to uphold you. I'm hoping our friend Pompey will be appointed by the Senate to be your legal guardian, for he will certainly support you."

"This is a wise policy, dear Father," I said.

"Let's hope it works!" Father said with a grunt, taking another sip of wine. "I thank the gods that Crassus, the one member of the Triumvirate who has always favored annexing Egypt, is dead. If he had succeeded in conquering Parthia last spring, it's probable that he would be in Egypt now, for I believe the rumor that, after Parthia, he planned to turn his legions on Egypt."

"Now that Crassus is dead," I said, "only Caesar and Pompey remain of the Triumvirate."

"Yes, and eventually one will eliminate the other."

"Who do you think will come out on top?"

My father stared into his wine goblet as if to find the answer. "Only the immortal gods know, but I think it is best to back Uncle Pompey. Of course, if we back the wrong horse, it could prove fatal!" He gave a rueful chuckle at the fickleness of fate.

"Tell me more about Caesar, Father," I prompted.

"Caesar was born to do great things," Father explained. "He is the most ambitious man I know and has a restless passion for fame. He has a genius for politics

143

and war, and he covets wealth. He's my age, and except for the falling sickness his health is good. He should be around for many more years."

"What do you know of his private life?" I asked.

"Well, I remember a few years ago when I was in Rome, everyone laughed when Caesar divorced his third wife, Pompey's sister the Lady Pompeia. Caesar remarked at the time, 'Caesar's wife must be above suspicion!' This was a great joke, since Caesar is a notorious womanizer, and it is certain that few of the wives of his friends are above suspicion when he is around. He then married the Lady Calpurnia, daughter of Calpurnius Piso, for her money. Caesar is as unscrupulous in his personal life as he is in his political life. Never oppose him, Cleopatra, never! In war he is implacable. He will give quarter to no one who opposes the might of Rome. In his campaign in Gaul he had thousands massacred, and hacked off the right sword hand of thousands of others who had fought against him. He is one of the great men of our time, and will grow greater in the coming years. With all his ruthlessness and ambition, he is charming, though it is a cold charm. Now that I think of it, Caesar has all the qualities you have, Cleopatra. Charm, ruthlessness, ambition, brilliance. If ever the two of you meet, when you are Queen, you will be well matched and the sparks should fly. I would love to be there to see that!" He laughed with pleasure at the thought.

"And Antony, Father?" I probed. "What do you think of Antony?"

"Of course I adore him! A charming, burly ruffian. When he was young, he played the effeminate fop because it was the fashion for young men to do so. Then he matured into a masculine giant, playing the great soldier because it is a part which nature has outwardly endowed him for. Yet at heart he is suited for neither role, being too rough for the one and too tender for the other." Father paused in thought. "After Pompey and Caesar, however, the world will be his. There is no one else worthy in the younger ranks."

I paused to consider all that my father had said.

144

"Well, in the future," I said, "I hope Pompey will win over Caesar, for he seems more warm-hearted."

My father smiled. "There is a spark inside you that urges you to greatness, Cleopatra. You have the drive and the intellect to leave your mark on the world and to write history. I am positive that whichever Roman triumphs, you will be able to handle him. You will be worthy of the dreams I have of you."

"I pray I prove to merit your faith in me, beloved Father," I replied.

As he had decided, my father drew up his testament a few days later. It was sealed in the presence of the majority of the councillors and nobles, who all assented to the arrangements that had been made for the succession. The will was sent off to Pompey in Rome and was deposited in the state archives of the Vestal Virgins. The Senate accepted the appointment as guardians of my father's successors and promised to perform the duties of the trust.

Not long afterward, when I turned seventeen and my brother Ptolemy Magus was twelve, it was our duty to submit to the Rite of Identification, an ancient and compulsory court ritual. For this ceremony we wore golden robes over our naked bodies.

"I don't know why I have to go through with this idiotic ceremony," Ptolemy pouted outside the Throne Room.

"It is a traditional custom from the days of the pharaohs," I said placatingly. "If Ramses the Third did it, so can you. When you become King, there will be many things you won't want to do, but it will be your sacred duty to Egypt to perform them willingly."

"When I become King I am going to change all that!" Ptolemy cried nastily. "I will do only what I want and not a thing besides."

I cringed, realizing that my brother with his silly wrongheaded temperament would probably attempt to do just that.

Trumpets sounded and Posidonius, the chief court chamberlain, announced us.

"Come, Ptolemy, we must go in now," I said.

Ptolemy and I marched side by side into the Great Hall. I could not remember a more brilliant and crowded gathering. Every courtier and noble had turned out to scrutinize us. We marched solemnly the length of the hall, with the mass of nobles on both sides, to the dais where our father sat his throne. Ptolemy and I then stood in front of two stately chairs and faced the assemblage.

A group of priests disrobed us, and we stood naked before the whole court. I stood regally, proud of my body, staring unseeingly ahead, like a beautiful statue, as Lady Charmion told me later.

I could see nobles whispering frantically to one another, their debauched, greedy eyes assessing us, wondering if they would ever have the chance to sample the royal flesh that they now so avidly viewed.

Prince Ptolemy and I sat down on our chairs. I did so with dignity, but my brother squirmed. He had been given explicit instructions not to cross his legs.

The High Priest of Karnak and the Chief Physician approached in their robes, and stood beside us.

"My Lord Physician," the High Priest said in a loud voice, "have you completed your physical inspection of the most sacred high Prince and Princess?"

"Yes, Lord High Priest," the Chief Physician said.

"Do you testify that Prince Ptolemy Magus is of the male sex?"

"The prince is incontrovertibly of the male sex," the Chief Physician affirmed, "and he is extraordinarily sound in all his members."

"Is the Princess Cleopatra of the female sex?"

"The Princess Cleopatra is undeniably female in all her parts," the Chief Physician solemnly ratified.

"They have no deformities of sex or body?"

"No, sire, they are perfectly made by the gods in accordance with their sex," the Chief Physician corroborated.

"Will they be able to produce children to fulfill the destiny of Egypt?"

"I certify, my Lord High Priest, that with the help of the gods they will be able to perform their sacred duty of procreation."

There was a blaring of trumpets as my brother and I rose and the priests came to dress us in our golden robes. The priests sang praises, prayers, and incantations, and waved wands and thuribles of perfumed incense. At last the ceremony came to a conclusion, and with our father the King, Ptolemy and I left the Great Hall, and the ordeal was over.

My seventeenth year was to be a time of grim realities for me, so unlike the previous year when my life had been so joyously enriched by my happy friendship with Charmion. I now spent less time with Charmion, for my father's health was not good and I must be at his side. As his body weakened, his will hardened, and he drove himself even more fiercely in ill health than he had in good health. He accepted his physical deterioration with grace, was never ill-tempered, and never spoke harsh words to anyone.

At my father's side I weighed foreign policies, took the pulse of the times, and prepared myself for the day I would assume the throne. My father taught me everything about kingship and the administration of the government. I now sat always at the council table. Pothinos disapproved, and I could see that he barely tolerated me. I feared the day when my father would die and I would be Queen, but could only hope that when that day came Pothinos would show more respect for my sacred position and that we could work together in harmony.

My brother and co-heir Ptolemy Magus took part in all court and religious ceremonies, but he was too young to sit on council. He took little interest in his studies, and was always with his coterie of little Greek playmates. Pothinos went out of his way to make a great fuss over him, while my father continued to give all his attention and affection to me. Ptolemy responded to the solicitude of Pothinos, extending the, high regard he felt for his pedagogue, Theodotus of Chio, to him.

Both Pothinos and Theodotus were typical ubiquitous

147

eunuchs about court, gross and overweening, obnoxious and unctuous, cunning and crafty. They were as base in birth as in deed and spirit. I could never decide which of the two I hated more. I knew that after my father's death they would control my brother and Egypt, and my position would be difficult to maintain.

To celebrate the third year of his restoration, my father had a splendid ceremony in the Great Hall in which he conferred many honors on those who had been particularly zealous in their services to king and kingdom. Charmion and Apollodorus were given the second order of the court's hierarchy, First Friend, and my father presented them with the great gold collar which goes with this title. The highest honor, the title of Royal Kinsman, was conferred upon Protarchus, Pothinos, and Theodotus.

During the autumnal equinox of my seventeenth year, Charmion's grandfather, the elder Kallimachos, died suddenly at his desk while discharging his duties as finance minister. This was a shock since Kallimachos, although in his sixties, had appeared to be in excellent health.

This death disheartened my father and made him acutely aware of his own mortality. In the succeeding weeks his health declined rapidly. The year came to an end, and the long-faced physicians told me privately that my father would not last long.

Just before my eighteenth birthday, the Theater of Dionysus presented *Bacchae* by Euripides, my father's favorite play. Against the advice of his physicians, he decided to attend a performance. I accompanied him with his lover Cleombrotus, my Charmion, and a small party of courtiers.

The company of actors gave a stirring performance that night. After the play, my father was too ill to go greet the actors, so he sent a message and a gold ring studded with a huge ruby from his own hand to Zenophantus, who had brilliantly acted the role of Dionysus.

As my father walked with labored effort to his litter, the crowds cheered him riotously, and this demonstration of affection warmed his heart. In the four years that had passed since his restoration, the people had grown quite fond of him, and perhaps felt guilty for their part in the troubles that had forced him into exile.

The royal party returned to the palace and my father was put to bed. Attending the theater had exhausted his body, but had stimulated him mentally. I lingered by his bedside while he sipped heated wine.

"Why is *Bacchae* your favorite play, Father?" I asked.

"Because it perfectly illustrates the universal, almost primal force of Dionysus," Father explained. "I am Ptolemy the Twelfth, the New Dionysus, and I am not afraid to die. I am a true man of Hellenistic culture. I cling to the promise of the divine Dionysus that his devotees will not be rewarded in this life, but after death when eternal salvation will be ours."

"But of course," I said, truly believing that my father was indeed the reincarnation of Dionysus.

"Dionysus is not only the god of wine but the patron of drama and the arts," Father went on. "That is why I've strongly identified with Dionysus and feel an affinity for *Bacchae*. My whole life has been spent in an anguished eagerness to escape my physical body, to go beyond myself into the rapturous embrace of mystic union with the Dionysiac rituals of wine, music, dance, and love." A small smile played on his mouth and his blue eyes glittered. "Soon my soul will slip away into tranquillity, freeing my spirit from the animal body that has been its guest, and I will escape into a glorious, new life."

"Dying is a rebirth," I said.

Father smiled fondly at me. "You are a true Hellenistic child."

After that night my father rarely left his bedchamber. I watched him dying, unable to help. He was much afflicted with his old pain in his belly and by insomnia. I commanded a flutist be stationed outside his bedchamber to sweeten the long anguished hours of the night when sleep would not come to him.

I was elevated to my father's side on the throne. Each

day I spent a few hours in the morning in the council chamber on affairs of state, while the rest of the time I was by my father's bedside. Charmion rarely left him, giving him solace and care. He had grown deeply attached to her and prized her beauty and spirit.

To celebrate my eighteenth birthday, my father, briefly revitalized, gave a small banquet in the Great Hall. Two Nubian slaves carried him in a chair to the dais as he could no longer walk because of the painful sores on his legs.

Diodorus did his dance of *Dionysus*. My father knew it would be the last dance he would ever see. It was only fitting that since the last play he had seen was *Bacchae*, so the last dance he should see would be *Dionysus*. Diodorus must have known this, for he danced supremely well that night. He was in his early forties and had first created this dance twenty years before in honor of my father. The last years Diodorus had lost much of his artistry and had become a caricature of his former self, but then often dancers and actors have a habit of relying on self-parody as they advance in years. People, too, come to think of it, although I hope as I grow older I will avoid this fate.

On this particular night of my eighteenth birthday, however, Dionysus shed all the tricks he had relied upon to replace his lost technique, and he danced as he had at the acme of his powers, ten years before. He gave a breathtaking performance, going beyond technique to great artistic heights. He had been famous for his gift of expanding himself physically in space, but of late had barely left the floor, but on this night he once again defied the laws of gravity. All the guests in the hall were mesmerized as he jumped fiercely to incredible heights, portraying a god against whom all circumstances conspired—for yes, even gods and goddesses are sometimes conspired against by the fates. Images of his dancing that night are indelibly impressed on my memory.

At the end of the dance, Diodorus acknowlededg the hysterical applause, then he approached my father's couch, his body dripping with perspiration and his chest heaving.

"Beautiful, so beautiful, Diodorus!" Father declared tearfully.

"The dance was for you, O King!" Diodorus cried breathlessly, kneeling and kissing my father's hand.

"Come, join us for a drink of wine," Father said.

Diodorus kissed my hand as I gave him a grateful, gracious smile. He took a seat adjacent to our couch, and a servant gave him a goblet of wine.

"No one touches you in Terpsichore's art," I said warmly. "You serve the muse with such dedication, and you dance with your soul."

"You dance as if your body is on fire!" my father exclaimed. "For the glory your dancing has brought to Egypt, Diodorus, I confer upon you the title of First Friend!"

"I am unworthy, O King!" Diodorus cried, tears springing to his eyes.

"Who in my kingdom deserves the title more?"

Consternation broke out among the guests at this action. A few years before my father had made Diodorus a Friend which gave him the gold armband, but elevation to First Friend with the great gold collar was an honor which no dancer had ever been given. There was jealous mumbling among the nobles about my father being senile. As a youth Diodorus had been briefly one of my father's lovers, and many maliciously held that his past carnal talents had prompted this honor, but this was absurd. Diodorus was honored for his achievements as the foremost dancer of our time, and no man ever wore the collar of First Friend more deservedly. He left the banquet deeply moved by his title.

My father then begged his guests to continue with the birthday banquet and to eat and drink to their hearts' content. I accompanied my father back to his bedchamber and helped his servants put him to bed.

"I'll never see Diodorus dance again," Father said, but there was no sadness in his voice, only resignation and acceptance. "Promise me, Cleopatra, to see that Diodorus, when he can no longer dance, will never want."

"I solemnly promise, Father," I avowed.

In the days that followed my father's condition sharply worsened, and he never again left his bed. He was sinking fast, and throughout the palace there were shocked whispers. The doctors ministered vainly to a body whose deterioration was far beyond their help. His life was trickling away, yet his mental faculties remained clear. Finally one day the physicians told me what I already knew, that he had only a few days to live.

I decided it was necessary to have an interview with my brother Prince Ptolemy Magus. I sent a message to him saying we should meet in the palace gardens, where he usually spent his afternoons with his brother and playmates.

We were to meet at a marble bench by a bronze statue of Ptolemy the First. I was there at the appointed time with a scroll of poetry. I sat reading for some time before Ptolemy came. I looked up to see him approaching slowly with a surly expression on his face. I spotted his foster father Theodotus in the distance among several courtiers.

I forced a pleasant smile. "Greetings, Ptolemy."

"Sister, you have called me away from my friends," he said resentfully. "I always play after my lessons."

"It was our father's wish. Come, sit with me for a little while."

Ptolemy was tall for his twelve years and growing into a handsome boy, and he knew it. He was vain and conceited, full of himself beyond endurance. He sat as far away from me as the length of the bench permitted.

"You know that our beloved father is gravely ill," I began.

"Yes, I know," Ptolemy replied matter-of-factly.

"Do you see this statue?" I asked.

Ptolemy squinted his eyes against the sun as he gazed up at the bronze head. "It is Ptolemy the First, the founder of our dynasty, and when Father dies I will be King Ptolemy the Thirteenth."

"And I will be Queen Cleopatra the Seventh!"

A silence fell as Ptolemy stared at a peacock that roamed by.

"Father says that we must rule wisely together," I said. "I hope that Theodotus is instructing you carefully in the importance of being a king. A great position will bring great responsibilities."

"One thing is certain," Ptolemy said with a smirk, "when I am King I will not lick the asses of the Romans like Father!"

"An honorable intention, Ptolemy, but perhaps you should study history. Mithridates of Pontus and Antiochus of Syria had that same idea, and they were destroyed by the Romans. Perhaps our father has catered to the Romans, but he succeeded in keeping the throne and has preserved the kingdom for us to inherit."

"I detest the Romans and will have nothing to do with them when I am King," Ptolemy declared churlishly. "They will not get our wheat unless they pay for it in gold. I will drive a hard bargain when I am King."

"The affairs of the kingdom will be more complex than that," I proceeded patiently. "Kings, more than other men, are driven by circumstances, as you will discover soon enough."

"I want to go back to play with my friends," Ptolemy said, squirming.

"Very well, Ptolemy," I said, rising with him and taking him by the shoulders. "I don't want you to be afraid of being King. It may happen any day now. It is our destiny and we must accept it. You will make a fine King."

"Yes, I know I will," he said with cocky certainty.

He submitted to my sisterly kiss with coldness, his body stiffening. "Goodbye, dearest brother."

Prince Ptolemy turned and walked away. He saw Theodotus in the background, and then, as if reminded of something, he turned back to me with a grim expression on his handsome little face. "Theodotus says, according to our laws, a king and queen can be associated together on the throne, just as you are with Father, but the will of the king always takes precedence before the will of the queen. Is Theodotus correct about this law, sister?"

I lifted my chin high. "Yes, Ptolemy, Theodotus is correct about the law."

Ptolemy nodded. "Just so you know the letter of the law, so there won't be any misunderstanding when Father dies." He abruptly turned and walked back to where Theodotus and his friends were waiting.

I was much chagrined by this encounter. When Charmion and Apollodorus joined me, I was silent with melancholy musings. We walked about the gardens between artfully placed trees, along winding paths between marble pools where fabulously colored fish swam, and where dolphins' heads sprouted water. I was too depressed to be solaced by the tranquil beauty, and finally I returned to my father's bedchamber.

The old pain in my father's bowels was now unremitting, and the medicines of the physicians could not dull it nor ease his fever or sleeplessness. With my own loving hands I changed the dressings twice daily on the running sores on his legs and did not flinch at the stain and smell.

One morning as I slept on the couch near his bed, the Chief Physician awoke me, crying, "Your father the King calls for you!"

Groggily, I jerked myself awake and hurried to my father's side and gazed down at him. The pallor and smell of death were unmistakably on him.

"Beloved daughter," he whispered hoarsely.

I sat on the edge of the bed and kissed his blotched, bloated face. "Yes, beloved Father my King?"

"I am thirsty," he said. "Wine."

"Yes, Father." A servant poured wine into a goblet, which I held to my father's lips. I wiped the fevered perspiration from his face and the wine that spilled down his chin.

"Cleopatra," he said, struggling with his voice. "The gods are about to close my eyes."

"No, Father, not yet!" I cried with anguish.

154

"Be calm, Cleopatra. The thread of my life has been spun. Call my councillors and the children."

Within a short time the councillors and the children came crowding into the bedchamber. My father was propped up upon pillows. Pothinos, Achillas, and Theodotus were there with my two brothers, the Princess Arsinoë and her tutor Ganymedes, a weeping Aunt Aliki, and a congregation of priests and nobles.

"Cleopatra, take Ptolemy's hand," Father commanded.

Theodotus gave Ptolemy a push, and my brother reluctantly approached the deathbed. I took his hand, and we looked down upon our dying father.

"My children," Father cried, "Neoi Theoi Philadelphoi, New Gods Brother and Sister Loving One Another!"

This was his title to us, his hope, his command, his plea.

"Heed the voice of your destiny," Father admonished in a croaking voice, speaking the pure Greek he usually employed only from his throne. "Rule together in harmony in accordance to the divine will of the gods. You must be closely linked, a strong chain against Rome, a chain that must not break. The more strongly you are united, the safer you will be against any interference from Rome."

"Yes, beloved Father," I cried firmly.

"Remember to revere the gods always."

"We will, Father, we promise," I pledged solemnly.

Prince Ptolemy stared coldly at our father, his lips pressed together, his hand straining in mine.

My father looked at the councillors hovering in the background. "Royal Kinsmen," he cried.

Pothinos, Achillas, Theodotus, and Protarchus advanced to the foot of the bed, looking askance at their king.

"I order all my councillors and nobles to assist in the orderly transference of power," Father said, "and I oblige you on your sacred oath to support Queen Cleopatra and King Ptolemy in their accession. This is my last command. There must be no power struggles or squabbling amongst any of you, and one and all must support the new King and Queen."

The nobles all raised their voices in protestations and oaths.

"You may take your last leave of your old King," Father said, falling back against the pillows, his last strength spent on these exhortations.

Everyone left the chamber except for a few praying, chanting priests. The pillows were taken from behind my father and his body stretched comfortably on the bed. He had done all he could, and now he was sinking to death.

This would be the death day of my father, I thought, yet he lived into the night. When nightfall came, a few lamps were kindled. Still my father breathed and even sipped spoonfuls of warm herb juice.

In the middle of the night the death rattle began. Courtiers scurried about the palace to call the councillors and members of the royal family to witness my father's dying moment. As they crowded into the bedchamber, everyone knelt on the floor. Priests murmured their incantations and incense was wafted about. Aunt Aliki and Cleombrotus wept uncontrollably. I longed for the relief of tears but did not weaken as I sat there holding my father's hand.

The dead hour of dawn came. Many of the flames had flickered out in their own oil.

The pupils of my father's eyes had contracted to brilliant points. His chest heaved as he fought for breath. His lids fluttered open, and his dilated eyes searched for mine.

"Cleopatra!" my father gasped.

"Yes, beloved Father?" I leaned my ear close to his mouth.

"You will challenge the gods," he whispered. "I hope you will be triumphant."

I kissed his fevered blistered mouth, and smiled at him. "I love you, Father," I said in a voice throbbing with emotion.

The rattle in his throat increased, shaking his body. I held his hand tightly as I watched the life going out of him. His hand fluttered weakly in mine. The sight slowly faded from his eyes, his chest gave one final heave, rattling his body, as all the air left his lungs, and then he stilled with a great sigh as he met death.

The Chief Physician put the silver mirror against his mouth, but I knew there would be no mist. The physician checked the mirror, and turned and whispered to Pothinos.

"The King is dead!" Pothinos cried in a voice swelling with exaltation. "Long live the King!"

"The gods have received King Ptolemy as one of their own!" the High Priest of Karnak cried. "He has gone to Olympus to be with the immortals!"

A soft cry of pain issued from my throat. I wanted to throw myself across my father in an agony of despair, but I held myself upright, although my eyes overflowed like the Nile at floodtime.

"Long live the King!" all the voices in the bedchamber cried out.

I let go of my father's dead hand and stood up with all my regal bearing. Protarchus came and sank to his knees at my feet, kissing my hand.

"Long live the Queen!" Protarchus cried loftily.

Charmion and Apollodorus with their agile steps were at my feet, crying, "Long live the Queen!"

"Long live the Queen!" other voices rang out, although these cries were not as loud as they had been for my brother.

And so I was Queen at eighteen years and one month of age, and my brother was King at twelve.

I walked over and stood before him. "We share each other's great sorrow, King Ptolemy," I said.

King Ptolemy the Thirteenth nodded grimly, but gave no reply. He turned and strutted out of the room, followed by Pothinos, Achillas, and Theodotus, the three most powerful personages in the kingdom. All the other nobles followed them, and I was alone except for Apollodorus, Charmion, Protarchus, Aunt Aliki, and Cleombrotus.

"You must rest in your chambers now, Queen Cleopatra," Apollodorus said.

"I want to sit with my father for a while," I said. I sat on the edge of the bed and held his hand. His jaw hung slack with the obscene indifference that death achieves.

Out in the garden the birds were beginning their drowsy twittering. The first quiet of early morning held a semblance of peace, and the first pink flush in the east painted the beginning of a beautiful new day, a day my father would not see. Sunlight suddenly poured into the bedchamber in golden shafts across the marble floor, but even with the sunshine the chamber was cheerless and bereft.

I looked up and saw a raven, the bird of death and prey, perched on the balcony terrace. A Nubian slave chased it away.

For a long time I sat beside my father, holding his hand. Now that the priests had gone with their incense, the smell of death became oppressive.

"O Queen, you must come and rest," Charmion begged.

"Farewell, beloved Father," I said, leaning over and kissing his stilled face, the skin warm still from the high fever at death.

Charmion and Apollodorus led me back to my apartments. In the privacy of my bedchamber I wept with grief. A numbness overwhelmed me, and despair trickled drop by bitter drop into my soul. I took a mild anodyne in an herb drink to sedate my nerves. Charmion and I bathed together, then went to bed for a few hours of rest.

In the afternoon I arose and donned regal array and went to the Great Hall where all the court was assembled. My brother and I sat stiffly on our thrones as the Lord High Priest of Karnak proclaimed us King and Queen. Enthroned and robed in our royal state we were clothed with godhead. The nobles prostrated themselves in reverence for our royalty, proclaiming their allegiance by kissing the floor.

I went to the council chamber. Deep in despair, I rallied my will and made many decisions that day, taking charge of the government and planning for my father's funeral.

Heralds went about the city, and couriers were sent with proclamations to all the provinces of Egypt, announcing my father's death and the beginning of a new reign.

It took ten days for my father's body to be properly embalmed. The corpse then lay in the Great Hall for three days within a circle of a hundred tall candles. Fanbearers stood sentry and fanned the flies away. Priests and singing eunuchs paced in a circle around the catafalque. Companions of the King never ceased their vigil nor priests their prayers.

The coffin was placed on a gilded catafalque, on a dais hung with precious purple cloths, in the square before the palace. All the citizens of Alexandria filed past and paid their last respects.

There was a magnificent funeral. The service was held with every solemn rite and full royal pomp in the presence of every noble of the court, foreign ambassadors, leading citizens, and army commanders. The procession traveled through the boulevards of Alexandria. Five hundred soldiers mounted on black horses with high black ostrich plumes on their helmets led the cortege out from the palace gates. Then a team of ten white stallions pulled the huge coffin through the streets under the brilliant sunshine. This was my father's last journey through his beloved city. King Ptolemy and I were carried in a litter behind the coffin, and Ptolemy Philippos, Arsinoë, Aunt Aliki, and leading chamberlains and nobles were carried behind us, their order marked by ancient hierarchy.

With an effort I maintained rigid self-control as I was conveyed in this high procession, with the sad dirge of priests and the uncontrollable sobbing of Alexandrian women ringing in my ears. The people forgot the flaws and failings of my father and were content to remember his virtues and achievements, and cried out with grief at their loss. They prostrated themselves as the cortege went by, in a final farewell to my father, and in obeisance to my brother and me, their new King and Queen.

At last the cortege reached the Sema. The gilded coffin was carried inside, and my brother and I followed, with the nobles and priests coming in after us. After the sunshine of the streets, the dark tomb chilled me to the bone.

Inside the mausoleum the priests waved their wands and thuribles of incense and chanted their last incantations. I placed my father's favorite Boeotian flute inside the coffin before the lid was covered. The coffin was then placed in a sarcophagus carved from Thracian marble. The maw of the sarcophagus neatly swallowed the coffin. An effigy of my father, carved from the same marble, was placed on top, sealing the sarcophagus.

The chilling finality of it smote my soul. My father would lie there through the long cold centuries to come, his speechless, sightless effigy staring into time as yet unborn, among the dusty violet shadows of the Sema.

The chants and funeral songs died away in a series of lovely, diminishing echoes that pursued each other upwards, and at last the funeral was over.

As I dictate these words to a scribe a decade later, I lie stretched on my couch. My father and mother stare at me from the unseeing eyes of their blue basalt busts, which are sitting on a table nearby. The busts were done before I was born, and I am told are fine likenesses of them as they were then. Sometimes when I am alone and dispirited, I kiss the cold stone with tears in my eyes, remembering my parents and wishing I could talk with them. I came from their womb and loins. I am their true daughter, and have inherited many of their faults and virtues, weaknesses and strengths. Their memories are alive in me; I can recall even my mother, who died when I was only five. Yet their voices I cannot hear in my mind. Their voices have somehow gone and I cannot remember the timbre and inflection, the sound of their speech. It is said the voice is always the first to be forgotten after a loved one departs, but I yearn to hear those dear ones speak again.

CHAPTER VIII

MY CORONATION DAY was one of the most solemn and splendid days of my life, the day for which I had been born. The ceremony followed just two weeks after the royal remains of my father had been deposited with his ancestors in the Sema. My father, knowing his end was near, had begun the preparations for the coronation a few months before his death, so it was not an event hastily thrown together as had been the crowning of Berenice and Cleopatra Tryphaina seven years before, but a magnificent affair. We Ptolemies have always known how to excite the imagination of the people, and my father thought that a coronation with all the traditional pomp and parade would have an emotional effect in bending the people to our will, and in getting our joint reign off to a glorious and propitious start.

The sacred service, conducted amid all the arcane pageantry handed down to us, took place in the Great Throne Room. This hall, with its pink marble walls, mosaic floors, and huge columns of purple porphyry, overflowed with chamberlains and nobles, the priests, officers of the army, and dignitaries from all the provinces of the Two Kingdoms.

I insisted that a hundred common Egyptian peasants also be invited to the coronation, which caused consternation among my councillors. Pothinos claimed it would be sufficient for the people to see my brother and me in the streets during the procession after the ceremony, but I was adamant that a delegation of street-cleaners, dock workers, and market vendors witness their sovereigns in the sacred ritual of anointment. The

163

council acquiesced, and one hundred peasants were selected by lottery. I had won my first battle with the council.

At court the Egyptians, who are a minority in the ruling class, are generally snubbed by the Greeks, but never by me. Even as a little princess I went out of my way to be cordial to Egyptians, and I speak their tongue fluently. This has always aroused resentment against me from certain quarters, but when I became Queen I vowed I would be Queen of all my peoples.

On the day of the crowning, I was so filled with the anticipation and excitement that I had trouble sleeping the night before, and had slept but a few hours when Charmion shook me.

"Cleopatra, wake up or you will be late for your crowning," she cried.

I arose and began preparing for the momentous day. I took a rose-scented bath, was massaged with precious oils, my fingernails and toenails were lacquered with gold, my eyes were rimmed meticulously with kohl and the eyebrows blackened. I took a little nourishment, and then my ladies robed me in a gown of beaded gold. Over this I wore a rich purple cloak, secured by a gem-studded clasp, which fell behind me in a long train. Over my blonde hair I wore a straight black Egyptian wig.

Gazing into a long polished silver mirror, I saw a resplendent regal figure staring back at me.

"You look every inch a queen!" Charmion cried.

At the appointed time I left my apartments, and Apollodorus and a squadron of guards escorted me through the long corridors. At the portal of the Great Hall I found my brother waiting. The ceremony had been in progress for some time, and now it was our turn to play our parts.

"Dearest brother," I said, "I tremble at the hallowed burden the gods have thrust upon us."

"Have no fear, sister," King Ptolemy said with his usual arrogance. "We have the three wisest men in Egypt to aid us." He nodded to the men in question,

164

Pothinos, Theodotus, and Achillas, who stood beside him in thir colorful robes of office.

I was speechless, thinking that if these were, in my brother's opinion, the wisest persons in our kingdom, we were poorly equipped to begin our joint reign, and I involuntarily shuddered.

Mighty trumpets in fanfare rang out to announce our entrance. We were led by high officials of the council. King Ptolemy, taking precedence, entered the Great Hall before me, bearing himself like a proud little peacock, dressed in a gold dress exactly like that worn by the pharaohs of yore, and tied to his smooth little chin was the long false blue beard. He also wore a black wig and a purple cloak, whose train was borne by his brother, eleven-year-old Ptolemy Philippos. My train was held by thirteen-year-old Princess Arsinoë, who in her new gown was as pretty as a little nymph on a Greek vase.

An involuntary gasp of awe escaped from a thousand throats, a great breath like a sighing breeze, as I entered the hall. Everyone sank to both knees as we walked the length of the Great Hall, in a slow and solemn gait, and with cymbals clashing to our measured steps.

At the end of the hall we were greeted by all the officiating priests, led by the august and austere Pshereni-Ptah, the High Priest of Memphis, the supreme prelate of Egypt who had crowned our father thirty years before. Pshereni-Ptah was well advanced into his sixth decade of earthly life, stooped with age, and his voice broke as he read the Egyptian incantations. The ceremony was long and arduous, and although Pshereni-Ptah was assisted by many younger priests, it was a stupendous task for a man of his age to perform. There were moments when I feared he would not get through it.

My brother and I knelt on gold cushions to receive Pshereni-Ptah's blessings. The priests moved about, swinging their thuribles of rich burning incense and waving their wands which bore the emblems of the stars. The fumes from the incense clogged my nostrils and made my head dizzy. My eardrums vibrated to the clashing cymbals, but the music of lutes, lyres, and harps and the sacred songs from a chorus of eunuchs were all most pleasing, inspiring, and beautiful.

At last my brother and I rose from the cushions and were led up the six steps to the dais where the twin thrones, fashioned from gold and encrusted with gems, were mounted. Over the thrones hung the cloth of state, the royal escutcheon, and a great golden disk of the sun. Our cloaks were removed and Ptolemy and I sat our thrones, flanked by a contingent of splendidly clothed Royal Fanbearers. Ptolemy's throne was overbig for him but I fitted mine perfectly.

From my throne I looked out over the whole assemblage of chamberlains and courtiers, brightly garbed attendants, soldiers in Macedonian mantles and high boots, priests, with their heads shaven like eggs, in robes whose design had not changed in four thousand years, and nobles in Grecian dress. Everyone wore a special headdress, coronet, or wreath to signify rank and title. It flashed through my mind that Egypt had lost much of its grandeur, but no one could tell from the ostentatious ceremony that was unfolding before my eyes, with my brother and me at the center.

The coronation itself was an artful blend of the rituals handed down by the pharaohs, with a few touches from the Macedonian and Persian crownings. After my brother and I were enthroned, the Royal Chief Cupbearer advanced with the holy oil. The moment of sacred anointment had come. Pshereni-Ptah dipped his fingertips into the oil to anoint our foreheads as music filled the chamber.

The Royal Regalia Bearers now came forth, carrying the insignia on gold silk cushions. Pothinos bore my brother's crown, Protarchus carried mine, Achillas brought the whips, Theodotus the crooks, and Aunt Aliki held a cushion with the sacred uraeus. Ptolemy Philippos held Alexander the Great's scepter, the symbol of the connection of our royal house with this great god.

The adornment of the sacred uraeus came next. A

priest took the golden asps and handed them to Pshereni-Ptah, who placed them, first on Ptolemy's head, and then on mine, the cobra heads jutting out from our foreheads. Then we were invested with the crook and the whip, which we held crisscrossed in front of our breasts.

The music stopped at the hallowed moment of crowning.

The multitude assembled prostrated themselves, foreheads touching the mosaic floor. No eye must witness the moment of crowning lest it be cursed forever.

Silence reigned in the great room. Not a whisper could be heard.

Pshereni-Ptah, his hands shaking under the weight of the double Pharaonic crowns, placed them on our consecrated heads, the red cobra crown of Lower Egypt, the Lady of Spells, and the white, conical, bulbous-tipped vulture crown of Upper Egypt, the Lady of Dread. The implacement of the crowns and the investiture of all the emblems of supreme power signified that we were now officially in possession of Egypt.

I trembled, not from fear or the weight on my brow, but with the weight of responsibility the double crown represented, and the awesome significance of the trust that the high immortal gods were placing in me. I thought of the long train of my ancestors who had worn the crown before me.

Pshereni-Ptah murmured an exalted incantation in his old voice, and the multitude was now free to rise and look upon their crowned monarchs. Cymbals clashed, trumpets blared, and the chorus burst into a triumphant song.

The coronation oath followed the crowning. My brother took the oath first, speaking in Egyptian learned by rote, his voice unclear as he stumbled over the words, several times being prompted by a priest. When my turn came, I spoke in the perfect Egyptian I had learned at Tamaratet's knee, speaking in a voice that carried to every ear in the Great Hall, each syllable

167

clear as a bell. The oath itself is bold and brief, and the words are engraved upon my heart.

"I, Cleopatra the Seventh, Fatherloving and Brotherloving Goddess, the Everliving Isis, solemnly pledge my sacred troth that as Queen and Liege Lady of the Two Lands I will keep and defend, uphold and govern with all my godly powers the laws and customs of my realm, pledging my life to my gods, my country and my people, with the help of Osiris and Isis and all other Egyptian gods, until the day they call me to their bosom as their own. All this do I, Queen Cleopatra, solemnly vow."

Having pledged ourselves, my brother and I received in return, through their representatives, oaths of fealty from the Three Estates made up of the priesthood, the nobility, and the people. These notables advanced to the thrones and gave the prostration and made their vows to their liege lord and lady. This exchange of oaths comprised a sacred compact between the rulers and the ruled.

Now that my brother and I were invested with the crowns of Egypt by the good order of the ancient laws of the kingdom, Pshereni-Ptah read our titles aloud, the same titles that had been borne by Ramses the Great, Thutmose the Third and Queen Hapshepsüt. Living Image of the God Amon, Children of the Sun, the Chosen of Ptah. I, the Fatherloving Brotherloving Goddess, the Young Isis, my brother the Fatherloving Sisterloving God, the Young Osiris. Pshereni-Ptah uttered our titles in his weak voice, and then the priests and the congregation repeated them.

At last the whole assemblage, with one voice that shook the Great Hall, cried out, "Hail, King Ptolemy! Hail, Queen Cleopatra! May you live forever!"

My brother and I rose from our thrones. Our regalia, except for our crowns, were taken from us. Our long robes were clasped around our shoulders, and we moved slowly out of the Great Hall past our kneeling subjects.

Outside Ptolemy and I crossed the courtyard to the Temple of Isis. We were given an armful of lilies, which we took inside and placed on the altar as an offering.

Side by side we prostrated ourselves on the floor in mute gratitude for having been raised so high. For some time we prayed, then stood to throw rich incense on the sacred altar fire.

We returned from the temple to the palace and appeared on the Balcony of Appearances which faces the huge square in front of the palace. The square was filled with citizens who sank to their knees as we made our appearance.

In full view of the people, Aunt Aliki brought a pillow with a wreath of gold studded with sparkling gems. King Ptolemy took the wreath and placed it on Pshereni-Ptah's shaven head. Princess Arsinoë handed me a bag filled with costly gems and gold, which I gave to Pshereni-Ptah. These gifts were a thanks offering to him for having crowned us. The crowd cheered their approval.

The King and I retired to our separate apartments for an hour of rest and repast. Then we met in the courtyard, climbed onto a great gilded litter, took our seats on two golden chairs, and the procession started out into the streets of Alexandria, our litter being carried by giant ebony Nubian slaves.

The royal road was strewn with flowers. The order of the procession was ordained by protocol. A thousand marching soldiers led the way. Then came Pshereni-Ptah in a litter, surrounded by a hundred walking priests who carried thuribles and religious emblems. Next came the litter which carried my brother and me, and after us those of my little brother and sister, my Aunt Aliki, and then the high nobles and chamberlains of the court. A contingent of Macedonian Household Guards drew up the rear.

The sun was great and golden that day, shining its benediction upon us. My brother and I, as custom dictated, were stiff as statues of idols. As the sun caught our golden dress, we flamed like fire and must have indeed appeared to the people a golden god and goddess and children of the sun.

The procession followed along the wide boulevards

that cut across the four miles of the city, past all the massive, marble, Grecian buildings built by my forefathers. Crowds of excited citizens lined the way, fighting and jostling to catch sight of their monarchs, held back by a phalanx of soldiers. The people, loving the pleasures of pageantry, and with all the atavistic pull of the monarchy, acclaimed us with hysterical rejoicings. The procession seemed interminable, but the wild cheers of my people inspired me, I knew the true meaning of exaltation, and a spiritual ecstasy upheld me and gave me endurance.

Late in the afternoon the procession slowly wound its way back into the palace courtyard. In my robing chamber my ladies divested me of my royal mantle and insignia. My neck ached from the weight of the double crown upon my head all those long hours. With relief I relaxed in a hot perfumed bath, had a body massage, and rested an hour. There was still the coronation banquet to attend in the evening.

The Banquet Hall was magnificently bedecked for the feast that night. I appeared in a Grecian gown with just a few ornaments, and my blonde hair hung loose to my shoulders. I shared my couch with Charmion, Protarchus, and Apollodorus.

My court feasted splendidly, Diodorus and fifty dancing girls danced, Lysandridas and Zenophantus declaimed, tumblers performed their feats, and jesters coaxed laughs from the guests.

It was midnight before I was able to retire to my apartments with my beloved Charmion, ending the most glorious day of my life, a day I had gone through as if it had been a beautiful dream.

Long had I been bred for queenship, and so it had come to pass. I am the seventh Queen of Egypt to bear the name of Cleopatra, and there were several Macedonian Queen Cleopatras. More than one soothsayer has assured me, however, that I will stand out as the Cleopatra of history.

I had longed to be a great monarch, greater than Thutmose the Third, Ramses the Second, Queen

Hapshepsüt, and Ptolemy the First. I longed—dare I say it?—to be as great as Alexander! But I realized from the outset that I was faced with forces that could prevent my working effectively to bring about the political objectives that would fulfill my destiny.

In the palace of the Ptolemies I lived and reigned. The palace, like Alexandria itself, is a splendid monument to the greatness that had been our dynasty and the splendor of my inheritance. I knew more than anyone, however, that this was a facade. I assessed my country, which was weakened and threatened by outside forces. The rapacious Rabirius had looted the land, and the dignity of the dynasty had deteriorated to the lowest level. Finding myself the only free monarch descended from the world of Alexander of three centuries ago, I vowed I would fight to my death for Egypt to endure as an independent state and not to become, as had all other civilized countries, a Roman province. Despite their military might and powers of organization, I felt I could stave off the Romans, and that I could arrest and even reverse the declining trend of my house.

I was Queen and had been invested with the title of earthly viceroy of the gods sent to rule Egypt, but it was a meaningless title, for I could not act as the absolute monarch the gods meant me to be. I was saddled with a half-brother, and three councillors of the Council of Regency held the reins of government in our names. I was accountable to them, for no law could be decreed unless they approved. I was rarely in concert with their ideas. They were all base and lacked insight and breadth of vision. During council sessions I was forced to listen to their ideas and I could always see through the self-seeking speciousness of their arguments.

Of the three most powerful councillors, the one I hated most was Pothinos. As Prime Minister under my father, he had been compliantly obedient, but now his true colors came out. He took complete control with the blessings of my brother, who felt an avuncular affection for him. He became a domineering despot, determined to rule unheeded, and he was unscrupulous in accomplishing his ends. Although I was a mature and intelligent queen at eighteen, he preferred to look upon me as a child because he was unwilling to pass any power into my hands.

During council debates, my brother, Achillas, and Theodotus always agreed to every proposition Pothinos put forth. When I voiced disagreement, Protarchus, who had a seat on the council, would feebly back me up. Although Protarchus was a great scholar, his gentle nature prevented him from being ruthless and he had not the spirit to fight for his beliefs.

The jealousy and ill will which Pothinos felt toward me increased as he found that I was advancing rapidly in strength of character, and that I could pose a serious threat to his influence and ascendency. Pothinos impeded me, and I knew that eventually one of us would have to go.

I was also hampered by the court system with its archaic customs which had become static. There was a complex hierarchy of duties jealously guarded by each chamberlain, who had his own functions and privileges. I wanted to eliminate the dead weight and corruption, but I was thwarted at every turn by tradition-bound nobles. I realized I had to move prudently and that my aims would not be achieved overnight.

In my first year as Queen I carried myself with the isolation of majesty, seriously discharging my sacred duties, denying myself all pleasures. During this time it was not the specter of Rome I feared as much as the insidious nature of my own house and council with their stupidity and lack of foresight.

My father had left four children, two on the throne and two others who automatically became claimants. King Ptolemy and his brother, a year apart, had been the best of friends, growing up in the same wing of the palace and sharing the same governesses, tutors, and playmates. "They are as different as day is from night," Father had said, describing his two sons, and indeed they were. The older was aggressive and insensitive, with a surly, bullying manner, while the younger was frail and delicate. Now that the elder was King he began treating the younger with arrogant scorn, as sometimes happens between siblings. Ptolemy Philippos, who was extremely sensitive and who had always adored his older brother, was deeply hurt by this treatment, and a hatred for his brother took root in his heart.

I felt a fondness for Prince Ptolemy Philippos, and often asked King Ptolemy to treat his brother with more gentleness, but this suggestion was ignored. I realized an underlying motivation for the King's treatment was that he now saw his brother as a threat. This was absurd, for Prince Ptolemy had no ambitions and the last thing he wanted was a throne. Much had always been made of his older brother, so he had always been given short shrift at court, which had left its mark. His nervous disposition, fragile nature, and dainty pretty blondness often prompted the remark that he should have been born a princess. His extreme nervousness soon manifested itself in a slight stutter, which increased as he advanced into puberty.

My little sister Princess Arsinoë was a miniature of her late mother, Queen Arsinoë, and that alone made me feel unkindly toward her. In temperament she was much like our brother-King, although while he was rather stupid, she had a better than average intelligence; and when she wanted to apply herself at her studies she excelled. She also had her mother's conniving and clever nature. I did not fear Arsinoë yet, although I suspected that as she grew older she might prove to be a threat, since she was gathering a cabal of adherents around her made up of her mother's relatives and her tutor, Ganymedes, who was an adept practitioner of the palace intrigue I deplored.

There was little love between my father's progeny. We were not a closely knit family and were torn by jealousy and mistrust. I thought it proper, however, that we all show civility to one another before the court. My brother-King, with the encouragement of Pothinos, was particularly hostile to me. I ignored this and treated him kindly, atlhough it was difficult to do.

I greatly enjoyed all the machinery of the government, and even the most minute matters did not bore me. Each day I sat with my councillors in the chamber where all issues of state were discussed and decided upon. The decrees were signed by me and sealed with the great signet seal of the Sphinx. My brother-King sometimes sat at council in the morning, but soon would grow bored and go off with his playmates or to his lessons. I had shown a keen interest in the kingdom's affairs even as a little princess, but it was apparent that my brother, even when he came of age, would relegate such matters to others.

At first I made an effort to avoid any contention with my council, although I realized that sooner or later I would be drawn into a dispute with Pothinos which would be too important to let go by. This finally happened when news came from Hermonthis, a holy city near Thebes, that their sacred bull Buchis had died.

My father had reared me to respect all the religious rites of my people, and since childhood I had taken an interest in all their cults. I understood their attachment to the past and their devotion to their traditions. My people from earliest times have worshipped, among other animals, the bull. Four Egyptian provinces have the bull as their sacred emblem. There is Apis at Memphis, a white-spotted black bull whose cult is associated with Serapis, and the warlike holy brown bull Buchis at Hermonthis, honored by the people as the living soul of Amon-Ra. I was proud to inherit my father's religious policy and wanted to associate myself with these customs. The Greeks, however, like the Romans, are appalled by the worship of animals. My father had been a restorer of the temples and had given aid to the upkeep of the Temple of Hermonthis, so I was concerned at the death of their bull.

"A letter must be issued to the High Priest of Hermonthis," I announced to my council, "informing him of the sadness of his sovereigns at the death of his sacred bull."

"This will be done, O Queen," Pothinos said briskly.

"A new bull has been selected from the bull pen of the city to be their new god. It is a brown bull and extremely well endowed, qualifying him as a successor to Buchis. As is customary, a royal proxy will be appointed to conduct the bull to his shrine."

"Yes," I said, my imagination captured, "and issue the proclamation to say that the Lady of the Two Lands will personally row the new bull in the royal barge of Amon to the Temple of Hermonthis."

"Yes, O Queen, the proclamation will read so," Pothinos said impatiently, "but I've chosen a proxy, one of Princess Arsinoë's governesses, who will discharge this tiresome duty for you."

I knew that he meant the Lady Thaïs, who was one of his cousins. I stared coldly at him. "I see no reason why I should shirk my duties. It is my wish to officiate at the installation ceremony myself."

"This would be without precedent, O Queen," Pothinos cried.

"If we do not change, Pothinos, we atrophy," I said.

"The installation ceremonies are next week, and you are still in mourning for your late beloved father," Pothinos said with a smirking smile.

"My father would be the first to urge me to go," I argued politely.

"May I point out to you, O Queen, that it would be unworthy of you to personally take part in this idiotic rite, this fertility cult?" Pothinos cried.

"The Pharaohs did!" I said vigorously.

Theodotus sneered. "The ancient pharaohs were heathens! Remember that you are a Greek queen sent by the Greek gods, the true gods, to rule over these barbarian people."

"The Egyptians were a great civilization when we Greeks were living in hovels!" I rejoined with spirit.

Pothinos clicked his tongue tetchily. "It is the custom of the Ptolemies always to appoint a proxy to officiate at these obscene rites."

"It has been the custom for the Ptolemies to never leave this palace, to spend their days drinking and debauching," I cried. "I wish to make improvements in my reign."

Theodotus grimaced. "It would be most unseemly, O Queen."

"It was seemly enough for Alexander the Great!" I retorted, pointing to a bust of Alexander sitting in a corner niche. "Alexander liberated the Egyptians from the hated Persians, who tried to stamp out the Egyptian gods during their brief occupation, but Alexander did not make the same mistake. He was looked upon as a savior and he worshipped all the native gods. Our dynasty followed in this tradition, contenting the people by paying tribute to their religious customs, and that is why we have survived three centuries. If my people felt I thought their worship of bulls was ridiculous, I would not remain long on the throne. I think it will have a special significance if I go to Hermonthis myself in a royal procession up the Nile, so that the people along the banks see me on the way to perform a sacred rite. Perhaps a few haughty nobles at court will think ill of me, but the people will love me for it."

Looking around at the faces of Pothinos, Theodotus, and Achillas, I could see that the last thing they wanted was for the people to love me.

"The people should fear their monarchs more than love them!" Pothinos declared.

"I disagree, Pothinos," I cried. "The monarchy will survive only if we are popular and are loved, not hated and feared. In my reign I am going to make every possible concession to the native population to win their goodwill."

"And what of the ruling class, O Queen?" Pothinos asked belligerently.

"I have their interests at heart," I replied. "I want to bring Egyptians and Greeks closer together. I want to eradicate all the hatred the natives feel for us, and all the racial and social hostilities. As you point out, my Lord Pothinos, we are Greek and our dynasty is Macedonian, and we have imposed to some degree our civilization on Egypt, but we have always respected the traditions of this ancient land, and this has been our greatest strength. The two cultures have intermingled and have been revitalized by the merger. In the manner of Alexander, I will honor all the native divinities."

"By all means, O Queen," Pothinos said angrily, "let us adhere to the Ptolemaic policy of tolerating the people's strange worship of animals, for in their ignorance they need these absurd practices, but our divine Queen cannot demean herself by participating in these heathen rites."

"That is why your council," Theodotus interjected, "advise that you be content to have a royal functionary as your deputy to take your place in this barbarous ceremony. It was acceptable when as a little princess you fed the sacred crocodiles. It impressed the masses and amused the nobles, but you are no longer a child but a woman and our divine Queen."

"Yes, I am Queen, Queen of the Egyptians—"

"But you are Greek, and only the wigs you wear are Egyptian!" Pothinos interrupted testily.

"To the people I am an Egyptian goddess!" I retorted. "The people see the Ptolemies as a link with their old pharaohs who are offspring of Amon-Ra. If the people believed that my wigs were my only Egyptian trait, I would not be Queen for long, and you, Pothinos, would not be prime minister but a rug merchant like your grandfather!"

At this remark Pothinos blanched and bristled, for it was true, although he hated to be reminded of the origins of the house of Pothinos.

"I should also like to point out that Hermonthis is in Upper Egypt," I resumed, "where our dynasty has never been popular. There are few Greek settlers there, and the region has often been the seat of seditious rebellions. If you know our history, you will recall that in the days of my grandfather, Ptolemy the Ninth, who ruled during the time your grandfather sold rugs in the bazaar, Lord Pothinos, there was a native revolt at Thebes that took three years to be quelled. Let us hope there won't be any uprisings during my reign, for I have enough trouble keeping the Romans at bay. My going to Hermonthis will endear the people to me. I am Queen, sent here by the gods to be their viceroy over Egypt, and the gods tell me that I must install the new bull Buchis myself."

A great silence fell on the chamber. I looked around at my councillors, and my eyes fell on Achillas, the general of all the armies. Achillas was the only true Egyptian on the council, although he had a Greek name and tried to be more Greek than the Greeks, but I suspected that in his heart of hearts he was a native son.

"What say you, my Lord Achillas?" I ventured, staring deeply into his brown eyes set in his serene, brown face.

"I think, O Queen," Achillas replied slowly, "that if you went to Hermonthis, the act would appeal to the native sentiment and content the people."

"Yes, the gods urge me on this course," I cried in a triumphant, swelling voice. "I am the living god and the living law." I glared at Pothinos daringly. "Pharaoh has spoken!" I added for good measure.

There was a heavy silence, but no one dared gainsay me.

Pothinos shrugged in acquiescence. "Of course, if you insist, O Queen, what harm can there be in it?"

It was with enthusiasm that I made arrangements for the progress to Hermonthis, and at last the day came for departure.

On the landward side of the palace which borders the blue shimmering Lake Mareotis, I boarded the royal barge of Amon. Musicians played and the whole court stood assembled on the palace terrace bidding me farewell. The barge sailed across the freshwater lake and entered the canal which gives access to the Nile. The traffic of merchant ships that generally plies the canal was halted to allow my barge to make its way unimpeded. I stood on the garlanded deck with Charmion and Apollodorus, touched at the sight of thousands of citizens lining the banks of the canal to cheer me.

The floating palace of the royal barge, propelled by

178

golden sails and a hundred galley slaves, left the canal and sailed into the broad expanse of the great mother river Nile. I was eighteen and had never been outside Alexandria before. Alexandria is a Greek city and no more Egyptian than old Carthage was African; and it was a moving experience for me finally to sail down the Nile into the heart of Egypt and to become acquainted with some of my native cities.

The mighty Nile, which fertilizes my land, flowed beneath the barge and the sun shimmered on the full majestic river. I was deeply impressed with the mystery and greatness of the Nile, whose waters come from the cataracts of Nubia, distributing its fertilizing waters through the canals and locks built more than two thousand years ago. The Nile is the source of all life, supplying Egypt with nourishment and food, and each day during the voyage I poured generous libations of wine into the river as a thanks offering.

I was Queen and this land was mine. All the people I passed were serfs of my state, and a portion of all they produced belonged to me. The whole machinery of my kingdom was set in motion by my will, and taxes were collected to fill my treasury. I felt tremendous emotion at seeing my country, and became acutely conscious of my duty toward my people, feeling that I was as much their serf as they were mine.

Within a few days I came to Memphis, a city sleeping at the foot of the Pyramids. This was a thrilling sight, for now I was truly in one of the cities of the old pharaohs. I stopped briefly and visited the Great Temple of Amon-Ra, which my father had restored to his great credit. I visited the High Priest Pshereni-Ptah, who had crowned me just a few months before, and who now lay on his deathbed.

As the royal barge proceeded up the Nile, I made stops at other cities and visited the temples on the river-bank. Here was the Egypt which had not changed in thirty centuries. There are thirty thousand towns in my realm and I wanted to know them all, but in that short week's journey to Hermonthis I could only stop at a few of them: Memphis, Naucratis, Heracleopolis, Hermopolis, Lykopolis, Panopolis, and Ombos. The priests and the people always gave me a heartfelt welcome as their goddess Queen descended from the gods, and I was deeply touched.

I wore only Egyptian dress on this pilgrimage, and the people saw me attired as Hapshepsüt and Nefertiti in the pictures on temple walls. I often sat on a throne on deck with Charmion, my ladies and Royal Fanbearers grouped around me, while musicians played their flutes and pipes. I watched fertile fields slip by, and the irrigation ditches lacing the land, spreading out from the river. I passed fields of wheat and papyrus. Peasants lined the banks as my blue barge sailed along, carrying two sacred passengers, queen and bull. The bull had an enclosure all to himself at the stern of the barge with a canopy to shield him from the blazing sun. I emptied buckets of food ceremoniously into his trough three times daily. From the shore, farmers and herdsmen knelt, and even goats and cattle seemed to pause in obeisance, raising heads to watch the royal passing.

After a week I came to Thebes, which in ancient times had been the great seat of power, but now is a city in ruins. It is still a glorious, breathtaking sight, however, with its four great temples and the City of the Dead. It was Homer who wrote that Thebes was the city of a hundred gates.

We sailed past Thebes to navigate the fourteen miles further southward, and arrived at the holy city of Hermonthis, called the glory of the Two Heavens, on the west bank of the Nile. The barge stopped at the landing near the gates of the temple. A contingent of the temple priests and priestesses, all in white linen robes, led by their High Priest, Antuk, met me as I stepped off the barge.

"Greetings, my Lord High Priest," I said in Egyptian. "It is with great honor that I bring your new bull to his sacred shrine."

"Queen Cleopatra, daughter of the gods, we bid you

welcome!" Antuk cried, kneeling at my feet and kissing my hand. "The last time we met, when I went to court on an official visit, you were a princess, and now you are our goddess-Queen. Your father our late sovereign lord King Ptolemy was our friend, and we pray that you will look upon us with similar affection."

"Rest assured, Antuk," I said, "that I feel the same reverence for you and your holy temple as did my beloved father."

I was led across the walks of the temple, past enormous statues of animals, the cat, the crocodile, the jackal, and the bull. In the cool interior of the temple, I threw incense on the fire at the altar and knelt in homage and prayer.

In the afternoon, people from miles around crowded the temple to witness the installing of the new bull and were held in check by soldiers. Ablaze with jewels of lapis lazuli and carnelian and wearing a gown of purple silk slashed with tissue of gold and buttoned with pearls, I ceremoniously conducted Buchis from the barge in formal ritual to his new home in a pen behind the temple. A cluster of priests and royal officials assisted me, and there was a medley of chants and sacred songs. I gloried in performing this magical ritual which had been hallowed by four thousand years of sacred usage.

When the ceremony was finished, I was served chilled wine and stuffed dates. Then the High Priest Antuk took me on a tour of the temple.

"Your father favored us with gold to restore our temple to the glory it had known during the time of the old pharaohs," Antuk said.

"Yes, my beloved Father always did his sacred duty," I replied, thinking that despite all the vast sums he had given Romans, he had given far more to Egypt, placating the priests and fostering national culture. He had died with an empty treasury, but he knew that gold is something to be spent, of little use if it is hoarded.

Antuk showed me all the art and ancient writings deposited in his temple. In Alexandria we have the library and museums which house Greek works, but it is the temples, with their stores of art and holy books, which are the seats of Egyptian civilization. I admired the collection at Hermonthis and realized how imperative it was that it be preserved.

"In my reign, my Lord Antuk, as in my father's," I said, "lavish benefactions shall be conferred upon the great temples so that our culture will survive."

"You are great in wisdom and generosity, O Sacred Radiance," he cried.

As I was led around the temple, I read aloud the hieroglyphics on the walls, which impressed the priests, for I am the only Ptolemaic monarch ever able to do this.

Finally Antuk guided me to a wall, and I gazed upon a bas-relief depicting my beloved father in the guise of an ancient pharaoh on a chariot whipping his enemies to the ground. He wore the tall crowns with the horns and feathers of Amon and the royal serpent on his head, just like a Ramses or a Thutmose. It was a highly romanticized portrait of my father, certainly, but it had been done with honor and love, and a lump lodged in my throat and tears filled my eyes as I looked upon it.

"It is very beautiful, my Lord Antuk," I said.

"We had deep reverence for your father," Antuk explained. "Our grief was great when news came of his death, but we rejoice that his beloved daughter is now our Queen and will pursue his policies."

In the evening my royal party took dinner with the priests in the Great Hall of the Temple. Sacred songs were sung by a chorus and religious poems were recited. After the banquet Charmion and I retired to a sleeping chamber appointed with every comfort and luxury. When we left the hall there was a league of admiring younger priests encircling Apollodorus, whose avid attentions he received with sheepish charm and delight, and I do not know how he spent the night.

"Is it true, Cleopatra," Charmion whispered as we lay abed, "that all the local young virgins will be given to Buchis to be deflowered?"

We giggled like two little girls and snuggled close.

In the morning I laid blazing gems as votive offerings on the altar. The overjoyed priests chanted prayers and did homage to the gods. I was then led to the pen of Buchis and prostrated myself on a rich carpet that symbolized his status as a god.

My departure was witnessed by a great gathering. A little local girl presented me with an armful of lilies and I kissed her cheek to the delight of the mob of onlookers. Flowers were strewn on the walk by the priestesses as I made my way to the river bank with my party, said farewell to the venerable Antuk, High Priest of Hermonthis.

The news of my royal progress to Hermonthis quickly spread throughout the Two Lands, and my people were touched that their young queen should honor them in this manner. Back in Alexandria, Pothinos and Theodotus received the reports of my success with coolness, unhappy that I was capturing the love and the imagination of my people, and undoubtedly they planned to use all their power to thwart this trend in the future.

A few weeks after I returned to Alexandria a new calendar was presented at court. Sosigenes, the oldest and most famed of all the astronomers, came with his colleagues from the Academy of Sciences. Sosigenes advanced to the thrones, knelt to my brother and me, and presented a copy of the calendar to each of us.

"We are praying that Your Divine Majesties will be pleased with the work of your humble servants," Sosigenes said.

"We thank you, my Lord Sosigenes," I said with a gracious smile.

Later that night, in my bedchamber before retiring, I scrutinized the calendar and saw that it was hopeless. It was now the end of the winter equinox when the weather is characterized by heavy winds coming in off the sea; but while the winds told me it was winter, the calendar did not corroborate this.

I sent for Sosigenes for a private audience in my chamber. I did not want to embarrass him before the court with what I had to say. He had been my father's boyhood friend, and I always showed special kindness for those who had been close to my father.

Sosigenes came in a flowing jade robe, reeking of perfume, and wearing the gold collar of First Friend which my father had conferred upon him. Now in his early fifties, he was in excellent health; for although he was known for indulging the pleasures of the flesh, he took good care of himself, and with his position at the academy lived a privileged life. His advancing years did not please him, and he made a pathetic attempt to disguise his wrinkles with thick paint, just as an aging waterfront whore might do.

"Most Sacred and Divine Queen, I am honored by your invitation," Sosigenes cried, sinking to one knee and kissing my hand.

"The honor is mine, too, Lord Sosigenes," I said. "Rise and do sit." I pointed to a chair that was identical to my own a few feet away.

After wine and honeyed cakes were served, I waved the servant away.

"I have been looking over the new calendar, Sosigenes," I said, picking the scroll up from a table beside me.

"O Queen, are you pleased with the gold-embossed numbering?" he cried,

"I find no fault with the numbers," I said.

"Oh, we had hoped you would be pleased with this calendar, the first to inaugurate your glorious reign!" Sosigenes said.

I stared silently at him for a moment, then ripped the calendar apart and flung the pieces to the floor. "That is what the Queen of Egypt thinks of your calendar, Lord Sosigenes," I cried.

Sosigenes gulped, his face registering shock. "Beloved Queen!" he stammered, aghast.

"This calendar is totally inaccurate and must be reformed," I said. "As the foremost astronomer of the world, you know that. The seasonal and solar dates do not match the calendar and lunar dates."

"Yes, Sacred Majesty, the calendar has these many

years fallen into a dreadful state of confusion. The sun is angry with us. The sun is in error."

"I, as Queen, come from the sun!" I cried, my eyes blazing with authority. "I am the incarnation of Amon-Ra. The error is not in the sun, Sosigenes, but in the idiots who composed this calendar."

Sosigenes gulped painfully. "Each year, O Divine Radiance, it seems the stars in their heavens go further off course."

"The course of the stars are perfect, Sosigenes. Amon-Ra has organized the constellations and their effect on the earth in perfect harmony. This calendar, because it has been made by charlatans and fools, is misinterpreting the stars and the sun."

"O Queen, the gods are angry with us! They send winter for summer. It is a sign of cosmic disorder!"

"It is a sign of your stupidity!" I rejoined harshly. I took a deep breath and resumed in a softer tone. "There is no fault in the stars, Sosigenes, but there is a human error. I would expect such an absurd rationalization from my lowest peasant, but not from my august astronomer and astrologer, Sosigenes. You have at your disposal a repository of charts and books of astronomy collected through the centuries by the ancient Egyptians and Greeks from which to conduct your research. If you studied this material, you would be able to devise an accurate calendar."

"Yes, Gracious Majesty," Sosigenes put in, "but you will allow that our Egyptian calendar is more accurate than the one used by the Romans?"

"Well, I should certainly hope that our great civilization should be able to produce a less confusing calendar than the barbarian Romans!" I cried indignantly. "That's not the point. We must get our calendar into perfect order, and then the country will be run on a more proper course. The farmers must know when to harvest, when the Nile'will rise and the seasons change."

The strong winds blowing in off the sea billowed the curtains at the windows of my chamber.

"Look," I cried with a gesture toward the windows,

"the winter winds blow, yet, according to your calendar, it is the autumnal equinox."

"Yes, O Queen, you are right," Sosigenes said shame-faced.

"Ancient Egyptian astronomers tell us," I went on with authority, "that the sun's motion is neither exactly parallel with that of the heavens in general, nor diametrically opposite, but in an oblique line the sun steers its course in a gentle curve, dispensing light and influence in annual revolution, producing several seasons in just proportion to the whole creation."

"Yes, Great Queen, that is so!" Sosigenes eagerly bobbed his head.

"I, Queen of Egypt, represent the sun, a giver of all good things, in the form of the Greatest Goddess Isis. As Queen I share in the power of the sun as supreme deity, and I concentrate in the state the radiant sun power. You will see on my new coins that my image is crowned with the rays of the sun. Yet, sun goddess that I am, I do not have a calendar that accurately interprets the sun. I demand a reform of the calendar for Egypt, and then later we will give it to the Roman world and show them the way."

"O Divine Radiance, I shall do as you command," Sosigenes cried. "To serve my Queen and country is my life."

"Give me a perfect calendar, Sosigenes, as perfect as the sun itself!"

Sosigenes and his colleagues went into a fever of activity at the Academy of Sciences. Tremendous research was done and all the ancient books were consulted in the composition of the new solar calendar. It was estimated that the old calendar had been in error by seventy days. It was decided that the new calendar should be divided into twelve months representing four seasons. It was calculated that there should be three hundred and sixty-five days in the year, with an extra day every fourth year, which I called a Leap Year. It took only a few months to compose this calendar, during which I went to the academy often to check on the progress. When it was completed I felt a sense of gratification, for it had been achieved at my instigation, and was a perfect synchronization of the sun and the stars and the moon.

In my first year as Queen, I fought desperately to gain a stronger position than was possible in the prevailing power structure. I turned nineteen and I thoroughly enjoyed being Queen. I applied myself most conscientiously to my duties and never stinted in performing them. I had rare moments of leisure. In the evenings in my apartments I studied reports and papers, while Charmion and Apollodorus, my two favorites, played chess with competitive zeal. They always took their meals with me, and their nearness was a comfort. Aunt Aliki visited me regularly, and I enjoyed her inconsequential chatter.

Once a week there was a court banquet, usually held for foreign ambassadors and distinguished guests. The table was sumptuously served and the entertainment lavish. There was music and dancing, and poets read their latest work. My brother and I sat on the royal dais, but on separate couches.

King Ptolemy was thirteen and down had appeared on his chin and cheeks, the first beginnings of manhood. In a few years Ptolemy and I would have to marry, conforming to the ancient Egyptian usage of marriage between brother and sister. Dynastically the custom is as old as Egypt itself, because of the right of the female line to succeed, for the only parent a royal prince can really be positive is his own is the mother.

One of my duties was to review my troops. The army was composed at this time of three divisions, and once a week in rotation I reviewed one of these divisions. I knew that a monarch was only as strong as the army was loyal. The army had supported my father's throne, and now that I sat in that regal but unstable chair, the soldiers were indispensable to me. They adored me and I always gave them a radiant smile, and personally distributed gifts to them at festival times.

As I often told my army, "You belong to me, and

I belong to you!" We all knew where we stood.

My favorite division of the army was the one composed of the Gabinian soldiers who had liberated my father five years before. Most of them were blond, blue-eyed barbarians from the far north. Many had married local girls and had children or had settled down with boys to their liking. They had taken to the free and easy ways of the city, and were now true Alexandrians. My father maintained that these blond Germans shared many characteristics of Macedonians. They too love to drink, are quick to quarrel, are fierce fighters and make the best soldiers. A strange lot, ignorant and totally lacking in subtlety of mind, they like to band together in groups and follow a leader; and once they choose a leader, they follow him to the death. An admirable trait, certainly, although not always sensible.

Apollodorus liked to fraternize with these Germans and had many friends among them, for being dark he has a penchant for blonds. He always accompanied me when I reviewed the Gabinian troop, and I would stop and talk to them and knew most of them by name. Of the three divisions of my army, the Gabinian soldiers were my most loyal and devoted.

The other two divisions of my army were recruited almost exclusively from foreign mercenaries made up of runaways from all the four corners of the world: highwaymen, freebooters, convicts, exiles, and escaped slaves. They come to Alexandria to gain employment and, by becoming soldiers, receive citizenship, find a home and are happy. The general Achillas, oddly enough, was one of the few Egyptians in the Royal Egyptian Army. Egyptians have always made deplorable fighters, and even the old pharaohs invariably recruited foreign mercenaries such as Greeks, the Phoenicians, and the like.

The first year of my reign passed without any major catastrophes; and then, fourteen months after my accession, I was presented with a cataclysmic crisis. As was inevitable, I suppose, it involved the Romans. A few years before, when Crassus had been defeated and killed by the Parthians, my father had predicted this eventually would have repercussions on Egypt, and he was right.

Gabinius had been replaced as proconsul of Syria by Marcus Bibulous. I learned that Bibulous, a stern and serious man, on reaching the province where he was to govern, found part of the Parthian army entrenched within the Syrian borders. He was short of troops, and felt that his only hope was to regain the soldiers that Gabinius had taken to Egypt with my father.

Bibulous sent his two young sons to Alexandria to retrieve these troops, and I received them in my audience chamber. They were both handsome boys and I liked their direct, honest manners on sight.

"My father is in desperate need of soldiers," the eldest son told me, "and so with your permission, O Queen, he wants to recall the Gabinian soldiers to Syria."

"We remember with sympathy the fate of Crassus, Lord Bibulous," I cried. "Since your father assumes he has a right to the Gabinian troop, I will vouchsafe his appeal. I've given the soldiers citizenship and honors, but if they wish to return with you to Syria, they go with my blessings. I will also give you a gift of supplies to help you against the Parthians, for any enemy of Rome is an enemy of Egypt."

The loss of the Gabinian soldiers would reduce my forces by a third, but I had no choice but to comply with the wishes of Rome and to fate.

The barracks of the Gabinian soldiers was outside the city walls. Since Apollodorus was on intimate terms with the leading Gabinian officers, I had him accompany the sons of Bibulous, who would present the document ordering the transfer of the unit to Syria. The leaders received the sons, taking them inside the headquarters' chamber, but making Apollodorus stay outside. When the German officers were informed of the order, they became heated in their objections, since they had no desire to leave Alexandria to return to the rough discipline of the Roman army or to fight the fierce Parthians. There was much passionate arguing, and the Germans all the while were heavily drinking.

In the heat of anger and drunkenness the Gabinian

officers had the two sons of Bibulous run through.

Apollodorus was told by the leaders what they had done, and he was instructed to return to the palace and inform me that they would not leave my service. I was their leader and they would serve no other and would die for me.

At first I was struck dumb. It seemed impossible that the two handsome youths I had given audience to in the afternoon were now dead. In a state of shock, I realized that my first major crisis as Queen had been thrust upon me.

At midnight I convened an emergency session of my council and reported the alarming news. Pothinos and Theodotus, both Roman-haters, could barely conceal their delight that two Romans had been murdered.

"What shall we do, O Queen?" Pothinos asked.

Pothinos who always had an answer for everything, now suddenly he was asking me what to do, eager to put the problem entirely in my hands so that I would be responsible for the outcome.

"What do my sage councillors advise?" I asked.

All the councillors remained silent with grave, perplexed faces.

"Rest assured, O Queen, that we will support you in whatever measures you wish to employ in this matter," Pothinos murmured in his unctuous voice.

Suddenly I was an autocratic monarch with his blessing. I forced my expression to remain impassive, maintaining rigid self-control.

"We cannot condone mutiny and murder," I finally said. "I command that the culprits be arrested."

The order of arrest was drawn up immediately by Pothinos. When the document was presented to me to be signed, I saw that it bore my name only and not my brother's with it. Whatever the outcome, I would have to accept full responsibility. I signed my name, Pothinos stamped it with the Great Seal, and it was given to Apollodorus to carry out. It was a difficult assignment for him since he was a bosom companion of the officers he would have to arrest.

190

At dawn Apollodorus took a detachment of soldiers and left the palace. The German ringleaders, all whom I knew personally, were rounded up and brought back in chains to the palace.

"They are in the dungeons, O Queen," Pothinos told me in the afternoon. "What is our next course of action in this matter?"

"You have no suggestions, my Lord Pothinos?" I demanded harshly.

Pothinos bowed. "The council will abide by the wisdom of your wishes, O Sacred Radiance."

"We must at all cost avert the wrath of the Romans," I warned. There was a heavy silence while my thoughts whirled. A moment of immeasurable import had befallen Egypt, and my words and decisions had to be right. I did not want to prosecute the soldiers, but at the same time I could not let the murderers go unpunished.

"I am in a quandary, yet I have little alternative but to act," I said. "Out of political necessity I must resolve the issue by having the four German murderers sent in chains to Syria to Marcus Bibulous, the father of the murdered boys. Bibulous can decide their fate and it will be out of my hands."

Pothinos smiled coldly. "You are your father's daughter in this matter, for you are doing what he would have done."

"Yes," I said with a proud toss of my head.

"This gesture will placate the Romans," Theodotus reminded me, "but will be intensely unpopular in Egypt and especially with your army."

I stared into his glittering, gleeful eyes. "Pharaoh does what Pharaoh must!" I answered.

I had the two victims carefully embalmed and sent with the murderers to Bibulous. In my accompanying letter, I wrote that he only could decide justice for the culprits.

Bibulous was heartbroken at the loss of his two fine sons, but he met this tragedy with stoic endurance, refusing to punish the murderers, and within two months my detachment of soldiers returned from Syria with the prisoners. Bibulous sent a message saying that only the Roman Senate and its officers redundant had the right to arrest Romans and to decide their fate.

Pothinos insisted that this was a slap in my face, and of course he was happy about that, but I was not so certain about the motives of Bibulous.

"What shall we do now, O Queen?" Pothinos asked expectantly.

Again the matter was put in my hands. I had been Queen for a year and a half and this was the hardest decision I had yet to make.

"The four murderers must be punished for their crime," I said stiffly.

"What will be the punishment, O Queen?" Theodotus asked, his whole body shaking with uncontrollable anticipation.

"Death," I replied.

I saw the look of absolute exultation in the eyes of Pothinos and Theodotus, for they knew that the troops would hate me for this act.

I ordered the condemned men to be put to death mercifully, not by decapitation which their crime warranted, but by the bite of an asp applied to the chest, which is quick and painless.

After this I still reviewed my troops with Apollodorus by my side, but I saw only hostility in the eyes of my soldiers.

"They have good reason to hate me, for they feel I have betrayed them," I lamented to Apollodorus. "I acted as circumstances forced me to act, for my position depends upon the friendship of Rome. On the other hand, however, I need the friendship of my soldiers." I gave a deep sigh. "I would have been damned by either choice."

"You will win the soldiers over again with your smiles," Apollodorus assured me. "This will pass over in time, my Queen."

I could only hope that Apollodorus would be proved right.

CHAPTER IX

THE THIRD YEAR OF MY REIGN began ominously with a low rise of the Nile, a bad harvest, and a crop failure. There were tensions mounting in the country, danger of famine, and murmurs of riots and rebellion. My position was seriously weakened, and although I was officially a joint ruler with my brother, it was his councillors who held tightly to the reins of the kingdom. I was fighting with all my guile to gain a stronger position, but I was caught between antagonistic forces and it appeared at times to be a losing battle.

At the same time that there was intense rivalry between my brother and me in Egypt, the Roman world was torn asunder by the rivalry of Pompey and Caesar.

"Julius Caesar has crossed the Rubicon with his legions," Pothinos announced one day at council, "and he has become sole master of Italy."

"And Pompey, what of Great Pompey?" I asked desperately.

"Pompey and his followers have been ousted from Italy and have sailed across the Adriatic to Macedonia," Pothinos explained.

"So my father's prediction has come true," I said. "There is no stopping this monstrous madman Caesar. After his conquest of Gaul, he is bloated by power and riches and now seeks to control Italy and then finally the world."

"Caesar must be stopped!" Protarchus cried.

"He will be stopped," I said with conviction. "Pompey will not dally in Macedonia, but will be making preparations to continue the struggle. He will undoubtedly be sending envoys to all the eastern kingdoms where he has great influence. Eventually a great battle will be fought between Pompey and Caesar which will decide the fate of the world."

"Pompey will be victorious!" Protarchus said.

"Do you really believe so?" Pothinos asked skeptically. "I suppose we must pray so, for if Pompey is defeated, it will bode ill for Egypt. I wonder if it is wise to adhere to this policy of espousing Pompey's cause which we inherited from our late sovereign lord King Ptolemy."

"Pompey always espoused the cause of my father and of Egypt," I reminded him. "It wasn't always wise for him to do so, but he did."

"A policy Pompey always found immensely profitable," Pothinos said.

Just as I predicted, Pompey busied himself in Macedonia recruiting forces and drumming up military, naval, and financial aid from all the eastern countries on the Levant. His eldest son, also named Gnaeus, came to Alexandria as his envoy, and I received him ceremoniously in the Great Throne Room.

As the young Gnaeus approached the thrones, I saw that he was just a few years older than myself. He was exceptionally tall and had an imposing, well-developed physique, fiery brown eyes, and a handsome head with curly brown hair. He sank a bit awkwardly to one knee, not accustomed to royal courts.

"August King and Revered Queen!" he said in Greek that was deeply accented by his Latin tongue. "I come in friendship and bring greetings from my father, Gnaeus Pompeius Magnus."

"Rise, son of Pompey!" I replied. "Egypt is honored to receive the son of the greatest Roman, who is our greatest friend and ally."

"My father has always held the interest of Egypt nearest his heart," Gnaeus said. "My stepmother, the Lady Cornelia, also sends a message expressing her deepest affection."

"We accept your kind messages with heartfelt appreciation," I said. "Egypt is allied to the Roman commonwealth, and we consider your father the true representative of Rome."

After the audience, my brother and I retired to an antechamber where Archimedes, the Keeper of the Crowns, took possession of our royal regalia.

King Ptolemy had just turned fourteen and had begun shaving. "I wonder, sister," he said as he took off his pharaoh's blue beard, "if our Roman policy is wise. Pothinos says we should not kiss the ass of Pompey's son."

"Pothinos is a fool!" I snapped impatiently. "If it weren't for Pompey restoring our father, you would not be wearing the crowns, little King!"

Instead of handing the blue beard to an attendant, Ptolemy flung it to the floor. He glared at me malevolently and stomped out of the chamber.

"Little monster," Charmion whispered beside me.

At high noon my majordomo conducted Gnaeus Pompey into my reception room. Protarchus and Charmion were with me, so there were just the four of us and a few attendants. The atmosphere was relaxed, a harpist played sweetly in a corner, and delicacies were served. Gnaeus lost the stiffness of manner he had exhibited during the audience that morning, he ate with appetite, and he was charming company. We conversed in Latin at which Charmion is weak, so she simply sat gorging herself. I discovered that his education had been excellent and scholarly, and I liked him immensely.

"My father used to talk with fascination about Rome," I remarked, "and I am most curious to one day go there."

"Rome would be greatly honored by your visit," Gnaeus said.

"Much has changed in Roman politics since my father's stay there," I said. "When Crassus was killed by the Parthians three years ago, my father predicted this civil war."

"This war is not my father's wish," Gnaeus avowed. "It is Caesar's doing. His ambition is relentless."

"Caesar's only child, the Lady Julia, was your step-mother," I prompted.

"The Lady Julia was the loveliest of ladies," Gnaeus explained. "I was a boy and she treated me with all motherly love. Her death in childbirth severed all connections between Caesar and my father. If Julia were alive or if her child had lived there would not be this impending war. My father wishes only to rule in peace with Caesar and to build a greater Rome, but Caesar will not be content unless he destroys the Republic and becomes dictator of Rome and master of the world." He paused. "My father has commissioned me here with instructions to request aid and reinforcements."

"Never fear, Gnaeus, your father never failed my father in his hour of need," I said, "and I, my father's daughter, will return that favor."

Gnaeus smiled broadly, his teeth brilliant against his brown beard.

After Pompey was dismissed, Charmion and I took a bath.

"Gnaeus is as handsome as a Greek god," I cried.

"He is not a Greek god," Charmion disagreed disgruntledly, "only a Roman pig! Perhaps your brother is right that this policy of courting the Romans will have disastrous results for Egypt."

"I love you dearly, Charmion, but you have no head for politics," I scoffed lightly. "My only hope is to have a powerful Roman behind me."

"It is your brother you need behind you," Charmion said. "You will need princes by his seed."

"Yes, but I also need an understanding with a leading Roman," I explained. "A bond of friendship and trust."

"And to acquire these bonds," Charmion demanded with flashing green eyes, "does it mean you must flirt like a harlot with every Roman that comes along?"

"You forget yourself, Charmion!" I rejoined sharply.

Charmion's lips quivered, her nostrils flared, and she looked away. She had a stubborn pride and knew she

196

had overstepped her bounds, but she did not apologize since she was so secure in my affections. I knew it was jealousy that had provoked her lapse of respect and let the matter drop, for I could never stay angry at Charmion for long.

The matter of aid to Pompey was discussed at council.

"It is wise, O Queen, to keep aid down to a minimum," Pothinos said, "since we are uncertain of the outcome of this war."

"Certainly Great Pompey will be the victor," I cried. "I think we should send one hundred cargos of corn to help feed his legions."

"Fifty!" Pothinos countered. "Remember the reluctance of the Nile this last season."

"That would be an insult," Protarchus maintained, coming to my aid. "Seventy-five ships of grain would have to be the absolute minimum."

"We should not send more than sixty at the most," Pothinos submitted, "or there may be famine and riots. The last time the people rioted, your father lost his throne and went into exile. The council will accede to your demands, O Queen, but you must bear the responsibility for this action."

"All right, sixty ships of grain," I relented. "Of course, I accept as always full responsibility for my decisions. Now I also propose that we send soldiers from the Gabinian division."

A great silence reigned and all eyes veered to me.

"Obviously we cannot afford a repeat of last year's predicament," I said, "so I will have Apollodorus talk with the Gabinian soldiers and recruit volunteers. No soldier will be ordered to go against his will."

"My Lady Queen, in this grave hour for Egypt," Pothinos said, "I am praying that you do not err in judgment or arouse the ire of the people."

"Sometimes a queen must take actions which incur the displeasure of her people," I advanced, "which only a queen in her divine wisdom can comprehend."

As I had hoped, the Gabinian soldiers, while they

had been unwilling to go combat the Parthians the year before, found the possible rewards of a war against Caesar more tempting, and a thousand of them volunteered to go fight under the greatest general of the age, Great Pompey. Sixty merchant vessels were prepared to carry these soldiers and supplies of grain, under the command of the young Pompey, to Syria to Marcus Bibulous, who was Pompey's Admiral of the Adriatic.

I gave Gnaeus a hospitable reception while these arrangements were under way. I showed him the landmarks of Alexandria, and one night I took him to the Theater of Dionysus to see Aeschylus's *The Persians*, which was admirably given. Gnaeus and I placed ourselves upon terms of trust and affection, much to the annoyance of Charmion. He was enamored of my beauty, and I certainly was not indifferent to his glorious looks. Finally even Charmion forgot her jealousy and warmed up to him, for no one could resist his unpretentious manners and magnetic personality.

All the organization of the transport of soldiers and provisions was finally completed. The night before Gnaeus Pompey and the officers of the Gabinian forces were to depart, a feast was held to bid them farewell. There were a hundred couches spread for the occasion, and all the leading nobles were invited.

I generally time my entrance to banquets so that I will be the last to arrive, and as I walked along the Great Hall, I noticed that half the couches were still empty. As I took the steps to the royal dais, I saw that my brother-King had not yet arrived. I reclined on my royal couch, and Charmion and Apollodorus took chairs near me.

My eyes veered over the hall to find Gnaeus Pompey, and I beckoned him to approach. He came and kissed my hand, a gallantry he also performed on Charmion, and he clasped the hand of Apollodorus. A servant passed us each a goblet of wine, and the four of us fell into convivial conversation. I was in a gay mood and felt certain that it would be a festive feast, for arrangements for dancing, singing, acrobatics, and the finest foods and wines had been painstakingly planned.

One of my brother's chamberlains, Aristodemus, suddenly approached my couch and sank to one knee. "O Sacred Radiance," he cried, "King Ptolemy has charged me to convey his deepest regrets that he will not be able to attend the banquet tonight for he has come down with a sudden fever."

My eyes quickly swerved over the couches that were reserved for Pothinos, Theodotus, and Achillas, which were all empty. I glanced at the shame-faced Aristodemus, who was unable to meet my eyes. "Send the King my brother my best wishes for a quick recovery," I said.

After Aristodemus had gone, I turned to my friends with a smile. "Well, if this fever is fatal, it will wipe out half my court."

"And good riddance!" Charmion cried.

I had tried my best to hide all dissensions at court from Gnaeus, but here it was unmistakably declared for him to take back to his father and the Roman world.

"My Lord Gnaeus," I said with a smile, "I should be obliged if you would share my couch with me."

"O Queen, the pleasure and honor is mine," he said.

As Gnaeus sat his large handsome frame beside me, there were gasps from the guests, for this was a breach of protocol. I blithely ignored the shocked stares, and gestured with a smile to my chief chamberlain of banquets to start the entertainment and the serving of food. Servants came forth carrying golden plates laden with oysters, fish, roast kid stuffed with mussels, broiled chicken, grilled bream, peacock's livers, imported Falernian wine, and an assortment of fresh fruit.

Gnaeus and I ignored everyone else as we sat side by side on the royal couch, and all through the banquet he never even glanced at a dancing girl, but had eyes only for me. At my prompting we discussed mostly politics.

"We have had a low rise of the Nile," I said, "so I

199

must apologize for our limited supply of grain we are giving you, Gnaeus."

"I have no words to express my gratitude, Queen Cleopatra," Gnaeus said.

"Tell me, on which side does Mark Antony stand in this coming conflict?" I asked.

"Antony is on the side of his cousin, Caesar."

"Well, he was once our friend, but he is henceforth our avowed enemy," I cried.

The hour was late when I decided to take my leave. Gnaeus anxiously implored me to stay longer, but I demurred, held out my hand for him to kiss, and then with a last look into the feverish longing of his eyes, I left with Charmion. As I walked from the royal dais, Apollodorus clasped the elbow of Gnaeus and eagerly suggested a game of dice to end the evening. During the three weeks that Gnaeus had been at court, Apollodorus had unabashedly demonstrated the same feelings for Gnaeus that Gnaeus had for me, but as I left the Great Hall I reflected that neither Gnaeus or Apollodorus would get what they pined for.

The following morning there was a farewell ceremony in the Great Throne Room before the departure of Gnaeus. I sat my throne, but the throne next to mine was empty. Gnaeus and the Gabinian officers approached the royal dais. I made a speech, giving my best wishes to the departing soldiers.

"You are Alexandrians and my citizens," I declared. "I am pleased that you have volunteered to aid an ally of Egypt and I willingly release you. When your noble task is done, you will be welcomed back as valiant heroes."

The leading officers arose from their knees, saluted me and stepped back. Then Gnaeus Pompey approached my throne. I looked at him with the impassive, stony face I always exhibited from my throne, but there was an unmistakable warmth in the expression of my eyes under the heavily kohled lids.

"My Lord Pompey," I announced, "tell your father that we appreciate the esteem he feels for Egypt, and

200

that in this struggle between Caesar and Pompey, our heart and hopes are with Pompey. May the world know that Egypt espouses the noble and righteous cause of Pompey the Great!"

"Queen Cleopatra," Gnaeus said with emotion stirring his voice, "I hope the day may come when I can use my sword in your service."

"Lord Pompey," I cried, "Egypt's Queen bids you a tender farewell!"

Gnaeus backed ten paces from the throne, then sharply turned on his heels, and with his attendants following him, marched out of the huge chamber to the blast of trumpets.

My brother-King and his triumvirate of eunuchs had not chosen to attend this farewell ceremony, their absence unequivocally signifying that they had no part in the support given to Pompey. If eventually Pompey should be vanquished, then all the onus would be mine.

From my chamber windows I watched Gnaeus embark on his galley. The sixty ships sailed away on the late afternoon tide. I had grown fond of him and I was deeply moved at his departure, wondering if we would ever meet again.

Reports reached me that in Italy, Caesar was making the most intense military arrangements since Hannibal a century before. Every battalion was being brought up to strength with picked recruits. Meanwhile, across the Adriatic in Macedonia, Pompey was also engaged in frantic preparations. Pompey, who had defeated King Hiarbus of Numidia at the age of twenty-five, was now fifty-eight and some said he had grown flabby and his mind was not as keen as it had once been. Caesar was a few years younger and had won a string of victories the last ten years. The world was wagering as to which of these two giant lions would be the victor. Each day I said prayers and made sacrifices to the gods in behalf of Pompey.

A large proportion of the Roman Senate, who had accompanied Pompey into exile, held council at Thessalonika. They were grateful for the assistance I had given Pompey, and they passed a resolution of thanks to Egypt. Pompey sent a letter addressed to me thanking me for my generosity, which I read in council.

"For the moment, O Queen," Pompey wrote, "I am too engrossed in this war with Caesar to take any active steps in respect to the duties as your guardian, as the agent of the Roman Republic, a post I hold sacred. Rest assured, however, that when my troubles with Caesar are at an end, and if the need arises, my sword will be at your service. The house of Pompey would lay down their lives for the house of Ptolemy.

"I send a kind message to your little brother, King Ptolemy.

"Farewell in devotion, from the Triumvir, your foster uncle, Gnaeus Pompeius Magnus."

My brother scowled. "I am not little any more," he fumed, "I am fifteen!"

The triumvirate greeted this letter with impassive, unimpressed faces.

As time went by, my position became increasingly unstable. When I had first come to the throne my accomplishments and charms had combined to give me a certain personal power, but then Pothinos and Theodotus had contrived to awaken my brother's jealousy of me and turned him against me. They had the upper hand and circumvented me at every turn, keeping me in what they considered my proper place, and there was nothing I could do about it. Theodotus and Pothinos molded my brother to their wishes, which they could not do with me.

Protarchus and I were naturally concerned about my waning influence, and we discussed ways to regain it.

"May I speak frankly, O Queen?" Protarchus asked one day.

"Of course, my dear Protarchus," I replied.

"It is time you married your brother," Protarchus said. "Your position would be secured if you kindled from the king's seed and begot children to continue the line of the Lagidae."

I gave a deep sigh, knowing Protarchus spoke sage

words. I would have to capitulate to my sex and rank. Women are born to be maidservants, women of pleasure, or dowered brides, pawns to be bartered, regardless of their personal feelings, to the interests of cementing relations between men or foreign alliances or dynastic obligations. My fate and birthright decreed that I be Queen, yet I was still a woman and must do what men decreed as if I were a slave girl or a farmer's daughter.

King Ptolemy was fifteen now, physically a man, although mentally still a child. Apollodorus heard from the grapevine of guards and soldiers of the palace that my brother already indulged in an active sex life. His relations had begun at the age of twelve with his play-fellows shortly after he became King, and his appetites and activities had broadened with maturity to include both sexes. His debauched advisors had never been overly concerned about his mental development, but they assiduously encouraged his sexual precocity.

Gossip had it that my brother was never the catamite with boys but always the sodomizer. In this respect he was our father's true son, for our father even in his dying days always took the active role. Unlike our father, however, Ptolemy liked women as much as his own sex. My father had been exclusively homosexual in preference and the only two women he consorted with were his two queens, by whom he fathered six children.

At this time I was twenty and as is the custom for Greek women I was preserving my maidenhead for the day I married. It was ordained that my maidenhead was to be for my brother-King, and that we would produce high-bred Lagidae stock. I was willing to perform my duty, but my brother was not. He was a typical Greek youth, spoiled, vain, and arrogant, and he thought the world revolved around him, as indeeed Egypt did. Since he had no great liking for state matters and loved pleasures, I thought we perfectly complemented one another. While he dallied, I could look after the affairs of the kingdom. I knew I could bring Egypt to greatness again, but only if I could conclude a conciliation with my brother and diminish the power of the eunuchs. As Protarchus clearly pointed out, I must now endeavor to get my brother to marry me.

Gathering my resolve, I went to my brother's apartments and demanded that we share a noonday meal. It was almost as if I had gone to court him. His reception room was filled with his rowdy Companions of the King.

"I would like to hold private speech with you, brother dear," I said.

"But these are my brotherly friends!" Ptolemy protested with a pout.

"And I am your sister-Queen and beseech you that we be alone."

King Ptolemy reluctantly sent his companions away, and we were alone but for a few eunuchs and servants who served the food.

I had always endeavored to be charming, and of late even seductive, toward my brother, but he met my advances with hostile aversion. He looked upon me as a hated sister, and as for my being a woman, I was not to his taste. It was said that he preferred only palace slave girls or waterfront whores, and as for boys, only guards and soldiers of the most common stock. All the elegant highborn men and women about court who hoped to become his lovers were given short shrift. He had a great need to be superior to his bedmates, as if being King was not enough. He would never be able to derive pleasure from me, but duty is not always a pleasure. Somehow I had to convince him that he would have to do his duty by me, no matter how painful the prospect.

My brother ate in hostile silence, washing his food down with gulps of wine. It was apparent that he had a weakness for the grape, a trait of our line which I am glad I do not possess. I made polite conversation, but as always in my presence he lost his tongue, except for a few interjected grunts and monosyllables. Finally, as we finished our meal, I realized I could delay no longer the issue at hand.

"Dearest Ptolemy, you are fifteen now," I said proudly, smiling.

"So?" Ptolemy demanded in his surly way.

"There is Egypt to be considered," I said gravely.

"In what way?" he asked fearfully.

"You are fifteen now and are capable of producing an heir!" I saw him grimace with revulsion, but I bravely went on. "Just think, peasants and farmers are fathers at your age. If you had a prince, you would prove your manhood."

"I prove my manhood in many ways!" he attested.

"Yes, with slave girls and daughters of Venus, but they cannot give you a prince," I cried with spirit. "I suggest you drop your seed where it can do good for Egypt." He began trembling at this suggestion, and so was I at saying it. I took a breath and went on. "Our father ordained that we marry and have children to carry on the dynasty, Ptolemy."

"There is plenty of time for all that," he shrilled, horrified.

"I know that you don't love me, but it doesn't matter," I went on. "You are my brother and King and I will love you always. I want us only to rule wisely together. Your eunuchs have turned you against me, but these family dissensions will be the ruin of us, Ptolemy, can't you see that? Our dynasty faces extinction. These internal squabblings must stop, for a dynasty divided against itself cannot survive. We must show Rome that we are united, and what better way than to have a prince to preserve our royal heritage?" There was a long pause, and then I added, "We must marry, Ptolemy."

At last he looked at me, his eyelids fluttering nervously. "I am too young yet," he said with a childlike wail.

"We are never too young to accept our royal responsibilities."

"My foster fathers have said nothing of this to me," he stammered.

205

"Must we always do the bidding of our councillors?" I cried. "Do what they suggest, when they suggest? Should it not be the other way around? Are we not descended from Osiris and Isis? Should it not be for us to tell the councillors that we will marry, and for us to dictate policy?"

"Our father selected them to guide us," Ptolemy temporized.

"You are the King and I am the Queen and it is ordained that we are the rulers of Egypt," I said passionately, "and everyone in this kingdom, including the councillors, should be answerable to us."

"I have no objections to what my council does," Ptolemy cried. He sprang up from his couch and began to prowl about the chamber. "My foster fathers follow my wishes precisely. You are but a woman and for all your knowledge you are inferior. Women are naturally inferior to men. I suggest you go bury your nose in a scroll, sister, and leave matters of state to more learned folk."

I suppressed a sigh. "Be that as it may, Ptolemy, we both have our duty to Egypt to marry and have children. You are the King and it is for you to decide when we shall marry."

"There is time enough!" he said, all aquiver.

"Don't you think the summer would be a good time for a royal wedding so the people can celebrate?" I demanded.

"I said there is time enough!" he shrieked. "We will speak of this matter no longer. Leave me, sister!"

Ptolemy turned his back on me. I walked over in front of him. He met my eyes fearfully, his body trembling.

"My dear brother, already you are half a head taller than I am and so handsome," I said gently. "It is my fervent wish to be your dutiful wife." I kissed him beside the mouth, feeling his body stiffen with revulsion. I drew away and looked softly into his frightened, hateful eyes. "Goodbye, dearest brother-King," I whispered.

Thereafter my brother shunned me. He saw me only

at council sessions or court ceremonies, and he always avoided my eyes. It was apparent he despised me and any thought of marriage to me. At council sessions both Protarchus and I were sneered at or ignored.

"What am I to do, Protarchus?" I asked in despair.

"If Pompey wins, as he assuredly will since his army from all accounts outnumbers Caesar's, then all will be better for you," Protarchus explained. "Pompey is your champion, and greater respect will be shown you in Egypt when he is victorious."

My twenty-first birthday drew near. A few weeks before, when my Sagittarian brother had turned fifteen, the event had been celebrated with much fanfare and proclamations had been sent to all the nomes in the kingdom to announce the occasion. There was no mention of my birthday, since the council wished to ignore me. Protarchus and I discussed the matter at length and decided that I would make a desperate bid for my rights and power.

On the morning of my birthday I went to the council chamber to attend to the affairs of state for the day. My brother stayed until the end of the session instead of leaving early as he generally did, so perhaps he expected something was afoot.

After the King and I signed all the day's decrees, they were stamped with the Great Seal of the Sphinx which Pothinos, as Regent of the Realm, controlled. Ptolemy and I could sign all the documents we wished, but to be valid, they had to be sealed by Pothinos. The royal signature could be forged, but not the Great Seal, so it was Pothinos who had the final say in the kingdom and who was the real ruler.

The session was about to be adjourned when I made my bid. Assuming my most regal manner, I said, "My noble councillors, what is the number of my years?" I looked around at all the startled faces and shifting eyes and met silence from one and all. "As of today," I replied to my question, "I am twenty-one years of age."

Pothinos gave a nervous laugh and bowed toward me. "O Lady Queen, I had forgotten! All best wishes."

"Yes, sister, all felicitous greetings!" my brother-King piped up.

I glanced at Protarchus and gave him a grave nod.

Protarchus cleared his throat. "According to our Egyptian sacred laws and usages, both Pharaonic and Ptolemaic," he said sententiously, "a king comes of age at eighteen and a queen at twenty-one."

A great heavy silence settled over the chamber. The councillors exchanged wary, uneasy glances between them.

"I have been these three years past the grateful, humble recipient of the excellent guardianship of my council," I stated, "and I hope in the many years to come still to benefit from the sagacity you have all zealously exhibited on my behalf. However, according to the letter of the law, a queen must at her majority take into her personal possession the Great Crown Seal." I looked squarely at Pothinos, who involuntarily clutched the seal.

I saw my brother look desperately at Pothinos.

"O Glorious Queen," Pothinos cried, his voice quavering, "I control the Great Seal in the name of the King!"

"Yes, and according to our laws," Ptolemy cut in vigorously, "the king takes precedence before the queen!"

"You are fifteen," I said patiently. "When you become eighteen I shall turn over the Great Seal to you."

My brother, who was lacking in his lessons and in particular mathematics, moved his lips as he calculated and came to the deduction—three more years! It would be an eternity, I could see him thinking wildly. He shot Pothinos a frantic look.

Pothinos spread his hands toward me. "O Queen, the people still think of you as a child—"

"The people are suffering from a gross misconception," I said sarcastically. "A proclamation must be issued at once to dispel this delusion."

"O Sacred Radiance," Pothinos cried nervously, "your learning brings great honor to Egypt, yet in matters of politics you are not always the soul of caution, but are wont to be in need of wise counsel. Your late father sensed this reckless streak in you and appointed us to be your guardians. It was his dying wish that we serve you and correct your faults and follies."

"Yes, Pothinos," I said impatiently, "and you have for three years served me well, but your guardianship is at an end, for as of today I have reached my majority!"

"The task of ruling requires not only age but discretion," Pothinos pursued frantically. "It is the wish of the Regency Council to continue to serve you and for you to rely on our wisdom. We are servants to the King and we protect his interests. There have been many times, against our better judgment, that we gave you free rein in foreign policy, which proved disastrous."

"Whenever you gave me free rein in foreign policy," I cried with exasperation, "it was with the hope that my policies would fail and you could discredit me before the people. As for the matter of aid to Pompey, that will not be disastrous since Pompey will be victorious over Caesar."

"We pray so to the gods, but only time will tell," Theodotus cried in his annoying, high-pitched eunuch's voice.

Controlling my voice, I said, "I do not wish to discuss this further, Noble Councillors. I am Queen, the chosen instrument of the gods, their viceroy over Egypt, and I demand that the Great Crown Seal of the Sphinx be placed in my hands today!"

A pregnant silence fell over the chamber. I heard only the sounds of heavy breathing from all around me.

Pothinos looked at Theodotus for reassurance and aid, and Theodotus took his cue and stood. I stared at Theodotus, at his heavy, phlegmatic, thick body, his bull-like neck, and found him repulsive.

"O Divine and Sacred Majesty," Theodotus said in his rasping wine-besotted voice, "we cannot in good faith comply to your wishes."

"Then you are depriving me of my lawful rights!" I cried, outraged.

"We are acting in the best interests of our King and kingdom," Theodotus said in a sanctimonious tone.

"In your own best interests, you mean!" I cried.

"We wish only to safeguard the sovereignty of our King against bad decisions which could lead Egypt to ruin," Pothinos said. "There is unrest in Egypt and in the Roman world, and it is no time for a young woman to take absolute control of the kingdom. I shall continue to hold the Crown Seal which your father entrusted to me. In a few years when King Ptolemy is eighteen I shall turn the seal over to him. I am acting legally in this, for it is Ptolemaic law which follows the customs of the pharaohs that queens, even when they are co-monarchs, take second place to the kings who are their colleagues."

"Yes, you do not share equality with me!" Ptolemy cried in a malicious, triumphant voice. "Your rank is inferior to mine."

"That is why," Pothinos proceeded, "we as foster fathers and regents of the King take precedence over you, O Queen. We appreciate hearing your opinions, but you have no final say in the judgment of Egypt."

"Yes," Ptolemy cried. "I want you to continue to possess the Great Seal in my name, foster father."

I heaved a deep sigh. I had taken the plunge and had lost. I looked around at all the faces at the council table. Protarchus could not meet my eyes. He was my only friend there, my good-natured, kindly tempered, gently dispositioned Protarchus, a benign voice of rectitude, but he could not support me when I needed him.

This refusal to surrender the seal was tantamount to anarchy, but there was nothing I could do about it. I stared with fury at Pothinos and Theodotus, these contemptible spayed catamites, yet with an effort I got myself under control.

"So be it," I mumbled softly. I stood up, and mustering all my regal dignity, left the council chamber.

Once again I had made a miserable botch of things. From the beginning of my accession I had had a difficult time of it, using a mixture of charm and craft to assert myself, sitting at the council table trying my best to go along with this corrupt coterie of councillors, trying to concentrate some semblance of power into my hands, yet power had proved elusive and what little power I had exercised in the beginning had now totally slipped through my fingers. I had tried to avoid open clashes with my council, but now I had overshot my mark and had brought about an open rupture, an imbroglio of the most deplorable sort.

The Nile was due to rise again about this time. I made sacrifices to Demeter, goddess of the fruitful soil, but she deserted Egypt as she had in the previous rise. The measures were taken daily and the reports brought to the palace and anxiously checked. The Nile can rise as much as twenty-seven feet, but rose only to eight feet, which is disastrous. There was gloom in the council chamber as the calamitous low rise was discussed.

"There will be famine and riots!" Pothinos cried, glaring at me as if I were the cause of the low rise.

"The people will remember those sixty cargoes of corn you shipped to Pompey!" Theodotus said perniciously.

All the councillors gave me the evil eye.

"What Egypt needs is a great high dam!" I cried fervently. "This is the great dream of my reign. I want a dam to provide year-around water for my millions of acres of land, that will eliminate forever the floods and failures of the Nile. The old pharaohs built the Pyramids, but I think it was absurd to build such a great house for one dead body. A dam will be a greater monument to me than the Pyramids. When I die, my body can be thrown to the crocodiles for all I care. I want a dam as my monument. I am not a necrophiliac like the Egyptian pharaohs, but as a Greek I am a worshipper of life. This dam will live forever as—"

"Yes, yes, O Queen," Pothinos interrupted testily. "It's a commendable dream, this great dam, but what are we to do now? A dam cannot be built overnight."

"Nothing is built overnight, my Lord Pothinos," I replied. "Such enterprises take a lifetime of dreams."

"Such enterprises will take a great amount of gold!"

Theodotus responded. "The treasury is almost empty. Our immediate pressing problem, however, is the famine that will be surely coming."

"We will evenly distribute the wheat in the royal granary to alleviate the famine," I maintained. "I have all the granary figures in my head. A crisis awaits us, no doubt, but with foresight and fortitude, we will deal with it."

In the streets of Alexandria people gathered, murmuring discontentedly. Pamphlets were distributed urging sedition, and riots erupted. Hordes of people congregated outside the royal granary, demanding free distribution of grain to hoard even before the famine. Achillas sent out platoons of soldiers to disperse the rioting by force.

My heart was heavy and my dreams disturbed. A voice within me, a feeling in my bones, told me that a calamity was about to strike, but I did not know in what precise manifestation.

One morning all my intimations suddenly proved valid.

As I lay sleeping in Charmion's arms, a slave girl awoke me saying that Apollodorus had urgent tidings.

"Cleopatra," he informed me, "the King's guards broke into the apartments of Protarchus an hour ago and arrested him."

Waves of horror swept over me. "No!" I cried, torn by anger, grief and confusion. I forced myself to be calm so I could attend the council session in a controlled state that morning. Meanwhile, I had Apollodorus bribe guards to get a message to Protarchus saying I would soon have him free.

I wore my most regal attire and jewels to give me confidence, and as I entered the council chamber I saw my brother was already in his chair. The councillors scarcely deigned to rise for me. I took my seat opposite my brother, who was flanked by Pothinos and Theodotus.

"Dearest Brother and Noble Councillors," I got right to the point, "I have been told that the most high

Chancellor Protarchus, who is closest to my heart, has been arrested. On what charges, pray tell?"

Pothinos, smug and inflated, shuffled various scrolls in front of him. "I deem it my unfortunate duty to inform you, O Queen, of the lamentable circumstances."

"Why has he been arrested?" I screamed, trembling with rage, losing the composure I had vowed to maintain.

"There are charges of bribery, extortion and theft, and abuse of his exalted position," Pothinos said placidly.

"Well, wonder of wonders, miracle of miracles, who at this table is not guilty of such crimes?" I demanded sarcastically. "If there is a councillor at this table who is not corrupt, please let him rise."

"Protarchus has been pocketing royal funds," Pothinos said, "and has given gifts of gold to various youths. We have depositions from ten soldiers who testify to this. He also used bribery to obtain government positions for friends. The council must be purged of this perfidious, false traitor."

"My ears are deceiving me!" I cried. "My Lord Protarchus is my dearest friend, the most wise, cultured, honest—"

"He is a thief and a traitor!" Theodotus interrupted rudely. "And his policy of selling out to the Romans is only one of his heinous crimes. He is a Roman-lover, and the people hate the Romans. In all the city squares the citizens are calling for his head."

"Because instigators tell them to do so," I cried.

"There is a universal outcry of hatred against the odious Protarchus," Pothinos said, "for it was he alone of the royal councillors who advised that the murderers of the Bibulous sons be sent to Syria, and he supported aid to Pompey. The people are restless with anticipation of the coming famine, and they demand that Protarchus be tried for his crimes."

"You mean you are demanding a sacrificial scapegoat," I cried.

"Pothinos, you have not told Cleopatra of the most

213

damaging charges!" King Ptolemy suddenly screamed out.

"You mean there is more?" I demanded.

"Your beloved Protarchus was plotting to murder me!" Ptolemy screamed shrilly. His voice had changed to a deep tone, but when he was hysterical it reverted back to a boy's falsetto.

"Protarchus commit regicide?" I cried with a laugh. "That's ridiculous!"

"We have evidence, O Queen," Pothinos said.

"What evidence?" I inquired sharply.

"His conspirators have made their confessions."

"A man will confess anything if his fingernails are yanked out," I countered.

"I know these truths are as bitter as gall for you, O Queen," Pothinos said, "but it's all too horribly true. Protarchus was in league with persons to murder the King. We thank the gods that we found no evidence implicating you. From all that we have learned, Protarchus acted on his own, although in what he considered your best interests."

"He was going to have me cut down at the baths!" King Ptolemy cried. "Assassinated!"

"Such absolute nonsense!" I said. "Protarchus wouldn't conspire to murder a fly, let alone his King."

"There will be a trial, O Queen," Pothinos informed me. "Protarchus will have due process of law."

"You have trumped up enough charges against him that would send ten men to their deaths!" I cried.

"I don't want anyone on my council who is a Roman-lover or a king-killer!" Ptolemy said vehemently.

Staring at my brother, I sighed, knowing it was all hopeless. Protarchus had met a cruel destiny. His trial would be a mockery of justice and he would be sentenced to death. Perhaps at my intercession the sentence would be commuted, and he would be allowed to go into exile.

"When will the trial commence?" I whispered.

"Tomorrow, O Queen," Pothinos explained. "The

people are demanding immediate justice. We must eliminate traitors."

"Protarchus is a would-be king-killer and must die," Ptolemy screamed. "Kings are greatly affronted by regicide."

With a great check on my emotions, I saw the session through and calmly discussed all other affairs of state that were pressing that day. When the council adjourned, I retired to my apartments. The rage inside me bubbled like lava. There was a black lump of fury in my heart, a throbbing pain assailed my temples, and I wept at my impotence. All I could do was try to see to it that Protarchus received honorable treatment in his dungeon cell.

The trial, which was held in the Hall of Justice next to the Temple of Isis, was a travesty of justice. People gathered in the square in front of the building chanting for the death of Protarchus.

There is a labyrinthine network of secret passageways that had been built into the palatial complex, whose plans my father had passed on to me alone. I walked through these subterranean tunnels, and from a hole in the wall observed the interior of the court chamber, witnessing the proceedings of the trial with Apollodorus and Charmion at my side.

A parade of a dozen soldiers gave nefarious witness that Protarchus had given them stolen presents. I had in the last year been missing several jewels and had suspected my ladies of itchy fingers but had never pressed the matter, for I have many jewels and one less never mattered to me. This is in stark contrast to my sister Berenice, who once had the hand cut off of one of her ladies who had stolen a bracelet. My missing jewels now turned up as evidence; Protarchus was said to have stolen them to give to his soldier favorites, which is utterly absurd.

Another round of witnesses came forth testifying that they had been given government franchises in perfume and shipping, arranged by Protarchus in exchange for bribes. This procedure was customary at court, but

Protarchus never practiced it, for his honor was unimpeachable. All these charges were false, and the witnesses bought by Pothinos who masterminded this whole charade.

The most damning witnesses were those who limped in, their joints out of their sockets, their fingertips bloody and without nails, and testified that they had been hired by Protarchus to kill the King when he visited the public baths.

The trial lasted three days. Protarchus bore himself with dignity throughout, declining to defend himself, refusing to dignify the charges by a denial. The judges found him guilty and passed the death sentence. Protarchus did not flinch at the sentence, and neither did I as I watched from my secret passageway. I was insulated by the state of shock that held me in its grip.

The six prisoners who had signed confessions under torture that they had been in on the conspiracy to kill the King also received the death penalty. A few of them hysterically tried to recant their confessions now, but were hauled off to their cells to await execution.

I got a message to Protarchus telling him that I would see to it that the sentence was never carried out.

The next day I went into the council chamber prepared to plead for the life of Protarchus. The judges had found him guilty, but my brother and I would have to sign the decree of execution.

Pothinos wore an expression of triumph as he looked at me. "Since we appreciate the tender feelings you have for Protarchus, misplaced as they were, O Queen," he said, "you will not have to sign this decree of death. The King alone will sign the warrant."

"Surely, my Lord Prime Minister," I spoke up clearly, "for past services rendered to the state, to my father and to myself, there will be a royal pardon for Lord Protarchus."

"Impossible!" Ptolemy shrilled. "The people are demanding the head of this king-killer."

"Brother dear, we are the living gods of Egypt," I cried, "and it is for the people to yield to our demands."

"Yes, and I the King-god demand that the head of this traitor be chopped off!" Ptolemy screamed. "Give me the decree to sign, Pothinos."

Pothinos passed the King the scroll. My brother hastily affixed his signature to it, and looked at me with glistening, gloating eyes.

My heart stopped and I clenched my hands tightly. I rose to my feet. "Surely, my brother-King, in honor of past efforts Protarchus has made in his long service to Egypt," I cried in an impassioned voice, "he can be pardoned and sent into exile, to Cyprus perhaps or a village in Upper Egypt or a town in the Trogodytes."

"Will anyone at this table raise his voice for clemency for our former colleague?" Pothinos asked.

All the councillors had been handpicked by Pothinos, and they sat in silence. I did not have one adherent on the council now that Protarchus had been removed. This was a deep insult to my sacred person, and waves of humiliation washed over me.

"So it will be done!" Pothinos cried in triumph.

The papyrus was laid out across the table. A secretary spread a blotch of warm wax by the King's signature, then Pothinos pressed the Great Seal into the wax, officially sealing the death warrant.

As I watched helplessly, a shiver passed through me.

Pothinos looked at me, his gross, heavy face elated. "The sentence will be carried out tomorrow at noon!"

"I want the head exhibited on the city gates!" Ptolemy cried ghoulishly.

Bitter gall rose from my depths to flood my mouth. I rose and left the chamber, and not one councillor got to his feet as I did so.

Apollodorus, waiting for me outside, accompanied me back to my apartments. Once there the full flood of my suffering gushed forth in tears. Despair overcame me and I collapsed on my couch. Charmion forced me to take some herb broth with a sedative which somewhat calmed me.

"I will go to Pothinos tonight and beg for the life of Protarchus," I declared.

217

"Oh, Cleopatra, you mustn't!" Charmion cried. "You cannot sacrifice your dignity."

"I don't care a fig for dignity," I said. "I will get on my knees if need be, anything to spare Protarchus."

I took a long soothing bath, my ladies royally robed me to give me confidence, and I wore the asp diadem to remind Pothinos of my sovereignty. I sent a note proceeding me that the Queen had urgent business with her Prime Minister, and Apollodorus and a guard of honor escorted me to the east wing of the palace where Pothinos lived. I was forced to wait outside his reception room for an hour before I was admitted.

This was the first time I had ever been in his private quarters. I saw at a glance that they were far more richly appointed than either my brother's apartments or mine, filled with rich furnishings and works of Grecian art.

Pothinos sat in an ivory and ebony chair, and after I entered he slowly got to his feet. Protocol demanded that he sink to one knee, but he merely inclined his head. "Greetings, O Queen," he said in a bored voice.

I held out my hand. He looked at it a moment askance, but then bent over and kissed the royal ring.

"Do sit down," Pothinos said as he settled his huge body into the chair. "To what do I owe the honor of your visit, O Queen?"

"The reason I have come must be fairly obvious under the circumstances, my Lord Pothinos," I said. "I have come to beg for the life of my friend."

His face wore a shadow of scorn. "I do only the bidding of my King, as we all must do in Egypt, including the Queen, and it is the King's adamant wish that—"

"The King does your bidding!" I cried, chafing. "You are the most powerful man in Egypt. The King obeys you in all matters. I ask only that Protarchus be permitted to go into exile."

"That would be impossible, for the people and the army are demanding his head," Pothinos said. "It is out of our hands."

"You have the power to change that, Lord Pothinos,"

218

I insisted. "Show the people that you can be merciful."

"If we spared Protarchus, the people would say it was the intervention of their Queen, and their hatred against you will increase."

"I will deal with the hatred or love of my people. I beg you, Lord Pothinos, to show mercy."

"Do not press this matter, O Queen. Rest content."

I then forgot all my dignity. My eyes spilled over and I stood up. "Do you want me to prostrate myself in supplication? Then I shall!" I fell on the floor in full prostration, the diadem from my head falling off as I did so and rolling on the marble floor. I stretched my body toward him and lifted my face in entreaty. "Please, Pothinos, your Queen begs for mercy for Protarchus!"

Pothinos glared at me with his bulbous face twisted with contempt. "Rise and retrieve the diadem which signifies your sacred rank," he chastised me. "Show some restraint and remember that you are Queen. I thank the gods we are alone and no one is witness to your shame."

"If you wish me to do this in front of the whole court I shall!" I sobbed. "I will do anything if you spare the life of Protarchus."

"My Lady Queen, you are being hysterical," Pothinos said sneeringly. "Where is your dignity? It is said in many quarters that you should share the same fate of your friend."

I stopped sobbing, stunned at this news, and silently I stared at my tormentor.

"We have kept this from you, O Queen," Pothinos went on in a rapturous voice, "but it is true, everywhere the people are demanding your head."

Somewhat sobered, I rose and replaced the diadem on my head, mustering my dignity. I stared into the face of the fat, pompous catamite who was my Prime Minister and greatest enemy.

"The people are demanding blood," Pothinos went on gleefully. "Let us hope tomorrow's sacrifice will slake their thirst. Remember how the people hated your father for his Roman sentiments? They know you also

219

love the Romans, and they believe you were a party to the conspiracy to murder your brother their King. We are doing everything we can to protect you, my Lady Queen. I suggest you look to other affairs that are more important."

I knew it was hopeless. "Then will you grant your Queen one small concession?" I asked in a hoarse, lifeless voice. "For past services to Egypt, will you permit Protarchus to die, not by decapitation, but by the more humane form of death, the application of an asp to his chest?"

Pothinos heaved a deep sigh. "Your brother the King and the council and judges think the means of death specified is most suitable."

"Even the most common criminals and slaves are given death by the asp and not the ax," I pleaded.

His mouth curled cruelly. "O Queen, be content that we do not nail his body alive to a tree as a feast for ravens. I suggest you retire to your temple and say prayers for your own head."

Involuntarily my hands went to my neck and I shivered. Pothinos had been responsible for my mother's downfall sixteen years before, and now he had brought down Protarchus. He would not be content until he had also brought me down. I did not speak another word, but simply turned and like a sleepwalker made my way out of his chambers.

Apollodorus accompanied me back to my apartments, where I threw myself on my couch and wept bitterly. Charmion doused my forehead with spirits, and my physicians administered a potion to numb my grief.

I had a tray of rich food sent to Protarchus, but it was turned away by the guards. It was feared that the food was poisoned so Protarchus could cheat the executioner, but I just wanted him to have a good last supper. Not that he cared much for food, unlike most eunuchs who, deprived of their manhood, become gluttons as a compensation.

All that night I could not sleep and paced the cold

220

marble floor by my bedchamber. A brazier gave off a little heat. When dawn came I resolved that somehow I would have to get through the guards to visit Protarchus one last time.

Charmion and I put heavy cloaks around us, and escorted by Apollodorus, made our way down into the dungeons.

"Make way for the Queen of Egypt!" Apollodorus kept calling to the sentries in his deep, commanding voice.

"We have orders that no one is to pass, O Queen," each sentry and guard would say.

"Of course you do," I would reply with a smile, and then nod at Charmion.

Charmion held a pouch filled with rich gems. She would take out a ruby or pearl and offer it to the guard, who would then let us pass. In this fashion we made our way along the passageways and staircases that led down into the dungeons.

At last we confronted the Captain of the Royal Dungeons, a brutish giant of an Egyptian.

"Greetings, O Captain," I said in Egyptian, smiling.

"Greetings, O Sacred Queen," he said in a gravelly voice.

"My father King Ptolemy often spoke warmly of you. You have served us faithfully these many years."

"To the death, O Queen," he cried.

"I would like to give you a solid gold figurine of Sobek which was my father's," I said, taking out the figurine of the crocodile god which I knew would appeal to his Egyptian heart.

"Oh, my Lady Queen," he cried, inspecting the little gold crocodile, which glistened in the torchlight. "I am very happy to receive such a precious gift from my Queen."

"Your Queen wishes to be taken to the cell of her High Chancellor the Lord Protarchus," I cried.

The Egyptian raised shifty, wary eyes to me. "O Queen, I beg that you make your visit brief."

I was led down a dank, dark corridor of cells that

reeked of urine and mildew. At last we stopped, and the Captain got out a set of clanking keys and unlocked a cell door. I entered the cell and found Protarchus on his knees in prayer. A lone candle burned. Protarchus turned his calm blue eyes on me. My lips moved to speak a greeting, to say his name, but no sound issued from my lips. I fell to my knees in front of him, flung my arms around him, and began sobbing.

"Now, now, my litttle Queen, I want no tears," Protarchus said, his hands gently patting my back.

With a great effort I stopped crying. Protarchus stood and raised me to my feet, and led me to a hard couch where we sat holding each other close. Protarchus had always used wonderful scents, but now that he was deprived of his perfumes he had an acrid odor about his body. He was my beloved Protarchus, however, and I did not care.

"I did all I could to prevent your fate, Protarchus." I cried.

"We must all accept our fate, my Queen," he said, smiling stoically. "The gods have a plan for us all."

"I love you so much, Protarchus," I said with deep emotion. "Only to my mother and father have I given such love."

"Let us not speak of what we already know, Cleopatra," he said. "We must speak of more serious matters. In the months to come you must be most prudent in your affairs. Divert your mind from my fate and concentrate on your own. Seek not my revenge, lest it bring harm to you. Henceforth guard your tongue well, be self-effacing, moderate the impetuosity of your spirit, beware of poison, and try to avoid all traps that will be set for you."

"Yes, Protarchus, I will heed well your words."

"If you finally find it impossible to maintain yourself on Egyptian soil, escape into exile with Apollodorus," Protarchus advised. "Breathe not a word to Charmion, for she has a loose tongue, and do not take her with you, for she would only be a hindrance in such circum-

222

stances. Take a ship to Pompey, for he is your champion and will reinstate you as he did your father."

"Yes, I know you speak sage words, Protarchus."

"As I am about to enter the door of death, my thoughts are of you. I have not always been the greatest help—"

"Your wisdom has shown me the way," I cried, "and you have been my greatest strength. I will say many prayers for your soul in the Infernal Kingdom, where you will surely be given a great welcome as a friend to a goddess Queen."

At length I took from a sleeve of my cloak a small phial of poison. "It is quick, Protarchus, and painless. If you find you do not have the strength to go through with the public execution, drink this."

"I will accept my fate, Cleopatra, as we all must," Protarchus said. "It is man's fate that every hour wounds, and the last hour kills, so what does it matter the form?" He smiled and touched a hand to my cheek. "How beautiful you are, my Queen. I will be watching from the Infernal Kingdom with great interest your progress as Queen. You will outwit them, one way or another. It is in your stars that you will be triumphant!"

"If so, I will owe much to your training," I exclaimed.

The Captain knocked nervously on the door.

"You must go now, O Queen," Protarchus said. "To tarry longer would be foolish."

Once again my tears started flowing. Protarchus drew me into his arms and held me close. With great effort I controlled myself, since I wanted Protarchus to see the last image of me as a brave, composed Queen.

I kissed him on both cheeks. "I will carry your memory alive in my heart until the end of my days, beloved Protarchus!" I pledged.

"Farewell, Beloved Queen!" he said, his eyes glittering, a fixed, forlorn smile on his lips.

"Farewell, beloved Protarchus!" I cried, and smiling tremulously, I walked out of the cell.

At the end of the corridor I collapsed and Apollodorus and Charmion led me back to my apartments where I fell on my couch. Sunlight poured in, bringing a day which was one of the most mournful of my life.

Protarchus did not make use of the poison I had left with him. At noon he was led in chains to the place of execution in the great square in front of the palace. Not far from the block, my brother-King sat on a golden chair under a canopy of state, flanked by his evil triumvirate. Soldiers held back the raging mob that overflowed the huge concourse. As he had always done, Protarchus bore himself tall and straight. I had made arrangements through Apollodorus to give the executioner a gold armband so that he would do the job skillfully with one stroke. Generally the executioner, to appease the crowd, deliberately botches the job, butchering the condemned victim, hacking away with several strokes while the populace screams in ecstasy. I did not want this to happen to my beloved Protarchus.

In my reception room I heard the long blast of trumpets from the square, and then the deafening silence as the moment of decapitation came.

The executioner earned his gold armband, for as Protarchus calmly laid his head down on the block, the neck was severed with one swift slash of the ax, much to the disappointment of the crowd, who booed vociferously. But as the head was held high, dripping blood that shone bright red in the sunlight, the crowd cheered their approval.

At the sound of these roaring cheers I knew that the deed was done.

"Protarchus, Protarchus, Protarchus!" I shrieked hysterically, flinging my body to the floor in a frenzy of despair. Charmion and my ladies hovered around me, and at last carried me half-conscious to my bed. My physicians mixed a sedative and forced it between my jaws and I slept.

Apollodorus, who had witnessed the execution, came to me that evening.

"Protarchus bore himself with dignity and died well," he said.

"Of course he did," I murmured. "He possessed a courage superior to the affronts of fortune."

The tragic fate of Protarchus was a shattering blow to me, and it preyed on my mind. I moved about in the days that followed in a spell of grief, much disordered with despair. It was all a cruel jest of the gods, and I realized we were all playthings of fate. I did not question the gods, however, for perhaps they had a purpose for all that they did. I did not neglect my sacrifices and prayers, for I well knew that those who are nearest to the gods are most at their mercy.

Nemesis, the Goddess of Retribution and Vengeance, received many costly sacrifices from me, and I said fervent prayers to her, begging her assistance that one day she would aid me in punishing my enemies. In spite of the last admonishings Protarchus gave me, vows of vengeance seared my soul. A little red coal of hatred and bitterness flamed in my breast, and it would not be burned out until I could somehow measure out the same fate to Pothinos that he had cruelly meted out to Protarchus. I had also not forgotten that Pothinos had been the architect of my mother's end. He was undoubtedly making plans to bring me down next, but I had every intention of eluding any traps he was setting for me. I was positive that although my future had never appeared so grim and uncertain, I would eventually triumph over my enemies, and I vowed with all my passionate Ptolemy heart that vengeance would be mine.

CHAPTER X

"SATURN, THE RULER of your sun, is retrograde," Sosigenes told me after a careful reading of my stars, "and until it goes direct your life will be ill-omened and full of bad auguries. You are under the shadow of a malevolent aspect, O Queen. You must be prudent in all your affairs and choose wisely your words until this evil influence passes."

"Am I walking in the shadow of death, Sosigenes?" I asked anxiously.

Sosigenes hesitated at such a lethal prognostication. "You are walking a perilous path," he temporized, "so you must negotiate each step with caution."

"But will I survive?" I demanded, holding my breath.

Sosigenes shrugged. "Your lifeline and your chart do not indicate that your life will be short, so it is safe to assume that you will survive this difficult period."

I expelled my breath, breathing easier. I would survive, I thought, but the question was how.

Sosigenes had become my friend since the reform of the calendar three years before, and I invited him to my apartments frequently. He was a master of astrology and astronomy, of the occult and magical formulas and potions, and he was versed in all the cultures. We had a great deal in common and I enjoyed his company and relied upon his wisdom.

In the days that followed the arrest, trial, and execution of my beloved Protarchus, I suffered through the House of Hades. Not even my father's death had torn me with such despair, for I had seen his end coming and prepared myself for it. The end of Protarchus had been unpredictable and had left me with an intimation of my own doom. My senses were sharpened by premonition, and I was anxious for occult help to assist me in thwarting any fatal nets which were being woven for me. Sosigenes was not much help, however, for any slave in the palace knew I was walking a perilous path. I wanted to know more specific omens about my fate and future, and so I sought a seer.

Apollodorus learned from the soldiers about an old Egyptian soothsayer who dwelled in a small house on the edge of the city.

"The soldiers swear by her," Apollodorus said. "She has a reputation for accurate prophesy. Shall I bring her to the palace?"

"No, she will know that I am the Queen and she may lie to me," I said. "I will go to her in disguise."

Apollodorus made an appointment for the middle of the night. He told her that she would be visited by a highborn lady. Most of the Alexandrians knew me from processions when I was carried in a litter and my profile which graced the coins. Yet I hoped that if I went heavily veiled she might not recognize me and would not fear to tell me the truth.

We left the palace by a secret exit. Charmion and I rode in a litter with curtains drawn, escorted by the bearers, Apollodorus, and two trusted soldiers. We made our way quickly through the dark, deserted streets. When we reached our destination the litter was set down, and I found myself in a street of dilapidated old houses. Apollodorus led me to the soothsayer's house and knocked on the door. After a moment the door creaked open. From the torch that one of the bearers carried, I saw the haggard face of an old woman staring out at us.

"Greetings, Wise Woman," Apollodorus said. "I've brought my lady."

I shuddered as I looked into her wrinkled face. She was dressed in a shapeless, ragged black dress, and a shawl covered her slumped shoulders. I took a breath

228

and stepped toward her and gave an uneven smile. "I seek my future, Lady Soothsayer," I said.

She gave a nod. "Enter alone," she said in a hoarse whisper.

Apollodorus gave me a nod of encouragement, and I followed the seer into the house. I shrank at the stench of the room, but, with an effort, controlled my nausea. The room was sparsely furnished, with a small table in the center. There were cabinets heaped with old yellowed scrolls which I presumed concerned astrology and the occult. The corners of the room were littered with amulets.

"Sit down, my lady," the old harridan told me.

I sat at the table, which held a large crystal ball and a small burning taper.

The Egyptian soothsayer sat opposite me. "Take off your veil," she demanded.

I did as I was told, wondering if she recognized me. Her face was emaciated, the skin wrinkled like old dried brown leather, but her big brown eyes were bright and took in everything.

"I hope you can predict my future, dear lady," I said nervously.

She stared sullenly at me. "The gods and the stars give you the future and I cannot do anything about that," she said in her croaking voice. "You cannot change the course of the stars or alter fate."

"Yes, I know, but I will be grateful for whatever signs or portents you can give me to help me meet my future."

"Do you pay me in yellow money or white money?" she asked.

"Yellow money, Lady Soothsayer," I replied.

She smiled at this, revealing gleaming red upper gums. She still had her bottom teeth, but they were yellowed and spaced with black cavities.

Her gnarled hands began roving about the crystal ball, invokingly, and her eyes stared deep into its depths.

I sat there, waiting with dread. She seemed almost to

doze as she stared into the crystal ball, and a long time went by.

"What do you see?" I asked fretfully.

"Be patient!" she hissed.

I willed myself to be still and waited.

Her hands kept circling the ball, her eyes staring deep down into it, as she summoned all her powers to discern the secret of my future. At last she took a quick intake of breath and raised her head and stared at me.

"Yes?" I asked fearfully.

"I see in your future a black bull," she announced.

"A black bull?" I asked, confused. "What omen is this?"

"A black bull that will mean death!" she cried.

"Death?" I asked, trembling. "My death?"

She looked once again into the crystal ball, endeavoring to extract further truth. "When the black bull appears," she added, "you may be able to avoid your death."

"How?" I asked with a stopped heart.

She looked at me with her hypnotic eyes. "You must be courageous and audacious and you will avoid death."

"But what must I do?" I beseeched.

"You must be wary as a wolf and as bold as a lion!" she cried.

"What other counsel can you give me?" I begged.

"I can tell you no more," she said, dismissing me. "I have told you enough, and the rest is up to you."

I took from the pocket of my cloak ten gold pieces and laid them on the table. All the coins bore my father's profile. "Please accept this gratuity for your wise counsel, Lady Soothsayer," I said.

Her sharp eyes glanced at the shiny coins. "You have given me money with your father's image and not your own, O Queen," she said.

I was surprised, but only for a moment. My respect for her powers increased.

As I made my way to the litter on the street, she called from the doorway, "Remember, O Queen, beware of the black bull!"

230

I climbed into the litter beside Charmion, the bearers hoisted us upon their shoulders, and we were swiftly carried back to the palace.

In the days that followed I was keenly alert for any signs pertaining to a black bull, for I had faith in the soothsayer's counsel and I had no doubt that this was a key to my salvation.

The internal dynastic struggle between my brother and me was reaching a rupturing point. Pothinos had agents sowing sedition against me in every quarter. Verses in uncertain meter vilified me, and salacious scribblings appeared on public buildings. Street speech-makers declared to the people that I had given Pompey's son not only grain and soldiers and ships, but my body to seal the bargain, and that at the same time I denied my brother's rights by marrying him. Apollodorus and his soldiers went about the city and washed the slanderous graffiti from the walls, but just as quickly they appeared again.

"It wounds me deeply that you are the victim of vicious, deprecating falsehoods," Charmion lamented. "You are a golden Queen, a daughter of the gods!"

"Go tell that to Pothinos, Theodotus, Achillas, and the people."

"According to the laws and traditions," she went on fervently, "your person is sacred, your power indisputable."

"Few seem aware of that now," I replied sadly.

The palace was dividing into two opposing factions. My brother and his trio had secured all the official politicians and government deputies and the army in their camp, while I stood alone with Apollodorus and a small band of men that made up my Macedonian Household Troops. As matters were taking shape, it was hardly a contest. I did not have any adherents of which to speak. The whole court was lined up against me. Waves of animosity, coming from all sides, were sweeping me off the throne.

I was intensely disliked in all the leading political circles, having alienated all the powerful nobles. I had been too liberal in my treatment of Egyptians, which the ruling class resented. I had looked after the interests of Egyptians, demanding that great numbers be enrolled in the universities and promoting several to positions of high rank which previously only Greeks had filled. Yet even the Egyptians I had favored were turning against me. They saw which way the wind was blowing and bowed to it.

When I made my bid for the Great Seal, I realized I had made a mistake and I braced myself for a period of upheaval, but I had no idea, as I now found out in hindsight, that it would seal the doom of Protarchus and perhaps of myself.

During these days my nerves were frayed. In the power of antagonistic forces, I was filled with seething frustrations and fears, yet I went about court masking my insecurities by a show of serenity. Walking along the marble corridors of the palace, I passed groups of grim-faced chamberlains, who shunned me with insolence and made sinister whisperings behind my back. I was barely acknowledged as Queen. Only a few sweet-faced eunuch boys smiled at me when I gave them smiles. I bore all this adversity with the dignity of my sacred rank, although inside a paralyzing sense of peril gripped me.

A month after the execution of Protarchus, harnessing my courage and stifling my pride, I decided to go to my brother and make one more attempt at a reconciliation, courting his favor in the manner of the meanest suppliant. A squad of tall guards, handpicked by Apollodorus, each armed with a sword, javelin, and shield, formed a cordon around me as I left my apartments and traversed the long corridors to my brother's wing.

King Ptolemy's reception room was full of his boisterous Companions of the King, who were playing dice on the floor. I requested that we be alone, and my brother reluctantly sent his friends away.

My brother at fifteen was a seductive stripling, with a boyish-mannish intensity. He had just come from a session of swordplay, and his body was gleaming with perspiration and his handsome face flushed.

I wore a diaphanous dress and had painted my face alluringly.

"Some wine, sister?" King Ptolemy asked coldly.

"Yes, that would be lovely. A loving cup!"

Ptolemy ignored this request and poured wine into two goblets. He handed me one and then took a seat some distance from me. He waited until I drank first, out of perversity, and I feared poison for a moment. I was relieved when he too took a sip from his goblet.

Gazing on him, I noticed that his thick, curly blond hair had darkened slightly to a light golden bronze, much like mine. His features were finely carved with high cheekbones, and he had well-shaped thick lips, although he had a habit of disfiguring his mouth by a perpetual petulant smirk.

"I have been busy mastering the craft of swordplay," he cried.

"Yes, and your physique has developed beautifully from the exercises."

Ptolemy lifted an arm and flexed a bulging bicep. "A King must know how to handle a sword," he boasted.

I thought that his mental growth had been shamefully neglected, but his body had been splendidly looked after. I observed his muscles with a look of admiration. "Your thighs are especially beautiful and well-developed, Ptolemy," I said glowingly.

A smile of satisfaction, in the manner of a woman who has been complimented on her bosom, lit his face. He took a drink of wine during a lull, and then gave me a look. "You seem troubled, sister."

"I am troubled, Ptolemy," I replied. "I am troubled for Egypt."

"Why? Egypt is in strong hands. The low rise of the Nile is unfortunate, of course, but my councillors are taking measures to deal with the famine which is coming."

"Egypt will be strong only if we the King and Queen are strongly united," I cried, my voice vibrating with urgency. "I know you care little for history, Ptolemy, but once we were a great kingdom."

"I remember enough history, and some not so ancient!" he said in an unpleasant voice. "I recall the Roman Rabirius. I was nine years old, but I remember when he was finance minister and looted the treasury. I also remember your Roman friends Mark Antony and Gnaeus Pompey, both of whom you hold highly in the affections of your heart. Well, I hate all the Romans and their greed, and I intend to keep Egypt free from their domination. Egypt will no longer be a plaything of Roman lust. The Roman policy which Father and you advocated has been ruinous, and is at an end!"

I knew that he was parroting his pedagogues, and I suppressed a sigh. "Our father was compelled to deal with the Romans to safeguard and perpetuate the dynasty, and he did it for us," I explained patiently. "I do not love the Romans, but they must be recognized as the mightiest power of the world and we must deal with them."

"My foster fathers think otherwise," Ptolemy said, scowling.

"Rome is a giant octopus spreading global tentacles," I cried with a ring of desperation. "Our only hope in preventing one of its thick tentacles from squeezing Egypt to death is to come to an understanding with this octopus by showing that we are united and are not enfeebled by internal squabbles. Can't you see that our differences will only destroy the dynasty, destroy Egypt?"

"As long as there is the Nile, there will be Egypt!" Ptolemy said, with surprising wisdom. "Dynasties come and go, Cleopatra. The Nile goes on forever. Egypt and the Nile will endure. You, so versed in history, should know that."

"I know Egypt will go on without us, but where will it go?" I said sadly. "It is not my wish that we be the last of the Lagidae."

Ptolemy drained his goblet, then excitedly went and refilled it. "Whatever squabbles we have are caused by you!" he snarled viciously. His fine young body strutted arrogantly to a desk. "I have something that Theodotus found in the Great Library which might be of interest to you."

"Oh?" I murmured curiously.

He picked up an old frayed scroll and unrolled it. "It's a Hellenistic treatise written during the reign of Ptolemy the Sixth called *The Questions of Ptolemy* by Alcibiades. For your elucidation, sister, I wish to quote this passage. 'Remember, O King, that womankind is headstrong, hot in the pursuit of its own wishes, apt to change readily for want of sound reasoning, and naturally weak and inferior to men. They are eternally false and not to be trusted. Women are emotionally unpredictable and unstable. For these reasons women should be prudently handled and kept in their proper place. Women are born to serve, O King, while men are born to rule.' "

My brother let the scroll fall on the desk, and stood there, his legs spread apart, his arms akimbo, giving me a superior smile. "I think these are words of wisdom, Cleopatra."

"You take so little interest in literature, Ptolemy," I rebuked in rebuttal. "How much of the *Iliad* and the *Odyssey* have you read? Yet this idiotic thesis written by a tenth-rate hack essayist a century ago has captured your imagination."

"His dissertations abound in classic truth!" Ptolemy cried belligerently. "Women are inferior to men, as Egyptians are inferior to Greeks. As Greeks rule over Egyptians, so should men rule over women."

Ptolemy moved nervously around the chamber, struggling with his insecurities and a rising hysteria. As a Greek woman I had been taught to control my emotions, whereas my brother, in the manner of a typical Greek male, had been encouraged to be expressive and excitable. In his pacing he suddenly stopped at a marble bust of Alexander on a pedestal. "Look at this work of art by Lysippus! Since when did womankind ever produce a Lysippus or a Praxiteles? Since when did wom-

235

ankind ever produce a Homer or a Sophocles or a Euripides or a Plato? Of course, your sex did produce that tenth-rate poetess, Sappho, whose lovesick verses make me want to vomit!"

"I don't wish to discuss literature with you, Ptolemy," I began, but then stopped, refraining from adding that he was not qualified to discuss the subject. With caution I resumed, "But I will talk about the differences between the sexes, which is a worthy topic. Both sexes have their good and bad points, and both sexes cannot do without the other."

"Women are good only for one thing," he cried nastily, "and one thing only!" Cockily he took a drink of wine.

"Ptolemy, I understand that you have certain fears about me—"

"I fear you?" He barked a nervous laugh. "Don't be ridiculous!"

"Yes, you fear me, which is ridiculous."

"I fear nothing about you, but there are certain things I hate about you, and one is that you do not want to be a woman. You want to be a man. You are a demented Amazon who wants to be a facsimile male!"

"Who gave you that idea, Pothinos?" I demanded.

"Not all my thoughts are from Pothinos!" he cried, but caught himself too late. "I have a brain of my own!"

"Of course you do, and you should use it to tell Pothinos what you want," I insisted. "He is your servant. You are not his servant."

"Pothinos and I are of the same mind on matters," Ptolemy retorted. "Whenever he proposes something contrary to my convictions, I shall command him to do as I wish. So far we have been in accord. I don't know why you've always hated Pothinos. At least, unlike your late Protarchus, he has never conspired to commit regicide and have you murdered."

"And neither did Protarchus. Those were all trumped-up charges."

"There was proof produced at the trial!"

I gave a sigh, seeing no point in offering a rebuttal.

236

"Ptolemy," I resumed with fervent feeling, "you must free yourself of these foolish fears you have of me. I am not an Amazon. You must remember that I am an ordinary woman—"

"I remember it, but it is you who forgets it!" he snapped. "You make such an effort to be extraordinary, which is unseemly in a woman. Remember, Cleopatra, I like women, but I like them to act their parts and to know their proper place. Women should be sisters, wives, mothers, or whores, but nothing else. You've always thought yourself to be so superior just because you've read a few books and speak a few tongues, but for all that you're still nothing but a—a woman!" he cried with infinite disgust.

"I've never shown a superior attitude toward you, Ptolemy," I protested patiently. "I've always shown you respect and devotion."

"But you never meant it," he cried in a whining voice. "You want me to remain a boy for the rest of my life, but I am fifteen now and a man. And I am the King! I am no longer just your little brother."

"Don't you think this pleases me, Ptolemy?" I asked. I rose and crossed over to the divan where he sat. "I have longed for the day when you would come into your manhood, so that we could fulfill our ordained destinies." I sat beside him, and as I did so he crossed his legs and his body stiffened.

I turned the full force of my will on him. "I want you to be a man, Ptolemy, don't you know that? It is your foster fathers who want to keep you a boy so that they can rule for you. Can't you see that you are only a toy in clever, evil hands? Can't you see that it is they who are dividing us and destroying our dynasty?"

"They are the wisest men in my kingdom!" Ptolemy railed at me. He jumped from the divan as if I were a leper, moved away, and glared down at me. "They will keep my country free from the Roman stranglehold and will not sell Egypt out to the Romans the way you would. You are a reckless and unpredictable woman, and because you're not given your way, you make mis-

237

chief. Until you resign yourself to your proper place, things will bode ill for you, sister!"

"Ptolemy, you say a woman should be a sister," I persisted. "In me a more faithful and loving sister no brother ever had. You say a woman should be a wife and a mother. If I could be these things, with princes to look after, a nursery to rule over, I would be content. When I ruled and used my influence, you were a child and it was your interests which concerned me, but you're a man now and soon will come into your majority. This is as it should be. It is now our duty to have children who will one day follow us on the thrones."

A look of utter revulsion transformed his face. "I hate you! You want me to be your stud bull, but I will never bed you, Cleopatra. I would sooner copulate with a camel or a crocodile than with you."

He was almost sobbing with this outcry of hateful words. He went and poured wine and drank gulps of it.

I sat, stung and shocked, deeply humiliated by this repudiation.

The chamberlain Aristodemus entered the room and thumped his staff on the marble floor. "O King, the Princess Arsinoë requests an audience with you."

Ptolemy turned with a relieved look spreading across his face. "Good, Lord Aristodemus, let her enter!"

I was stunned as I watched Princess Arsinoë come into the chamber. She was sixteen now and a budding beauty. She was outstripping girlhood, and womanhood was developing in her, with curves showing where her body had been flat or straight. She wore a dark black wig over her blonde hair, and her face was painted garishly.

"Arsinoë!" Ptolemy cried, running toward her.

"Ptolemy, I'm sorry I'm late," she cried as he embraced her.

As she looked over his shoulder, held in his arms, she saw me and the smile disappeared from her face. "Oh, I didn't know Cleopatra was here!" she said with a pout.

Protocol demanded that Arsinoë come and give me my proper due as her Queen by bending the knee, but she overlooked such homage.

"Greetings, little sister," I said with forced bravado.

"Greetings," she said coldly, as Ptolemy led her to a couch.

I watched as the two of them sat side by side. I noticed that Arsinoë had the temerity to wear a Grecian dress the color of royal purple the shade of which only reigning monarchs were entitled to wear.

"Arsinoë, I like your dress," I said, smiling.

"Purple is my favorite color," she said confidently.

"It matches her violet eyes," Ptolemy said proudly.

They began ignoring me, talking of silly things, giggling and sitting close together. I sat at a distance from them, excluded, feeling conspired against, and waves of humiliation washed scaldingly over me.

Finally I could endure it no longer. "I must be going now," I cried. I walked over to them and kissed them in farewell. They received my kisses with a turned, cold cheek. After I kissed Arsinoë, my eyes lingered on her face. "You're looking more like your mother each day," I observed.

"I wouldn't know," she said resentfully. "I can't remember her." She gave me a look of hatred, as if I had been the agent of her mother's death, which is absurd.

I left them alone together. Why had I not perceived this outcome before? Arsinoë was taking my brother away from me, just as her mother, whom she resembled, had taken my father away from my mother sixteen years before. Fate seemed to be repeating itself.

Ptolemy and Arsinoë were constantly together now. The triumvirate was undoubtedly behind this as part of a plan to get me out of the way. They hoped that, if Ptolemy and Arsinoë were married and sharing the throne, they could continue to wield power for several more years. What they could not see was that Arsinoë in time would be troublesome, for she was as ambitious and willful as I, but without my superior intelligence. I was able to rule without strong advisers, for I did not lack spirit and wisdom. I would never be a malleable monarch in the hands of others. My brother's trio had always known what a threat I posed for them and had done their best to keep me down, and now it seemed they were in the final stages of my complete overthrow.

I would not be the first monarch of my dynasty to be murdered by a sibling co-ruler. In the past there have been many Ptolemies who met horrendous deaths. There are few left with Ptolemy blood, for the Royal Kindred has been thinned out, decimated by family bloodletting. Not one in ten kings of any dynasty recorded in history has died a natural death. I myself was used to living close to death, having done so since babyhood, but the fear of doom had never been so oppressive. They were moving in for the kill, but when, where, how? I was alert now to every shadow, for death could come from any source—a guard, servant, food, drink. I slept with a dagger beneath my pillow, and Apollodorus slept outside my door with a dozen trusted soldiers. I kept desperately searching for signs of the black bull, looking everywhere for it to show its head, for the black bull meant death, the death I could avoid if I showed courage and audacity.

One morning, early in the summer equinox, I was at a council session. My brother sat at one end of the table while I was at the other. I was totally ignored, for what authority I had once exercised was gone. Pothinos held sway, looking at my brother only for agreement to whatever measures he put forth. Ptolemy never ventured an original idea of his own. No councillor meanwhile ever turned toward me for my thoughts, and when I did express an idea I was barely acknowledged. This situation dispirited me, and I sat helplessly while Pothinos made ridiculous decisions that became the law of the land.

At this particular session, Pothinos suddenly fixed me with his beady eyes, which quite startled me, for he rarely looked my way.

"My Queen," he began, forcing a benign smile.

I stiffened with apprehension. "Yes, Lord Pothinos?"

"We have received a letter by courier from Anchoreus the High Priest of Memphis," Pothinos explained, "informing us of the sad tidings of the death of Apis, their reigning black bull."

A cold chill shot along my spine. Beware of the black bull, the Egyptian soothsayer had warned me, for it would mean death.

"A new black bull will be taken to the temple," Pothinos went on in his oily voice. "All Egypt recalls how you personally conducted Buchis to his shrine at the Temple of Hermonthis, and Anchoreus is hoping you will install the new Apis at his temple."

My thoughts were whirling. "I see," I murmured.

"You must go, Cleopatra," King Ptolemy cried encouragingly, with wide-eyed anxiousness. "You loved going to Hermonthis three years ago, remember? Here is another opportunity to show yourself off to the people. It isn't every day that one of the sacred bulls dies, since there are only four of them."

"Anchoreus is the supreme prelate of all Egypt," Theodotus cried in his fluty voice. "What you did for Hermonthis you certainly must do for Memphis."

"You were all against my going to Hermonthis," I reminded them bitterly.

Pothinos nodded. "Yes, O Queen, we did not think highly of the venture, but you proved us wrong, for the people were deeply impressed."

"You do want to go, don't you, Cleopatra?" Ptolemy cried desperately.

"When will it be?" I asked in an inaudible voice.

"In five days' time," Pothinos said. "A new black bull has been selected to succeed Apis and all the arrangements are being made."

"This will give you another chance, O Queen, to pay respects to the religious customs of our natives," Achillas said.

"You can't disappoint the supreme prelate or he will take umbrage," Ptolemy declared fiercely. "You must go, Cleopatra!"

241

Pothinos gave a pained look and glanced at the King warningly. It certainly was out of character for my brother to insist that I take part in a ceremony that excluded him and one which would bring me glory. This anxiety on his part that I go to Memphis was most suspicious in itself.

"The decision, of course, is yours, O Sacred Radiance," Pothinos said, giving me a placid smile.

Sphinxlike I stared straight ahead for a long time. All eyes were fixed on me. "Of course I will do my duty and go," I finally said.

I saw my brother hiss a sigh, his face registering relief. He was a bad king, for a good king never shows his thoughts and feelings.

When the session adjourned, Pothinos took me aside. "O Queen," he said, "I hope you are looking forward to your visit to Memphis."

"I am always happy to fulfill my royal obligations," I said.

"Of late there have been strained relations among us, but we have not wished it so, O Queen," Pothinos said. "Perhaps the visit to Memphis will bode good for all of us, and when you return hopefully the air will be cleared between us."

The air would be cleared between us, all right, for I would be dead. I forced a smile, knowing his words and smile were as false as his heart.

"Yes, my Lord Pothinos, I still have hopes that we can work harmoniously together for the glory of Egypt," I cried.

"We must set aside our differences for Egypt's sake," Pothinos said piously. "We have often been in conflict, but our differences have been honorable ones. And we are united in our dream of a great Egypt!"

"My Lord, I am touched by your words," I cried.

Outside the council chamber, Apollodorus and my guards met me and accompanied me back to my apartments. My legs were weak and could barely carry me.

They were definitely plotting my assassination in Memphis. Protarchus had been dead two months and every day since I had been wondering what fate they were planning for me, and now I knew. They did not want the deed committed inside the palace or in Alexandria, for that would not look good to the people. They thought it best to have me done away with in Memphis in such a manner that no blame would be laid on them or the King.

It was only later, of course, that I learned the details of the projected conspiracy. A fanatic had been selected to approach me with flowers as I stepped off the Royal Barge of Amon at Memphis. Inside the flowers would be a hidden dagger to be plunged into my heart, ending the life of Queen Cleopatra the Seventh.

At this time, however, I did not know what plans they had for me, but only that if I went to Memphis I would certainly die. The black bull meant death. Was I the chosen victim of the gods? Had I lived out my time on earth after twenty-one years? Or could I, as the soothsayer said, avoid my fate if I were as wary as a wolf and bold as a lion? I was determined to foil whatever conspiracy was planned to kill me.

I realized that the triumvirate wanted me dead and out of the way before the battle in Macedonia, for Pompey my patron would surely be victorious and become master of the world. Pompey's victory would vindicate my pro-Pompey policy, and they would not dare touch me then. No, I would have to be gotten out of the way now with no delay.

That evening I closeted myself with Apollodorus and discussed the situation.

"I see it as if it were hieroglyphics on the wall," I cried. "I can go to Memphis and meet certain death, or make my flight into exile. It is impossible for me to remain on Egyptian soil and live."

"Having pledged my troth before the high gods to serve you faithfully as long as I draw breath," Apollodorus said fervently, "I will go where you go, my sword at your service."

"If I were a soldier," I cried, "we could flee to Pompey and offer our swords at his side against Caesar."

Apollodorus shrugged and gave a sighing smile. It was his great regret in life that I had not been born a man.

It was decided to leave Charmion behind, since she was spoiled and used to luxuries and would only be a hindrance to us. I had known nothing but palatial splendors myself, but I felt out of necessity I could function in the outside world in difficult circumstances.

For some time we talked over the idea of temple asylum. Although the Alexandrians had been turned against me, I still retained widespread allegiance in Middle and Upper Egypt. Like my father I was popular with the priesthood, since I always welcomed the leading High Priests at court. From a temple sanctuary I could gain supporters and at least be within the confines of my country. However, if I sought refuge in a temple it would in effect be my prison, and my brother and his triumvirate might still have me murdered there, so I ruled out the possibility of staying in Egypt. I felt it was safer if I went into exile, out of reach of my brother and his army. From outside Egypt I would be free to enlist help for my restoration, as my father had some years before.

At first we thought of going to Rome, but realized it was senseless to go there to seek the protection of the Senate when all the leading senators were in Macedonia preparing for the great battle between Pompey and Caesar. Besides, it was my dream to go to Rome one day, but I wanted to go on a splendid state visit and not as a homeless fugitive as my father had gone.

After much deliberation we decided in favor of flight to Syria, the nearest place of refuge. We would go to the Syrian proconsul, Bibulous, who would remember that it was I who had sent the murderers of his sons to him. He would undoubtedly give me a warm reception, aid, and advice. From Syria I could gain an army of mercenaries, and also await the outcome of the battle in Macedonia. With Pompey the victor, as I was positive he would be, I could obtain aid from him to effect my restoration.

244

While I was apparently busy preparing for my journey to Memphis, Apollodorus arranged secret passage for us on a merchant ship bound for Syria that was set to sail at dawn on the day of my scheduled departure for Memphis. Not a soul knew of our plans.

Two days before my supposed valediction to Memphis, Charmion came to me with her jade eyes tear-stained.

"Cleopatra, my father is dreadfully ill with a bowel complaint," she said. "He has asked that I not accompany you to Memphis, that I stay behind and nurse him since he draws great comfort from me."

I studied her carefully, realizing that her father Lord Kallimachos suspected that some calamity awaited me in Memphis. I daresay everyone on the council knew about the conspiracy. If I was to be assassinated he did not want his daughter there when it happened, lest she too might come to harm.

"Of course, Charmion, stay with your father," I said. "I will miss you, but I will have my other ladies with me."

"I remember what fun we had going to Hermonthis and I had looked forward to this journey," Charmion cried.

"There will be many journeys in the years ahead, Charmion. Your father needs you now more than your Queen."

The night before my planned flight, I had a longing to visit my aunt the Princess Aliki. Accompanied by Charmion and Apollodorus, I went to her apartments. Only the immortal gods knew how long my exile would be. I hoped I would be gone only a few months, but my father had thought the same thing when he fled to Rome and three years passed before his return.

In Aunt Aliki's anteroom, her chamberlain, Timolaus, lumbering slowly with age and obesity, approached me. He made to bend the knee, but I clutched his elbow and refrained him.

"Greetings, my Lord Timolaus," I said with a gentle

245

smile. "Would you tell your mistress that her niece Queen Cleopatra would like to visit with her?"

Charmion and I sat on a marble bench while Timolaus went inside the apartments. It was some time before the old eunuch returned.

"I am sorry, O Queen," Timolaus said, his high-pitched voice breaking with age, "but the Princess Aliki has a cranium torment and begs that you excuse her."

I sensed by the way he could not meet my eyes that he was lying. My aunt was suffering from the fear of associating with one who was out of power. I covered my pain with a smile.

"Take your mistress the message that her niece the Queen wishes her a quick recovery and she sends all her love, my Lord Timolaus," I said.

I never held this against my Aunt Aliki, for I knew she was only being prudent. It would be unwise for anyone to associate with me under the present circumstances, and perhaps even she knew of the conspiracy. After all, she was a Ptolemy and we have a sixth sense about such things, inbred through the centuries. The fact that she had been close to me put her in an unfavorable position as it was. She had never been fond of Ptolemy and Arsinoë, since she hated their mother, but if they were to be the joint sovereigns of the future she had best not antagonize them further.

Every chamberlain and guard in the palace I knew by name, and I was courteous to everyone. I especially went out of my way to be kind to native Egyptians. In contrast my brother strutted around arrogantly, never called anyone by name or gave a greeting or a smile, and treated slaves and nobles alike with extreme rudeness. He was polite only to his evil trio, his companions, and sister Arsinoë.

Where had all my kindness and courtesy gotten me? All my fair-weather friends now changed coats in the foul weather I found myself in, and I was being eschewed by everyone from slave to Aunt Aliki, while my nasty brother and his ruthless gang carried the day. Let it be duly noted that I learned something about human nature during this period of my life.

The eve of my departure came. From my window I could see the ship in the harbor that would take me to Syria. I would not be sailing on the Royal Barge of Amon to Memphis as everyone expected, after all.

Charmion and I supped together. Her father was still ill, supposedly, and after our meal I bade her to return to his bedside.

"While you are gone I will sorely long for you," Charmion said.

"Your father needs you more than I do, Charmion. Go to him now."

I embraced her and sent her off. I then dismissed all my other ladies except for Daphne, who resembled me in physical proportions.

"Come, Daphne, have a drink of wine with me," I said invitingly.

Daphne's blue eyes glowed with happiness, for she had longed to be singled out by me. I gave her a goblet of wine with a potion which would induce a death-like sleep that would last for almost a day.

"The wine is delicious, my Queen," Daphne said serenely.

"I do not wish to sleep alone tonight, Daphne," I said.

"Yes, my lady," she said with a tremulous smile.

"Bring your goblet," I told her.

Daphne followed me into the bedchamber.

"Lie on the bed and be comfortable, Daphne my dove," I said.

"As you command, my lady," Daphne said submissively. She drained the goblet and stretched languorously on the bed. She put a hand out toward me. "Come, rest with me, my mistress."

"Soon," I said in a voice of promise. Nervously I paced the marble floors that were strewn with rich carpets and furs.

Daphne closed her eyes and surrendered to the potent power of the potion. I threw a damask coverlet over her.

From her size, one could not tell that it was not I who lay beneath the covering.

Apollodorus and I went and stood on the uppermost terrace of my palace. I looked out on my city, doomed and fortified, slumbering peacefully in the night. The marble monuments glittered silver under the moon and starshine. On the other side spread the silvery sea, which at dawn would provide my escape from death to Syria.

I knew Bibulous would give me a sympathetic welcome, but I wondered if I would be able to raise an army to return and defeat my brother and resume my rightful place. Would Pompey be victorious and be my champion? Or would he let matters rest in Egypt, with Ptolemy raising Arsinoë to his side? Would I then spend the rest of my days, a wanderer in strange lands, an outcast living on charity? At first I might be a novelty, a young, beautiful deposed queen carrying about her a poignant glamor, but if I did not regain my throne in time, my glamor and novelty would wear off. I would not be marriageable, for who would want a deposed queen? I would be poverty-stricken and live the remainder of my days as a homeless fugitive.

With a rallying of my will, I pushed all negative thoughts from my mind. I would return triumphantly, somehow, I vowed, and act out the glorious destiny which the high gods had in store for me.

In the middle of the night, Apollodorus and I left the palace by a secret passageway, dressed as a soldier and his woman. We carried a pouch filled with gold pieces, and rich gems were sewed into the linings of our cloaks. I took my favorite gold uraeus and, as a talisman, a small scarab of a sacred dung beetle carved out of carnelian, which fourteen hundred years ago belonged to Amonkotep the Third.

An underground tunnel took Apollodorus and me out onto the harbor. All the taverns along the waterfront were closed, and only a few harlots and bitch boys roamed in search of customers, and a few drunken sailors lurched about.

We boarded an old, rickety ship with patched sails and rotting timbers, which surely must have been launched during my grandfather's day. We had a small cabin with one bunk to ourselves. I had been accustomed to large palatial chambers, and I now discovered I had claustrophobia, but with a great effort I controlled it.

As dawn approached, we heard the ship come to life with sailors calling and running on deck above us. The anchor was weighed. We went up on deck and stood watching the sailors hoisting the gangplank. The sails caught the breeze, and the ship sailed off with the morning tide.

Apollodorus put his arm around me and held me close against his tall, strong body. We stood there, the wind whipping against us. I looked out at the sea, which was turning rose-colored with the rays of the rising sun. The raucous squalling of gulls overhead gave me the shivers. I turned back and saw the glorious, splendid monuments of Alexandria receding in the distance as we sailed past Pharos and moved out into the open sea.

Tears filled my eyes as I suddenly wondered if I were looking upon my capital for the last time, but then I immediately rejected such a preposterous, unthinkable thought, and vowed I would return and with the help of the gods defeat my enemies and regain my rightful throne.

For several hours I stood watching from the deck as Alexandria grew smaller. At high noon the horizon swallowed up the last dome of the city, and there was nothing but a space of sea all around me. Apollodorus and I returned wearily to our small cabin and snuggled close together on the small bunk bed, holding one another with trust, devotion, and love. We gave in to our exhaustion and fell asleep.

In the middle of the afternoon we awoke to the sound of torrential rain. A violent storm had broken out over the sea. The old ship, which groaned under the gentlest of waves, now listed dangerously. Apollodorus and I were thrown off the bed, as the ship tossed violently in the whirlpool of the tempest sea, and when the storm was at its most turbulent, I thought surely the ship would sink and drown us.

Just as suddenly as the storm had come up, it subsided, and the sea grew placid again. Apollodorus and I struggled up on deck. The sun came out and the clouds disappeared. All around was the sea in regained tranquillity. The great ball of the sun disappeared over the horizon in a bright scarlet red sunset. The storm was over, and the sun shone brilliantly again. So it would be with my life.

Life had gone down on me but I did not despair. Defeat would not overwhelm me for long. I realized the gods were being seemingly perverse with me, yet I never doubted for a moment that this was not a part of a higher plan they had for me. The gods are sometimes wise in their cruelty. I was carried along by a kind of mounting ecstatic fever. I had youth and audacity and courage, and I was never more sure of my destiny, feeling positive that I would pull myself up out of exile and raise myself to the pinnacle of the world.

BOOK II

CHAPTER I

THE SHORES OF SYRIA were sighted on the sixth day at sea. A southerly gale blew us along the shore until we came to the port city of Raphia near Gaza, where we docked. It was good to be off a swaying ship and on firm ground. Apollodorus and I took rooms at a small inn on the waterfront. Water was brought to my room by a serving girl and, in a small basin I washed my hair, which was caked with sea brine. I had left the comforts and luxuries of my palace behind me, but I bore all these deprivations with good spirit. I was sure I would not for long be a wanderer in the wilderness.

The fortress where Marcus Bibulous, the Proconsul of Syria, was stationed with his army was located outside Raphia. I sent a message to him saying that I, Cleopatra, Queen of Egypt, unjustly driven from my kingdom, sought his hospitality.

Within a day a squadron of his soldiers came to the inn to escort Apollodorus and me to the fortress. Although I wore a simple dress, on my brow was the gold uraeus I had brought with me into exile.

Bibulous met me at the fortress gates. He was a tall, slightly stooped, graying man well into his fifties, with a neatly trimmed beard.

"On behalf of Rome, I welcome you, O Queen," he cried in a rough-edged voice.

Apollodorus and I were each given a chamber in the fortress, and the old general assigned me two of his Persian female slaves. I bathed and rested, and then that evening Apollodorus and I attended a banquet in the bleak rustic hall which was presided over by Bibulous.

The features of Bibulous were stamped with a melancholy aspect, a mark he bore from the tragic loss of his two sons who had died in Egypt the year before. I was grateful that he still had a living son, Lucius, who was serving in another part of the empire. Bibulous looked kindly upon me since I had executed the murderers of his sons, and he sympathized with my dire plight.

"I will help you rally supporters, Queen Cleopatra," he promised.

His old blue eyes, yellowed and veined, warmed as he gazed at me, and perhaps my youth and beauty stirred his sluggish blood a little.

Far into the night we discussed politics, for not only Egypt, but the Roman empire, was in turmoil. In far-off Thessaly, on the plains of Pharsalia, the armies of Caesar and Pompey were encamped opposite each other.

"Who will be the victor, Lord Bibulous?" I asked.

"Only Mars knows," Bibulous replied. "Pompey has never lost a battle, but Caesar's men are hardened with ten years of fighting in Gaul."

Bibulous had frequent reports that came in by ships, and he explained to me that Caesar had been desperate to take the offensive, but he was obliged to postpone this intention since he was outnumbered and needed reinforcements. Mark Antony, who commanded in Italy, then marched with his legions to provide Caesar with aid. As matters stood, Pompey had forty-five thousand infantry and fourteen thousand cavalry, against Caesar's twenty-two thousand soldiers.

I settled down at the gloomy fortress and began making my own military preparations. The fortress was made of stone and cedar, there was no marble or gold anywhere. From this cheerless place Bibulous administered the province of Syria for Rome in a stern but just manner. My serving girls told me that Bibulous suffered from rheumatism, and he slept with adolescent twin Persian eunuchs, whose warmth assuaged the pains in his legs. I could only surmise that he no longer craved the pleasures of Aphrodite.

A report came from Egypt that as soon as I had fled,

I was formally deposed by a court ceremony and my brother proclaimed sole sovereign. Plans were being made to raise Arsinoë to the double throne and to marry her to Ptolemy. In the streets of Alexandria agents stirred up the people to rejoice at these announcements. I naturally took these tidings with a bitter heart.

I wrote to Pompey at Pharsalia, wishing him speedy victory. I explained my predicament, and expressed the hope that when the battle was won against Caesar, he would come to my aid, for as the executor of my father's will it was his duty to restore me to my rightful place in Egypt.

Bibulous helped me recruit soldiers from the Arab tribes outside the eastern frontier, and from Jewish and Syrian mercenaries. Some of the gems I had smuggled out were sold to pay these mercenaries. My command of Aramaic, Hebrew, and Persian came in good stead, for I was able to converse with my soldiers and win them over. I had studied the history of these peoples and knew their customs, and established a rapport with them. Bibulous himself could not act as my general without the sanction of the Senate, but he did assign me his lieutenant, Lucius Lucullus. I had three commendable commanders, Apollodorus, Lucullus, and Zamblichus, the young nephew of the great Arab king from Hemesa. Zamblichus commanded the five hundred Arab soldiers in my little army. He was dashing and exotic in his colorful robes, and he fervently pledged his life to my cause.

I had not been the first Ptolemaic queen who had been forced to withdraw from Egypt. Sixty-five years before, my great-grandmother Cleopatra the Fourth had quarreled bitterly with her son, Ptolemy the Ninth. She had fled to the Seleucid court where her sister was queen. Antiochus the Eighth, her brother-in-law, gave her an army which she led back into Egypt, but she died in battle. I could only pray that I would be more fortunate.

In the middle of the summer equinox, I bade farewell to Bibulous. With my small force of two thousand men and my two Persian serving girls, I marched across the desert like an Amazon, following the path of my father seven years before.

After a week we crossed the desert to Mount Cassius, a few miles from Pelusium, where we set up headquarters, encamped on the raw, exposed windswept plain between the mountain and a cliff that fell to the sea.

Back in Egypt, Achillas mobilized his forces, and with Pothinos and my brother, he advanced to the frontier fortress at Pelusium. The armies of Ptolemy and Cleopatra, brother and sister, faced each other at the eastward edge of Egypt, poised to do battle for the oldest throne on earth.

My army was a pathetic rabble of renegades and Asiatic adventurers, but they were brave and had vowed to die for me. With the odds against us, they would surely get the opportunity to test their vows, for my brother's host was vastly superior. It was apparent that I was on the brink of a losing battle and that I would die with my soldiers. I was not afraid of death and I was willing to throw myself into battle in the courageous manner of my great-grandmother, but I prayed to the immortal gods for salvation.

The eyes of the world were fixed not upon Egypt but Thessaly where two far greater armies prepared to do battle, not for a mere realm, but for the world.

At last Antony arrived at Pharsalia with his legions, and Caesar was able to take the offensive against Pompey. A great battle was fought, with Antony commanding on the right. Pompey, my beloved Pompey, was decisively defeated, meeting ruin on the Thessalian plain. He fled from the battlefield, by ship with his sons Gnaeus and Sextus and a remnant of his mighty army. Caesar went to Pompey's camp and found the empty tents garlanded with flowers and the tables laden with food and wine for the victory feast.

Left behind on the battlefield was Marcus Brutus, who went to Caesar and appealed for clemency. Caesar, who believed that Brutus was his son by Servilia, granted the pardon. Brutus then betrayed Pompey, telling him Pompey was bound for Lesbos and then Egypt. Caesar left in hot pursuit of Pompey with just three thousand men, leaving Antony, his Master of the Horse, to take his legions back to Italy to hold Rome in his name.

The news of Pharsalia flew like the wind across the seas and along the shores of the Mediterranean and reached my camp within a week. I trembled to think that my adored patron and friend, the brave Pompey, had been conquered. I knew that my brother and his triumvirate would recall with malicious joy my sending Pompey aid some six months before.

Pompey had provided for his wife the Lady Cornelia a mansion on the island of Lesbos, where she awaited the outcome of Pharsalia. Knowing that Pompey would be going to her, I quickly wrote a letter to him, and Apollodorus took it to the nearby port and sent it off in a ship bound for Lesbos.

"Salutations, my dearest Uncle Pompey," I wrote. "My brother and his councillors are at the fortress of Pelusium, but I beg you not to trust them. The events of Pharsalia can be redressed. Combine your soldiers with mine for a fresh fight. Your loyal, powerful fleet remains intact. Pharsalia was not a defeat but a postponement of victory. Goddess Fortuna has plans for us. You will yet be the ultimate victor and you and your worthy sons will rule the world."

I was positive that, with the great Pompey as my general, I could easily defeat my brother.

"The world has not heard the last of Pompey!" I told Apollodorus, Lucullus, and Zamblichus.

"Nor of Cleopatra!" Apollodorus cried fervently. "Your Divine Majesty will rule once again in Egypt, as surely as the sun is in the heavens."

At fabled Lesbos there was a sorrowful reunion between Pompey and his wife. Cornelia took my letter with her on board Pompey's vessel, and they hurriedly sailed southward. Rather than submit to Caesar, Pompey decided to flee to Egypt in the hope of asylum. He pondered my letter, and the Lady Cornelia, I later learned, urged him to throw in his fortune with me. Pompey, however, decided to seek refuge with my brother, the reigning ruler, rather than to join forces with an exiled ruler who was a fugitive like himself. He was confident that, even in his fallen state, he would be welcomed by a country that owed him much for services rendered.

The little fleet carrying Pompey sailed over the serene summer waters of the Mediterranean toward Pelusium. Nearing shore, the ship sailed toward my brother's camp. Because of the shallow water, the ship dropped anchor at a distance from land, and Pompey sent a messenger to my brother to request his protection.

There was consternation at my brother's headquarters in the fortress, and a council was convened by Pothinos, Theodotus, and Achillas, with my brother present, to decide Pompey's fate.

"The thought of Egypt becoming a battlefield for foreign invaders is appalling," Achillas cried. "I am all for sending an order for Pompey to be gone."

"I think we should accord the fleeing Roman general an honorable reception," Pothinos said, "since I fear that Pompey, instead of departing, could easily make an alliance with Cleopatra, who is just a few miles from here. The last thing we want is for his military genius to assist her."

"If we receive Pompey," Theodotus declared, "we will have Caesar for our enemy and Pompey for our master. If we dismiss him, we offend Pompey with our inhospitality, and Caesar will hate us for allowing his enemy to escape. The most expedient course would be to send for Pompey and take his life. This will do the victorious Caesar a service and curry his favor, and we will have nothing to fear from Pompey, since dead men don't bite."

The advice of Theodotus carried the day, and the deed was assigned to Achillas. An invitation was sent to Pompey with a promise of protection. Achillas took with him the soldier Lucius Septimius and the centurion Salvius, and they went to Pompey's galley in a small fishing boat.

Lady Cornelia had a premonition of evil and begged her husband not to go, but Pompey brushed her fears aside and bade her farewell as she clung desperately to him. His sons Gnaeus and Sextus embraced him, and he left the flagship and descended into the fishing boat, accompanied by his favorite attendant, the faithful freedman, Philippos.

As the boat rowed ashore, Pompey prepared an address in Greek that he intended to make to King Ptolemy at the approaching interview.

The little boat advanced in a solemn silence, with no sound but the dip of the oars in the sea and the gentle splash of the waves along the shore.

At last the boat touched the sand. Philippos alighted first, and gave his master a hand. As Pompey stepped onto the beach, Septimius stabbed him in the back, as Achillas and Salvius struck with their swords. Pompey, feeling the wounds and knowing all was lost, took up his toga and covered his face. He uttered no cry, although Cornelia's shrieks from the deck of the ship were so loud that surely he heard them on the shore. He sank to his knees and, gathering the mantle over his handsome head, he fell dead.

The assassins cut the head from Great Pompey and held it aloft in triumph. Taking his gold signet ring and his head as tangible proofs for Caesar, they rushed off, leaving the trunk bleeding on the beach dyeing the sand red.

Pompey's sons, with all speed, hoisted sail and fled with their grief-stricken stepmother. A strong breeze from the shore came up, as if from the gods, assisting their flight, and they sailed out into the open sea.

Philippos, who had been unmolested, sobbed beside the body of his master. Later when the first rage of grief had spent its force, he performed the solemn duties of sepulture. He washed the body in sea water, and found an old fishing boat upon the strand, from which he obtained wood for a funeral pyre. He burned the body, and the following morning gathered the ashes in his cloak. Later he bought an urn for the ashes and made his way back to Rome, where Lady Cornelia buried the ashes at the Pompeian estate at Alba with bitter tears.

The life of Pompey, the greatest general and admiral of all time, was over. The moment his head was hacked from his shoulders, Caesar's triumph at Pharsalia was sealed and he became master of the world.

One of my spies at the Pelusium fortress heard the details of this tragic event and slipped across the frontier and came to my tent to break the news to me. I burst into tears, for although I had never met Pompey, we had exchanged many letters since my childhood and I tendered a deep affection for him. He had been my father's friend and had restored him, and I maintain that gratitude should have a high place on the list of political virtues. It shamed me that my brother would assassinate an old friend and patron of our house.

A few days after Pompey's murder, Caesar, not knowing to what part of Egypt Pompey had fled, arrived at Alexandria with thirty-five ships and three thousand men. He dropped anchor, landed his soldiers and established himself in the palace, trusting to the fame of his exploits.

King Ptolemy, with Pothinos and Theodotus, rushed off to Alexandria to greet Caesar, leaving Achillas with the army at Pelusium to prevent my entering the kingdom.

I marvelled as I sat in limbo in my tent beside Mount Cassius that these two events, the assassination of Pompey on the eastern extremity of the Egyptian coast, and the arrival of Caesar in Alexandria, should burst upon my country like simultaneous claps of thunder.

King Ptolemy arrived at the palace and found Caesar ensconced in my private apartments. Roman troops were posted at all the city and palace gates. My brother was back in his palace, but he must have felt himself a prisoner in his own house, with Caesar his jailer.

Hastily outfitted with all the regalia of royalty, he received Caesar in an audience in the Great Throne Room.

"I have come to set order in Egypt," Caesar announced. "It is my honored obligation, for it was in my previous consulship that your father King Ptolemy entrusted the Roman Republic to be the guardians of Egypt's rulers."

It was obvious that Caesar was taking up Pompey's duties as patron and protector to the Ptolemaic court.

"Great Imperator," Theodotus cried, grinning with oily servility, "our sovereign lord King Ptolemy has a gift for you!"

A gold bucket was brought forth, and a soldier lifted out, by the hair, the freshly embalmed head of Pompey. Caesar stared, and recognizing the famous features, forced tears and groans to disguise the joy he felt.

"A Roman lion done to death by Egyptian jackals!" Caesar sobbed.

Ptolemy and his councillors were disconcerted, for they had thought Caesar would be pleased with such a gift.

"If I had been defeated in Thessaly," Caesar cried, "you would be pulling my head out of a bucket as a gift for Pompey. The risks at Pharsalia were far greater than either Pompey or I imagined. I dreaded only exile and my former father-in-law's angry threats and public opinion at Rome. Yet all the time the penalty for defeat was to fall into the hands of Egypt's Pharaoh. King Ptolemy, you have denied me the chance to make peace with Pompey. I never desired his death. I prayed for the privilege to crush him, so that I might embrace him in forgiveness, renew our old friendship, and rule the Republic in harmony."

Not a word of Caesar's speech was believed by those at court, but I myself think the tears were genuine, for my brother had robbed Caesar of the vengeance which he had promised himself.

261

"King Ptolemy," Caesar cried, "I command that you ask forgiveness of Pompey's ghost, that you cremate his head on a pyre with rich incense, and send the sacred ashes to Rome to be delivered to his widow."

"Our god-King, Son of the Sun, will do as Caesar wishes," Pothinos said.

"If I did not know that you hated your sister Cleopatra so, King Ptolemy," Caesar added, "I would show my contempt for your gift by tracking her down and cutting off her head as a gift for you."

Caesar was presented with Pompey's ring, a gold band bearing the signet of a lion holding a sword in its paws.

My brother and his triumvirate must have hoped that when Caesar discovered his enemy dead, he would not prolong his visit, but they were wrong. Caesar was in need of money. Pompey was dead, but his sons and supporters would renew the fight. Wars were costly, and Caesar had to pay his soldiers. Caesar, with his greedy eyes, saw the wealth of Egypt, but he needed a pretext to seize the kingdom.

Caesar announced that he had come to collect his debts. My father had paid only half of the six thousand talents which he had promised Caesar for procuring the treaty of alliance some eleven years before. Caesar decided he would consider the debt settled by an immediate payment of half the balance due and cancel the remainder.

"So Caesar is on a fund-raising mission!" Pothinos said sarcastically. "Surely Caesar has urgent affairs that require his immediate attention in Rome."

"I need no advice from Egyptian eunuchs," Caesar retorted.

In the coming days, Pothinos and Theodotus did not conduct themselves in a hospitable manner toward their unwanted guest. They had inferior grain served to the Roman troops. When the soldiers complained, they pointed out that since there had been a low Nile rise, they were fortunate to have anything when Egyptians were starving. Pothinos also hid all the gold plate and set earthen pottery on King Ptolemy's table, suggesting to the people that Caesar had confiscated the precious royal plate.

Gossip travelling fast via ships and caravans informed me that Caesar and his soldiers were being met with a hostile reception, which did not surprise me, for I knew my people and their pride and rebellious nature. The evil eunuchs were up to their old tricks, fomenting agitation and stirring up the touchy Alexandrians. I wondered what demented policy my brother and his regents were pursuing and to what purpose. They had killed Pompey, and I thought they also might be planning to make an end to Caesar.

Because agitators in the pay of Pothinos were whipping up hostile sentiments against the invaders, Caesar thought it wise to make a second entry into Alexandria. Leading his two legions, he marched along the boulevards in the manner of a conqueror, with the full insignia of a Roman consul. My people considered Caesar's march a blatant insult to their royal house and national sovereignty. Soon outbursts flared. Caesar's soldiers quelled the tumultuous crowds, but disturbances continued to erupt in the city in the days that followed.

While Caesar slept in my bedchamber in comfort, I froze in my tent on the edge of the desert, huddled near a little brazier for warmth. For years Caesar had exercised the most despotic power wherever he had gone, conquering lands and dethroning kings, and now with the prestige of his Pharsalian victory and Pompey's death, he considered himself the autocrat of the world.

Caesar was totally captivated by Alexandria, even if the Alexandrians were not so charmed by him. He knew at long last that the legends of my capital had not been exaggerated. He climbed to the top of Pharos, strolled through the Park of Pan, examined the tomb of Alexander, viewed the temples of the Olympian gods and Egyptian deities, toured the schools and the library, and marvelled at the monuments which my forefathers had built. Caesar, who had conquered half the world for Rome, now had his eyes fixed on the star of the east, and he was panting to annex the land of the pharaohs, but circumstances forced him to bide his time.

At length Caesar announced that by the will of my father, it fell upon him as the representative of the Roman people to settle the dispute between Ptolemy and me, and we were ordered to disband our troops and submit to his arbitration.

In my tent beside Mount Cassius above the sea, I paced on Persian carpets strewn on the ground, anxious and uneasy. It was imperative that I return to my capital, but insurmountable difficulties barred the way. I could not march at the head of my small army for my brother's forces were at the fortress of Pelusium, barricading the border, and if we tried to break through we would be massacred.

"At this very moment," Apollodorus said anxiously, "King Ptolemy is in direct communication with Caesar, laying before him a statement of his claims and grounds on which he maintains his right to the throne to your exclusion."

"Yes, I know," I said fretfully, moving about my tent like a caged tigress. "Ptolemy is cultivating Caesar's favor, while I am far from the scene, my cause unheard."

"Out of sight, out of mind," Apollodorus said. "How can Caesar's arbitration be carried out unless both sides are presented to him? You must get to Caesar and use all your personal and political skills in pleading your cause, Cleopatra. The crown of Egypt is at stake."

"But how am I to get back to Egypt?" I wondered aloud.

"You'll think of something," Apollodorus said, flashing his winning smile. "You are not a Lagidae for nothing."

I called Lucullus and Zamblichus into my tent for supper. As my two Persian girls served us, we sat cross-legged on the carpets and discussed what methods I might employ to return to Alexandria. The night wore on, but no one came up with a safe solution. At last I showed Lucullus and Zamblichus out of the tent, while Apollodorus lingered behind.

The waning moon lit the dome of the sky, and the stars had a cold glitter like diamonds. Soldiers sat around the campfire, singing softly and drinking wine.

I let the tent flap fall back and went and sat on the carpets near the brazier, and Apollodorus sprawled nearby idly eating grapes.

Since leaving Alexandria, Apollodorus had grown a luxuriant beard, and the sun had baked his skin dark during the long hours he worked in the open field drilling the soldiers. He had taken to wearing Persian clothes, the pants, colorful jackets, turban and flowing robes.

"With your new style of dress and great height, Apollodorus," I cried, "you look every inch a romantic Persian!"

Apollodorus smiled abstractedly and took from his pocket a handful of Roman coins which he had gotten from a money-changer in Raphia. He threw the coins, which were stamped with Caesar's profile, on the carpet.

I picked up several of the silver denarii and studied Caesar's portrait. He combed his hair from the back of his head over the bare pate and hid his baldness further by wearing a laurel wreath. His face had sharp, stern angles, an aristocratic nose, a thin, cold, calculating mouth and deeply sunken cheeks.

"Caesar does not have a kind face," I murmured.

"If Caesar were kind," Apollodorus said, "he would not be what he is today, the indisputable master of the world."

"When my father was alive, he often told me about Caesar and Pompey," I said. "I always thought Pompey would triumph."

"Pompey is dead," Apollodorus replied. "Long live Caesar."

I remembered all that my father had said about Caesar. He was a consul, a general, a dictator, a conqueror. Apollodorus and I discussed his campaigns and victories, his unscrupulous politics, his several wives. Calpurnia was his fourth wife, yet he had no son. His first wife, Cornelia, had given him his daughter Julia, who had died in childbirth while married to Pompey.

"Caesar is fifty-two now and they say that is a dangerous age for a man," I remarked. "If I were to get in to see Caesar, I might be able to charm him."

"They say Caesar has a hard heart," Apollodorus said.

"I could soften it," I cried confidently.

"Cleopatra, you are exquisitely beautiful, but you have had no experience with men," Apollodorus said.

"So much the better," I explained. "My innocence and youth will appeal to Caesar's jaded flesh."

"Yes, but in the meantime," Apollodorus said, "perhaps Caesar's jaded flesh, at this very moment, is being stirred by the youth and beauty of King Ptolemy."

I stared at Apollodorus, surprised at this statement.

Apollodorus shrugged. "Well, Ptolemy would not be the first king to bed with Caesar. They say Caesar is the most Greekified of all the Romans. The world remembers the story of Caesar and King Nicomedes of Bithynia."

"Yes," I recalled with a sigh.

Indeed the world well knew the story. When Caesar had been twenty-three the Roman government had sent him on a diplomatic mission to the Hellenistic court of Bithynia. Caesar had been a handsome and elegant young man, and Nicomedes a cultured monarch of middle years, celebrated for his perverted proclivities. Nicomedes became enamored of Caesar, and it was said that Caesar's official duties at the palace were confined to the royal bedchamber, that he was the catamite and the King the sodomite. Caesar stayed in Bithynia for six months, and when he finally returned to Rome, Dolabella called him "The Queen of Bithynia." Caesar's intimacy with Nicomedes became a lasting reproach, which had laid him open to ribald jests ever since. Once while Caesar was addressing the Senate on his obligations to Nicomedes, Cicero cried out, "Yes, yes, we know, it's common knowledge what Nicomedes gave you, and what you gave him in return."

"It is said," Apollodorus cried with a little laugh, "that Caesar is known as every man's woman and every woman's man."

"Yes, my father once told me that Caesar has the reputation of a notorious man-and-womanizer, and is called 'the bald adulterer.' "

"Pothinos might be urging an intimacy between Caesar and Ptolemy," Apollodorus said.

Such a possibility filled me with agitation. If Caesar and my brother were to enter into an intimate alliance, I would be excluded and lost.

"I must get back to Egypt!" I cried desperately, springing to my feet and nervously pacing my tent. "Caesar is not in Alexandria to arbitrate for peace; that is just an excuse for his invasion of Egypt. He is there to steal our gold and grain, to enrich himself, to collect the remainder of the bribe my father owed him. The monstrous evil of this man!"

"Caesar is a consummate politician," Apollodorus observed admiringly.

"Well, so am I!" I cried. "Great Pompey was murdered and Caesar could meet the same fate. I must see him before that happens. To send him a message would be fruitless, for it would only be intercepted. I must get to Caesar alive, and while he is alive!"

The dark brows of Apollodorus knitted in a hard knot. "The border is blockaded, so we must go as we came, by sea," he suggested.

"Yes," I agreed. "We can find a ship leaving the port of Cassius bound for Alexandria, but once we get to Alexandria it will be dangerous. My brother's fleet will be blockading the port to prevent our return."

"We will go disguised," Apollodorus said. "I will be

267

a Persian rug merchant, and you will be my slave girl. With a veil over your face, who will ever know that you are the Queen of Egypt?"

"Oh, how clever you are!" I cried, throwing my arms around his neck.

The two of us laughed happily together, excited about our audacious plan.

In the morning I held a council in my tent with my officers. It was decided that Lucullus and Zamblichus would stay encamped with my small army, while Apollodorus and I made our way to Alexandria. As soon as feasible I promised to send them an order to march to Alexandria to serve me. Lucullus and Zamblichus vowed to keep my plan secret so that no word would reach my brother's headquarters.

One of my lieutenants went to Cassius and obtained passage on a ship sailing to Alexandria the next day. With a rush of excitement I prepared for the journey. My two Persian girls gave me their brightly colored clothes and veils to use as a disguise. In his beard and turban and robes, no one would doubt Apollodorus was a Persian. We had the dozen carpets that were strewn inside my tent bundled up as merchandise to complete our disguise as a merchant and his slave.

At dawn the following morning, I waved farewell to my soldiers, who were told I was going to Raphia for a few days to parley with Roman officers. I rode off on a red-gold Arabian mare, accompanied by Apollodorus, Lucullus, Zamblichus, and my two Persian girls. After riding all morning over bleak countryside under a blazing sun, we arrived at the teeming little port of Cassius at high noon. We ate at a harbor tavern while our carpets and a few belongings were taken on board an old Syrian merchant vessel.

I kissed the two Persian girls farewell, and Lucullus promised that he would make arrangements to have them returned safely to Bibulous at the fortress in Raphia. I embraced Zamblichus and Lucullus, and covering my face with a veil, I went on board the old ship with Apollodorus.

As the late afternoon tide came up, the ship weighed anchor and sailed out to the open sea.

Apollodorus and I shared a small cabin without a porthole deep in the hull of the ship. A single lantern gave off a little yellow light. The small room stank, but I did not mind. If the winds were favorable, after a few days' voyage I would arrive at last at the harbor of Alexandria.

As night came on, Apollodorus and I lay close in our bed in our cabin, as the ship plowed through the turbulent waters.

Except for my father and Protarchus, Apollodorus was the only man I had ever loved, but it was the affection of a sister for a brother. I had never known physical intimacy with a man. Though I was an innocent virgin, I felt confident that Caesar would not be indifferent to me. The court poets had praised me in poems, and though Caesar was a conqueror, he was also a man of flesh and blood.

"In a few days," Apollodorus whispered as we lay in each other's arms, "we will be back in Egypt, and you will again be Queen."

"If Great Caesar wills it," I remarked soberly.

"The holy cat of Egypt and the Roman wolf!" Apollodorus muttered thoughtfully. "That will be an interesting encounter. Let us hope that back in the palace tonight Caesar is not sharing his couch with Ptolemy."

My heart missed a few beats at such a repugnant thought, but I well knew that this could be possible. "Could you be attracted to Ptolemy, Apollodorus?" I asked.

"King Ptolemy is not to my taste," Apollodorus replied, "but he is a good-looking stripling with a beautiful body which might appeal to an old rake like Caesar."

"I too have beauty which I can use as a weapon," I said with pride and confidence. "For all his glory and victories, Caesar must be filled with sorrow not to have a son to inherit his name and power and fortune."

"Yes, I am sure he is," Apollodorus agreed.

"I can give Caesar what my brother could never give," I cried, my voice vibrant with inspiration.

"What, Cleopatra?" Apollodorus asked with a little laugh, but knowing the answer.

"A son!" I cried ecstatically.

CHAPTER II

THE BEACON OF PHAROS, glowing like a fiery meteor in the darkness of the night, told me my beloved Egypt was less than a hundred miles away. Pharos, which Ptolemy the First had built, so famous for its splendid architecture, ornamented with balustrades and galleries and columns, was offering us guidance as mariners and voyagers.

A favoring northwest wind blew against the sails as the galley sailed toward the guiding light, toward Alexandria, carrying me to Caesar and to my destiny.

"The captain says we will reach port in the middle of the night," Apollodorus said, standing beside me on the galley's prow as we took the fresh air.

"The gods have watched over us these days at sea," I said gratefully.

An Egyptian sailor came lumbering toward us along the deck, and I quickly lowered the veil over my face. I shivered in my thin Persian dress, and Apollodorus threw his colorful cloak over my shoulders.

"Tomorrow you will be back in your palace, and ruling your people as the gods ordained," Apollodorus whispered reassuringly.

"With the help of the gods," I said, "and Caesar."

I had mixed emotions of excitement and apprehension. My brother and his triumvirate expected me to return to Egypt and were undoubtedly watching for me. If my disguise was penetrated, I would be murdered.

Apollodorus and I returned to our small, dark, windowless cabin and lay on our bed, but we were too nervous to sleep.

A few hours later the galley reached the entrance to the Harbor of the Happy Return and dropped anchor. I heard much stirring and talking above on deck. Presently Apollodorus, who had been on deck, returned to our cabin.

"A boom has been placed at the entrance to the two harbors," he explained, "and no ship is allowed in until it is searched. Soldiers will come on board sometime before noon."

My heart raced wildly. I knew we had to get off the ship before dawn. We decided to bribe the captain to let us use a small boat to take us to nearby Pharos Island. We could go to the Temple of Isis, near the lighthouse, and take sanctuary. From the temple it would be an easy matter to get across the Great Harbor to the palace.

I still had a dozen priceless gems left in my pouch. Three of the choicest ones were selected, and Apollodorus took them up to the captain. While he was gone, I collected our few belongings. In a short time Apollodorus returned with two sailors to carry our Persian carpets. Heavily veiled, I made my way up on deck. It was not yet dawn. I pulled the hood of my cloak tightly around me against the chill morning breeze. Across the harbor I could see a few flickering torches in the city. My heart warmed as I gazed out at the marble splendor of my Alexandria.

We bade farewell to the captain and descended the ladder into the boat. A lone sailor rowed the boat across the short distance to Pharos Island, where I stepped once more onto Egyptian soil.

Dawn broke and the fires in the lofty tower of Pharos above us paled. The sun god rose, turning the sea to a glowing vermillion as Apollodorus and I entered the forecourt of the Temple of Isis and approached a slumbering priest who sat sentry at the door.

"Greetings, Father," Apollodorus cried, rousing the priest. "I am a Persian merchant travelling with my lady, and we wish to give sacrifice and say prayers to the great goddess Isis."

"Welcome, friends from Persia," the priest said and led us into the temple. We prostrated ourselves before the monumental marble statue of Isis that stood behind the altar. The statue held the sistrum and the looped cross, the symbol of eternal life. We lay on the cold marble floor for a long while, giving our prayers to the goddess of whom I am the earthly reincarnation, beseeching her to watch over us in the precarious hours ahead.

After our prayers, Apollodorus went to the priest and gave him a rich gem.

"Our voyage has been long and rough, Father, and my lady has been ill," he explained. "We beseech the priests of Isis to give us sanctuary for the day, so that we may rest before entering upon our labors in the city."

"The Goddess Isis is honored to give solace and shelter to two of her children," the priest said.

In a small chamber off the temple courtyard, a priestess brought me water and I undressed and sponged the dirt from my body. Presently Apollodorus returned with two dockworkers carrying the carpets, which they piled in a corner of our chamber.

From the men, he had learned that the city was indeed in the hands of the Romans, with centurions and soldiers patrolling the streets. There was a mood of anxiety and tension in the capital.

Honeyed cakes and hot herb juice were brought to our chamber, and Apollodorus and I spent the entire day there. We realized that we would have to take a decisive step, for I had to get in to see Caesar. My life and throne depended upon my winning his support.

We spread on the floor our remaining half-dozen gems and gold coins. We hoped we had enough to bribe our way into the palace.

Apollodorus learned that it was Caesar's habit to stay up late into the night in my apartments, writing reports, while most of the palace was asleep. It would be easier to get into the palace at night than during the day. We knew the palace well, every corridor and passageway, but we would have to get through the guards without being detected. By the time my enemies discovered that I had returned from exile, I wanted to have laid my case before Caesar. The question remained how to accomplish this.

"I could get in to Caesar in my disguise as a Syrian merchant," Apollodorus said. "I could bribe his sentries and say I have a message from the Syrian Proconsul, Bibulous."

"Yes, but I could never go with you," I said. "Your face is disguised by a beard and a turban. My veil need only to be lifted by a curious guard and the game would be lost." Sighing, I sat on the floor, my hand idly caressing the Persian carpets piled in the corner.

"Somehow I've got to smuggle you inside the palace with me," he said.

My eyes fell on the carpets. "I wonder if I could be rolled up inside one of these carpets, and then you could carry me inside. Is that possible?"

"Of course!" Apollodorus exclaimed. "I'll roll the carpet around you, swing you over my shoulder, and walk into the palace saying that I have a gift from Bibulous which I must personally deliver to Caesar."

We decided to test the plan. Selecting the rarest, richest carpet, we spread it on the floor, and Apollodorus rolled it around me, hoisted the bundle over his shoulder and walked around the chamber, laughing triumphantly. When he put the carpet down and unrolled it, I sat up happily and threw my arms around him.

"These carpets will have more value than we ever imagined when we brought them from Syria," Apollodorus cried, laughing. "When shall we put this plan into action, Cleopatra?"

"Tonight after nightfall," I said. "To delay would be folly."

Late that afternoon, Apollodorus left the temple and made arrangements for a small fishing boat to be ready after dark to row us across the Great Harbor to the palace dockside. I rested in the tranquillity of our chamber, gaining strength for the night ahead.

When Apollodorus returned, we went to the temple altar and said fervent prayers, beseeching Isis to guide and protect us in the night ahead.

Outside darkness fell as we prepared for our journey. I dressed in a simple Persian tunic, and I fastened on my uraeus crown.

"The time has come to go, Apollodorus," I said.

"Yes, Cleopatra," he said gravely. "I pray to Isis that I will not fail you."

"You won't fail me, Apollodorus. Isis will watch over us."

Once more we embraced tenderly. I stretched out on the end of the carpet, and Apollodorus carefully rolled the carpet around my body.

"I'm glad that you have a slender figure and are not well-fed like Charmion," Apollodorus teased as he went about his task.

"I'm as slim, after this sad exile, as a reed growing on the banks of the Nile," I answered.

"Can you breathe all right, Cleopatra?" he asked as he tied the bundle.

"Yes, Apollodorus, let's get on with it," I said impatiently.

Apollodorus hoisted the carpet over his shoulder. His strong, sturdy arms held onto me as he carried me outside the temple into the night.

To the fisherman at the dock who helped him Apollodorus said, "This is the rarest of rugs, my friend. Lay it down gently."

I lay inside the rolled-up carpet on the boat bottom, listening to the oars splashing in the waters, and my blood coursed at the thought that I was nearing my palace.

Finally the boat slid against the marble dock. Apollodorus paid the fisherman, and shouldering his royal burden, stepped onto the quayside. It was a short walk to the eastern gates of the palace, where we were stopped by a Roman centurion.

"Halt!" the centurion barked. "Who goes there?"

"Antiochus, a Persian merchant," Apollodorus cried.

Inside the carpet I lay over his shoulder, trembling with fear.

"Noble Roman," Apollodorus said in Latin, "I am an ambassador from General Marcus Bibulous, Proconsul of Syria, who has sent me here on a secret mission, with this gift for the Imperator Caesar."

"From Bibulous?" the centurion cried. "Any news of Cleopatra?"

"I've a message from Bibulous regarding the Queen," Apollodorus said firmly, "but it is for Caesar's ears only."

"Where is your diplomatic seal and letter?" the centurion demanded.

"General Bibulous thought it best that I travel without papers," Apollodorus said, "in case I should fall into the hands of King Ptolemy's men. Bibulous asked that I give a gift to the centurion who assisted me in getting to Caesar."

Apollodorus offered silently his last coins, which were as silently accepted and pocketed.

"Antiochus, I will see that the Imperator Caesar receives you," the centurion said. "Come with me."

The centurion called some soldiers to act as an honor guard, and we were escorted into the palace. Apollodorus carried me easily along the corridors to my royal apartments.

"Wait here, Antiochus," the centurion said. "I will see if the Imperator Caesar will receive you."

As we waited, Apollodorus surreptitiously patted the carpet to reassure me. Then the great bronze doors opened, and the centurion came out.

"Caesar will receive you, Antiochus," the centurion cried, and Apollodorus boldly carried me inside my reception room which had been appropriated by Caesar.

"Great Caesar, this is the Persian Antiochus who says he is an emissary from Lord Bibulous," the centurion said.

"My Lord Caesar, I bring greetings from Lord Bibulous," Apollodorus cried.

"Greetings," said a cool and imperious voice, a voice that unmistakably could belong only to Caesar.

"I have a gift for you, my Lord Caesar, the greatest gift!" Apollodorus said brightly.

"Yes, I know, from my friend Marcus," Caesar replied impatiently. "And a message regarding Queen Cleopatra?"

"My Lord Caesar, it is not Bibulous who sends this gift, but Cleopatra, Queen of Egypt!" Apollodorus announced dramatically.

Although muffled by the carpet, the startled cries of Caesar's aides and soldiers reached my ears.

"I beg leave that I may present you with the gift from Cleopatra in private, Great Caesar," Apollodorus cried urgently.

"You may be an assassin!" a harsh voice protested.

"You will give me the gift now," Caesar said peremptorily.

"As Caesar commands, although Queen Cleopatra wished that I give it to the Imperator privately," Apollodorus said.

"At the moment, Cleopatra's wishes carry little weight in Egypt," another Roman commented coldly.

"Let us see this gift from Egypt's fugitive queen," Caesar remarked.

Apollodorus carefully set the carpet down on the marble floor. "I do not have a knife to cut the cord," he said.

"Rufio, use your dagger and cut the cord for our Persian friend," Caesar instructed.

I heard the dagger severing the knotted rope. Then Apollodorus, pulling at the end of the carpet, unrolled the rug, spinning my body over and over until at last I was unwrapped. For a moment I lay still, quite dizzy, my head filled with blood, and then regaining my equilibrium I sprang to my feet, dishevelled, with one sandal lost. Apollodorus reached out and took my elbow to steady me.

Around me I saw the astonished faces of Roman

277

soldiers, heard their surprised gasps, and at last my glance found Caesar's. His dark brown eyes fixed me with a penetrating gaze, and I knew that here was the most powerful man on earth. Almost in spite of himself, he was charmed by the spectacle of my coming.

"What have we here, a pretty courtesan for my couch?" Caesar laughed in admiration and amusement.

"Great Caesar, you blaspheme the Divine Majesty of Egypt," Apollodorus cried, deeply affronted.

I took a step toward him, the cobra head of my uraeus crown jutting forth from my forehead. "Greatest of all Romans and world conqueror," I cried, "I, Queen Cleopatra, Lady of the Two Lands, salute you!"

"Beware that she is not an imposter, Great Caesar," a soldier cried.

Caesar drew closer to me, a cynical smile on his face. I stood there, my head uplifted defiantly, and then I turned to show the profile that matched the image stamped on my coins.

"As Aphrodite rose out of the sea with all her beauty and grace, so Queen Cleopatra has risen from a carpet!" Caesar cried. "Welcome, O Queen."

I inclined my head toward Caesar in a graceful nod.

"Lord Rufio and the rest of you, begone," Caesar said. "Queen Cleopatra and I wish to have a private audience."

"Be prudent for she may compromise your safety, Great Caesar," a centurion said anxiously.

"Who is your cautious friend?" I asked disdainfully.

"Queen Cleopatra," Caesar said amiably, "may I introduce Rufio, the Roman commander of our garrison here in Alexandria."

Rufio acknowledged his introduction with a stiff, hostile salute.

"Leave us, all of you," Caesar demanded.

I smiled to Apollodorus, and he knelt and kissed my hand.

"Thank you, Apollodorus," I said softly.

The great bronze double doors banged shut after Apollodorus and the Romans.

278

Caius Julius Caesar and I, Cleopatra, were alone together.

For a long moment Caesar and I stood assessing each other. I saw that he was tall of stature, with a spare, lithe body and shapely limbs. His face was much like the bust in my father's collection, sharp and keen, with a broad full brow, a pale complexion, a long, sinewy, proud neck, delicately molded lips and chin and many deeply etched wrinkles. He wore his hair combed forward over his balding crown. His Senator's toga was fringed with purple and had gold sleeves to the wrist, which he fastidiously draped in folds about his body.

Caesar gazed upon me with the appraising and mocking eyes of an old rake. I was slightly dishevelled and plainly dressed, my hair all awry and one sandal missing, but I could see that he was intrigued and charmed by the twenty-one-year-old girl challenging him to deny her beauty.

I turned from Caesar and with cool dignity I walked to a table and poured a goblet of wine, deliberately moving seductively in my silk Persian sheath. As my back was turned, he quickly placed his gold laurel wreath on his head to camouflage his baldness. I took a long draught of wine, which I sorely needed after my long ordeal of being bundled up in the carpet.

"I hope you don't mind my having made myself comfortable in your beautiful apartments, Queen Cleopatra," Caesar said in his deep voice.

"Certainly not, my Lord Caesar," I cried, facing him. "You should live like a monarch, for you are one." I saw that this remark pleased him, and I walked over to him. "Imperator Caesar," I resumed in Latin, caressing the vowels, "perhaps birth accounts for little measured against achievements such as yours, but I am a lineal descendant of King Ptolemy, the brother of Alexander the Great. I have been treacherously driven from my throne. You are the supreme master of the world, and you have the power to give me back my crown and restore order to my wretched country."

"That is what I have come to do," Caesar explained.

279

"It is to Rome's interest that this feuding between the Ptolemies be stopped."

"I commit my cause into your hands, Great Caesar, and I surrender to your august power."

"I pray to the gods that I merit the unbounded confidence you place in me," Caesar said.

"If the Pharaoh Ptolemy were his own master," I cried passionately, "he would show that he loves me, but he is a tool of corrupt eunuchs. I beg that you rescue Egypt from their unworthy stewardship. Remember, Caesar, that they ordered Pompey's head to be cut off, and may plot the same fate for you."

Caesar gravely nodded and took my elbow. "Come and sit, Queen Cleopatra, and have more wine." He guided me to a couch where I reclined, and he fetched me my goblet.

"Remember too, Great Caesar," I continued earnestly, "his tutors have instilled in King Ptolemy Philhellenic ideals and a bitter hatred against Rome. Princess Arsinoë also loathes all Romans. I am the only member of the royal house of Lagos to adopt my beloved father's Roman sentiments. With me on Egypt's throne, Rome will be assured of a faithful friend."

Again Caesar nodded. "How did you get here from the desert?" he asked curiously. "How did you enter the city when all the gates are closed and the port watched?"

"I came out of the night," I replied lightly. "I flew like a falcon!" Then assuming a grave tone, I told him of my flight and return with Apollodorus. As I talked, I noticed Caesar moving ever closer, bewitched by my manners, my voice, my audacious anecdotes.

"Cleopatra, I am enchanted by your daring," Caesar said. "You could easily have ended up with a dagger in your belly if you had fallen into the hands of enemies."

"That danger was part of the fun," I said nonchalantly. "Besides, I am a Lagos. The queens of my line are celebrated for their courage."

"Years ago when your father was in Rome, he often

talked about you," Caesar remarked with his thin smile. "He said that even as a child you were as full of cunning as a tigress and as stubborn as a bull. Your father loved you well, O Queen."

"As I loved him, Caesar, for my name is Cleopatra Philopator," I said, my voice hoarse with sudden emotion.

"You must be weary from your travels, Cleopatra," Caesar cried. "Surely you would like to bathe. In an hour let us meet for a little repast. In the meantime, I will finish writing reports that must leave by galley for Rome on the morning tide."

I stood and walked over to Caesar. "Are you writing my old friend, Mark Antony? I remember his visit to Alexandria seven years ago."

"Yes, I am, as a matter of fact," Caesar said.

"Give Lord Antony a greeting from me," I said, "and write the Senate that I place my trust in their custodianship."

"I shall do that," Caesar promised.

I put my hand out to Caesar, and after a moment's consideration, he leaned over and kissed it.

Turning from Caesar, I went to my bathing chamber and roused the slaves. I ordered a bath prepared and Charmion brought to me. I sat at a table filled with my ointments and perfumes and was pleased to see that nothing had been disturbed during my four-month exile.

Inhapi, one of my most devoted Egyptian ladies, a Coptic with a little brown face like a cat's, solicitously came to me and knelt at my feet.

"My Lady Queen, my soul has been filled with longing for you," Inhapi cried. "My prayers to the gods have been answered, for you have returned."

"Beloved Inhapi," I cried, touching her cheek. "You are more beautiful than ever. How I have missed your attentions to my hair."

"Do you wish me to brush it now, my Queen?"

"Yes, dear Inhapi," I said.

I stared into polished silver mirrors as Inhapi stood

281

behind me and brushed my hair. "Tell me, Inhapi," I said, "how fares the Lady Charmion?"

Inhapi stopped with her brushing, and I could see in the mirror that her face took on an evasive expression.

"Answer me, minx!" I said sharply.

"Oh, Divine Majesty, the Lady Charmion has been most unhappy in the long days of your absence," Inhapi cried.

"Yes, Inhapi, go on!" I demanded, knowing she had more to tell me.

"What I have to say will not please your divine ears, O Queen," Inhapi said. She took a deep breath and blurted out, "The Lady Charmion has been finding solace in the arms of the Lady Daphne."

"I see," I said, staring at my reflection in the mirror.

"Yes, my Lady Queen," Inhapi said, and then gaining courage, continued in a voice rising with gloating glee, "Charmion and Daphne have hardly spent an hour apart since you left, day or night."

I sat, unmoving and expressionless, as Inhapi brushed my hair. Suddenly the brush caught in snarls and pulled sharply at my scalp.

"You bitch!" I cried out, my anger breaking as I slapped her face.

Inhapi backed away from me, covering her face as she began sobbing. "Please, forgive me, my Queen!" she cried, sinking to her knees.

I glared at Inhapi, who had always loved me devotedly. I was sorry she had borne the brunt of my anger with Charmion.

"Leave me, Inhapi, begone!" I ordered.

I covered my face with my hands, filled with remorse to think that, while I lay alone all those months of bleak exile, my beloved Charmion had lain in the arms of another. I almost broke into sobs, but then I realized that I could never be a slave to my emotions, to any man or woman. After all, I was Egypt and had higher matters to claim my heart.

Charmion came rushing into the bathing chamber, dressed in a robe, having been called from her bed. A bed she shared with Daphne. She knelt at my feet and threw her arms around me.

"Oh, my beloved Cleopatra," she cried, embracing me, "at last you have returned! My prayers to Isis have been answered."

"Charmion," I murmured.

She gazed up at me, and then we kissed tenderly. There were tears in her green eyes. In a torrent of words she expressed her despair at my absence and her happiness at my return. I smiled, holding her hands, taking in her words.

When my bath was ready, I said, "Come, share my bath, dear Charmion."

Holding hands, we walked to the pool and climbed into the warm perfume-scented water, submerging our bodies to the chin.

After my bath, I submitted to a massage, and then my ladies daubed my body with perfume. My hair was toweled dry and brushed.

"Shall I braid your hair in the classic style?" one of my ladies asked.

"No, let it fall simply to my shoulders," I replied.

"In the fashion of a virgin!" Charmion cried. "Oh, Cleopatra, your brother will be pouting and fuming when he finds out you have returned."

All my ladies giggled at this remark.

"I know Ptolemy won't be overjoyed," I said.

"Caesar has been using your bedchamber," Charmion cried. "Where will you sleep tonight, O Queen?"

"For the last two months I have been sleeping on the floor of a tent in the Syrian hills at the edge of the desert," I explained. "Tonight any couch in the palace will be an improvement."

"You must order Caesar out of your apartments!" Charmion insisted. "Do not forget that you are Egypt's Queen."

"I am Queen only if Caesar says I am," I said.

When my hair had been brushed to my satisfaction, I went to my robing chamber and asked for my gown of Isis.

283

"I am going to sup with Caesar," I told Charmion.

"Ah, you are going to dress as Isis to impress him," she said brightly. "Shall I wear my gown as a priestess of Isis?"

"You won't be joining us, Charmion," I told her.

"It would be unseemly for you to sup alone with Caesar, Cleopatra," Charmion protested painfully.

"I have a great deal to talk about with Caesar in private," I said.

"At this hour of the night?" Charmion countered. "What will the gossip wags of the palace have to say about that?"

I made no reply as my ladies laced my golden sandals and robed me in the white Sidonian silk gown of Isis. Charmion placed the gold uraeus crown on my head and clasped gold snake bands around my arms. I was handed the symbols of Isis, the sistrum and the looped cross.

I walked out of the robing chamber and down the corridor to my reception room, with Charmion and my ladies walking respectfully behind me. At the door, Charmion came close to me.

"O Cleopatra, shall I wait until you have finished supping with Caesar?" she asked.

"There is no need, Charmion," I replied crisply. "I dismiss all of you for the night."

My ladies bent to their knees, murmured farewells and rushed off, all except Charmion.

"This is unseemly, Cleopatra," she fretted. "Surely you will have need of me later. Oh, how I have missed you!"

"Run along back to your chamber now, Charmion," I said coldly. "The Lady Daphne will be sorely longing for you."

A look of surprise flashed across Charmion's face.

I held her eyes. "I am pleased to know that you were able to find consolation in Daphne's arms during the anguish of my absence."

"But Daphne and I are merely friends!" Charmion protested desperately.

284

"Good night, Charmion," I snapped.

"My Queen, please believe me!" Charmion cried.

"Open the doors and that will be the last duty I require of you for the night," I said sternly.

Charmion, with a great effort, controlled her emotions and opened the doors to my reception room.

"Good night, my Queen, love of my life!" Charmion whispered urgently.

I entered my reception room, and Charmion closed the doors behind me. I saw Caesar sitting at my desk. He put down his pen, and looked at me in amazement.

"Why are you marching around dressed as Isis in the middle of the night?" he laughed.

"I am Isis!" I retorted firmly.

"Well, Queen Cleopatra, I know that you're supposed to be the reincarnation of Isis, veiled in flesh, and if you've been told that since childhood, of course you believe it. It's a lovely thing to believe."

I stood there, the symbols of my divinity trembling in my hands.

"My mind has no room for silly superstitions," Caesar went on. "Mind you, it's good for the common people to believe you're Isis, and you are the most beautiful goddess the Egyptians worship. Egypt is such a weird land with its worship of vultures, bulls, crocodiles, and cats."

"If you find Egypt so repulsive with its customs, Caesar, leave tomorrow!" I said. "No one invited you here."

"My Royal Lady, I am here to fulfill my duties to Rome and to bring about peace between you brawling Ptolemies."

"I know what motives brought Caesar to Egypt!" I cried vehemently.

"Come, O Queen, let us not bicker," Caesar said, placating yet condescending at the same time. "Put down those things and forget that you're a goddess and remember that you're a mortal with a stomach, and eat with me."

I placed the sistrum and cross on a table, and

stretched myself on the cushioned divan. It was pleasant to relax in my favorite chamber, with its rose-colored porphyry pillars, its exotic blend of Egyptian and Greek furniture, its art works, the walls decorated with a frieze of ancient pharaohs making offerings to deities, golden hangings from India, and Persian carpets strewing the marble floors.

"You've probably been living on dates these last weeks in Syria, so I've had delectable foods prepared," Caesar said, serving me as if he were the host and I the guest.

I took a sip of wine. "Speaking of Isis," I said, "is it not true that in Rome she has many worshippers?"

"Only among the rabble and a few patrician ladies," Caesar explained. "Even my wife worships her. There was a guild of Isis followers when I was a boy, and the consuls had the altar of Isis on the Capitoline hill destroyed, so it is all done secretly. The Senate is wary of these hysterical eastern cults."

"I don't know why Roman leaders believe that the worship of Isis is a source of subversion," I cried.

"Have some peacock liver, Cleopatra," Caesar said, changing the subject.

As Caesar hovered over me, I found myself warming up to him. He was dignified, regal, courteous, and polite, a man of breeding, a little cynical, with a sharp wit and a brilliant mind. I sensed instantly that he was hard and unbending, with his thin mouth and cold dark eyes. Pompey's enemies could always expect magnanimity, but not Caesar's enemies. One could never tell what Caesar was thinking, for his face was inscrutable like his busts, concealing more than he would ever reveal. Time had not diminished his magnetism nor reduced his charm.

As the night wore on, we conversed easily in Latin and Greek. We matched wits, and I was conscious that Caesar found me enchanting, enjoying my knowledge of the arts and sciences and my grasp of politics. At last I broached what was uppermost in my mind.

"The burden of the world is on Caesar, the Atlas

286

holding up the world," I cried. "I know that Caesar will do his duty by Egypt and save us from the tyranny of Pothinos. He is a base scoundrel with no sense of world affairs."

"I've been told that Pothinos won his way into your father's heart by supplying him with a stream of beautiful boys," Caesar said. "I must say, speaking of your father, I greatly admired the way he hung onto his throne all those years by shamelessness and sheer wits."

"All power is achieved and retained by shamelessness and wits," I cried with mild rebuke. "You, Great Caesar, of all people, should know that."

"Yes," Caesar agreed, taking a sip of wine.

I stood and paced around the chamber, gazing with quick admiration at beautiful statues, the works of Praxiteles, Myron, and Phidias, and at last I stopped before a bust of Alexander by Lysippus that rested on an alabaster pedestal.

"Caesar, are you an admirer of Alexander?" I asked.

"Alexander was my boyhood hero," Caesar replied.

"You remind me of Alexander, Great Caesar," I lied, shamelessly.

Caesar smiled with pleasure. "Coming from a Greek and a relative of Alexander's, I take that as a supreme compliment."

"You are a great conqueror in the tradition of Alexander," I said, walking toward him. "Who but that mad Macedonian has conquered more? The world has been waiting three centuries for a man to come along to finish what Alexander began. You are master of the world, while I am a Queen of a mere realm."

"A land which is the breadbasket of the world," Caesar said.

Reaching his couch, I sat beside him and took the goblet he offered me.

"Your dynasty is gnarled and hollow," Caesar said, "but you are a bright flower blooming on the dying Ptolemaic tree, and perhaps you will go down in history as the greatest of your line."

"Only with Caesar's help," I said, staring deep into

his eyes. "Oh, I feel that you are my friend. Not since my father died four years ago have I had a true friend. I've had a troubled time on the throne, but now I feel in you I have someone to protect me."

"Rest content, Cleopatra, that I shall espouse your cause," Caesar said. "I am impressed by your spirit and intelligence, and with your superlative beauty which is celebrated in distant lands."

"Is it really, Caesar?" I asked with a smile.

"In Gaul and Britannia they talk of the Queen of Egypt as a living Venus and the Aphrodite of the Nile," Caesar said.

Caesar's voice and eyes had a compelling power, and I felt myself deeply stirred. "You know how to talk to please a woman, Caesar," I said.

"Well, I should, since I too am descended from a goddess," Caesar said with a laugh. "Venus began the Julian line, you know."

I laughed affectionately. "Well, if they have told you that since childhood, Caesar, I'm sure it's a nice thing to believe and no harm done."

Caesar's smile faded and a serious gravity came over his face as he moved closer to me on the couch.

"I have never touched a goddess before," Caesar said, raising a tentative hand over me.

"A goddess is also a woman, Caesar," I said warmly.

Holding my face carefully between his hands, as if it were a precious object, Caesar stared intently into my eyes. "Your eyes resemble the blue waters of the Rhine more than the brown waters of the Nile, Cleopatra."

I was kissed by Caesar, and I trembled under the influence of his kiss.

"I have never kissed a goddess before," he whispered, sighing.

"And I have never kissed a man before," I said in a trembly voice.

Caesar gave me a skeptical look, challenged by the remark, and then he determined to accept the challenge. Rising, he took my hand and, without a word, led me into my bedchamber.

Outside my windows the sea shimmered under the glow of moonlight. I sat on the edge of the huge bed and looked up at Caesar hovering over me.

Caesar tenderly touched my face and whispered, "Ah, so very beautiful!"

I lay back across the bed, smiling provocatively at Caesar. "You will have to undress me, Caesar, for I've never undressed myself before."

Slowly, tantalizingly, Caesar removed the snake bands from my arms and my gown of Isis, his hands exploring my body.

"Now you are naked as Venus fresh from the waves," Caesar said, his hands roving over me, "and as exquisite as all those centuries of careful breeding destined you to be. Ah, but I won't let your delicate body fool me, Cleopatra, for I know that inside you are hard as marble and as strong."

Caesar stood up and undressed, his toga falling to the floor, and then he climbed onto the bed beside me. I lay trembling and anxious as he gathered me into his arms, and my heart throbbed like a bird's as he caressed my vulnerable breasts.

Great Caesar, fifty-two years old, battle-hardened and scarred by life, proved that he was still the great lover. That I was a virgin surrendering herself to him surprised and touched him deeply. From the corners of my bedchamber, marble statues of Aphrodite and Venus looked on approvingly as I won Egypt back, not with an army but with my body, not on the battlefield, but in my bedchamber. On that fateful, magical night, instead of conquering Egypt for Rome, Caesar became my lover and returned my kingdom to me.

I, Cleopatra, conquered Caesar the Conqueror.

CHAPTER III

CAESAR WAS MY LOVER, and by morning everyone in the palace knew it. In one night I had completely won Caesar's heart, forming a coalition with him, and it was a tacit conclusion that he would restore me to my throne. All the nobles had been against me, supposing that they could control my brother more easily, and I had always been surrounded by implacable foes. Now a protector had arisen to support and defend me, the most powerful man in the world.

When we awoke, Caesar and I had breakfast served to us. We acted perfectly at ease with one another, as if we had known each other a long time instead of just a night, so great was our mutual sympathy and trust.

After we ate, Caesar went to my reception room to be with his officers to labor over official matters, and I went off to my bathing chamber. I sent for Charmion to join me, and she came, all wan and puffy-eyed.

"Is Caesar for or against you, Cleopatra?" Charmion asked anxiously.

"Caesar is my lover," I whispered in her ear.

"Oh, Cleopatra, I am jealous, yet I am happy!" she cried, embracing me.

Together we submerged ourselves in the bathing pool.

"Caesar has bedded with kings before," Charmion remarked, "but you must be his first Queen."

"So you know the story of Caesar and Nicomedes of Bithynia," I said.

"Doesn't the world?" Charmion asked. "King Ptolemy, urged on by Pothinos, has been playing the coy, seductive boy around Caesar these last weeks, but so far Caesar has been polite but indifferent to his charms. Bets were being taken around the palace between the nobles and guards whether Caesar would succumb to the seductive young King."

"If I had delayed in reaching Alexandria by a few days, perhaps things would not have worked out as they have."

"Ptolemy and his regents will receive this news with the greatest indignation!" Charmion cried gleefully.

"Yes, and their dismay is my pleasure," I said.

"So Caesar is ensnared by the spell of your beauty!" she continued happily.

"Like me," I said coolly, "Caesar is all head and little heart, more brain than body, as all must be who wish to be great."

"And Caesar the lover?" Charmion whispered.

"He was considerate and capable, but he did not fire my heart and body."

"Then you will not be falling in love with Caesar?" Charmion asked.

"Power and my destiny are more important and intoxicating to me than love," I answered. "Whether Caesar and I can love one another, I know not, but I know I need him to help me fulfill my destiny."

"What will your people say when they find out you are Caesar's mistress?"

"They will call me a whore," I replied, "but they have called me that for years, and until last night I was a virgin."

I learned that statues of me in the palace had been removed during my exile, and I ordered them brought up from the cellars and restored to their pedestals.

News of my return to Alexandria quickly spread to the people, and as the morning wore on, a huge snarling mob assembled in the square in front of the palace, their anger against me whipped up by agents in the pay of Pothinos.

Although Caesar had only a small force in Alexandria and was unable to enforce the superiority which he assumed, he immediately set to work to secure my restoration.

At high noon, dressed in a golden gown and wearing my regalia, I went to the Great Throne Room, accompanied by Apollodoros, Charmion, and an escort of household guards. The whole court had assembled in that immense room. As I passed the nobles on my way to the throne, they sank to their knees with forlorn expressions, not happy to see me back. I sat upon my throne as Caesar stood near me smiling encouragement.

My half-sister Princess Arsinoë, her pale, delicate face wearing an air of peevish assertion, sat in her chair of state with its gold lion claws to the right of the royal dais. Beside her in identical chairs sat her little brother, Ptolemy Philippos, and our aunt the Princess Aliki. Caesar's officers and soldiers lined the hall in strict attention.

Posidonius, an aged chamberlain, leaning on a staff, announced the King in his croaking voice. To the blast of trumpets, Ptolemy strode into the chamber with Pothinos, Theodotus, his companions, and an entourage of sycophants and soldiers.

King Ptolemy had obviously been awakened during the night and informed of my coming. He was dismayed at confronting me, and he could see at a glance, with Caesar standing beside my throne, that the rumors about us were true. His face was sulkily hostile, and his eyes flashed hatred at me. He had grown another inch in the four months of my exile. Almost sixteen, he was increasing in looks, stature, and arrogance, if not in composure and intellect. He had enjoyed being the sole sovereign, and he did not look upon my return with joy.

"Greetings, King Ptolemy," Caesar said.

Ptolemy stopped a few feet from the dais, glaring up at me. I stiffened on my throne, my eyes taking him in with a cold, calm contempt.

"Go sit on your throne, King Ptolemy," Pothinos urged.

293

"Yes, by all mean, King Ptolemy," Caesar said with a grand gesture.

King Ptolemy took the six steps to the dais, and without a glance my way, sat his equal golden throne.

Caesar faced us with a cold smile. "I have come to put a stop to this civil war between the two sovereigns of Egypt."

Pothinos, his enormous body swaying in a purple silk robe, approached the dais. "I would think, Caesar," he cried, his voice thick with snide innuendo, "that the attachment you have overnight formed with Cleopatra has wholly disqualified you to act impartially in this matter."

"Yes, and furthermore," Theodotus cried, waving a fat beringed hand at Caesar, "we the officers of state of King Ptolemy's government question your right to meddle in Egyptian affairs."

"Theodotus, teacher of kings," Caesar said imperiously, "I assure you that I am acting quite legally, for if you will read the testament of the late King Ptolemy the Twelfth, you will learn that Rome was made the executor of his will, and it is Rome's duty to see that its terms are carried out. The double throne was left jointly to Cleopatra and Ptolemy. Queen Cleopatra was unjustly expelled. As guardian of the kingdom, I insist that you lawfully restore Cleopatra to her rightful place."

"We run the affairs of Egypt and the people support our opposition to Cleopatra," Pothinos said harshly. He raised a hand to the raucous noise that came through the windows from the mob outside.

"I am here to reinstate Cleopatra," Caesar replied sternly. "I am determined with all the power at my command to see that King and Queen, brother and sister, declare themselves honorably reconciled."

King Ptolemy, unable to control himself any further, sprang to his feet, exploding in a childish tantrum. "I will not have Cleopatra at my side!" he screamed with rage. "I will not have it, my ministers will not have it, and my people will not have it!" He took the six steps from the throne in two leaps, and stormed out of the Throne Room, moving so quickly that he was gone by the time the nobles sank to their knees in obeisance.

"We must go attend our King!" Pothinos cried hoarsely. "You will excuse us." With a negligible bow, he scurried out, his gross body waddling with surprising speed considering his bulk. He was followed by the huffing and puffing, and equally fat, Theodotus.

Caesar came to my side, gazing after the two departing eunuchs calmly.

"My Lord Caesar," I cried, gripping the sleeve of his toga, "I'm sure they will be inciting the King to some foolish act."

Caesar nodded gravely. I rose from my throne as trumpeters blasted away. With Caesar, Charmion, and Apollodorus following me, I swiftly left the Throne Room as all the nobles sank to their knees. On reaching the Great Alabaster Hallway, I saw Ptolemy leave the portals of the palace. He stormed down the long flight of marble steps to the square to meet the mob, undoubtedly at the instigation of Pothinos and Theodotus.

"I am lost!" King Ptolemy shouted to the people. "My cause has been betrayed!" In a spectacular rage, he tore the uraeus from his head, threw it on the ground, and trampled on it. "My sister, my Queen, prostitutes herself to Caesar! Cleopatra is Caesar's whore! Caesar will depose me and make his whore sole sovereign! My people, I implore your help!"

Ptolemy's rhetoric was simple but effective, and his hysterical harangue kindled the wrath of the mob.

"You must get the King back inside the palace!" I told Caesar.

Caesar sent out a detachment of legionnaries to recapture Ptolemy. The soldiers, disciplined and determined, fought through the crowd, seized the King, and brought him, kicking and screaming, back into the palace.

"Don't think, Caesar, that you can get away with this!" Ptolemy shrieked. "My people will not take this treatment of their sacred sovereign lightly. You and your whore will be sorry for this outrage!"

My brother was right, for at this daring presumption, the tumult in the square increased. I trembled, knowing the fury of the Alexandrian mob, the mob which had forced my father twice to flee his kingdom.

"I will address the demonstrators to calm them down," Caesar decided.

I drew a tremulous breath, clutching his elbow with alarm.

Caesar smiled reassuringly. "I've faced many great armies, Cleopatra, and I have no fear of a bunch of screaming civilians."

Despite his assurance, I refused to allow Caesar to go out into the square, but instead led him up the staircase to the Balcony of Appearances, which is high enough so that missiles from the mob could not reach him. I waited inside, out of sight, while Caesar walked onto the balcony.

"Citizens of Alexandria!" Caesar declaimed in excellent Greek. "I do not pretend to judge between Queen Cleopatra and King Ptolemy as a superior, but only as a representative of Rome, assigned as guardian by the late King Ptolemy. My only wish is to settle this question equitably and to arrest the progress of this civil war. I therefore counsel you, good people, to disperse peacefully. Tomorrow I will consider the issue at hand and affect a settlement to the satisfaction of all."

This speech, made in a persuasive, eloquent voice, and in an imposing, dignified manner, had a calming effect and the mob dispersed.

King Ptolemy sulkily withdrew to his apartments with his councillors and companions, and Caesar and I retired to our chambers.

In the evening, while Caesar and I supped, I expressed the fear that my brother might send a message to Achillas ordering him to march with thirty thousand soldiers at Pelusium to Alexandria. Since Caesar had only three thousand men, I urged him to obtain reinforcements. He dispatched a messenger into Asia Minor to his trusty confederate, Mithridates of Pergamum, with orders that the legions under his command should march speedily to Alexandria.

While we ate and drank, my head buzzed with ideas.

"The people must be placated, Julius," I ventured. "Why don't you perform an act of bounty and give them back Cyprus?"

"Cyprus?" Caesar asked incredulously. "Cyprus belongs to Rome!"

"Ten years ago Cyprus was a piece of Ptolemaic property," I reminded him. "Cato annexed Cyprus and caused my Uncle Ptolemy to take poison, which offended national feelings. Tell the people you will restore Cyprus, and you will win their instant goodwill."

Caesar took a reflective sip of wine. "Rome will be angry if I give away imperial property without the sanction of the Senate."

"Hasn't the Senate just appointed you Dictator?" I retorted. "Must you consult the Senate before every move?" I watched while Caesar squirmed under these words. "Besides, you can pacify an angry Senate later. In the meantime, there are a million angry Alexandrians outside who must be appeased."

"You are a politically astute young lady," Caesar said with admiration. "I shall do as you suggest."

I smiled with pleasure. "You can tell the people that Princess Arsinoë and Prince Ptolemy Philippos will be sent to Cyprus to rule as joint sovereigns."

"What a splendid idea!" Caesar said.

I was pleased with the idea myself, for it would get Ptolemy, Arsinoë, and their scheming tutors out of my way.

Caesar and I retired early to our bedchamber to spend our second night together, in which Caesar, a tutor of vast experience, resumed his lessons in love to a willing pupil.

I was under no illusions, however. Caesar's dominant idea was to control Egypt by a skilled play upon my heart and body, but I also knew what without Caesar I was nothing and only with his consent could I live and reign.

An assembly was convened the following morning in the Great Throne Room with all the chamberlains of state, army officers, and nobles, so that Caesar might arbitrate the issues at stake. In high state my brother and I marched to our thrones. Near us in seats of honor sat Arsinoë, who at sixteen was ravishingly beautiful, Ptolemy Philippos who was thirteen, and my dear Aunt Aliki.

Caesar moved in front of the royal dais, carrying himself with careful dignity. Like me, he had a pleasing consciousness of his own good looks, presuming that all eyes were turned toward him.

The original will of my father's, which had been brought from the royal Alexandrian archives in a golden box, was presented to Caesar. He removed the scroll and gave it to Theodotus to read aloud.

"Officers of state and citizens of Alexandria!" Caesar announced when Theodotus had finished, "the provisions of this will are perfectly explicit, requiring that the sovereign power be settled between Cleopatra and Ptolemy. It recognizes Rome as ally of Egypt, and names the Roman government as executor of the will and guardians of the King and Queen. The reading of this document by Theodotus is in itself a decision of the question at hand. Therefore, I have a duty to see that Cleopatra shares the supreme power with her brother. Is there any voice to be raised to question my decision?"

Silence reigned in the immense hall as Caesar's penetrating gaze searched the sea of faces.

"The King and Queen must swear by the sacred will of their father," Caesar announced, "that they will reign according to its terms."

Posidonius brought the box to me first, and I placed my hand on it. In a strong, clear voice, I cried, "I, Cleopatra Philopator, by the holy gods, Serapis and Hathor, swear that I will reign beside my brother King

Ptolemy Dionysus and be obedient to the will of our father and to the guardianship of the Roman Republic."

Then Posidonius took the golden box to my brother, who scowled at it a long while before reluctantly putting a hand on it.

"I, King Ptolemy, do swear that—" He broke off irresolutely.

"That you will reign alongside your sister in peace, in love and trust," Caesar prompted.

Ptolemy glowered at Caesar, and in a strained voice repeated the words.

"So be it," Caesar said, and then faced the assemblage. "As the chief officer of the Roman Republic, I now present as a gift to Egypt a portion of the Roman Commonwealth, the island of Cyprus!"

A stunned murmur grew to shouts as the full impact of Caesar's announcement gripped those assembled.

Caesar lifted his hands for silence. "Furthermore, nobles and citizens, I deem it only fitting that Princess Arsinoë and Prince Ptolemy Philippos reign jointly as king and queen over that fair isle."

Shouts and acclamations rent the air. From my raised throne, I glanced at Arsinoë, seeing her pretty face radiant. She then turned to look at her conniving tutor, Ganymedes, who stood nearby. Suddenly her face darkened. She had thought it would be lovely to be queen of a rich island of pines, cedars, lemon groves, copper mines, and sparkling harbors, but in his gaze Ganymedes reminded her that they shared a higher ambition to reign over a larger realm. Arsinoë was my sister and a Ptolemy to her fingertips in her craving for power.

Anexandridas, an aged, venerable noble who had been one of my father's favorites, stepped forward and cried, "Great Caesar, Egypt is gratified at your decisions today, and by your generous gift from Rome!"

"There will be a series of festivals to commemorate the reestablishment of a good understanding between Queen Cleopatra and King Ptolemy," Caesar announced.

299

This decision also met with spirited approval.

The assembly was adjourned in high state, and my brother and I left the Great Throne Room. As we reached the great corridor, I turned to Ptolemy with a conciliatory smile.

"Dearest brother, I wish to share a loving cup with you," I said.

Ptolemy gave me a hostile look as Charmion dispatched a servant to bring a goblet of wine.

"How could you do this, Cleopatra?" Ptolemy whispered intently.

"Do what, brother dear?" I rejoined.

"Prostitute yourself to Caesar, to bed with a barbarian?" he cried incorrigibly. "They say you seduced Caesar by using a love potion."

"What I do, as always, I do for Egypt," I declared self-righteously. "A queen is not as other women, as a king is not as other men."

"You've become Caesar's slave and you want your people to follow suit," he pressed on wrathfully. "You know how the people hate the Romans. You became unpopular because of your Roman-loving ways. Do you think becoming Caesar's whore will help you win back the people's favor?"

"When I returned to Alexandria, Ptolemy, I heard that Pothinos was trying to push Caesar into your bed."

King Ptolemy forced a laugh. "Such a preposterous idea! Where did you get such a ridiculous notion?"

"It seems to be common gossip about court."

Lady Charmion came with a golden goblet of wine.

"Let us lay aside our differences, brother dear, and become reconciled," I cried. I took a sip of wine and gave the goblet to Ptolemy.

King Ptolemy took the goblet, whether in good faith or simply to quench his thirst, I know not, and drank heartily.

"Dearest brother," I said firmly, "we must set aside our hate or we will destroy each other and our dynasty. It is our fate to rule together and we must accept that. We have the protection of the master of the world.

Caesar has been good to us, for he restored Cyprus. If we rule together wisely, we can restore our empire to its former glory, but we must stop this infernal squabbling. Cast off the evil tutelage of your triumvirate."

"And listen only to you and your Roman paramour?" Ptolemy asked in a querulous voice. He dashed the loving cup to the floor. Turning his back on me, he swaggered down the corridor, followed by Pothinos, Theodotus, and the Companions of the King.

As Caesar came up to me, I remarked, "You see how irrational and unstable, foolish and unpredictable King Ptolemy is."

"Becoming a god-King so young has obviously affected him, but he will mature in time," Caesar said forbearingly.

"His head is too little to wear such a big crown," I cried.

Princess Arsinoë, Prince Ptolemy, and Aunt Aliki came up to me, and I kissed them all in turn.

"Dearest Arsinoë and Ptolemy," I said warmly, "I hope that you will reign in health and happiness over Cyprus."

"I shall go without question where my destiny and duty calls me, Cleopatra," Arsinoë said gravely.

"Cyprus, they say, is the most beautiful spot on earth," I said. "You are so beautiful, Arsinoë, it is appropriate that you should reign over the birthplace of Aphrodite." I turned to my young brother and smiled fondly. "Dearest Ptolemy, you have grown taller since I last saw you," I said.

Ptolemy Philippos made an attempt to say something, but a fit of stuttering attacked him, and his fair face crimsoned and contorted as he sputtered the same syllable repeatedly.

"Dear Ptolemy," I cried, coming to his rescue by interrupting him, "you will make a fine king for Cyprus."

His blue eyes blinked at me and he gulped painfully.

"My prayers to the gods have been answered, dearest niece," Aunt Aliki gushed. "The gods have returned you to Egypt."

"I owe it, not only to the gods, but to Caesar!" I smiled at Caesar, and he approached and made a few courteous remarks. I then kissed my kin, and promised Aunt Aliki I would send for her soon for a game of chess. I did not hold it against her that before going into exile she had refused me at her door.

With Caesar I returned to my apartments. Charmion deftly divested me of my robes and regalia, and I put on a simple shift of Indian silk. My opalescent rounded breasts showed through the diaphanous material, all the better to entice Caesar.

I settled on a couch facing Caesar, and we were served wine and food.

"For the most part, Julius," I said, "the people seemed satisfied with your decrees today. Ptolemy and I are ostensibly reconciled, but it is only a temporary armistice."

Caesar grunted. "Ptolemy was his usual sulky self, but Pothinos and Theodotus put on pleased faces."

"It was all an act!" I said fervently. "They are suppressing discontent, but they are my inveterate enemies, and my restoration could mean their downfall. They had hoped to rule Egypt for years to come and they now fear their days are numbered. They are now doubtless representing to all quarters that you design to depose Ptolemy and make me sole monarch. We must keep a careful eye on them and not forget for a moment that just a short time ago they struck down noble Pompey."

Caesar reflectively fingered Pompey's signet ring, which hung on a gold chain from his neck. "No, Cleopatra," he said soberly, "we won't forget."

"Even if they don't murder you, after you've sailed back to Rome, I will not be safe," I said. "They will be seeking to overthrow and murder me. Today I was restored, but my enemies are playing for time."

"Never fear, Cleopatra," Caesar said, "after winning the world, I do not plan to be murdered in Alexandria, and neither will you be. If this is a game to the death, I assure you we will be the winners."

302

Comforted by his words, and with a beckoning smile from him, I left my couch and went and sat beside him, laying my head on his shoulder.

"Oh, Caesar, in you I feel I have a friend and a protector, a man of noble and generous spirit, and of the highest station. If you stay by my side, in a week I will love you with all my heart!"

"In that case, Cleopatra, I will not hasten off. After ten years in primitive Gaul fighting barbarians, and those long months of campaigning in Thessaly, I want to settle down in tranquillity beside the Nile in a luxurious palace, held in thralldom by a dazzling enchantress who happens to be a queen."

"Do you really believe the coming months will be so tranquil?"

"Whatever happens, we will meet the future together," Caesar avowed.

Sitting up, I reached for a goblet and took a long drink to gain courage to broach a delicate subject.

"Tell me about your wife, the Lady Calpurnia," I said. "I am told she is a great lady of noble and impeccable character."

"Yes, Calpurnia is a perfect lady," Caesar affirmed stiffly. "For twelve years she has been my devoted wife, unostentatious, patient with all my faults. She has proved to be the best of my four wives."

"Yet she has not given you a son," I said.

"No, she has not," Caesar admitted in a voice filled with regret.

"She is of barren stock and has passed the age of birthing," I said.

Caesar gave an inaudible sigh and closed his eyes. I moved closer to him, my mouth pressing against his ear. "I can give you a son, Julius," I said in a soft, seductive voice. "I can give you a prince!"

"A prince," Caesar murmured wistfully.

"Any son of mine would be a prince," I went on in a mellifluous tone. "I can give you a son from a daughter of the Ptolemies, who for three centuries have been kings in Egypt, and before that for five centuries kings in Macedonia. I am the product of eight centuries and thirty generations of a direct line of kings!"

"Thirty generations of incestuous degenerates, you mean!" Caesar said with playful scorn. "Why, Ptolemy the First was no more than an upstart who planted himself in Egypt."

"The son of King Philip and half-brother to Alexander the Great!" I cried. "Besides, even god-kings must start somewhere."

"True, and despite all the madness in your family, I do not overlook the glorious achievements of the Ptolemies."

"The oldest dynasty in existence," I said with pride.

I pressed my lips on Caesar's mouth, kissing him tantalizingly. "Come, Julius, let us go to bed. It is almost the time of my monthly flowers, which I am told is the most propitious time to conceive. I gave you my virgin jewel, and now I long to give you another great gift, a son! It is the least I can do since you restored me to my throne."

"You are sparking emotions inside me which I had thought were long since chilled by the years," Caesar said in wonder.

I led Caesar to my bedchamber and we joined our bodies in erotic loveplay, in which I desperately hoped my womb would kindle from his seed. I prayed to conceive a son who would bind Caesar to me and who would become in time king of the world.

This was the third night that I had lain with Caesar, and I had come to know his habits. In the middle of the night he would arise from bed, plagued by a weakness in his kidneys, and pass water in the golden chamber pot that was kept under the bed. True enough, this happened again, and I stirred in my slumber as he did so.

I was startled by a sharp groan from Caesar, and I sat up, jerking myself fully awake. I saw Caesar clutch a bedpost, and then fall back, sprawling across the floor. He lay there helplessly, his body writhing spasmodically.

With a rush of horror, I realized a seizure of the sacred sickness had attacked him. I jumped naked from the bed and crouched beside him, deeply alarmed as I watched his body thrashing about. He was foaming at the mouth, and the veins were enlarged on his forehead and neck.

This was my first experience with an epileptic, but I knew that his mouth had to be stuffed to prevent his tongue from being chewed off with the uncontrollable clenching of his teeth. With my hands, I forced his jaws apart and stuffed the ends of a leopard coverlet into his mouth. I cradled his head on my lap, holding his face between my hands, as his body jerked under the force of the convulsions.

On the marble floor, in the middle of the night, Julius Caesar, the Dictator of Rome, Master of the World and my lover, lay the helpless victim of an epileptic fit, with all his physical control and mental reality severed.

After some minutes, which seemed a small eternity, the paroxysms tapered off and lost their force, his muscles ceased to twitch, the attack subsided, and his mental faculties returned. I pulled the ends of the coverlet from his mouth, and Caesar released a moaning sigh.

I leaned over and kissed his wet, feverish forehead. "Oh, my beloved Julius," I cried with emotion, "you have the sacred sickness Alexander had!"

Caesar was too weak to speak. A rush of tenderness for him possessed me, and I kissed his face. He lay on the floor, gasping, depleted of all energy. He was as weak as a small child, and it was some time before I was able to help him up onto the bed.

I poured a goblet of wine and held the rim to his mouth as he drank.

"The day will come," he whispered weakly, wine trickling down his chin, "when the sickness will befall me in front of my troops before a battle, or during a public ceremony before the people."

"Your soldiers and the people will know that the

sacred sickness is a malady of the gods!" I cried, impassioned. "A sign of your divinity!"

I took a drink from the goblet and put it aside. With a cloth I wiped the sweat and wine from his ravaged face. His body was shivering, and I pulled a cover of leopard skins up to our chins and snuggled close to give him warmth.

"I'm sorry, Cleopatra, that you saw me in that state," Caesar said.

"Nonsense, Julius," I scoffed gently. "You remind me more than ever of Great Alexander. You are my beloved, and there should be no shame or falseness between us, ever!"

Caesar, exhausted, soon slept in my arms. I lay awake, holding him, intense feelings burgeoning inside my heart.

With Caesar as my lover, my position at court drastically changed. All the powerful nobles had been in King Ptolemy's corner, and for three years I could not count my friends on one hand and at my expulsion I stood alone. Now with my restoration and Caesar in my bed, the personages of the court and city, thinking that I had a future after all, began making flagrant overtures toward me. They sent me letters and gifts, vowing friendship and begging audience. I accepted the gifts and distributed them among my ladies and guards, but postponed any meetings, for other affairs and Caesar took up my time.

It was wonderful to be back in my rightful place at court, with its color and pageantry, its music of flutes and trumpets, the array of the finest finery, and the whispering and intriguing of the nobles and priests. I grew in confidence, secure in my relationship with Caesar, who was charmed by my beauty, my wit, and my imperial pride.

Once again I was Queen, but I lived with the apprehension of assassination. Although Caesar scoffed at me, I took precautions to guard us against being poisoned or daggered to death, having our quarters surrounded by a strong contingent of soldiers. Ptolemy was equally cautious, and a thousand guards stood sentry in the corridors leading to his apartments.

In the hectic days following my restoration, I prepared a celebratory banquet to mark my so-called reconciliation with Ptolemy, a banquet on a lavish scale to impress Caesar with the magnificence of my court.

On the night of the banquet, I paid close attention to my dress, wearing my most beautiful golden gown encrusted with pearls and several pearl ropes around my neck. I made my entrance into the great hall after all the guests had been seated and the sight of my resplendent appearance elicited a chorus of gasps from the gathering.

The hall, large as a temple, was spread with two hundred gold couches and ebony tables laden with precious foods. The guests, consisting of Greek and Egyptian nobles and Roman army officers, were dressed in their richest raiment. Everyone had received wreaths of roses, and the air was filled with intoxicating incense.

Caesar stood as I walked up to the royal dais. "Royal Egypt is gloriously beautiful tonight," he cried.

"Greetings, my Lord Caesar," I said warmly.

"You have a fatal Grecian beauty," Caesar went on, sitting beside me, "a beauty reminiscent of Helen who laid Troy to ashes."

"I hope if I am to be remembered in history it will not be for causing the havoc wrought by Queen Helen," I cried.

"I have conquered King Vercingetorix of Gaul and Pompey at Pharsalia," Caesar said, "but surely the conquest of Egypt's Queen will go down in history as my greatest victory."

A laugh of pleasure rippled out of me, and then my eyes veered to my brother who sat on a couch to my right. He greeted me with a sullen nod. Pothinos, Theodotus, and the king's young companions were grouped around this couch, while Arsinoë, Ganymedes, and Aunt Aliki shared the couch to my left.

Servants moved about gracefully, carrying golden plates heaped with food, and dancing girls rushed out to the sound of music and began dancing in the open space on the onyx flooring in the center of the hall.

I noticed that Apollodorus was absent. Since our return to Egypt, he had been jealous of my relationship with Caesar, and I thought it was because of a childish whim that he was absenting himself this night.

"Do you like this little room, Julius?" I asked.

Caesar's eyes scanned the chamber, observing the fretted ceilings encrusted with precious stones, the gold-plated rafters, the walls of marble, and the pillars of porphyry. "My villa on the Tiber could fit into this room," he observed with a trace of envy in his voice. He took a sip of wine. "I notice you have a passion for pearls, Cleopatra."

"I have been told Caesar admires pearls," I remarked. "Is it true that the Lady Servilia, the mother of Brutus whom many say is your son, loved pearls, and the real reason you conquered Britannia was because you heard pearls were to be found there in great abundance?"

Caesar gave a throaty laugh. "Quite often, Cleopatra, legends die hard!"

The dancing girls ran off, and Diodorus did a solo dance about the death of Socrates. Most of the revellers were too engrossed with each other and in gorging themselves to watch, which was their loss, for Diodorus danced this creation only once. I vividly recall the dance, which perfectly dramatized the piteous torment of Socrates, the touching moment of drinking the hemlock, and the dance of death which was executed with stirring poignancy.

When Diodorus finished, there was only slight applause from the insensitive guests. Diodorus, rising from the onyx floor, came to the royal dais and knelt at my feet.

"This is your greatest dance, Diodorus," I cried, hanging a wreath around his neck.

"Alas, my Queen," he said, "I can no longer fly into the air like Icarus, so I did a dance as an old man in which such feats would not be necessary."

"Diodorus, age has robbed you of technical feats," I said, "but your artistry grows richer with the years."

"The fame of your Icarus is known throughout the world," Caesar remarked, "and I regret never having seen it."

"I cannot perform the same physical deeds I did ten years ago, Great Caesar, but then what man can?" Diodorus asked.

Caesar frowned, not appreciating this remark, and Diodorus, after kissing my hand, left us.

A variety of entertainment followed, acrobats and singers, and the servants were kept busy carrying trays of food and wines.

I had Sosigenes brought to the royal dais.

"My Lord Sosigenes," Caesar cried, "your calendar brings the solar and lunar forces into harmony. I may use it for the Roman world, and we will owe you a debt."

"The credit belongs to our Queen," Sosigenes said. "The calendar was prepared at her instigation."

I waved a dismissive hand. "I requested a revised calendar, Sosigenes, but the work was yours."

A little later I invited Pothinos and Theodotus to sit on chairs near our divan.

"Theodotus," Caesar said, addressing him pleasantly, "word has it that you are the most learned man in Egypt."

"Caesar has a gracious tongue," Theodotus said, his tiny pig eyes gleaming as he smiled with pleasure.

"Yes, Theodotus, Egypt is fortunate to have your wisdom at her service," I cried, lying in my teeth. "And you, too, Pothinos! I'm overjoyed that we are all joined in friendship to benefit Egypt!"

Pothinos and Theodotus smiled insincerely, disbelieving my every word.

"I am wondering where the waters of the Nile come from," Caesar remarked curiously.

"Ah, mankind has always been puzzled by this question," Theodotus cried.

"Do the waters come from mountain snows melting in Ethiopia?" Caesar asked.

"Such an idea is absurd, Great Caesar," Pothinos said, but then remembered to smile. "The Nile floods come because the gods have ordained them for the benefit of the Two Lands."

"It is a secret kept by gods and nature, Great Caesar," I remarked.

"Did Alexander the Great ponder this question during his stay in Egypt?" Caesar inquired.

Theodotus smiled and waved a fat hand in my direction. "This is a question for our beloved Queen, noble Caesar, for I doubt if there is any scholar living who knows more about her ancient relative."

"Indeed Alexander did," I explained. "He sent explorers up the Nile into Ethiopia, but when the heat became too hot, his soldiers rebelled and the party turned back. Alexander was annoyed that the secret of the Nile should defy him. Five centuries ago Cymbases the Mad sailed up the Nile in a similar quest, but he also met with failure and the secret of the Nile eluded him. To this day the source of the Nile remains a mystery.

"My Sacred Queen," Caesar said, "perhaps we could journey up the Nile to discover the source of this great river. Where Alexander and Cymbases failed, could not Caesar and Cleopatra succeed?"

A wave of emotion swam through me, and I was profoundly moved by this notion which Caesar so eloquently put forth. Caesar was linking himself with me, and I detected the envy in the eyes of Pothinos and Theodotus.

At midnight Caesar and I left the banquet. In my apartments my ladies relieved me of all my jewels and clothes, and then I went to my bedchamber where Caesar was already abed waiting for me.

"It was clever of you to call Pothinos and Theodotus over for a pleasant talk," Caesar said. "We must remember they are highly thought of by people, and it is to our advantage that we be reconciled with them."

"Yes, Julius, but never forget that leopards do not change their spots. Circumstances compel them to be with us for the moment, but behind our backs they are plotting to betray us."

"Cleopatra, your suspicions bode ill for the future," Caesar scoffed. "You must work with them for the common cause of Egypt. But let us not talk any further of these dreary affairs."

Just as Caesar gathered me into his arms, there came a pounding at the door with Charmion calling for me.

"What does that little harlot want?" Caesar asked irascibly.

"I will see, Julius," I said, extricating myself from his arms. I slipped on a robe and went and opened the door.

"Cleopatra, please forgive me!" Charmion cried with distress. "Apollodorus begs to have a few words with you."

I glanced back at the bed. "I'll return soon, Julius," I cried, and then went with Charmion into my reception room.

"Apollodorus, why weren't you at the banquet?" I demanded. "Your absence was noted and I take umbrage that you did not honor me with your presence."

"Cleopatra, I saw fit to serve my Queen in other ways," Apollodorus said solemnly, sinking to one knee.

"Pray rise and explain yourself," I commanded.

Apollodorus stood and came close to me, his eyes burning. "Following your instructions, Cleopatra, I have had my men guarding all the palace exits to keep a watch over anyone leaving who might be a messenger going off to Achillas at Pelusium."

"Yes, yes?" I cried impatiently, my curiosity rising.

"Tonight I thought with the excitement of the banquet the soldiers on guard would be lax, resentful at not being able to carouse, and they would be passing the wineskin around. I suspected our enemies might take advantage of this situation, and I myself was extra alert. While the banquet was in full swing, I went to the Gate of the Sun and found the soldiers half-drunk.

311

I recognized Demaratus, one of the favorite sodomizers of Pothinos, mounted on a swift Arabian charger. The soldiers were about to let him pass when I detained him. I took him to my quarters for questioning. He told me the unlikely tale that he was going to ride to the western end of the city to visit a brothel. I had him searched and discovered a letter sealed in a leather tube inserted in his rectum."

"Leave it to you to find it there, Apollodorus!" I cried with an admiring laugh. "Who wrote this letter?"

Apollodorus handed me the rolled papyrus. "It is from Pothinos to Achillas, O Queen," he cried, smiling triumphantly.

I unrolled the letter with trembling hands, my heart pounding, and the words danced before my eyes.

"Salutations, Achillas," Pothinos wrote. "We are awaiting you at the head of your army to arrive at Alexandria in three days' time to make a surprise attack on the palace to liberate King Ptolemy and Egypt from the clutches of Caesar and Cleopatra. The bright star which brought Caesar to the pinnacle of the world does not dazzle us. Pompey's ghost is proof of our power. Caesar, like Pompey, is merely a man. Great Romans like Cato and Brutus will be grateful to us for having rid Rome of these despots and dictators. Caesar, without his army, can easily be eliminated, along with his whore, Cleopatra. We in the palace will do our part. We have a foolproof plan that will be executed to make an end to this pair as soon as you arrive with your army. Hasten, beloved friend, in the name of the gods and in accordance with our vows of friendship. Farewell, Pothinos."

I was breathing heavily, yet a cold calm befell me. I threw my arms around Apollodorus. "Oh, my valorous, stalwart Apollodorus! Once again you have saved my life, and you are my most faithful friend."

Clutching the letter in my hand, I went into the bedchamber. I found Caesar on the bed with the coverlets thrown off him, and it was evident the call of Venus

312

was strong upon him. Wordlessly I handed him the letter.

Grumbling, Caesar sat up to read the letter, and I watched while the urge of Venus waned in him. Muttering a curse, he rose from bed, and we went into the reception room.

"Apollodorus," Caesar said stiffly, "your service deserves our praise."

Since Pothinos had his apartment in King Ptolemy's wing and was heavily protected by the King's Macedonian Guards, it would be impossible to arrest him there during the night, so in the morning the King and he were summoned to a meeting in the Great Throne Room.

I was already sitting my throne when Ptolemy and Pothinos entered. The King, in a peevish, sleepy-eyed mood, mounted his throne. A few chamberlains and nobles drifted in, although most of them were still sleeping off the food and drink from the banquet the night before. Caesar's soldiers stood stiffly on duty.

"Where is Theodotus?" I demanded of Pothinos.

Pothinos, grinning fulsomely, approached the dais. "Lord Theodotus overdrank last night, O Queen, and begs to be dismissed."

"What matter calls us here so early, sister?" Ptolemy demanded.

"An affair of grave import, King Ptolemy," Caesar cried. He took the letter and handed it to Pothinos. "I ask your indulgence to read this letter aloud to your King, Lord Pothinos."

Pothinos smiled obsequiously at Caesar and took the letter in his hands. Because of his myopia, he held the scroll close to his face, his pig eyes squinting. "Salutations," he read aloud, but then stopped, his face paling with recognition, and he let out a startled groan.

"Read the letter, Pothinos!" I cried imperiously.

"This is a forgery!" Pothinos protested, as the letter fluttered to lie upon the gem-inlaid mosaic of the Ptolemaic phoenix. "I never wrote this letter," he cried,

313

his fat jowls palpitating. "It's a forgery, a clever forgery, I must say, but I swear by the gods it's a forgery nonetheless."

"It is your characters, Pothinos," I cried. "This letter is proof of your guilt. This is no false charge such as you invented against Protarchus. With your own hand you have signed your death warrant."

"Let me see this letter," King Ptolemy said.

Rufio picked up the letter and passed it to the King.

"If this letter is true," King Ptolemy cried cleverly, "it was certainly written without my cognizance!"

I sensed my brother was lying. Perhaps I had misjudged him and he could, if events pressured him, display the Ptolemaic precocity for which our house had long been famed.

An uncontrollable wave of hysteria possessed Pothinos. "No, I am innocent, O Queen," he shrieked. "Innocent!"

"You stand condemned by your own hand for plotting to murder your Queen and me," Caesar cried. "For your treachery you must be punished. Shall I cut off the hand that composed this letter?"

Pothinos let out a piercing scream and fell to his knees. "Oh, mercy, Great Caesar, mercy!"

"For such an offense, Caesar," I said, "more than just the amputation of a hand will be warranted."

Pothinos flung himself against the steps leading to the thrones, his hands reaching up toward me. "Oh, mercy, Divine Majesty, show me mercy!"

"We cannot cut off his manhood," Caesar said sarcastically, "since that has already been done."

There were a few sniggers from the soldiers at this remark.

"I think it is only just and fitting that Pothinos have cut off what my Lord Protarchus and Pompey had cut off!" I cried emphatically.

Pothinos screamed, his hands clutching his neck. He rolled down the steps and lay on the floor, his gross body quivering as if he were seized with the falling sickness. He then crawled up the steps to King Ptolemy.

My brother sat, clutching the arms of his throne, a gleam of sweat on his upper lip.

"Oh, my King, intercede on my behalf!" Pothinos sobbed, clutching the King's ankles. "Do not let them harm your foster father!"

My brother sat his throne, still as a statue, mastering his emotions.

"King Ptolemy," I spoke up, "just six months ago I went to Pothinos begging on my knees for the life of my beloved Protarchus. Will you not now raise your voice on behalf of your foster father, Pothinos?"

Ptolemy lifted his gaze from the pathetic heap at his feet and stared sightlessly ahead as if he had pulled a veil over his eyes and a curtain over his emotions.

"Please, my King, save me!" Pothinos screeched, his hands, sparkling with rings, pulling at the King's legs.

Finally Ptolemy's face contorted with contempt, and he moved to kick Pothinos away. "Farewell, Pothinos," he cried with annoyance. "Stand up and prepare to meet your fate. Do not shame your King so, I beg you, show a little dignity!"

At Caesar's signal, Apollodorus and a few soldiers marched to the dais and pulled Pothinos from the King and dragged him away.

"Judgment in Egypt is mine, to be decreed as I see fit!" I declared with majesty. "Strike off this man's head without delay."

"Shall the execution be public as was the one for Lord Protarchus, O Queen?" Apollodorus asked, his words barely audible over the screams of Pothinos.

I reflected a moment, thinking that for years Pothinos had been the great minister of state, the real ruler of Egypt, king in all but name, and evil as he was, he was popular with the people. A public execution would only inflame the inflammable populace.

"Perform the deed in a palace courtyard," I decided.

Pothinos, sobbing hysterically, was held up by several soldiers. I motioned for them to wait a moment.

Pothinos hung limp, unable to look at me, tears streaming down his fat cheeks.

"Pothinos, remember my beloved mother Queen Cleopatra Selene and how bravely she met her fate which you designed for her sixteen years ago? And do you not recall the solemn dignity with which Protarchus went to his execution which you also masterminded? Let their courage in the face of death be an example for you."

Apollodorus saluted me, and the soldiers dragged the struggling, screaming fat eunuch from the Great Throne Room.

Without a word, King Ptolemy rose from his throne and hurried out of the chamber to the blast of trumpets, followed by his companions.

"Theodotus is to be found and placed under arrest!" I ordered.

Within an hour, Pothinos met his doom. With Charmion beside me, I watched from an upper window down on the courtyard where the execution was performed. Pothinos had been given a sedative to calm his nerves, but still he kicked and writhed and screamed, as he was dragged to the block. The thought of stepping into eternal life terrified him. The courtyard was crowded with officials and soldiers, all eager to witness the decapitation, and I could only surmise how the people outside would react when the news reached them.

The black-clad executioner who came up from the dungeons to perform the task was the same man who had decapitated Protarchus. At that time I had bribed him to do a swift, neat job on Protarchus, but no one tickled his palm now. Pothinos, squealing like a fat pig, was butchered. Three strokes of the ax were required to sever the gross, fatty neck. As the executioner held the dripping head aloft in the sun, I thought I saw the mouth still moving in protest and the eyelids fluttering in shock and disbelief.

A tight, tense feeling inside me relaxed, replaced by a buoyant rush of exultant triumph.

Pothinos, my mortal enemy since childhood, who had long plotted to bring me down, met his ignoble doom, and my beloved mother and Protarchus were avenged. I had dreamed of someday crushing him like a fat crawling worm beneath my sandal, and so I had, and he was consigned to the House of Hades deep within the bowls of the earth.

The wily Theodotus could not be found, for somehow he had heard news of events afoot and during the night escaped from the palace. I sent soldiers searching the city for Theodotus, but only learned later that he had made his escape in disguise and become a vagabond. For the death of Theodotus I would have to wait six long years, during which he wandered a poor fugitive through Asia Minor. At last he was recognized by Marcus Brutus, who crucified him ignominiously for having given counsel to murder Pompey.

After Pothinos was beheaded, I felt the greatest threat to my power had been removed. A sense of security settled over me, even though I was aware that Achillas was marching with thirty thousand soldiers to Alexandria against Caesar and me, and we had only three thousand men by which to defend ourselves.

Caesar was by my side and together we faced the future fearlessly.

CHAPTER IV

"YOU HAVE WON THE WORLD, beloved Julius, and hold it in your hands," I said one night as we lay abed, "but do you realize you risk it all by being in this bed with me?"

"A risk well worth taking, Cleopatra," Caesar gallantly replied.

"I pray to the gods your relationship with me does not bring you dishonor, or worse yet, death," I cried.

"It is not the Nile I plan to die beside, but the Tiber," Caesar said. "I have no choice but to stay here and fight it out, since the winter west winds prevent my leaving by ship. Besides, I'm confident that my life is safeguarded by four royal hostages."

The danger of Achillas marching with thirty thousand men against us only enhanced our feelings for one another during those anxious days and tender nights.

Messengers were sent off in galleys to Cyprus and Rhodes where Roman troops were stationed, ordering the authorities there to forward their troops with the utmost speed to Egypt. Mithridates of Pergamum was already on the march through Syria with the Thirty-First Legion. My little army was waiting at Mount Cassius, and I sent a message to Lucullus and Zamblichus to wait until Mithridates joined up with them.

King Ptolemy, now that he was deprived of Pothinos and Theodotus, matured overnight. He no longer burst into childish tantrums, and had a strong hold on his emotions. One day he approached Caesar and me with a shrewd suggestion.

"Please understand, Great Caesar and Beloved Sister," he cried cleverly, "I had nothing to do with that dastardly order issued by Pothinos demanding that Achillas march on Alexandria with my royal host. I didn't even know about it!"

"I'm sure you didn't, my boy," Caesar said courteously.

"If Great Caesar is in agreement," Ptolemy said cunningly, "I would like a new order sent in my name, forbidding Achillas to approach the city and ordering him to return with his army to Pelusium."

"Ah, that might prove to be an excellent maneuver!" Caesar said.

I thought possibly Arsinoë's tutor, Ganymedes, had put Ptolemy up to this scheme, although it could have been his own idea. I did not think it would be effective, but Caesar thought it worth a try. I had Diosorides, a distinguished courtier who had served my father, sent to deliver this counter command.

Diosorides rode eastward, encountering Achillas encamped some two days' ride from Alexandria. Instead of listening to the King's message, Achillas had Diosorides slain, suspecting that whatever commands Diosorides brought originated not from Ptolemy's own free hand, but had been dictated by Caesar or me.

Achillas and his army continued their progress toward Alexandria.

The whole palace was occupied with the tidings of the advance of the army and by the preparations required to meet the impending contest. The death of Pothinos had alarmed a great many people in the palace who were hoping that Achillas might prevail. The Alexandrians, already stirred up by the execution of Pothinos, were dangerously edgy.

Caesar and I held power in a delicate balance. We would be hopelessly outnumbered, for our three thousand men were too small an army against the overwhelming force which was advancing to assail us. With his customary bravery, boldness, and genius, Caesar made the best arrangements to encounter the crisis, and established his command post at the Theater of Dionysus, not far from the palace.

The first measure to be adopted was the strengthening of our position of defense against Achillas until reinforcements arrived. We withdrew all our soldiers from other parts of the city and established them in the palace complex. I assisted Caesar by suggesting defense measures, going over maps and pointing out parts of the metropolis where attacks were to be expected. The palace complex, comprising the palace, the university, the gymnasium, the theater, the arsenals and granaries, became a citadel, and all the streets leading to these points were barricaded and the gates fortified. Prodigious military engines, made to throw heavy missiles, were set up within our lines.

In the middle of November, as these frantic preparations were in progress, I realized that I was with child. At first I thought my time of the flowers was late because of the emotional excitement I had been under, but then I realized my female rite had always come with perfect regularity even during times of great upheavals.

"I am with child, Julius," I said simply one night as we climbed into bed.

Caesar was silent, and I could see that he was calculating. "If so," he said, "you conceived during one of our first nights together."

"Yes, it was by the divine will of the gods," I said. "In the summer of next year, beloved Julius, I will bear you a son, a prince, a divine child!"

"We shall see," Caesar said. "Who else knows?"

"No one, Julius," I cried. "Only the gods and you."

"Tell no one," Caesar said, and then with great tenderness he gathered me into his arms.

Now that I was pregnant, our fortunes and honor were inextricably intertwined.

A few days later Achillas and his infantry column of twenty-eight thousand soldiers and two thousand cavalry reached the outskirts of Alexandria. As the army advanced into parts of the city from which we had

321

withdrawn, the populace rose up, declaring themselves for Achillas. Not only were Caesar and I confronted by the formidable Egyptian army, but by the ferocious Alexandrian mob. We were penned into the palace and subjected to a siege.

The Alexandrian War, as Caesar called it in his *Commentaries*, began.

Since the enemy did not possess siege equipment, they were unable to do us much damage, other than to shoot flaming arrows over the walls. They had inferior rams with which they tried to beat down our gates, but we eliminated this danger by throwing hot oil from overhead battlements. Caesar's soldiers were used to battling in the open field, but they adapted themselves remarkably to city fighting.

I strongly suspected that Ganymedes had been involved in the conspiracy to murder Caesar and me which Pothinos had mentioned in that letter to Achillas. Now that Pothinos was dead, Ganymedes appeared alarmed. Several courtiers and soldiers were questioned in an effort to get to the bottom of the conspiracy, but no one would admit to anything, not even in the torture chambers. It was apparent, however, that Ganymedes realized the palace was no longer a safe place for him, and he longed to escape.

Apollodorus had long been the chief of my bodyguards and First Friend, and to reward him for his services to me in exile, for having smuggled me in the carpet into Caesar's presence, and for his discovering the conspiracy of Pothinos, I gave him noble status and created him a lord of the kingdom. This caused quite a stir among the effete hereditary lords, who were mostly of Macedonian descent and whose forebears had come to Alexandria with Ptolemy the First. These lords considered Apollodorous, the son of a Greek Sicilian merchant, an upstart. Apollodorus was proud of his title, which he richly deserved, for he owed it to his own deeds and not to those of his ancestors.

Caesar was impressed by Lord Apollodorus and entrusted him with the responsibility to see that none of the courtiers escaped from the palace to go over to Achillas. Since Apollodorus had detained Demaratus, the agent who had attempted to go to Achillas with that message from Pothinos, Caesar thought that he was eminently qualified in the discharge of this duty.

Suspecting that Arsinoë and Ganymedes were resolving to make their escape to Achillas, I told Apollodorus to make sure that if they should attempt to flee, his soldiers were to look the other way.

Just as I expected, a few days after Achillas had encompassed the city with his army, Arsinoë and Ganymedes accomplished a hazardous escape from the palace during the dead of night.

In the morning, while Caesar and I were taking our breakfast, Appollodorus was admitted to us with this news.

"How dreadful!" I cried with feigned shock and surprise. "Arsinoë, that little bitch, that subtle serpent!"

"And King Ptolemy?" Caesar demanded sharply.

"The King is in his apartments, Imperator!" Apollodorus cried.

"I entrusted you with the responsibility of seeing that no one escape," Caesar said reproachfully, "and now you have allowed a princess to get away!"

"Please forgive me, Great Caesar," Apollodorus said abjectly.

"How did this happen?" Caesar asked impatiently.

"I don't know, Great Caesar," Apollodorus said meekly.

"They did not sprout wings like Icarus and fly over the walls, did they?" Caesar asked mordantly.

Apollodorus silently hung his head in shame.

Caesar trembled with rage. "You have our leave to go, *Lord* Apollodorus!" he cried, giving a caustic intonation to the title I had just bestowed upon my friend.

Apollodorus saluted stiffly and walked to the door.

"See that King Ptolemy is kept under surveillance and he is not to get away to join his sister," Caesar called after him.

I could sense that Caesar had no inkling that

Apollodorus and I had connived in allowing my sister and her tutor to get away.

"You still have three other royal hostages, Julius," I cried.

"Arsinoë, that impudent minx, is so much like you, Cleopatra," Caesar said with mixed bitterness and admiration. "At seventeen she is pulsing with that insatiable ambition which seems to form the character of every child of the Lagidae, and I am sure growing up in this palace with its intrigues has taught her a few lessons. I made her Queen of Cyprus out of the goodness of my heart, but she wasn't satisfied with that. Here inside the palace she was insignificant, but outside at the head of an army she may become Queen of Egypt."

"Caesar will never let that happen," I cried.

"Let us hope so for your sake," Caesar said.

"And for the sake of our son I carry in my womb!"

Events were proceeding exactly as I anticipated them.

That very afternoon Princess Arsinoë and Ganymedes met Achillas and the army and were received with acclamation. Ganymedes had been in contact with all the merchants and money-lenders of the city, who offered to support Arsinoë if she did away with taxes once she became Queen. With this agreement concluded, the army officers decided that, as all other members of the royal family were held captive by a foreign general and were incapable of exercising the royal power freely, the crown devolved upon Princess Arsinoë. My half-sister accordingly was proclaimed by the army Queen Arsinoë the Fourth.

Riding a white mare, she reviewed her troops.

"Long live Queen Arsinoë!" the soldiers and the people cheered.

Everything was now prepared for a desperate contest for the throne between Arsinoë with Ganymedes as her minister and Achillas as her general and me with Caesar as my general and minister.

King Ptolemy, remaining in the palace as Caesar's prisoner-of-state, was confused by the intricacies of events and scarcely knew which way to turn now that

Pothinos and Theodotus were gone. He was closeted in his apartments with his silly, rowdy companions, a dozen boys who all put together did not make up one good brain between them.

"When I came to Egypt in pursuit of Pompey," Caesar told me, "I took only three thousand soldiers. I had no idea that I would end up embroiled in a war; but here I am in a military undertaking against an enemy ten times my strength, fighting for my very life in the streets of Alexandria."

"There is no need to fear the Egyptian army, Julius," I said. "It is a mongrel horde composed of slaves and criminals, refugees and runaways, and is not to be matched against your hardened legions. Who is Achillas against the greatest general since Hannibal and Alexander? Besides, aren't you accustomed to extricating yourself from complicated perils? Did not Pompey's forces greatly outnumber yours at Pharsalia? As for me, I have no fear of the final result of this contest."

"Come to think of it," Caesar said smugly, "in ten years of campaigning in Gaul, I took eight hundred towns by storm, subdued three hundred states, killed a million men, and made another million slaves. I certainly have no fear of the Alexandrian mob or this mongrel army."

During these days of the war, I stimulated Caesar's spirit and energy, and he took special pride in encountering the difficulties which beset us. I believe my pregnancy was a source of inspiration for him. I watched him cope masterfully with each new obstacle. He had passed his prime, but I rekindled his youth and made him feel young again. My heart was full of boundless admiration for the champion who had restored and defended me. I confided everything to Caesar, he understood me, and I felt free to be perfectly honest with him. My wildest dreams and ambitions never seemed to surprise or shock him.

I was in love with Caesar, and the emotions I felt heightened my natural charms. The native force of my character was softened by the love I felt and the child I carried in my womb, and Caesar was indubitably fascinated with me.

Life in the besieged palace during the war was an exciting time. Caesar and I dined and slept together every night, and shared all the troubles and tribulations of the war side by side. Several times it seemed we would not survive, but our spirits never flagged. We were committed to one another, Caesar and I, to the death.

As the days passed, the enemy kept launching full-scale attacks on the palace. Our soldiers, amid savage fighting, held off these attacks, but it soon became apparent that the warfare at sea would be far more serious than any fighting in the city.

One evening in early December, after Caesar and I had supped, we sat on the terrace overlooking the Royal Harbor. Gazing across this harbor, I could see the fortress situated at the head of the Heptastadion, the marble mole a mile long which leads out to the island of Pharos and which separates the Royal Harbor from the Harbor of the Happy Return. Achillas commanded the entrance to the Heptastadion mole. Pharos island and the fortress at the end of the mole was still in possession of Egyptian authorities who held it for Achillas. On the island itself, besides the lighthouse and the fortress, there was a small town inhabited largely by fishermen and sailors, with a long avenue of marble villas where wealthy Alexandrians lived. In the Harbor of the Happy Return, on the west side of the Heptastadion mole, lay a fleet of seventy-two Egyptian vessels, twice the size of Caesar's fleet in the Royal Harbor.

"If Achillas takes possession of the Egyptian fleet," Caesar said, "and if his adherents continue to command Pharos, he will be master of all approaches to the city and to the sea. We will be cut off from reinforcements and supplies from abroad."

"We must protect ourselves from such a danger, Julius," I said.

"Exactly, my Queen," Julius said with a nod.

The following twilight, with Apollodorus and

Charmion, I watched from the terrace as Caesar led a small expedition by ship around the mole to the west harbor to take possession of the Egyptian fleet.

I was suddenly startled to see a ship in the harbor go up in flames, then another ship, followed by yet another, as Caesar had his men hurl resin-dipped torches at the sails and decks, setting the ships ablaze. Within the hour all seventy-two ships of the fleet were burning, lighting up the harbors with a brilliance which outshone the lighthouse fire above.

Egyptian sailors and soldiers were swimming for their lives, burning ships began capsizing and sinking, and the night air was filled with smoke, screams, and the acrid smell of scorched flesh.

One of the burning ships, driven by a sudden wind that had sprung up, sailed close to the dockside, and sparks flew and set fire to a building on the waterfront. The fire spread and many buildings fell prey to the flames.

This disaster relieved the pressure against us, for Achillas and his soldiers formed a brigade to fight the fire. While they were fighting the fire, Caesar and his troops easily took the small fort on Pharos, expelling the Egyptian soldiers and installing a Roman garrison. Pharos island and the fortress now came into our command.

The Roman soldiers went running in a rampage and ransacked the row of luxurious villas on the island. Highborn ladies were raped. Since these were the residences of Alexandrian nobles who had always been my enemies, I cannot say I was terribly grieved at this outrage of plunder and rapine.

I witnessed these exploits from my terrace with mixed feelings, buoyed with admiration for the valor my Roman adherents displayed, but disquieted at the burning of Egyptian ships.

It was midnight when Caesar returned to the palace, begrimed and exhausted.

"Why did you burn the fleet?" I exploded nervously.

"I had no choice, sweet Cleopatra," Caesar ex-

327

plained. "I realized we do not have the men to hold the fleet, and better the ships be destroyed than to fall into the hands of our enemies."

"Seventy-two ships!" I cried in despair.

"It was a dreadful necessity," Caesar said sternly.

I stifled my feelings of despair and misgivings, but when Caesar and I were served a late supper, I had no appetite.

Suddenly, Apollodorus hurried into the reception room. "Queen Cleopatra," he cried excitedly, "the flames from the dockside have spread to the great library."

My heart stopped and I cried out in anguish. I rushed to one of my chambers which commands a view of the library, and I was horrified to see one side of the building engulfed by giant, curling, yellow flames.

I turned with blazing reproach as Caesar came up behind me. "How dare you!" I cried in a rage of grief. "The greatest library in the world! Ships can be rebuilt, but we have priceless volumes there that cannot be replaced. The original manuscripts of Euripides and Aristotle! The loss of one book is a greater tragedy than the loss of a thousand men. Are you such a barbarian, Caesar, that you burn books? It is books that will make you immortal, for otherwise you'll be forgotten like your lowest soldier!"

"Caesar is no barbarian!" he cried with annoyance. "I've scribbled a few books myself and have the highest reverence for them. Tonight the scales have tipped in our balance; we are winning the war, and you stand there weeping hysterically about some old scrolls. I'll send off to the libraries at Ephesus, Athens, and Antioch, if you like, and bring you back shiploads of manuscripts to replace whatever is lost."

At the force of my rage and feeling a little guilty, Caesar hurried away.

I wanted to flee to the library to help put out the blaze, but I could not cross enemy lines. I was deeply unsettled and did not sleep all that night, staying by the window and watching the ghastly spectacle of the holocaust. All through the night, Achillas to his credit had his soldiers working as a brigade, and by dawn the fire was put out.

As I was to learn later, a fourth of the books in the library was lost that tragic night, over one hundred thousand volumes. Among the priceless manuscripts destroyed were the original of Ptolemy the First's memoirs and his biography of his brother, Alexander the Great, the Old Testament as translated by Ptolemy the Second, a copy of the Odyssey which had been in Aristotle's personal library, several original scripts by Euripides in his own hand, and Egyptian books with the Pyramid calculations.

Perhaps I was unreasonable, but I held Caesar responsible for this arson and I could barely speak civilly to him for days.

The destruction of the Egyptian fleet in the west harbor and the taking of Pharos did have one positive result, for Achillas met his doom.

From the time of Arsinoë's arrival in the camp there had been a power struggle between Achillas and Ganymedes, and two parties had formed in the army, each declaring either for Achillas or for Ganymedes. When the fleet was burned, Arsinoë furiously charged Achillas with having been, by his neglect, the cause of the loss. That very afternoon Achillas, who just weeks before had helped to murder Pompey, was condemned and beheaded.

"I now appoint Lord Ganymedes to be my minister of state and the commander-in-chief of my army," the self-styled Queen Arsinoë proclaimed.

When this news reached me, I was elated, for Achillas, although not a Caesar, was an experienced general, but Ganymedes had no military experience.

Arsinoë and Ganymedes, astride white horses, galloped through the boulevards of Alexandria and were cheered by the people.

Much to my surprise, Ganymedes soon showed ability to deploy power. He brought up his troops on every side of the walls of the royal citadel and made preparations for an assault. He constructed engines for battering down the walls, and established forges to manufacture darts and spears. He built towers supported on huge wheels with the design of filling them with armed men when ready to attack the palace. The rich were taxed for war funds, and the poor were pressed into service as artisans and laborers. Ganymedes sent messengers into the interior of Egypt, summoning citizens to arms and calling for money and aid.

Heralds warned the people that the independence of Egypt was in danger. The Romans, the heralds cried, had extended their conquests over all the civilized world, and were now interfering in Egyptian affairs, which would end in the subjugation of Egypt unless the people chased out "the foreign dictator and his harlot Cleopatra."

Banners were carried by the heralds and soldiers proclaiming, "Romans Go Home!" and "Egypt for the Egyptians!"

One late afternoon Charmion and I went to my bathing chamber.

"I'm surprised at the vigorous measures Ganymedes has been taking," she commented as we were disrobed. "I didn't think the perfumed catamite had it in him."

"I suspect Arsinoë should be credited for many of these propositions," I said. "She is not my sister for nothing. Do not worry, though, Charmion. Caesar and I have possession of Pharos and the harbor and are carrying the day!"

"One thing is certain," Charmion said, "you have cast an irresistible spell over Caesar." She reflected a moment. "Or perhaps he is in love with Egypt."

"But I am Egypt!" I exclaimed.

I submerged myself under the water, and then brought my head sharply up, tasting salt on my lips.

"By all the gods!" I cried, licking the water off my hand.

"What is it, my Queen?" Charmion asked.

"This is sea water!" I cried balefully.

I hurried out of the bath, and with a robe thrown

around me, I rushed back to my reception room and sent for Apollodorus.

"The water aqueducts have been tainted by sea water," I cried. "Investigate the matter, Apollodorus."

"Yes, O Queen," Apollodorus cried, saluting and going off.

I was filled with fear, suspecting what had happened before investigation verified my fears. There are vast cisterns underground which convey fresh water from Lake Mareotis to the palace, where it is raised by hydraulic engines for use in the palace and to feed the numerous fountains in the gardens and city squares. Arsinoë and Ganymedes, knowing this, had conceived the design of digging a canal to turn the sea water into the palace aqueducts.

Within an hour, Apollodorous returned to confirm my suspicions. We went to Caesar's study, finding him surrounded by his court of young handsome Roman officers and a harried Rufio.

"My Lord Caesar," Rufio cried, "the soldiers are panic-stricken about the poisoned water supply. What will they drink?"

"We will all live on wine, my good Rufio!" I cried with bravado.

"The soldiers are afraid they will perish without fresh water," Rufio went on, ignoring me. "We consider it hopeless to hold out, and your officers urge you to evacuate the city and embark on our galleys and proceed safely to sea."

My heart stopped at the thought of being deserted by Caesar.

"I came to Alexandria in solemn pomp," Caesar retorted grandly, "and I will leave in the like manner. I will not be ousted from Egypt until I have fulfilled my duties here. The soldiers, instead of grumbling, will go to work and dig for wells of fresh water."

I breathed a sigh of relief and my heart lightened.

The soldiers, under the direction of various officers, dug wells in every part of the palace complex. Apollodorus was the first to hit upon a pool of water at the depth of about forty feet. In the succeeding days new wells were dug, yielding pure, abundant water.

A week after this obstacle was overcome, a small sloop came into the harbor bringing the intelligence that a group of transports carrying the Thirty-Seventh Legion had anchored off the coast and were unable to come up to the city harbor because of the contrary easterly winds which always prevailed during the winter. This windbound fleet had sent forward the sloop, propelled by oars, to acquaint Caesar of their dire situation.

Caesar decided personally to supervise the operation of bringing this fleet into the harbor. He went on board one of his galleys, and ordering a few ships to follow, sailed secretly away in the dead of night.

I waited anxiously during Caesar's absence, aware as I was that my hero was exposing himself to great danger.

Somehow, Arsinoë got word of this expedition and hastily collected all the vessels which could be obtained from the various branches of the Nile and anchored them in the Harbor of the Happy Return. At the same time, she launched another full-scale attack upon the palace. Missiles came crashing over the walls, and the gates were rammed so vigorously that I thought they would not hold, but Caesar had firmly reinforced these defenses.

Caesar arrived at the anchorage place of the fleet, and taking the transports in tow, brought them up to the harbor. On his return, he found the formidable navy which Arsinoë had assembled to dispute his passage. A severe sea battle ensued, in which his brave admiral Euphranor perished. Caesar was victorious, and the navy which my sister had hastily collected was destroyed, her vessels burned, sunk and captured.

Caesar triumphantly brought the transports into the Great Harbor, docking them at the moorings beside the palace. He was welcomed by the cheers of his soldiers, and still more warmly by me. I was in a highly emotional state, having watched the sea battle from my terrace, and as I clasped Caesar in my arms I wept with joy and relief.

I was saddened that Euphranor had died, and I realized that it could just as easily have been Caesar to perish. I knew that if Caesar were dead I would have no chance to live and rule as I dreamed. It was times like this that I was acutely aware of how deeply I loved Caesar.

The arrival of the Thirty-Seventh Legion greatly improved our circumstances, and Arsinoë and Ganymedes realized they must possess the harbor if they intended to keep Caesar and me from receiving further reinforcements. They sent along the coast and ordered every ship in all the ports to be sent to Alexandria. In a few weeks, to my amazement, they assembled over twenty ships, which occupied the Harbor of the Happy Return. It was obvious that they intended to launch an attack on the Royal Harbor where our ships lay at anchor.

Although we occupied Pharos island, the Heptastadion, the mile-long marble mole, was still in the hands of my sister. Caesar went forth himself to take an active part in capturing the mole, sailing out from the palace dockside and landing with a troop of soldiers on the pier.

From my terrace I watched this operation, full of excitement at the dangers Caesar was facing. Commanding his men, he proceeded along the mole to the point where it joins the fortress on the mainland which was in my sister's hands and started to seal it off by erecting a barricade.

While this work was in progress, one of my sister's ships sailed from the Harbor of the Happy Return and landed a contingent of soldiers on the mole, attacking Caesar from behind. His warships, which had been accompanying the operation, started to sail away. This caused great alarm among Caesar's men, who believed they were being deserted. They abandoned their unfinished fortification and boarded any available boat, or dived off the mole into the sea in a mad rush to get to their ships.

It was a scene of dreadful confusion and din. Caesar exhorted his men not to give up, but when he saw that

333

they were all giving way, withdrew to his own vessel. He was followed by a crowd of men who began forcing their way on board, making it impossible to steer the ship or to push off from the mole. Caesar then jumped overboard and swam out to another ship farther off in the Great Harbor. Eventually this ship began sinking under the weight of soldiers climbing aboard, so once again he dived into the sea and swam for his life. Wearing armor, he swam two hundred yards until he reached another ship, which I thought was a remarkable feat of stamina.

Caesar returned to the palace, drenching wet and with seaweed matted in his sparse gray hair.

"I left my Imperator's purple cloak on the mole," he said wearily.

"A trophy for my sister!" I replied.

We laughed, but this was an ignominious defeat. We lost four hundred men, and the mole was still in the hands of the enemy.

I learned during a brief cessation of hostilities that my sister was having her problems. The people and the army, judging the virtues of their leaders solely by the criterion of success, had become discontented.

About this time we received a message that Mithridates and his army were nearing Pelusium. Within a week they would reach Alexandria and we would crush all resistance; but, in the meantime, we had to stall for time.

"In the moment of Roman victory, Julius," I pointed out, "if King Ptolemy is still under your protection, you will be honor-bound to see that he retains the throne jointly with me, and I will be right back where I started. For four years I tried to reign beside Ptolemy, but I now realize that is hopeless. He does not have the intelligence or inspiration to be a great monarch, and I do! We must accept the fact that he is a nuisance and he must be gotten rid of!"

"What do you propose we do, Cleopatra?" Caesar asked.

"The people are tired of Arsinoë and Ganymedes, and they're clamoring for King Ptolemy," I said. "Send them word that you are willing to release the king into their hands so that he can negotiate a peace. Of course, once at the head of the army, he will be sure to renew hostilities. In that case, it will be more honorable for Caesar to fight against a King than a usurping Queen and her eunuch."

"We shall broach the idea to the King," Caesar decided.

Ptolemy was sent for and he came into our reception room, leaving his companions and guards waiting in the anteroom. I had not seen my brother for two months, and he appeared wary, taut, and troubled.

"Beloved sister and Great Caesar, it is good to see you!" Ptolemy cried with a diffident smile.

"Dearest brother," I said warmly, kissing his cheek.

Caesar embraced the King. "How have you fared these last weeks, Ptolemy?"

"I have been preoccupied with Latin studies," Ptolemy said. "Someday, Caesar, I hope to converse with you in your native tongue."

This remark pleased Caesar, but it was difficult for me to imagine my brother unrolling a Latin scroll.

The three of us settled on divans heaped with cushions.

"Would you like some wine and dates, Ptolemy?" I asked pleasantly.

"Oh, Cleopatra, I have just stuffed myself to the gills and couldn't take a thing," he cried nervously, fearing poison.

"Ptolemy, the Egyptian army wishes you to serve them," Caesar remarked.

A gleam of fear appeared in my brother's blue eyes.

"We need your help, my boy," Caesar said. "We are in a stalemate. Your name carries weight with the people, and I am entrusting you with the grave duty of bringing peace to Egypt."

"Oh, please, do not send me away, Great Caesar!" Ptolemy protested. "I feel the strongest attachment to you, and I prefer to remain under your benevolent protection."

"We are hoping for a negotiated solution which only you can achieve," Caesar said urgently.

"Yes, dearest brother," I cried, "you must bring the people to their senses and secure a settlement and a restoration of order."

"You are only sixteen and this is a great undertaking for one so young," Caesar said, "but sometimes fate forces a king to perform enormous tasks beyond his experience and years. The gods will help you rise to the occasion, never fear."

"Caesar and I have tremendous faith in you, Ptolemy," I said sweetly, "and we know that you will be able to promote peace to our kingdom."

King Ptolemy nodded, trembling, knowing he had no choice. "If you insist, Great Caesar, with the help of the gods I will try."

"Then it is settled," Caesar said. "You will leave the palace in the morning."

During the night, the King must have had misgivings, for in the morning when Caesar and I went to the great corridor to bid him farewell, he appeared distraught and torn. Part of him longed to escape, yet part of him longed to remain. Perhaps he had heard reports about the reinforcements on the way to us, and realized that once they arrived he would be defeated and meet death, or be forced to flee the country as he had once obliged me to do.

"Great Imperator!" Ptolemy cried, weeping, flinging his arms around Caesar. "I don't want to go!"

"King Ptolemy, your people know of your coming and are waiting for you," Caesar said firmly. "It is your duty to build a lasting friendship between Egypt and Rome. If you succeed, you will have great honor before the gods."

The king's companions, all eager to be gone, exhorted him to leave, and Ptolemy reluctantly released Caesar from his embrace.

"Brother dear," I cried, "if you are sincere in your sentiments, this separation will not be a lasting one."

"Farewell, Cleopatra," King Ptolemy cried coldly.

336

The great gold-plated doors of the palace were opened, and the companions, grabbing hold of their king, rushed him down the steps into the center courtyard and out through the gates into the square, where they were eagerly received by the people.

I sighed with relief at seeing my brother, who had plotted to kill me and had driven me into exile, leave the palace, and I prayed to the gods I would never see him again.

King Ptolemy was received by the army with a riotous welcome. My brother, for all his defective education and his lack of discipline, was beloved by the people and the troops. He was after all a man and their young King, and they wanted to fight under his banner. Instead of promoting peace, Ptolemy began making preparations for a vigorous prosecution of the war.

On my twenty-second birthday, I learned that Mithridates of Pergamum had arrived at Pelusium with the Thirty-First Legion, which had been swelled by a Jewish contingent of soldiers commanded by Antipater, and my little army I had left behind beside Mount Cassius. These combined forces had smashed through the fortress at Pelusium and were marching on the road to Alexandria.

At the same time, this news also reached the enemy camp, and a large part of the Egyptian army under Ptolemy and Ganymedes left Alexandria and marched eastward to meet the invaders. A small force remained behind to hold the city under the command of Arsinoë.

During the night, Caesar slipped away with a small force, leaving the remainder of his army to man the defenses and to protect me. He moved across the country so quickly that he joined Mithridates before the forces of King Ptolemy encountered them.

When the two armies met, King Ptolemy, to his credit, showed some of the old Macedonian spirit of his forebears and fought bravely, but his army was routed and he was obliged to flee the field. With several of the Companions of the King, he galloped to the Nile and in a crowded small boat pushed off from the shore.

337

The boat, overloaded with fugitives, sank and my brother, not knowing how to swim and weighted down by gold armor, drowned, as did all his young friends and Ganymedes.

Caesar sent a fast courier to the palace with the message of his victory and the death of my brother.

After two long months, the Alexandrian War came to an end.

Caesar collected his forces beyond Lake Mareotis, and two days after the battle the gates of the city were opened to him and he entered Alexandria triumphantly at the head of his legions. He was crowned with laurel wreaths and rode in a chariot. Mithridates, Antipater, Zamblichus, and Lucullus rode in chariots behind him, followed by their marching soldiers.

In great majestic pomp Caesar led the way down the Canopic Boulevard. The Alexandrians, having laid down their arms, came out into the streets, begging for mercy and forgiveness, kneeling and holding up effigies of their deities as a token of submission.

I stood in my robe of Isis at the top of the long flight of marble stairs leading up from the great square in front of the palace, the uraeus crown on my forehead and the cross of eternity in my hand. Charmion and Appollodorus stood behind me, and arranged on the marble stairs were the courtiers and nobles of the court, who had overnight become my fast friends and adherents.

Caesar's chariot rattled into the square and he alighted.

A great silence prevailed in the city as all the citizens crowding the boulevards watched us.

I stood motionless as a statue of Isis at the top of the marble stairs. Caesar slowly ascended the steps toward me. Silence reigned in the entire city. Caesar stopped on the step below where I stood.

I held out toward him the looped cross of Isis.

Caesar bowed his laurel-wreathed head and kissed my hand in a gesture of forgiveness for the sins of my people.

338

A great roaring cheer went up from the crowds so loud it could have been heard in Thebes.

An exultant pride swelled my bosom. I wanted to fling my arms around Caesar, but I could not forget my dignity in public.

"My conquering hero, my savior," I whispered solemnly, all the while keeping my goddess-like rigidity, "I shall reward you with a son, this I promise you in the name of all the gods!"

Caesar gave me a thin-lipped smile, but his silence was touching and full of eloquence.

The intoxication of victory and power and hope pulsed through my veins like potent wine, as I took the smiling Caesar by the hand and led him into my palace as my people cheered.

CHAPTER V

ON THAT DAY OF TRIUMPH my elation was tinged with a certain sadness, for this was the first time my beloved Alexandria had fallen to a foreign foe. It was a complex situation, for I regarded the Alexandrian War, not as a Roman campaign against Egypt, so much as an Egypto-Roman suppression of an Alexandrian insurrection, and I considered it my victory as well as Caesar's.

My sister Princess Arsinoë, after having been a queen of sorts for two months, was found hiding in a building in the Jewish quarter. She was brought to the palace and confined to a chamber and kept under scrupulous supervision. There would be no more escapes for her. It was Caesar's design to take Arsinoë with him to Rome to walk in chains in his triumphal march. As distasteful as it was for me to see a princess of the Lagidae humiliated in such a fashion, I could not gainsay Caesar's command.

"It is a fitting death for King Ptolemy to have drowned in the Nile," I pointed out to Caesar, "for such a death bestows upon its victims the blessings of Osiris. However, Ptolemy's body must be recovered. I want Ptolemy proved positively dead so there won't be any divine resurrections to haunt me later, or imposters to lead rebellions against me. The man-child I carry inside my womb, Julius—your son!—will be King of Egypt one day, and I do not want anything to endanger his rights."

Caesar saw the logic of my reasoning and sent a group of soldiers to have the body dragged up out of the muddy base of the Nile.

The body of my brother, who had resembled a statue of a young Greek contestant in the Olympics, was bloated beyond recognition by the Nile water. The embalmers, with their ancient arts, worked the corpse into a familiar form, mummified it and wrapped it with linens, and then the gold armor was reattached. I had the corpse placed upon a catafalque in front of the palace for all the Alexandrians to see, to erase all doubts that their King was no longer among the living.

A funeral of some pomp was given Ptolemy, for he had been after all my half-brother, fellow-monarch, and fellow-deity. The burial was performed under the strict guard of Roman legions to keep down the emotions of the people, and I even permitted Arsinoë to attend the service in the Sema, where she wept copious tears in an hysterical display of grief.

Just before the body was to be consigned to the sarcophagus, Caesar ordered the gold armor removed so that he might carry it as a trophy in his triumph. I was shocked at this heartless action, but I did not contradict Caesar's whim.

Winter had ended along with the war, and spring was in the air. The seas were calm again and ships arrived daily, bringing dispatches from Rome urging Caesar to annex Egypt. In the case of my father, the leading Romans had preferred to take huge bribes rather than the drastic step of annexation. With this in mind, I gave Caesar the remainder of the money my father owed and, in addition, settled a fabulous fortune upon him. He had his soldiers to pay, and there would be more fighting in the future, for Pompey's sons were preparing to continue the struggle in Spain.

"I reject the idea of annexing Egypt," Caesar wrote to the Senate, "because Queen Cleopatra has been my ally all through the war, and I will not jettison her now."

Caesar also realized that if he made Egypt a Roman province, a strong governor might use the wealth of the country to effect a rebellion and become his rival.

"There is no proconsul whom you will be able to trust

342

to govern Egypt, Julius, except me!" I stressed to him.

My guardian gods had been looking after my welfare. My rivals were gone and now I was a reigning sovereign in Egypt like the mighty pharaohs of ancient days.

It was my wish to rule Egypt as an exclusive monarch. There have been more than two hundred and seventy monarchs who have worn the double crown since Menes the First of the First Dynasty of the Archaic Period of the Old Kingdom, of which four have been female sovereigns who reigned without a male associate. I wanted to be the fifth.

I have always been deeply fascinated by these four queens: Queen Meryt-Nit of the First Dynasty, Queen Khentkawes of the Fourth Dynasty of the Pyramid Period, Queen Sebekneferu of the Twelfth Dynasty of the Middle Kingdom, and Queen Hatshepsüt of the Eighteenth Dynasty of the New Kingdom.

One evening soon after the war had ended, while Caesar and I supped, I told him the stories of these four queens to show him that it was not unprecedented for a queen to rule Egypt alone.

I emphasized the remarkable story of Hatshepsüt, the daughter of Thutmose the First. She married her brother Thutmose the Second, and when he died they had only two daughters. There was an illegitimate son, Thutmose, by a concubine, and it was arranged that this bastard boy should marry one of the princesses and take the throne as Thutmose the Third. Until he came of age, however, Hatshepsüt, his aunt and mother-in-law, was to rule as regent.

"This did not sit well with Hatshepsüt," I explained. "So she told the people that the gods had transformed her into a man. She put on the blue beard, girded her waist with the lion's tail, was crowned Pharaoh, and even took a wife as queen-consort. She was accepted as a man, ruled for twenty years, had a glorious reign, and is known as one of our four greatest monarchs."

"Hatshepsüt sounds like a woman after your own heart, Cleopatra," Caesar said with a smile, refilling my goblet.

343

I took another draught of wine. "Perhaps I can tell the people I have become a man, change my name to Ptolemy, put on the blue beard, become Ptolemy the Fourteenth, and take Charmion to be my queen."

Caesar guffawed with amusement. "I can just see your obstreperous Alexandrians swallowing that!"

"I am clothed with godhead!" I exclaimed. "Who would gainsay me?"

"The million citizens of Alexandria!" Caesar cried. "My little Queen, I admire your audacity in all things, but this would be going too far. The wine has gone to your head. What worked for Hatshepsüt fifteen centuries ago would not be feasible today. These are civilized times, and the people are not so ignorant and gullible. Besides, you make such a lovely woman, so why do you want to be a man?"

"Because if I were a man, I could be Alexander the Great!"

"Yes, and we would be meeting on the battlefield instead of in the bedchamber," Caesar cried.

"Oh, I wouldn't be so sure of that!" I replied.

Caesar had no retort for this fillip.

My wish to be an exclusive monarch was not to be fulfilled, however. A contingent of nobles and city fathers came forth and pointed out to Caesar and me that, according to the laws of Egypt, a male co-monarch was needed, and that my half-brother Ptolemy Philippos would have to be elevated to my side.

Having just gotten rid of one troublesome brother, I did not relish being tied to another, but I had no choice but to acquiesce. The leading nobles were still antagonistic toward me. My brother at thirteen was too young to share in the exercise of royal power, he did not possess a strong intelligence, and I felt he would not oppose me as my other brother had. Besides, I was rather fond of this feeble, sensitive sibling.

"I don't want to be k-k-k-k-k-k-k—" Ptolemy Philippos stuttered, unable even to say the word, let alone be one.

"It is your duty and destiny, dearest brother, for you

344

are the last prince of the blood royal and you must become the good god Dionysus-Osiris for your people," I said, gently touching his pale, trembling face. "We will share the sacred burden together."

A simple coronation stripped of all the complex pageantry was held in the Great Throne Room. I thought that after the costs and tragic circumstances of the late war it would be unseemly to have an elaborate ceremoney. My brother, who was frail, did not have the strength to endure a long ritual and was grateful for this. He was swiftly robed, consecrated with the holy oil, and crowned. The coronation oath had been abbreviated for him, but still he stumbled over the words. It was a pathetic sight and everyone breathed a sigh of relief when, after much prompting from the High Priest and struggling and stammering, he got through it and became Ptolemy the Fourteenth.

I gave my brother's tutor, Mardian, the titles of foster father and the King's Regent and a seat on my council. I had long admired Mardian for his intelligence and temperance. He had a small, elegant body and a handsome face. His beardless eunuch's skin and creamy complexion were the envy of many women about court. His huge brown eyes possessed a compelling power, and in spite of his mincing gait, one could sense that if he had not been deprived of his manhood by the scalpel at the onset of puberty, he would have developed into a man who could have had his way with many a lady.

"Royal Queen," Mardian said after I had conferred his new titles on him, "may I suggest that there be coins minted with King Ptolemy's profile stamped on them?"

I gave him a penetrating look. "That will not be necessary as yet, my Lord Mardian," I replied crisply.

Mardian inclined his head. "As your Sacred Radiance wishes."

In the days that followed, I subtly indicated to Mardian that if he wished to enjoy further favors from me, he should do my bidding. Mardian, clever and ambitious, adopted all my policies. He was my brother's foster father, but he was my servant first. He never made another suggestion to me, but simply carried out my wishes, and became one of my dearest friends.

The war had violently affected my capital, but now that it was over, the commercial pursuits of Alexandria resumed and trading with the world began anew. As I entered into the peaceful possession of my power, I began to use the royal revenues, which poured in abundantly upon me, to enter upon a career of accomplishing all my ambitions and dreams.

My beloved Alexandria bore many scars from the war, and I set about repairing the damages. The barricades were cleared from the streets and the wreckage along the harbors removed. The broken streets were mended, smashed buildings rebuilt, and the floating charred ship masts and sails and bloated bodies were raised from the two harbors. My capital was speedily restored to its former beauty, and once again my lively people filled the streets.

The loss of one hundred thousand manuscripts in the library fire was the most heartbreaking part of the war for me. I wept for my dead people, but I also shed bitter tears for those lost books. I sent away to libraries at Antioch and Athens to have copies made of some of the missing volumes, but the collection of original manuscripts could not be replaced.

"Antony writes that my presence in Rome is urgently required," Caesar told me, after the war ended.

"Oh, please, Julius, linger until I give birth to our son," I urged. "Pompey was a great favorite in Rome and there will be resentment against you. You should allow that resentment to abate before returning, and in the meantime, Antony can hold Rome for you."

"Antony is my right hand," Caesar said. "He has the audacity of a charging bull and about as much subtlety. He is genial and unable to resist any temptation. He isn't satisfied unless he makes love to three women and a boy every day and gets drunk while he's at it." Caesar expelled a long sigh. "But perhaps he will be able to hold order in my name with Dolabella's help."

"Just five more months, Julius, until I give birth," I pleaded.

"I would dearly like to see our child born," Caesar said wistfully.

"Our son!" I amended with emphasis.

"How can you be so sure, Cleopatra?"

"I just know, Julius," I said with a serene smile.

We heard from Rome that Antony went about the streets in a litter drawn by a pair of tame lions, eating grapes with his mistress, the notorious actress Cytheris. The plebeians rejoiced at the sight of such vulgar display. The Lady Fulvia, Antony's formidable wife, was not so amused, and jealous of Cytheris, she took Dolabella for her lover. Antony, outraged, fought a public duel with Dolabella, although neither of them drew blood. Since Antony and Dolabella were the leaders of Caesar's party in Rome, their scandalous behavior caused Caesar anxiety.

A celebratory and conciliatory banquet was held in my palace in early February, which all the prominent nobles and citizens attended. On the royal dais there were two large divans, one which Caesar and I occupied, and another where the newly crowned boy King sat with Mardian and Aunt Aliki. Just below the royal dais, on couches of honor, sat the military commanders who had played a part in our victory—Mithridates of Pergamum, Antipater, Lucullus, and the Arab princeling Zamblichus, who had fallen madly in love with Charmion. Although she had no interest in Zamblichus, Charmion flirted outrageously with him, fanning the fires of his ardor recklessly, which disturbed the Lady Daphne. I found all this rather amusing.

Although the food was excellent and the entertainment superlative, the nobles were subdued, for they had been my avowed enemies and were having a difficult time adjusting to my success. These nobles for the most part were of Macedonian descent, proud of their fairness and blue eyes and barbarian accents, and belonged to the Pan Hellenic party at court which detested everything Roman. While they came to the banquet and lounged indolently on couches, eating and drinking everything in sight, they looked not at Caesar and me but smiled winningly in the direction of the new King.

For this banquet I wore a loose-fitting and flowing gown, ungirdled, for I was four months pregnant. I could no longer conceal the secret from my ladies.

At last I issued official word to my people that a divine seed had kindled inside me. Since I am a goddess-Queen I made much of the fact that the father Caesar was a descendant of Venus and the reincarnation of Jupiter-Amon who had come to visit the goddess of Egypt, just as in the days of antiquity when the gods had fathered offspring on earth to further their divine designs. In the villages of Egypt, I was regarded with profound reverence, and the Egyptians accepted the news of my divine pregnancy with grave awe.

In Alexandria, however, it was a different matter. Poets, their minds still harboring the lies of Pothinos and Theodotus, fashioned vilifying verses about me and pasted them on public buildings. I recall one poem which went:

> Egypt now belongs to Caesar,
> And how did this come to pass?
> He burned our Great Library,
> Drowned our young King,
> And copulated with our Queen, alas!

I have always had a sense of humor and the gift of self-mockery, and I thought some of these verses clever, no matter how lame their meter or derogatory to my character. Caesar, however, took himself with deadly seriousness. He used his scathing wit as a pathway to disparage others, but this was not a two-way boulevard with him.

Caesar was incurring censure in Rome also for having turned aside from his duties as Dictator to embroil himself in the quarrels of a remote kingdom. Despite

348

requests that he return home, he continued to linger by my side.

If I had not become pregnant, I knew Caesar would have left Egypt when the Alexandrian war ended, after having annexed the kingdom as a client-state; but he did not now want the Ptolemaic dynasty to be destroyed if his son were to be its heir. During the months of my approaching motherhood, he was concerned and affectionate with me. His feeling for me might be called love, if indeed Caesar was capable of such an emotion, cynic that he was. Or perhaps, like me, he could love only power and glory.

A month before the summer solstice, Caesar and I decided to make a pleasure progress up the Nile. The voyage was planned as a matter of policy and ritual. Because of the famine the previous year, I wanted to pacify my people by a goodwill tour, which would also fortify my Roman alliance. My people would become acquainted with my lover, the great Master of Rome, who was their friend. I also wanted Caesar to see the wonders of my kingdom so he would have visible verification of the wealth which as my lover and ally he would have at his service.

Thalameyos, the royal state barge, was prepared for the journey. This splendid ship, of enormous size such as no pharaoh ever possessed, contains colonnaded courts, stately saloons and shrines dedicated to the gods. The floors are all mosaic, the royal bedchamber has walls with a frieze of gold-leafed scenes from Homer, and the decks have sheltered awnings and exotic plants.

"It's a floating palace!" Caesar exclaimed in amazement.

Leaving Mardian and Lord Kallimachos in Alexandria as regents, and bidding my brother to continue his studies so that one day he should not stand in awe of my intellectual superiority, I set off on my journey. Half of Caesar's legions stayed behind at the capital under the command of Rufio, while the rest, numbering twenty thousand soldiers, followed the royal barge in a fleet of four hundred ships. Caesar was prudent about the safety of our lives and the life of our unborn child, and thought it best that such a force accompany us.

The voyage was conducted with great pomp, music, and feasting. Dancing girls and actors came along to entertain us in the evenings. Never had Caesar known such luxury, and as austere as he liked the world to believe he was, he savored every comfort. After the rigors of the Alexandrian War, the battle of Pharsalia, and ten years spent in Gaul, he was entitled to a few pleasures.

The royal cruise travelled into the nearest branch of the Nile and sailed southward. The barge, propelled by the steady rowing of a hundred Nubian slaves, carried us swiftly upriver, leading the train of accompanying vessels. This made a spectacular parade along the legendary river, gliding between miles of flat fields with growing papyrus. Peasants came rushing to the banks to wave at us and pay homage. After a few days we reached an area where the vegetation was scarce, with vast stretches of sand gleaming under the sun.

Caesar and I sat under deck awnings, and fanned by slaves, watched the land drift by, seeing farmers at their ploughs and camels resting under palm trees. I recall the browsing cattle and donkeys grazing, herdsmen with goats, workers on riverbanks at water wheels and irrigation ditches, women carrying pails of water, and fishermen in the marshes. Wind tumbled the poppy fields and bent the marsh reeds. We passed little villages, sometimes just a cluster of huts, where my people toiled, loved, and died. We stopped at as many towns along the Nile as possible, meeting with the rulers of the various provinces, and we toured the ancient temples and made offerings to the gods.

"Alexandria is a modern city, and so Greek that it might be Athens," Caesar commented, "but this is truly the land of the pharaohs."

Litters carried us under heavy guard from the royal barge to the temples, where people always gathered, murmuring their adoration and falling flat on their faces at the sight of me, their god-begotten Queen who stood

350

next to the sun, the stars, and the immortal gods. Caesar was impressed with the reverence my Egyptians gave me, which was in stark contrast to the begrudging obeisance paid me by the Alexandrians.

On these temple visits I wore my white robe of Isis, and on my head the golden horns supporting the disk of the sun, wrought in gold, which rested on my vulture cap, whose blue wings covered my ears to shut off all earthly sounds.

Caesar, my companion-consort, wore his laurel wreath, and in the Ptolemaic fashion, a garland of flowers around his neck. He was recognized as a god, which greatly flattered his vanity.

Venerable High Priests, leaning on staffs carved with hieroglyphics, greeted us at the temple portals.

"Hail, Lady of the Two Lands, Our Motherloving Savioress, welcome!" And then with a bow toward Caesar, "Hail, Jupiter-Amon, Beloved of Isis!"

"Hail, my Lord High Priest!" I would declaim. "I come bearing our child Horus in my womb."

I would enter the vast temples and approach the great altars, bearing lotuses in my hands as an offering. I would say a prayer of purity. In my advancing motherhood I could not stretch out flat on the floor in reverence, so knelt humbly on my knees and stretched out my arms.

"Hail, Beloved Osiris, Lord of the Dead and the Living!" I would cry out. "I beg blessings for my child."

The priests behind me would prostrate themselves on the stone floor, their faces hidden, chanting loudly their Egyptian prayers. Listening to the prayers and the songs and the rattling of the sistrums, and with incense wafting all around me, I would become almost hypnotized, as I whispered the prayers I had known by heart since childhood.

Before leaving, Charmion would hand me a sack made of gold cloth filled with gems, which I would hand to the High Priest. Then I would leave the temple, enter my litter, and be carried back to the barge, showered with flowers by the peasants, which deeply moved me.

As we voyaged upriver, the whole history of Egypt unrolled before our eyes. On about the tenth day of the journey, Memphis appeared and we dropped anchor in front of the long line of the Pyramids, stretching for miles along the western ridge of the hills. Litters carried us to the gigantic tomb of Ramses the Great rising from the plateau.

"By all the gods!" Caesar cried, as we stood beside one gigantic statue. "This pharaoh's little toe is bigger than I am!"

We gazed in wonder upon the great Sphinx, sitting majestically on a bed of sand with the sun setting behind the Libyan hills.

"Cleopatra," Caesar said, "your beauty exceeds that of the Sphinx."

"Cleopatra has a more enigmatic expression, too!" Charmion cried.

At Memphis I fed the sacred bull Apis at the temple, and then we proceeded on our voyage.

At Abydos, the city sacred to Osiris, with its awesome antiquity and decaying temples, Caesar observed, "Alexandria sparkles with brilliance and novel life, but the weight of centuries hangs in the air over these old cities."

On the third week we reached the old capital of Thebes-the-Hundred-Gated City, where the priests and people received us with great ceremony. Caesar was curious about all the monuments, the three temples bordering the river, and the decrepit but still marvelous city which is nine miles long.

"Just think, Julius," I said, "this city of Thebes was the seat of the world before there ever was an Athens or a Rome."

"Is it true, Cleopatra," Caesar asked, "that in accordance with venerated Egyptian custom, young virgin princesses are brought here, and in a sacred ritual, they are deflowered as an offering to Amon-Ra on an altar by priests using a golden dildo?"

"You of all people, Julius, who found me a virgin,

should know that such a custom was done away with before my time," I replied.

The spell of the Nile captured the cynical Caesar. He was amazed at the spectacle of miles upon miles of fields growing papyrus and wheat. Caesar saw that the Nile was the source of fertility. As a country without rain, we rely upon the rise of the river and its constructive conservation. Whenever I came across a badly kept canal or irrigation ditch, I reprimanded the supervisor in charge and ordered repairs to be made at once.

In the evenings we always had a small banquet with Charmion, Apollodorus, and Caesar's officers in attendance. Sometimes a High Priest or provincial governor would be invited on board. In my state of pregnancy, I reclined on divans covered with precious tapestries, and slaves waved peacock fans to keep me cool.

While being served our supper, we had entertainment of singers and jugglers, but the best amusement was always Caesar, who loved to talk. Certain tales he told more than once. He liked to remark, after a sumptuous feast, how he had lived on boiled roots in Gaul for weeks, although sometimes the time span became months. He was given to exaggerated figures. The number of right hands hacked off from vanquished warriors after Gallic battles varied greatly. For the most part, I enjoyed hearing stories from the Homeric saga of his life. There was one battle he never mentioned, however, and that was Dyrrachium, the only battle he ever lost. I was more curious about this defeat than all his victories, for I think there is more to be learned from a debacle than from a triumph, but Caesar never mentioned Dyrrachium and I never prompted him.

Caesar and I slept in a large bed in the royal stateroom. Before going to sleep I would read him the history of Alexander the Great written by his half-brother Ptolemy the First, hoping that this would inspire Caesar to further conquests.

These moments, when we were alone abed, were my favorite times. Each day as we journeyed on the river, the child inside me was growing larger, forming, stirring, and displaying vigorous signs of life in the warm cell of my womb. Before going to sleep, Caesar liked to put his head on my swollen belly to feel our son kicking.

On the river we passed many cargo-carriers laden with luxury goods from the east. I informed Caesar about our flourishing trade with India, describing how our merchants journey up the Nile to the city of Koptos, travel by caravan across the desert to the seaport of Berenice, and then sail over the Red Sea.

"I hold in my hands the keys of the vast and mysterious Orient!" I proudly explained. "Like Alexander, Julius, you must one day expand your empire all the way to India."

Caesar remained silent, but I knew he agreed with me, for a dreamy look appeared in his brown eyes.

We passed Elephantine, and a few days later reached the island of Philae in the middle of the great river, with its temple built by Ptolemy the Second, reserved for the priests and priestesses of Isis. I stopped at this holy isle and made sacrifice. A few days afterward we reached Aswan, the first cataract of the Nile, where the river is filled with crocodiles.

Caesar and I were willing to proceed further into Ethiopia and if possible to gain the source of the Nile itself, but our voyage had to be curtailed by the mutinous mood of the soldiers.

"My fearless soldiers who have never quailed at any enemy," Caesar scoffed, "are now frightened by the rapids of a river!"

"Obviously your soldiers do not find this pleasure cruise as pleasurable as we do," I said.

The hot south winds were blowing hard, the blazing heat during the day was intolerable, and I began to suffer discomfort as I entered my eighth month of pregnancy. We began the journey downriver homeward. After a voyage of ten weeks, we reached Alexandria in midsummer.

The memories of this journey on the Nile, with its

serene and colorful days, and with Caesar at my side, I will treasure all the days of my life.

My return was none too soon, for my physician Olympus told me my time of deliverance was nigh. We arrived at the palace at high noon, and after a short rest and repast, I went to the Temple of Isis near the palace to give thanks to the goddess for my safe return and to beseech her protection in my imminent travail.

In my carrying chair I was taken to the temple, escorted by Apollodorus, Charmion, and my attendants. Dressed in my gown of Isis, I entered the temple as trumpets and timbrels sounded a solemn song.

Heavy with child and moving slowly, I advanced through the length of the temple as my people arranged themselves respectfully on either side of my procession.

A group of priests, their heads shorn and robed in immaculate garments, chanted hymns to a flute accompaniment, as I walked to the huge white marble altar with the statue of Isis rising behind it. It gave me solace to once again look upon the sacred statue of Isis, painted in many colors and clad in gorgeous golden draperies and studded with precious jewels.

The Temple of Isis is one of my favorite places in all the world. It is always cool and peaceful, and worshipping there invariably invests me with serenity and strengthens my spirits.

Upon the flagstones in front of the altar there are engraved the twelve signs of the zodiac in a circle, surrounded with the mystic signs, and no one can set foot within this magic circle, not even a goddess-Queen. I walked around the circle and climbed the dozen marble steps to the altar, and then with the help of Apollodorus, I slowly sank to my knees.

Behind me, all the worshippers prostrated their bodies on the marble floor, murmuring their prayers.

On my knees, I stared at the eternal flame rising from the altar amid a cloud of scented fumes. As I beseeched the goddess to help me bring my son safely into the world, the priests chanted a grave melody and moved about me, sprinkling me with costly holy perfumes.

I rose slowly to my feet and approached the altar. Charmion handed me costly objects destined for the sacrifice. All music stopped and silence reigned in the great temple, except for my prayers which I made in a clear voice. I consecrated the offerings on the sacred fire and waited reverently for the flames to do their work.

When the sacrifice was consummated, the trumpets rang out afresh and I raised my arms to the heavens.

Just as the sacrifice was completed, a sudden stab of pain cut through me. It was as if a bolt of lightning had struck me, and I doubled over. Charmion caught my elbow and I fell forward, clutching the altar.

"My son is about to be born!" I cried ecstatically.

I considered it a good portent that my labor had begun in the temple, as if Isis herself had ordained it.

In my carrying chair I was rushed back to the palace and put abed. My bedchamber had been prepared as a birth chamber, and all was in readiness. Slaves brought in cauldrons of hot water. The physicians and midwives hovered anxiously over me, preparing me for the birth.

Another assault of sharp pains attacked me, and now that I was no longer in the temple I felt free to scream out in anguish.

"Bear down, my Queen," my chief physician Olympus ordered.

For nine months my child had grown and shaped and stirred and turned inside my womb, and now he was ready to come, head first, into the world.

"Oh, Olympus," I cried gaspingly, "I feel my prince hitting his head against the walls of my womb, impatient to be born."

"It will not be a long labor, my Queen, because the babe is already very low," Olympus told me.

Caesar was beckoned, and he came to me and held my hand.

"Your physicians assure me that you will come through the birthing with no difficulty," Caesar said. "Forgive me if I do not stay, Cleopatra."

"This is the work of women and eunuchs and physicians, Julius," I said. "You have already done your work."

Caesar kissed me and went off. He was highly nervous, perhaps remembering that his daughter Julia had died in giving birth to a dead son to Pompey. I also remembered that, and feared for my life and the life of my son.

At my invitation, several nobles crowded into the chamber to witness the birth, and also Caesar's trusted friend, Aulis Hirtius. I wanted no one to claim that I had borne a girl and had replaced her with a boy babe. There was also a contingent of priests and priestesses, adorned with masks and insignia to represent various gods and goddesses, assisting in the ceremony of birth. My father's old favorite flutist made sweet melodies to lull my pain.

All the rest of the afternoon and into the evening I was in labor. Charmion never left my side, holding my hand and giving me comfort.

"Where is Caesar?" I asked.

"The Imperator is in the reception room playing dice with Rufio," Charmion explained.

"When my son is born," I cried, "take him immediately and place him at Caesar's feet. This is the Roman custom. If he picks up the child, he will acknowledge his fatherhood."

"Mistress Queen," Olympus said sternly, "this is Egypt, not Rome, and you are Queen of Egypt. Caesar will come to you!"

"Do as I command!" I cried imperatively.

"Your wishes will be carried out, O Queen," Apollodorus assured me.

The pains kept coming and the chants of the priests and the sound of flutes offered me no comfort from the searing agony that convulsed me. Finally when the torment grew into an all-engulfing, tearing pain that tore me asunder, all but obliterating my senses, my child was born.

"You have a son!" Charmion cried out rapturously.

The cry was taken up by all those assembled in the chamber, an excited babble of ecstatic voices.

"You have a son, my Queen, a son!"

"A prince for Egypt!"

"A son for Caesar!"

My senses returned, and I opened my eyes dazedly. "But of course I have a son," I whispered weakly. "Why is everyone surprised?"

I gazed up as Olympus held the little babe, all red and wet and crying and wriggly. "O Sacred Radiance, you have a fair and beautiful prince and he is perfectly proportioned!" he cried, placing the babe in my arms.

A surge of tremendous joy suffused me.

Apollodorus was waiting in the anteroom and I sent for him. The cord was cut, the babe was washed and wrapped in cloth-of-gold and placed in the arms of Apollodorus to take to Caesar.

The afterbirth was attended to, I expelled all the waste from my womb, and my body was purified and sponged off with rosewater. My Nubian massage slave rubbed oil of almonds over my stomach to ensure that my skin would not wrinkle or scar from having been stretched during the pregnancy.

While this was happening, Apollodorus brought the child to Caesar, who was on his knees playing at dice.

"Great Imperator, Queen Cleopatra has borne you a perfect child," Apollodorus said, placing the basket at Caesar's feet.

Caesar lifted the cloth-of-gold to scrutinize the sex of the babe. "I have a son!" he cried jubilantly. "I have a son!" He picked the babe up in his arms, acknowledging his paternity.

Carrying the child in his arms, Caesar came to my side. I had been placed once again in my freshly made bed. His face was flushed with happiness, and tears sparkled in his eyes.

"I have had a great life full of conquests," Caesar said with emotion, "but this is the greatest gift I have ever received. My time has not been wasted in the land of the pharaohs, for I have a son!"

"Julius, I told you all along that I carried a son," I said.

"I was nineteen when my daughter Julia was born," Caesar said. "I have waited a long time for another child, and this time it is a son!"

Caesar sat on the side of my bed, holding the babe in his arms, beaming with pride, his face flushed with tender joy.

"He has blue Lagos eyes like you, Cleopatra," Caesar remarked.

"All infants have blue eyes at birth," the Egyptian midwife cried. "Perhaps in time, Great Caesar, his eyes will turn brown like his father's."

"He has tufts of blond hair, too," Caesar observed. "He is a Ptolemy, but I grant there is some Caesar in him which will come out in time."

Caesar placed the babe in my arms, and the little mouth sought and found almost by instinct my full nipple, and the milk spilled forth into his greedy little mouth as he took his first drink.

"I have a son!" Caesar kept repeating. "You have accomplished a great victory, Cleopatra, and the spoils of victory shall be yours."

"I will name him Ptolemy," I said, "and he should bear the surname of Caesar."

"Certainly," Caesar cried expansively. "Ptolemy Caesar! He will carry our names like a glorious standard across the world!"

Midnight came and everyone left us. Caesar lay down on the bed. Ptolemy Caesar, having drunk his fill, slept soundly. The lamps were put out, the last servants left, and we were alone. Soon Caesar and I fell asleep with our child between us.

Although I had almost died in the travail, I was filled with unbounded joy and pride. I had borne a son, and this was the happiest day of my life.

CHAPTER VI

THE BIRTH OF MY FIRSTBORN man-child was the means by which I hoped to forge an unbreakable link with Caesar. The Master of Rome, who was indisputably the most powerful man on earth, could not in good faith desert me after I had given him a son. Never had I felt more certain of my destiny, and vistas of immortal triumph opened before me. One day my son would be King in Egypt, inheriting all the glory of his goddess-Queen mother, and I thought it only right that he should receive as a legacy the powers possessed by his father.

I have always been committed to the advancement of my dynasty and country. I had a dream which the birth of my son made feasible. Egypt would not become a slave to Rome, but would be the equal of Rome. The star of Egypt would glitter alongside the star of Rome. The two empires would be united over all the nations of the earth, and a descendant of mine and Caesar's would sit upon the throne of the world.

For over a century Rome had been angling to take over Egypt, but now it was possible that I, Cleopatra, an Egyptian Queen, would one day sit in judgment in Rome as Caesar's imperial consort.

There was no turning back now that I had Caesar's son. The die was cast, and I was completely committed to Rome.

I knew that the news of Caesarion's birth would not be received joyously by Caesar's seventeen-year-old great-nephew Octavian in Rome. Octavian, the son of Caesar's sister's daughter, was now eclipsed by a genuine male heir who was a prince of the oldest kingdom on earth.

The birth was hailed with great rejoicing by my people, who accepted the child as the legitimate offspring of their goddess-Queen with the god Jupiter-Amon in the guise of Caesar. Bonfires were lit in all the squares, and festivals were organized to honor the event. Although my child was named Ptolemy Caesar, the Alexandrians immediately dubbed him with the Greek diminutive of Caesarion, Little Caesar.

At the Temple of Hermonthis the birth was recorded with drawings and hieroglyphics sculptured in bas-relief, in the manner of the old pharaohs, and the babe was hailed as a young god by the priests and nobles.

My son was born on the last day of the month, just two days after the birthdate of his father. I issued a decree changing the name of the month to July in commemoration of Julius, for it was only fitting that the month be named in honor of the father of my son. This appealed to Caesar's vanity, and he began to consider adopting my calendar for the Roman world.

I had fresh coins minted, showing my portrait in profile with an infant suckling at my breast. To the Greeks the image of mother and son implied Aphrodite and Eros, and to the native Egyptians this picture represented Isis and her baby god Horus.

About a week after the delivery, as I lay abed breastfeeding the newborn Caesar, the old Caesar came to me in an anxious state.

"It is said that Princess Arsinoë refuses all food and is wasting away," Caesar cried with vexation. "I have her heavily guarded so that no poisons can be supplied to her, so she is trying to kill herself by starvation. I don't want her dead, Cleopatra!"

"I see," I murmured weakly.

"I keep remembering the suicide of your uncle the King of Cyprus," Caesar said uneasily. "Arsinoë must be reserved to grace my triumph in Rome. Tell her that she need only to walk in my triumph and she can become Queen of Cyprus afterward."

The thought of my sister-princess being humiliated in a triumph was abhorrent, and I understood her longing to die. Yet I had to do as Caesar commanded, although a confrontation with my headstrong and highstrung sister was not something to which I looked forward.

Arsinoë was duly informed of my coming. As I was taken in a carrying chair along the corridors to the chambers where she was closeted, my mind was filled with the contemplation of her sad predicament. Not only had she lost all her hopes of wearing the Pharaonic crown, but she had lost the two people dearest to her, her brother and Ganymedes. It was said that she had been in love with Ganymedes, a handsome, elegant eunuch in his mid-thirties, and that she had offered rich sacrifices to the gods to restore his lost testicles. She had quacks concoct magical brews which she slipped in his food so that the testes would grow back. As we all know, however, once the knife has cut the eggs away, not even the power of Eros and Venus can restore them.

I was led to believe that Arsinoë had kept her virgin jewel intact. She had been close to King Ptolemy and it had been their plan to marry once I was out of the way, but this design had been thwarted. Several of her ladies were deeply attached to her, but there was no special favorite. She was in a lamentable state, and I could not help but feel sympathy for her.

As I entered Arsinoë's reception room, several of her ladies sank to their knees and begged me to get their mistress to take sustenance.

With trepidation, I stepped into the bedchamber which Arsinoë had not left for weeks. I had not seen her for six months, not since she had been taken prisoner after the Alexandrian War, and I was shocked. She was bone-thin, a ghost of her former self. Her skin was the color of white marble, and she had an ethereal aura that was quite becoming. She sat in a chair beside her bed and fixed me with a haughty stare.

"Sister Queen," she said, "forgive me for not rising and prostrating myself at your feet, but I have been ill and haven't the strength."

I gave a small smile and shrugged. "In the custom of our beloved father, Arsinoë, I've always dispensed with protocol with my family in our private chambers." I poured two goblets of wine and handed her one. "Let us take wine together."

She took the proffered goblet with a listless gesture, and I sat on a divan near her and sipped wine to give me the strength to endure the meeting.

"In spite of your thinness, Arsinoë, you are more beautiful than ever," I said.

Arsinoë ignored the compliment. "I must congratulate you on the birth of your natural son," she said.

I ignored the insult the word natural implied, and merely nodded and again nervously sipped from my goblet.

"Is it true that your babe is really Caesar's son?" she asked skeptically. "For decades he has had no children and it has universally been believed that he is sterile, and now this child you claim is from his seed! Some vicious tongues about court insist that Apollodorus is the father, but then perhaps the potions you fed Caesar worked this miracle. I suppose only Caesar and you and the high gods know the truth. It will be a riddle for future historians to ponder."

"Sister, I have not come here to defend the paternity of my child," I cried with annoyance.

"Oh, no, then why have you come?" Arsinoë flashed back.

"Because I am concerned about you," I said helplessly.

"Yes, I'm sure you are!" she retorted with a bitter little laugh.

With an effort, I met her eyes unblinkingly. "Arsinoë, why haven't you been taking your daily walks in the palace gardens?"

"Because I detest walking escorted by Roman dogs, that's why!" she cried incorrigibly.

"You must get exercise and fresh air, Arsinoë."

"Why?" she demanded belligerently. "To keep in

physical form for my marathon walk on the Roman streets?"

My jaw dropped and I was speechless. She was the prisoner and I the jailer, yet it was I who was cast in the role of supplicant.

"Caesar sent you here!" she cried vehemently. "I find it disgusting, Cleopatra, that you do his bidding, that you are indeed his slave in bed and out!" Her voice rose with contempt. "You have your throne, but you got it not by standing on your feet and fighting for it, but by lying on your back and spreading your legs like a whore to a Roman barbarian, an old, weary, wrinkled, bald-headed profligate who takes fits!"

I was gasping, yet I could not argue this cruel but apt description of Caesar. The goblet trembled in my hand and I struggled to maintain my composure. "My sister," I said, my voice barely a whisper, "I know the last six months have been a time of grief for you, but surely you are not beaten. You are only seventeen and your life has just begun. Caesar, when he first came to Alexandria, promised you Cyprus, and you rebelled against him. As a reckless gambler, you threw the dice and lost. Caesar admires your gambling spirit, and he is magnanimous in victory. The Cypriot crown is still yours."

"But first I must be exhibited as a trophy in his triumph in Rome. You wear the crown and I wear the chains."

"The chains will be golden," I put in placatingly.

"I would rather die!" she said tremulously. "After all, I am a Ptolemaic princess, a lady of the Lagidae, and, unlike you, I have dignity. There is nothing you would not do to satisfy your greed, Cleopatra. You sold your body and your country to our inveterate enemy. You betrayed your people and led them into the den of Roman wolves. You are without a shred of decency or shame."

"I care little about the opinions you or the Alexandrians entertain of me," I snapped, losing patience and standing up, "and I do not care to sit here all day squabbling with you. Stop wallowing in pity and starving yourself, submit to your fate stoically, go to Rome and walk in the triumph, and Cyprus will be yours!"

Arsinoë looked at me with flickering, frightened eyes. "How will I be able to trust Caesar and you?"

"We swear a sacred oath to the high gods that we will honor our pledge," I said firmly.

"What an outrageous egotist Caesar is!" she said thoughtfully. "One daughter of Lagos his whore, and another his prisoner. I think it is more honorable, however, to be his prisoner than his whore and the mother of his bastard. If given the chance, Cleopatra, I would not change places with you for all the crowns and gold in the world."

I did not think Arsinoë was being entirely honest with me in the discharge of this noble and outrageous statement, but the saying of it gave her tremendous pleasure.

Arsinoë sat drinking from her goblet, and I could see by her expression that she was relenting a little, mulling over my proposition.

"You have tasted ashes, Arsinoë, but you are not finished yet," I said softly. "There is still sweet nectar to be drunk from life. Are you or are you not a Lagos?"

"I will consider the matter," she said waveringly.

"Caesar will be leaving Alexandria in a week for Pontus," I explained, "and at the same time he wants to send you on to Rome. You may take twenty members of your household with you. You will be lodged at a grand villa on the Tiber."

"You mean, instead of a dungeon I will have a villa, but it will be a prison nevertheless, to stay in until I am needed to walk the dirty, dusty streets behind Caesar's chariot," she said bitterly.

"I gave birth to a son and almost died in the travail," I told her, "but I was rewarded with a beautiful prince. Sometimes we must pay in pain, blood, tears, and sweat for the riches we crave. Endure the agony of the march, Arsinoë, and you will be rewarded with an island kingdom all your own."

Her blue eyes took on a dreamy, abstracted look, and

I knew that she had decided to live and take another gamble at life.

I stood and bent to take in my hands her pale oval face that glowed with the beauty of a jewel. "Farewell, my dearest sister," I said, kissing her compressed lips.

Enervated by the encounter, I collapsed into the arms of my attendants. I was put into my carrying chair and rushed back to bed.

It was reported to Caesar and me that evening that Arsinoë had taken her first solid food in weeks.

"I deem your mission this afternoon a success," Caesar said with a stern smile of approval.

"Yes, Arsinoë will go to Rome with you, Julius, never fear," I said.

There was a lull while Caesar sat sipping wine and listening to a flutist play a sweet and haunting song from a corner.

Taking a drink of wine and a deep breath, I asked as casually as possible, "Beloved Julius, will you marry me in the Egyptian rites before you leave Egypt?"

If Caesar felt any surprise at my proposal, he did not show it. "If I married you, Cleopatra, such a union would not be recognized in Rome, for Roman law forbids marriages of her citizens with easterners."

"I should like to point out to you, Julius," I said, bristling, "that I am eminently suitable to be your wife in the eyes of Rome, for not one drop of Egyptian or eastern blood flows in my veins. Like Alexander the Great, my relative, I am pure Macedonian. Other Greeks are not pure Greeks, for their blood has been polluted by centuries of eastern and Doric invasions, but these mongrelizing migrations never reached Macedonia in the north, and our bloodlines have remained pure. I am also the richest woman in the world and the most royal lady of the most royal dynasty in existence, which makes me, if I am not too presumptuous to say so, a wife worthy of the man who is master of the world."

Caesar gave me his thin-lipped smile. "Unquestionably desirable qualifications in a wife, my dear."

"Besides, Julius," I resumed in a soft tone, "I have

given you a son, which all four of your legal Roman wives failed to do. Let us hope our son will rule Egypt one day. If you married me in the Egyptian rites, this would legitimatize our son and exclude the possibility of his rights ever being contested in Egypt."

Seeing the cold logic of this, Caesar nodded. "We shall marry then in the Egyptian rites, but for the moment this must be a private and not a state affair, for I dread the reaction of Rome."

"So be it, beloved Julius," I said with a nod.

The marriage took place a few days later in my small private temple in the palace. Anchoreus, High Priest of Memphis, the highest prelate in the kingdom, officiated at the ceremony. Caesar invited only a handful of Roman officers, and a dozen of my Greek and Egyptian adherents witnessed the event.

My prince, a week old, was held in the arms of his great-aunt, the Princess Aliki, who beamed happily. Caesarion did not utter a cry throughout the rite, but with open eyes and mouth lay fascinated by the swirl of incense and soothed by the sound of the chants and hymns.

Caesar stood with an arrogant posture, his nose in the air, sniffing the incense with an unpleasant face and an air of contempt. He heaved a noticeable sigh of relief when the ceremony was over and affixed a scrawling signature to the marriage documents. I insisted that a Roman witness the document, and he selected Rufio. This was an insult, since Rufio was a freedman, but I did not protest.

I had given Caesar one of the greatest dowries in history, an immense fortune, and he knew he could always depend upon me to supply him with gold and grain, the sinews of war, for all his future campaigns.

In Egypt Caesar was recognized as my legal husband, and my brother was my co-monarch. It was an intricate situation, but I was not daunted by it.

Now that our son was born, Caesar realized he could no longer delay his departure from Egypt. As anxious as he was to return to Rome, he first had to go to Asia Minor to suppress an uprising in Pontus.

The day before Caesar's sailing, I took him to visit Alexander's tomb. We rode in a litter down the Canopic Boulevard to Sema Square. Upon entering the great mausoleum, we quickly traversed the long rows of sarcophagi and headed toward the staircase leading down to Alexander's crypt. A soldier, carrying a torch to light the way, preceded us down the dark stairs to the underground chamber. The torch was placed in a holder on the wall and the soldier departed.

Caesar and I were alone with the golden corpse of Alexander.

I took Caesar's hand and led him to the bronze catafalque with the gold coffin and its covering of crystal. We stood in silent reverence, gazing upon the beautiful corpse encased in gold-plated armor, a tutelary body composed of beeswax, cosmetics, spices and human clay, which had once housed the greatest spirit the world has ever known.

"The body looks three days dead instead of three centuries," Caesar said.

"So must your body be preserved in a like manner, Julius, when your mortal time comes," I replied. "It is a heathen custom for Romans to burn the bodies of their great men like garbage."

"One can see that Alexander was, as Callisthenes wrote, a powerfully built man of medium height," Caesar observed, staring transfixedly.

I gazed upon the face with its mask of gold covering the features. "Such a beautiful face," I murmured in a hushed tone.

"Yes, a delicacy of feature," Caesar said a bit envious. He turned his head and gave me a penetrating look. "I see a marked resemblance between the two of you. Indeed, Alexander could be your twin, for you have his looks as well as spirit."

I exhaled a sigh, blushing with pleasure at the compliment.

"You both have faces that embody romantic Hellenistic sculpture," Caesar resumed. "You have the same stamp of beauty, the same dreamy, veiled and remote look, the same vague cast of melancholy on refined features."

"Alexander's face is refined but manly," I emphasized. "But I know what you mean, he has the face of an artist rather than the greatest general who ever lived—until you, of course, beloved Julius!"

"He was a mad yet glorious adventurer," Caesar said reflectively, "and perhaps his ashes should have been scattered over the world he conquered, yet here they are in this consecrated shrine, perfectly intact."

"Yes, Julius, but this preserved corpse gives evidence," I exclaimed, "that the great artists who portrayed him in life, Apelles, Lysippus and Leochares, did not exaggerate his glamorous and heroic beauty, and the likeness represented in marble and bronze, on gold and silver coins, in busts and statues, on plaquettes and cameos, was not falsified."

"Yes, perhaps it was a blessing," Caesar replied, "that he was cut off in his prime, when nature called a halt to his restless feet in conquered Babylon, before his face became ravaged with wrinkles and his hair fell out."

I reached for Caesar's hand and squeezed it. "Your blood has been mixed with the blood of Alexander, Julius," I cried passionately, "for our son has the blood of Alexander in his veins."

"Yes, and it's a nice thought, too, for Alexander was the hero of my youth," Caesar said wistfully.

"Alexander was my hero, Julius, until I met you," I cried with adoration.

"You are always rhapsodizing on about your beloved Alexander and his exploits," Caesar said resentfully, "but then you must remember that he was King of Macedonia at the age of twenty, so why should he not have become king of the world at twenty-six with all his advantages? When I was born, my family was at low fortune, and I had to fight my way up to power. I was forty before I had a province to rule, and Gaul was a barbarian province at that. My dear friend Pompey, on the other hand, had the whole rich Asia Minor under his thumb, but he was always rich and famous, a noble among nobles, the darling of the gods and the people and the Senate, with everything served him on a golden plate." Caesar paused and heaved a deep sigh. "It was just three years ago that I stood outside Rimini, hesitating whether to take the plunge and cross the Rubicon, march against Pompey, and be proclaimed an enemy of the fatherland. Antony, disguised as a slave, rode out of Rome and joined me and gave me the courage to take the risk, and the Rubicon was crossed."

"You crushed Pompey," I cried exultantly, "and now you are Dictator of Rome and Master of the World."

"I won at Pharsalia, but all glory is short-lived. It is not long before death reduces victors to the equal of the vanquished."

"You have many more years left, Julius, and many more glories," I protested. "You are the greatest soldier since Alexander, the greatest statesman since Pericles!"

"Yes, I am at the top of the world now at the old age of fifty-two," Caesar said cheerlessly. "My son, thanks to the gods, will not have to fight the way I did. No, my son, like his kin Alexander, has been born with a regal rank and will have as his legacy the oldest throne in the world and will become King of Egypt."

"And King of Rome!" I added fervently.

Caesar caught my gaze, and his eyes narrowed. "Oh, Cleopatra, such fantasies you have!" he said with a sigh.

"Why should you not be King of Rome, and your son after you?" I demanded ardently. "Are you not King by achievement, just as my forefather Ptolemy the First was when he made himself Egypt's King? You are of noble blood and a divine descendant of Venus. Return to Rome, Julius, have the Senate cower before you and proclaim you their King. Rome has long outgrown its republican form of government. It requires the dignity of a dynasty of divine kings ordained by the gods. Who

371

else should be King of the Roman empire but you, Julius, the guardian genius of the world?"

Caesar gave me a smile. "And you will ascend the throne of the world at my side, Cleopatra?"

"Yes," I said, nodding gravely, "and our son will inherit our combined glory, the Roman-Egypt Empire!"

"Could it be possible to have all my achievements settled on my son, or are you just a wild dreamer, Cleopatra?"

"I am like Alexander, that rare combination, both a visionary and a realist, Julius," I said. "A future which makes political sense cannot happen unless it has been imagined, for imagination is the prerequisite of all historical achievement. You of all people should know that."

Caesar shifted restively before me, but I could detect by his dreamy gaze that he agreed with me.

"Return to Rome, Julius, and lay the foundations of the dynasty which will rule the earth and endure a millennium," I said earnestly, looking into his eyes. "Only if you are king will you be able to accomplish what you must for Rome. You see how smoothly the affairs of Egypt's government are conducted by my decrees. I have no Senate to satisfy. I am the living law, and so must you become the living law of Rome, of the world!"

"*Yes!*" Caesar breathed in ecstasy, caught up by the fever of my words. Then suddenly something collapsed within him and he groaned. "Oh, if only I were twenty years younger!"

"You have fifteen, twenty years of mortal life before you, Julius!" I cried intoxicatingly. "You are in your prime!"

"The Senate will never make me King," Caesar insisted.

"Make the Senate cringe before you!" I said forcefully. "Take up the dream of Alexander and finish where he left off. Teach the world to cower before a sole conqueror! Have every senator and every nation grovel at your feet. Alexander reduced Parthia to a tranquil

Macedonian province, and you can make it a tranquil province of Rome. Let nothing bar your advance or impede your dreams. Go east and conquer India, and then the Senate will have no choice but to make you emperor of the world that is yours!"

I moved swiftly to the catafalque where Alexander lay under his crystal cover. "I will give you Alexander's gold armor for luck!" I cried.

"It's much too small," Caesar retorted, stiffening with pride.

I saw the gold-plated sword which was clutched in Alexander's hand. "I will give you his sword which he carried in all his victories!"

"I have my own sword, Caesar's sword!"

"Yes, but of course you do," I said, walking back and standing in front of him. "You need nothing of Alexander's, Julius, but you can take his dream. The dream of a new kingdom of earth to embrace east and west. Alexander decreed that Greeks and Persians should be brothers. You will decree that Romans, Greeks, Egyptians, and Persians should likewise be brothers."

Caesar walked to the catafalque and gazed as if mesmerized by the golden corpse. "The glory of your dreams is easier to contemplate than to accomplish, Cleopatra," he said.

"You are another Alexander, Julius. You are greater than Alexander!"

"They said that to my uncle Marius, to Crassus and Pompey, but will there in truth ever be another Alexander?"

"You have already conquered Britannia and Gaul and Iberia, where Alexander never set foot," I said. "You have conquered me, and Egypt is yours. Conquer Parthia and our boundaries will be measured by the sun!"

For a long while Caesar gazed upon the face of Alexander, and then he shifted his eyes to mine. "You not only have his beautiful looks, Cleopatra, but his madness!" he whispered intensely. "The gene of his divine madness, dormant all these three centuries, has come

373

down the line of the Lagidae and sparked in your soul like a sacred flame."

I held his eyes. "Yes, I know."

"Your madness is contagious," Caesar admitted with a sigh. "You are my inspiration."

I moved closer to Caesar until our faces were an inch apart. "Return to Rome, Julius," I said with intensity, "and overthrow the Republic and set up our imperial dynasty."

"This glorious game must be played skillfully," Caesar said.

"We will play it so and win the throne of the world in just a few more years," I said.

"I will do it, Cleopatra, not for myself and not for you," Caesar cried, "but for my son!"

"Yes, beloved Julius, for our son!"

Caesar and I kissed, a kiss of tremulous ecstasy, standing before the body of Alexander the Great, and with that kiss we sealed a sacred pledge.

With a last look at Alexander, we left the tomb and returned to the palace.

Caesar, living by me all those months, had been deeply awed by the proximity of royalty and dazzled by the glamor of all the trappings of my court. For months I had fostered with care his aspirations toward monarchy. Since he detested the thought of subordination to any other being, he had observed my autocratic manner with envy. His relationship with me inspired him to be a king himself, and now the birth of our son gave his dream a greater impetus.

When we had first met, Caesar had scoffed at my divinity. For nine months I had constantly fed his mind with the idea of his own divine origins, until he had come to actually believe that he too was divine. Since he was a man of soaring ambitions my task had not been difficult, and his sense of divinity had developed into a fixed fantasy. I felt that only if he believed he was clothed with godhead like myself could he attempt to accomplish the dreams I had for him, for me, and for our son.

The day of Caesar's departure from Egypt arrived. It was a beautiful luminous day with the sun sparkling from the eternal blue sky. Despite the beauty of the day, it was a sad, emotional time for me.

The leavetaking ceremony was conducted with great pomp, which I masterminded, knowing how fond my people are of spectacle. A distinguished deputation of court officials and nobles gathered on the dockside, and the crowds of citizens were held back by guardsmen with crossed javelins. The priests chanted their prayers and waved their thuribles of incense, sacrifices were made to the gods, and trumpets blasted as the soldiers marched on board the galleys.

At last only Caesar and a handful of his closest officers remained on shore.

I stood beside Caesar in front of his flagship's gangplank.

"The world is waiting for Caesar," I cried.

"Yes, Royal Egypt," Caesar said solemnly.

"Bid farewell to our man-child, the fruit of our loins and our love, Great Caesar," I said, motioning for the Royal Egyptian Nurse to bring Caesarion forth.

For a long moment Caesar held Caesarion in his arms. In awed silence the enormous crowd watched Caesar kiss his son and roared with approval as the babe was given back to his nurse.

Caesar turned to Rufio, who was staying behind in Alexandria as the commander of the Thirty-Seventh Legion. Since my popularity was still questionable, Caesar was leaving this force of occupation to secure my sovereignty.

"Lord Rufio, guard Queen Cleopatra and Prince Ptolemy Caesar with your life," Caesar exhorted.

"I vow to the gods to do so, Great Imperator!" Rufio cried, clasping Caesar's hand.

"Queen Cleopatra, Rufio is my most faithful officer and friend," Caesar said, "and you can trust him in all matters."

"I shall look upon Lord Rufio as you do, Julius," I avowed.

As Caesar embraced me, I had the premonition that the fates were parting us forever, and I clung to him. "Oh, beloved Julius!" I cried.

Caesar extricated himself from my embrace. "Farewell, my cherished love," he said softly. He gazed a long moment into my eyes, then abruptly turned and walked away.

Intense emotions cut off my voice and I could not call out a final word of farewell, but only stood there in a desperate daze.

To the fanfare of trumpets, Caesar went on board his flagship, then stood on deck waving his sword in the air as the flagship and accompanying vessels sailed out of the two harbors.

I collapsed into my litter, and my bearers swiftly bore me up the long marble stairs to the palace. Back in my apartments, overcome by emotion, I sat in a chair, with Caesarion in a crib beside me, looking out a window that commanded a view of the harbors. I watched Caesar's galleys, burdened with Egyptian gold and treasure, their oars rhythmically dipping into the sparkling blue water, gliding out to sea. I sat there until the last of the ships disappeared over the horizon as the sun was setting.

The dockside became deserted, the two harbors were empty, and the city was strangely quiet after the bustle of the great departure. I too felt deserted and empty. Caesar had departed from me, and I realized that all alone I would have to deal with my child, my unruly people and my kingdom.

Great Caesar was gone, but little Caesar lay in my arms, and I had the hope in my heart that Caesarion would be greater than his father, greater than Alexander, and that one day he would wield the scepter of the world.

After Caesar left Egypt, we were in constant communication by courier. Even if I were in a council session with my ministers, I would stop the moment a letter arrived, break open the seal, unroll the scroll, and read it. Our letters were written in Latin, since his Greek was poor. His letters were brief, stern and severe,

376

stripped of ornamentation. With his pen Caesar was laconic, but with his tongue he could be as verbose as any Greek. My letters to Caesar were florid and full of details, but then I am a Macedonian Alexandrian and we are freer with our tongues and pens than the Romans. In my letters I wrote Caesar of my affairs of state, and all matters concerning our child, his first words, his growing weight, and each new tooth. I did not dictate these letters, but wrote them in my own beautiful, bold hand, using high-quality papyrus smoothed with pumice.

Through Caesar's letters I followed his travels and battles from the time he left Egypt to quell an uprising led by King Pharnaces of Pontus. Pharnaces, taking advantage of Caesar's prolonged stay in Egypt, had crossed the Black Sea into Asia Minor and defeated Caesar's friend, Domitius Calvinus. Pharnaces pursued his victory so eagerly that he became master of Bithynia and Cappadocia, and he was encouraging all the kings of the east to rise against Rome.

A favorable wind had carried Caesar across the Mediterranean, and he landed his three legions at Tarsus at the end of July. Marching into Asia by the same road which had been used by Alexander, Caesar met Pharnaces and his army outside the city of Zela, four hundred miles north of Tarsus. The opposing forces engaged in battle, and Caesar was victorious, fighting a brilliant battle that lasted only four hours.

"*Veni, vidi, vici*," is the way Caesar expressed it in a letter. I came, I saw, I conquered.

I was exhilarated at Caesar's victory, but part of me was disconcerted, for the king Caesar had defeated killed himself after the battle. I always tremble at the fall of a king. I belong to that small, select circle chosen by the gods, and Pharnaces had been a civilized, cultured, rare breed of a king. This illustrated to me once again, however, the folly of any monarch rising against the power of Rome, or the will of Caesar who was Rome.

In a triumphant mood, after having restored Roman

rule to the east, Caesar set sail for Italy. When the news of his victory at Zela reached Rome, enemies like Cato and Scipio, realizing that Caesar would soon be returning, fled to North Africa and established a resistance government-in-exile. With the assistance of King Juba of Numidia, they gathered ten legions.

Arriving in Rome in October, Caesar found the city in a state of unrest. There was anxiety about the food supply and rioting in the streets. Caesar promised that a fleet carrying wheat from their ally, Egypt, was on the way. The Tenth Legion was in a state of near mutiny. Caesar met these hardened, embittered veterans on the Field of Mars, calmly listened to their grievances, and dispensed to each soldier a sum of gold—gold which had come from my treasury—and won them again to his heart. He would need them in the battles ahead.

Meanwhile, in North Africa, Cato, Scipio, and other fugitive friends of Pompey were preparing an invasion of Italy, resolved to destroy Caesar at any cost.

"I long to settle in Rome at my desk," Caesar wrote me, "employing my efforts in the tasks of administration, but fate is forcing me in a direction I loathe. Pharsalia and Zela should have been the last battles, but that final triumph eludes me. I must go to North Africa and exterminate my enemies before they come and destroy me. Only when this business is out of the way will it be feasible for you to come to Rome with our son."

The winter solstice commenced as Caesar sailed across the stormy Mediterranean with five legions. After a rough crossing, he arrived at Hadrumetum, and on landing he wrote me saying that this adventure would be quickly taken care of as at Zela, but unfortunately events proved otherwise.

After setting up camp, Caesar marched inland with three legions. He came across the armies commanded by Petreius and a bloody battle followed. Caesar, defeated and routed, got back to his camp with his life. A greater part of his army had been massacred.

Caesar wrote me requesting aid, and I sent him off a

fleet filled with supplies, grain, and wheat to feed his soldiers.

It was a long, arduous winter while Caesar waited for reinforcements to be sent by Antony from Italy. In these months his army endured harsh exposure and fought several engagements with the desperate enemy. More than once Caesar nearly lost his life.

In the spring five legions arrived from Antony, and Caesar was able to resume the offensive on a grand scale.

At Thrapsus on the sixth of April, between the lagoon and the sea, Caesar took up a strategic position. The enemy forces came against him, reinforced with sixty elephants, and a battle was fought.

It was said that Caesar was taken by the distemper on the day of the battle and did not participate, but Caesar told me later this was a fiction of his enemies. He said he perceived the approach of a fit, but withdrew to his tent to compose himself. Having recovered, he joined the battle in the thick of the fray, and fought it to a victorious conclusion. He sacked the camp of Scipio and King Juba. Scipio escaped, but was intercepted at sea and killed, and King Juba committed suicide.

"The battle was a dreadful scene of slaughter," Caesar wrote. "Neither I nor my centurions could restrain the fury of our soldiers. Fifty thousand of the enemy were butchered. I lost fifty men."

After this battle, Caesar set out for the enemy base at Utica where Cato had been left in command. Cato, my old enemy, who had annexed Cyprus when I was a child, stealing the possessions and the kingdom of my Uncle Ptolemy and causing his suicide, now opened his veins.

Caesar, coming into the tent and gazing upon the body, said, "Cato, I begrudge you your death, as you begrudged me the honor of sparing your life."

I do not believe Caesar was honest with these words, for all of the men of praetorian rank who were taken into custody were put to death, except for those who anticipated Caesar by killing themselves.

The death of Cato was a triumph for me. I had waited thirteen years for this, and I felt a bitterness in my heart at last expunged.

Numidia, a rich kingdom, was annexed by Rome, and King Juba's five-year-old son, Prince Juba, was taken prisoner to grace Caesar's triumph in Rome, in the manner of my sister Arsinoë. Caesar appointed Sallust in command of this province and ordered him to capture the wild animals of the land, including the giraffe, to be exhibited in triumph along with the little prince.

After the victory at Thrapsus, I expected Caesar to return to Rome, but instead he went and stayed two months at the court of King Bogud of Mauretania. While there he engaged in an affair with the King's wife, Queen Eunoë, apparently with the willing consent of her husband. Queen Eunoë, I was told, was my senior by several years, rather plump, and not known for her beauty. She was also not as rich as I and could not give Caesar great presents, and instead Caesar presented her with extravagant gifts.

"These gifts were undoubtedly paid for by gold from your treasury," Charmion said with agitation. "And to think that Caesar never gave you the meanest trinket!"

"Caesar gave me a son," I said.

"A mutual gift," Charmion retorted.

I could not admit even to Charmion that I was hurt by these tidings.

"I am visiting the royal family of Mauretania to insure myself of their goodwill to Rome," Caesar wrote me, although I thought he was going to extraordinary lengths in the pursuit of this policy. "I am hoping King Bogud will assist me next year when I go to Spain and fight a campaign to crush the sons of Pompey. If you hear rumors about my friendship with Queen Eunoë, do not overly concern yourself, Cleopatra, for she is merely a trifling fancy."

If Caesar had taken to bed with a woman of ordinary rank, I would not have been so offended, but it was another Queen, my equal, whose paramour he became.

"Evidently Caesar has taken a fancy to queens,"

Charmion said bitterly, "and has added another one to his list."

Caesar had spies in my court, but no shred of scandal about me ever got back to him. I was mistress of a great palace and presided over a corrupt court where no one had the same bedmate two nights running, yet I slept alone. Beside my bed was the crib where Caesarion slept, for I was afraid that if he had his own bedchamber some misfortune might befall him. During the night, faithful household guards, handpicked by Apollodorus, patrolled the corridor outside the chamber to guard our lives with their own against any possibility of a palace revolt.

At the end of July, Caesar was back in Rome after an absence of seven months, victorious and wreathed with glory, and his fifty-fourth birthday was celebrated with extravagant feasting.

A year had passed since I had bade farewell to Caesar, and during that time I had followed his actions with pride as he moved from continent to continent to conduct brilliant campaigns.

"I have been received with riotous rejoicing by the people," Caesar wrote me. "My powers as Dictator have been officially prolonged for ten years, and my statues are being set up all over Italy."

Caesar was indeed King in all but name.

I longed desperately to join Caesar in Rome, and in his letters he hinted that it would not be long before he would send for me, since he wanted me by his side during the celebration of his triumphal festivities.

From the time Caesar had left me, my nights may have been empty, but my days were filled with the all-consuming activities as Egypt's sacred sovereign. I took a great share in the affairs of administration, conscientiously applying myself to my burden, sitting at council each day, with no one to oppose my will as in the bygone days of Pothinos and Theodotus. Now, with my handpicked council, all my wishes were immediately carried out. I was present at the legal debates that took place in the gymnasium, and I judged in public all important cases.

About this time, in an elaborate ceremony, I elevated Apollodorus and Charmion, my two most beloved friends, to the highest rank in the court's hierarchy, the title of Royal Kinsmen, making them my "brother and sister."

Apollodorus, who was now twenty-eight, in addition to being the Commander of the Queen's Household Regiment, was also appointed to be my treasurer-general. In this capacity he restored order to the public finances and wiped out all corruption. Huge sums were no longer skimmed off the top from the government monopolies, and my royal revenues suddenly increased twofold.

I put these riches to good use. I began building a great fleet to replace the one which Caesar had burned, which I entrusted to my admiral Serapion. I wanted to have the greatest fleet of any nation on earth which would be used to conduct our trade and, if fate so decreed, the prosecution of war against Egypt's enemies.

In my capacity of High Priestess, I presided daily at religious ceremonies, sometimes in the Temple of Isis near the palace, and occasionally I would be rowed over the Great Harbor to the Temple of Isis on Pharos island. The mystic charms of these rites enhanced my mystery and shrouded me in a supernatural atmosphere in the eyes of my people. These rituals also gave me a feeling of tremendous solace, for the prayers were like a spell that instilled in me a spiritual sustenance and reinforced my spirit and faith, which ultimately gave me the strength to perform my temporal duties.

My obligations to the state were manifold and ceaseless, and although I had a co-monarch, I received no help from him. The new King Ptolemy, for whom I had always felt a certain fondness, was a pathetic, sad figure. While his older brother had been robust, the younger Ptolemy since birth had been beset with ill-health, and as he entered adolescence his constitution became even more delicate. I was chagrined to discover that Ptolemy had become addicted to the juice of the poppy, of which a few sips renders reality a reverie.

"Why do you take this poison?" I once demanded of King Ptolemy, finding him lost in another world.

"Because," he said, and then faltered, lapsing into a fit of stuttering that prohibited his elucidating the reason.

"Don't you know that the poppy is extremely addictive and undermines the health?" I cried.

King Ptolemy only hung his head in a dazed state.

I was told that it was his foster father, Lord Mardian, who had introduced Ptolemy to the poppy, but perhaps this was a fiction of Mardian's enemies. My enemies, on the other hand, insisted that I introduced Ptolemy to this poison, but this is ridiculous. Poppy is plentiful around the palace and many of the courtiers are addicted to it, but generally they are in their dotage and past all other pleasures. For my brother to be a slave to the poppy after just leaving childhood was a sorry state indeed.

As a little boy, Ptolemy had enjoyed playing with dolls and acquired a habit of putting on female tunics and wigs and kohling his eyes, but I thought surely with puberty these silly pastimes would be put aside. I was mistaken, however, and I was told that in the company of his effeminate companions, Ptolemy would spend hours sitting before a mirror, experimenting with cosmetics and trying on various wigs.

My father often told me that, as a young prince, he had a habit of dressing up as a young lady of fashion, and in this disguise would tour the taverns, but only as a lark. These habits were discarded once he put on the manly toga. My father had never been effeminate, and with his comely young favorites who were facsimile females, he was very much the manly lover.

It was obvious, however, that his youngest son possessed a different persuasion. Once Ptolemy became King at thirteen, he developed a sexual precocity, taking lovers from the palace guards. Later he acquired a taste for dark Nubian slaves. I was alarmed at this development, for some of his favorites appeared to be as sturdy

383

as bulls, and I feared that Ptolemy with his frail physique, and in his role of a surrogate female, might become physically damaged.

Alexandria is a melting pot of the vices of the world, with the stark sensuality of Greeks mated to the feverish eroticism of the east. The streets are filled with whores of both sexes, many of whom are little more than children. It is the custom for Greek boys to be sexually precocious, but I was still scandalized at the precocity both my brothers exhibited in their early worship of Eros and Venus.

I myself have inherited the voluptuous hot blood of the Macedonians, and I can be extremely passionate, but I am not a slave to passion and look with contempt upon those who are, regarding them as weaklings.

King Ptolemy, like his older brother, had no interest in intellectual pursuits or studies, and his tutors could do nothing with him. With his delicate health he had never been able to participate in sports. He did not want to wield either the sword or the scepter, and became a slave under the power of the poppy and the pleasures of the palace guards.

"What can we do about this situation, my Lord Mardian?" I asked helplessly.

Mardian gave a sigh and a shrug. "The physicians say that the gods have not ordained King Ptolemy to live into mature years," he explained. "The King is tormented by many fears, and knows that he will never be able to live up to the burden of being a man and a king. Perhaps this explains his enslavement to the poppy and to the beguilements of Eros, whose euphoria and ecstasy allow him to forget his fears and inadequacies. In the few years he has left of earthly life, O Queen, perhaps we should be tolerant and permit King Ptolemy to live in the manner in which he wishes."

In dealing with my brother, I took Mardian's advice. When he would look at me with his dazed blue eyes, his curly blond locks falling over his frail, pretty face, I found it impossible to pursue harsh tactics with him. I resigned myself to accepting him as he was, perceiving the likelihood of his early demise. We must each of us act out the roles the immortal gods have assigned us to play in our life upon the stage of the world.

With this frame of mind, for his fourteenth birthday, I presented King Ptolemy with a large gold casket filled with fabulous jewelry from my collection, knowing that he adored to adorn himself with jewels in the privacy of his apartments. Oddly enough, I am told that when he had on his female attire, complete with jewels and a wig, with his face painted, he made a bewitchingly beautiful young maiden, and he never stuttered but talked easily in a lovely low voice.

In public, Ptolemy was forced to wear the dress of the ancient pharaohs or the Greek toga, which made him stiff and awkward. Whenever we appeared in public, however, he was always greeted with rousing cheers from the Alexandrians. They heard rumors of his peculiarities, but they were tolerant or skeptical of them. He was, after all, their young King, and the people, considering the cultural matrix which formed them, naturally gave King Ptolemy more affection and allowances than they accorded me.

While I waited impatiently for Caesar's invitation to come to Rome, I quietly made preparations for the state visit. My father had gone to Rome in a poor and needy condition, imploring aid and begging mercy from everyone. I, his beloved daughter, would appear in all the pomp and glory of a queen, with a fabulous entourage of court functionaries and nobles and servants in attendance, striking all by the dazzling splendor of my sovereignty.

Accompanying me would be my son, Caesarion, whom I was anxious for Rome to see. I also planned to take my brother, for I did not want any general to make an independent bid for the throne in his name during my absence. My brother had no ambitions, but he was too weak to withstand the ambitious schemes that might be perpetrated in his name. My faithful Prime Minister, Mardian, would stay behind as my regent.

I did not think it unreasonable to hope that Caesar

would divorce his wife Calpurnia, and with the Roman quick divorce laws, I thought this could be arranged; but I never pressed Caesar on this point in my letters. Caesar had divorced two other wives, so I could not understand why another one, of barren stock, could not be eliminated in favor of a fruitful vine.

As time went on, however, spies in Rome let me know that Caesar had ruled out the possibility of divorce for the present. Perhaps he feared the outrage of public opinion. As distasteful as it was for me, I realized that, although I was Caesar's wife in Egypt, I would have to go to Rome as his mistress.

Ammonios, the Greek banker who had been my father's agent in Rome, wrote me several enlightening letters on the subject of Calpurnia.

"Calpurnia is the lady decorum personified," one letter stated. "Since Caesar divorced Pompeia because his wife had to be beyond reproach, Calpurnia has no intentions of giving Caesar a similar excuse for divorce. Since the civil wars, moral turpitude has been rife in Rome, and all the young ladies are no more than whores, but not so Calpurnia. She is straitlaced as a Vestal Virgin. Interestingly and ironically, O Queen, she is a secret worshipper of Isis. It was during the long decade when Caesar was in Gaul that, repressed and frustrated, she found consolation in the new religion from the east. It is a sardonic twist of fate that you, the reincarnation of Isis, should hold such a place in Caesar's wife's heart. I am told that Calpurnia scoffs at your divinity, refusing to believe that you are in any way connected to the beloved goddess she worships."

Soon after Caesar had left Alexandria, I began erecting a temple in his honor and I helped the architects draw up the designs for this splendid shrine. The temple is not far from the palace, a large colonnaded structure rising high above the waterfront in the shadow of Pharos.

There are two things left in Egypt to remind my people of Caesar, his son Caesarion and the temple Caesareum.

I realized with bleak certitude that a nest of enemies awaited me in Rome, but I was anxious to go and overcome all obstacles, and I was certain my stay there would culminate in a glorious triumph.

At last I received a letter from Caesar and read with ecstatic joy the words which I had long been awaiting.

"Come quickly to Rome, my beloved and beautiful Queen, and bring our son to share my triumphs and to build our imperial future."

As I sailed out of the Royal Harbor on my way to Rome, standing on the deck of my flagship with Caesarion beside me, the cheers from my people thronging the dockside ringing in my ears, one of my beloved father's favorite old Macedonian sayings suddenly flashed through my mind.

A long journey begins with one step.

CHAPTER VII

THE SUN RISES IN THE EAST and I, Cleopatra, Daughter of the Sun, indisputably emphasized this point when I went to Rome in all my pomp and golden glory.

After a two-week voyage across the calm waters of the Mediterranean, my five galleys carrying me and my entourage arrived at the harbor of Ostia, sailed up the Tiber, and dropped anchor late in the afternoon at a dock outside the city limits of Rome.

A courier from Caesar was admitted on board my flagship, bringing me a letter of warm salutation, and explaining that the Senate had decreed a public reception to welcome me in the Forum the following day.

Ammonios, the Greek banker, came aboard to greet me. At last I met the man who had been my father's friend and agent in Rome, and who had long corresponded with me about Roman affairs. In his early sixties and wearing his years well, he was a man of portly stature and shrewd mentality. He wore a purple Greek toga and a rich mantle, and his fingers glittered with rings.

In my stateroom Ammonios and I sat and enjoyed a repast of honeyed cakes and wine, and we felt instantly at ease with one another.

"You are the talk of Rome, O Queen," Ammonios cried. "In all the villas along the Tiber and the Appian Way, in the streets and baths and taverns, among the patricians and plebes alike, your name is on everyone's lips."

I thanked Ammonios for having sent me the lists of

all the important families in Rome, their family trees and a breakdown of their wealth, and for the lists he had compiled, one of my friends who favored my cause, and one of my enemies who were against my alliance with Caesar.

"O Queen, don't worry about your enemies," Ammonios told me in his husky voice. "Remember, I have spent most of my life in Rome and I know, as your father learned years ago, that all Romans are greedy trollops and their favors can be bought."

I nodded gravely. "Taking your advice, my dear Ammonios, I have come with numerous chests filled with splendid gifts, prepared to pave my way into their mercenary hearts."

"The Lord Antony will arrive tomorrow morning with a large guard of soldiers to escort you into the city in great state," Ammonios said.

"How fares Caesar's first deputy?" I asked curiously.

"With his orator's tongue, Antony has excited the plebes with speeches extolling your beauty," Ammonios cried.

"Do Antony's views carry weight with the people?" I inquired.

"Oh, yes, the people love him in spite of, or perhaps because of his extravagance and debaucheries," Ammonios said. "They admire his courage and gift of oratory. When Cicero makes a speech, everyone goes to sleep, but when Antony declaims, the blood is stirred and soldiers march to battle."

"Then the common people are favorably disposed toward me?"

"Decidedly, Divine Majesty," Ammonios replied, nodding vigorously. "Antony has told them that you are the reincarnation of Isis, whom they all worship. He has also stressed that you are bringing Rome your trading routes with the Orient. The rich merchants, the bankers, the patricians and the plebes alike, all realize they can make money out of an alliance with Cleopatra and Egypt."

"Still, I have my enemies here," I remarked soberly,

"judging from that long list you sent me, headed by Brutus, Cassius, and Cicero."

Ammonios waved a hand. "Cicero is an old fool, O Queen. Flatter his vanity and he will be eating out of your hand. As for Brutus, that is another matter. As Caesar's bastard, he realizes if his father had married his mother, he would be the heir to Caesar's name and fortune. There is a resentment in him against Caesar, and against you, the mother of a son Caesar openly acknowledges, and that resentment will never be palliated. If all goes well, however, Divine Majesty, you will be Queen over Rome within a twelvemonth."

Mark Antony arrived the next morning and, when Apollodorus ushered him into my stateroom, he approached me with his swaggering gait, his purple tunic girded close to his huge thighs, the red cloak of his rank as Master of the Horse thrown carelessly over his shoulders. Nine years had passed since we had last parted. Now I was twenty-three and, although he looked years younger, he was thirty-six. Antony was as I remembered. Brimming over with abundant life, he was indeed the uncanny reincarnation of Hercules.

"Queen Cleopatra," Antony cried in his deep, booming voice, sinking to one knee and kissing my outstretched hand, "I offer all my greetings to the loveliest Queen in the world, whose beauty casts a brighter glow than the famed Pharos."

I laughed merrily. "Lord Antony, that orator's tongue inherited from your grandfather has grown even more adept with the years." I gestured to a chair near my throne. "Pray sit and have a goblet of wine with me."

"The Bacchic Antony never turns down a drop of the holy grape," Antony replied, his blue eyes gleaming.

A servant served us each a goblet of Samos wine.

"Much has happened since last we met, O Queen," Antony remarked.

"I've heard many tales of your fabulous exploits since, and all to your noble credit."

"You have become a great Queen, fulfilling your father's prophecy," Antony said warmly. "How proud my dear friend the Piper would be of his cherished daughter."

"I like to think so," I said softly. "Of course, Great Caesar had a hand in securing my destiny. Since his triumphs begin in two days, I am happy the seas were calm and my arrival not delayed, for I am anxious to grace his festivities with my presence to show the people that Egyptian sentiment is with him."

"There are half a million citizens in Rome," Antony cried, "and they are all in the streets now, waiting to see the Queen of Egypt light our streets with splendor. But of all the Romans, the one who most eagerly awaits you is her first citizen, Caesar."

"And Caesar's wife, the Lady Calpurnia, is she eagerly awaiting me also?" I asked, arching my brows.

"Calpurnia is a dutiful wife to Caesar and does as Caesar bids her," Antony explained.

"She is Caesar's wife and the first lady of Rome," I cried, unable to keep a bitterness from my voice.

"Yes, but you will eclipse her with your beauty, divinity, and royalty," Antony assured me.

I smiled thinly. "I dread meeting her, but I shall treat her with unfailing courtesy and do my best not to antagonize her."

"What man or woman could withstand your charms, O Queen?"

"I have been resisted more than once, Lord Antony," I said with a little laugh. "I am sure Marcus Cicero will resist me."

"Tell Cicero that he is a great scholar and intellectual and he will be at your feet," Antony advised.

"Cicero was my father's great enemy and I depise everything I know about him, but I will try to win him over for Caesar's sake," I said resolutely. "Caesar is embarking upon a difficult phase of his life, and he will need all the assistance of his devoted friends."

"I am Caesar's right hand, and I shall minister to him with my life," Antony vowed, draining his goblet.

"Well, my Lord Antony, Rome awaits me," I cried, rising from my seat, "so let them wait no further."

Antony left and then my ladies fussed over me, putting the finishing touches to my appearance. I left the flagship and the crowds along the dockside cheered me wildly.

At last, with my great retinue I began the elaborate procession through the streets of Rome. A holiday had been declared and the Romans thronging the streets were duly impressed by my display of wealth and power. I wanted to make clear that I was not an alien Asiatic siren, but a pure Macedonian-Greek Queen ruling in Egypt. With this in mind, only members of my court who were of the Greek type accompanied me on my state visit to Rome. I had left behind all my black Egyptian wigs I wore on state occasions in Egypt, and my blonde hair flowed freely for I was aware that the Romans consider light hair a mark of superiority.

Antony, striking a gorgeous figure in shining armor, and riding a beautiful white Arabian stallion, led the procession, waving and smiling at the crowds as he passed.

After him and an escort of Roman centurions, several Indian and Alexandrian merchants were carried on ornate litters. They were followed by a contingent of my chamberlains and chief eunuchs in their colorful robes. Sosigenes led a group of astronomers, their banners emblazoned with sacred symbols. A dozen of my most beautiful ladies were carried in litters, borne aloft by Nubian slaves who were naked but for colorful loinclothes, their ebony skins gleaming under the sunshine.

I was resplendent, carried all alone in the most ornate litter made of burnished gold and sparkling jewels and roofed with purple silk to guard me from the sun. I sat on a golden throne, wearing a gown made of golden scales, with a headdress of the solar disk wrought in gold gleaming above my head, and my golden bronze hair fell in rippling waves halfway down my back. Under my solar headdress, my snake of gold jutted forth on my forehead.

Caesarion, who was fourteen months old and the most beautiful babe in the world, was carried in the litter behind mine with the ladies Charmion and Daphne. The two women took turns holding Caesarion on their laps, occasionally lifting him up. Screams of delight rose from the excited onlookers at seeing Caesar's son. Caesarion never cried once during the long procession, but squealed happily throughout.

The stench of the streets was unbelievable, and it was with an effort that I showed no expression of distaste as putrid fumes wafted to my nostrils, coming from the garbage that littered the streets, not to mention from the plebeians. It was obvious that the common folk rarely took advantage of the public baths. It was a far cry from Alexandria, where street-cleaners are busily at work daily and where even the poorest citizen takes pride in cleanliness.

Rome struck me as a small, over-crowded city made up of twisting, hilly streets and small squalid squares. All the buildings were constructed of wood, largely five-story tenements built around dark courtyards. A revolting, ugly, teeming city, but a city of raw power, Rome is in stark contrast to white marble Alexandria.

I smiled graciously at the people, nodding as they screamed out greetings. I was thrilled at my enthusiastic reception from the plebeians.

At last my royal cortege passed the Capitoline hill, with the Senate and all the impressive government buildings built of marble in the Greek style, and with great flights of marble steps. The procession moved along the Via Sacra, and then passing under the Arch of Triumph, led into the Roman Forum. There amidst its temples and marble statues stood the great men of Rome and the citizens, tightly packed, cheering me.

To the sound of trumpets, all the litters were set down in the great square. My ladies, wearing simple Grecian tunics, came and formed two lines from my litter.

Caesar sat in his chair of state. On one side of him was the stand where the Senate sat, and opposite another stand had been erected where the Roman ladies were grouped—Calpurnia, Fulvia, Portia, Cordelia, and

394

all the Julias, Claudias, and Pompeias in their stiff silks, heavy curls, their faces painted.

The senators and their ladies wore golden medallions depicting an image of myself holding Caesarion in my arms. These medallions had been minted in Alexandria to commemorate my state visit to Rome and had been sent on ahead to be distributed. Many Romans wore them unwillingly that day, but they dared not offend Caesar. Even Brutus, I was told, had his dangling down his chest.

Amidst the roaring cheers from the mob, Antony led me to Caesar, who stood as I approached. Following suit, all the senators rose to their feet, and in the stand where the women sat, Calpurnia was the first to rise to do me honor, with her Roman sisters following her example.

With all the pomp and circumstance of the Republic, Caesar, surrounded by consuls and officials, came toward me in greeting. I was deeply shocked at his drawn, haggard face, for he had aged ten years in the fourteen months since I had seen him. His cheeks were more hollow, the forehead more wrinkled, and his neck more withered, yet his face still radiated an aura of power and greatness. With effort I camouflaged my stunned reaction with a warm smile.

"Greetings and salutations, Queen of Egypt!" Caesar cried. "On behalf of the Senate and the Republic of Rome, I welcome you!"

Caesar formally saluted me as trumpets rang out, and I solemnly inclined my head toward him.

Caesarion waited inside his litter on Charmion's lap. Caesar gave an anxious glance toward his son, but there had been no plans for him to greet our child during this ceremony, since he thought it would be in bad taste to flaunt the child in the face of the first lady of Rome.

Raising his hands for silence, Caesar made a short speech welcoming me, and at the finish of it the people cheered. When silence fell, I gave an answering speech in my best Latin.

"My joy is boundless in visiting this great city on the

Tiber in acceptance of the official invitation the Senate has extended to me to conclude a treaty of friendship and alliance which my beloved father King Ptolemy arranged with Caesar thirteen years ago," I declaimed. "I pray to the gods that this treaty, which combines the great forces and strengths of Egypt and Rome, will benefit the whole world, and that the Roman eagle and the Ptolemaic eagle will fly in the heavens side by side as brothers."

A roar of applause followed my speech. I was led to a marble table set up in the square, and Caesar and I signed the documents that legalized the treaty, the terms of which gave Rome annually a talent of gold, two hundred thousand attic bushels of wheat and three million pounds in weight of oil, which would provide Rome with three quarters of their bread and lamp fuel. We both pressed our signet rings into the hot smear of wax beside our signatures.

The Roman populace erupted into an ovation, as well they might. They were getting a tremendous bargain. I, on the other hand, had the guarantee that I would not be destroyed and that my people would not become slaves of Rome.

Antony next made a stirring speech, singing my praises. I stood with all my dignity and regal grace, gazing about the vista of the Forum with a grave smile, seeing many happy, glowing faces, but here and there among the patricians I found a few hostile looks.

"Julius, I hope my Latin did not offend Roman ears," I said.

"Cleopatra, your Latin could be your mother tongue and you know it," Caesar retorted.

Caesar and I stood beside my litter as the Forum resounded to cheers.

"You are a golden queen," Caesar cried, waving a gesture toward the mob, "and you have won the heart of all Rome! Your procession will continue now to the Tiber," he told me, "and a barge will take you to the villa in the Transpontine Gardens." Then, stealing a look at Caesarion sitting on Daphne's lap in the next litter, he promised, "Tonight I will come visit you and our son."

"We will be eagerly awaiting you, beloved Julius," I said warmly.

As trumpet blasts rent the air, I climbed onto my litter. My cortege of personal litters resumed the procession along the streets to the Tiber, where Apollodorus escorted me aboard a barge draped in banners. It was only a short cruise along the winding, flowing Tiber, and at last the barge was anchored to the landing place situated below Caesar's villa.

The villa, standing off the Via Campana, is set in lovely, rolling gardens on the right bank and west side of the Tiber. It is a charming, luxurious place of residence, secluded by vast gardens, within easy reach of the city, yet at the same time remote from its teeming bustle. The gardens are situated on the Janiculum Hill.

Ammonios was waiting for me on the landing place, and he escorted me up the flight of marble steps to the gardens behind the villa. As I entered the atrium of the villa, I found a scene of confusion and din. Soldiers and slaves, under the supervision of hysterical eunuchs, were busy bringing in my possessions from the ships anchored along the river and stacking them at random in the corridors and chambers. Ammonios accompanied me as I made a quick tour of the villa with Caesar's chief steward. It was a small palace with more than twenty-five rooms and three courtyards containing beautiful, sculptured fountains.

King Ptolemy, who was not physically able to join me in the procession, was already installed with his entourage in a suite of rooms in the east wing; and my son and I and our court took up residence in the rest of the villa.

"It is the most luxurious villa in Rome," Ammonios remarked.

"Caesar once said that his villa could fit into my palace banqueting hall," I said. "The Lady Calpurnia must be vexed to be shut out of her home."

"Their townhouse on the fashionable Capitoline Hill

near the Forum is almost as grand as this," Ammonios explained.

"O Queen," Apollodorus said with an air of urgency, "I think our ships must be docked on the banks of the Tiber below the villa at all times. May the gods forbid it, but if Caesar were to die, your life and the life of Caesarion would be in danger from Caesar's enemies. We must be able to escape by river to the sea if such a tragic event were to occur."

"Lord Apollodorus speaks sagely," Ammonios said.

"As always, and so it shall be done," I cried.

I took a leisurely, soothing bath, slept for an hour, and then my ladies dressed me for Caesar's visit.

At last Caesar arrived and I greeted him in the garden as he came up the steps from the riverbank. I wore a tunic of transparent tissue, spun like gossamer gold, and a tantalizing perfume.

"Beloved Julius," I cried, tenderly embracing him, "it's been such an eternity! I pray the gods never part us again."

"A sentiment I share, Cleopatra," Caesar said, kissing me on the mouth.

Taking Caesar by the hand, I led him to the chamber where Caesarion lay asleep in his crib.

"You may pick him up if you wish, Julius," I whispered.

"No, I do not want to wake him," Caesar said. He was content to lean over, examining our child closely. "My son, my very own son!" he said softly. "He has my chin, I dare say, and that sharp little nose is definitely Julian."

"Everyone says he has an uncanny resemblance to his father," I said pridefully. "He is the cub of the great lion of Rome!"

"I hope you will find the villa comfortable, my dearest," Caesar said as we reclined together at dinner. "I want to repay the hospitality you gave me in Egypt."

"I am sure I will be very happy here, Julius."

"And so, Cleopatra, after several years you have

renewed your acquaintanceship with my Master of the Horse, Antony," Caesar ventured.

"Oh, yes," I murmured, reaching for my goblet.

"What is your impression of him now?" Caesar inquired

I took a reflective sip of wine. "Antony is as I remember him, an overgrown boy," I replied. "If only he had a few more brains and a little less brawn! During our meeting on my flagship this morning, the conversation was rather trivial."

Caesar gave a throaty, pleased laugh. "Antony cares not a fig for our cherished intellectual pursuits, but the common people worship him. His wife Fulvia and his mistress Cytheris also are not paragons of intellect and are well suited to him."

"Your wife, the Lady Calpurnia, is the first lady of Rome," I said. "I do not wish to preempt her place, and I want to live quietly here."

"Yes, but you must witness the triumphs," Caesar insisted. "You will sit on the official stand beside Calpurnia."

I did not relish such a prospect, but smiled pleasantly. "As you wish, my dearest."

Two of my favorite lute players were making soft, romantic melodies, which stirred us to a sensuous mood. After we finished dining, Caesar gazed fondly at me, his eyes falling to my bosom.

"You must be tired from the long day, my darling," Caesar said.

"Yes, beloved Julius," I replied with a tremulous smile.

We rose and walked in silence to the bedchamber. I went to the robing room and my ladies undressed me. They held up a robe for me, but I shook my head and walked naked back into the bedchamber.

A slave had extinguished all the lamps and only a small taper glowed. I found Caesar sitting naked on the edge of the bed. I stood, in all my nakedness, as Caesar drank in the sight of me.

"Cleopatra, I must have Archesilaus fashion your

body and immortalize it in marble," Caesar cried with inspiration.

"Archesilaus, the greatest sculptor in Rome!" I exclaimed. "That would please me tremendously, Julius."

"Ever since I left Egypt," Caesar cried, gathering me against him with urgency, "I have dreamed of holding you in my arms."

As great tenderness swept over me, I embraced Caesar once again. It had been more than a year, and as my hands explored his body, I was shocked at how emaciated he had become. His epileptic fits now occurred more often, and had taken their toll. The act of love was a tremendous effort for him. I had studied all the books from the library on the art of love and erotic lore written by the ancient Greeks, Persians, and Egyptians, and I used every wile I had gleaned to stimulate his debilitated flesh.

When Caesar lay spent against me, I was overcome with love. I was surprised at the intensity of the feelings I experienced because Caesar, the master of the world, the father of my son, the man of my life, the only man I had ever known, was once again in my arms.

In the morning, Caesar rose early, and after playing with Caesarion on the floor of the reception room, and taking a little food, he had to leave. Holding Caesarion in my arms, I walked down the marble steps to the banks of the Tiber and saw Caesar sail off on his barge to return to the city and to the duties of state.

The following day, Caesar began celebrating his four triumphs to signalize his victorious campaigns over Gaul, Egypt, Pontus, and Numidia, and to illustrate the magnitude of his exploits. The spectacle of my entrance into Rome had been merely a prelude to the pomp and parade to which the Romans were now treated. The pride and vainglory of Caesar led him to make his triumphs more imposing than any former conqueror had ever enjoyed.

The triumph over Gaul was held first. At noon I was taken from my barge in a litter to the Forum, where I alighted with Charmion beside me as the crowd cheered. The Lady Calpurnia approached me and we were introduced by Ammonios. We inclined our heads and exchanged smiles and gracious greetings. To the roars and scrutiny of the huge assemblage, we were escorted to the official dais and sat beside one another on golden chairs of state, with all the ranking ladies of Rome sitting behind us.

"Lady Calpurnia, I am honored to witness the first great triumph of your husband," I cried, smiling.

"Caesar earned this triumph over Gaul fourteen years ago," Calpurnia explained in her thin, high-pitched voice, "but due to the ruses of Cato it has been many times postponed."

"What glorious weather for a triumph," I exclaimed. "All Rome seems to be in a jubilant mood."

I observed that what little beauty Calpurnia had once possessed had long since faded. She was clothed in a tunic of Vestal white, and looked more like an old Vestal Virgin than the first lady of Rome. She seemed stiff and ill at ease in my presence, and my youth and beauty obviously disturbed her.

The triumphal procession had begun early that morning, congregating in the Field of Mars outside the city, and had been making its way through the streets and now was proceeding along the Via Sacra into the Roman Forum.

A legion of soldiers was in the forefront, marching stiffly and arrogantly, their bronze helmets, shields, and breastplates glinting in the sun. They were followed by a contingent of senators and magistrates amid a fanfare of trumpets.

An endless train of wagons rolled by, overloaded with all the spoils of Gaul, gold and silver booty from the conquered cities, and statues of the Rhine gods. Lurid paintings depicting battles and other striking scenes, mounted on wheeled platforms, rolled by, a record showing Caesar leading his armies in one victory after another. The animals for sacrifice were paraded along, white bulls with their horns gilded and garlanded with flowers.

Next came the forlorn figures of Gallic captives, marching sorrowfully on foot and dragging their chains. There is a theory that Macedonians stem from Gallic tribes who had migrated south in the days that are time out of mind. I found it difficult to keep an impassive expression as I watched thousands of wretched Gauls pass by, chained to one another. They were, after all, merely patriots who had defended their fatherland against the Romans. Like these miserable captives, I, too, was an alien in Rome.

After the Gallic prisoners had passed through the Forum, I glanced over to the marble Arch of Triumph through which Vercingetorix, the King of the Gauls, now passed. I saw that Vercingetorix, who was only thirty years old, was a splendid specimen of a Nordic god. Tall, with massive bone structure and noble bearing, he had blond lank locks that fell to his shoulders, and indeed he looked as much a Macedonian as a Gaul. His feet and hands were bound with golden chains, and in spite of the weight of the chains, he walked tall and proud with a kingly bearing.

"Vercingetorix has lain in prison for six years waiting for this public appearance today," Calpurnia explained in a smug tone.

Those long lamentable years had not broken Vercingetorix, I clearly saw. "The way this King holds his head," I remarked in admiration, "one would think he was a hero instead of a captive."

Calpurnia bristled, not pleased with the dignified deportment of the King her husband had vanquished, and I knew that Caesar would not be too happy about this, either.

After Vercingetorix there came Caesar's official escort of seventy-two lictors. Beside them pranced a troupe of musicians playing flutes and zithers, and attendants walking with smoking jars of perfume to make the air aromatic for the god who was behind them.

402

At last Caesar's triumphal chariot, drawn by four white horses, passed through the Arch of Triumph and entered the Forum to resounding cries. Caesar stood stiff and tall in the chariot, wearing a purple robe embroidered with golden stars, and gold sandals on his feet. In his left hand he held the ivory scepter with the eagles of Jupiter at its tip, and he saluted his people with right hand uplifted. A golden laurel wreath crowned and camouflaged his balding head, and his face was proud. A troupe of clowns, dancing and singing in the Etruscan manner, rambunctiously cavorted around Caesar's chariot.

"Caesar today has become the living image of Jupiter!" Calpurnia exclaimed ecstatically.

"Yes, he so has the bearing of a god," I agreed.

Just as the victor's chariot was approaching the official dais where I sat, the axle of the chariot broke. Caesar staggered, but with an agile movement he leaped to the ground. The chariot twisted and fell to its one side. There was a great startled murmur from the crowd, and my heart missed several beats.

Caesar, regaining his aplomb, held his ivory rod in the air, and the people, recovering from their shock, cheered.

I glanced at Calpurnia, seeing that she had turned white. I myself shuddered, thinking an evil portent had occurred.

Caesar glanced our way, waving his baton, but it was my eyes he sought and not his wife's who sat beside me.

Mark Antony alighted from his chariot, embraced Caesar, and helped him onto his chariot. They continued, their arms around one another, to the other side of the Forum, where they were to sit with all the leading senators.

Several of Caesar's loyal legions marched by, singing bawdy songs referring to him as the "bald adulterer." There were obscene lyrics about his affair with me, and even his old relationship with King Nicomedes of Bithynia from his youth was dragged up. It was the custom for the legionaries to have the license to sing these salacious songs. Caesar took it all in good sport, and I was obliged to do the same.

Caesar, with Mark Antony, left the official stand and once again climbed onto Antony's chariot. To the thunderous roars from the people, the chariot passed out of the Forum.

The Lady Calpurnia and I rose from our chairs.

"What will happen to King Vercingetorix?" I asked anxiously.

"As custom decrees," Calpurnia said loftily, "he will be taken to the Marmentine Prison near the Tarpeian Rock and strangled."

"But King Vercingetorix is an honorable, brave enemy!" I cried, aghast. "Surely Caesar will spare him."

"He broke oaths of fealty, and his sins against Caesar and Rome are too great for him to hope for forgiveness," Calpurnia said dispassionately.

"Vercingetorix voluntarily surrendered to Caesar to spare his people from further punishment," I cried. "It will do Caesar great honor to now show him mercy."

Calpurnia shrugged indifferently, bored by this topic. "Queen Cleopatra, I pray your stay in Rome will be a pleasant one, and I hope that before the pressing duties of your kingdom call you back to Egypt I will again enjoy the charm of your company."

It was apparent that Calpurnia wished my Roman stay to be one of brevity, but I had no plans to leave.

"I entertain a similar wish, Lady Calpurnia," I said.

"I trust you are comfortable in my villa?"

"Very comfortable, my noble lady," I replied.

"Did you enjoy the triumph today?" she asked.

I had thought it a gaudy circus, cheap, offensive, and tasteless, but I smiled and cried, "It was a glorious spectacle and a day that will be remembered in history."

"Tomorrow Caesar's second triumph will be even more memorable," Calpurnia said with a touch of sarcasm.

The next day would be the triumph over Egypt, and as distasteful as it would be for me, I would have to lend my presence to the proceedings.

Apollodorus had my royal litter brought up, and with Charmion beside me, I bade farewell to Calpurnia and made my way down the steps of the dais. Charmion and I entered the litter and, with Apollodorus leading the way on a white horse, I was carried to my barge on the Tiber, as huge crowds that lined the route along the way cheered me.

For Caesar, however, the day did not end. After the procession had left the Forum, it continued to the foot of the Capitoline where Caesar officiated at the sacrifice, cutting the throats of the white oxen.

As darkness was falling, to the light of a thousand torches held aloft by loyal soldiers, Caesar ascended the marble flight of stairs to the Temple of Jupiter, with Mark Antony at his side. Inside the temple Caesar laid his laurel wreath and other trophies of victory in the lap of the statue of the god, and made sacrifice and said prayers to Jupiter and Jove the god-protectors of Rome.

In the evening I played with Caesarion and fed him with my own hands. We then went to the bedchamber and I placed him in the crib beside my bed. My nerves were as tightly pulled as the strings of a harp, and I took a draught to insure that I would sleep that night so that I would be better able to cope with the arduous day to follow.

The next day, at Caesar's wish, I went to the Forum and took my place beside Calpurnia on the official stand. It was an unbearably hot, sultry day. My heart was heavy, my head was aching, and my eyes watched unseeingly the immense columns of carts, flags, banners, and trophies which made up the parade that passed before me.

One cart carried an enormous gold-plated reproduction of Pharos, and another carried a model of the Sphinx. A statue representing the famous old god of the Nile, Nilus, was borne on a huge wagon. Several animals native to the Nile, lions, panthers, and crocodiles, were paraded in cages. A hundred giraffes and camels were led in the procession. The Romans had never seen these animals; and, in their ignorance, they laughed and jeered at these proud, beautiful creatures, thinking they were ugly beasts.

It was with some glee that I rested my eyes on the paintings of my dead enemies, Achillas and Pothinos. Their likenesses were done in caricature which exaggerated, if possible, their grossness and coarseness.

A wagon bearing a painting of my dead drowned brother, King Ptolemy, came next, and in front of the painting his gold armor, which Caesar had taken from his body, was displayed.

A long line of Egyptian prisoners, who had fought for the cause of Arsinoë and Ptolemy, filed by in chains.

I took several deep breaths to steady myself, for I knew that Arsinoë was not far behind. I must now witness the degradation of my sister-princess, and with an effort I showed no expression.

Calpurnia turned to me. "What a marvelous triumph it must be for you to see the sister who tried to steal your throne march in chains today," she cried.

I gave Calpurnia a noncommittal smile.

At last through the Arch of Triumph, Princess Arsinoë entered the Forum. The jeers with which the mob had greeted the paintings of Pothinos and Achillas were not to meet my sister. Caesar had put her in a plain brown homespun tunic and she walked barefoot. Although she had a slender, elegant body, she bore the weight of her heavy chains and walked proudly, her lovely head held high in the best tradition of our house, every inch of her a princess. At the sight of her, the crowd was struck with admiration. I was to learn later that all along the processional route, her courageous figure and dignity had overwhelmed the populace, and they were touched by the way she conducted herself in her sad state of sorrow. In their admiration they threw roses, meant for Caesar, at her.

Caesar had been intent on having a princess paraded as a trophy, but he had not expected that the people would lament the lot of the captive who had fought against him and that they would be moved by the valiant spectacle she made.

"Viva Princess Arsinoë!" the people cried out all along the way.

Behind Arsinoë, as Caesar's chariot rumbled by in a cloud of dust, I could see his unhappy scowl.

I felt a certain pride for my sister, for the sight of her walking courageously in chains was unforgettable and she turned her humiliation into a triumph.

"As you know, Queen Cleopatra," Calpurnia remarked, "it is the custom for royal personages, once they have walked in a triumph, to be slain at the end of it. However, Caesar has promised as a homage to your royal house to spare Arsinoë, unlike Vercingetorix, who was only a barbarian."

"Vercingetorix was slain?" I asked, shocked.

"Last night, according to custom, he was strangled."

I was horrified that Caesar would be so cruel.

"It's unfortunate that your consort, King Ptolemy, is not with you to enjoy Caesar's triumphs," Calpurnia remarked.

"King Ptolemy has stayed behind at the villa to play with his nephew, Prince Caesarion," I explained.

At the mention of Caesarion, I saw a nerve twitch in Calpurnia's cheek.

I made my farewells and was hastily taken back to the villa. Arsinoë was escorted once again to the small villa where she had lived as a prisoner of state for more than a year. I learned that Caesar had been greatly unnerved by the popular reception Arsinoë had received, and he was beside himself with anger.

Bored by the gaudy parades, I resolved to exempt myself from the triumphs of Pontus and Numidia the following two days. I sent a message to Caesar informing him of this intention. I knew that he was set with the idea that I should bear witness to all the glorious display of his popularity and power, but I felt that I had done my part by sitting through the first two.

For the next two days, I stayed in the villa, spending the humid afternoons in the shaded gardens playing with Caesarion. Apollodorus and Charmion, however, went to the Forum to witness the third and fourth triumphs and duly informed me of them.

The third triumph carried a painting representing Caesar plunging a sword into the chest of Pharnaces of Pontus, which was a mendacious interpretation since this Hellenistic king took his own life after defeat in the manner of the noblest of Greeks. A large banner was carried in the procession before Caesar's chariot bearing the arrogant declaration, *Veni, vidi, vici.*

For the fourth and final triumph over Numidia, Caesar could not march Cato, Scipio, and King Juba, for they had all killed themselves, so he had vulgar paintings depicting their suicidal scenes carried aloft. Little Prince Juba, six years old, was too small to walk in chains, so he was chained to a cart beneath a huge portrait of his father. This handsome dark-skinned boy won the admiration and pity of all as had my sister. Caesar remarked later that perhaps the custom of having royalty participate in triumphs was not such a good idea after all.

Several thousand Numidian prisoners, chained together, walked behind the cart that carried their young prince. Forty elephants obediently marched in the parade, linked together by tails and trunks, which excited the curiosity of the Romans, for elephants had not been seen in Italy since the days of Hannibal.

Caesar presided over these celebrations for days while I stayed quietly in the villa. He gave a banquet in which twenty-two thousand tables were set up in the squares for the people. The best foods were served, wine spouted from fountains, and the citizens became riotous and intoxicated.

Shows of every possible variety were exhibited to gratify the barbarous and cruel population. The Romans are especially fond of combats of all kinds, providing they end in bloodshed and death. They enjoy combats between wild beasts, of dogs against dogs, lions against tigers, of any animal that can be trained or goaded into fighting. The most abominable custom is the Roman gladiatorial games in which human beings, soldiers and slaves and captives, are forced to fight each other to the death to entertain the people.

In Alexandria we amuse ourselves with Greek sports and contests, of fine young athletes wrestling, running, throwing the discus, of equestrian games and dances and the theater, all of which are civilized entertainments. Needless to say, in all my time spent in Rome, I never once set foot in one of the gladiatorial amphitheaters.

Caesar, wishing to indulge the Romans in their barbaric tastes on an unparalleled scale, had a large artificial lake built near the Tiber and filled with water drained off from the river. The lake was surrounded by stands on which the populace could sit. Caesar had two galleys put on the lake, with a thousand fighting men on each ship. The galleys were manned with captives, one with Asiatics and the other with Egyptians. The two squadrons were ordered to approach each other and fight a real battle to amuse the spectators. Most of the soldiers were slain, and the dead bodies of the combatants fell into the lake and dyed the water with blood.

A land combat followed, held in the Field of Mars, in which five hundred foot soldiers, twenty elephants, and a troop of thirty horses were engaged on each side. Apollodorus attended this fierce, merciless, bloody encounter, but I begged him not to describe it to me.

As Queen of a great kingdom, I know that sometimes it is necessary to make war and to spill blood, but to do so only to amuse the mob is beyond my civilized comprehension. I was deeply shocked, but I refrained from condemning Caesar for his cruelty and reckless waste. He had obtained a great portion of the money to spend on these spectacles from my treasury. I did not mind giving money to Caesar to secure an alliance and to build our future, although I wished it to be put to better use for libraries and schools to serve as a more lasting benefit to the people.

The Romans are barbarians, but I feel that if a Roman-Egypto Empire can be created, with a Julian-Ptolemaic dynasty established, it would take two or three generations, but these barbarous customs can be

409

stamped out, and one day the Romans could be as civilized as any Greek.

At the end of the triumphal festivities, which lasted several days, Caesar gave donations to soldiers, centurions, and officers, and each citizen received one hundred denarii, ten pecks of corn, and six pints of oil.

My sister Princess Arsinoë had won many admirers during her walk in the triumph. All over Rome people spoke of deep compassion for her, and everyday citizens of all classes congregated outside her villa, struck by her beauty and moved by her misfortunes. They would call out her name, and she would step out onto the balcony and receive their ovations like a queen. Men in love with her laid flowers at her doorstep and would sleep in the garden beneath her window at night.

When Caesar came to visit me one evening, I brought up the subject of my sister.

"Julius, I think Arsinoë should be set at liberty and sent to Cyprus to take up her duties as Queen," I suggested.

"That would be an extremely unwise move, Cleopatra," Caesar said grimly.

"We promised her on oath that if she walked in the triumph she would be installed as Queen of Cyprus," I reminded him.

Caesar laid before me three letters. "These are for your cognizance, Cleopatra!" he said harshly.

I unrolled the scrolls and scanned them, shocked to my soul at what I read. The letters were in Arsinoë's hand and had been intercepted by Caesar's intelligence agents. They were addressed to certain nobles at the court of Alexandria and mentioned plans to make Arsinoë Queen of Egypt, a move that could only be accomplished with my death. Obviously there were plans being made to take care of that contingency.

"Twice I promised to make that incorrigible little bitch Queen of Cyprus," Caesar cried with umbrage, "but she is not content with that."

"No, the Cypriot crown would never assuage her ambitious heart," I said with a sigh. "She is obsessed with the thought of the Pharaonic crown blazing on her blonde little head."

"Her blonde little head ought to be put on the chopping block," Caesar said with a sneer.

"That would not be propitious, Julius, considering the force of public sentiment which seems inclined to sympathize with her," I remarked.

Caesar bristled, still outraged that she had been cheered instead of jeered when she had walked in his triumph.

"We could send her to Ephesus, a city far from Alexandria, Cyprus, and Rome."

"Send her where you wish," Julius said. "I wash my hands of her."

I made arrangements for Arsinoë and her household to be taken to Ephesus on one of my galleys. I had her brought to me before her voyage. The galley anchored below my villa, and Apollodorus and guards escorted her up the flight of steps into my reception room.

She carried herself with her usual defiant and prideful demeanor, walking toward me as she had walked in the triumph. When she reached the throne-like chair in which I sat, she reluctantly sank to one knee.

"Dearest Sister Queen," she murmured inaudibly.

I stood, and taking her by the shoulders, raised her to her feet. "Greetings, dear Arsinoë," I said warmly, kissing both her cheeks. "Pray, sit and let us take wine together."

Arsinoë took a chair near me. A servant gave us goblets of wine, and a tray filled with stuffed figs was set on a table between us. Several of my ladies in a far corner strummed lyres and harps, making sweet music.

"You're looking remarkably well, sister," I said sincerely.

"My skin was sunburned from walking in the triumph," Arsinoë remarked airily, "but I enjoyed the exercise. I received as many cheers as Caesar!" She gave a wicked little laugh. "I'm told Caesar was displeased."

"What actually displeased Caesar were your treasonous letters which were intercepted," I replied.

Arsinoë took a sip of wine and nonchalantly shrugged. "Yes, Cleopatra, I've been told about these letters which Caesar had forged to turn you against me. I won't even bother to protest my innocence."

"No, please don't bother, since we both know the letters were in your script, Arsinoë," I said firmly.

Her blue eyes narrowed at me. "Possibly it was you who forged these letters as an excuse to renege on your promise of Cyprus!" she cried with a flash of audacity.

"I promised you Cyprus, but I did not take into account your plotting my downfall," I cried. "One is not rewarded an island kingdom for treason, but punished by death."

"You would not dare to rouse the disfavor of the Romans by cold-bloodedly killing me," she cried defiantly. "Who would believe these trumped-up charges and those cleverly forged letters?"

I was breathing heavily, and I took a drink of wine to calm myself. "You are my half-sister," I resumed patiently, "and we share the same father. Although I detested your mother, you are a Lagos and there aren't many of us left of the blood royal. I do not want to kill you, Arsinoë, although I would be in my right to do so. You will be allowed to go to Ephesus. Our father stayed there, and the High Priest Megabysus at the temple who was his friend will receive you. I will send you a generous pension so that you will be able to live in the style according to your rank. Ammonios has arranged for you to have the villa in the groves of Artemis where Father lived."

"I thank you for all your kindnesses," Arsinoë said in a tone of harsh sarcasm, habitually arrogant and ungrateful as ever.

I had one of my eunuch chamberlains fetch King Ptolemy.

"Before you depart, I imagine you will want to see our brother," I said. "I take it Ptolemy had nothing to do with your treasonable schemes."

"What schemes?" Arsinoë retorted recalcitrantly. "I am at the mercy of whatever schemes Caesar attributes to me, and if he wishes to associate my poor, weak little brother in these absurd allegations, what can either of us do about it?"

I sighed, but deep down I admired her boldness.

When King Ptolemy came, brother and sister embraced. There was an awkward tension between the three of us. I tried my best to keep the conversation on a pleasant plane, but Ptolemy only stuttered uncontrollably each time he attempted to make a declaration, and Arsinoë did not relent an iota in her arrogance toward me.

"I hope Caesar will make an honest woman of you in the eyes of Rome," she said provocatively. "Caesarion is no more Caesar's legal son in Rome than is Brutus."

"There are many problems in the path of my future, but they will all be solved in time," I remarked calmly.

"Perhaps, with the help of the gods and the Senate," Arsinoë exclaimed sarcastically, "both of whom will have to be propitiated with munificent offerings!"

The time came for Arsinoë to take her leave. King Ptolemy and I bade her farewell at the top of the stairs leading down to the Tiber.

"Perhaps in Ephesus I will become a priestess at the Temple of Artemis," Arsinoë said with mock piety.

"Oh, I don't want you to become a priestess, Arsinoë," I said frankly. "In a few years I hope that you will be able to rule Cyprus as my vice-queen. However, there must be no more letter-writing to brew plots to disrupt my sovereignty, for rest assured I will come to know about them and you will suffer the consequences. I will not be so lenient the next time I am faced with your treason."

I embraced Arsinoë and found her body stiff in my arms, and the cheek she turned to my lips was cold. I stepped back and watched as she took our brother and held him close to her with warm affection.

"Farewell, dearest Arsinoë!" Ptolemy cried tenderly,

without stuttering. "I pray that Neptune gives you a pleasant voyage to Ephesus."

"Farewell, sweet Ptolemy!" Arsinoë cried with true emotion stirring her voice.

I saw tears sparkling in her blue eyes, but then once again she got a firm grip on her emotions. She relinquished her brother, and holding herself erect, was led down the marble stairs, escorted by Apollodorus and a guard of honor.

King Ptolemy and I stood, watching our sister descend the steps. She crossed the gangplank and walked onto the deck of the galley. The gangplank was pulled on board, the oars were dipped into the gray waters of the Tiber, and the galley began sailing downstream. Ptolemy raised a hand in farewell, and I would have done the same, but I saw that Arsinoë had disappeared below deck without even a backward glance our way.

The sun was setting behind the hills of Rome, and twilight was falling as we made our way in sad silence along the well-kept gardens leading back to the villa. King Ptolemy took leave of me, returning to his suite where he could once again put on cosmetics and female attire, and sip poppy juice and be at ease with his companions.

Although Ptolemy felt affection for Arsinoë, and there was a kindred spirit between them, I did not entertain for a moment the possibility that he could have been associated with her plotting. His health of late had been improving, and it occurred to me that perhaps he would outwit the predictions of the physicians and survive into manhood. If so, I hoped that in five years I could send him off to Cyprus to reign beside Arsinoë, since it was apparent that he could not go on being my co-monarch. I felt that, because of his timidity and the dilemma of his sexual identity, Ptolemy would be willing to give up sharing the double throne of Egypt, which he had assumed reluctantly in the first place, in exchange for the less demanding crown of Cyprus. Arsinoë and he were compatible and this would prove to be a solution to many dynastic problems that I could see arising in the future. I would then be able to make Caesarion my co-monarch and declare him Pharaoh of Egypt.

Life in the future would be an intricate chess game, but I felt certain that if I made the correct moves, I would win the world.

CHAPTER VIII

THE GREATNESS AND GLORY which Caesar had attained appeared to wipe out all open opposition to his power. Rome was grateful to Caesar for having won half the world, and the Senate vied with the people in rendering Caesar every possible honor. Statues of him were placed in public buildings and borne in processions along with those of the gods; he was given an ornamented gold chair to sit on during his official duties in the Curio—almost like a throne but not quite—and he was voted the privilege of wearing the purple boots of the old kings of Alba. Caesar was Dictator and Consul, the title of Father of his Country was conferred upon him, and he was commander-in-chief of all the armies of the Comomnwealth.

In everything but the name, Caesar was a sovereign and an absolute monarch, just as I am in Egypt.

"When will you be made emperor?" I asked Caesar.

"Patience, my dear Cleopatra," Caesar counseled.

"If I were a slave, patience would be a virtue," I cried, "but I am not a slave but a divine monarch."

I settled into Caesar's villa surrounded by my retinue of chamberlains, eunuchs, and guards. I conducted my life with tact and reserve and rarely ventured forth across the river into Rome. I sorely missed Alexandria with its cooling sea breezes. I hated the hot, humid, autumnal air of Rome, but Rome was the seat of the world where it was imperative I live for the moment to make myself known to the Romans, for one day I wished to be their empress. I had to be at Caesar's side to assist him in organizing the empire along the lines of an eastern monarchy. Through me, the most royal creature on earth, he could establish a dynasty. He certainly could not expect Calpurnia to play the part of an empress.

While I posed each morning for the Greek sculptor, Archesilaus, my chief chamberlain read me the dispatches from Alexandria, and I dictated my decrees to the scribes. At least twice a week ships sailed from the dock below my villa and carried my diplomatic pouches to Alexandria. In this fashion, from the villa on the Tiber, I ruled Egypt by constant communication with my ministers back at my Egyptian court.

I gave my first banquet in late October, and invited many of the leading Romans, although not all of them came. Brutus and his wife Portia sent their regrets. Caesar had just appointed Brutus, along with his brother-in-law Cassius, to the post of the praetorship of Rome. Although receiving this high office, Brutus did not deem it necessary to oblige his patron by accepting an invitation.

This first banquet was a small but splendid gathering of some fifteen couches. The best foods and wines were served, and for entertainment I had the great singer, Tigellius Hermogenes, whom I had taken under my wing, and the guests were treated to several lovely songs during the first courses.

Mark Antony came with his wife, the Lady Fulvia, and he also brought his dull-witted but charming younger brother, Lucius. Fulvia was a tall, well-made woman of striking looks. She was not overly feminine and lacked grace and even charm, but she had intelligence and strength of character, and I liked her immensely. Antony was happy with her and it was obvious that he was under her influence.

At this time Fulvia was in her mid-thirties and had been a widow with a thirteen-year-old daughter. Caesar had arranged Antony's marriage with Fulvia. For several years Antony had led a scandalous life, living with the actress Cytheris, and Caesar thought that marriage with a strong, respectable woman like Fulvia would be good for Antony. I agreed that she was just the sort of woman he needed. She had an inflexible seriousness, and Antony was constantly playing tricks on her, and all Rome laughed at his vain attempts to get a smile out of his wife.

Fulvia came to the banquet barely out of her confinement, having presented Antony with a son, Antyllus. I invited Fulvia to share my couch, thinking we could discuss motherhood, but this was not a topic that interested her. She was an ambitious woman and immersed in politics.

"I am not suited for domesticity, Queen Cleopatra," Fulvia frankly admitted. "Nor would I be content with a private husband. Marriage with a first magistrate interests me, and nothing less."

"If Antony is to realize the great potential within himself," I agreed enthusiastically, "he needs a strong woman behind him."

"Until I married him, he was always in the company of prostitutes and parasites," Fulvia explained. "I have put a stop to all that, and I see to it that he conserves his energies for the state."

"Fulvia, with you at Antony's side, only the gods know what pinnacle of power you may attain," I said.

"Well, I am certainly not like other Roman matrons," Fulvia cried. She gestured disdainfully at the ladies congregated on the other side of the room. "My sisters are only concerned about their latest lover or with swapping the latest gladiator or wrestler from Thrace. They do not consider adultery an act of which to be ashamed, and chastity is looked upon as proof of ugliness. I find it revolting the way they deceive their husbands."

"Including the Lady Calpurnia?" I asked.

"Divine Majesty, the barren, cold Calpurnia is the only faithful wife in Rome besides myself. No one wants her, not even her husband. She is faithful to Caesar and to her beloved goddess Isis, and the irony of that is lost on no one in Rome!"

419

I had every intention of being just as faithful to Caesar as Calpurnia, I reflected with resolution.

At length I dismissed Fulvia, and with a smile I beckoned Marcus Cicero and his wife, the Lady Tertia, to me. Cicero was nearing sixty; he had snow-white hair, and years of drinking had taken a toll on his body. Since he had a sharp tongue and pen, I knew I had to court and charm him.

"Great Cicero, you are the greatest intellectual in the world," I exclaimed with a glowing smile, "and I would be honored if you would one day come to Alexandria and lecture at the university."

"I will come, O Queen," Cicero cried with a fulsome smile, revealing yellow teeth, "but only if the time does not conflict with my duties to Rome. With Marcus Cicero, the Republic always comes first!"

"I would not want to be guilty of taking you away from your obligations as the staunchest, foremost Roman Republican, my noble Marcus," I responded.

At this banquet, at the theater and in several other events during my stay in Rome, I was approached by people who claimed that they had been my father's friends during his years of exile in Rome. There were several delicate fops, now past the flower of youth, who intimated that they had enjoyed my father's personal favors. I treated them with utmost courtesy, for I was grateful to anyone who had shown kindness to my father during that bleak time of his life. I was also sought after by several businessmen and bondsmen who insisted that my father had left Rome owing them money. I instructed Ammonios to pay those debts, some twelve years outstanding, with accrued interest and without any attempt to substantiate the bills, although I am sure many of them were not authentic or had been sizably padded.

Caesar came at least twice a week to visit at the villa, the trip taking less than half an hour by barge on the Tiber, and we resumed the intimate life we had enjoyed in Alexandria, interweaving love and politics, irrevocably bound by our son and our dreams. Caesar loved to play with Caesarion, and one of his greatest enjoyments was to bathe with his son. Caesar tremendously enjoyed these visits, for he was able to relax, enjoy our conversation, and escape from the dull, dour Calpurnia.

I continued to exert a strong influence over Caesar. We always talked over the affairs of Rome, and he owed many of his measures to me.

"There are no libraries in Rome, which is a disgrace!" I pointed out to Caesar. "As Ptolemy the First built the library at Alexandria, so must Caesar build a great library in Rome and be remembered for it."

"Yes, if Rome is to rival your beloved Alexandria, she will certainly need a library," Caesar agreed.

After mulling over several candidates, Caesar appointed his old enemy, the polymath scholar, Marcus Terrentius Varro, to the post of librarian. Under my aegis, Varro formed excellent relations with my chief librarians in Alexandria, who assisted him in getting together a great collection of volumes.

Caesar was forced to hire Greek architects to draw up the designs for the library, since Roman ones of any merit were not to be found. At the same time a Greek theater was designed and construction began near the foot of the Tarpeian Rock. Caesar planned many other public buildings of marble in a grandiose scheme of development which he hoped would exceed in scope and splendor all the edifices of the world.

"The Pontine Marshes must be drained," I earnestly told Caesar. "Pestilence is rife from the marshes and every year thousands die of fever. Remember, Alexandria was once marshland, but Ptolemy the First drained the site and constructed a city of marble over it."

"It will be a formidable task, Cleopatra," Caesar said, "but as always you are right, so it shall be done."

Canals were constructed to drain the marshes. Caesar also began revising the Criminal Code. He conferred citizenship upon doctors and artists, most of whom were of Greek origin, which pleased me. He made plans to cut a canal through the Isthmus of Corinth, and the harbor at Ostia was improved.

For every measure taken, however, Caesar had first to obtain the approval of the Senate.

"It's so absurd, Julius, that you must go before the Senate and ask their permission to do this, to do that, as if you were a pupil and they were your pedagogues," I said sarcastically. "The first three years of my reign I was hampered by my brother's triumvirate, but with your help, I overthrew them. Now when I want something done to benefit Egypt, I issue the decree and it is forthwith executed. The Senate has no imagination and only hampers you. What Pothinos and Theodotus were to me, the Senate is to you."

"Rome is still a Republic, my dear," Caesar said.

"That can be rectified," I cried.

The year drew to a close. I celebrated my twenty-fifth birthday quietly with a small banquet, and Caesar gave me a necklace of rubies and pearls.

I impressed upon Caesar that my Egyptian Eudoxian calendar should be adopted into the Roman world.

"The Roman calendar is off by six months from the seasonal, solar year, and must be reformed, Julius," I explained fervently. "There are not three hundred and fifty days in the year, but three hundred and sixty-five and a quarter days, which means there should be an extra day every four years, what we call a Leap Year."

"Our calendar corresponds exactly with the annual circuit of the sun, August Caesar," said Sosigenes, who had been called in to consult with us. "It has worked perfectly for the last six years in Egypt, and three thousand years will have to elapse before our calendar will be off by one day."

Sosigenes showed Caesar all the charts, and Caesar at last concluded that our calendar was indeed ideal. He presented the matter to the Senate, which after much debate approved, and the calendar was adopted in the name of the Julian calendar. Neither Sosigenes nor I received any credit for the calendar. I suggested that Sosigenes, the greatest astronomer in the world and the architect of the calendar, should be on hand in the Senate the day the calendar was officially adopted so that he could take an ovation from an appreciative assemblage, but Caesar brushed this suggestion aside.

"The fact that Egyptians have reformed the calendar will engender enough ill will in the Romans," Caesar said, "so we must not overstate this."

Rome detested bowing to the wisdom of the east, and for the time being I had to repress the resentment I felt.

A force of great strength was building up in Spain during this time of the two defeated sons of Pompey, Gnaeus and Sextus, who desired to avenge their father's cruel fate. Gnaeus and Sextus were young, yet they had managed to gather an immense army and showed they had the courage and conduct to command it.

"I feel this force puts me in extreme danger," Caesar told me one evening after we had supped. "I must go to Spain and destroy the last of the Pompeians."

"Do you really think it is wise for you to leave Rome," I asked, alarmed, "now that there is so much to be done in reform?"

"My administration is endangered as long as there is a Pompeian force menacing me in the rear," Caesar cried.

"Julius, I have been in touch with the Lady Cordelia," I broached softly. "She has great influence over her two stepsons, and she could write them in an effort to mediate between you."

"I, Caesar, negotiate with Pompey's sons?" Caesar bellowed.

"A negotiated truce would be a propitious move," I cried fervently. "If a little moderation, statesmanship, and common sense were applied, this could lead to a just solution to the civil wars. This is not the time for you to disperse your energies by running off to Spain."

"No!" Caesar cried. "The matter will be settled on the battlefield and my enemies will be exterminated to the man."

"You have forgiven so many of your enemies, Julius," I bravely went on. "Brutus, Cassius, Trebonious—"

"Pompey has been destroyed," Caesar interrupted hotly, "and so will all his seed!"

"It would be better for your cause to have certain enemies in Rome exterminated, instead of going to Spain to make an end of the fine sons of Pompey," I pursued recklessly.

"Of course, that is your counsel to me," Caesar said, stewing with dissatisfaction, his voice swelling with suggestion. "I recall your ardent friendship with Gnaeus some years ago when he lingered at your court on a mission from his father."

"Gnaeus and I were friends," I said calmly, "and the salacious stories wicked tongues invented about us were false, but then you of all people, who found me a virgin, know that."

Caesar bristled and stared past my shoulder. "I have already begun making plans to start off for Spain in a month," he announced adamantly.

I took a deep breath and made one final plunge. "I think it is best to conquer by tactics and diplomacy, beloved Julius, rather than by the sword."

"Not until the heads of Pompey's sons are cut off in the manner of their father will I know any rest," Caesar cried cruelly. "We will speak no more of this!"

Caesar was palpitating, and I feared that I had so provoked him that the distemper would seize him. I knew there was no arguing with Caesar, for he hated to be contradicted, and so I at last desisted.

"While you are in Spain, beloved Julius," I said in my sweetest voiec, "I will sorely miss you."

Caesar's anger began to abate a little at these tender words. "It will be a short campaign," he said crisply. "I do not anticipate any difficulty in wiping out the last of my enemies."

A few days before Caesar's departure, in early February, he came to the villa to spend some time with Caesarion and me. On a crisp, cool but sunny afternoon, he took his son out into the garden. They lay on a blanket on the ground playing together, while his soldiers and attendants stood nearby. I watched for a moment from a window, and content that father and son were in merry spirits, I resumed the chair at my desk to dictate letters that had to leave by special squadron for Egypt the following day.

After some time a servant rushed in unannounced.

"O Queen, Caesar has been hit by the falling sickness!"

Deeply alarmed, I raced madly out into the garden. I found Caesar writhing convulsively on the ground in the throes of a fit, and Caesarion was crying helplessly beside him. Caesar's aide, Aulis Hirtius, was kneeling beside Caesar, and had placed the ivory stick, which Caesar always carried in his pocket for such emergencies, in the mouth to keep the tongue from being chewed up.

"Take Prince Caesarion inside!" I cried, gesturing frantically to the nurses who hovered several feet away.

The nurses were terrified to approach Caesar in his condition, but at my command crept near, picked up Caesarion hurriedly, and scuttled away.

I knelt beside Caesar and took his trembling hands in mine. He had bitten his tongue and the foam streaming from his mouth was red. The convulsions were violent, but gradually the spasms subsided, and I knew that the fit was running its course. I observed closely, seeing that his eyes had rolled in the back of their sockets. I wondered if it were really true that the body is inhabited by a god when the divine malady seizes its victim.

At last the final tremors diminished, Caesar's body stilled, and the brown eyes rolled back into place. Caesar came back to himself, and his eyes looked up at mine with recognition.

I tenderly wiped a hand over his moist, wrinkled brow. "Oh, Great Caesar, every time you suffer an attack of the divine malady, I am reaffirmed of your divinity!" I cried rapturously, wanting to give him courage, knowing that the fits always demoralized him. "I think of Alexander, of Hannibal, and of our great Pharaoh Akhenaten who believed in one god, all who suffered from the same sacred sickness."

Caesar only gave a wearied sigh, as if he had just fought a tremendous battle, and closed his eyes.

I stood and motioned for his soldiers to carry Caesar into my bedchamber. I ordered everyone out so that we could be alone. With my own hands, I tended Caesar, removing the clothes from his frail body, sponging the sweat from his skin, and holding his head while he sipped wine.

"Beloved Julius, what do you experience under the influence of the divine malady?" I whispered.

"During the seizures," Caesar explained weakly, "I suffer hallucinations and divine manifestations!"

"Yes, yes?" I prodded eagerly.

"It is difficult to articulate my sensations," Caesar said with his usual tight-lipped reserve.

I sighed with disappointment, wondering if Caesar was withholding the truth.

"I pray to the gods that I will not fall prey to a fit in Spain," Caesar moaned. "The attacks have become more frequent and pronounced lately, and I feel myself wasting away under their strain."

"Only the greatest of men and gods suffer from fits," I cried. "This malady indicates emphatically your close relationship with the gods."

"Who will tell that to my soldiers if I have a fit on the field of battle?" Caesar asked. "And what will happen if I do?"

"You will have your soldiers around to protect you," I said. "Besides, the seizures never last long."

"The battle could be lost by the time the fit is over," Caesar remarked.

"Caesar has never lost a battle and never will!" I cried with spirit, choosing to forget the one defeat at Dyrrachium. "It is not in your stars, Julius!"

I lay on the bed and held Caesar close to me, and he soon drifted off to sleep.

A contingent of officers and centurions came to the villa the next morning. In the group was Caesar's great nephew, Octavian, whom I had never met before. Caesar was scheduled to leave Rome the day after, but I would not see him again. Caesar warmly embraced Octavian, who at seventeen was a short, thin lad with light, blotchy skin, straight blond hair, and a reticent disposition.

"Cleopatra, this is my nephew, Octavian," Caesar cried proudly.

I went up to the boy and smiled, holding out my hand. "Greetings, Octavian," I said in my most gracious manner.

"Greetings, O Queen," Octavian said shyly, taking my hand and inclining his head stiffly.

"Your uncle has often spoken warmly of you," I said. "You must be full of anticipation in going to Spain as one of his aides-de-camp."

"Yes, Majesty," Octavian replied.

I turned to Inhapi, who held Caesarion in her arms. "Octavian, I want you to make the acquaintance of your cousin, Caesarion."

Inhapi came forth holding Caesarion toward Octavian.

"Shake the little devil's hand, Octavian," Caesar encouraged expansively.

Octavian gingerly placed his fingers around Caesarion's little hand, and managed a pinched smile which did not quite mask a look of hostility.

"Do you see the resemblance to me, Octavian?" Caesar asked.

"Yes, Uncle Julius," Octavian replied morosely.

"Great Caesar, the time has come to depart," Aulis Hirtius cried.

The moment of farewell had irretrievably come. With a swelling heart, I walked down to the riverbank to Caesar's barge.

"Beloved Julius, return quickly from Spain," I cried in a quavering voice. "In your hour of triumph, be merciful and give clemency to your enemies."

"You couldn't resist a final good word for the last of the Pompeians, could you?" Caesar said. "We shall see, my love."

I threw my arms around him with a surge of desperation. "Oh, Julius, you are a giant among men, and all others are mere midgets!"

"Farewell, beloved Cleopatra," Caesar said, kissing

my mouth. He turned from me and kissed Caesarion, who was held in Charmion's arms, and then he hurried to the barge.

A cold wind came in off the river. I stood shivering, with tears in my eyes, watching Caesar go aboard his barge with Octavian and his officers. I waved as the barge sailed away. Caesar stood on deck beside Octavian; he waved briefly and then put his arm around his nephew's shoulder. Tears sprang to my eyes, blurring the sight of Caesar and his nephew standing shoulder to shoulder, and with a feeling of deep despair, I hurried up the steps to the villa, resigning myself to a time of anxiety until Caesar returned.

Travelling with his usual celerity, Caesar reached Spain in twenty-eight days, arriving in late February. There followed several inconclusive minor engagements before he was finally able to force the Pompeian army to a major confrontation.

"On the plains of Munda on March the seventeenth, the Day of Bacchus, a great battle was waged," Caesar wrote me. "Seeing my men hard pressed, and making a weak resistance, I ran through the ranks of my soldiers, and crying out, asked them whether they were not ashamed to deliver me into the hands of boys. At last, with great difficulty, I forced back the enemy, killing thirty thousand of them, and losing one thousand of my own men. I have often fought for victory, Cleopatra, but this was the first time I fought for life. Your old friend Gnaeus was slain on the battlefield, but his younger brother Sextus managed to escape. I am happy to report that the Pompeians have been decisively defeated."

I felt joy over Caesar's victory, but a sense of sadness at the death of Gnaeus overwhelmed me. I recalled the long lost days when he had come to Alexandria and we had felt each other's charm. We had been so young, and there had been the promise of glory about us and a sense of our young lives about to take shape. Gnaeus, the golden son of Great Pompey, had gone on to meet

Pompey's statues up again, Julius," I suggested one night.

Caesar grunted. "You always did have a soft spot for my greatest enemy, Cleopatra."

Pompey's statues went up again, and Caesar even had one placed in the Curio of the Senate and named the chamber the Hall of Pompey.

"Surely your countrymen will concede all to your fortune," Antony cried fervently to Caesar one night as we all dined together. "There is a move in the Senate, Julius, to make you all-powerful ruler in the hope that the government of a single person will give Rome time to breathe after so many civil wars."

"The time has come when Caesar will be made emperor of Rome!" I exclaimed hopefully.

"We must take one step at a time, Cleopatra," Caesar said.

By great conquests, public feasts and spectacles, by erecting glorious public buildings, by bribes and shows of clemency, Caesar had galvanized the people and bent them to his will. He had been made Dictator for ten years, and now the Senate changed this to Perpetual Dictator. I knew that his enemies would regard this as indeed a tyranny avowed, since Caesar's power was not only absolute but perpetual.

Caesar had celebrated his fifty-sixth birthday shortly before returning from Spain, but he looked well into his sixties. The weight of the world lay heavily upon his frail features, and his sickly appearance acutely distressed me.

"You are the unchallenged lord and master of the Roman empire which stretches from Britannia in the north to Asia Minor in the east," I told Caesar. "You are the master of the world that you conquered and united."

"Yes, so I am," Caesar agreed with an ecstatic sigh.

"Being proclaimed Dictator for Life is not enough, Julius," I cried with impatience and agitation. "You must be proclaimed emperor of the empire you carved out with your sword."

Closing his eyes, Caesar sighed and trembled, over-whelmed and lost in thought. He did not speak, and neither did I. The silence around us was pregnant with our thoughts, for we realized, given the state of Caesar's health, that our dreams of replacing the traditional Republic with a divine monarchy for our son to inherit must be realized or they would forever be just dreams.

Caesar and I were running a race with death.

CHAPTER IX

IT WAS A LOVELY AUTUMNAL DAY when the statue Archesilaus had done of me was publicly exhibited. The statue, all gilded in gold, is a beautiful likeness and shows me in a Greek tunic and with my hair caught in a classic style. Caesar and I were extremely pleased with the work, which so authenticated my beauty, dignity, and elegant proportions, and we rewarded the great sculptor handsomely for his labors. The statue had been completed soon after Caesar had left for Spain, but it was not until a month after his return that it was officially unveiled.

The Juliam Forum, the grandiose annex to the overcrowded Roman Forum, was filled that day with thousands of spectators who were anxious to see the statue and to gaze upon Caesar and his Egyptian mistress, the Queen whom they rarely saw in public. The statue had been placed on a pedestal in front of the Temple of the Venus Genetrix and was placed alongside the statue of Venus, the progenitress of the Julii. Workmen had erected my statue during the night and covered it with a cloth of gold.

To the sound of trumpets, and with Caesar at my side, I pulled off the cloth. The surging, excited crowd, held back by soldiers with crossed javelins, gasped with awe at the unveiling and rang out with resounding roars. I stood there, gripped with emotion, radiant, and transfigured at this glorious honor being bestowed upon me.

"It is only appropriate that your golden statue should stand beside my divine ancestress," Caesar told me with pride. "This is an act of homage to the woman I love who is the mother of my son, and may no Roman mistake it."

No Roman did mistake it, nor the political implications which the statue represented. Cicero and some other senators were indignant, although the plebeians accepted Caesar's glorifying me in this manner. The plebeians were partial to me, regarding me as a kinswoman of the gods and the reincarnation of their favorite Isis, the sister of Venus, a goddess of love and fertility. Unlike the patricians, the lower classes did not object to me as a foreigner. They were of a heterogeneous composition themselves, for Rome, in the manner of Alexandria, is one of the melting pots of the world.

The sovereign power of Rome for centuries had been divided to balance one interest against another. Terrible conflicts had often occurred among the various sections of society, but no one power had been able to gain the entire ascendency in the Republic until Caesar who, through his mighty exploits, had concentrated in himself all the principal elements of power.

Caesar was assuming autocratic powers, and this awakened jealousy in his rivals who hated him for having triumphed over them, and they began to be suspicious that Caesar wished to make himself a king. Many watched his rise with fright and envy, and I felt that they would stop at nothing to hinder his attainment of royalty.

The intoxication of divinity and the desire for a crown burgeoned within Caesar, and yet he hesitated to make the final moves to bring his dreams into reality. He was at the peak of his powers, and I urged him to make himself a king before his enemies gained strength.

"The people must offer me the crown," Caesar said irresolutely, with a mixture of pride and timidity.

"Did my forefather Ptolemy the First ask the Egyptian people for the crown of the pharaohs?" I asked goadingly. "No, he took it. Did his brother Alexander the Great ask the Persians to make him Emperor of Asia? No, he took it. Did my ancient an-

434

cestor Perdiccas the First ask the people eight centuries ago to make him King of Macedonia? No, he took it. And so, Julius, must you crown yourself Emperor of the Roman empire which you have created!"

The sagging jowls of Caesar's face twitched nervously. "If we are to bring our dreams into manifestation, Cleopatra," he temporized, "we must tread this path with prudence."

"Just think, Julius, once you are King, you will be able to wear a crown to hide your baldness," I said teasingly.

"Yes, I'm aware of that advantage, my dove, and I will have the crown, but patience!"

"I must be patient about so many things," I said with a trace of bitterness, deciding, while I was in one of my nagging moods, to bring up another unpleasant topic. "I am Caesar's wife in Egypt, but in Rome I am merely his whore."

Caesar reached for my hand, squeezing the fingers placatingly. "It is my fixed intention, Cleopatra, my love, that one day we will be legally married by Roman constitutional law, never doubt that."

"And our son?" I demanded. "You were married fourteen years to Cornelia, six years to Pompeia, and now fourteen years to Calpurnia, but only I have given you a son!"

"Yes, and Caesarion will be legitimized," Caesar assured me. "You will be my wife and Empress, but Rome was not built in a day, and you must bide your time."

"Time, time!" I cried, trembling with impatience. I felt the time had come to be frank, even at the expense of being cruel. "Time is not the greatest ally we have in the world, Julius!"

Caesar blanched at this remark, but he stiffened and nodded gravely. "Yes, and so you are right, Cleopatra. I am a god, but even gods are called in time to Olympus."

There were many points about which Caesar kept me dangling, but the question of Calpurnia was a burning issue that rankled deep. I knew that Antony was encouraging Caesar to repudiate Calpurnia and to marry me, but Caesar demurred, saying, "The time is not ripe," and "It will affront society."

A large crowd of flatterers assiduously frequented my villa, and all the great men of Rome came to pay their respects. I knew several of them hated me as an alien queen. Many lavished upon me the most fulsome of flattery, seeking Caesar's favor through me, and I had to use all my diplomacy to handle these situations.

My friend Ammonios was always at my court, and I grew extremely fond of him. The historian Hirtius, who had been with Caesar in Alexandria and had been his ghost-writer on the *Commentaries*, was a frequent guest. Gabinius, who had restored my father more than a decade before, had been in exile, but I interceded with Caesar to recall him. He was now an old, grizzled man, racked by rheumatism, and I invited him to all my banquets and treated him kindly. Atticus, Lepidus, Lentulus, Dolabella, and all their wives came to enjoy my hospitality. The wives received lavish gifts, such as little Sphinxes plated in gold, and I did my best to gain their goodwill.

Antony and Fulvia came often and were dear friends. Although Antony and I took each other's distinct measure and experienced deep feelings of sympathy, I never allowed us to be carried away into relations of a more intimate nature. We were never alone, although I had the impression that if we had been, he would have made amorous advances toward me, as he did with Charmion, who took it all as a joke. Antony had uncontrollable impulses and could be an impetuous fool if one gave him the slightest opportunity. I was too wrapped up in Caesar to even think of any other man, and what appealed to me most about Antony was his loyalty to Caesar and his advocacy of our cause.

In early October, Caius Octavian, having reached the age of eighteen, was sent off to Greece to study with a friend his own age, Marcus Agrippa.

"A year of study at Apollonia will do him the world of good," Caesar said with enthusiasm.

"His Greek is atrocious," I remarked.

"Yes, and his rhetoric is deplorable, but under the tutelage of the tutors at Apollonia, all that will be rectified," Caesar said.

I felt a deep loathing for Octavian, that pale, cold young man, and I could not understand why Caesar lavished such concern on the son of a niece when he had a genuine son in Caesarion. Every time Caesar came to visit, he brought up the subject of Octavian, and it took all my will power to control my resentment.

"Octavian served me well in Spain," Caesar said. "He will be a great politician. He is taciturn, but still water runs deep. He is ambitious and astute, and he should have a glorious future ahead of him."

"His health seems delicate," I mentioned.

"Yes, and that's one reason why he should spend a year in Greece," Caesar explained. "The Spartan discipline will be good for him, and although he is frail, he will toughen up with the regimen there. Octavian has a cautious streak and takes care of himself. It is men like Antony, blessed by the gods with Herculean strength, who abuse themselves and go to seed quickly and die young."

Rumors were rife in Rome that, while in Spain, Octavian had submitted to the desires of his great-uncle. I was naturally deeply disturbed by such stories, perhaps more so because, knowing Caesar as I did, such tales were not outside the realm of possibility.

I was pleased that Octavian was out of Rome, and I prayed to the gods that the weather would be quite severe in Macedonia that winter and would prove lethal for the boy's frail constitution.

"I sometimes fear for Caesarion's life," Caesar said to me one evening. "If something should happen to me before our dreams of a Roman dynasty are realized, Caesarion will still be the heir to the Egyptian throne. After we are called to Olympus, however, who says that

437

he will ever wear the crown? You may think your brother is a weak stutterer, but as long as he lives he poses a grave threat to our son's Egyptian inheritance."

"What do you suggest I do, Julius?" I asked calmly.

"There should not be too many Ptolemies in this world," Caesar replied coldly.

"Our son is named Ptolemy Caesar," I cried with emphasis. "I will make an agreement with you. I will eliminate any Ptolemy who endangers our son's Egyptian inheritance, if you eliminate anyone of your family who endangers our son's Roman inheritance."

I stared unwaveringly at Caesar as his deep-set brown eyes flashed fire at my words, for he knew well whom I meant. He looked away and gave no reply, for he dearly loved his nephew. After this exchange, Caesar never again made reference to the notion that I should do away with my brother.

Caesar was intent on winning Marcus Brutus over to our side. Several times I had invited Brutus to the villa, but he had always declined. Finally, Caesar prevailed upon Brutus to accept one of my invitations, along with his brother-in-law Cassius, whom Caesar had just made one of his legates.

"I do not relish entertaining Brutus and Cassius," I told Caesar. "As always, however, I shall comply with your wishes."

"You will like Brutus if you give yourself the chance," Caesar said.

"I don't understand people like Brutus," I cried. "Pompey had his father murdered, yet in the civil war between Pompey and you, Brutus was leagued on the side of Pompey, his father's murderer!"

"Brutus thought it the more upright cause," Caesar explained. "Brutus has inflexible integrity and the greatest honor."

"After Pharsalia, when you pardoned Brutus, he immediately told you that Pompey had fled to Egypt," I said. "And you say Brutus has honor and integrity? May the gods spare me from ever having such an honorable friend!"

438

"I pardoned Brutus in memory of his mother, Servalia."

"Yes, I know you believe him to be your son," I said bitterly.

"That is the one reason why you hate him so, because you wish to believe Caesarion is my only son."

"I hate Brutus because he is your enemy!" I cried violently. "He would rather kill you than see you realize your ambitions."

"Cleopatra, Brutus is coming to the villa, and you must hide your feelings," Caesar insisted. "You can win his sympathy in speaking of scholarly subjects, for Brutus is an intellectual like yourself. His writings and orations are always filled with maxims and axioms."

"All stolen from the Greeks," I interposed.

"Why, just the other day I was listening to one of his speeches in the Senate," Caesar remarked, "and I didn't understand a thing he said, but he said it all with such beautiful rhetoric."

Caesar decided that both Antony and he would stay away from the villa the night Brutus and Cassius paid court, on the excuse that matters of state called them away.

The banquet was held on a cold November evening. I had braziers burning all over the reception room, for I was not used to the severe Roman winters. It was a small party of only ten couches, and a delicious feast was served. Sallust recited his latest verses, and Horace, who had just turned twenty, read some dreadful, pretentious, flowery poems, all cribbed from Callimachos, and the Roman guests applauded enthusiastically.

Cicero was present that night. He had just divorced his old wife Tertia, and had married his seventeen-year-old ward, Publilia, in order to get her vast fortune and to renew his youth. I gave the new bride a wedding present of a ruby necklace, and she giggled with girlish delight.

"Illustrious Queen," Cicero said, smiling with fulsome ingratiation, "I am a great admirer of that masterpiece of Alexandrian literature, *The Argonautics* by

439

Apollonios. Is it true that you have the original manuscript in your library?"

I moved away from him a little, trying not to show my distaste at his foul breath. "Yes, my noble Marcus," I said. "I will send to Alexandria and have the original sent to you as a gift."

"The original?" Cicero cried gleefully. "Oh, Queen Cleopatra, your generosity is boundless."

"It is my duty to see that the original manuscript of one great writer should belong to another man of letters who is equally great, noble Cicero," I said without blinking an eye.

Brutus arrived late with his wife Portia and his brother-in-law Cassius and his wife Tertia. Brutus, although only thirty-four, appeared years older. His face was worn and he had a grave, austere aura. Portia was a pale and prim woman with a cold beauty and cool, aristocratic features. Cassius was tall, lean, and pale, with a fanatical fervor gleaming in his wild black eyes, and his wife was nondescript and totally submissive to her husband. The wives immediately went off to the side of the chamber where the ladies congregated to titter and gossip.

I moved around the room conversing with my guests. At last I took a seat in a chair surrounded by men. By this time I noticed that Brutus, Cicero, and Cassius were heavily into their cups, true to their reputations as the hardest drinkers in Rome after Antony.

"I pray I am not intruding, my noble Romans," I said pleasantly.

"Not at all, Queen Cleopatra," Cassius said.

"We were only saying how we Romans abhor the very name of king," Brutus announced churlishly. "We have had kings in our early periods, but they made themselves odious by their pride and oppressions."

"I am cognizant of Roman history, noble Brutus," I said serenely. "It was your ancestor, Lucius Junius Brutus, who drove out the Tarquin kings and founded the Republic and became First Consul."

"Yes, and his name and memory have been cherished

440

ever since as that of a great deliverer," Cassius asserted.

"In that legacy I am a staunch Republican and follow the principles of the Conscript Fathers," Cicero said haughtily.

"We Romans have for the last five centuries been persevering about our Republic," Brutus gravely resumed, "and though we have had our internal dissensions without end, we have persisted unanimously in our detestation of all regal authority, so that not one of our long line of statesmen, generals, and conquerors has ever dared to aspire to the name of king."

With a great effort I maintained a placid expression. "Yes, I am aware that you have little respect for crowned heads."

"Most high, most worthy, most puissant Queen," Cicero said facetiously, "please understand that our Roman dislike of kings is only a dislike of having kingly authority exercised over ourselves. As you see, there are a few statues of foreign monarchs in Rome, such as your golden image which graces the Juliam Forum. We are willing that kings should reign in our provinces, under our guardianship, but there is a spirit of democracy in Romans which is affronted at the notion of a monarch in Rome."

"We venerate the antiquity of your ancient line," Brutus said gruffly. "We admire the efficiency of your government, the grandeur of your empire, and your city of Alexandria, which is the flower of your dynasty. An ancient, fabled land like Egypt, filled with an ignorant people who worship animals, needs a monarch to rule with despotic wisdom over them. It would take a million soldiers, however, to place a king securely upon a throne in Rome."

"In Egypt we do not worship animals, but merely the spirit personified in them," I remarked calmly.

"It is said you celebrate all the sacred rites of Egypt," Cicero cried, "but surely, O Queen, you do not follow the heathen religions but do so simply out of political calculation."

441

"I am Queen of Egypt, and the ancient faith of my peoples is my own, noble Cicero," I said simply.

"Oh, dear gods!" Cicero murmured in dismay.

"When I was a little boy at school," Cassius cried, his voice high-pitched and sour, "Faustus, the son of the Dictator Sulla, bragged to me about his father's autocratic powers, and I punched him in the mouth. I was six at the time!"

"Cheers for you, my dear Caius!" Cicero cried.

Cassius beamed happily at the memory. "Yes, since childhood I've had a fanatical hatred against any form of autocracy."

I signalled to the wine steward, who passed more wine around, filling the goblets of these hard-drinking Republicans.

"Come, let us drink a toast," I said good-humoredly. "You will notice, noble Brutus, I am not serving a Greek wine from Samos, but a good Falernian. Will you kindly propose a toast to the Republic?"

"Certainly," Brutus cried, raising his goblet. "Long life to the Republic!"

Brutus, Cassius, Cicero, and several others drank with me.

I excused myself from this vicious circle to go bid farewell to several departing guests, among them Lady Fulvia.

"I saw you surrounded by all your devoted admirers," Fulvia said with a sarcastic smile. "Was the talk interesting?"

"Very, my dear Fulvia," I replied.

"My Queen, I have been so bored with the women," Fulvia moaned. "I must say, after more than a year in Rome, you have behaved like a perfect wife to Caesar, while the rest of the Roman matrons are nothing but whores. All they talked about tonight was their latest lovers and their jealousy of you."

I kissed Fulvia in farewell, and as she walked away, Brutus came to my side.

"Queen Cleopatra, may I have permission to speak honestly?"

"Of course, Brutus, as you have done all evening."

Brutus drew very close, his eyes narrowing at mine. "Many say that you are urging Caesar to make himself a king," he whispered gruffly. "Whether this is true or not, I do not know, but as long as you stay here, his life will be in mortal danger. Heed my advice, and return to Egypt, for your sake and for Caesar's sake."

"You are a valiant Roman, and I thank you for your presence this evening," I said coolly. "Farewell, noble Brutus."

At this I turned away, trembling inwardly with rage.

The whole evening had been more disastrous than I had anticipated. To be humiliated by my guests in such a fashion was reprehensible. I decided that Cicero would never get the precious manuscript I had promised him.

Many times I had suffered humiliation because of Caesar, but this ordeal was inexcusable. The next time Caesar came to the villa I reproached him bitterly for having subjected me to such a trial.

"Brutus will never be won over!" I cried vociferously. "It is folly for you to keep honoring the man who would rather kill you, emulating his famous ancestor, than to see you become king. If you had made an honest woman of his mother, however, Brutus would be the greatest advocate of the monarchy in Rome, for he would become king after you. This is your Brutus with his integrity and honor. And as for the fanatical Cassius, I cannot believe you have made him one of your legates. Why aren't you giving these positions to your friends who favor our cause? You will never be able to conciliate your enemies, Julius. You should murder them before they murder you."

A new year dawned, and I became fretful and anxious about Caesar's health, which was failing. Subject to fainting fits and nightmares, he became grouchy and bad tempered. My experience with my father in his last years had prepared me for dealing with old men with deteriorating health and ill-tempered moods, al-

443

though at times it took all my forbearance to handle Caesar.

Caesar was growing daily more short with his subordinates. "Men must look upon what I say as the law!" he would cry out in vexation. He harshly rebuked the Tribune Pontius Aquila for not standing when he walked in front of the Tribunician seats, and for weeks afterward he would sarcastically preface his statements in the Senate by saying, "With the kind permission of the Tribune Aquila!" Since Aquila was known for favoring our cause, I thought this was tactless.

At my suggestion Caesar had Roman coins minted with his profile stamped on them in the monarchical tradition. My Alexandrian coiners came and improved the minting plants and did the engraving on the coins, which showed Caesar's head crowned with the halo of a sun god. Caesar presented me with a necklace made of the first gold coins bearing this image. This was only one of the many gifts he gave me for my twenty-sixth birthday, but the one I most cherish.

In late January, as Caesar was returning from the Latin games in the Field of Mars, people in the street shouted, "Hail, O King, hail!"

"I am not king, but Caesar!" he retorted.

Caesar decided to elevate his surname to the significance of a royal title, since Rex was so repugnant to most Romans.

All this time Cicero, Brutus, and Cassius were making strong speeches against Caesar in the Senate.

"How long are we going to let Caesar play the king?" Cicero demanded.

Caesar remained indifferent to what I considered treason, and I heatedly argued against his tolerance.

"You are a divine monarch." Caesar told me patiently, "and of course you have the legacy which gives you the right to squash anyone who opposes you, but Rome is still a Republic."

"Yes, but let me warn you, Julius, that there will be dire consequences for you if you continue to permit men like Cicero and Brutus and Cassius to remain alive and to carry on against you in this manner."

It seemed our glorious dream of a monarchy was not emerging into reality, and Caesar lacked the courage to repulse by force all antagonists.

"I shall conquer Parthia," Caesar announced one evening, "and then they will make me king!"

A pause fell while I took this in, shuddering. "But a campaign in Parthia will take at least two years of your life, Julius!"

"Rome still rankles from the defeat of Crassus in Parthia nine years ago," Caesar said. "I will give Rome their revenge, return triumphantly, and in gratitude Rome will make me their king!"

"You have given the empire Gaul, Iberia, Germania, Britannia, and half a dozen other dominions," I cried with exasperation. "Is that not enough?"

"No, Parthia will have to be added to the list."

"Two years of your life, Julius!" I cried with despair.

"I know I am old beyond my years, Cleopatra, but I am always invigorated by campaigning," Caesar said. "I shall leave in the spring with my legions. I shall conquer Parthia through to India, and return to Rome, crowned with glory."

"May I go with you, Julius, as Princess Roxanna accompanied Alexander on his campaigns?"

"No, you must return to Egypt and keep my son in safekeeping and guard his interests there," Caesar said firmly. "The Parthian adventure will require enormous supplies of wheat and money from Egypt and the eastern kingdoms. You must control the supply lines to my legions during the campaign, and for your backing, my beloved, you will be rewarded."

"In precisely what way?" I demanded coldly.

"Why, you will become my empress, of course!"

"If you married me before you left and declared yourself king, I could stay in Rome as your regent," I suggested.

"That would be out of the question," Caesar said. "Rome will never accept the rule of a foreign woman."

"Shall you leave Rome in Antony's hands?"

"No, I will send Antony to be Proconsul of Macedonia, and Brutus will take charge of Gaul. Rome will be left in the care of Balbus, Oppius, and Lepidus."

Balbus, Oppius, and Lepidous were three weak, nondescript fools, I thought, but they would never dream of wresting Caesar's power away for themselves.

I was against the Parthian campaign for several reasons. For one, I felt sympathy for the east, being Queen of an eastern kingdom myself, and I did not share Caesar's anxiousness to crush Parthia for the disgrace they had inflicted upon Rome when Crassus was killed, for after all, Parthia had merely been defending itself against invaders who wanted to crush their freedom.

"Forget Parthia, Julius!" I cried fervently. "With one audacious, bold stroke, proclaim yourself king and be damned to Cicero, Brutus, Cassius, and the rest. You have Antony and many powerful Romans who would support you as their king. Have a coronation in the Forum, and we will mount the thrones of Rome, side by side, with our son beside us, and anyone who does not kneel at our feet will have their lives forfeited and their property confiscated."

"I cannot steal the crown, Cleopatra, it must be given to me," Caesar said timorously. "After Parthia, our dreams will be fulfilled and the Senate will invest me with the regal power."

After a pause of deep reflection, I sighed and remarked, "Well, Julius, never forget that in Egypt you are my husband, and you can always come to Alexandria and be my consort."

"I will never settle for being a pharaoh!" Caesar cried with a sneer. "I will be emperor of the world, and nothing less."

Preparations for the Parthian expedition proceeded rapidly, and since I could not discourage Caesar in his plans, I put a good face on the matter and encouraged him.

"You will become the equal of Alexander!" I cried with spirit. "My father told me years ago, Julius, that

446

you were born to attain great glories. After you have conquered Parthia, Clio, the Muse of History, will dub you Caesar the Great!"

I began to look upon the expedition with a lighter heart, and I realized that if Caesar were successful, his achievements could build a power structure that would last for centuries.

One evening in early February, Caesar came to the villa, bringing with him, as he often did, Mark Antony, and the three of us supped together.

"I have a brilliant idea!" Antony exclaimed, after he had eaten his fill and was flushed with wine. "It has been in my mind for several weeks, Julius, but I want to broach it in the presence of Queen Cleopatra."

"Let us hear what the idea is, Antony!" I cried eagerly.

"Yes, by all means," Caesar said.

"As we know, a good half of the Senate body would willingly see you crowned king, Julius," Antony explained, "and all of the common people, who love you as if you were their father, would be overjoyed if their Caesar, the father of their country, became their king and emperor."

Caesar nodded thoughtfully. "I have feasted the plebeians for years and passed legislation that protected them from being exploited by the patricians, and I have never doubted their loyalty."

"Once the diehards in the Senate see that the people are wholeheartedly for you as king," Antony went on, "they would have no choice but to knuckle under. I have a scheme to test the reaction of the people."

"Yes, yes, my dear Antony, go on," Caesar cried.

"In two weeks there will be the Feast of the Lupercalia," Antony said. "I think my young cousin Antoninus and I should be selected to be the two nobles from the Order of the Luperci to run through the streets and perform the sacred rites. You as Dictator will be sitting on your state chair in the Forum, which will be crowded with plebeians. When I reach the Forum, I will offer you a kingly crown. We will judge by the reaction of the people whether they want you to have a crown or not."

"An excellent idea!" Caesar cried, and turned anxiously to me. "What are your thoughts on this, my dove?"

I took a long thoughtful sip of wine. "My noble Lord Antony, you know that I hold you in the highest esteem, and I do not mean this as an offense," I said, looking at him sincerely, and then veering my gaze to Caesar, resumed, "but, Julius, the Senate should offer you the crown, not Antony with the approval of the dirty plebeians drunk on a day of festival. There will be no dignity in such an exhibition."

"Although as Antony says, it will test the response of the mob, and their opinion carries force with the nobles," Caesar said.

"We cannot lower ourselves in this coarse manner!" I cried passionately. "You are suggesting that we play games with a crown which to me is a sacred symbol."

Late into the night the matter was discussed. Both Caesar and Antony argued forcefully for the idea, and at last I gave my half-hearted sanction to the scheme, hoping against all my better judgment that perhaps the test would work.

The day of the Lupercalia, February the fifteenth, came. I stayed secluded at the villa with Caesarion all day, awaiting the outcome of the scene to be acted out in the Forum. Charmion and Apollodorus, dressed as Persians, with wigs and coloful clothes, mingled with the polyglot mixture of common folk who crowded the Forum that day, so that they could give me a detailed description of the proceedings.

Caesar had often sneered at some of our Egyptian customs, yet the Lupercalia struck me as an absurdly heathen rite. The annual festival is a feast of fertility in honor of the old god Lupercus, whose origins date back to Etruscan times when the day was celebrated by savage shepherds with lusty rites in fields and woods. The Lupercalia is a popular event in Rome, and for the common folk it is a day of rousing rough fun.

The festival opened in the morning as Antony and

Antoninus were cut on their wrists by a priest, and as custom decreed they had to laugh instead of groan. Antony and Antoninus sacrificed a nanny goat and a dog. The sacrificial priests skinned the two offerings and cut the skins into strips, which were soaked in the blood of the victims. Blood was then smeared on the bodies of Antony and Antoninus, who wore only loincloths. In ancient days the rite had been performed naked, and Antony had wanted to revert to this usage since he was inordinately proud of his beautiful physique and endowments, but he was persuaded by Caesar that perhaps it would be best to at least adorn his manhood with the loincloth.

"It is no secret that the gods of love, Eros and Cupid, Aphrodite and Venus, were all overly generous with you, Antony," Caesar had remarked, "but it would be in bad taste to openly parade their gifts in the streets and incite so much lust and envy."

The day was mild and pleasant, and the streets of Rome were filled with animated citizens. Antony and his young cousin, armed with the bloody fertilizing thongs, went tearing through the streets, striking in every direction at all the women who put themselves in their way, in the hopes that they would bear children for the state before the year was out. Antony, a devoted servitor of Eros, was regarded as aptly qualified to perform this rite of fertility.

The Forum was filled with an excited, boisterous mob. Caesar, dressed in a splendid robe, emaciated and with a deathly pallor on his face, sat on his throne on the rostrum surrounded by his officers.

A swelling crescendo of shouts rose from the people as Antony and his cousin made their way down the narrow, crooked street leading into the Forum. Antony, the image of a pagan god, came darting into the Forum, his splendid physique gleaming with perspiration. He ran up onto the rostrum and flung himself at Caesar's feet.

"Hail, great Lupercus, God of Fertility!" Antony bellowed. "Be benevolent in the year ahead to your devout subjects so that Roman cradles will be filled wtih healthy babes at the year's end."

Caesar clutched tightly at the arms of his throne, steadying himself to act the part assigned him.

Antoninus came up behind Antony and gave him a golden crown sparkling with gems and laced with laurel leaves.

"A crown for a king!" Antony cried, holding the diadem above Caesar's head.

Silence fell over the crowd as the people stood stunned, straining with expectation.

"Does the Divine Caesar, the Roman Imperator, accept this crown?" Antony demanded, his booming voice carrying to every ear in the Forum. "Does Caesar take this crown and crown himself with the royalty of Rome?"

The silence in the Forum was broken by a rumble of murmurs. There was a claque of Caesar's supporters strategically placed among the mob and they shouted out, encouraging Caesar to accept the crown. They were soon drowned out, however, by a far greater number of people who wildly dissented with a chorus of boos.

The vociferous marks of public disapproval obliged Caesar to shake his head, and he pushed the crown away. At this action, applause broke forth from the mob.

"The Roman people demand that their Julius-Jupiter take the crown for having served them!" Antony cried out, once again thrusting the diadem at Caesar.

Caesar trembled, and his hands made a tentative gesture toward the crown, but again the crowd screamed dissent, and he was forced to demur, shaking his head emphatically.

"The pleasure of serving the people is my crown!" Caesar announced, rising from his chair.

The plebeians ceased with their clamorous boos and erupted into a frenzy of cheers for Caesar, their Republican Roman.

"Take this crown to the Capitol and place it on

Jupiter's statue," Caesar cried out, "and have it set down on the official calendar that on the Lupercalia, the people twice offered Caesar, through their consul Antony, a kingly crown, but twice Caesar refused it."

Once again a storm of applause roared out over the Forum. Lepidus, beside Caesar, took the precaution of bursting into tears, which can be interpreted any way.

Antony handed the crown to one of Caesar's aides and picked up his bloody thong. "Come, dear cousin, let us resume our duties."

As Antony and Antoninus made their way out of the Forum, Apollodorus playfully pushed Charmion forward, and she received a stroke from Antony. Apollodorus and Charmion relayed to me all the details of this ghastly day, and at this part were greatly amused.

"Will I have a child before the year is out, Cleopatra?" Charmion asked gleefully. "And if so, who will be the lucky father?"

"They say it is a magical charm that always works!" Apollodorus cried with a mischievous grin.

I gave them both a stern grimace, seeing no humor in anything that day, for the event had been disastrous, although nothing that I had not expected.

Later that night Caesar and Antony came to the villa. Caesar looked dejected, and weariness weighed heavily upon his frail features. I was annoyed to think that Antony could have been so obtuse as to twice offer Caesar the crown, and I was convinced that Antony had talked about the plan. As a result, Brutus and Cassius had known of it and had placed people in their pay all over the Forum to cry out against Caesar.

"Our hopes of a throne will have to be set aside until after my conquest of Parthia," Caesar said sorrowfully.

"I had hoped to be Empress of Rome by this time," I said sadly, "and instead I must return to Egypt."

Since Caesar's return from Spain the previous summer, there had been vague but persistent rumors of a plot against his life, and after the Lupercalia I learned from my spies who were slaves in the great households that a conspiracy was being formed by a nexus of conservative senators and they were meeting secretly behind locked doors.

A sense of foreboding oppressed me, and I feared for Caesar's life. In February against my heated objections Caesar dismissed his retinue of guards when the Senate vowed to guard his life with their own.

"Without an armed escort, what is stopping your enemies from cutting you down?" I demanded, alarmed and shocked. "There are many men in Rome who are eager to see you dead, Julius."

Caesar gave a cynical, harsh laugh. "What a mess that would create!"

I was stunned, thinking that perhaps Caesar was going mad. "Your death would place your son in a gravely dangerous position, Julius!"

"I have no doubt that no matter what happens to me, Cleopatra, you would protect Caesarion like a lioness her cub," Caesar said.

"Julius, call it my sixth sense, my Ptolemaic prescience, or simply uncanny intuition, but I fear assassins!" I cried. "Your enemies do not want you to go to Parthia and return with more glory. I beg you, in the name of our son, until you depart, have a personal guard about you at all times."

"Roman law allows me to have only my lictors attend me," Caesar cried.

"Twelve men carrying a bundle of rods and sticks?" I demanded with infuriation. "What good would that be if you are attacked?"

"It is against Roman law to have soldiers guarding me," Caesar insisted.

"Then change the law! Are you not Dictator? How long do you think I would be safe if I went about the streets in my litter with twelve men carrying sticks? My life would not be worth a copper denarius, and neither is yours."

"I have lived long enough for nature and for glory, and I will not have a guard," Caesar said. "It is better to suffer death once than always to live in fear of it. Besides, I look upon the affections of the people to be the best and surest guard."

This statement struck me as stark madness, and I wondered if his bouts of epilepsy had damaged his brain. Trembling, I took a deep breath. "Julius, surely you know that there are inscriptions cut into the statues of Lucius Junius Brutus expressing the wish that he were alive once again, and each morning when Marcus Brutus goes to his tribunal desk, he finds letters left during the night saying, 'Awake, Brutus, to your duty!' And 'Are you a Brutus or a coward?' You have many enemies in Rome, Julius, but Brutus is at the top of the list."

"How ridiculous!" Caesar scoffed with a sneer. "Brutus has ambitions, but he has the grace to wait until the last breath leaves this old body. Brutus is wise, noble, and honest, and he would never bring me down."

"I have it on excellent authority, Julius, that Brutus and Cassius are plotting dark deeds," I cried vehemently.

"The authority of your friends who are slaves who worship Isis?" Caesar sneered scornfully. "You are having feverish fantasies, Cleopatra."

I gave a deep sigh, wondering if Caesar was being euphoric or fatalistic, but I knew there was nothing I could do to dissuade him from going carelessly about the city, tempting fate.

By this time I had become aware that I was an object of displeasure. My enemies had agents stirring up hatred against me. The public was engrossed by the political movements made by Caesar and the ends toward which he was aiming, and parties had formed for and against him. It was repugnant to many Republicans that sooner or later Caesar would repudiate Calpurnia and marry me and establish a royal dynasty. East and west would be united, and this offended conservative Romans who wanted the east to be eternally enslaved and not an equal.

I had always conducted myself in Rome with utmost dignity, although many of my chamberlains did not.

Alexandrians are noted for their overweening arrogance, and they were often offensively haughty with Romans, who were naturally infuriated. I implored my servants to comport themselves with courtesy, but behind my back they disregarded my admonishings, and this situation did my cause no good.

"Once Cleopatra is Empress she will treat us all as slaves," Cicero told anyone who would listen, and he found listeners aplenty.

Cassius cried, "Caesar is under the spell of Egyptian black magic, and he is besotted with Asiatic debauchery."

One day in the Senate, Caesar remarked, "There are still many laws left for me to institute for the good of Rome."

Cicero immediately stood and cried, "Yes, indeed, Caesar, I'm sure you are about to make a law permitting the practice of bigamy!"

This remark elicited a chorus of titters around the Curio.

There were many contemptuous comments on Rome attributed to me, and although I regarded Rome as inferior to my beloved Alexandria, I would never be so foolish as to say so in public. Rumors also circulated that Caesar was planning, at my insistence, to move the capital of the empire to Alexandria. Caesar knew that Rome was not the most suitable center for the commonwealth, whereas Alexandria would be, being ideally situated on the sea, but the move would be in the distant future and in all probability would take place during the reign of Caesarion, long after Caesar and I were dead. It was also said that I planned to make Italy Egyptian. Because of these various spurious rumors, I found myself increasingly unpopular in Rome.

To add to all my troubles, all was not going well in Egypt. There had been a low rise of the Nile again, and unrest was brewing with the anticipation of famine. The most disquieting news, however, was that a bold imposter, claiming to be Ptolemy the Thirteenth, had appeared in Alexandria, This imposter insisted that he had escaped in the battle of the Delta, eluding Caesar's forces, and had taken sanctuary in Upper Egypt for three years.

Having suspected such a possibility, I had insisted that my brother's body be dragged up from the Nile at the time of his death and publicly exhibited. Many people now insisted, however, that the body displayed had been a cleverly made-up dummy. Naturally, I was disturbed at this impudent assumption.

The false king collected a number of partisans, and a disturbance broke out in January, only to be put down immediately by the energetic action of Rufio and his legions. Ptolemy the Pretender escaped and made his way to Syria, which annoyed me. I wanted him dead so that he would be unable to make any more attempts at usurpation in the future.

I realized that my long absence from Egypt had grown dangerous, and I was anxious to return to my kingdom. I gave orders that a fleet of twenty ships were to meet me at the Bay of Naples to escort my flagship back to Alexandria.

As Caesar made preparations for Parthia, I prepared to journey home. Caesar was due to set out with his legions on March the seventeenth, and I was scheduled to sail two days later.

With a melancholy spirit I watched Apollodorus and Charmion supervise the packing of my belongings, which were carried down to my ships anchored along the Tiber. Despair burned in my heart, consuming my soul, for I felt defeated and dishonored in the eyes of the Romans.

Charmion was particularly bitter about the way fate had gone against me. She had hoped to be the first lady to the empress of the world, and the thought of returning to Egypt was a crushing blow to her.

"Caesar is a fool!" Charmion cried, quivering with rage. "For two years you have absented yourself from your people at his wish, and you have nothing to show for it but the contempt of Rome and unrest in Egypt.

Caesar will never survive two years of war in Parthia. He will perish there like Crassus."

"Only the gods know what will happen, and we must pray for their help," I said calmly.

Although the arrangements for the Parthian adventure took up much of Caesar's time, he still came often to the villa, and he brought many beautiful gifts for Caesarion and me. We had anxious discussions about the future, and there was a deep tenderness between us. We nostalgically recalled how four years before Apollodorus had brought me to Caesar in a rolled-up rug, and how Caesar had overnight transformed me from a deposed Queen to a reigning Queen. We fondly remembered the sunny days and starry nights on the Nile during the voyage when Caesarion had been growing inside me.

"We have many memories of the past and experiences shared, my love," Caesar cried, "and there will be many more in the years to come."

"I will miss you terribly, Julius," I said with emotion.

"And I will miss you," Caesar said stirringly. "To be quite frank, however, I am vexed by the carping criticisms from the Republicans, and I'm anxious to go to Parthia. After my victory there, the coveted crown of the world will be ours, and you shall become my wife, my only wife, and we will have the most splendid marriage celebration Rome has ever seen or the world will ever know."

"Oh, beloved Julius, I will be the happiest woman in the world on that day," I cried, kissing his deeply furrowed brow and holding his shrunken, withered body close to mine.

Lucius Aurelius Cotta, Caesar's old uncle, who adored me, looked up the Sybilline Books and found an ancient oracle which stated: "No campaign waged in Parthia will ever succeed unless the Roman legions are led by a king." Uncle Lucius immediately brought this matter up in the Senate. Caesar's enemies accused him of tampering with the sacred scrolls, but regardless, the implication was clear. Before Caesar left for Parthia, he

456

should be made king or else there would be another Roman defeat in that country.

A week before Caesar was scheduled to leave Rome, it was decided that the matter of the oracle would be debated in the Senate on the Ides of March. Caesar was scheduled to leave Rome two days after the Ides.

Antony, Dolabella, and several others of Caesar's adherents were frantically busy lobbying for our cause, trying to gain support for a final movement to have Caesar declared king. Once again I allowed myself to hope that all was not lost, although there were just a few days left to accomplish our ends.

On March the thirteenth, Caesar came to the villa to visit. It was a cold day, and for weeks the weather had been damp. A somber, oppressive mood had prevailed over Rome. Outside the city the legions were ready to march, and there was a feeling of general unease everywhere which the foul weather only accentuated.

Caesar spent most of the afternoon playing on the floor with Caesarion, who talked to his father in fluent Latin.

"My son, one day you will be king of the world!" Caesar cried.

"Yes, Father," Caesarion said, his handsome little face gravely set.

In the evening we shared a meal, and then Caesarion's nurses took him off to sleep. Caesar and I, alone, listened to a flute-player making sad, soft music behind a screen in a corner.

"The other day the old soothsayer, Spurinna, sent me a note," Caesar said, "telling me to beware of the Ides of March."

"Spurinna?" I asked. "Isn't he the Greek tutor to the children of Brutus?"

"Yes," Caesar replied. "These soothsayers are all a bit touched in the head."

A silence fell while we sipped wine, and I observed that Caesar, reclining on his favorite couch, appeared preoccupied.

"You seem engrossed with sad reflections, beloved Julius," I said tenderly.

"Yes, my love," Caesar replied with a vague smile.

"Shall I read to you?" I reached for a scroll on the table beside me. "Would you like to hear some Homer? Here, this scroll recounts the siege of Troy."

"Troy!" Caesar cried, his mind captured. "I was at Troy a few years ago, you know, after I left Pharsalia in pursuit of Pompey. I crossed the Hellespont and sailed along the coast until I came to the strait Helle named after the daughter of Nephele, who was drowned there when she fell from the back of the golden ram."

"Oh, yes," I cried excitedly, "the same strait where Leander drowned one stormy night when he swam the Hellespont on his nightly visit to his beloved Hero. When the guiding lamp in her tower went out, he lost his way and foundered in the rough sea."

"You might be interested to know, Cleopatra, that I went ashore and walked along the rocky beach where Leander's body was washed up, and where Hero hurled herself to the rocks beside it," Caesar explained. "I saw the remains of Hero's tower. My interest in the ancient glories led me to delay my pursuit of Pompey, and I visited the Sigean promontory with its memories of Achilles. I saw Rhoeteum where Ajax is buried, and the river Simois where so many heroes died. I walked around what is left of Troy, but which is now only a name. I looked for remnants of the great wall that Apollo built."

"Did you find it, Julius?" I asked anxiously.

Caesar shook his head sadly. "I found only a hill covered with decaying trees and aged roots embedded in the foundations of the ruins of the palace of King Assaracus. The natives showed me the cave where Paris sat when he judged the charms of the three rival goddesses, and I walked the spot from which the eagle carried Ganymede off to Olympus. I gazed upon the mountain where Oenone lamented her desertion by Paris. Every rock has its legend. I crossed a rivulet trickling through the sand, and someone remarked,

'This was the famous river Xanthus.' Then as I walked through a patch of grass, someone cried, 'That is where they buried Hector, Caesar, so be careful not to offend his ghost.' "

Such thoughts made me ponder pensively, and I was acutely aware of my own mortality. I felt an involuntary shudder ripple along my spine, and my goblet trembled as I took a sip of wine.

"After I had done enough sightseeing," Caesar resumed, "I built an altar, burned incense, and said prayers to the spirits of the dead who haunt the ruins of Troy and those sad shores."

"When we are emperor and empress of the world, Julius," I cried with urgency, "we will rebuild the walls of Troy and restore its buildings and repeople it with soldiers, as you did Carthage and Corinth, and Troy will be a great city once again."

Caesar stared into space, wrapped in a melancholy trance. "A great river becomes a trickling stream," he murmured morosely. "A great dynasty of kings—" He broke off, and then found my eyes and gave me an ominous stare. "My dear Cleopatra, the day will come when your great palace in Alexandria will be in ruins just like the palace of King Assaracus. Such is fate."

I did not reply, but inwardly I trembled.

"Troy rose and fell," Caesar went on pensively, "and so did the powers of Nineveh and Babylon. Persia flourished, only to see power fade away. In days gone by, Xerxes the Great wept to realize that his own generation was doomed to perish. Greece, led by Alexander, reigned far and wide, but later Greek might crumbled to bits. As for Carthage, when the great city blazed, Scipio wept for his defeated enemy because he had the vision to foresee Rome's ultimate doom."

"Yes," I said, remembering my Homer and quoting. " 'The day will come when holy Troy will be destroyed, and Priam of the mighty speak, and all of Priam's tribe.' "

"It is remarkable how the sacred labors of poets serve to keep events from oblivion," Caesar remarked reflectively. "We will live, Cleopatra, in chronicles, in scrolls, in libraries, in plays performed on the stage. It is writers who bestow immortality on those who participate in them. I am jealous of those great Greek heroes commemorated by Homer. What Latin Homer is there to write of my exploits and to make me immortal?"

I put down my goblet, stood up and went to Caesar, holding out my hand and smiling sweetly. "Come, beloved Julius, let us philosophize no further, and come to bed with me."

"Once again I give in to the wisdom of Egypt's Queen," Caesar said.

As we lay abed, I held Caesar's frail body close, and it took all my skill to bring him to the surging pitch of passion. I was hoping that in this desperate fusion he might gain sustenance from me, but I only sapped his strength as his seed seeped into my loins, and then he sagged in my arms. I wondered that if the labor of love was such a difficult task for his withered body, how could he conquer Parthia? Caesar fell asleep after lovemaking, and I lay there, overwhelmed by a sense of gloom.

I slept fitfully that night, listening to Caesar's labored breathing and the falling of rain outside. It had been raining for days from dark skies. I had suffered through two cold winters in Rome, but in a few days I would leave, and I began to long for the constant sun of Egypt.

Caesar slept late that day and then breakfasted with Caesarion. After eating they rolled on the leopard skins covering the marble floor, playing and laughing together.

In the middle of the afternoon there was a rattle of chariots outside on the Via Campana as Mark Antony arrived.

"Julius, all is well!" Antony cried excitedly, his handsome face flushed. "Dolabella and I have been hard at work among the senators, and a compromise has been reached. Tomorrow on the Ides the matter of the oracle will be debated and it is agreed that to insure victory in Parthia, you will be proclaimed king of all the

Roman dominions outside Italy, authorized to wear the royal diadem anyplace on land or sea, although not in Italy."

"You mean, I will be king of the Roman dominions, but not king in Rome?" Caesar cried, aggrieved. "It is all or nothing!"

Antony shot me a despairing glance, seeking my help.

"Julius, take whatever they give you," I said urgently. "If they make you king of a barren island in the Aegean or of a mountain in Asia Minor, take it. The rest will come later."

"King of Roman dominions, but only Dictator in Rome!" Caesar moaned.

"What does it matter?" I demanded. "You can establish your royal capital in Alexandria. You will be able to marry me and incorporate my kingdom with your eastern dominions. In a few years, Italy will come to us begging to be a part of our glorious empire!"

I was quivering with excitement, pondering the possibility. For a century Rome had been panting to annex my kingdom, but perhaps it would work out that in time I would annex Rome to the empire I shared with Caesar. Such a thought thrilled me.

"So it shall be done," Caesar said with a deep sigh.

"Dear Antony, you have done your work well," I said warmly.

Antony smiled at me. As Caesar went and knelt on the floor to kiss Caesarion goodbye, I went close to Antony and clutched his elbow. "Antony," I whispered desperately, "in the next two days, guard Julius with your life and never let him out of your sight for a moment."

"I promise faithfully, Cleopatra," Antony replied.

I accompanied Caesar and Antony out into the atrium.

"Tonight, Julius," Antony said, "Marcus Lepidus wants you to sup at his house. There will be several important senators there whom you must win over."

"Just as you say, dear Antony," Caesar said.

In the doorway I turned to Caesar and pulled the hood of his purple cloak up over his head. "There is a slight drizzle outside, Julius."

Caesar embraced me. "I shall come back the day after tomorrow," he promised.

"You will be a king then, Julius," I said happily.

"Half a king," Caesar remarked wryly.

Caesar kissed my lips, and then he rushed off with Antony. I stood in the doorway and watched the chariots race down the Via Campana through the fog and light rain.

I was filled with anticipation about the debate in the Senate the next day on the Ides, and a warm glow of hope swam through me that all would work out according to our dreams.

Late that afternoon Apollodorus came to me with an anxious expression.

"Queen Cleopatra, I have just heard a disquieting tale," he cried.

"Yes, what is it, Apollodorus?" I asked.

"One of the stewards has just returned from the city," Apollodorus explained, "and he learned that this morning a little bird, with a sprig of laurel clutched in its beak, flew into the Hall of Pompey in the Senate, pursued by a flock of other birds which overtook the little bird and killed it."

I shuddered. "This is a bad portent, Apollodorus."

"Perhaps it means nothing, my Queen," Apollodorus said.

A premonition infused me, destroying the feeling of optimism I had felt earlier.

Later I learned that in the evening when Caesar dined at the house of Marcus Lepidus, the talk turned to death.

"Julius, what kind of death would you prefer?" Dolabella asked.

"A quick and unexpected one," Caesar answered.

CHAPTER X

THE IDES OF MARCH dawned and still I had not slept all night, but had tossed in a fever of anxiety. The night, with heaven and earth at odds, had been punctuated by storms and thunderclaps, which had awakened Caesarion. I had taken him sobbing from his crib and placed him in my bed between Charmion and myself, and he had fallen back to sleep contentedly. Outside the rain, the wind, and the intermittent bolts of lightning continued, and I was too unsettled and full of misgivings to hope for any rest.

At last the rain ceased as another gray, ominous day dawned, and a thick mist, rising up from the Tiber, enveloped the city like a pall.

Charmion arose and went to her bath, and Caesarion's devoted nurses took him away to bathe and feed him. Apollodorus joined me, and as we sat sipping hot herb juice, I told him of my troubled spirits.

"I am convinced that Caesar should not go to the Senate today," I said fretfully.

"You should obey your instincts, Cleopatra, and advise Caesar accordingly," Apollodorus said strongly.

I called for pen and papyrus and wrote feverishly. "Beloved Julius, I beg you with a humble heart to stay home today. Let your dear Uncle Lucius and Antony take care of the matter of the oracle and the kingship for you. You are mighty and bold; you fear no one; you are as fixed in the firmament and as constant as the northern star, but please do not go to the Senate, for today is the last chance your enemies have to harm you before you depart. In the name of the gods and for the sake of our son, heed my counsel."

Apollodorus gave the sealed letter to one of my Nubian slaves, whose legs could run as fast as the speediest Arabian mare, to deliver to Caesar's house.

Later I learned that Caesar, in his town residence, as he slept beside Calpurnia—he hated to sleep alone because he had so many nightmares of late—had been abruptly awakened in the middle of the night as the windows of his bedchamber suddenly burst open with a massive gust of wind. This gale caused Caesar's ceremonial armor of Mars to fall with a crash from the wall where it had been hanging. Caesar noticed that Calpurnia, who had not awakened, was moaning as if in the throes of a nightmare. He shook her awake, and she told him that she had dreamed of seeing his statue running blood from a hundred spouts. They were both disturbed by this and slept no more, but lay there as it rained and thundered outside until a dreary dawn crept up.

As they had breakfast, Calpurnia beseeched Caesar not to stir out of the house that day, and Caesar was discomposed by her dream and entreaties. He also felt ill, and his physician examined him and advised that he should return to bed for the day.

A messenger arrived from the official priests with the report of the morning sacrifice, which had been inauspicious, for when the priests took out the entrails of a goat, the heart could not be found. This portent further agitated the Lady Calpurnia.

At nine o'clock, Antony, who lived not far away on the same fashionable street, arrived. Caesar discussed with Antony the idea of not visiting the Senate. Antony suggested that Caesar should not go, stating that he felt confident that he could sway the Senate to pass the decree of kingship without any mishap.

Caesar was due in the Senate at the tenth hour, and he sent word by a messenger that he would not attend.

There was consternation among the conspirators in the Senate with this news. They thought their plot had been discovered and Caesar would be moving his armies, from their encampment outside the city, into Rome to arrest them and declare martial law.

Marcus Brutus hurriedly enlisted Decimus Albinus to go to Caesar to convince him to change his mind. Decimus, whom Caesar had appointed to the consulship of Cisalpine Gaul for the following year, was one of Caesar's most trustworthy friends, and there were few whom Caesar esteemed more.

"Most mighty Caesar," Decimus cried, arriving at Caesar's house, "there is much state business for you to transact in the name of Rome before you leave for Parthia."

"My health is not the best," Caesar demurred, "and my wife had a bad dream last night and has beseeched me to stay home today."

"Divine Caesar, today we have agreed to cast the vote to confer upon you the title of king, which you richly deserve," Decimus cried coaxingly.

"Yes, and I trust this matter can be settled without my presence and in a more democratic fashion, too," Caesar said.

"Great Caesar, if you do not honor us with your presence in the Senate when the senators have agreed to make you king of all the Roman dominions outside Italy," Decimus argued passionately, "my colleagues may be angry and change their minds. Must I tell the Senate we must postpone making you king until Caesar's wife has better dreams?"

Caesar, after reflecting, thought he could not slight the Senate by staying away, and not wishing to jeopardize the kingship, he said, "Go and inform your august associates that I shall be there at noon."

Decimus, as he was leaving, bowed to the distraught Calpurnia. "May the gods give you sweeter dreams tonight, my noble lady," he said, and then he rushed back to tell his fellow conspirators in the Senate that they need not worry.

My slave arrived at Caesar's house, and after reading my message, Caesar sent him back with a short reply.

465

"My dearest one, your fears are groundless, for the long-sought-after moment has arrived. On this day part of our dreams will be achieved. I shall visit you on the morrow. As always, I tender my deep love and devotion to you and our son. Farewell, your Julius."

In the artium of their townhouse, Caesar and Calpurnia embraced, and again she implored him not to go, reminding him of the morning sacrifice and the missing heart.

"I am no coward in the face of bad auguries," Caesar remarked rebukingly. "I am not a beast without a heart, but mighty, divine Caesar!"

On the street, Caesar and Antony climbed onto a litter, and as they settled into their seats, Caesar said that his forebodings, gloom, and illness had all vanished and he was in high spirits.

The slaves bore the litter rapidly through the narrow streets to the Senate. Caesar stepped down on the marble pavement of the great square, and immediately noticed the Greek soothsayer, Spurinna, who stood out prominently among the crowd with his long gray beard and leaning on a staff.

"Ah, my good Spurinna, you warned me to beware of the Ides of March!" Caesar called out nonchalantly. "Well, the Ides has arrived."

"Yes, great Caesar, but not gone," Spurinna retorted pensively.

At that moment a man darted out from the crowd and thrust into Caesar's hand a scroll which warned Caesar of a plot, but Caesar, thinking it was merely another petition which he was always getting, thrust it unread into the pocket of his toga. The man begged Caesar to read it, but Caesar said he never read petitions in the street and brushed him off.

The fatuous senator, Popilius Laenas, approached Caesar. "Great Imperator, good morrow!" he cried obsequiously, bending to kiss Caesar's hand.

The conspirators, grouped on the great flight of marble steps leading to the Capitol and pacing nervously

466

about, had a moment of panic, thinking that Laenas was about to spill all.

With a fawning smile, Laenas informed Caesar that the official priests had just sacrificed two doves for the noontime sacrifice in the Hall of Pompey, and the livers were streaked with blemishes which signified a bad portent.

"Julius, these harbingers betoken the gravest misfortune," Antony suggested. "Perhaps I should take you back home."

Caesar had never paid much attention to omens and auguries, and laughed at Antony. "You were always as superstitious as a woman, my dear Antony," Caesar cried chidingly. "I have come this far; the Senate awaits me within. Now that they are about to acclaim me their king, I cannot disappoint them."

"Caesar, Brutus says that his wife is deathly ill this morning with hysteria and fainting spells," Laenas added.

"Can you blame a woman married to a humorless prig such as Brutus for suffering from hysteria and swooning spells?" Antony asked with a booming laugh.

"I will offer Brutus the services of my physician for his noble wife," Caesar said with concern. "Portia is with child and Rome will have need of the offspring of such patrician lineage."

Caesar and Antony began walking up the long flight of steps, with Caesar leaning on Antony's arm for support.

Popilius Laenas raced up the steps ahead of them and approached Brutus and Casca. "Good luck with your enterprise, my friends," he whispered, "but be quick about it, for people are beginning to talk."

As Caesar and Antony arrived at the portals of the Curio, Caius Trebonius came up and tugged at Antony's sleeve.

"I must attend Caesar," Antony said dismissively.

"Lord Antony, I beg you to lend me your ear for a moment," Trebonius said desperately.

"I shall see you presently within, Antony," Caesar said, releasing Antony's arm with a nod.

Caesar passed through the portals and traversed the great corridor of the Senate alone, his purple cloak trailing after him, and several senators followed him. He entered the Hall of Pompey, and the senators already seated stood in salutation. Caesar inclined his head at them as he walked toward his ornamented golden chair.

Suddenly Caesar was confronted by the senator Metellus Cimber, who stood in front of him, blocking his path.

"Most illustrious and honored Caesar," Cimber cried, "may I humbly make a request?"

"What is it, Cimber?" Caesar asked impatiently.

"Recall my beloved brother from exile," Cimber cried.

"That is out of the question," Caesar said testily. "The decree of banishment against Publius Cimber will never be lifted in my lifetime!"

Caesar was then somewhat taken aback to notice that he was surrounded on all sides by senators. "Stand back, all of you!" he cried peremptorily.

"I beg you, great Caesar!" Cimber cried, kneeling and reaching out as if to touch Caesar's toga in a gesture of supplication, but instead he grabbed the end of the purple cloak and yanked it with a tearing thrust to the floor.

This was the signal, and the senators closely crowded around Caesar in a tight circle.

Without his thick imperial cloak, Caesar stood with his frail frame clad only in a light toga. He was shocked, realizing that he had been stripped of the cloak which symbolized his power, and seeing the menacing hostility in all the eyes around him, he cried out, "Is this violence?"

Casca, whom Caesar had recently promoted, came from behind and struck the first blow toward the neck, but missing, pierced the shoulder.

Caesar wheeled around and caught Casca by the arm. "You villain, Casca! What are you about?"

In that awful moment, Caesar knew what Casca and all his friends were about.

The assassins came upon Caesar like a pack of wolves, crazed with malice, envy, and bloodlust, hemming him in on all sides. Casca's brother stabbed Caesar in the side, and then Cassius struck him in the face. Bucolianus plunged a dagger between the shoulder blades, and Decimus Albinus, who an hour before had persuaded Caesar to come to the Senate, struck him in the groin.

As the steel of daggers flashed all about him, my beloved Caesar fought for his life like a wild animal at bay. All his life from young manhood he had fought for everything he had obtained, for nothing had been handed Caesar on a golden plate. This was his final fight and the only one he ever lost. At first he desperately defended himself with his ivory baton, and then when that was knocked from his hand, he struck out in every direction with his arms and bare hands, and finally managed to break through the circle of plunging, stabbing daggers. Again he grabbed Casca by the arm and struck a fist at his face, and then he fell against Pompey's statue, clutching hold of the pedestal to steady himself, as his lifeblood gushed from ghastly wounds.

Brutus had hung back, but now he was urged by the others to strike a blow and they made way for him to approach Caesar.

Caesar looked up dazedly, seeing Brutus walking up to him with a dagger in his hand. "And you, too, my son?" Caesar said sadly, uttering the words in Greek, and then he lifted a fold of his toga and covered his head, in the fashion of all great Romans, so that none could see him pass.

The dagger of Brutus was plunged into the heart, and Caesar slid to the floor at the base of Pompey's statue and died.

The murderers rushed in again, falling upon the body, stabbing and slashing at the prostrate form, wounding each other in the frenzy of their bloodlust. At last they stood back, breathing heavily, and stared down at the massacred body in a pool of blood.

There were twenty-three dagger wounds, but the physicians who examined the corpse later said that only the thrust by Brutus was fatal.

Brutus took from his pocket a scroll with notes on it for a speech he had prepared to justify this deed, but to his astonishment he found himself alone in the Curia, for all his fellow conspirators had rushed outside.

Antony, who had been detained by Trebonius during the assassination, was stupefied when he discovered the tragic news, and he thought he would be next on the list. He raced down the steps to the marketplace, found a beggar, and giving the old man all the gold he had on him, bought the poor man's worn, patched homespun cloak, and throwing it over his shoulders to disguise himself, he fled through back streets. When he at last reached his townhouse, he locked himself within.

The word that Caesar had been murdered spread like wildfire across Rome, and all the citizens poured out into the streets and squares, full of hysteria, running amok with grief. A great mob collected in front of the Capitol. The murderers, calling themselves tyrannicides, collected themselves on the Rostra, waving daggers in the air and screaming out with words such as "Liberty!" and "Freedom!" and such phrases as, "Caesar is dead!" "Tyranny is dead!" and "The Republic lives!"

Brutus addressed the multitude and made a conciliatory speech to justify his actions, and the people were somewhat pacified, but then Cinna made a few disparaging remarks about Caesar and the loyal plebeians became enraged and unruly. The assassins were chased into the Capitol where they bolted the doors for protection. This was ironic, since they claimed they had acted on the wishes of the people; but instead of being hailed as Republican heroes, they had to run for their lives.

At the time of Caesar's death, I was sitting at my desk after having eaten a light noontime meal. I was dictating letters to my scribes which I planned to send, along with special gifts, to various Romans who had shown me friendship during my stay in Rome. The news, reverberating across Rome, hit the villa within an hour after the execution.

I was suddenly disturbed by wild shrieking from my eunuchs and ladies in the atrium.

Apollodorus came rushing into the chamber, his handsome face ashen, his massive body trembling all over.

"Queen Cleopatra!" Apollodorus gasped, falling on his knees, his head bowed, his lips moving convulsively.

"Caesarion, is he all right?" I demanded with a stopped heart.

"Yes, Caesarion is well, my Queen!" Apollodorus assured me.

My heart began beating again, slowly. "What is it, Apollodorus?" I asked. "Out with it!"

With a great effort, Apollodorus raised his head and forced the fatal words out of his mouth with gasping, choking sobs. "Divine Majesty, Caesar is dead!"

A galvanizing horror struck me, paralyzing me, and I sat there unmoving, trying to absorb the reality of the words.

Charmion came running into the chamber, her face whiter than a lily, and she looked at me with great eyes, her arms outstretched to me in a wild, helpless gesture.

"No!" I finally cried, shaking my head, denying the truth. "No, no, no, no!"

"Yes, it is true, Cleopatra!" Charmion cried, falling at my feet, sobbing hysterically. "One of the slaves was in the city, and he ran back to tell us. It happened at noon, less than an hour ago."

"How?" I cried out in frenzied despair. "How?"

"Caesar was daggered to death by Brutus and others in the Senate," Apollodorus explained.

"No!" I cried frenziedly, covering my face, my mind refusing to accept the truth which was sinking in, the truth which I had feared for months. "My ears deceive me, your tongues·lie! It is a false rumor. I don't believe it! It can't be true!"

Frantically I ran about the room, until I tripped on a fur rug and fell to the floor. I lay there like a wounded animal, groaning and crying, my body convulsing uncontrollably.

Charmion, Apollodorus, and my other servants gathered around me, trying to solace me, but I wildly hit out at them.

The dementia of grief and shock at last abated a little, and I allowed myself to be lifted onto a couch. My physician Olympus came and wanted to give me a potion, but I knocked it out of his hand. Although in that first hour after Caesar's murder I was tormented and grief-seared beyond endurance, I would not alleviate my pain by dulling my brain.

The whole villa was rent asunder by consternation and ferment. Apollodorus put all the guards on alert, surrounding the villa in case the conspirators came to murder Caesarion and me.

"In this hour of tragedy, all Rome will be torn by revolution," Apollodorus cried excitedly. "We must make our flight. Your life and the life of your prince are in danger, O Queen."

My flagship lay anchored on the Tiber below the villa, and we had been scheduled to sail in three days. Apollodorus said that after a few final preparations, we could leave during the night. Although I was feverish with deranged grief, my thought processes were lucid.

"The Queen of Egypt does not flee Rome like a fugitive coward!" I cried, spitting out the words, inflamed with pride and resolution. "I shall leave Rome as I came, with pomp and ceremonial state. I once left Alexandria under cover of night and I had to sneak back, as you well know, Apollodorus, but never again!"

Caesarion was brought to me. The poor boy was in a terrible state of confusion. At three years of age, he could not comprehend what was happening, but the hysteria and turmoil prevailing in the villa had deeply affected him.

"What is wrong, Mother, what is it?" Caesarion begged.

"Nothing, my brave, valiant little prince!" I cried, smothering his beautiful little face with kisses and smoothing his blond locks. "Soon we will be going on a sea voyage back to Egypt. You cannot remember Egypt because you were just a baby when we came to Rome, but you are a prince of Egypt and your people need you."

"Won't I also be a prince of Rome, Mother?" Caesarion asked, looking at me with his big blue eyes.

There was a sob in my throat and I could not reply, but only stared at the fine features that were so like his father's. "Caesar lives in you!" I cried with a burst of emotion. "You will be greater than Caesar!" With an upsurge of feeling, I held my son close to my bosom. "You will be greater than Alexander the Great!"

I released Caesarion into the hands of his nurses. I cautioned them to hide their grief for the child's sake, and they took him into the adjoining chamber for his afternoon nap.

"That little prince will be worth a hundred Caesars when he becomes a man!" I declared in a quavering voice.

It was this thought which gave me strength and sustained me during those first dreadful hours of the tragedy.

Nightfall came on, and the mob in the Forum swelled until every niche was filled wtih grief-torn, lamenting citizens.

Brutus sent word to Antony saying that no harm was intended him; and with this promise, Antony went to the Capitol. Caesar's body had been examined by the physicians, the death mask made, and the corpse wrapped in the purple imperial cloak. Antony, with his soldiers, conducted the remains to the Forum and placed them on the Rostra in front of the Temple of Jupiter. Antony stood there, staring sadly upon the body of his beloved cousin and friend and master, as the plebeians cried out with sorrow.

Leaving the Forum, Antony went to visit the Lady Calpurnia to offer his condolences. She put all her affairs in his charge, giving him Caesar's documents and a copy of his will.

Soldiers gathered around Caesar's corpse and thousands of citizens slept in the Forum that night to keep vigil.

A feeling of doomsday struck Rome. The body of Caesar lay in state in the Forum for five days, while the upheaval of the city raged on, and then at last on March the twentieth the funeral was celebrated.

Apollodorus and some of his companions went in disguise to witness the emotional event in the Forum. Charmion stayed by me at the villa to give me comfort, for I was in a stupor of grief.

A gigantic funeral pyre had been erected in the center of the Forum, and on the top Caesar's body was placed wrapped in his imperial cloak.

The Forum was filled with soldiers banging their javelins and swords against their shields, and the women lamented loudly.

Antony mounted the rostrum, with the consent of Brutus and the others, and gave the funeral oration. With plain, blunt words that stirred the emotions of the plebeians, he extolled Caesar as the greatest man who had ever lived in the tide of times. He quoted the line from Accius: "I spared those who gave me death." At one point he held up by the tip of his sword the tunic which had been removed from Caesar's body, pierced with holes and dyed with blood. At the sight of this macabre relic, the plebeians became inflamed with hatred against the assassins. Antony's eloquent speech fired them to grief and rage, and they wept copious tears.

A copy of the will was unrolled, and Antony read the clause which bequeathed to every citizen three hundred sesterces, and he told them that the orchards in the Transpontine Gardens were to be given over as a public park.

"Now you know how dearly Caesar loved you!" Antony cried, and the mob erupted into a frenzy of hysterical grief, vowing vengeance upon the conspirators.

Antony took a torch from a soldier and applied it to the pyre, which had been doused with oil. Flames speedily blazed, rising in a roar, and a consuming fire enveloped the corpse. All through the night the fire burned, and at dawn there was nothing left but embers and ashes.

I was crushed to think that the body of my beloved Caesar, the greatest Roman who had ever lived, should be reduced to ashes in a barbarian rite. Caesar had been deeply impressed by Alexander's body having been preserved as a sacred relic, and he had hoped to initiate this Hellenistic custom once his dynasty was established.

A comet blazed in the sky above Rome for the following seven days and nights after the funeral. When ordinary folk die there are no comets seen in the sky, for the heavens blaze forth only at the death of men who are touched with godhead.

I stood on the terrace of the villa with Caesarion in my arms.

"Look, look up at the comet!" I cried. "It is your father on his way to heaven."

Caesarion was too young to grasp the idea of death, or to understand that the father who came to play with him often would not come again. Yet he stared up at the blazing comet with a grave, wondering expression.

For several days a thick haze hung over the sun and the days were dark, and it was acknowledged by one and all that the celestial sun was clouded over by the approach of the divine Caesar.

The state official priests named Caesar as God in Truth and on all his statues the star of divinity was placed upon the forehead.

For days I was numb with dark brooding and impotent anger, in a fever of torment, and nothing could assuage the pain in my heart. I sat mute with unspeakable despair. I was morbidly obsessed with the assassination, and from various reports I learned every detail of the crime and made up a list of the sixty conspirators. All my suspicions had become tragically confirmed. I learned how the plotters had organized their band

and committed the murder. I slept little during the nights that followed, for my sleep was interrupted by nightmares in which I saw Caesar's body being daggered to death and lying in a pool of blood.

The greatest leader Rome or the world had ever known, after Alexander, had been murdered out of malice and jealousy. I lost my lover, my benefactor, my patron, the father of my son, and the man upon whom the fulfillment of all my ambitions had depended. My divine soul burned with the bitterness of betrayal and the ruin of all my dreams.

A tumultuous situation now prevailed in Rome. The day after the funeral the Senate convened. Antony, as Caesar's co-consul, quickly gathered up the reins of power. He realized that the upheaval could result in anarchy which could tear down the stones of the city itself, and so was effective in having a general amnesty and an Act of Oblivion proclaimed.

Antony dispatched Roman soldiers to reinforce my guard at the villa to protect me. If he had not taken power, it is possible that my life and the life of Caesarion would have been wiped out as Caesar's was. In the confusion and terror which prevailed in Rome, I looked upon Antony as my protector.

Although Antony was occupied with consolidating his power, he sent messages to me daily, and a week after the funeral he came to the villa. I rallied from my stupor to confront him with a calm composure.

"Welcome, Lord Antony," I said somberly, meeting him in the garden as he came up from his barge.

"Queen Cleopatra," Antony cried, clutching my delicate hands in his giant paws, "we share each other's tragic loss."

I led Antony into the reception room. There were a few of my ladies in a corner plucking lyres and harps. I gestured toward a couch for Antony, and I took a chair nearby. We spilled a dollop of wine on the mosaic floor in a libation to Caesar, and then took a sip ourselves.

"Will you ever forgive me, Cleopatra?" Antony asked with an imploring look into my eyes. "You begged me never to leave Caesar's side for a moment, and when Trebonius detained me at the door—"

"Do not blame yourself, dear Antony, for we are but playthings in the hands of fate."

"The assassins wanted to cut me down at the same time, you know, but Brutus insisted that I be spared," Antony explained.

"They feared your Herculean strength," I said with admiration. "It was a simple thing for them to dagger Caesar to death, for he was an old, feeble man, but you would have taken the whole lot of them on and torn them limb from limb."

"To keep order we must deal civilly now with Brutus and his fellow murderers," Antony said apologetically. "Rest assured, however, that the day of vengeance will come."

"I have a list of the sixty conspirators, and one by one they will all get their due," I said emphatically. "We owe Caesar that."

"The gods will assist us in this task," Antony said earnestly. He took a scroll from a pouch of his cloak. "For your cognizance, Cleopatra, a copy of Caesar's will."

"Caesarion and I are not mentioned, of course," I said in a placid tone, camouflaging my chagrin under a cool exterior.

"Regrettably no, Gracious Majesty," Antony said. "It is against Roman law for an alien to be left a legacy. Caesar's will as Dictator could only bequeath his private property, since his public offices cannot be inherited. Of course, if he had lived through the day and had been proclaimed king, things would have been drastically changed."

A pang of regret stabbed my heart at this thought, for then Caesarion would have become king after his father.

"The Lady Calpurnia was not mentioned in the will, either," Antony said.

"Well, I am told she is one of the richest Romans, with a vast fortune inherited from her father."

Antony laughed ruefully. "Yes, Calpurnius Piso

477

should definitely have been impeached for corruption when he was consul!"

I could not share Antony's amusement at the venal vagaries of his fellow Romans.

At length we discussed the will which Caesar had made after returning from Spain, in which three quarters of his estate was bequeathed to his great-nephew, Caius Octavian, and the other quarter was divided between two older nephews, Lucius Pinarius and Quintus Pedius.

"It is a sobering fact to realize that a good portion of Caesar's fortune came as a gift from me," I remarked grimly. Seeing a troubled frown touch Antony's face at this, I quickly added, "Of course, I gave Caesar and Rome only a small fraction of my fortune. Even Caesar never knew its precise extent."

"Then it is true, Queen Cleopatra, that next to you King Croesus of Lydia would be a pauper?" Antony asked.

Silently, I unrolled the will further and read the codicil in which Octavian was named as Caesar's official heir, to be adopted as Caesar's son with the right to bear the name of Caesar.

"Octavian's paternal grandfather was a provincial moneylender," Antony said contemptuously, "and of his other lineage, only the gods know."

"Surely Octavian, at his studies in Apollonia, will be hearing about the terms of the will and will board the first ship bound for Brandisium, to come to Rome to claim his inheritance," I said.

"Yes, he will be here, but he is a beardless boy of nineteen and without a marked intelligence," Antony said. "He will never be able to turn his inheritance into anything."

"Should I take the gamble and have Caesarion proclaimed as Caesar's official, rightful heir?" I broached.

"Not if you don't want Caesarion and yourself murdered," Antony replied. "Doubtless, Cleopatra, Julius made this will to protect you, knowing that if anything happened to him while Caesarion and you were in Rome, your lives would be in mortal danger."

"My son is Caesar's son!" I cried passionately. "Does Caesarion have no champions in Rome?"

"I promise you, Cleopatra, that I shall pass a law in the Senate acknowledging Caesarion as Caesar's son."

"Put forth the right of my son and you will be greatly rewarded, my Lord Antony," I said firmly. "My granaries and treasury will always be available to you in your campaigns in the future."

Antony's blue eyes glowed as they drank in my face. "I would outrage the memory of the deep love I had for Caesar if I did not champion your cause, O Glorious Queen!" he cried.

True to his promise, Antony made a stirring speech in the Senate a few days later, putting forth a bill which acknowledged Caesarion as Caesar's son. This was vehemently denied by Caius Oppius, who advocated Octavian's claims. Oppius made an odious speech, crying, "Everyone in Alexandria knows that Apollodorus is the father of Cleopatra's son!"

This comment caused a commotion in the Senate, but was not taken seriously by anyone, for all the senators had seen Caesarion and recognized the uncanny resemblance between father and son. Consequently the bill was passed by an overwhelming vote. For what it was worth, Caesarion was lawfully set down in the records of Rome as the legitimate son of Caesar, but not heir. Since Caesarion was not a Roman but an alien Egyptian prince, this meant nothing, for the time being at any rate.

The conspirators, realizing that their lives were in danger in Rome from the mob, were anxious to serve the commonwealth elsewhere. Antony, whose influence with the Senate was unbounded, persuaded them to send Brutus to Macedonia, Trebonius to Cilicia, and Cassius to Syria, to serve in the capacity of proconsuls. They summarily collected troops and hastily left Rome for their respective provinces, safely away from the irate plebeians.

The turbulent scene in Rome was further complicated with the news that Octavian was on his way to Rome.

The city was no longer interested in the conspirators, but began forming into two opposing factions, one championing Octavian, while the other espoused Antony who was working for the cause of Caesarion.

It was with a sad heart that I accepted the realization that I was no longer the presumptive empress of the world, but simply the Queen of Egypt, and sitting upon an unstable throne at that, with no Caesar to prop me up and protect me.

"Civil war will be breaking out, my Queen, and we must return to Egypt," Apollodorus cried. "From Alexandria you will be able to safely watch the outcome of the coming struggle."

Octavian was due to arrive any day. I rebelled at the thought of taking Caesarion away and permitting Octavian to fulfill the legacy of Caesar's adopted son, but I had no choice but to give in to the cruel joke the fates had played on me.

On the thirteenth of April, a month after the assassination, I left Rome. It was a bright, spring day filled with sunshine, and by this time I had somewhat recovered from the demoralizing grief which had been eating away at my soul. All my possessions had been taken on board my flagship and my ships were ready to sail. I took one last walk around the villa where I had spent almost two years of my life, remembering with sadness the days and nights of dreaming and arguing and lovemaking with Caesar.

Antony arrived with several officers to give my leave-taking a semblance of official pomp, although it did not compare to the grandeur of my entrance into Rome.

In the reception room of the villa, Antony and I shared a farewell goblet of wine.

"Pray, take some Egyptian dates and dried apricots, Lord Antony," I said in a soft, lovely voice.

Antony popped several of them into his mouth between swallows of wine. "I have a great passion for Egyptian things," he said, smiling.

"You may come to Egypt and satiate your appetite for Egyptian things to your heart's content," I cried.

"It has been more than ten years since I was in Alexandria, and I will accept your offer when my duties permit."

"Octavian will be in Rome any day now," I remarked, bringing up an unpleasant but imperative topic.

"I am told that his mother, Lady Atia, has written Octavian, begging him to embark on a private life and to avoid politics," Antony said hopefully. "Frankly, I don't think the youth has it in him to become a senator."

"Brutus will be in Macedonia soon," I said bitterly. "To think that Brutus, that villainous hypocrite, was Caesar's pet." My voice throbbed with rancor. "Brutus must be exterminated along with all the others!"

"In time I will march to Macedonia and destroy Brutus, I promise you that, Cleopatra," Antony said intensely.

The time to leave came. Without looking back, holding myself erect, I walked out of the villa. Antony escorted me along the path of the garden and down the marble steps to the banks of the Tiber.

The sky was radiant and the day was bright with spring after the long, harsh winter. My standard and colorful banners were flying from the masts of my flagship. Antony came on board with me. King Ptolemy, who was now sixteen, stood beside Caesarion on deck, where several chamberlains and attendants were gathered.

Antony picked Caesarion up in his arms, and my prince squealed with delight. Antony put the child down and then turned to me with a grave expression.

"Oh, noble, brave, wise and valiant Antony!" I cried fervently. "The moment of farewell has come."

"The gods in their infinite wisdom will ordain that our stars will cross again, Queen Cleopatra," Antony cried with flashing eyes. "Never fear. I shall be your champion and Caesarion's champion."

"After two years in Rome, I leave at least one friend behind," I said sincerely.

Antony's handsome face lit up with pleasure and he

gave me an irrepressible smile, his great white teeth sparkling in the sunshine.

As Antony's eloquent eyes burned into me, I knew he was fighting the temptation to draw me close in an embrace, but I drew myself up with rigid dignity, cutting off such an action.

"Farewell, my Lord Antony," I said with solemnity.

"Farewell, Royal Egypt!" Antony cried, his voice resonant with emotion. Although it was my mouth he wanted to kiss, he settled for my hand. Then he stood erect, nodded curtly, and left the flagship to the sound of trumpets.

My flagship began moving down the Tiber. I stood on deck with Charmion, Apollodorus, my son, and my brother beside me. On the dock, Antony stood waving his sword in the air. As his figure grew smaller, I was conscious of a deep emotion and a warm glow spreading through me, and in my heart there grew a buoyant feeling of promise.

By late afternoon, we left the Tiber and sailed into the sea. We poured an offering of rich wine overboard, propitiating Poseidon and Neptune so that these gods would aid us in easing the terrors of the voyage ahead. They proved generous, for the waters were placid as my flagship, escorted by twenty squadrons, serenely sailed across the blue beautiful Mediterranean.

I had leopard skins spread on deck, and each day I would lie on them with Caesarion, playing and laughing with him. I loved the sun-dappled, dazzling waters all around us, and the fresh, invigorating breezes did much to restore my spirits. The soft lisp of the sea, falling and rising to the rhythm of the sea gods, made marvelous music.

At first I felt I was drifting in a sea of uncertainties, but gradually the voyage had a rehabilitating effect on me. After Caesar's death I had felt all my hopes had been cruelly obliterated, but I was young and I had a resilient heart, and once again I felt my life held glorious promise. Caesar was dead, but he lived in Caesarion, and Antony was our friend. I was still Queen of Egypt, the most powerful and richest kingdom on earth. I vowed that our dream would not die with Caesar, and my mind was full of plans.

After a two-week voyage we reached my cherished city of Alexandria. Rufio and his legions who were still loyal to me lined the docks, and Alexandrians crowded the jetties and the great marble stairs and squares near the seafront, waving banners and cheering thunderously.

As I sailed into the Harbor of the Happy Return, I was dressed as Isis, my face radiant and showing no sign of defeat, and I held the hand of Caesarion. My heart overflowed with tremendous joy at the tumultuous reception that greeted me. My homecoming was truly one of the happiest days of my life.

I was to learn later that an unfounded rumor had run through Rome to the effect that my flagship had gone down in a storm at sea, drowning Caesarion and me, and many of my enemies there had celebrated. Many Romans thought they had seen the last of Cleopatra and Caesarion of Egypt, but I swore by the Holy Isis of whom I am a part that I would return to sit in judgment and to rule mightily over Rome.

BOOK III

CHAPTER I

EGYPT WAS MY KINGDOM and I returned and retreated to her after the catastrophic Ides of March, and the palace on the promontory, in the city built by my forefathers, became my refuge and lair. At first I was assailed by memories which struck me with acute distress. In my reception room I was reminded that on the marble floor I had been rolled out of a carpet at Caesar's feet four and a half years before. In my bedchamber, where I now slept alone, I had given my virginity to Caesar, and nine months later, had borne our son. As I looked out the windows upon the harbors, I remembered watching Caesar swim for his life from a sinking ship during the Alexandrian War.

I was haunted by Caesar's memory. For all our conflicts, we had shared a tremendous bond. We had been bound to each other by political designs and the fulfillment of mutual dreams, but with all considerations aside, we had shared a great love. When I looked over the effete men of Alexandria, I longed sorely for Caesar, for as weakened as he had been in his last year, still he had been a paragon of a man.

The huge, vaulted chambers of the palace echoed with memories, and I was overcome by nostalgia. There had been six of us Lagidae siblings growing up in the palace, and although there had been rivalry and dissension between us, at least there had been excitement. Now there was only my brother King Ptolemy Philippos, but he kept to his apartments with his companions, and he offered me little comfort.

I found my aunt, the Princess Aliki, much fatter and

older, which saddened me. Often I would have her brought in a litter to my apartments so that we could share a meal. Her brain was always clouded with poppy juice, Egyptian barley beer or wine, and she could no longer concentrate on chess or conversation, but her presence gave me great solace.

The sound of a flute moved me painfully with memories of my beloved father, the flute-playing king. I recalled with nostalgia his lavish banquets. I remembered how close we had been, and all the advice he had given me. Caesar and my father had been the two most important men in my life, and their loss left a void in my heart.

Caesarion now filled this emptiness and motivated my existence. When I had taken him to Rome he had been unable to walk, but now he ran through the corridors of the palace. I carefully supervised his education, appointing tutors to mold him, and he became the inspiration of all my future dreams. I had been grief-worn, but time did its work and my spirits revived in new hopes which I placed in my son, and I vowed to live solely for him.

A few months after I returned to Egypt, I discovered that Caesarion was afflicted with the sacred sickness. He suffered his first fit just before his fourth birthday. I was deeply distressed to learn this, but it proved to the skeptics that Caesarion was indeed the son of Caesar, resembling his father not only in physique but in this divine malady. I was beset with anxiety at this development, and I had Caesarion watched closely by attendants at all times. The fits never lasted long, and months passed between them. Caesarion, like a brave little god, suffered them stoically.

When I was carried in my consecrated chariot, my people cheered me wildly. Some of my ministers and the merchant potentates of Alexandria, however, were not so happy to see me back. There had been a corrupt bureaucracy during my absence, which my regent Lord Mardian had been unable to put down. Now that I had returned, everyone knew that I would tolerate no more swindling or perversion of power.

I was alarmed to observe the dissatisfaction that certain nobles entertained for me. I was still accused of having decoyed the alien conqueror and of having compromised the honor of the kingdom, but as a dauntless ruler I had always defied public opinion. I wondered if I would be able to withstand the snares and threats which faced me. Caesar had made Egypt respect me, and his might had been my shield, but Caesar was dead now and I stood alone.

My first summer back in Egypt, the Nile inundation failed, bringing the threat of famine and pestilence. In spit of this crisis, I forged ahead in building a hundred ships. I was obsessed with having the greatest fleet in the world to use along with my gold and wheat as pawns in the chess game of Mediterranean politics.

I felt grave anxiety over Cyprus, an important possession of my empire. I feared that Cassius, the Proconsul of Syria, might attempt to annex Cyprus with the Roman fleet. To safeguard against this possibility, I sent ships to blockade Cyprus under the command of my admiral Serapion, making him Viceroy of Cyprus. I still hoped that eventually Arsinoë would be installed in Cyprus as my vice-Queen, but for the moment I could not trust her.

One afternoon in early summer, about a month after I had returned to Alexandria, I was overcome by melancholia. I had spent the morning in council, and the affairs of state were weighing heavily upon my heart. I took my noontime meal with Charmion, and although I was surrounded by a coteries of my lovely ladies, I was oppressed by loneliness.

I could barely touch the food sitting before me, having no appetite at all. I stared past Charmion's shoulder, out a window which commands a marvelous view of Pharos and the sea.

Suddenly I was drawn from my melancholia, beguiled by one of Sappho's songs being sung by one of my ladies. In the corner sat a young girl plucking a five-stringed harp as she sang.

I stared at her, enraptured by her vibrant, throbbing voice. She had great dark eyes set in her small, beautiful face, and she sang on, unaware of my scrutiny, her fingers working with deep concentration on the tight strings.

Charmion, noticing my attention, ceased her chattering, and all my attendants, becoming aware of my absorption in the girl, stilled. Now there was not a rustle or murmur in the chamber, and the girl's voice intensified.

At last she noticed she had a rapt audience, and her voice throbbed as she sang the last verses which described the broken heart of a woman who had lost a great love. As she finished the song, her voice swelling to an emotional crescendo, my eyes clouded and I felt tears sliding down my cheeks. There was a tightening at my throat, and I could barely speak.

"What a beautiful song," I whispered at last, deeply moved.

"A great song, but the rendition overstressed," Charmion said disagreeably.

I reached for my goblet with a shaking hand. I took a sip of wine, thinking I had noticed the girl before, peripherally, for she had entered my service soon after my homecoming. She was a small, shy girl who kept in the background executing her duties quietly. She was a daughter of one of the leading Alexandrian families, who as is the custom generally enter my service for a few years until their parents find suitable husbands for them. It was not until that afternoon however, that I was struck by the force of her beauty.

The girl had resumed plucking on the harp, making wistful, enchanting music, although no longer singing. I gave a quick glance in her direction, seeing her head bent over her instrument.

I wiped the tears from my cheeks with a silk scarf. My heart had lost its proper rhythm and was beating rapidly. "Who is that girl, Charmion?" I asked.

490

"It escapes me, O Queen," Charmion said with cold indifference.

I beckoned Polydemus, one of my eunuch chamberlains, to my side and instructed him to bring the girl to me. Polydemus waddled his gross body over to the girl and whispered to her. She stood, nervous at being singled out, and left her harp.

She approached me, her small, exquisitely shaped body moving with lambent grace, and as she reached me she fell to both knees.

"Yes, my lady Queen," she cried timorously, staring downward.

I reached out and put a hand under her chin, lifting her face. I gazed into her face, seeing she was incredibly beautiful, with olive skin, eyes glowing like huge black pearls, and black ringlets falling over her forehead.

"What is your name, my sweet one?" I asked gently.

"Iras, of the house of Epaphroditus," she replied.

"Your father was once my father's Lord Treasurer," I cried.

"Yes, he had that esteemed honor, my Queen," Iras said softly.

"Last year in Rome," I explained, "I was saddened to hear that the gods had called your father to eternal life."

"My mother treasures the letter of sympathy you sent her from Rome, my Queen."

"Were you thinking of your dear father when you sang Sappho's song of lament for a lost love, Iras?" I asked quietly.

"Yes, my Queen," Iras murmured.

"We have both lost a beloved, my little Iras. You sang that song with such feeling that my heart was stirred."

"The credit is not all mine, O Queen," Iras said humbly, "for the words were by Sappho."

I smiled tenderly. "Yes, you are so right. As Plato said, 'There are more than nine muses, for surely Sappho is the tenth.'" I reflected a moment. "Although

491

I must say, I have heard that song sung many times, but it has never moved me so deeply."

Iras raised her black-orbed eyes to me and gave a radiant smile.

"Your family fares well, Iras?" I asked with concern.

"Yes, O Queen," Iras replied. "My three brothers have the honor to serve as officers in your army."

"The house of Epaphroditus has a long hereditary attachment to my dynasty, and its loyal services to the Lagidae have been a true blessing," I cried.

Iras gave me a tender and timid smile. "I live only to serve you, my Queen, in the tradition of my house, in whatever way you command."

"Besides being a singer of songs and having a divine touch on the harp," I said smilingly, "do you possess any other talents?"

"I am clever at dressing the hair, O Queen," Iras said brightly.

"Oh, that is a talent of which I shall make use," I said. "Are you happy at court?"

"Most happy since you have returned," Iras said, "although while you were away the court was like the earth without the sun."

I smiled at her ingenuous compliment. "Do you have comfortable quarters, sweet Iras?"

"Yes, my Queen, although they are in the east wing, far from your sacred presence," Iras replied.

"Well, if you are to tend my hair, I will want you closer to me in a chamber in this wing of the palace."

"Oh, thank you, my beloved Queen," Iras cried, her face flushing like a rose petal, her dark eyes dancing with delight.

I rose, and as I took a step away I paused, looking down at Iras who still knelt on the floor. I laid a hand on her soft, lovely face.

"Farewell, my Lady Iras," I murmured.

As I was about to move away, Iras clasped my hand and kissed the fingers ardently. With an effort, I withdrew my hand from her grasp, and with a furiously

492

beating heart, returned to my council chamber to meet with my ministers.

From that day onward, I had the Lady Iras always by my side, and she became my dearest, devoted friend. She gave me unstinted loyalty and love. At this time my life was full of shadows, and Iras became the sunshine in my life, brightening my days. Her childlike charm, her delicate tenderness, the brillance of her beauty, always lifted my spirits. She proved not only to be gifted at singing and the harp, but she also worked miracles on my hair, styling my long tresses in any fashion.

Charmion, who for eleven years had been indisputably my foremost friend, was jealous of my new favorite.

"Can't you see that she is part Egyptian?" Charmion cried with venomous disdain. "She is not pure Hellene. Her father, Lord Epaphroditus, was impotent, and her mother took Egyptian lovers and not always caring where she found them. For all the gods know, Iras could be the daughter of an Egyptian dockworker."

"If Iras is half-Egyptian, that makes me even more predisposed toward her," I said placidly. "After all, I am Queen of the Egyptians. To have a favorite with Egyptian blood should please my people."

"The common people perhaps, but not the Greek patricians."

"My snobbish nobles should not object if Iras brings joy to their queen who has suffered so much," I declared.

Charmion, who has wisdom and common sense, soon overcame her hostile feelings toward Iras, and a warm and sisterly bond formed between them.

About this time I used all my persuasion to get Charmion, who like myself was twenty-six, to marry Apollodous, who had just turned thirty-one. It would have been gratifying for me to see my two oldest favorites linked as man and wife. Marriage in Alexandria has been generally a utilitarian institution, with both partners going their separate ways and with Egyptian servants to rear the children. Marriages are invariably arranged, but this was one marriage that even I, the Queen of Egypt, could not bring about.

"I would die for you, my Queen," Charmion cried, "and although I love Apollodorus like a brother, I will not marry him or any beastly man."

"I am fond of Charmion," Apollodorus told me for his part, "but I don't think that after my long years of service to you, you should sentence me to a cruel fate as to marry such a windbag."

My dear friend Ammonios, that old faithful servant of the Lagidae, wrote me gossipy letters from Rome which enabled me to keep abreast of all turbulent events happening there. I was pleased to hear of Antony's political elevation since Caesar's death. Indeed, Antony was Rome, and he lived in great splendor and style with Fulvia at his side.

When Octavian arrived in Rome after my departure, the first thing he did was to visit Antony. He wanted a share of his great-uncle's legacy of political heritage and fortune, which Antony found various excuses to delay in giving. Octavian was too young yet, Antony insisted, to assume such enormous responsibilites. There were bitter arguments between the two, and Antony accused Octavian of having secured his adoption by his uncle through their immoral relations during Caesar's last campaign in Spain.

Octavian was a pompous, unimpressive, silly boy of no account, with an ignoble and irregular birth and a borrowed name, yet at the same time there was something tenacious and tricky about him. With resolution he applied himself to Cicero, who was rejoicing in Caesar's death and lamented that the conspirators had not let him in on the murder.

"I am the son of Julius Caesar!" Octavian, the grandson of a village moneylender, announced grandly to one and all.

With Cicero's backing, Octavian stood for the office

of Tribune and was able to draw together loyal legions who had served Caesar and who now pledged to fight under the banner of their dead leader's adopted son.

Accommodating himself to the issue at hand, Antony was forced to give Octavian a meeting in the Capitol. The two exchanged a kiss of peace and reached some sort of rapprochement, but not for long. Within weeks Antony heard that Octavian was plotting to assassinate him, and the breach between them widened. Both of them hurried through Italy engaging by great bribery the old soldiers who lay scattered in their settlements.

Cicero stayed in Rome and made use of his orator's art to denounce Antony with venomous invective in ten speeches. He persuaded the Senate to declare Antony a public enemy and to make open war upon him. Octavian was sent the rods and axes, and orders were issued to the two consuls, Hirtius and Pansa, to lead the Roman legions and to drive Antony out of Italy.

As all these tidings trickled in from Rome, I was horrified that civil war was brewing again. I prayed to the gods that out of the chaos, Antony would emerge triumphantly.

Antony, with a small force, met the armies of his enemies, and the Battle of Mutina was waged. Octavian, feigning illness, stayed in his tent. Antony's forces were completely cut to pieces; with a handful of followers he fled northward.

Crossing the Alps, Antony joined the legions encamped in Gaul and won Lepidus to his side. A month later they returned to Italy with seventeen legions and ten thousand horse.

Realizing that he was not a general, Octavian thought it best to come to an understanding with his adversary. Antony, with such a host at his disposal, had the strength to obliterate Octavian from the face of the earth. For some imponderable reason, however, Antony desisted and agreed to meet Octavian.

The conference was held on the banks of the Po in northern Italy. Antony, Octavian, and Lepidus decided to form the Second Triumvirate to last for five years. The three of them would wield the supreme command in the Roman world, with Lepidus taking North Africa, Octavian Italy, Spain, and Gaul, and Antony holding sway over Greece and all the Roman provinces in the east.

The first item on their program was to draft a list of proscriptions to avenge Caesar's murder and to preserve their own political skins. The execution of a hundred enemies was ordered and their properties confiscated. Antony demanded that Cicero be placed at the top of the list, and Octavian obligingly agreed without a murmur.

The blood bath that had begun with Caesar's death, I knew, would not end until the wars of the rivals waged the length of Italy and the breadth of the Mediterranean.

To complete the reconciliation, the soldiers demanded that confirmation should be given to it by some alliance of marriage, and Octavian agreed to marry Antony's thirteen-year-old stepdaughter, Clodia.

Antony gave orders to the soldiers who were sent to murder Cicero that the head and the right hand were to be cut off. Later, when Cicero's head and hand were brought to Antony in Rome, he regarded them with joy and had them hung above the speaker's rostra in the Forum.

I could not help but experience a great rush of triumph and pleasure at these tidings, for I felt Cicero deserved such a fate.

Soon after the Triumvirate had been formed early in the autumnal equinox, which was some six months after I had returned to Egypt, the annual Festival of Serapis, our ruling deity, was celebrated in Alexandria.

On this day of festival, the city is always full of visitors from all parts of Egypt, Memphis, Hermonthis, Pelusium, and even from far-off cities in Syria, and for a week the boulevards are always full of boisterous merrymaking.

The morning of the festival, Charmion came rushing

into my chamber. "Cleopatra, King Ptolemy has sent a chamberlain to say that he is ill today and will not be able to assist you in the rites at the Temple of Serapis."

My brother had often been ill since his return to Egypt. I was annoyed that he did not feel up to assisting me in the temple ceremony, which as my co-monarch and fellow deity it was his duty to do.

Since it was essential that I pay homage to Serapis in a purified state, I had fasted for three days and did not eat that morning.

A venerable old priest, The Purifier of the Pharaoh, came into my chamber and washed my hands and feet with holy Nile water. Charmion and Iras, as the Ladies of the Royal Vestiture, put on my clothes of Isis. The Keeper of the Crown Jewels put on my uraeus and double crown, and I was robed in a mantle of golden sheathes. I left the palace, accompanied by Caesarion who was dressed like a little Pharaoh.

The October sun was shining brilliantly over Alexandria, and all the streets of the city were filled with people. The main boulevard of the Canopic Way had been reserved for the royal cortege and soldiers held back the cheering multitudes ranged along the sidewalks. The royal procession, winding out of the courtyard of the palace, made its way down the Canopic Way with Rufio and the Gabinian troops in the forefront. A congregation of musicians playing trumpets and clashing cymbals came next, followed by the Royal Astrologers, then priests carrying the statues of the gods, Apis and Anubis. A chariot bearing a great statue of Serapis was in front of my golden litter, which was surrounded by a phalanx of my Macedonian Guards. I sat with Caesarion, who bore himself with grave dignity. Behind us came my Aunt Aliki, Charmion and Iras, and several councillors and nobles in ornate litters and chariots.

The heat of the sun was unbearably intense, there was no breeze coming in from the sea, and I felt perspiration prickling my skin under my heavy golden robes, as we made our way slowly along the boulevard.

The Alexandrians swarming the sidewalks, propelled

by their deep-rooted, mystical feeling for their royalty, wildly cheered Caesarion and me, calling out our names in a wave of exaltation.

I was weak from fasting, and I prayed under my breath to the gods to give me the strength to endure the long procession.

After what seemed an eternity, we reached the Temple of Serapis at the farthest end of the Canopic Way. The temple is the most noted one in Egypt, a mighty monument built on the model of the ancient temples at Thebes. As my litter was carried into the temple courtyard, my Royal Macedonian Guards stayed outside on the street, since no danger could ever befall me in the temple precinct, a house of holies.

In the center of the courtyard, Caesarion and I alighted from the litter.

"Caesarion, my son," I cried with a gesture, "look at the terrifying watchdogs who protect the temple."

"Yes, Mother," Caesarion cried, gravely pointing to the granite, monstrous statues. "I see the wolf, the jackal, and so many lions!"

Holding hands, we walked toward the temple steps. I glanced up and saw soldiers stationed between the pillars, and in their immobility, I thought they resembled groups of statues.

"So many steps, Mother!" Caesarion said with a sigh.

"Yes, one hundred of them," I agreed, looking up at the flight of marble ascending before us to the temple portals. "Oh, well, my little god, let us take a deep breath and start."

We began the ascent to the heavenly kingdom of the temple. The steps were covered with the petals of lilies, which were soft against my golden sandals. Directly behind me followed my Aunt Aliki, Charmion and Iras, and as always, Apollodorus, who walked with his right hand on his sword, and behind him there were a few other guards.

A feeling of vertigo possessed me as I was halfway up the steps. I went slowly, weighed down by my robes and held back by Caesarion's little legs which had difficulty in negotiating the steep stairs. I beseeched Serapis to give me the strength to go on.

There were about a dozen steps left to go when suddenly I heard shouting and shrieking erupting all over, which snapped me out of my vertigo. I turned to see Apollodorus running and pouncing on a soldier who had sprinted from his station between two pillars, darting in my direction with a drawn sword. Apollodorus intercepted and attacked him when he had gotten but a few feet from me. They fell onto the stairs, engaged in a fierce struggle. Soldiers quickly rushed up and formed a cordon around Caesarion and me. It seemed to me that a few of the soldiers between the pillars were about to come, not to my aid, but to the rescue of my attacker, but they thought better of it and desisted. Apollodorus and half a dozen handpicked guards had the situation under control, and my would-be assassin was thoroughly subdued with Apollodorus astride his chest.

"We want him alive!" Apollodorus screamed, seeing that a soldier was about to run a sword into a vital lower area of the attacker.

I was transfixed with horror, clutching Caesarion's hand. He never moved nor uttered a cry.

Apollodorus stood and got the soldier to his feet. I saw that he was a young man with dark good looks and a powerful physique.

"I will question him thoroughly, O Queen," Apollodorus cried.

I saw that Aunt Aliki, behind me, had fainted on the steps, and her ladies were hovering anxiously around her.

"Take the Princess Aliki back to the palace," I commanded.

"You must also return to the palace where you will be safer, O Queen," Apollodorus cried urgently.

"I will return to the palace after I have paid homage to Serapis," I announced in a weak but steady voice.

"O Sacred Radiance, you were almost assassinated!" Apollodorus shouted.

"Yes, but you, my valiant Apollodorus, with the

divine intervention of Serapis, saved me," I said placidly. I glanced down at my son. "Come, Caesarion."

Together, holding ourselves erect, Caesarion and I climbed the remaining stairs and entered the temple. In the vestibule the High Priest of Serapis greeted us with outstretched arms.

"Welcome, Daughter of the Gods, O Isis the giver of eternal life!" the High Priest cried.

"Greetings, Beloved Father!" I said warmly.

Iras, coming in behind me, was crying softly.

"Control yourself, Iras!" Charmion hissed.

I turned around and gave Iras a soothing look, tenderly touching her cheek, and she regained control.

"Iras, we have our duties to perform," Charmion said.

Charmion and Iras removed my golden robe, and I heaved a sigh of relief. Dressed in the gown of Isis, white as shimmering wheat, I entered the cool, dark temple and walked with Caesarion through a colonnade of immense pillars which support the roof. Thick incense lay heavily in the air.

A flame leaped in the great altar that was carved with hieroglyphics. Behind the altar stood a gigantic statue of Serapis carved in marble and painted in gold. Beside it was a table laden with the objects destined for the sacrifice. Charmion and Iras took the objects and handed them to me. Absorbed in the sacred rite, I was able to put out of my mind the unfortunate happening on the temple steps. I gave a handful of wheat to Caesarion, and lifted him up as he threw the wheat into the holy fire. I poured oil on the flame, then water from the Nile, and blood from the doves that had been sacrificed by the priests that morning.

I uplifted my hands to Serapis, and Caesarion followed suit. I gazed up at the statue which stood three times the height of the tallest man, serene majesty written on his features, his beard spread over his knees, the seal of kings on his forehead, his hands extended with a gesture that embraced the whole world. A shaft of sunlight came in from an opening in the roof and fell on his enamelled lips, producing the effect of a kiss from heaven.

"O mighty Serapis, all-powerful god, whom the winds obey, be favorable to my prayers," I exhorted in my loudest, most vibrant voice. "You, who are the god who gives life and health to all, liberate your blessed waters of the Nile so that the river will rise mightily and their abundance flow over the Two Lands with fertility. Let no sedition breed in my cities, nor alien enemy come to destroy us. Hear my prayers, O Beloved Serapis!"

Caesarion and I prostrated ourselves on the marble floor, and I gave silent prayer to Serapis for having saved my life. The priests, lying on the floor behind us, chanted loudly their incantations. After my prayer, I stood and Caesarion rose with me. I nodded at my son, who looked up at Serapis with an expression of pious gravity.

"I thank you, Serapis, for your blessings!" Caesarion cried.

The throng in the temple chorused its fervent benediction.

Caesarion turned to me with an anxious look, and I smiled down at him with approval. His hand in mine, we traversed the long temple, and the golden robe was once again put over my shoulders. I made my farewells to the priests and walked outside. The heat of the sun struck me with great force after the coolness of the temple.

Apollodorus came toward me with an anxious look. "Queen Cleopatra, may I humbly suggest that you return to the palace not in your slow-moving litter, but in a swift chariot."

"I shall return in the manner in which I came, Apollodorus," I cried. "It would be unseemly for me to show any fear on this day, and the people must see that I am unshaken and staunch."

Apollodorus was about to protest, but controlled himself. "Yes, Great Queen, as you wish," he said with a resigned sigh.

I took hold of Caesarion's hand, and we began the

long descent down the hundred sacred steps with body-guards forming a circle around us.

"O Queen, I am told that the assassin is one of King Ptolemy's lovers," Apollodorus told me. "I will get him to tell me all."

"I am sure you will, Apollodorus," I said confidently.

When we reached the courtyard, Caesarion and I climbed onto the litter. The redundant procession back to the palace seemed interminable. The crowds, who had learned quickly about the attack on my life, gave me a rousing reception. These cheers strengthened my spirits.

Back at the palace, Mardian and I closeted ourselves in my apartments, which were doubly secured by guards. Apollodorus took my attacker into a room for questioning. The interrogation lasted only a short while, and then Apollodorus came to me, his face flushed.

"Queen Cleopatra," he cried, "his name is Seleukos and he is one of the king's boyfriends. He was acting for King Ptolemy, who promised to raise him to great honors and ennoble him if he succeeded."

I sat stupefied. I could not believe that my sickly, stuttering brother, who dressed in female clothes, could plot an attempt on my life.

"The King is in his apartments," Apollodorus cried, "protected by his contingent of Macedonian Household Guards. I could take my soldiers and fight through his guards to his person and apprehend him."

"He must be taken alive," I insisted. "I want him brought to me unharmed. I want to face him and question him personally."

"Yes, O Queen!" Apollodorus saluted and rushed off.

While the din of revelry and holidaymaking drifted into the palace from the streets outside that afternoon, a short but fierce battle raged within. My brother had barricaded himself within his private apartments. Apollodorus, leading my soldiers, massacred my brother's bodyguards who were stationed in the corridors of the King's wing. My brother's soldiers were slack and un-disciplined and no match for my hardened and ruthless men. In less than half an hour, amid savage fighting, my brother's guards were overwhelmed, several hundred slaughtered, and the marble corridors were strewn with butchered bodies and running with blood.

Breaking into Ptolemy's apartments, Apollodorus found the King surrounded by his retinue of squealing companions.

King Ptolemy was brought to my reception room. He stood before me, dressed in a toga. His usually pale face was crimson and his forehead beaded with perspiration, and I was struck instantly by the fact that his usual timidity was gone. He stood before me, and his stance and the tilt of his head bespoke a certain defiance.

"Everyone out, except you, Apollodorus," I commanded.

All my chamberlains, servants, and soldiers reluctantly filed out of the chamber. Apollodorus stood near the King with a drawn sword. After the double doors had closed, I walked over and stood before my brother.

"Pray, sit down, brother dear," I said stiffly.

"I will stand," Ptolemy cried harshly, breathing heavily.

He had not stuttered, I noticed, but then often when he had only a few words to utter he could manage them without faltering.

I paced around him, noticing that he held himself erect, and his delicate shoulders, generally sloped, were manfully squared.

"Your friend Seleukos says that he was acting on your wishes," I cried. "After he had killed me, he said that you promised to make him a noble. I imagine you then planned to bring your dearest sister Arsinoë from Ephesus and make her your Queen. A foolishly conceived plot, and badly, clumsily executed, brother dear." I paused, hoping for some reply. "Of course, he was acting in what he thought would be your best interests, but was he in fact acting in concert with you?" His gaze eluded mine, and I noticed that his face no longer seemed so girlishly pretty. Suddenly he had a

503

manly aura about him. "Answer me!" I demanded hotly.

"I have nothing to say," Ptolemy replied in a bored tone.

"Well, do you deny that you had a hand in this attempt on my life?" I demanded.

"I refute nothing," King Ptolemy rejoined, and then his mouth curved with contempt, "and I confirm nothing!"

A realization gripped me, and I stepped back, shocked. "You—you have lost your stutter!" I cried gaspingly.

King Ptolemy replied with a bored sigh and looked away.

"You have lost your stutter!" I cried again, stunned and surprised. "Where is your stutter?"

Ptolemy met my gaze with a look of sneering hatred, and tears welled in his eyes. "I could have saved Egypt!" he said chokingly. "You will destroy Egypt, you and your barbarian Romans, but I could have saved her!"

"Your stutter!" I reiterated with amazement. "It was a fake, a ruse, a trick! You never had a stutter, did you? You have fooled me all these years, haven't you?"

The look of insolent haughtiness deepened on his face, twisting his features. "I have lived to be seventeen," he declared. "If I had not had a stutter, I would have been dead years ago."

A violent glow of bristling anger coursed through me. Arrogant and audacious, and even in his defeat, Ptolemy looked at me with disdain, so reminiscent of the impudent looks his sister Arsinoë had always given me, even in her defeat. It was unendurable. For years Ptolemy had outwitted me. I, Cleopatra, who prided myself on having presience and a sixth sense, had been made to appear like a sentimental fool.

Apollodorus raised his great broadsword over Ptolemy. "Divine Majesty, let me have the honor of hacking him to death before your very eyes!" he cried zealously, saliva dripping on his chin.

"No!" I cried, pacing the room, in a turmoil of emotions.

"He must be killed without delay, O Queen," Apollo-dorus cried.

I went to a cabinet and took out a vial of poison that I kept handy. I walked over to my brother and laid the vial on a nearby table.

"There, a potion that will put you to sleep forever, brother dear," I said softly. "It is painless and quick."

King Ptolemy stared derisively at the vial, picked it up, looked at me with a smirk, and then threw the vial against the wall. The crystal broke, and the lethal liquid ran down the marble wall.

"If you want my life, dear sister, you must take it and be responsible for the action," he cried scornfully.

I stiffened, smarting, boiling with rage. "So be it!" I hissed. "Apollodorus, take him away and finish him off, and make it as painful and as messy as possible, and take your time about it, for there is no rush!"

"Trust me, Queen Cleopatra!" Apollodorus cried, feverish with excitement. "Guards!"

The double doors opened and a dozen guards ran into the room.

"Seize this little monster," Apollodorus cried, point-ing his sword at Ptolemy, "and bring him with me."

The soldiers fell over themselves rushing to Ptolemy, all trying to grab hold of him.

A wild, crazed fervor blazed in Ptolemy's face. "You will be the ruin of Egypt and our house!" he screamed stridently as the soldiers held him. "Before you are through, you will make Egypt one whole stinking grave because of your ambition and madness. Arsinoë and I could have saved Egypt, we could have saved Egypt!"

"The immortal gods have decreed otherwise, brother dear!" I cried triumphantly.

The soldiers dragged Ptolemy out of the chamber, and as he went he kept repeating the words, "We could have saved Egypt!"

All my ladies rushed in and surrounded me as I sank onto a couch, numb with fatigue and shock.

My brother's last words—*We could have saved*

Egypt!—kept echoing through my mind as he was dragged down the corridor, out of sight, out of earshot.

I was deeply shaken. I lay on the couch, tossing in a delirium of anguished emotions. Iras knelt at my side, clutching my hands, and sobbed quietly. I also spilled a few tears, assailed by misery.

Later in the afternoon Mardian came to see me. "The situation is under control, O Sacred Radiance, and you are securely on your throne," he cried. "It seems your brother attempted to murder you on this holy day, thinking that the people would look upon the event as having the divine blessings of Serapis."

"An inspired plan," I murmured with weary irony.

"O Queen, justice is being meted out to Ptolemy now," Mardian cried. "Shall Seleukos be executed, too?"

"No," I replied thoughtfully. "I must show clemency." I felt a certain gratitude to the boy for having bungled the job, revealing the treachery of the brother I had trusted, but I could not set him free unpunished. "Have both his legs cut off above the knees," I commanded coolly. "As for the right arm that held the sword that was about to strike a mortal blow at me, have that cut away at the socket. Leave him his left arm. Have the royal physicians tend him carefully, for I don't want him to die."

Mardian's brown eyes glowed with perverse pleasure. "And his manly eggs, Divine Majesty, shall they be cut off, too?"

I paused, thinking that since Mardian had had his testes cut away as a boy, he was eager that my assailant should meet the same fate. "No, Lord Mardian, that won't be necessary," I explained, noting the disappointment showing in his face. "When the boy has recovered from his amputations, he is to be set out on the streets to be a beggar."

"Is it wise to show such clemency to one who tried to murder your Sacred Radiance?" Mardian asked incredulously.

"He is a poor boy and crazed," I exclaimed compassionately. "I have given the order, Lord Mardian, so let it be carried out."

"There is a statue of Ptolemy Philippos in Sema Square," Mardian declared. "Shall it be torn down tomorrow?"

I ruminated briefly. "No, when Seleukos has recovered, I want him placed beside the statue with a beggar's bowl."

Mardian sank to one knee, inclined his head, and then left me.

Night fell over the city, and evening came on. The festivities of the day continued. All the theaters, the circus, and the stadium had free admission that day. To secure the favor of my people I gave a public banquet in the square in front of the palace, and I had given orders that no expense be spared. The fountains in the square ran red with wine, and long tables were set up and covered with meats, cheese, and pastries. The common people filed by for their food, and order was carefully preserved by soldiers.

An hour before midnight, Polydemus came and told me that Apollodorus was in the anteroom requesting audience.

"His mission has been accomplished, O Queen," Polydemus said.

A bitter joy suffused me and I trembled, but I felt that I could not bear to see Apollodorus with blood all over him from the day's slaughter.

"Tell Lord Apollodorus that I will see him in the morning, Polydemus," I said shakily, "and say that his Queen sends her deepest appreciation for his services on this fateful day."

Polydemus left, and I lay there in the grip of painful emotions.

"By all the holy gods," I cried out in despair, "what malicious games are the fates playing with me?"

I lay back on pillows and Iras pressed cold cloths to my forehead. I was tormented with the thought that I had seen four of my siblings die unnatural deaths, and now there was only Arsinoë left. I had to face the fact that she, too, as long as she lived, would be plotting to overthrow me from her villa in Ephesus. For the moment I realized she was out of my reach, but I resolved on that bitter night that she too would have to pay for her conspiracies against me. As long as she breathed, no matter how far from Egypt, my life and the life of my son were endangered.

"The people are calling for you, Cleopatra," Charmion whispered.

I could hear the people gathered in the square chanting my name. It was royal custom that at midnight on the Festival of Serapis I would appear on the Balcony of Appearances to receive the thanks of my people for the hospitality I had lavished upon them. I was in a stupor, but I realized that it was my duty to go out there. I took wine to give me strength, and then I went out and stood on the balcony.

It was a night of the full moon, and the moon hung like a ball of gleaming silver in the sky. As I looked down, I saw a sea of surging people filling the square and all the streets that branched off. The square was a beautiful spectacle illuminated by torches and lanterns. The people waved their arms and cheered me heartily.

I uplifted my arms in an all-embracing gesture as the waves of shouting cheers washed over me.

"Hail, Cleopatra!"

"Long live Cleopatra!"

"Cleopatra! Cleopatra! Cleopatra!"

My gaze drifted over the wide avenues, the marble temples, and all the precious monuments. Three hundred years before, my ancestors had come down from the north and had built this most glorious of cities. Now they all lay in the Sema, whose bronze dome stood out in the moonlight. My mind revelled in the vastness of my heritage. I shivered, realizing that I had almost died that day, and I wondered if Alexandria would be mine tomorrow, and if Caesarion would ever inherit all my riches and glory.

A tremendous clamor swelled from thousands of

throats like the roar of a hurricane. Solaced by their applause, I returned to my apartments.

In my bedchamber my ladies undressed me, covered me with a silk robe, and gave me a glass of warm honeyed milk. I dismissed all my ladies. Exhausted by the events of the gruesome day, I sat on the side of my bed, sipping the warm, sweet milk.

Suddenly I heard a sound from the other side of the bed, and stood up, startled.

"Who is there?" I whispered, my heart stopping.

"It is only I! Oh, please, my Queen, I want to be with you, to comfort you!" Iras cried beseechingly. "It is not right that on this horrible night you should be alone!"

A deep sadness gripped me as I gazed on her lovely, grief-torn face and saw the tears sliding down her cheeks. I walked over and stood in front of her. "Iras," I whispered softly.

On her knees before me, she embraced me, passionately pressing her face at the conjunction of my thighs. "Oh, my beloved Queen!" she said with a cry bursting from her heart.

Tenderly I laid my hands on her head, caressing the lovely curls. "Yes, you are right, Iras," I said in a whispering voice. "I should not be alone tonight. I have been alone for so many, many nights . . ."

In the six months since I had returned to Egypt, I had slept alone, with Caesarion in the chamber adjacent to my bedchamber. As Iras clung to my knees, I gazed around at the busts and statues of Caesar which stood sentry in the corners of my room. It was as if my bedchamber were a tomb with Caesar's ghost watching me.

A deep sigh escaped me, and as Iras breathed hotly against my navel, I felt a heat spreading through my loins. "Iras, my beloved!" I cried, leaning down to press my lips against hers. Her mouth was soft, wet, and searching. We kissed for a lingering time, and an ecstasy seized me.

"Oh, my Queen!" Iras cried in a voice quivering with

509

passion. "I have been waiting for this night of favor for so long, for you are my lady whom I was born to serve and to love until death!"

An inexpressible joy swelled within me at these words. "You need wait no longer, my beloved Iras," I said, taking her to my bed.

The mournfulness of my solitude and celibacy had weighed heavily upon my body and soul, but it was lifted on this night as Iras brought the tomb of my bed-chamber alive with the pulsing urgency of her love.

"Of all the rich raiment you wear, my Queen, your white skin is your most beautiful and precious garment," Iras cried in wonderment, as her lovely little hands explored my body.

The soft but eager touch of her fingertips induced a sensuous intoxication. The fires of Venus caught at us, burning through our bodies, making our hearts beat and our blood throb, and Iras and I were consumed in the flames. My body, which had felt little but emptiness and pain for so long, ached with convulsive ecstasy under the sensual solicitations of Iras, as she beguiled me with voluptuous pleasure. In her love, I was able to forget my despair and exhaustion and the specter of the slaughter of my brother and so many of his bodyguards on that macabre day. I forgot that I had almost been murdered on the temple steps. I was grateful that I was alive, and lost myself in the enchantment of Iras, and became absorbed in the delicious delight of tasting the bitter sweetness of the secret places of her body.

In the morning, after little sleep, I arose, and in a daze of supreme happiness, and with an effort, I went about my duties as Queen. I had to stir out of my enchanted state and pursue more worldly matters. It was my difficult task to issue a proclamation stating that my brother, King Ptolemy Philippos, had been seized with a sudden attack of the pox, and that Almighty Serapis had seen fit, on the day celebrating his birthday, to call Ptolemy to his bosom.

The proclamation fooled no one, of course, for every Alexandrian knew of the attempt on my life on the steps of the temple and that my brother had instigated the action.

The corpse was too unsightly after Apollodorus had finished with it, and was not emblamed, but simply placed in a silver coffin and buried in the Sema in the dead of night.

My brother's last words to me often haunted me. "We could have saved Egypt!" At times I wondered if my policy of dealing with the Romans would eventually destroy me, and that perhaps Alexander's desire to unite east and west was an impossible dream. My father's words, however, would echo in my mind: "Never go against Rome!"

I saw no other way than to pursue the policy which my beloved father had bequeathed me.

In a lovely marble square on the seafront, not far from the palace, there is a beautiful statue of me. It stands on a pedestal facing northwest, gazing out to sea in the direction of Rome. I have always thought the placement of this statue had a symbolic significance.

CHAPTER II

IT WAS WITH PLEASURE AND PRIDE that, after the death of Ptolemy Philippos, and in compliance with Egyptian state-law which forbade a queen to rule alone, I raised my beloved son Caesarion to the double throne of Egypt beside me. There was a beautiful court ceremony which declared him King Ptolemy the Fifteenth, and I gave him the surnames of Philopator and Philomator, Fatherloving and Motherloving. Caesarion was five years old and bore himself during the ceremony with preternatural aplomb. There was no coronation, however, for when Caesarion submitted to the sacred act of anointment, to be consecrated of the gods, I wanted it to be as emperor of the world.

Even with the removal of my brother, I still felt insecure about my position, for there was still the threat of Arsinoë plotting to overthrow me from the sacred groves of Artemis. I had no great power to protect me, and Rome was in terrifying chaos. I also felt frightening waves from Asia Minor, where two of Caesar's assassins, and my most hated enemies, held sway.

Brutus as Proconsul of Macedonia, and Cassius as Proconsul of Syria, were during this time concentrating their forces and forming alliances with the various eastern powers. They raised troops and brought over to their side the Roman legions which were stationed in the eastern quarter of the world, and gathered contributions from all who could be induced to favor their cause. All the eastern monarchs were in league with them, and I feared that I might be forced to follow suit.

A great wave of love for Caesar was washing over

513

Italy, and Antony was hailed as Caesar's true successor. The people pleaded with him to make war against Brutus and Cassius and to avenge the murder of their beloved Caesar.

In Macedonia, Brutus put to death Antony's younger brother, Caius who was Praetor, in retaliation for the execution of Cicero. I hoped that this dastardly deed might spur Antony to action against Brutus.

Cassius, who held eight legions, sent an ambassador to me, demanding that I turn over the five Roman legions which Caesar had left in Alexandria under the command of Rufio. I listened impassively to the envoy and then dismissed him.

"The temerity of Cassius!" I cried angrily to Mardian. "Does he think I will aid the murderer of my son's father?"

"Egypt is once again being faced with a dilemma," Mardian said, "as in the days when we had to side with either Pompey or Caesar. Now it is either Cassius or Antony. It would be best if we could remain neutral."

"To pursue such a policy will be easier said than done, my noble Mardian," I said soberly. "Circumstances will force me to choose, and I am inclined to espouse Antony."

The situation became more complicated when, a few weeks later, an envoy called Alienius arrived from Cornelius Dolabella, the Proconsul of Phoenicia-Judaea, making the same request as Cassius. Dolabella was planning to conquer Parthia, as Caesar had intended to do. A year before, Dolabella had executed Caius Trebonius for having been one of Caesar's assassins, so I was naturally predisposed to aid Dolabella if anyone.

In helping one supplicant, I would inevitably make an enemy of the other, but I felt obliged to gamble by taking sides. I told Alienius that he could have four legions if Dolabella promised to defeat Cassius before setting out for Parthia. The four legions marched with Alienius, and I was left with only one legion in Egypt, the faithful Gabinian troop commanded by Rufio, and my Royal Macedonian Household regiment to protect me.

Soon I learned that Serapion, my Viceroy of Cyprus, sent his fleet of fifty ships over to Cassius in Syria. I was outraged to discover that Serapion was in league with Arsinoë. They had plans to declare her Queen of Cyprus, but that would be merely a stepping stone to the throne of Egypt. After I had been done away with, she would become Queen, marry Serapion, and make him King. I also learned that Arsinoë was courting Brutus and Cassius.

"Place me on the throne of Egypt, and all the royal granaries and treasury will be yours," Arsinoë wrote them. "From Cleopatra you will get not a gold piece or a bushel of wheat, for she will only aid your enemy, Antony."

Arsinoë had always insisted that she was a Phil-hellene and hated Romans from the depths of her soul, yet here she was making application to Brutus and Cassius, willing to surrender the wealth of Egypt to Rome in exchange for the throne of the pharaohs.

I expected this treachery from Arsinoë, but not from Serapion, whom I had trusted and had raised to great power. I took his betrayal with a bitter heart. I vowed that Arsinoë and Serapion would pay for their perfidious treason with their blood.

Distressing news reached me that Dolabella had been attacked by Cassius before Alienius and my four legions reached him. He was defeated and shut inside Laodicea. Serapion and his fleet blockaded Dolabella by sea. Dolabella, completely penned in by land and sea, opened his veins. When Alienius and the four legions arrived, they had no choice but to go over to Cassius.

The shadow of Rome was once again falling over sunny Egypt. I received reports that Cassius, outraged that I had attempted to aid Dolabella, determined to proceed at once to take possession of Egypt, kill me and Caesarion, and place Arsinoë on my throne.

These events frustrated all my hopes. I was alarmed, for I had no sizable force to protect me. In desperation

515

I wrote Antony, urging him to hasten to Macedonia for his final reckoning with Brutus and promising him that I would come to his assistance.

In the middle of the summer equinox, Antony transported eight legions from Italy across the Adriatic to Macedonia and joined the Roman encampment at Amphipolis. Octavian was with him, while Lepidus stayed in Rome to maintain the government.

Brutus, learning of these movements, dispatched a messenger to Cassius. The messenger caught up with Cassius in Judaea as he was marching to Egypt with Arsinoë. Cassius read the letter which ordered him to turn around and meet Brutus in Lydia. Cassius regretfully renounced his hopes of conquering me, since he had more important things to do than place Arsinoë on the Egyptian throne. He sent her back to Ephesus, against her hysterical protests, and hastened to join up with Brutus in Lydia.

I gave a great sigh of relief, realizing that, for the moment, I was out of danger.

Late in the autumnal equinox, Brutus and Cassius concentrated their forces to meet the armies of the Triumvirate. From Sestos they crossed the Hellespont and marched into Thrace.

I resolved to join Antony in the coming war, and fitted out an expedition of thirty ships, loaded with grain and supplies. I decided personally to command this fleet.

"You are the first woman to take a fleet to sea since the ancient days when Queen Artemisia of Halicarnassus, who accompanied Xerxes in his invasion of Greece," Philostratos proudly told me.

Mardian begged me not to go. "I have learned from intelligence reports, Divine Majesty, that Brutus has sent his admiral, Lucius Murcus, to intercept you as soon as you appear on the seas off Greece."

"I am not afraid, Lord Mardian," I said resolutely. "I am determined to run the gauntlet of the blockade to reach Antony."

After giving sacrifices and saying prayers at the

516

Temple of Neptune which stands near the harbor, I boarded my flagship and amid great fanfare and cheers from my people, sailed out to the high seas.

Two days later the north winds came up, and my fleet encountered a sudden, violent tempest. My fleet was thrown into confusion, the masts and sails of many of my ships were destroyed, and several ships sank. I was obliged to turn back. My ships, beaten and battered, sailed sadly into the two harbors, guided by Pharos. I was seasick and distraught, and all my dreams of emulating Queen Artemisia and of aiding Antony were shattered.

"The gods surely sent you that storm, O Queen," Mardian told me. "You must sit by while the Roman situation resolves itself."

"Yes, and pray to the gods that out of the prevailing chaos, Antony will come out the victor," I cried. "If Brutus and the tyrannicides win, then Egypt will become a colony of Rome."

I settled back in my palace and fretfully waited while, once again in far-off Macedonia, the land of my forefathers, Roman armies congregated to engage in the struggle for world empire. I was in constant consultation with my councillors. Several maps of Macedonia were spread across large ebony tables, and from intelligence reports I learned the movements of the armies and placed markings on the maps to denote their positions.

In early October, the armies of Brutus and Cassius converged upon the vicinity of Philippi. Antony, encamped with his legions a few miles away at Amphipolis, broke camp and advanced with his men to Philippi.

The cold winds of October settled upon the flat and barren plains as the two great armies confronted one another.

On the Ides of October, the battle of Philippi was fought. Octavian, who lacked personal courage and military talents, feigned indisposition and stayed quaking in his tent. It was Antony who overwhelmed the enemy with the irresistible onslaught of his charges and the deployment of his great military skills and strategies.

Cassius, aware all was lost, had his freedman, Pindarus, run him through with the dagger he had used on Caesar. Brutus, seeing thousands of his soldiers lying dead, their weapons glittering in the cold afternoon sun, fled the battlefield like a coward with his friend Strato.

As night came on, in the dell where they had taken refuge, Brutus begged Strato to finish him off with the dagger with which he had pierced Caesar's heart. As Strato held the dagger in the air, Brutus rushed upon the point of the weapon with such force that he fell and immediately expired.

Not long after Antony arrived, eager to make Brutus a prisoner, but found him dead. He gallantly took off his military cloak, a magnificent and costly garment, and spread it over the corpse.

At length Octavian was brought up in a litter, and miraculously recovering from his illness now that the battle was over, pranced about raging against his fallen enemies, and insisted that the head of Brutus be severed and sent to Rome to be exhibited by Caesar's statue in the Senate. Antony, a generous foe, ordered that the remaining body be cremated with all military and religious honors, and that the ashes be sent to the mother of the deceased, the Lady Servilia.

All the glory of the brilliant victory at Philippi was credited to Antony. He was worshipped by thirty-two legions and hailed as a hero, while Octavian was cursed as a coward. Philippi marked the termination of the conflict between the friends and foes of Caesar which had agitated the world in the two years since that fateful Ides of March.

"The battle has secured for Antony the first place in the Republic," I pointed out to Mardian. "Indeed, he is the most powerful and conspicuous man in the world."

"As you are the most powerful and conspicuous woman in the world, O Queen," Mardian said with a solemn bow.

All alone, I had led a nation to its destiny during

these years, and my kingdom had enjoyed the blessings of peace. Industry had propered, agriculture had flourished, and commerce had thrived. Our schools were as famous as ever with students from all over the world, and artistic life was vigorous under my patronage. I took care to see that my subjects had freedom and the joys of prosperity. I kept a stern hand upon the government of the provinces, tolerating no abuses, and I punished the least extortion. Thanks to my rigorous administration, revenues from imports filled up my treasury, enabling me to pour enormous sums into the restoration of monuments and temples, and the construction of hundreds of new ships. I also squandered fortunes in amusing my people, giving them entertainments, maintaining the greatest theater in the world, and no expense was spared in celebrating religious festivals and in the display of my splendor.

As prosperous as Egypt was, however, I was still threatened by peril from within and without. I suffered anxiety at the pervasive fear that parties could at any moment be formed to bring about a palace revolution. Many of my ministers and the bankers and merchants of the city, who could not do as they wished under my authority, wanted me toppled. The rich would get richer and the poor would get poorer if I were removed. Greeks have a passion for intrigues, and I knew that many Alexandrian potentates were busy hatching plots against me behind my back.

I learned the disquieting tale that Ptolemy the Pretender had gone to Ephesus and met Arsinoë, and that she declared unequivocally that he was indeed her long-lost brother. Before the Temple of Artemis, they embraced and wept. Our dead brother had been blond and the pretender sported badly dyed hair that was orange, but this did not deter them. They were in touch with many prominent Alexandrians who wished to see me dethroned, and they made plans to one day come to Egypt, oust me, and sit on the double throne.

Apollodorus and Rufio took extra precautions to guard against a palace conspiracy or an uprising. If an attack were made on my life or Caesarion's, and if successful, Arsinoë was the only person alive with a claim to the throne, except for my dear old Aunt Aliki. I had always been tolerant of Arsinoë, but I now formed a burning hatred for her. I decided that Arsinoë, my incorrigible and indomitable sister, would have to be eliminated. I could no longer hedge on this crucial point.

I was a woman alone, threatened by opposition and plots, and deprived of troops. Under the weight of responsibility and in the absence of strong support I lived in forlorn desolation.

It is no wonder that I dreamed often of Caesar, remembering when the strength and passion of the mightiest man in the world had been mine, and now that Caesar was gone, my thoughts often turned to Antony.

I was overjoyed, of course, that Antony was the victor and the most powerful Roman of them all, for I felt he would always advocate my cause. He had become an object of universal interest distinguished by his eccentric manners, the vicissitudes which marked his life, and now by the supremacy of his power. I would need Antony, I perceived, and perhaps in time he would need me.

After Philippi, Octavian, who was twenty-three and shaved once a week, was sent back to Rome to hold order there. He was so sickly that it was thought he would soon die, but I felt his ill health was about as genuine as my late brother's famous stutter. Lepidus crossed over to Numidia to hold the North African provinces. Antony, as the most powerful of the Triumvirs, claimed as his share of the spoils the mighty provinces of the east, Macedonia, Greece, Bithynia, and Syria.

The Roman treasury was empty, and the soldiers were clamoring for pay. With a great following, Antony, the hero of the day, made a triumphant mission to gather taxes and to assert the authority of Rome. He first went down into Greece. In Athens he was acclaimed as Dionysus, attended public games, sat for lectures at the university, and underwent initiation in the Eleusinian Mysteries. Admired by all as a true Philhellene, he moved from city to city, from festival to festival, and was received everywhere with obsequious ovations.

Crossing the Aegean, Antony came to Ephesus. When he made his entrance into the ancient city, the women met him dressed as Bacchantes, and the men and boys like satyrs and fauns. Throughout the town the air was filled with the sound of harps and flutes making merry music.

In the spring, Antony left Ephesus and travelled to several provinces with the brilliant pomp of a Hellenistic king. He went to Syria, to Pergamum, to Bithynia, to Pontus where all the monarchs and satraps received him with unheard-of homage and honors. In Rome Octavian might proclaim himself the adopted son of a god, but in the east Antony truly was a god. He accepted the homage eagerly and greedily inhaled the incense of flattery, enjoying the privileges his glory conferred upon him.

In the beginning of the summer equinox, Antony came to Tarsus on the Cilician coast and set up his court there, surrounded by courtesans and acrobats. He was tired of travelling, and decided it was more in keeping with his dignity to summon the kings and vassals to him, rather than for him to go to them.

All along the roads leading to Tarsus, cavalcades of Oriental pomp brought the kings of Antioch and Sysima, the satrap Polemon, Herod and Mariamme from Judaea, Adallas of Sidonia, the tetrarchs of Laconia and Commagene, and the rulers of Thrace and Arabia, who came to seek Antony's favor. He received and charmed them all.

Antony, the Autocrat of Asia, dealt out favors, giving, taking back, and restoring at pleasure and whim, provinces and kingdoms. The personal attractiveness of the supplicant occasionally influenced his decisions. Princess Glaphyra of Cappodocia, who had passed her prime but was still a ravishing beauty, had an affair with Antony.

As a reward for her favors, he restored her dynasty, and her son became King of Cappodocia.

After some weeks, Antony began making preparations for a campaign against Parthia, which he felt would bring him even more honor. Although tribute had made him wealthy, the Parthian campaign could not be waged unless he had the aid of the richest kingdom on earth.

My kingdom. Egypt.

I had sent him a greeting of congratulations after Philippi, and he had acknowledged it with a short missive. Other than that, there had been no communication between us during the eight months of his eastern progress. I knew that he would need my help for Parthia, however, and I expected that he would soon contact me.

In the middle of June, a ship arrived in the Great Harbor bearing a Roman flag, and I was told that the vessel carried Antony's ambassador, Quintus Dellius. He had long been one of Antony's hangers-on. I had known him briefly in Rome. He was in his forties, short of stature, and had refined, handsome features, an acerbic wit, and pompous manners. He was fond of boasting that once he had been Antony's catamite for a night, but Antony always replied, when questioned on the veracity of this statement, that he must have been drunk and could not remember. I was told that Dellius wrote a weekly letter to Fulvia in Rome, describing all that Antony said and did and with whom, for which he was paid a handsome sum.

With great pomp I received Dellius in my Throne Room. Beside me sat Caesarion in the dress of a Pharaoh. He was six years old and his handsome, bright face bore the features of his father.

Dellius entered the immense chamber, resplendent in Roman helmet, breastplate, and flourishing cloak. Flanked by an escort of Roman centurions, he walked to the steps of the thrones and sank to his right knee, giving me the Roman salute with left hand on his breast and right hand uplifted.

"Hail to the Queen of Egypt!" Dellius declaimed in greeting. "And to the Pharaoh Ptolemy Caesar!"

"Welcome, Lord Dellius, and salutations," I said.

"Greetings, Lord Dellius," Caesarion said clearly.

"O Majestic Queen, I come from my master, Mark Antony," Dellius declared, "to salute you and your young consort, wishing you both glory, happiness, and health."

"You may take your master our greetings in return, Lord Dellius," I responded, "and tell him that Royal Egypt rejoices at his triumph at Philippi eight months ago."

Late that afternoon, I received Dellius less formally in my reception room. He relaxed on a comfortable couch, and I sat in a stately chair. Servants served us food and wine, and we were more at ease, each eager to be agreeable to the other.

"I am happy to be in golden, legendary Alexandria, O Glorious Queen," Dellius cried graciously. "I can now see how in this voluptuous city, and in this sumptuous palace, Great Caesar fell a victim to love."

I was not interested in the past, but the future. "Do you bring me a letter in your master's hand?" I asked.

"No, Divine Majesty," Dellius replied.

I was offended that Antony had not done me the courtesy of a letter, but not a flicker of an eyelash betrayed my disappointment.

"Antony has sent me on a mission to summon the goddess-Queen of Egypt to Tarsus to hold counsel with him on the affairs of the east," Dellius said grandly.

"Great goddess-Queens are not summoned, my Lord Dellius," I retorted, as I swept a haughty glance over him.

Dellius lost his composure. "Please, a thousand pardons, O Queen," he stammered. "My master, the Triumvir Antony, has sent me to invite you to be entertained by him at his palace in Tarsus."

"Do not dissemble with me, Lord Dellius," I said bluntly, meeting his eyes boldly. "Speak plainly, I command you."

Dellius took a breath. "Lord Antony wishes to question you about your equivocal behavior in the late wars."

523

"Equivocal behavior?" I demanded. "I took a fleet to his aid, and only a bad storm forced me to turn back."

"Many say that you gave assistance to Cassius and Brutus in the spirit of revenge after Antony reconciled with Octavian," Dellius cried, "but I am sure once you answer these accusations against you, Great Queen, all will be well between my master and Royal Egypt."

"If your master wishes to fabricate charges to call me to account as a pretext for me to go to him, he is using the wrong approach," I cried. "If the august Triumvir wishes to discuss any matter with Royal Egypt, he has only to come to Alexandria and be my honored guest."

"Divine Majesty, Antony's pressing duties to Rome keep him at Tarsus!"

"The pressing duties of Egypt keep me at Alexandria!"

"It is essential, O Queen, that Antony and you should meet," Dellius insisted. "A means must be found."

"I am told that the Princess Glaphyra threw herself at the conqueror's feet to gain a throne for her son," I said disdainfully. "Well, I have a throne of my own, and I do not need to go crawling to any Roman for one. These last months many vassal kings and queens went begging to Antony and climbed into his bed for favors, but I am Queen of the oldest and wealthiest kingdom on earth. Egypt is an independent kingdom and not a client state of Rome. I take my sacred duties seriously, and I cannot leave my people at present."

"My lord and master is most anxious to renew his ties of friendship and affection for you, O Great Queen," Dellius persisted eagerly.

"I have no doubt that he is, Lord Dellius," I rejoined. "To be blunt, Antony needs the support of Egypt for his future plans."

"Yes, Gracious Majesty, and you need more Roman soldiers to insure the stability of your seat on the throne." Dellius pursed his lips in a satisfied smile. "Lord Antony can give you this."

I offered no reply to this statement, but busied myself at digging a mussel out of a shell and eating it.

"O Divine Queen," Dellius resumed, "I think it is wise to tell you that your sister, the Princess Arsinoë, has written many letters to Lord Antony, who has perused them with interest."

Dellius had struck a vital blow. I did not fail to recognize the warning inherent in his revelation that Arsinoë was up to her old tricks again. Antony could place Arsinoë on the throne, as Cassius had been thinking of doing, as a more subservient slave to Rome. Anger boiled within me, but I controlled my fury, for I had been cleverly checkmated by the wily Dellius.

"Most Gracious Sovereign," Dellius resumed, "in the three years since I last saw you in Rome, you have grown even more beautiful. Your figure has filled out and has taken on the most voluptuous curves."

"From your reputation, Lord Dellius," I said sarcastically, "I did not think you were an authority on female pulchritude."

"Divine Majesty, I am an expert on beauty and art," Dellius avowed, "and your face and form embody the refinement of the most splendid example of Grecian sculpture. Antony has a weakness for beauty, especially when it is united with intellect and charm. I advise you to go to Tarsus in the Homeric style and in your best attire and with great pomp. Antony is the kindest and most human of generals, and you would be like Hera who, by displaying her charms, converted the wrath of Zeus into love."

I did not choose to reply, but my silence suggested that I was seriously considering his advice.

After he had gone, I called Mardian to my side and we discussed the situation at length.

"I have faith in the words of Dellius, O Queen," Mardian said thoughtfully, "but more in your charms, which formerly recommended you to two Romans, the young Gnaeus Pompey and the Great Caesar, and which should prove yet even more successful with a third, the Triumvir Antony."

"You speak sagely, my noble Mardian," I remarked. "Antony has always been strongly influenced by beautiful women and was always attracted to you, even when he first met you fifteen years ago when he was a young cavalry officer and you were a princess of fourteen. Now that you are at the pinnacle of womanhood, with your beauty at its height, he will not be able to resist you. Go to Tarsus and put your experience to the test, and Lord Antony will be yours."

"I never for a moment forget my motto, *Everything for Egypt*," I cried passionately. "My sense of duty to my kingdom and my people dictates all my actions, and if Egypt will benefit from the voyage, of course I shall go, but it must be done in great style and dignity befitting my sacred station."

"O Queen, I humbly suggest you not give Dellius a set time for your departure," Mardian said. "The longer you delay, the more the Triumvir's appetite will be whetted."

Dellius was kept at court for two weeks. I entertained him lavishly, took him to the theater to see a Roman comedy, and then at last bade him to return to his master.

"Tell the Triumvir Antony that when my duties permit, I should very much like to visit fabled Tarsus," I said.

"May I tell the Triumvir when he can expect you, O Queen?"

"When the Egyptian gods give me respite from my royal responsibilities, my Lord Dellius," I said evasively.

Dellius knelt and kissed my hand. "I pray to the gods that you will come soon for the sake of my master," he said, and then rising, added with an ominous ring, "and for your sake, too, Divine Majesty!"

My royal barge was magnificently outfitted, and Apollodorus helped me plan the expedition. Our ardent imaginations were fired with the idea that for a second time I should conquer the greatest general alive in the world. To prepare for the voyage, all the resources of my kingdom were procured for the most glorious means of display. Splendid dresses, rich services of plate, ornaments of precious stones and presents in great cost and variety were loaded onto my ships. I selected a large retinue of attendants and entertainers to accompany me.

While these preparations were going forward all that summer, I received frequent communications from Antony, soliciting me to undertake the journey with all speed, but I did not reply to these messages.

"I took you to Caesar rolled up in a rug, Cleopatra," Apollodorus told me with his flashing smile, "and I will take you to Antony in a golden barge."

CHAPTER III

MY BARGE OF BURNISHED GOLD with purple sails and silver oars, and with a statue of Venus at its prow, escorted by a fleet of twelve triremes loaded with treasures, and propelled by sharp southerly gales, carried me swiftly across the Mediterranean to the coast of Cilicia. After a week's voyage we reached the mouth of the river Cydnus one lovely September dawn, and I stood on deck as a mist of silver floated between the sea and sky. A sudden light gleamed through the haze, the horizon was transfused with rose-colored clouds, and through the limpid light shot the gold and scarlet of the rising sun.

Leaving my escort of ships at the mouth of the river, my beautiful barge sailed serenely up the Cydnus toward Tarsus, which stands twelve miles inland. Dressed as Venus rising from the sea, I reclined on deck in a divan set in a giant man-made seashell which was covered in mother-of-pearl, with a canopy of gold shading me from the sun. Pretty boys, painted to resemble cupids, stood beside me waving peacock fans. The loveliest of my ladies, clad as nymphs, took charge of the ropes and steered the rudder, for all men were banished below deck. The silver oars dipped rhythmically into the river to the beat of music from flutes, pipes, and lyres. Kaphi, an incense compounded, according to the sacred books, of sixteen precious ingredients, burned in bronze bowls on deck and the scent wafted to the banks. People came rushing to the shores, thronging both banks, cheering and hailing me, and following the barge upstream as we sailed along.

529

At high noon when the domes of the old city of Tarsus came into view, I rose from my seashell and went to my stateroom below deck. Presently the barge reached the port where the city stood, situated amid the most enchanting scenery and beneath towering mountains, giving the city a breathtaking and romantic backdrop. I had not sent any messenger ahead, and my coming took the town totally by surprise.

In the public square of Tarsus, not far from the dock, Mark Antony sat enthroned under a canopy of state beneath a cluster of sycamore trees, holding court as Proconsul, dispensing justice according to Roman law. The crowd was listening attentively to the speech of one of Antony's praetors when men came running up from the dock with the tidings of my arrival. The agitation spread quickly, and my name was on everyone's lips.

The town square was rapidly deserted as the curious crowd rushed to the dockside. They had been jostling one another in the square to get closer to Antony, and now they pushed one another along the harbor to get a better view of my barge. In a frenzy of excitement, they kept calling out my name, begging me to make an appearance.

Antony, sitting practically alone in the square, called Quintus Dellius to his side.

"Go, Quintus," Antony said, "welcome the Queen of Egypt and tell her that she may come to me in a litter to pay me homage."

Dellius rushed to the barge and was admitted on board. I did not receive him, but had Apollodorus greet him. Apollodorus explained that Egypt's Queen was overcome with seasickness and could not leave her bed.

Dellius hurried back to the square, finding Antony sitting under the canopy, fidgeting and perspiring in the afternoon sun. Antony, who thought that his title of Triumvir outranked that of all monarchs, was deeply affronted that I would not go to him, but he put a good face on the matter.

"Return to the Queen of Egypt," he said, "and invite her to my palace tonight for a banquet."

Again Dellius returned to the barge and had conference with Apollodorus, who told him that his mistress was too fatigued from her voyage to journey to the palace. Apollodorus added that if Antony wished, he and all the lords of Tarsus could come to a banquet on board the royal barge that evening.

Antony, who had waited for me all summer, conceded gracefully and returned to his palace to prepare for the evening ahead.

The sun set behind the western mountain slopes of Tarsus, and a purple dusk fell softly over the city. The congregation of citizens along the harbor swelled, the people admiring my ship and hoping for a glimpse of me. On the deck of my barge, musicians played flutes and harps. A hundred torches were lit, and a thousand lanterns hung from the masts and sails. The barge glittered and glimmered with a glorious constellation of lights.

All the lords and ladies of Tarsus came on board and were conducted to the banqueting salon below deck.

In my stateroom I had taken a long perfumed bath and had been massaged by a Nubian slave. Charmion and Iras carefully thickened my long lashes with kohl and painted my mouth with carmine. Iras arranged my hair flowing to my shoulders, threading pearls in the curls. I was dressed in a diaphanous silk blue dress that clung seductively to my body, and my wrists and neck sparkled with sapphires and rubies from India.

"You are a heavenly vision, Cleopatra," Iras cried. "Antony will be in love with you before the night is over."

"Queen Cleopatra," Apollodorus announced, "the Triumvir Antony has arrived on the dock."

After my ladies gave the finishing touches to my appearance, I went up on deck. As I appeared the enormous crowd cramming the waterfront erupted into ecstatic cheers.

"Welcome, Venus, who has come to visit Antony, the Roman Dionysus, for the good of Asia!" a claque of voices cried out.

I cast a placid eye over the waving crowd, and then

my eyes fell on Antony as he alighted from his litter. Accompanied by Dellius and his praetors, he crossed the gangplank and came on board, walking gracefully as a lion.

My eyes calmly glanced over him as I wore a mysterious smile. At forty-two he was more gloriously good-looking than ever, dressed in a golden breastplate which depicted Achilles being dipped in the river Styx by his mother. With his massive and majestic bearing, he made a heroic figure, and I smiled into the handsome, dark face framed by a splendid beard and masses of great curls. His blue eyes glowed as they drank in the sight of me, and he returned my smile with a flash of white teeth.

"Hail, noble Triumvir," I cried out. "Welcome to Egypt!"

"Egypt?" Antony responded, a bit taken back. "But Queen Cleopatra, you have come to Tarsus!"

"Lord Antony, you have come on board my barge, which is Egyptian, so you have come to visit me in Egypt."

"So I have, Queen Cleopatra," Antony said, flashing a smile. "Ah, the beautiful Lady Charmion!"

Charmion went forward, standing in front of Iras and blocking the younger, smaller girl from Antony's view. "Greetings, my Lord Antony!" She smiled seductively.

Antony peered over her shoulder. "And the tiny, fair maiden behind you, Charmion?" he asked with bright-eyed curiosity.

Charmion, with a look of displeasure, moved aside.

"The Lady Iras," I said serenely, "who has a special place in the affections of my heart, noble Antony."

Antony's great eyes appraised Iras as he held out his hand, and Iras took it somewhat reluctantly.

"Queen Cleopatra, you have always had an eye for beauty," Antony cried.

I saw that the compliment did not win Iras over, for she stepped back, with no display of pleasure.

"Come, let us feast and be merry," I said pleasantly.

I led Antony down to the banqueting salon, and I

saw that he was entranced by the spectacle that greeted him. The chamber was hung with purple, gold-embroidered tapestries and mirrors, and the floor was strewn with roses. There were twelve gold couches with an ebony table before each, spread with golden goblets and plates studded with precious jewels, and mounted pieces filled with a profusion of exotic flowers and fruits. The air was filled with rich incense, and flaming torches glowed from their holders on the walls, reflecting in the mirrors which lit the room with an incredible brilliance.

Antony introduced me to his chief officers and to the learned teachers from the school of oratory for which Tarsus is famed, and I also said greetings to several local merchants and magistrates. Antony and I then went and stood at the table on the dais. There were two golden crowns studded with gems on the table, and I picked one up.

"Triumvir Antony, the fame of your incomparable valor and victories have already given you a crown of glory, and I now want to give you a golden crown," I cried. I placed the crown upon his head, and then Antony set my crown upon mine.

The guests gave approving applause. I hoped that this mutual crowning would have a symbolic significance for our future.

Antony and I sat on our chairs, and the guests, wearing crowns made of flowers which my servants had distributed, resumed their places on the twelve couches spread before us.

"I am very pleased to sit beside Cleopatra," Antony cried, "where once my cousin Caesar had the honor."

The banquet began as I saluted my guests in the custom of Egypt by drinking from a goblet filled with a holy wine. Antony drank from this goblet, and it was then passed from guest to guest as everyone took a sip. Antony responded by offering, in the Roman style, the libation of the garlands. A great goblet was filled with a golden wine from Samos. Antony dipped a flower in the goblet and took a sip, and I did likewise. The goblet then went from couch to couch, as each guest took a flower from their crown, dipped it into the cup, pronounced a prayer for good health and happiness, and drank.

I had used all my imagination to arrange a banquet of prodigal abundance, designed to dazzle the greatest of Romans so that he could see that the daughter of the Lagidae lived in a luxury which made him a provincial by comparison. Antony had always craved splendor, but the incense that Asia had burned at his feet had intoxicated him. He was obsessed with the love of ostentation and riches, which I personified, and that night I saw that he was satiated with it.

Handsome slaves dressed only in loincloths distributed the food of rare delicacies, and the finest wines filled the golden and translucent obelisk-shaped crystal goblets. Acrobats performed in the space in the center of the salon, and dancing girls moved to sensuous rhythms. Antony, however, sitting beside me, rarely glanced at the dancers. He was overcome by my feast, my heady wines, and by me.

"Your impeccable wife, the Lady Fulvia," I asked at one point, "how does she fare?"

"Fulvia is in blooming health," Antony replied.

"You are most fortunate to have a faithful wife and your devoted brother, Lucius, to look after your interests in Italy."

"Fulvia is indeed a remarkable woman," Antony said. "She reminds me a little, in her strong character, of the long line of formidable women who have marked your venerable dynasty."

"Do they remember me in Rome, my Lord Antony?" I asked, turning a serious gaze upon him.

"Assuredly, Great Queen," Antony declared. "The legend of Caesar and Cleopatra has grown."

"Yes, I know, Caesar who had the falling sickness and the Cleopatra sickness," I said cynically. "I am the Egyptian siren who embodies all the shameful depravity of the Orient." I took a sip of wine and then gave him a long, searching stare. "We were friends in Rome, Antony, do you remember?"

"Yes, and I hope we still are, O Queen," Antony cried.

"O greatest of Romans, I have never done anything to hurt you," I cried passionately, "and that is why I was aggrieved when Dellius suggested I had given assistance to Cassius. Surely you know that such an accusation is unfounded. Twice he demanded recruits from me and each time I refused and was threatened with invasion. I sent off the legions to your friend Dolabella, and on their own they went over to Cassius."

"I thought you were my best ally, Cleopatra, and I was expecting your fleet to come to my aid," Antony said reproachfully.

"The gods thwarted my plans," I cried. "My fleet had scarcely been put to sea when a tempest scattered my ships, sinking several, and I was forced to return in a leaking ship to Alexandria. When my fleet was reassembled, you no longer needed it, for you had won at Philippi and had become the most powerful man in the world."

Antony placed a huge hand on my wrist. "Now that you have explained yourself, Cleopatra, I am moved by the heroic dangers you endured on my behalf. Your conduct as my ally is worthy of all praise."

I smiled at his words and at his touch and drew closer to him. "I knew that, face to face, we would clear up any misunderstandings between us."

"All summer long I waited for you to come, Cleopatra," he whispered hoarsely, leaning nearer still. His words bespoke a mixture of reproach and desire.

"My obligations to my people detained me."

"It has been three years and five months since we last saw one another."

"Yes, and during that time while you have been busy running the Roman empire," I exclaimed, "I have been occupied with the affairs of my small kingdom, a task which has filled all my days."

"And your nights, Cleopatra?" Antony asked with curiosity and fear.

"My nights have been lonely," I replied with a sigh. "My life has been full of dreams. Dreams do not only come at night, Lord Antony. In this world of misery they come to us during the waking hours."

"Caesar always said your head was full of fantasies," Antony said with wonder. "He regretted he did not have the strength, will, and the youth to bring all your glorious dreams to consummation."

"My beloved Caesar, unfortunately, was at the end of his life when I loved him," I said. "But you, Antony, are in the prime of life. Philippi was only the beginning, and future historians will mention it only in passing in their works of the life of Antony the Great."

Antony drank in my words, as intoxicated with them as with the wine I poured with my own hand. For a long while he only sat there, silent, drinking in my dreams.

I ran a finger over the rim of my goblet, staring out at the guests in front of me, who were all discreetly avoiding looking at us.

"In the three years since we last saw one another, Cleopatra, you have changed immensely," Antony said softly.

"How have I changed?"

"You have grown even more beautiful than you were in Rome," he replied in a quavering voice.

"And you have grown even more handsome."

"You are the rarest creature on earth and your beauty is beyond compare," he said. "You are indeed touched by the gods."

At the end of the banquet, my chamberlain Theopompus stood beside my table, and with a nod from me, turned to the assemblage.

"Honored guests," Theopompus cried in a grandiloquent voice, "my mistress Royal Egypt wishes that you take the golden plates and goblets you have used tonight as souvenirs of this banquet."

The guests gave out with shouts of delight.

"Dearest Cleopatra," Antony cried, "you must do me the honor of attending a banquet at my palace tomorrow evening."

"My Lord Antony, I shall come with pleasure," I

said, giving him a smile that invoked a sensuous invitation.

I walked with Antony up on deck, and the crowd along the harbor erupted with frenzied cries as we appeared.

Antony turned to me, and I saw myself reflected in his sparkling eyes.

"Today has been a day of days, Great Queen!" he cried.

"Tomorrow will also be a day of days, most mighty Triumvir!" I answered warmly.

Antony kissed my hand, and the crowd responded with cheers. Antony went ashore, and as he stood waving at me, I disappeared below deck.

"With your voice and manners," Charmion said happily, "and with your wit and conversation that so charmed Caesar, you have now totally beguiled Mark Antony."

"He is so gross!" Iras said scornfully, pouting. "My precious Queen, he resembles a brute gladiator or a wrestler with all those muscles and all that coarse, curly hair."

"Never mind, Iras, he is the most powerful man in the world!" Charmion cried with her usual practical point of view. "Oh, Cleopatra, it was apparent that Antony was drunk tonight, and not with wine. You possess the gift of fascination which can steal the reason of men."

"Not only men, but women, too!" Iras cried, her dark eyes adoring me.

I was drowsy with food and wine, and I went to sleep that night recalling the ardor and my reflection in Antony's fiery eyes.

My twelve triremes docked at Tarsus the following dawn, and slaves carried the gifts I had brought Antony, his Roman officers, and the Tarsian lords through the streets and up the hill to the palace.

In a shroud of blue twilight, a cavalcade of golden litters took me and my retinue up to the palace. It had been the seat of the Seleucid kings, and although not so grand as my palace in Alexandria, it is still an impressive residence with a magnificent view.

"Cleopatra, Queen of Queens," Antony cried in a booming voice as he greeted me, "the precious gifts you have lavished upon me and my officers have delighted us all."

"The pleasure has been mine in giving, my noble Roman."

"Yesterday," Antony remarked, "with the glorious vision of your sailing up the Cydnus to visit Mark Antony, was a day that will be remembered, as we remember the visit of Queen Makada of Sheba, who in all her splendor came to King Solomon in Jerusalem seven centuries ago."

I laughed softly. "Do you really believe the world will be talking about us seven hundred years hence, my Lord Antony?"

"As long as the world endures, Cleopatra, we will be remembered!" he cried with pride.

Antony, perhaps as an homage to my Greek heritage, was dressed in a short Greek white tunic, which revealed his powerful, hirsute chest and magnificent legs to full advantage, and on his feet he wore white leather sandals. On his head he had a garland of ivy and vine leaves. A golden robe of gauze clung to my body, and I observed Antony's great eyes appraising the length of me, lingering upon my breasts under the transparent tissue.

"Your dress is surely made of spun gold," Antony cried. "And your hair, too!" With a spontaneous gesture, he touched the ends of my hair.

"And you look like the Greek Dionysus in your dress," I said admiringly.

"That's the idea, for I've always enjoyed playing the Greek," Antony said with a twinkling smile.

Antony took my hand and led me down a long corridor, while our attendants followed in our path. As we entered the great hall, all the guests sitting rose to their feet and trumpets blasted. At the table of honor on the dais, we sat down, the guests resumed their couches, and the banquet commenced.

A group of mimes, who went everywhere with Antony, came on and, invoking Thalia of the Comic spirit, performed a skit, *The Unfaithful Wife*. It was vulgar and crudely performed, not the sort of theater one got in Alexandria, but I laughed good-naturedly since I did not want to insult my host. Next Charmides, the Greek mime, recited lascivious limericks. Xandos, the dancer, did a dance of Bacchus. Anaxador, the famous flute-player, blew several lovely songs, and his musicianship was almost as good as my father's.

The highlight of the evening for me was when a dozen Syrian dancing girls, each more beautiful than the other, performed a sensuous dance to the music of oboes and harps. The guests, concentrating on their food, applauded languorously at the finish, but I was enraptured. The dancing was not of the caliber to which I am accustomed, but I am always fascinated by any form of Terpsichore's art, and these lovely girls made up in enthusiasm and grace what they lacked in training.

Medradro, Antony's majordomo in charge of the table, had supervised the food, which lacked delicacy, and the wines were of an inferior cask. This did not discourage any of the guests, however, who all gorged and drank themselves to the fill.

"I am afraid the splendor and refinement of your feast last night puts me to shame, Cleopatra," Antony said apologetically.

"Oh, not at all, dearest Antony," I rejoined politely.

Sitting beside Antony, I sensed that my presence was working like a charm upon him, and that an ardent passion for me was burgeoning within him. Every time I turned, I saw the glow of desire sparkling in his blue eyes. While I ate with lanquid gestures, he ate with uncontrollable nervousness, his body coiled and trembling with tension.

The voluptuousness of Asiatic cities like Tarsus appealed to Antony's sensual character. At the banquet, he was surrounded by gay companions and flattering libertines, and he permitted them every liberty. Charmides came up beside him, and the two jested together, throwing their arms around each other affectionately.

"You seem to enjoy these days of revelry, Lord Antony," I remarked with a certain reproach in my voice.

"Last winter the needs of war compelled me to endure the cold and the harsh army camps of Macedonia where I wore the skins of wild animals," Antony explained defensively, "but after my hard-earned victory there, I am entitled to enjoy the warmth of these lands, to wear silk and to have a little relaxation."

"Oh, indeed, great General!" I cried. "Your fame and heroic deeds are known all over the world. However, while you play at being a god here in the east, Octavian is becoming a god in Rome. It is ten long months since Philippi."

Antony's smile became a scowl. "Is it time to buckle on my sword again, great Queen?"

"One should not rest on one's laurels," I said. "There is Parthia to be conquered."

"I am busy making preparations for a Parthian invasion," Antony attested. "All the plans are being worked out, the number of soldiers, the roads to be taken, the logistics, the costs."

"You can rely upon me to aid you in this undertaking," I promised. "However, I will lay down certain conditions for my support."

Antony lifted his great eyebrows quizzically.

I took a long drink of wine and set down the goblet. I met his eyes calmly. "For one, my Lord Antony, my sister the Princess Arsinoë must be disposed of." Antony blinked at me, refusing to comprehend my meaning. "As the Triumvir of the eastern provinces," I continued, "your word is law around these parts, is that not so?"

"By all the gods, yes! Need you question it?"

"You have power over every creature in Asia?"

"Indisputably!" Antony avowed firmly.

"Arsinoë is residing not far from here in Ephesus," I said. "What is good for me is good for you. I want you

540

to send a detachment of soldiers to Ephesus and have her executed."

Antony stared at me with astonished eyes. "I, Antony, murder a royal princess of the house of Egypt? On what grounds?"

"You know of the plots she has fomented to bring me down," I explained heatedly. "In Rome I intervened with Caesar to spare her, but I was a fool. Since then she has betrayed me more times than I have fingers. I can no longer be sentimental about my sister. As a matter of self-preservation, I must have Arsinoë put out of the way. She is caught in a net woven by her own fingers. If you are my ally, Antony, and if I am to be yours, you will oblige me in this matter."

Antony gave out with an uncomfortable laugh. "Cleopatra, I shrink from committing such a dreadful act."

"If you want my aid, it is my condition," I said obdurately. "I also want Ptolemy the Pretender, the admiral Serapion, and the High Priest Megabysus of Artemis executed, too!"

"You want Antony to murder a holy High Priest?" he cried. "Such an act would be reprehensible."

"Great rulers must sometimes commit abhorrent acts in compliance with the dictates of their great positions."

"O Glorious Queen, I spent several joyful weeks at Ephesus and the citizens loved me. To murder their High Priest would make the Ephesians my enemies."

"Their High Priest and my sister are in league with some of my nobles in Alexandria, hatching plots to finish me off," I cried. "You say you want me as an ally, but if Arsinoë succeeds in her designs, I will be crushed. Do you want Arsinoë to be Queen of Egypt?" I flashed him a reproachful look. "I know she has been writing letters to you, Antony!"

Antony guiltily avoided my gaze. "I grant that Arsinoë has been guilty of treason, Cleopatra. She will be indicted on charges of conspiracy and imprisoned."

"As long as she lives and breathes, my life is in mortal danger," I cried vehemently. "I demand a more definite solution to this vexing problem. The way I see it, I must strike before I am struck."

"Arsinoë has taken sanctuary in the Temple of Artemis," Antony temporized. "I would profane the sacred grounds if I harmed Arsinoë there."

"My sister must be done away with, Antony," I insisted. "Send your soldiers into the temple, and if need be, drag her out and execute her. If there is to be a grand alliance between Antony and Cleopatra, this must be done. You murdered Cicero and hundreds of your fellow Romans as a protective measure. Can you not do this to protect Caesarion and me?"

Antony took a gulp of wine and swallowed hard. "It shall be done, Cleopatra," he sighed in capitulation.

I felt the pleasure of triumph course through my veins.

"The matter is settled, Cleopatra, so let us discourse on happier topics," Antony said, refilling my goblet.

I nodded and smiled. "As you wish, my noble lord."

Antony looked longingly into my eyes, and touched my hand. "All those years in Rome, Cleopatra, I longed to touch you, but you were always beyond my reach."

"I belonged to Caesar," I said. "A woman is not worth her weight in salt if she cannot be faithful to the man she loves."

"All the gods and the Romans know that you never gave Caesar the least grounds for jealousy," Antony said. "I have always wanted you, but Caesar's exalted position restrained me, for I was an inferior officer who owed everything to my cousin Caesar. My deep devotion to Caesar prevented me from expressing my admiration openly, but surely you knew my eyes spoke to you with that eloquent look a woman always understands."

"Any woman under sixty, Antony, can understand the eloquence of your eyes," I said with gentle mocking. "And every woman in the Empire knows of your great appetite."

Antony gave me his frank, sensual smile. "There is no woman on earth like you, Cleopatra. Now that Caesar is dead, I stand in Caesar's place and know no master for a rival, and I can reveal my feelings. These last three years your beauty has haunted me. Last winter, on the cold plains of Philippi, alone in my tent at night, shivering, I dreamed of you, conjuring you up in my feverish mind. You have become an obsession with me, Cleopatra."

His words swayed me, and his nearness tempted me, but I had to prevent fulfillment of his desires until he came to Alexandria.

"Your voice thrills me and your beauty makes me drunk, Cleopatra," Antony said hoarsely.

"Are those the same words you used to seduce the Princess Glaphyra?" I asked with a smile.

"Please, don't mock me, O Queen!" Antony cried in a strangled voice. He gave a deep sigh. "Your hair is so luxuriant and golden, and your great blue eyes are flecked with gold."

Antony caressed my hair, but I had decided I would grant him no other liberty. I could not permit myself to be undermined by his overpowering presence and passion. I had to keep a firm grip on my emotions.

I felt his hot breath blowing on my cheek, and then his warm lips.

A sense of panic seized me and I abruptly rose. "It is late and I am tired, Lord Antony," I cried. "I must return to my barge."

"So soon?" Antony asked, perplexed, rising after me.

"Yes, my lord," I replied firmly.

"Will you come back to the palace tomorrow so we can discuss our terms of alliance?" Antony asked desperately.

"Tomorrow my ships hoist sail with the morning tide to take me back to Egypt."

"Great Queen, you only arrived two days ago!"

"Yes."

Tormented by such unaccustomed resistance, Antony's desire turned to exasperation. "You came clear to Tarsus to spend two days?"

"It was worth it, Lord Antony," I said placidly. "I cannot remain outside Egypt any longer, however, since there is danger of an uprising there as long as Arsinoë remains alive."

"I will have her slaughtered tomorrow!" he bellowed excitedly.

"Do that," I said. "I am also not only a Queen, but a mother, and I must return to Caesarion."

"Cleopatra, stay just one more day!"

"My plans, mighty Triumvir, are made!" I turned from him and walked down the steps from the dais. The guests stood as I swept out of the hall, and my ladies, chamberlains, and Antony trailed after me.

At the palace portals I turned to Antony.

"Oh, Cleopatra, I beg you, stay!" he cried, impassioned, seizing my shoulders. "I am intoxicated, and not just with wine, but with you. I am master of the world, but with you I am not master of myself. You are not only a queen above all other queens, but a woman above all other women!"

"Well, Antony is a man of men," I said sincerely. "You must remember, however, that as Queen I cannot always do what my heart wishes. It is true that I succumbed to Caesar the first night I met him, but I was young and innocent then. In the seven years since, I have endured many experiences and tragedies, and I have learned a few lessons. Frankly, I have come to put a great price on my favors. I am determined to grant whatever gifts you ask of me, Lord Antony, but first you must make certain promises."

"All that you wish will be granted, Cleopatra," Antony said fervently. "I promise in the name of all the gods!"

I met his eyes coldly, challengingly. "Antony, you are the new Caesar and you hold in your hand the fate of great countries, millions of people, and dozens of monarchs. You are Atlas holding up the world. I am a great Queen, inspired by my kinfolk the gods, and I know that with my riches and your military genius, we could rule the world together. Caesar realized this, but he was too old to do much about it. You will be greater than your cousin Caesar, for you are at the peak of your powers. If our destinies are linked, the world will belong to Antony and Cleopatra!"

"I agree, Cleopatra, so stay a few days longer and we will discuss our glorious future," Antony pleaded.

If I stayed one more day, I knew that Antony would force the issue between us. For my second Roman I wanted to choose the time and the place.

"My duties command that I return immediately to my kingdom," I said. "When Arsinoë, Megabysus, Serapion, and Ptolemy the Pretender are in the shades, come to Alexandria and we will plan our alliance and seal the bargain. And bring the corpse of Arsinoë with you so that I may give her honorable burial with her ancestors in the Sema. Farewell!"

Antony's strong hands clamped my shoulders. "A kiss," he whispered feverishly, "do I not warrant a mere kiss of friendship from the lips of Royal Egypt?"

I trembled as his strong hands held my face, drawing me close. His sensual mouth pressed passionately against my lips, and I yielded myself up to the kiss with closed eyes. He forced my lips apart and I felt his hot, fiery tongue invading my mouth, creating a fire within my whole body that made me dizzy.

With a great rallying of will power, I tore my mouth from his and writhed free. "Do not let me forget myself in public, Triumvir Antony, I beg you!" I cried. "I am a great ruler, but I cannot always rule my emotions."

With flashing eyes, I turned away and raced outside to my litter, and Antony trotted at my heels.

At the litter I turned to him, once more in possession of myself, cool and commanding. "Come to Alexandria, my noble Antony, as soon as possible, and leave your legions behind. Come as a private citizen and do not make the same mistake as Caesar, who came with his soldiers, for my people are easily offended and it would only stir them up."

"I shall come, Cleopatra, as soon as the affairs of Asia are put in order," Antony said, kissing my hand.

"Farewell, noble Antony," I said, pulling my hand free.

My litter began moving as Antony stood there, disappointed and baffled, tortured with frustrated desire.

"I shall come soon!" Antony cried, running alongside my litter.

No other woman before, not even a queen, had ever denied Antony her favors.

The litter carried me down the hill and through the streets of Tarsus, and the people strolling the sidewalks cheered me as I passed by.

"Oh, my Queen," Iras cried. "Antony is under your spell, as I am, for you are a bewitching sorceress."

As the sun rose at dawn, my barge broke away from the dock. I heard galloping horses resounding through the deserted streets of Tarsus. I looked out the window of my bedchamber and saw Antony riding up to the dockside to bid me farewell. I realized that surely he had not slept all night, but had lain awake tossing in frustration.

"Cleopatra, should you not go up on deck to wave farewell to Antony?" Charmion suggested.

"No," I replied complacently, lying back in bed.

The barge and the accompanying triremes sailed down the Cydnus with the sharp currents, leaving Tarsus behind.

I came, I saw, I conquered.

With a triumphant rush of feeling, I realized that, although I had not given in to Antony, I had won him.

"Like Caesar, my Queen," Apollodorus remarked to me later that afternoon as we strolled on deck, "Antony has completely capitulated to the charms of Cleopatra, the Aphrodite of the Nile."

"We have come to an understanding," I said confidently. "My journey to Tarsus will change the course of history."

A flood of hope rose within me, washing away all my insecurities and doubts. Antony would come to Egypt and my cherished dreams of world empire, which had been murdered on that Ides of March, would be revived again. A glorious future lay ahead, with Antony.

The prows of my ships cut the blue waters of the

Mediterranean, speeding southward, and I returned to Alexandria after an absence of two weeks. Cheering citizens and a distinguished deputation of nobles awaited me on the dock as I stepped ashore.

Caesarion broke down as I embraced him, sobbing like a baby instead of the six-year-old Pharaoh that he was.

"Oh, Mother, why did you go away?" Caesarion cried.

"I went to see a great general, my darling," I replied, kissing his wet cheeks. "You are too young yet to fight our battles, and I am only a woman."

"Never leave me again, Mother, please!" he pleaded.

"I promise you I never shall, my son," I cried.

It soon became evident that my trip to Tarsus had been worthwhile, for in the following weeks Antony complied with all my requests. The goddess Nemesis answered my prayers, and I had vengeance on three of my enemies, with Antony the agent of retribution.

Antony sent a centurion, Caius Catiline, with a squad of soldiers to Ephesus. They found Arsinoë in the great temple, where she was serving the goddess as a novice. Catiline walked into the huge, colonnaded temple, one of the wonders of the world, and a priest led him to Arsinoë as she stood serving a small altar.

"Are you the Lady Arsinoë Lagos?" Catiline asked.

Arsinoë drew herself up with all her dignity. "I am the Princess Arsinoë, liege lady of Egypt, daughter of the Ptolemies and a child of the gods!"

Catiline unrolled a parchment and read the order of arrest, which listed the several conspiracies she had been involved in against me.

"You are ordered to come with us, Lady Arsinoë," Catiline said.

"I have taken sanctuary in this holy temple, and I will not leave," Arsinoë replied boldly. "Mark Antony has no jurisdiction over me while I reside with the Mother Goddess Artemis."

"If you do not come willingly, Lady Lagos," Catiline said harshly, "we must take you by force."

Arsinoë, panic seizing her, turned and ran off through the immense temple, and up the marble steps to the main altar. The temple echoed with the tramping of the soldiers who pursued her.

Behind the altar, Arsinoë flung her arms around the statue of Artemis. "Great Mother, protect me!" she screamed.

Catiline and his four soldiers, with their swords drawn, stopped a few feet away from her, hesitating to act.

"You will not dare harm me here!" Arsinoë cried.

"Lady Lagos, we ask that you come with us!"

"You will not damn your souls by committing the sacrilege of harming a divine princess in this precinct," Arsinoë sobbed.

"Take the lady by force," Catiline commanded his soldiers.

The four soldiers pulled Arsinoë by the shoulders, but she clung so strongly to the arm of the statue that they could not pull her free. One of the soldiers, in a frenzy of impatience, brought his sword down and severed her hand at the wrist, releasing her hold from the goddess.

The temple reverberated with Arsinoë's tortured screams. The priests, priestesses, and worshippers all scurried away or fell on the floor, horrified, as Arsinoë was pulled through the great house. The marble and mosaic flooring was spattered with the blood that poured from the bleeding stump at Arsinoë's wrist. She was dragged outside and down the cascading flight of steps and thrown on the street, where she lay writhing, screaming with pain and shock, her one hand clutching at her bleeding stump. Catiline then mercifully thrust the point of his sword into her breast, eliciting one final, agonized groan from her throat.

The sad life of my spirited, restless half-sister, Princess Arsinoë, was over at the age of twenty-three. To the very end she showed indomitable daring and energy. I was naturally affronted by the butchery of the Roman soldiers and the cruel manner in which they carried out their duties, but Arsinoë had not made their task easy for them.

When I received news of her death, I was relieved to know that there would be no more plots to topple me and put her in my place. At the same time, however, I shed a few tears and prayed that Arsinoë would find tranquillity in the Infernal Kingdom such as her ambitious, restive heart had never permitted her to find on earth.

Serapion, my traitorous governor of Cyprus, was apprehended by Antony's soldiers and executed. Ptolemy the Pretender, hiding in the Phoenician town of Aradus, was ferreted out and killed. Megabysus fared better, for an Ephesian deputation visited Antony and begged mercy for their High Priest, and Antony gave in to their demands, which displeased me.

Antony wrote me of these actions, and to say that he would soon join me in Alexandria. He industriously applied himself to governmental tasks from morning until night. He deferred the war against Parthia, and entrusting Asia Minor to two of his generals, he set out for Tyre, where a small fleet awaited him.

In the middle of November, Antony set sail for Egypt. The heavens were dark, the sea was gray and rough, but this did not deter him. The north winds drove his ships straight to Alexandria.

Antony sent a ship on ahead with a messenger telling me that he would not be far behind, and so I was expecting him. The splendor I exhibited at Tarsus had charmed Antony, but now I wanted to entrance him totally with the rich brilliance of my court. I hung my palace with flags, colorful ribbons blazed across the two harbors, and a great banner, made of white silk, was hung down the marble walls of Pharos, with WELCOME ANTONY written in gold over it.

On a bright, sunny day in late November, Antony sailed into the Royal Harbor. Though he disembarked unpretentiously as a private citizen, oriental carpets were strewn on the dockside where he walked. He was met by Apollodorus and a contingent of my councillors who led him under a triumphal archway to a golden chariot.

Antony was taken on a circuitous route to my palace so that my people could see him. With Apollodorus standing beside him on the chariot, he made his way along wide boulevards and at last down the Canopic Way to the palace. Cheering citizens shouted enthusiastic greetings all along the way.

With Caesarion beside me, I descended the great marble staircase of the palace, followed by priests and my councillors, who were dressed in colorful garb. As I reached the bottom step, Antony's chariot, drawn by six white horses, raced into the square.

"My Lord Antony, welcome!" I cried as he alighted from the chariot and rushed up to me.

"Salutations, Royal Egypt!" Antony cried, sinking to one knee and saluting me with his right hand.

Charmion handed me a garland which I draped around Antony's neck. I took his uplifted hand in mine, and as he stood we embraced.

"I am so happy you have come to Egypt!" I said.

"Cleopatra!" Antony cried, the name issuing from his lips as if in exaltation. He then noticed Caesarion, and smiling broadly, squatted in front of him. "Ah, my little cousin, Caesarion!" he said. "Do you remember me from when you were a little boy in Rome?"

Caesarion scowled unpleasantly. "No!" he blurted out coldly.

Antony was taken aback but continued to smile. "I can see that you are the image of your great father, my boy!"

Seeing that Caesarion was not responding to Antony's charm, I took him by the hand, saying, "Come, my noble Antony," and we three walked up the steps to a fanfare of trumpets.

"How wonderful it is to be in Alexandria again after all these years," Antony said enthusiastically.

"My people regard you, the hero of Philippi, as my greatest ally, Lord Antony," I said.

"You must go back to your studies now, Caesarion!" I said as we entered the main corridor.

Caesarion shot Antony a final, hostile look and then went off sadly in the company of his tutors, nurses and attendants. At the entrance to my reception room, Antony stopped and studied a huge statue of Hercules.

"It's by Praxiteles," I explained placidly.

"What a glorious specimen of Greek art," Antony cried, and then his feverish eyes focused upon me. "The most stunning example of Greek art, however, is the living statue of you, O Beauteous Queen!"

I accepted the compliment with a graceful smile. The huge bronze doors of my apartments were opened, and I led Antony inside. Melodious, seductive music from harps and lutes was issuing forth from corners.

"Pray sit, dear friend," I said, pointing to a divan heaped with richly embroidered tapestries and pillows.

Antony took off his cloak and indolently arranged his huge body on the divan. He gave himself up with a sigh to the luxury and comfort of the room. Golden streams of sunshine poured in through the windows. The incense, the music, the rich surroundings, all enveloped him like a web, ensnaring him.

I sat near him as servants brought forth delicacies and cool wines.

"The corpse of Arsinoë is on my flagship," Antony said softly.

A sad sigh issued from my lips. "My sister has returned to Egypt, not as Queen but as a corpse, not for her coronation but for her burial. In the tradition of the Princess Antigone, I will not offend the gods by neglecting to bury my sibling. She shall have honorable rites in the Sema with our ancestors."

Antony hardly spoke, but ate heartily and drank great quantities of wine from a gem-encrusted goblet as he appraised covetously the statuary and furnishings and Oriental hangings on the walls.

"Tell me of the political scene in Asia Minor, Lord Antony," I asked.

"I want to put all thoughts of Asia Minor, Rome, Fulvia, Octavian, and Parthia out of my mind," Antony cried. "There is only one thing I want to concentrate on and that, O Queen, is you."

His glowing eyes held mine, and I acknowledged their message with a solemn smile.

Antony soon became drowsy with wine, food, and the

rich, intoxicating incense that wafted about the chamber.

"My Lord Antony," I said at length, "you should rest in your apartments for the banquet to celebrate your arrival tonight."

"Cleopatra, I hate to part from you so soon," he said, at the door of my chamber.

"Until tonight, dear Antony," I said firmly, yet with promise in my eyes and voice.

At the eighth hour of the evening, I met Antony in the corridor outside the banqueting hall. Holding hands, we entered the huge vaulted chamber. We looked indeed like a god and a goddess. He wore a blue tunic covered with silver stars, and I wore a dress of gold silk. Gold dust was sprinkled in my loose flowing hair. As we made our entrance, the music of harps and flutes increased their tempo and all the guests stood. We passed through the long hall, walking on the floor covered inches deep with rose petals, and all the guests knelt as we passed them. We sat side by side on the dais facing the assemblage.

So that Antony might know that Alexandria was the capital where the greatest luxury reigned, and that I, Cleopatra, eclipsed all other monarchs in my splendor, I gave the greatest banquet of my life that night. The hall was decorated with garlands, lighted by flaming torches supported by brass arms and silver tripods sprouting forth giant flames. The libations were performed, and Lord Mardian made a speech welcoming Antony. Then the courses were served, an assortment of flesh and fowl, sea fish and river fish, spiced meats, and the rarest of wines.

"The perfume from the roses on the floor is so strong the food is flavored with it," Antony cried happily.

After an hour of eating, I comanded Diodorus to begin the dancing. To the lovely music of harps, flutes, and lyres, twenty-four beautiful dancing girls performed the *Dances of the Hours*. The first girl was a Nubian with skin the color of blackest night, and her dance was haunting and mysterious with the eeriness of the first hour. Each successive girl grew lighter in pigmentation, one rosy as dawn, the next bright as day, and then successively they took on darker hues of twilight. After each girl executed her dance, she would run up and kneel to kiss my feet, whose gold-lacquered nails were exposed prettily in my sandals. The twenty-four dances took more than two hours to complete, then all the girls, with Diodorus, their master, lined up, hand in hand, to receive wild applause from the appreciative guests.

"Ah, Cleopatra, your father would have been proud of his daughter for this night's magnificent banquet," Antony declared.

"He would have enjoyed it more than anyone," I said wistfully. "I remember sitting on this dais beside him for the banquet that celebrated his restoration. You were my father's pride, a young officer who had bravely helped him win back his throne." I smiled solemnly. "I was fourteen and impressionable, and I thought surely Prince Paris of Troy had not been as handsome as Mark Antony."

Antony gave me a stirring look. "I had the love of a thousand girls in Alexandria during those days, but it was you, the ranking princess of the land, whom I wanted above all others."

"I told my father my first love would always be Egypt."

"You were hopelessly beyond my reach in those days," Antony said painfully. "After that, there were all those years when you belonged to Caesar. Oh, how I envied Caesar, not for his glory and conquests, but for his conquest of you!"

I reached over and laid a warm hand on his. "My dear Antony, the tale of Caesar and Cleopatra ended," I cried with emotion, "but the tale of Antony and Cleopatra is just beginning."

For a long moment Antony and I only stared at one another, and then the tension between us intensified.

"Oh, I am so warm, Antony," I said at last. "Let us walk in my paradise garden."

"Yes, Cleopatra," Antony agreed eagerly.

Antony and I rose, and taking his hand, I led him out through a door. With Apollodorus and a few guards not far behind, we descended a flight of marble steps into the gardens.

The gardens were bathed by the light of a full moon and fanned by sea breezes. We traversed terrace after terrace, connected by marble steps and dotted with fountains. The crickets and fountains made lovely music, and the scent of many flowers filled the air.

I stopped and picked a rose, inhaling the scent, and smilingly handed it to Antony.

He cast the rose to the ground and gathered me into his arms. "The perfume of your body," he cried huskily, "enchants me far more than the fragrance of a rose!"

Fiercely he kissed me, his tongue like fire, and I began trembling.

"Shall I take you here in this Babylonian garden?" Antony demanded, a wild, glazed look in his eyes.

"No!" I protested. "Come!"

Taking his hand, I led him through the gardens to a small staircase which led to the balcony off my bedchamber. In a few breathless moments we were inside the bedchamber itself.

A small taper burned, which showed statues of Venus and Aphrodite in places where once marble Caesars had stood.

My sandals pattering on the marble floor, I led Antony to my large bed.

"Is this the bed where you lay with Caesar?" Antony demanded.

I faced him boldly. "Yes!"

Antony reflected a moment, and accepted the challenge. "I will show you that I am a hundred times the lover Caesar was!" he cried, pulling me against him in an all-engulfing embrace.

On fire with passion and impatience, Antony tore the clothes from my body and ripped his own tunic away, and he threw me back across the bed. I swooned under his savage ministrations as he thrust his manhood inside me, and I thought at first I would die from the agony of it, but then the pain gradually dissolved into infinite pleasure. I had the sensation of a shaft of fire penetrating

554

the core of my womb, to the center of my being. In white heat, I lay beneath his gigantic body, my senses swimming, tossing in a blind sweet torment, under the pulsing and purposeful thrust of him, moving in a tidal rhythm of ecstasy.

I felt a burgeoning of urgent passion such as I had never known. I accepted Antony's ravishment joyously, as he penetrated me, becoming an inseparable part of my being, of my flesh. I heard harsh little cries that I knew were my own, and deep-throated animal wails from Antony, as he mastered me with his passion and manhood.

A quaking tremor began deep within the universe of my being, a cascade of spasmodic tingles, an intensification of feelings, and I felt a vast explosion wheeling close. Antony, astride me, continued his inexorable thrusting, his motions frantic as he reached for the pinnacle of pleasure.

Fiery meteors rained and the solar system shook, as Antony took me with him to a universe of swirling colors. In an explosion of unbearable gratification, in a giant convulsion, my body melted with pleasure and warm waves of bliss washed over me.

After a moment of infinity, I broke through to reality, panting for air. The waves of pleasure gradually receded, leaving soft flutterings of feelings lapping gently at the boundaries of my senses.

Antony and I lay there, wet and panting, as if we had fought a great duel. We were silent with languorous stupor and fatigue, our bodies a tangle of arms and legs.

"Cleopatra!" Antony cried at last, saying my name in a voice of bewildered amazement. "My love."

My hands idly stroked the thick hair curling about his magnificent head. "Yes, Antony, my Roman lover!" I cried.

"Will you have me killed in the morning, O Queen?" he asked seriously.

I gave out with a delighted laugh. "Why should I?"

"In Rome they say you have a different lover every

night," Antony explained. "They say that you are like the praying mantis who, as soon as she has been satisfied, devours the male, making him pay with his life for his pleasure."

"Well, they are right!" I cried flippantly. "I will let you live a little longer, since I enjoyed you so much and want to repeat the experience a few more times."

"I thank you, O Queen," Antony said. He propped himself up with one arm, and with his other sword-calloused hand he caressed my body, the callouses making me shiver with their own special titillation. "Oh, Cleopatra," he said in a voice filled with wonder, "you are a woman unparalled in the shapeliness of your lovely breasts, the slenderness of your waist, the symmetrical contours of your hips, the roundness of your thighs, the delicate line of your legs, your slim ankles, your lovely hands, and your perfectly shaped feet!" He hissed a deep sigh. "You are indeed the most perfect woman I have ever known."

"Your words are sweet to my ears, Antony," I said with a soft, enchanted laugh, "but do you make the same speech to all your conquests?"

"There is no other woman like you," Antony vowed solemnly. "Oh, my Egyptian Sphinx, you are the elixir of enchantment." He held me close. "To have conquered you is better than having conquered a kingdom."

"Oh, my Herculean Roman, you have conquered a kingdom, for I am Egypt!"

"Yes, so you are," Antony said, his voice marvelling at the thought. "And in my arms I hold Royal Egypt who is Isis-on-Earth."

My arms encircled his massive neck. "And in my arms I hold the master of the world!" I cried ecstatically.

An indescribable feeling of happiness possessed me. Before dawn, Antony and I made sacrifice two or three more times to Aphrodite, rapturously rejoicing in each other's bodies. Antony proved to me that his reputation as a great lover was honorably won.

As the morning rays of the sun began slanting into the bedchamber, Antony, exhausted after his amorous

556

labors, fell asleep in my arms, but I was too excited to sleep.

A flood of hope swelled my heart, as I lay there, my body bruised and spent from lovemaking. I closed my eyes and drifted in a reverie of dreams. For the second time I had won the greatest Roman soldier of the day to my heart, and once again I had powerful protection and love. My name had been coupled with Caesar's, and now it would be linked with Antony's. All now lay within my grasp, and the future, full of glorious, beautiful vistas, spread out before me.

CHAPTER IV

THAT GLORIOUS WINTER when Antony and I became lovers was a time of magical enchantment for me. After years of loneliness and insecurity, I was eager for happiness, and I yielded to the passionate love of this powerful protector. In the first heady flush of our love, I was joyously happy and savored to the point of intoxication the delights of ecstasy. Antony gave himself up wholly to the seductive pleasures of my love and hospitality. Everything seemed to unite to bring about perfect felicity, and the world smiled upon us.

Antony decided to stay in Alexandria until the spring, conducting himself as a noble courtier. I was inordinately pleased at this, although some of my friends were not. Iras pouted in jealousy, and my faithful Apollodorus had many misgivings, which he expressed one morning as we strolled in the palace gardens. I had spent a delirious night of lovemaking, and I was in a blissful state as I sauntered along.

"May I speak frankly, Cleopatra?" Apollodorus asked, his face grave.

I touched Apollodorus on the arm. "You are my oldest and dearest friend, Apollodorus, of course you may speak freely."

"I have been thinking of Antony," he said hesitantly.

"Yes," I said, encouraging him to continue.

"Antony is debauched, addicted to all the vices, changeable and inconsistent!" he said harshly.

"Yes, but he has enormous abilities, character, and a deep intelligence," I said. "He is the greatest general in the world, worshipped by his soldiers and the people."

"He is vain and boisterous and is incapable of controlling his intemperate blood," Apollodorus resumed. "His unbounded pride could lead him to commit disastrous follies."

"The world tolerates the vices of the great, Apollodorus," I said calmly. "Such exalted personages as Antony are judged differently from ordinary folk."

"Yes, but you are not ordinary folk, you are a great goddess-Queen and you must judge Antony with uncompromising objectivity."

"In other words, my friend, you are telling me that love must not blind me to the vices and follies of Antony."

Apollodorus nodded soberly. "To fall in love with Antony would be fatal, my Queen."

"I am not in love with Antony, Apollodorus," I cried, but as I spoke the words I knew my voice lacked the ring of conviction. "My first love is Egypt, always has been, and always will be. I am a woman and a lover, but I am foremost a sovereign. I need this alliance with Antony to keep Egypt independent, which is my creed and my oath. I must bind myself to Antony, as I did to Caesar, to fulfill my destiny."

"Caesar was a great disappointment to you."

"Antony will not be," I said confidently. "I am mistress of myself. I give Antony my body, but not my soul. I am ruled by my head and not my heart. I am in thrall to the most irresistible of all passions, the passion for power. My womanhood is my weapon. I have no choice, considering the scheme of the world. Antony loves me, I am his Egeria, and through his love I can effect my salvation. An alliance with Antony, the foremost Roman, will stem the tide of Roman enslavement which has threatened Egypt for a century."

Apollodorus gave a long sigh. "I pray that your second Roman will not fail you as did your first, O Queen."

I knew that Apollodorus was jealous of Antony, and much of what he said was motivated by this jealousy. His concern for me, however, was genuine, and I knew that he was concerned with my best interests.

Charmion, on the other hand, ever ambitious for me, approved of my relationship with Antony. He always flirted with her, and she was gratified by the attentions of the greatest lover in the world, and her feelings for Antony were warm. She saw that, through Antony, I could be mistress of the world, instead of just a small kingdom. I was perfectly aware that Charmion had always loved me for my place and power, whereas Iras loved me for my person. I never considered, however, the love of one more important than the love of the other.

Winter deepened, a galaxy of golden days and tender nights, as Antony enjoyed my palace of delights and our love grew.

"I love your beautiful city, Cleopatra," Antony exclaimed. "It is a city of unparalleled grace and gaiety, a splendid setting for the enjoyment of life and a great love."

"That pleases me, Antony," I cried. "Rome has always been jealous of Alexandria, and many Romans wish to destroy my city as they did Carthage and Corinth. As long as you remain the greatest Roman I feel secure that Alexandria will be safe."

I had totally aroused Antony's physical passion for me, but I did not wish to captivate him merely with my caresses. I wanted him to appreciate the refinements of Hellenic civilization. He already had strong Philhellenic tendencies, but I wanted to make him wholly Greek, in order that he might more easily break the bonds that bound him to Rome. I lavished every luxury upon him and spoiled him with all the tendernesses of my devotion. We were never apart, day or night. He wore Greek dress at all times, which Caesar never did. We visited the theater, attended lectures at the museum, and philosophers and orators came to the palace for informal debates.

My beloved Alexandria is not only famous for the greatest university in the world, but also as the center of depravity. The enormous fortunes made in Alexandria have produced unlimited luxury, and with it unlimited debauchery. My people are devoted to sensuality, herbs and drugs, and refined pleasures, all of which perfectly suited Antony's hedonism. Although he was interested in the intellectual influence of the daughter of the Lagidae, being a man of culture himself, he also had an earthy nature that was not to be ignored.

We formed the Society of Inimitable Livers, a club composed of the cream of Alexandrian society and notables from the artistic and scientific worlds. Feasts and revels followed one another night after night, and I entertained with an extravagance beyond measure. I gave banquets where nobles, professors, actors, and dancers all mingled, dedicating themselves to pleasure under my royal auspices.

Antony became immensely popular with my people from all walks of life, and my popularity flowered to a degree I had not enjoyed since my earliest childhood. Blessed with magnetism, Antony possesses all the gifts to make life a thing of joy for himself and all those about him. His gaiety is infectious, and his conviviality and spirits lend themselves perfectly to mixing with my capricious and brilliant Alexandrians.

Perceiving that his raillery was bawdy, more that of a soldier than that of a courtier, I rejoined in the same vein, falling easily into his ribald manner without reserve. I decided to beat Antony at the game of pleasure and gave myself up to being a pleasure-loving Greek pursuing the noble art of life, doing anything to satisfy Antony's whims and my own. I became as free as a harlot, but as Antony said, "Coarseness, ruthlessness, even cruelty, my love, all become beautiful through your indescribable charms!"

If Antony was serious I responded in the like manner, and if he were disposed to mirth, I had some new delight to meet his wishes. I played at dice with him on the floor, drank with him, and we took pleasure cruises on Lake Mareotis and the Nile. Antony, being a soldier, never neglected his exercises. Every morning he had a swordplay session with a selected soldier in a palace courtyard, and in the afternoon he would ride his favorite Arabian charger the four-mile length of the Canopic Way, from one end of the city to the other, which took him less than an hour.

Antony and I would go out on nocturnal escapades, scampering about the streets of Alexandria, he disguised as a burly servant and I a serving lady. One night in a city square I danced a dance taught to me by Diodorus when I was a child, and coins bearing my image were thrown to me by drunken sailors. During these excursions Apollodorus and a handful of soldiers never were far behind, just in case mischief should befall us. Antony, deep in his cups, liked to pound on the doors of houses, disturbing the sleepers, and he was often rudely answered.

The people knew who we were, and they loved us for our cavortings. Such behavior established sympathy between me and my subjects. Before, I had always been remote, but now I became more human, touchable, vulnerable, and I became beloved in the hearts of my people.

The Alexandrians adopted Antony. Caesar, with his imperial and domineering manner, had kept them at a distance, but Antony, with his friendly temperament, mixed with the people, watching the street shows, shopping at the market stalls and buying trinkets, going into taverns and buying wine for everyone.

"You are more Alexandrian than my Alexandrians, more Greek than the Greeks," I told Antony.

"That is the greatest compliment, my love," he cried.

Day followed day, and night after ecstatic night, in which nothing was too high or too low to add to our amusement. We were truly inimitable in our pursuit of gaiety and life.

At this time there was a certain vagabond prince at my court, Prince Alexas, the son of King Alexander of Laodicea who had been deposed years before by Pompey. Alexas had won my friendship and favor with his good looks and charming ways. For a time Apollodorus and he had been lovers. During this winter Antony took a keen liking to him, since they shared many of the same interests and both had an avid appetite for life.

563

Winter came with its fogs and sea storms. Ships were moored in the harbors, bobbing up and down in the choppy waves, and navigation was suspended, with no ships bringing in any news from Rome or Asia. We were cut off from the world. Antony and I were completely possessed and caught up with one another, bathed in bliss and enjoyed our time of happiness.

For my twenty-ninth birthday, the gods gave me a truly magnificent gift, for my physician Olympus confirmed that I was with child. This meant that I had conceived on one of the first nights I had spent with Antony, just as I had with Caesar. I was overjoyed, for I hoped that through a child I could better bind Antony's love to my heart, as I had held Caesar's.

I broke the tidings to Antony as he came into my chambers, flushed and sweaty from his afternoon equestrian exercise.

A look of supreme joy spread across his face. "Cleopatra!" he cried, embracing me and lifting me into the air. He then gently put me down and took my face tenderly between his hands. "Oh, my love, I have dropped my seed in many places, but this will be the most honored and hallowed spot!"

"I will give you many children, Antony!"

"The world will be ours," Antony cried, "and Caesarion and our children will sit on the most exalted thrones."

To celebrate my birthday, Antony gave a lavish banquet for me which cost an exorbitant sum. There were oysters from the Red Sea, nightingales from India, and several other expensive, exotic courses served. Antony presented me with a great gold ring set with a sparkling, enormous sapphire.

"I shall treasure this ring always, Antony," I cried, bestowing a kiss on his mouth to the titillation of all the guests.

"In eight months I want a gift from you," Antony cried. "A beautiful child!"

A dispute arose between us as to how much could be

spent upon a single banquet. Antony wagered I could not spend more than he had just laid out.

"Tomorrow night I shall give a banquet that will cost ten million sesterces," I declared.

"I'll wager you cannot," Antony said arrogantly.

"If I win the wager, I want Phoenicia," I cried, recalling that this land had once belonged to the Ptolemies, with its rich towns of Tyre and Sidon.

"The wager is accepted," Antony said, "but if you lose, I want Cyprus for Rome."

The next evening the same guests came and filled the hall, all excited about the wager. As the banquet unfolded with the same gorgeous display of flowers, gold plate, rare foods and wines, it seemed to everyone that there was nothing to justify the great sum that I had announced.

"There is no way this feast could cost ten million sesterces," Antony cried. "You have lost Cyprus, Cleopatra."

I wore a serene expression and nodded at Agathocles, the Royal Cupbearer, who brought me a golden cup, a marvel of workmanship which had once belonged to Pericles. The cup was filled with vinegar.

Antony peered curiously into the cup. "A magical charm?"

Every eye was upon me. I wore many jewels that evening, but the most valuable were the pearl earrings that hung from my ears by an almost invisible string of gold. I calmly removed one earring. "This pearl, Antony, was sent by Alexander from Persopolis to his mother Queen Olympias."

"The value must be inestimable," Antony said, awed.

I tore the pearl free from the gold string, and dropped it into the cup. I watched calmly, while Antony gaped aghast, and excited murmurs filled the hall as the pearl dissolved in the vinegar.

"A drink fit for a queen!" I cried, lifting the golden cup to my mouth. "I drink to your health and happiness, Antony!"

Cries of consternation sounded in the hall as I drank

the mixture, grimacing at the acid taste of the vinegar. I then nonchalantly proceeded to remove my remaining earring.

"Queen Cleopatra, you have won the wager!" Antony cried. "Spare the other pearl. I acknowledge defeat. Phoenicia is yours."

Since then this night has become legendary as the Banquet of the Pearl. Many say that my gesture was foolish, but it is not in my nature to do anything that is frivolous. In sacrificing the precious pearl I had demonstrated to Antony that my wealth was measureless.

All my reassurances to Apollodorus notwithstanding, as the winter weeks went by, I had to admit to myself that I was in love with this handsome beast of a Roman, whose child I carried within me. I had willed myself to be cool and removed, but at long last, with a pain in my heart, I recognized the supreme surrender of my soul. Against all my prudent judgment, I fell violently in love, and I enjoyed an emotional fulfillment such as I had never known. My seduction of Antony had been a snare, but I found myself caught in my own trap. I had gone to Tarsus out of political reasons, to gratify my ambitions, but I ended up enmeshed and entangled. In Antony's arms, I experienced feelings of unparalleled rapture, such as Caesar, Charmion, and Iras never had evoked. Caesar had been a gentle lover, but Antony was a lover of incredible endurance, and he took me to heights of peerless ecstasy. There were times when he made my heart pound with such passion I was frantic that it would burst. My love was like a fever tormenting me. At night I abandoned myself to love, but during the day, with a great effort, I regained possession of myself and tended to my royal obligations.

I love rarely, but when I do, it is greatly. When I set my passionate Ptolemy heart, it is forever.

Antony, for his part, admitted quite frankly from the very beginning that he was deeply in love with me.

"I feel a tyrannical love and a consuming passion for you such as I have never known before, Cleopatra," he cried unabashedly. "I've been a slave to my senses often, but never to love. You enchant and terrify me at the same time. I want you to be my slave, as I am yours."

"I am your slave, Antony!" I avowed. "I ran after you to Tarsus, with the world watching, recording it for history. I know no shame where you are concerned. Rome and history will call me a whore, but I don't care. Need you doubt the sincerity of my love?"

The age of forty-two is a crucial time for a man, and after having lived a life of sexual excess, Antony was ripe for a great love. That winter he surrendered to this experience with me without reservation or restraint. I was also prime for an overpowering passion, and my body was ready for these new sensations which Antony provided for me.

I was enthralled by his magnificent body, which neither the privations that he had endured, nor the excesses to which he had given himself up since youth, had in any way impaired. His manly beauty and prodigious strength truly confirmed his descent from Hercules. The gods had endowed him with remarkable physical gifts, and his capabilities in the art of love astonished and delighted me.

"Sensuality does not last forever, Cleopatra," Antony announced expansively. "I am very Greek in my appreciation of the whole gamut of human enjoyments. To enjoy life is my creed, like the followers of Epicurus, whose aim was to enjoy every passing hour."

I was not the only one struck by Antony's good looks, for several Alexandrian artists under my patronage used his handsome head and body as models for busts and statues that winter.

To justify his lengthy stay in Egypt, Antony busied himself with the task of revising the Treaty of Alliance between Egypt and Rome, and the clauses were written according to my desires. Antony gave me two Roman legions to help me maintain order, and these legions, stationed in Asia Minor, marched to Alexandria. I rode beside Antony as we reviewed these soldiers. At this display of military might, everyone saw that once again

I had the support of Roman forces to shield me against insurrection.

Spring came, and as I entered my fourth month of pregnancy, a restlessness possessed Antony and he started straying from my arms. Although he could have had his every whim and wish satiated within the walls of the palace, he made outside excursions. In the company of his degenerate friends, Dellius, Philotas and Prince Alexas, he would ride to Rhakotis outside Alexandria and there visit the taverns and houses of sin.

In Rome, I am told, it is said that I accompanied Antony on these outings, dressed as a common trollop, but since I was growing heavy with child, this is preposterous vilification.

Antony liked to visit the Garden of Ceramincus, where hundreds of courtesans traffic their favors. He also enjoyed running up to the Park of Pan, the public gardens on the hill above Alexandria, where he would engage in provisional pleasures. At night whores of both sexes stroll these lovely grounds and people meet in the moonlight for carnel coupling behind bushes and under trees.

One of Antony's daytime pleasures was fishing. He liked to go behind the palace and sit on the marble embankment bordering Lake Mareotis. I recall one morning in late March when Antony caught nothing and was extremely vexed, especially since I was watching from a nearby bench. I was sitting there reading while Caesarion played at my feet.

Glancing up from my scroll, I saw Antony go over and put his arm around a young Egyptian boy who was the son of one of the palace cooks. They huddled in conspiratorial conversation, and then Antony returned to his fishing rod. I soon perceived the boy slipping into the water some distance down the lake.

From then on Antony kept pulling up fish with rapid regularity, making great cries of joy as he did so.

"How wonderful, Antony!" I cried.

Antony stopped fishing to take a noonday repast with me. Carpets were spread on the garden grounds, and servants served us a picnic. While we were eating, I had

Apollodorus go to the Egyptian boy and give him a command from me.

"Back to fishing!" Antony cried when he had eaten.

"And I back to Zeno!" I cried, settling onto a bench and unrolling the scroll.

Antony threw his line into the lake, humming happily, and shortly, feeling his line give, he drew up his prey. "Another catch!" he cried proudly, examining the catch, but then his nose screwed up, for the fish was a dead, rotten salt fish.

A look of consternation crossed Antony's face, and laughter ensued from all the attendants around us.

Antony took it all good-naturedly, shrugging, but turned and gave me an accusing look.

I leaned forward, throwing my arms out. "Antony, greatest of all generals, leave the fishing rod to us petty rulers, for your sport is the catching of cities, provinces, kingdoms, and the mastership of the world!"

Antony threw down his rod. "So it is, my Queen."

As the winter passed in play and diversion, I recognized that there were two elements fighting for mastery in Antony's ardent yet weak spirit, ambition and sensuality. Ambition had inspired his valorous deeds and conquests. A spark of Caesar glowed in his relative Antony, and I hoped to ignite that spark into a great flame.

As spring approached, ships began sailing into the harbors, bringing dire news, which awakened Antony from his apathy of indolence. Storm clouds were brewing everywhere. King Orodes of Parthia, anticipating that his country would be invaded by the Romans, sent his armies into Asia Minor and subjugated Syria. The Parthians then advanced into Judaea and captured Jerusalem.

"You will compromise your future irretrievably if you linger in Alexandria, Antony," I told him fervently.

"Now that your belly is flowering from my seed, you would cast me off?" Antony asked with a small smile.

"Need you doubt my great love? Part of me will die when you go, but to stay here would be conceding the world to Octavian."

"Yes, I hate to go but I must," Antony agreed. "I can see why Julius lingered here all those months, caught by the spell of you and Egypt. I am squandering what the orator Antiphon called that most precious of gifts, time. I must shake off the fumes of wine and leave the comfort of yours arms, and remember that I am not only the lover of the Queen of Egypt, but the Triumvir of Rome and the Autocrat of Asia with obligations to fulfill."

Roman ships brought letters from Fulvia, describing a disturbance which had broken out because of her machinations. Four years before, Octavian had agreed to marry Cloudia, Fulvia's daughter by Clodius, when the Triumvirate had been established, but now Octavian repudiated Cloudia without consummating the marriage and sent her back to her mother. Fulvia, with her restless spirit and in league with Antony's brother Lucius, was collecting an army to make an attack on Octavian. I suspected that Fulvia was motivated by a mixture of ambition and jealousy, and was forcing an issue which would tear Antony from my arms and back to Italy and her.

At the same time, Octavian was menaced by Sextus Pompey, who controlled the seas as a roving pirate, making raids along the southern coast of Italy.

I prayed to the gods that Fulvia and Sextus between them would crush Octavian.

Although events were demanding Antony's attention in both east and west, Antony decided that the east was more important.

"Fulvia wants me to come to Italy to avenge the affront of Octavian to her daughter," Antony said with annoyance. "I don't like my hand being forced in this manner. I will fight Octavian when I am strong enough, when I have conquered Parthia, and not before."

"Follow in Alexander's path and plant your eagles in the east," I urged him. "Conquer Parthia and become emperor of the east, and then with me at your side, and with the wealth of my kingdom at your disposal, you will be able to eliminate Octavian in the struggle for world supremacy. Either Octavian or you will rule the world, for it cannot be both of you."

"I am aware of that, my love," Antony said bleakly.

"Oh, Antony, why didn't you kill Octavian at Bologna, instead of reconciling with him and forming the Triumvirate?"

"At the time, I had no choice. The next time I confront him, however, I will not hesitate to strike a mortal blow."

"Ammonios writes me that Octavian is filling Italy with terror, torturing and crucifying thousands," I said. "They call him The Executioner, and he scandalizes Rome with his debauches. As the gods know, what you do, you do openly, but the hypocrite Octavian conducts his vices behind closed doors. He cannot perform sexual concourse unless it is with a virgin, and he demands the virgin daughters of all the senators." I trembled as a wave of embittered anger swept through me. "Oh, I cringe to think that he calls himself Caesar."

"It doesn't matter, my sweet dove, for no one will ever confuse him with the other one," Antony remarked.

"My son is Caesar!" I cried with deep emotion.

My hatred for Octavian, who had stolen my son's name and inheritance, obsessed me. I counted on Antony to destroy Octavian, and the first step toward that goal was for Antony to go to Asia Minor and bring the eastern provinces under firm control.

"The coming separation fills me with anxiety, my darling Antony," I said sadly. "It will mean loneliness for me, but I am resigned. You will become master of Persia, and then no human power can prevent our carrying out a grand design of a new world, uniting east and west, a world ruled by us. Oh, Antony, you will be greater than Alexander or Caesar!"

"Plato said there are four sets of flattery, but you have a thousand," Antony said with a merry chuckle. "Most women stale after a night, but you possess unparalleled variety. I believe in your faith in me, and I will place the imperial crown of the world on your head."

At the beginning of the spring equinox, after a stay of

five months, Antony left Alexandria. Although the day was bright with sunshine, I was overcome with sadness as I accompanied Antony down to the dockside. All the marble steps and squares on the seafront were crowded with my people and my whole court was present to bid Antony a grand farewell.

As Antony and I stood before the gangplank of his flagship, he unsheathed his sword.

"The Philippian sword that brought me great victory, Cleopatra," Antony cried. "A gift for the child you carry within you."

I took the sword, tears flooding my eyes, and handed it to Apollodorus. I gave him in return a new sword, bright, sharp and shiny, fashioned in Alexandria, gold-plated and bearing both our crests on either side of the handle.

"With this Alexandrian sword," Antony cried, "I will carve out a great empire for our children. Julius was with you when Caesarion was born, and it saddens me that I will not be here when you birth my child. It may be a year before we meet again."

"A year!" I exclaimed tearfully. "Oh, Antony, how will I live without you for so long?"

Antony took me into his arms. "I will miss your embracing arms, warm lips, and the enchantments of your flesh."

"Oh, Antony, I will always love you!" I cried, clinging to him. "I don't ask that you be faithful to me—"

"My thoughts will always be of you, my Egyptian Sphinx, no matter what body my restless nature obliges me to go with," Antony avowed.

"I ask only that you come back to me," I cried.

"We part with the promise that our separation will be no more than a year's duration," Antony said.

Before thousands of my people, I covered Antony's face with kisses, in a wild display of love and grief at his departure. My hot-blooded people, who understand emotion, cheered and cried with me.

"Antony, may the gods bring you back to me!" I declared.

"Never fear, I will come back, my goddess," Antony cried. "I will never be able to escape from your spell."

I lifted my face as Antony bruised my lips with one last kiss.

"Farewell, my little Greek girl!" Antony cried, turning away from me.

"Antony!" I whispered painfully, anguish gripping my heart as I watched him march across the gangplank to board his flagship.

With a sense of overwhelming sadness, I stood on the dockside and watched the fleet sail out of the harbor past Pharos. Antony stood on the deck, staring shoreward, waving his new sword in the air.

All around me, the Alexandrians screamed out their farewells to their favorite Roman. I shivered with emotion, and my ears rang with the resounding roars from thousands of throats.

"Come, O Sacred Radiance," Olympus said in a stern, commanding voice. "With your delicate condition, I humbly beseech that you return to the comfort of your palace."

I sank wearily into my carrying chair, and two Nubian slaves swiftly conducted me up the marble steps to my private apartments in the palace. I lay abed, sobbing heartbrokenly, and then in the afternoon I went to the Temple of Isis and gave sacrifice and said prayers to Isis, asking that she intervene with her fellow deities to see that Antony would return safely to me.

CHAPTER V

ONLY EROS COULD KNOW of the misery I suffered after Antony left me that spring. I was subject to severe melancholia. I could not sleep at nights, and finally, although I generally avoid all drugs, I allowed Olympus to give me a sleeping draught, distilled from the poppy, before bedtime. Growing heavy with childbearing, I was overcome with fretful anxiety, and in my innermost being, discontentment reigned. Antony filled my thoughts with such preoccupation that Caesarion, affairs of state, everything, held little importance for me.

In late May, Antony landed at Tyre and learned to his chagrin that all of Syria and Phoenicia had fallen into the hands of the Parthians. He realized that before he could deliver the eastern provinces he would need reinforcements, and so he resigned himself to abandoning the east for the time being. On receiving further pressing letters from Fulvia, he made his way with two hundred ships toward Athens.

The army that Fulvia and Lucius Antony had gotten together was besieged at Perugia, and was massacred by Octavian's army which was commanded by Marcus Agrippa. Octavian, of course, made it a point never to fight his own battles. Fulvia fled across Italy to Brandisium where she took ship and sailed toward Athens, where she hoped to meet Antony. In the Peloponnesus, a messenger from Octavian caught up with her, persuading her that Antony would not meet her in Athens after all, but had sailed back to Alexandria to join me. This was an outrageous deception. Fulvia, so full of manly ardor that she went about with a sword girded to her side, died, her heart broken. Some said she died from being ravaged by grief and jealousy, but I believe that she was poisoned by someone in the pay of Octavian. Only the gods know the truth.

"Lady Fulvia is dead!" Charmion cried gleefully. "If only Calpurnia could have died so conveniently years ago in Rome."

"We must offer Fulvia many prayers and sacrifices," I said solemnly. I was saddened by the death of a remarkable woman I had liked and admired, but I knew that her death would make my future with Antony easier.

Octavian had struck out at Antony, creating a rupture in the Triumvirate. I felt positive now that Antony and I would marry, and together we would face Octavian and defeat him. Antony could then persuade the Senate to ratify a marriage with a foreign Queen, and our children would be legitimatized in the laws of Rome. People had called Caesarion and me Caesar's bitch and her pup, and I did not want that to happen with Antony and our children.

It was one of the longest summers of my life. I was proud of my impending motherhood, but the pregnancy was not a smooth one. My breasts enlarged and the veins showed blue and were tender to the touch.

A gentle lethargy enveloped me as the summer ended, and when my confinement drew near, I took to my bed. As I lay there my imagination ran riot. I was lost in fantastic dreams. I had visions of sitting in judgment in Rome, humiliating all those who had murdered Caesar and had scorned me. I saw a multitude of Romans passing before me, prostrating themselves and begging forgiveness and hailing me as their empress.

On September the third, I gave birth to twins, Cleopatra Selene and Alexander Helios, the Sun and the Moon. The confinement was a long one, lasting two days. The effort was so difficult that it brought me to the door of death, but at the last moment, my soul stepped back. I had almost walked into the netherworld of eternal life, but I returned, like Persephone floating up from the underworld.

My recovery from the travail was slow. The pregnancy, the birth, and the long summer months of waiting for news from Antony had worn me down physically and spiritually.

At last in the second week of November, a Roman merchant ship from Brandisium sailed into the harbor at dawn. A messenger called Germanicus came to the palace. Trembling, I put on a robe and rushed to the small receiving chamber in my private apartments, and the young Roman was ushered into my presence.

"Divine Majesty," Germanicus cried, kneeling at my feet, "I bring tidings from Brandisium, where I sailed from two weeks ago."

"Yes, my young Roman friend?" I asked in an eager voice.

"The Triumvir Antony reached Brandisium but was denied entrance," Germanicus explained, "for Octavian had the gates of the port closed. Sextus Pompey came with his fleet to aid Antony, and civil war was about to break out, but the soldiers refused to fight and demanded that Antony and Octavian reconcile their differences."

My heart stopped with those startling words, *reconcile their differences*. "Yes?" I demanded, fear squeezing my heart.

"Lord Antony sent Pompey away and then went ashore and struck hands with Octavian," Germanicus cried. "A great pact was sealed."

An agonized groan issued from my throat and my eyes closed.

"The Treaty of Brandisium has renewed the Triumvirate for another five years, O Queen," Germanicus added.

I was staggered by these tidings, and I clutched the arms of my stately chair. A dizziness engulfed me, and I thought I would faint.

"They divided the empire between them, with the Ionian Sea as the boundary," Germanicus went on. "Octavian has taken the west and Lepidus the provinces of North Africa. Antony has the east and has been given two more Roman legions to command."

As my vertigo and pain subsided a little, I opened my eyes, trying to focus on the Roman messenger. My heart lightened a little to think that Antony was still lord of the east, and I realized that now since Fulvia was dead, Antony and I. . . .

I managed a small smile. "I thank you, Germanicus, for your tidings. You will be rewarded for your news."

Germanicus stood and was about to depart.

"Wait, there is more!" Apollodorus cried, standing beside me.

Germanicus hung his head. "No, that is all, Divine Majesty!"

I looked closely at Germanicus, seeing fear on his face. He was avoiding my eyes, staring down at the floor.

"You have not told Queen Cleopatra everything!" Apollodorus accused with stern authority.

"Yes, I have, my lord!" Germanicus protested wildly.

I perceived that the young Roman was holding something back. I peered at him, and he met my eyes with fright.

"Is there more, my friend?" I asked gently.

Germanicus reluctantly lifted his head, struggling to meet my eyes.

"The treaty was secured by a sacramental marriage of state," Germanicus said gaspingly, and then faltered.

"Yes?" Apollodorus prodded.

"On the Ides of October, a marriage between Octavian's sister, the Lady Octavia, and the Triumvir Antony was celebrated in Rome," Germanicus cried, and then he threw himself prostrate on the floor. "Forgive me, Divine Majesty, for bringing such tidings!"

I sat on my chair, transfixed with shock, as the first rush of agony engulfed me. I was immobile with stupefaction, my head spinning, and I tried to absorb the reality that the messenger's words imparted.

Germanicus was sobbing, fearing my wrath.

In a state of shock, I rose weakly to my feet. Apollodorus reached out and took my hand as I negotiated the few steps from my throne-like chair. As I passed Germanicus, I stopped beside his prostrate form. I slipped from my finger the great sapphire ring which Antony had given me, and I dropped it to the floor. As the ring fell with a thud, there was a chorus of gasps sounding from my attendants.

"A gift for you, my friend," I muttered.

Like a somnambulist, I walked from the audience chamber with Charmion, Iras, and Apollodorus following me closely. At the door of my bedchamber I stopped.

"Leave me!" I uttered intensely. "I want to be alone."

I went alone into the bedchamber and closed the door. I looked over at the bed where Antony and I had lain, and my skin turned cold. I gazed at the naked statue of Antony that stood in a corner. I took the Philippian sword from the wall and stood before Antony's statue, the sword heavy in my hands. I stared at the statue for a long time, and then, anger swept through me like a hurricane, I furiously hacked at the genitalia. After I had mutilated the manhood away, I struck at the nose, ears, and hair, sobbing hysterically all the while.

Apollodorus, Charmion, and Iras came rushing into the bedchamber. Apollodorus tore the sword from my hands. I struck out blindly and then fell to the marble floor in a transport of demented despair. I lay sobbing with grief as Iras and Charmion knelt at my sides, holding down my body as I thrashed about in the throes of torment.

At last I was picked up and placed in bed. Iras put cold wet cloths on my temples and the scent of aromatic spirits under my nose. Olympus came and forced a potion down my throat, and a blackness engulfed me. I slept, but nightmares came and went like ghosts, haunting me.

When I awoke, I found that Antony's mutilated statue had been removed from the bedchamber. I ordered that all the busts of Caesar, which had graced my bedchamber but which had been removed before Antony's arrival, were to be returned to their pedestals and niches.

This was truly one of the blackest times of my life. Not even the murder-day of Caesar had been so excruciatingly painful for me. Deserted and debased by the betrayal, I found myself in a condition of utter disillusionment. All my dreams were shattered, and it seemed all my grand designs were destined to failure. I was torn with jealousy and anguish, and my vanity and pride were mortally wounded.

The spring of hope that had carried me through so many tragedies had run dry. For days I lay prostrate, unable to eat, to sleep, longing for death. I bitterly chided myself for having gone to Tarsus, and for having given Antony my love and my trust.

"Octavian stipulated that Antony should marry his sister as a bond of fidelity and to prevent him from coming back to you," Apollodorus assessed. "They were anxious to put a chain around the lion's neck and to force Antony to cleanse himself of the guilt of Fulvia's rebellion."

"Yes, Apollodorus," I agreed with bitterness, "and so Antony had a chance to redeem himself for having dallied so long in Alexandria with his Egyptian whore!"

"Antony's hands were tied, Cleopatra," Charmion argued, endeavoring to find excuses for him. "He was without legions. He had no alternative but to make terms with Octavian, who has control of Italy and Gaul, while Antony's eastern territories have been tottering. This is merely a political marriage, and Antony did it only to gain time. He will come back to you, Cleopatra, at the propitious moment, I know he will."

"I will not have him, ever again!" I proclaimed passionately, despair twisting my heart. "Twice I have trusted a Roman, and twice I've been tricked and betrayed. The gods on Mount Olympus and the Romans along the Tiber must be laughing now at my absurd follies."

My heart was like a wound in my breast, and for days, overcome with remorse and unable to function, I could not leave my bedchamber.

"My precious queen, you must pull yourself together," Iras begged tearfully. "For the sake of Egypt, and for your children!"

It was my children who finally pulled me up from the dark depths of despair.

"Mother, I will be a man soon," Caesarion cried, all of seven years old, "and I will lead armies and you will not need Antony."

For several days I had refused to see my newborn twins, hating their father and cursing the day I had lain with him, but at last Iras prevailed upon me to see them. The two-month-old infants were brought to me. My heart melted as they were laid in the bed beside me.

The twins were beautiful babes. Antony had given them to me. I was filled with an overwhelming rush of love for the twins, realizing that all the humiliation I had suffered from their father had been worth it, for I now had a precious prince and princess.

Despite my disillusionment, I resolved to meet the situation with the grace befitting my sacred and regal rank. I went through all my jewels and selected a gold necklace studded with precious gems. I sent the necklace off as a gift for Octavia, and with it went a letter, composed in my own hand. This letter, devoid of all recrimination and rancor, wished the marriage all happiness and reaffirmed the goodwill of Egypt with Rome. It was a letter of state, and the twins I had just given birth to were not mentioned.

Mortified by these blows of fate, I was ravaged by jealousy and obsessed with thoughts of Octavia. I had met her a few times in Rome, but she had been so lackluster that I had barely noticed her. She was the half-sister of Octavian, seven years older than he, and two years older than I. At fifteen she had married Caius Cloudius Marcellus and had given him three children. Octavia had been a widow for six months when she married Antony. She did not possess one drop of noble blood, for while Octavian did have patrician blood through his mother Atia being Caesar's niece, Octavia's mother, Ancharia, was as plebeian as their father.

"To think that Antony has married a woman who is not worthy to tie the laces of your sandals, my Divine

581

Queen," Iras said scornfully. "Thanks be to Isis that you are rid of that monster."

"Octavia at thirty-two and after three children has lost the freshness of youth, O Beauteous Queen," Ammonios wrote me from Rome in one of his gossipy letters. "She has good features but no sparkle in her face. Endowed with a plebeian nature, she enjoys spinning and makes her own clothes, as well as her brother's, which are ill-fitting. She is as pale and as cold as her brother, but she is virtuous in life as her brother is in pretense. We all know what that little hypocrite, for all his mouthing of high morality, does behind closed doors. Octavia is not a passionate lady, nor does she inspire passion. To be frank, O Queen, Antony needs a strong woman to compensate for his weaknesses. Devoted to his mother the Lady Julia, he has always liked stalwart females. One needs only to recall the actress Cytheris, the Princess Glaphyra, the late redoubtable Fulvia, and you, my goddess, all of whom are more suited to his temperament. Octavia is not Antony's type, and I wager my fortune that the Triumvir will soon be bored with her."

In the deep recesses of my royal soul, there glowed an ember of hope which this letter had rekindled, that in time Octavia would be discarded and Antony would return to me. Gradually, the lacerated wound Antony had dealt my heart ceased throbbing and healed. The marriage, which had been devised to hold Antony and Octavian in "perpetual amity," would one day fall apart. My twins, my grain, my ships and gold, would bring Antony back to me. I was still in love with Antony and with the dreams that I could accomplish only with him, and it was not my nature to relinquish my hopes so easily.

I knew precisely how Sisyphus, King of Corinth, felt when he was condemned to Hades and made to roll a heavy stone up a steep hill. Every time he got to the top, the stone rolled down to the bottom, and he had to start all over.

Once again I was at the bottom of the hill.

In the meantime, there was nothing to do but continue my life as Queen and mother to my children and subjects. I governed my kingdom, and although my days were full, my nights were filled with loneliness. After those passionate five months of ecstasy with Antony, I withdrew into a life of celibacy. There were no revels in the palace, the Society of Inimitable Livers was disbanded, and only an occasional decorous banquet was held. The time for frivolity had ended.

I watched with dark despair the complicated events ensuing in the Roman world in the following months. Letters from Ammonios and other friends in Rome, who all discreetly gathered information for me, described the progress of affairs, all of which disconcerted me.

Antony was unable to settle affairs to his own advantage with his ally. Octavian was on bad terms with Lepidus and at open war with Sextus Pompey, and Antony could easily have checkmated him. Making peace with Octavian and marrying Octavia was the wrong course for Antony to adopt. Though Antony was a man of great physical strength and courage, he lacked political perspicacity, and he did not have the moral strength to brave the sarcastic taunts of the Romans about his love for "the Egyptian" and "Caesar's widow." As a result, I and the children I had just borne him were repudiated, and Antony lost the chance to become the sole master of the world.

Sextus Pompey, styling himself the Son of Neptune, and in league with the notorious pirates Menas and Menecrates, had controlled the seas the last several years, gaining possession of Sicily. His ships had so infested the Italian coast that no Roman ship dared venture into these seas. To my joy, and out of the friendship his father Great Pompey had shared with my father, Sextus never touched a ship flying the flag of the Ptolemaic eagle.

Since the plebeians regarded Sextus as a hero, public opinion demanded that the Triumvirate come to terms with him, and so Antony arranged that Octavian and he should meet with Pompey.

At Mount Misenum, a promontory off the Bay of Naples, the conference was held in the spring after Antony's marriage. Pompey's fleet lay at anchor in the bay, while the forces of Antony and Octavian were drawn up on the shore. The treaty of Misenum was signed between them, signifying that Pompey would enjoy the control of Sicily on the condition that he would use his ships, not to harass the supply routes, but to keep down pirates.

The agreement signed, they invited one another to supper, and by lot it fell to Pompey to give the first entertainment on his six-banked flagship. Antony, Octavian, and their officers passed on board for the celebration.

During the banquet, Octavian told a coarse joke about Antony and me. Antony gave a feeble laugh, and the rest of the guests laughed uproariously. Emboldened, Octavian later made a second ribald remark about me. Antony, not so genial now, erupted in anger and drew his sword, and his friend, Ahenobarbus, prevented him from running Octavian through.

While this commotion was going on, Menas the pirate went up to Pompey and whispered, "Shall I take up the gangplank and make you master, not only of Sicily, but of the whole Roman empire?"

"Menas, you should have done this without telling me," Sextus remarked, "but now we must leave matters as they are."

It was apparent from this decision that Sextus was a man of honor and was a worthy son of his great father.

"And so Antony and Octavian were saved from assassination," Charmion cried. "If they had been murdered, the course of history would take a different turn."

"Oh, how so, Charmion?" I asked.

Charmion gave me a cryptic smile. "An alliance between Cleopatra and Sextus Pompey, the master of Rome, would be a fortuitous thing for the world."

I smiled bitterly. "You're incorrigible, Charmion!"

After the Treaty of Misenum, Antony went back to

Rome. He sent his lieutenant, Ventidius, into Asia Minor to fight the Parthians. Antony was often with Octavian, and they behaved themselves with much friendliness.

Athenagoras, the most noted astrologer in Alexandria, made his way to Rome at my instigation and attached himself to Antony. Antony, as superstitious as a child, paid heed to whatever Athenagoras said.

"Great Triumvir," Athenagoras told Antony, "although the star of your fortune is bright in itself, it is obscured by Octavian's, so keep yourself distant from that young man, for the genius of your life dreads his. When absent from him, yours is proud, but in his presence it is dejected."

"Egyptian diviner, you are known for calculating the nativities wisely," Antony retorted, "but when you speak, are you being true to your ancient art, or has your tongue been sweetened by Egyptian gold?"

"Let events that follow judge me, Great Antony!" Athenagoras cried self-righteously.

Incidents that occurred later showed Antony that Athenagoras had great skill. When Antony played at dice with Octavian, he always lost, and in games of cockfighting it was Octavian's champions which proved superior.

At the end of the summer equinox, taking the advice of Athenagoras to put as much distance as possible between Octavian and himself, Antony decided to go to Athens and from there administer the eastern provinces.

In Athens, a city Antony loved, he settled into a luxurious villa beside the Acropolis with Octavia, her three children by Marcellus, and his two boys by Fulvia. Soon after their arrival, in September, about the time my twins were a year old, Octavia bore Antony a daughter, Antonia. The gods answered my prayers that Octavia not give Antony a son.

The Athenians hailed Antony as the god Dionysus come to earth. He ruled with kind despotism and genial good humor. He abolished the Roman governorships of the eastern provinces under his control and converted

585

them into vassal kingdoms. Herod was reinstated as King of Judaea and Darious the son of Pharnaces became King of Pontus.

There were courtiers in Antony's court who hated me, accused me of being a sorceress, laughed at my religion, mocked my love for Antony, and strove to efface the thought of me from Antony's mind. The chief of these intriguers was Quintus Dellius, the hypocrite who had originally coaxed me to go to Tarsus and form a relationship with Antony.

Prince Alexas of Laodicea, whose royal house had been deposed years before, and who had been living on charity at my court, offered me his services.

"Cleopatra, let me go to Athens and attach myself to Antony," Alexas suggested, "to remind him every now and then of you."

I was gratified that Alexas should volunteer to perform such a duty, and since Antony liked him, I felt he was suitable for this employment. I gave him a trunk of clothes and a great bag of gold, and he sailed off to Athens. Alexas rapidly won Antony's confidence and was always at his side, taking every opportunity to remind him, as if by chance, of the gay times he had spent at Alexandria basking in my love.

Antony threw himself into the life of the Athenians with as much gusto as he had among the Alexandrians.

Prince Alexas wrote me often, informing me of all that Antony said and did. "Antony has formed a Society of Inimitable Livers," he wrote, "and we have banquets in all the rich houses beside the Acropolis, but they are heavy affairs without your graceful guidance, my Queen. The other night at a party, Antony remarked, 'Athens is the second loveliest city in the world.' Dellius piped up, 'And which is the first loveliest, our beloved Rome?' Antony made no reply, but merely sipped sadly from his goblet. O Cleopatra, Antony enjoys Athens more than Rome, but not as much as he did Alexandria two winters ago. At the very mention of your name or Alexandria, he falls into a deep trance and his eyes mist over."

"As for the Lady Octavia," Alexas wrote on, "she is always primly complaining about Antony's drinking and his other women. Cold and conventional as she is, I sense that he is growing tired of her. Do not abandon hope of one day recovering his love. One day it will flame again and burn brighter than ever."

A great hope flared within me at this letter. However, with it I received Athenian coins bearing the profiles of Antony and Octavia. It had been my desire that my profile should be coupled with Antony's on coins, and tears sprang to my eyes as I gazed upon this Greek money.

That winter Antony received the news that Ventidius had defeated the Parthians. The Parthians were compelled to retreat into Mesopotamia. Ventidius went to Rome to celebrate his triumph. I could well imagine that Antony, drinking and debauching in Athens, heard this news with jealous uneasiness.

At times I faced my destiny bravely, absorbed in governing my kingdom, but at other times I had a relapse of resolve, falling into trances of melancholia and ardent longings. On these days I felt a torment of spirit that nothing could assuage. For periods I could not eat or sleep, and I became emaciated. I made no secret of my grief, and Antony heard of these tidings. Dellius told him that I was starving myself as a means of arousing his concern, but these fits of depression were not feigned.

At about the same time I lost Antony, Apollodorus found the love of his life. After being promiscuous for years and flitting from soldier to sailor to eunuch boy, he settled down with a beautiful young scribe, Demetrius of Delos. They are deeply devoted to one another, and I find their love touching. I took Demetrius on as one of my private secretaries. He has a quiet and gentle disposition, he worships me, and I find his presence soothing.

It was after Antony left me that I began the writing of these books of my life, sitting at my desk often at night when I cannot sleep, or dictating them to Demetrius, whose hand moves swiftly with his pen across the parchment, taking down all that I say. His discretion is beyond reproach, and his service, skills, and devotion are both unimpeachable and indispensable.

Life went on in Rome, where Octavian annulled his marriage to Scribonia, with customary callousness, on the day she bore him a daughter, Julia. He then married the Lady Livia of the old house of the Claudii. Ammonios wrote me that Livia was recently divorced and had a young son named Tiberius, for whom she has great hopes. Ammonios added that Livia is as cold and calculating as her new husband, and if any two people ever deserved one another, Octavian and Livia do.

I rejoiced to learn that Octavian's admiral, Agrippa, was defeated in the sea battle of Mylae against Sextus Pompey. While Octavian met with this reversal, Antony's general, Sosius, led Antony's legions and drove the Parthians out of Phoenicia and took Damascus and captured Jerusalem.

Octavian was in dire straits, having lost most of his ships to Pompey, and he was no longer able to supply Rome regularly with food. The capital was threatened by famine. Not knowing what course to adopt, Octavian implored Antony to come to his aid. Antony had little desire to help his rival, yet he yielded to his wife's entreaties. After a year and a half in Athens, he sailed to Italy with three hundred ships.

Reaching Tarentum, Antony left his fleet in the harbor and went ashore where Octavian stood against the stately spectacle of his vast army lined up on land. The two brothers-in-law overwhelmed one another with embraces and declarations of brotherly love.

The Treaty of Tarentum was sealed, by the terms of which Antony handed over to Octavian a hundred and twenty vessels to make war upon Pompey. Also, although the second term of the Triumvirate had two more years before expiring, it was agreed to be in effect for another five years. Agrippa sailed off with Antony's ships to fight Pompey in Sicily, and Antony went off to Rome with Octavia and Octavian.

The spring the treaty was signed marked the third

year since Antony had left me. It was that same spring that I lost my beloved Aunt Aliki. She fell prey to a torturing malignant dyspepsia. For weeks I sat by her bedside, nursing her, neglecting my royal duties. Except for my children, she was the only relative I had. My physician Olympus tended her with herbs and drugs to keep her alive.

"If I were an animal, darling niece, you would have me put out of my misery," Aunt Aliki told me in a rasping, weak voice. "Please, no more medicines, I beg you!"

I was ashamed of myself for keeping her alive when she was suffering so severely, and I had the physicians desist from their ministrations. I stayed with her for two days, holding her hand, while she shook with the death rattle, and then at last she stepped into eternal life. It had not been an easy death.

Grief paralyzed my mind, and I took her passing very badly. It was hard for me to accept that my beloved Aunt Aliki was gone.

A few days after I buried my aunt in the Sema, I heard the news of the Treaty of Tarentum. This was a crushing blow which further intensified my low spirits, and pangs of mortification flared afresh within me.

A languishing melancholia possessed me. I could not eat and pined away. The condition of my health sharply worsened. I was tormented by violent headaches, pains in my abdomen, nocturnal insomnia, and spells of complete prostration. My strength was stolen by fevers, and several times I swooned in the council chamber, and once in the Temple of Isis when I was making sacrifice. Olympus gave me herbal infusions, but I did not respond to treatment.

"These ailments come from the mind, Olympus," I told him. "Our minds and bodies interact in a strange way sometimes."

"I advise that you go on a voyage on the Nile, O Queen," Olympus suggested. "Take Caesarion and the twins with you. A cruise on the holy river may do what all my arts learned in Kos cannot."

Taking this advice, and leaving Alexandria in the hands of Mardian, I sailed off on the royal barge in early summer.

I spent most of the days on deck, lying on a divan with an awning overhead, as we made the voyage upriver. Lulled by the sound of harps and flutes from musicians on deck, the gentle river breezes, and the movements of oars, I fell into a state of tranquillity and my health slowly improved. The banks of the Nile passed by, and Caesarion sat at my feet, seeing his first vision of the land the gods had chosen him to one day rule over. He was fascinated by the landscapes, the rugged and desolate Libyan plains, the land dotted with asses and goats, the long line of Pyramids, and the farmers and workers who, at the sight of the royal barge, came rushing to the banks to kiss the ground.

"Eleven summers ago, Caesarion," I said, "on this very barge, when I carried you in my womb, your father and I made a progress on the Nile. It was one of the loveliest times of my life. This voyage with you, my son, will be just as memorable for me."

Caesarion, who celebrated his eleventh birthday in July during this voyage, was extremely precocious, as befitting the son of Caesar and Cleopatra. I had overseen his education with great care. His health was good, except for an occasional fit. He understood perfectly his destiny and he took his divine royalty seriously, just as I had when I was a child. As we sailed along the river, I told him stories of the ancient pharaohs.

"You will be the greatest pharaoh in history!" I cried. "At the time you received the gift of life, your fate was ordained."

The twins, Cleopatra and Alexander, three years old, scampered playfully around the barge, but Caesarion sat always near me, grave and serious.

We wore traditional Egyptian dress and headdresses, stopping at Memphis and Thebes and Karnak, and several other temples along the way, meeting the High Priests, saying prayers, and making sacrifices.

"Great goddess Queen," the High Priest of Abydos

told me, "you are as great as any of our pharaohs. While you have been Queen, no human being or animal in Egypt has gone without his daily ration. You have made many just laws, and the lowest peasant has been able to go before court to seek justice. You have placed peace and prosperity like a wreath over the weary brow of Egypt, and you will be remembered for it."

In the middle of the summer equinox, after a two-month voyage, I returned to Alexandria. I had not had a headache or a fever during the whole time, and my health was restored. I decided to forget Antony. I had spent three years harboring the hope that he would return, but that had been a foolish dream. I did not need Antony, for in a few more years Caesarion would be a man. Antony had been a colossal mistake. He was the past, and I resolved to forget the past.

I was serenely happy to be back in my palace. As soon as I settled into my apartments, I called Mardian to my side so he could report on the affairs of state.

"Divine Majesty," Mardian said, wearing a somber countenance, "for one month Fonteius Capito, ambassador from the Triumvir Antony, has been waiting for an audience with you."

"What does this mean, Lord Mardian?" I whispered.

Mardian merely shrugged, but we both knew, in that pregnant moment, what it meant.

"Bring Lord Capito to me now," I said, trembling.

"Sacred Queen, may I suggest that you first receive Lord Capito with ceremony in your Throne Room?" Mardian said.

"That will take too long," I cried. "I have waited three years for this moment, and I won't wait a moment more! Bring him in."

The long sought-after moment was at hand.

Capito wore the richly embroidered tunic and the gold-bordered toga of an ambassador. He was patrician and decadent, and in Rome he had come often to my villa. He had always been enraptured by Apollodorus, and I think he favored my cause with Antony, not because of me, but because of my first friend.

"Welcome to Egypt, Lord Capito," I cried as he knelt at my feet and kissed my hand. "I trust you have been well cared for."

"Queen Cleopatra, I have been treated like a prince," Capito assured me in a deep, rich voice.

"Pray sit, Lord Capito, and take some figs and wine," I said with a gracious smile.

Capito sat on a divan near me, and we drank each other's health.

"You are as beautiful as I remember you in Rome, O Queen," Capito said. "And Lord Apollodorus is just as handsome. By all the gods, he looks like a mere youth."

"Apollodorus has seen thirty-eight summers," I remarked.

"A youth potion or a pact with the gods?"

"Apollodorus simply takes care of his health and never overindulges in food, drink, or his pleasures," I replied.

"Is it that simple, O Queen?" Capito grinned.

"I am pleased that Lord Antony sent you as his ambassador," I said, "for if Dellius were here in your place I would feed him to the crocodiles."

Capito shrugged and sighed. "Dellius has not been favoring your cause these last few years, O Queen."

"Prince Alexas has written me that you have, and I give you all my thanks for that, my noble friend."

"My master, the Triumvir Antony, sends you affectionate greetings, O Divine Queen," Capito declared.

"When you return to Antony, give him my congratulations for having renewed the Triumvirate for an additional five years," I said, not without a trace of bitterness in my voice.

"Ah, that was in the spring, O Queen," Capito said quickly with a knowing smile, "but much has happened since then."

"Oh, really, my lord?" I asked, searching his eyes.

"Your friend, Athenagoras, consulting his horoscopes and charts, told Antony, 'You will cover yourself with unparalleled glory by the conquest of Parthia, but you must not delay,' " Capito explained.

I nodded, thinking that Athenagoras was earning his pay.

"Rome has been filled with talk about a war against Parthia," Capito went on. "Everyone is anxious for it."

"Why not?" I retorted. "Romans, ruined by years of civil wars, hope to get rich with the spoils of a vanquished east."

Capito paused, flustered by this remark, but bravely went on. "Lord Antony realized that, if he did not want to lose the advantage of the successes of Ventidius and Sosius in Asia, he must take prompt action, and so in early summer he set out for the east."

I calculated that this was about the time I had begun my journey on the Nile.

"Antony and Octavian parted in Rome with expressions of friendship, and Antony set sail with his wife and family," Capito resumed. "He planned to install Octavia and the children in Athens and proceed to Syria alone, but on the way, he stopped at Corfu. Even I, who was in the suite, do not know what transpired, but at Corfu Antony decided to send Octavia back to Rome with the children."

My heart began beating furiously. I gazed upon Capito, my wide eyes imploring him to go on.

"The Lady Octavia, with many tears and entreaties, begged that she not be sent back," Capito said, "but Antony was adamant, putting forth many reasons why she should be in Rome. One reason was that from Rome she would be able to hasten the despatch of reinforcements. Another reason . . ." He faltered and fell silent.

I eyed him challengingly. "Yes, and another reason?"

"The Lady Octavia," Capito replied uneasily, "is expecting a child and is some four months gone."

I closed my eyes in anguish. Another child, her second to Antony. I could only pray that this child also would be a girl.

593

"Did she comply with Lord Antony's wishes?" I asked, forcing my voice to be calm.

"Yes, O Queen, Antony, unmoved by her tears, insisted that she go," Capito confirmed, his voice rising. "Antony has been in Antioch for more than a month now, alone, making preparations for the Parthian invasion. All the legions in Asia and Greece are concentrating in Antioch, and the vassal kings are leading their men into Antony's camp. When he is through, Antony will have the greatest army since Alexander the Great."

"Fonteius, my friend, such an army is worthless if they are not paid and fed," I said pointedly.

We exchanged a look of bleak and perfect understanding.

"Queen Cleopatra, I assure you that Antony has totally repudiated his wife and brother-in-law," Capito cried. "Remember the words of Plato in *Phaedrus*, 'Like a restive and rebellious horse his soul has broken loose.'"

"Did Antony tell you to quote Plato to me?"

"Oh, Great Queen, all these years the memory of your love has burned in Antony's heart, which has never been effaced by the frigid Octavia."

"Fonteius, my friend, spare me your silly words," I cried. "You have long favored my cause, and you shall be rewarded by both Antony and myself."

Capito's brown eyes gleamed. "Then you will come to Antioch, O Queen, to discuss an alliance with the Autocrator of Asia?"

"I will go, Lord Capito," I replied with a nod.

Capito sighed with relief, realizing his mission was successful, and he took a gulp of wine.

After I dismissed Capito, I sent for Apollodorus. Sitting there on my divan, I shook with emotion and held back with difficulty the flood of sobbing that threatened me.

"This is life, Apollodorus," I cried in a tremulous tone after telling him the news. "Suddenly, out of nowhere, the gods give you a gift!"

594

"Shall I start making preparations and outfitting the golden barge with lavish pomp, Cleopatra?" he asked excitedly.

"My dear friend, there will be none of that nonsense," I said firmly. "I shall not go to Antioch as a seductive Venus, loading Antony with gifts, as I did in the folly of my youth. These three and a half years have taught me wisdom. I shall not take gifts but councillors to help me work out an alliance, and this time I will drive a hard bargain. I shall also take with me the High Priest of Memphis."

"The High Priest Anchoreos, my Queen?" Apollodorus said.

"Yes, to perform the marriage rites," I cried. "I shall bind Antony's fickle heart to me forever. I must marry Antony, as I married Caesar, in the Egyptian rites. I will sully my honor and debase my house by marrying a Roman beneath my station, but circumstances force me to trade my ancient rank for brute power."

Later I told Charmion and Iras the tidings.

"I always said Antony would come back to you!" Charmion cried happily.

Iras began weeping bitter tears. "Oh, my precious Queen, don't go back to him, I beg you in the name of Isis!" She threw herself in a transport of supplication at my feet. "Caesar and Antony used your divinity and riches, trampled you in the mud, and broke your heart. Antony will only use you again and betray you again."

"As I will use him, sweet Iras," I cried, pulling her to her feet and embracing her.

"Cleopatra knows what she is doing, Iras," Charmion snapped.

"Come, let us all bathe together," I said.

I was undressed, and then I stood before a full-length polished silver mirror and gazed critically at my naked thin body.

Charmion came up behind me, smiling. "Never fear, Cleopatra, you are more beautiful than when last Antony saw you. In spite of your suffering and sickness, your beauty has not been impaired."

"I am a skeleton covered with skin," I said ruefully.

"Your body is beautifully proportioned, my lady," Charmion said in wonder. "You are as when I first knew you when you were a maiden of fifteen, eighteen years ago."

"My face has lost flesh, and is all bone," I cried.

"But such beautiful bones, and skin with the sheen of marble!" Charmion avowed. "No artist has ever sculpted a more perfect face, such high cheekbones and noble sweep of brow."

"Antony has a penchant for voluptuous women," I said dolefully.

"When you have won Antony back, you will flesh out again, O Queen, never fear," Charmion assured me.

I scrutinized the reflection in the mirror. "It takes all my effort to wear a mask of serenity on my face to disguise the bitterness and resentment which has raged within me all these years," I said mournfully. "But my eyes! A glow of bitterness burns in my eyes and I cannot camouflage that."

"When Antony and you meet, your hearts will open up and these years will never have happened," Charmion cried.

I decided to take the twins with me, so that Antony could see his children by me, but Caesarion would stay behind in the care of his tutors.

Caesarion, an incredibly intelligent boy, stoically accepted my going to Antioch, even though he knew I was returning to Antony, whom he saw as a rival for my affections.

"Do you think I should go to Antoich, Caesarion?"

"You must do what your duty commands you to do, Mother," Caesarion replied gravely.

Under the brilliant benediction of the rising sun, I sailed out of the Royal Harbor with the morning tide. My heart was racing wildly with excitement and anticipation. For three and a half years I, Cleopatra, Aphrodite on Earth, had been without a mate, but now I knew that in a week I would be in Antioch, face to face with Antony, and I would win him back.

CHAPTER VI

MY HEART BLAZED WITH EMOTION as my flagship and a dozen accompanying vessels sailed toward Antioch, the capital of Syria, the third city of the world after Alexandria and Rome, a city famous for the retreat of Daphne and celebrated as a center of art and voluptuous pleasure. At the end of September Mount Amases was sighted, the landmark of the river Orontes. We passed the harbor of Seleucia on the coast, and after a short voyage upriver, we came to Antioch, which spread out in glorious splendor from the banks of the Orontes.

My ships, loaded with gold and war provisions, dropped anchor along the harbor. I stayed below deck, but peering out of a porthole I had my first glimpse of the picturesque city of superb monuments and temples, great houses, broad boulevards, and laurel gardens. I was astonished to see the whole metropolis surrounded by gigantic military forts which scaled the rocky slopes of the Coryphean mountains and crowned the summit with their crenellated walls and high towers.

Antony was in residence in the ornate palace high above the city. Capito went to tell Antony of my arrival. For the next three days Capito ran between the palace and my flagship. At first Capito told me that Antony was waiting for me in his palace, but I was determined that Antony would first come to me. I made it clear that I was quite willing to raise anchor and return to Egypt if Antony did not make this gesture.

I had the banqueting salon of my flagship turned into an Audience Chamber, with a throne on a raised dais.

When Antony greeted me, it would be as a suppliant and I would be a queen seated on my throne.

Finally, after three days Antony acquiesced and in a frenzy of impatience and umbrage, he came to my flagship. He was kept waiting, pacing fretfully on deck, while Charmion and Iras carefully dressed me. At last I mounted my throne, and on either side of me my three-year-old twins, dressed in Egyptian court dress, sat on chairs of state.

I took my symbols of royalty from Charmion and Iras and nodded to Apollodorus to allow Antony to enter. I was in a ferment of feelings, afraid that Antony and I would be two strangers or two enemies meeting, but with an effort I assumed a cool and regal composure.

"The Triumvir Mark Antony begs an audience with the Daughter of Amon-Ra, Her Sacred Radiance, Queen Cleopatra of Egypt!" my chamberlain, Theopompus, announced in a haughty, grandiloquent voice.

The double doors at the end of the chamber swung open, and Antony entered, flanked by several officers carrying the eagles. I sat upright, holding the crook and the whip across my chest, my head weighed down by the double crown. Antony strode across the chamber and stopped at the steps that led to my throne. I saw instantly that he was strained with nerves.

"Hail, Queen Cleopatra!" Antony cried, breathing heavily, raising his arm in a stiff salute.

I sat like a statue, staring with no recognition in my eyes, although my heart was pounding furiously. I noted that his glance took in the twins beside me. Their presence disarmed him, and he blinked with sudden tears.

"All those who approach the throne of Royal Egypt must kneel in homage!" Theopompus cried, his voice throbbing with arrogance, as he gave his staff a loud thump on the floor.

Antony bristled, but gazing at his children, he relented with a sigh and slowly sank to one knee.

"Greetings, noble Triumvir," I said in a formal recognition.

Antony raised his head and peered sadly at me. My heart wrenched as I took him in, and my royal rods trembled in my hands. Three and a half years had wrought their toll on him. His huge frame had become stouter; layers of fat thickened his neck; there were puffy bags under his eyes, and his curly hair had grizzled at the temples. For all these ravages, however, at forty-six he was still incredibly handsome and he retained his old magnetism and nobility.

"What business does the Triumvir have with the Royal Daughter of Isis?" Apollodorus demanded, standing beside me.

"I have come to revise the Treaty of Alliance between the Roman Commonwealth and the Kingdom of Egypt," Antony said loudly in an overwrought voice. "I am about to conquer Parthia, and I have the biggest military horde since the time of your relative, Alexander the Great. I wish to extend to you the honor of leaguing your kingdom with Rome in this historic adventure."

"You have sixty thousand soldiers to feed, for soldiers cannot fight on empty stomachs, and they will not fight for glory alone but for gold," I cried in a swelling, triumphant voice. "You have a great army but no war chest, my noble general. All your eastern provinces have been squeezed dry. I was amused to hear that Hybreas, the celebrated orator in Cappadocia, said to you, 'If you demand a triple tax from my poor country, will you kindly provide a triple harvest?'" I paused, giving Antony a superior smile, and with pleasure I watched him squirm. "Triumvir of the East, your colleague and beloved brother-in-law will not help you. I, Cleopatra, Queen of Egypt, who alone might be your beneficent goddess at this crucial hour, will aid you in your colossal campaigns, but only in exchange for certain concessions."

"Certain concessions?" Antony bellowed, taken aback.

"Yes!" I rejoined confidently. I read from a scroll that Apollodorus held before me. "By your authority as Proconsul of the east and Triumvir of Rome, you will grant to Egypt the following territories: the islands of Crete, Samos, and Simi, Petra, the Sinai Peninsula, Galilee, Samaria, Lebanon, the part of Jordan lying between the Dead Sea and Jericho, the whole of the Phoenician and Syrian coasts, the towns of Sidon, Tyre, and Damascus, and the principality of Chalcis."

I looked down at Antony from my raised throne, seeing his outraged reaction.

"This is preposterous!" Antony cried belligerently, the veins in his temples swelling purple. "You ask that Rome give up a fourth of the empire."

I shrugged. "Without my aid you will not be able to keep the possessions you have," I said stolidly, "and with this agreement you will be able to gain Parthia, which I think is a fair exchange."

"Royal Egypt, you drive a hard bargain," Antony said with a deep sigh of capitulation. "I will grant all of your wishes, Cleopatra, but I ask only that you come down from your throne so that I may kiss you and my beautiful twins."

I stared at Antony for a long time, sensing that I had him in the hollow of my hand. I stood and he reached out for my elbow as I negotiated the steps from the throne. I then looked up at the children, saying, "Come, Cleopatra and Alexander, meet your father."

The twins got off their chairs and came down the steps. I watched with emotion as Antony squatted and his children approached him. Cleopatra Selene, so jovial, warm and outgoing like Antony, was the first to rush into his arms, crying, "Father!"

"My little Cleopatra!" Antony cried, overcome with emotion as he embraced her. At last he let her go and turned to Alexander Helios, who was as serious and dignified as I had been as a child. "My son, Alexander!" he cried, holding out his arms to the blond and blue-eyed prince who was a little image of me. The boy went up to his father. "My beautiful son!" Antony cried chokingly, engulfing the boy in his arms.

Tears welled in my eyes as I gazed upon this poignant scene and there was a painful swelling in my throat. I walked out of the chamber and into my reception room. Antony followed, leading the twins by the hand. As Charmion and Iras took away my royal regalia and robes, Antony sat on a divan with the twins, talking softly to them. My ladies draped a silk robe around me, and then I walked over and stood before Antony.

"You have given me two beautiful children, Cleopatra," he said hoarsely.

"I think so, Antony," I said with emotion.

I gestured to the nurses of the twins, who came forward.

"Run along, my children," I said, "and later you can come back and sup with your father and me."

Antony and I kissed the twins, and then we watched as they went off with their attendants.

At last we were alone. I turned my back on him and went to a table and poured two goblets of wine.

"You are as beautiful as ever, Cleopatra," Antony said. "You are more beautiful than Homer's Helen. You wear your beauty like a glorious garment, and your hair is just as golden."

"The roots of my hair are no longer spinning just gold, but a little silver, too." I handed Antony a goblet.

"The years have grizzled us both a little," he said, taking a drink.

"How is your superior, the Triumvir Octavian and your beloved wife, the Lady Octavia?" I asked with sarcasm.

"Yes, Cleopatra, out with it!" Antony erupted. "Let's get your storm of tears and reproaches over with!"

I flashed him a fierce look. "I am a royal princess of Macedonia and Queen of Egypt, not some silly girl in love!" I cried, but my voice trembled with emotion, belying my words. "I have not come here to speak of the kingdom of Eros, but my kingdom of Egypt!"

Antony gave me a smile of admiration. "Spoken like a true Queen, Cleopatra, but even if you are a Queen, with that royal snake on your head, you are still a woman. I hurt your womanly pride and caused you pain, and I beg your forgiveness. From today onward we will forget the past and think only of tomorrow. Be that as it may, I have never stopped loving you, and you have never stopped loving me."

"There is no love between us," I insisted, my voice throbbing. "What you do you do for your own glory and for Rome, and what I do I do for Egypt. I have lived every moment of my life endeavoring to be a worthy servant of my people, although Rome foolishly thinks of me as a servant of their Triumvirate and Republic. I have played off one crude, arrogant, stupid Roman against the other all these years, and by doing so kept my country free. They say Cleopatra has had two great loves, Caesar and Antony, but they are grossly mistaken. The two great loves of Cleopatra are Caesarion and Egypt!"

"Yes, drive the dagger to the hilt into my heart," Antony cried, tears springing to his eyes. "I deserve it, for I've wronged you, but I know you speak with a false tongue, for you told me a thousand times that winter that you loved me."

"It was that winter I spoke with a false tongue!"

"Your body did not lie," Antony said, as his hand reached out and encircled my breast, squeezing hard.

My body shivered with the touch, but I stiffened, meeting his eyes defiantly. "Whatever love I may have entertained for you was killed when you went off and married the granddaughter of a common, country moneylender," I said in a quavering voice, "and when you renounced me and the children I had just borne you."

I pushed his hand from my breast and moved away.

"It was a temporary measure," Antony retorted wildly, following me around the chamber. "I was without troops and my eastern provinces were toppling. When I arrived in Brandisium, the legions demanded that there be no war and the Triumvirate be renewed and secured by a marriage of state."

"You married to beg forgiveness for Fulvia's having gone against Octavian and for having stayed that winter in Alexandria with your Egyptian whore," I cried bitterly. "You stabbed and scorned me."

"I am cursed by the wrongs I have done you, and I beg that the past be forgotten and that we start afresh."

"Until I die I will never forgive or forget."

"I have cast off Octavia and her brother," Antony said with desperation. "That gesture signifies that in time I will make my move against Octavian. All my life is yours, and I have no thought but to love and to serve you, Cleopatra."

"Your heart is inconstant, and I will never take you seriously again," I cried vehemently. "After Caesar's murder you said that Octavian did not have it in him to become a senator, and a year later instead of killing him at Bologna, which you could have done, you formed the Triumvirate with him. You spent a winter with me in Alexandria, declaring that we were the greatest lovers since Prince Paris of Troy and Queen Helen of Sparta, and then you went off and married the sister of the man who had usurped my son's name and rights, and for three years you have licked the feet of Octavia and her vile, vicious brother."

"True, I have made blunders, but that is all finished now," Antony cried. "I am throwing my lot in with you, and the next time I go to Rome it will be as a conqueror." He grabbed my shoulders, his fingers digging into my skin. "Oh, my divine one, there is no woman on earth who has your majesty and beauty, your pride and courage. With your love and inspiration I can do anything. All the dreams we had can still be made good."

I breathed heavily, searching his face. "My royal rank obliges me to insist that you accede to all my demands."

"I solemnly vow an oath to the gods that I will consent to all that you desire of me," Antony said stoutly.

"Very well," I said, sighing, "and in return I will give you gold, grain, and ships."

"And your heart and soul, Cleopatra?" Antony asked in a supplicating voice. "I control the whole of the east, but do I control the Queen of the east? Will you ever love me again as you did that winter?"

"You will never again have my love!" I cried, pushing him away and walking across the chamber.

"In Alexandria you were my kitten," Antony cried teasingly, pursuing me, "but now I see you are a tigress."

Antony backed me against the wall, enclosing me with his powerful arms. My heart was beating fiercely, and I turned my head away. I felt his breath striking hot blows against my cheek.

"Oh, Cleopatra, your eyes are still deep and unfathomable like the blue sea," Antony cried, taking my face in his hands, "and your mouth is still appetizing like a red, ripe pomegranate!"

"Antony!" I gasped as his mouth engulfed mine in a passionate kiss which stirred my senses. All my coldness melted under the fire of his kiss, and my need for him burst into flame. When he took his mouth from mine, I sobbed, unable to control my emotions. Antony swept me up easily in his massive arms, as if I were a child, and carried me to a couch. He gently laid me down, and then hovering over me, covered my face with kisses, his hands tenderly fondling me.

My body was on fire as desire flared within me. I lay panting in waves of ravenous need, my bosom heaving, my heart throbbing and the blood pounding in my ears. Antony impetuously tore all my clothes from my body. He impatiently tore off his toga, and with that animal force and insolent sensuality I had known so well, he took possession of me.

"Oh, Antony, I have been yearning for you all these years!" I said sobbingly, once again pliable and yielding with relief and joy. Again I knew rapture and fulfillment, as transports of ecstasy burst from within me.

The joy of desire having found surcease, we clung to one another with intensity, as though to obliterate all thought of time lost and wrongs done to each other.

"Oh, Cleopatra, my little Greek girl, a great hunger

for you has gnawed inside me all these three years," Antony groaned.

"A hunger the lovely Octavia could not appease?" I asked.

"Octavia should have been a Vestal Virgin," Antony said. "You are a warm, delectable feast after that cold diet. She's a noble woman, but not for me. You have a heart all woman and a mind all man. You are the only woman who has ever understood me. I thank the gods we are together again, and from today onward everything will be different."

"Yes, things will be radically different," I said coolly.

Antony happily bounced off the divan and went across the chamber to pour himself a glass of wine.

I sat up, watching his great, hairy body move with the grace of a panther. "You will marry me, Antony," I announced in a calm, clear voice, in full possession of myself.

There was a long silence while I watched Antony take a big gulp of wine, the goblet trembling in his hand.

"Octavian would be outraged!" Antony cried, yet bemused by the thought. He sat beside me and gravely considered my proposal.

I sat waiting, my heart pounding, my body shaking.

"Very well, my tigress!" Antony cried, kissing my mouth and patting me as if I were a child. "When I have conquered Parthia, I will come to Alexandria and marry you."

Antony stroked my breast, but I pushed his hand away. I stood and clothed my body in a robe and faced him obdurately.

"You will marry me here in Antioch," I cried, "for it is one of the conditions of my aid. I will raise anchor and sail immediately unless you agree to all my requests."

"But my Egyptian Venus!" Antony muttered help-lessly.

"Don't try to dissuade me!" I rejoined fiercely. "You married Octavia for political reasons, and you can marry me for political reasons. Octavia married you because her brother wanted her to, and she loved being sister to one Triumvir and wife to another. While I, Cleopatra, Queen of a great kingdom, had to be content with the name of whore! Well, no longer, my Roman eagle. We are both without illusions now, and we will speak no more of love. I am no longer a fool, for life has taught me wisdom. If I am going to deplete my treasury so that you may conquer Persia and become the most powerful man since my kin Alexander, I will be at your side as your wife when you ride in triumph through the streets of Rome. I cannot trust you, so I must bind you to me with a sacred marriage."

"There are obstacles to be considered," Antony cried, temporizing. "I am married and bigamy is against Roman law, as is marriage between Roman rulers and foreigners."

"We will be married by Roman law later," I said, "but we will marry in the Egyptian rites now. Caesar was married to Calpurnia and he faced the same obstacles, yet he married me in Egypt and planned to divorce Calpurnia and declare me before the Republic as his lawful wife."

"Yes, but Caesar planned to do that on his return from Parthia when the song of triumph would drown out all opposition," Antony cried. "After I am master of Persia, I will do the same."

"That could mean two more years, and who but the gods know whether you might die in Parthia as did Crassus?" I asked harshly. "Besides, without marriage to me, there will be no Parthian campaign. If thousands of my talents in gold are to be sunk into this enterprise, I am going to get something in return besides your goodwill, a promise, and a kiss. I have not come here to badger you with recriminations, Antony, but to state my case and my requirements. You say we are bound together from this day forward. Well, if I mean so much to you, I would think you would be overjoyed to make me your wife."

"To marry you would be a scandalous, revolutionary act!" Antony cried blusteringly. "Public opinion would be outraged, and Octavian's fury over an affront to his dear sister will pass all bounds. Who can foresee the consequences?"

"The consequences will be war and the overthrow of Octavian and the supremacy of Antony!" I declared. "Isn't that the game we are playing and the destiny we are reaching for? I am implacable, Antony. Shall I sail with the evening tide for Egypt?"

There was a long pause while Antony went and poured a goblet of wine. He drained the goblet, as if to take courage, and when he turned to me I saw capitulation sagging in his every muscle.

"I will marry you, Cleopatra," he sighed.

A feeling of triumph and a glow of satisfaction coursed through me. "Very well, we will marry here in Antioch," I said softly.

"If you will only forgive me for all my sins, I will do all that you want," Antony said, sitting on a couch. He spread his arms out and gave me an imploring smile. "Come to me, Royal Egypt."

I went to Antony, realizing that I had come to Antioch to win him back on my terms and I had succeeded.

Often in the past I had dazzled the world with my carefully staged displays of royal pageants, but I wanted to conduct myself with dignified simplicity in Antioch. Antony, however, insisted that I at least make an imposing ceremonial entrance into the city. A full legion marched in parade. Antony drove a chariot in front of my golden litter, in which I sat with the twins. My litter was surrounded by a cordon of bodyguards in resplendent regalia. The procession made its way down the Corso, the immense main thoroughfare which is bordered from one end to the other by quadruple lines of marble columns, truly a breathtaking sight. It seemed that the whole population of half a million lined the Corso that glorious October morning, welcoming me with thunderous ovations.

I was led to the old palace of the Seleucides, and conducted to the apartments where once Antiochus the

Great had lived, the chambers which had been made ready for me with a splendid luxury.

A few weeks later my marriage to Antony was performed in the grand hall of the palace. It was decorated with lotus flowers, and rose petals were strewn in profusion upon the multicolored mosaic flooring. My Grecian dress was made of light gauze dyed a Tyrian purple and encrusted with hundreds of small sapphires. I wore golden sandals, and my head was encircled by the white crown of Upper Egypt, bearing the uraeus and surmounted by a headdress of the solar disk wrought in gold.

Antony and I were seated beside one another on identical square taborets, and behind us hung a great golden disk of the sun. The twins sat in chairs of state nearby.

Anchoreus, the High Priest of Memphis, with the help of several other priests in white robes and with leopard skins thrown over their shoulders, performed the Egyptian nuptial rites. The priests moved about, chanting incantations and waving wands. Finally, Anchoreus dipped his fingertips into a bowl of sacred perfumed holy oil, and spread the oil over our lips. Antony and I rose and embraced, our oil-smeared lips meeting in a sanctifying kiss, as trumpets blared.

The ceremony complete, I sat on a raised throne, and Antony took a chair of state beside me. My Egyptian ministers advanced and prostrated themselves before us, kissing our feet. The eastern satraps did likewise, although the Roman officers merely came and saluted. I vowed under my breath that the day would come when these Romans would kiss my feet when I was crowned their Empress in Rome.

Antony and I went to an ebony table where the scribes awaited us with their scrolls. We signed various documents ratifying the treaty and marriage and declaring our twins legitimate, fixing forever our names together.

I, Cleopatra, the greatest of the Lagidae, and Antony, the greatest of the house of the Antonines, were man and wife and joint rulers of the eastern world. Invested with sovereign power, Antony gave me the nuptial gifts of all the Roman territories I demanded. At last I received Phoenicia, which was owed me for the famous wager at the Banquet of the Pearl. With all these new territories, my possessions stretched around the eastern Mediterranean. I realized with emotion that my name would be remembered as one of the handful of the greatest monarchs of Egypt, if not the world. I would be more than a queen. I would be the Cleopatra of history. Twice before, by Caesar's murder and by Antony's repudiation, I had been cast to the nadir of despair, but now I found myself at the summit of the world with all my hopes rekindled.

"When news of this Treaty of Antioch reaches Rome," Antony said flippantly, "Octavian and his sister will be surprised."

"No more surprised than I was with the news of the treaties of Brandisium and Tarentum," I rejoined caustically.

Antony and I and our twins, holding hands, left the hall and entered the huge, vaulted banqueting chamber. We reclined on richly ornamented couches on the dais, and the guests took their places on a hundred couches spread out before us.

The nuptial banquet began as a flurry of slaves brought forth a variety of dishes and wines. Dancing girls made a dazzling diversion, and a troupe of pantomimes acted out scenes from mythology. Music ran through the chamber, and the wine flowed as if from fountains. Antony's officers and mine drank toasts to love, loyalty, and brotherhood in a dozen languages.

"Wine enjoyed in moderation is the gods' gift to us, Antony," I observed, perceiving that he was drinking too much. "The gods, however, did not mean for us to abuse their precious gift."

Antony took the hint. Now that he was my husband, I meant to dissuade him from his old degenerate vices.

The marriage was inscribed on the civil registers at Antioch and Alexandria, but there was no notification made to the Roman Senate. By Roman law Antony, a Triumvir and Proconsul, was still the husband of Octavia and had gone through an illegal, heathen rite to placate a rich Egyptian mistress so that he could obtain assistance to carry out a campaign which would benefit Rome.

Many of Antony's Roman officers reproached him for the marriage.

"My ancestor, Hercules," Antony told them nonchalantly, "trusted not to the fertility of one woman, and by various connections with the opposite sex he became the founder of many families. And so shall Antony."

In Antioch coins were struck, with Antony on one side with the inscription, *Autocrator of the East*, and with my portrait on the reverse side as *Queen of Kings*.

Under my influence, Antony assigned various provinces to vassal kings in the coming months. These Asian countries had been conquered by Rome, and they were chafing under the harsh administration of Proconsuls. I pointed out that under the princes of the soil, these vanquished nations would be more willing to assist Antony in his conquest of Parthia. Antony saw the wisdom of this policy.

These were golden days for Antony and me in Antioch, and we settled down to spend the winter. Antioch is declared to be a city famous for its scandalous living, where morals and manners are inordinately lax. The depraved atmosphere had no effect on Antony, for he had drunk the goblet of depravity to the dregs. He left his retinue of libertines to their own vices and spent all his evenings with me and the twins. We rejoiced in recovering each other's love and were blissfully happy.

A month after the marriage, I was greatly overjoyed to find myself with child.

"Many future kings and queens will be the fruit of our loins, Cleopatra!" Antony said pridefully.

"If I were not with child, Antony," I said wistfully, "I would go with you to Parthia in the spring."

"I would never permit you to endanger yourself,"

Antony said stoutly. "You will return to Egypt and have our child safely in your palace."

News came in from Rome saying that Octavia had given birth to a second daughter by Antony. Once again my prayers to the gods that she not give Antony a son had been answered.

Athenagoras, well skilled in the casting of nativities and the auguries, told me that the child I carried would be a son, which would make a second son from my body for Antony.

My heart soared like a freed bird at once again having Antony's love. He had grown older, and so had I, and a new understanding came between us. We belonged to one another, body and soul. Our spirits no longer clashed, and a harmony drew us together. Our flesh was integrated in the twins and in the child in my womb. Antony cherished his new-found children and delighted in spending hours playing with them every night after we took the evening meal together. He once again fell prey to my daily habit and affectionate intercourse.

The winter in Antioch was a gloriously happy time. For three years I had taken my frustrations out on my ministers and servants, being short-tempered and snapping at them acriminously, but now I regained my sense of serenity, and laughter became an easy thing for me. The court at Antioch was not as complex and rigid as that at Alexandria, and I relaxed in the simple atmosphere.

Antony and I made an occasional public appearance at the theater, the gymnasium, the circus, or the racecourse, where we were always greeted with thunderous cheers. We made these appearances to content the people, who were anxious to see us, but we preferred spending quiet evenings with the children or a few guests. There were no revels as there had been at Alexandria four winters before.

During daytime, Antony and I were busy with the preparations for the Parthian campaign which was to be launched in the spring. We administered in concert the management of the eastern provinces, making territorial appointments, settling boundary disputes, acquainting the vassal princes with the new order, and trade agreements were set up so that our empire would flourish.

There were quiet evenings when I read to Antony from Zeno of Citium, the founder of the Stoic School, who had been a great inspiration to Alexander.

"We will have a sun state, Antony," I cried hopefully. "It was Zeno's scheme of world union and Alexander's vision. We will be the rulers over a united world. I, a Greek Queen of Egypt, and you, a Roman Autocrator, will proclaim a brotherhood of peoples. Rome will be the first of states, but only the first among equals. We will give common citizenship to all. In Alexandria, any runaway slave can come to Egypt and I grant them citizenship. Such a custom is unheard-of in Rome, but we will change that when we rule jointly over the world."

Antony smiled affectionately. "As Caesar so often remarked, my love, you are a revolutionary."

"Caesar was a conservative," I said sadly. "Yes, I am a revolutionary, and so are you, and together we will transform the world and unify mankind. To Caesar there was only Rome, the conqueror and exploiter of the rest of the world, with everyone slaves to Rome, but we will bring about the brotherhood of man and build in harmony one world, the sun state, for that is our destiny."

"The blood that bubbles in your veins is too strong and hot ever to be satisfied," Antony remarked reflectively. "If you think there is one little thing you desire that you do not have, then you feel that you are totally impoverished."

"Yes, but of course," I agreed with a shrug.

Antony gave me a fond smile. "Of all those of Alexander's line, Cleopatra, only you have been touched by his fire and genius. And like Alexander, with his concept of royal servitude, you believe that you have a mission from the gods to bring men into harmony and to reconcile the world, and perhaps you might."

"We will do it together, Antony," I said stirringly.

612

The winter passed quickly and spring came. Antony had drunk little all those months and was in excellent health and active in body and mind. He was elated by hopes and anxious to set out for Parthia. I was aware that this campaign might take two years and I had certain misgivings about the expedition. The Parthians had been pushed back and were giving no trouble to the Roman provinces, and I felt there was much to lose and little to gain by conquering a country of barbarians. I was also haunted by the thought that Crassus had met his doom there, and although Athenagoras assured me Antony would return alive and victorious, the wisest soothsayers are sometimes thwarted by the fates. Antony, however, was set on the campaign and I could not deter him, any more than I could have dissuaded Caesar, and so I gave my support to the project.

I was pleased that Eros, the young, beautiful Athenian youth, an orphan but whose family was of noble blood, was going with Antony to Parthia. Antony had found Eros in Athens a few years before. Eros deeply loved his master and was always at his side with constant devotion. The love of a man for a boy has always been the fashion with the Greeks, and the Romans have been taking it up. I realized that Eros, a sweet, gentle boy, would be a plaything for Antony's idle hours during the bleak, harsh campaign in Parthia, but better he than a camp follower who carried the pox of Aphrodite. Eros had grown deeply attached to me that winter, and he promised to write me letters describing Antony's health and welfare.

The day before our separation, I stood beside Antony as we reviewed the army that had been assembled on the plains outside Antioch. Legions marched with fearless step across the vast parade ground, making the earth shake. My heart trembled as I looked over the multitudes of chariots, mules, and troops.

"No human eye has ever witnessed such an army," Antony cried proudly, his face radiant with the divine energy of Mars. "Sixty thousand foot soldiers and ten thousand cavalry of Romans, Thracians, Persians,

Greeks, Macedonians, and Gauls, all fighting under my banner! I am on the road to victory, and I will return crowned with glory!"

I had thought of returning to Egypt by the overland route, stopping off at Jerusalem. King Herod had sent me messages offering hospitality, but since I was in an advanced state of pregnancy, I thought that travel by caravan might endanger my child and decided to return swiftly and smoothly by sea.

It was a spectacular sunny day in March when Antony and I took our sorrowful leave of one another on the deck of my flagship. Antony would be marching off with his army eastward the next day. I was disturbed at the thought of separation, which I knew would be long and beset with uncertainties, and it was with a great effort that I kept my composure.

"How I shall ache with longing for you, my love," Antony cried, clasping me close.

"To fulfill our golden destiny we must part," I said. "Oh, Antony, the Parthian moon will be eclipsed by the Roman sun. When I look upon you, I recall lines from Aristotle: 'Wonders are many, but none is so wonderful as man himself!' And you are a wonder of a man, Antony. You will place great victories on the altar of Zeus, and nothing can stand in the way of your divine destiny."

"In our destiny, Cleopatra," Antony cried. "In a year I will have conquered Parthia, and we will go to Rome to celebrate my victory and it will be the most stupendous triumph ever celebrated in the seven-hilled city of Romulus and Remus. My power, as the victor of Philippi and Parthia, will be exalted over Octavian's, and he will be forced to retire. I will annul my marriage to Octavia and we will have a great marriage. All your dreams will be realized with me, and we will rule over a greater empire than Alexander ever dreamed of doing."

"Dearest Antony, I love you!" I cried tenderly.

Antony embraced the twins, and once more we kissed and held onto each other passionately. Then with a stifled cry, he tore himself from me and left my flagship with his retinue of staff officers.

"Farewell, Antony, farewell!" I called out, a sad echo throbbing in my voice.

A fanfare of trumpets sounded from the dockside as my ship drifted away, and the multitude of soldiers and citizens along the riverbanks cheered and waved their farewell. The wind sprang up, billowing the sails, and the Orontes pulled the ship quickly away in its swift currents. I stood on deck, watching Antony standing on the dockside against the backdrop of the glorious city of Antioch, growing smaller, and then a bend in the river obliterated him from my view.

At last the sun-dappled and white-capped blue Mediterranean stretched out before me, and I was on my way home to Egypt.

CHAPTER VII

WITH A BUOYANT SPIRIT I arrived in Alexandria that spring after an absence of eight months, the great marble watchtower of Pharos looming up to greet me. My belly was swelling fruitfully, making me heavy, but I was light of heart and full of optimism and hopes for the future.

I was overjoyed to see that my darling Caesarion, the rejuvenated spirit of his father, had grown taller during my absence. He was approaching his twelfth year and was a beautiful stripling.

"Caesarion looks like Queen Cleopatra's younger brother instead of her son!" was the remark which all the courtiers were making.

I was relieved to learn that Caesarion had taken few fits during my time in Antioch. He was no longer so emotionally dependent upon me. Just as I had as a child, he conscientiously applied himself to his books, and was precocious in learning, languages, maturity, and wisdom. He was perfectly aware of his destiny, that he would be emperor of the world as his father would have been if he had lived. Caesarion was my firstborn, and I loved him more than anyone in the world. If I could only see him crowned Emperor of Rome, then I will die happily.

To my delight I found that, with Antony as my husband, all opposition toward me in Egypt ceased. I had secured for Egypt the help of the most powerful man in the world, I had increased Egyptian possessions so that once again Egypt was an empire, I was empress of the east and mistress of the Mediterranean, and I enjoyed a power unmatched by any prince in the world.

My days were busy as I saw that new ships were built and the old ones overhauled, and I reorganized the army. As always, I improved the condition of my people, guarded against famine, and saw that the irrigation canals were properly maintained. Trade with the four corners of the world steadily increased, bringing Egypt immeasurable riches.

In the early part of the autumnal equinox, I withdrew to the confinement chamber with my physician Olympus and the royal midwife, and went into labor. My previous confinements had been protracted, bringing me close to death, but this time I easily gave birth to my third son. I named the man-child Prince Ptolemy Philadelphus.

The courtiers and priests offered prayers to the gods for the safe delivery. A few days later the priests performed the circumcision on the prince in a ceremony witnessed by many nobles and magistrates.

Although I was blissfully happy with my new prince and with my new security in Egypt, I was beset with anxiety from external affairs. There were ramifications from Rome for one thing, since my marriage to Antony was galling to the vanity of Octavian, and the gift of territories was a source of envy to the avaricious Romans. The fire of hatred against me grew more fierce, fanned by Octavian's propaganda mill.

Octavian laid plans that summer to have me murdered. I had spies at King Herod's court in Jerusalem, and I learned from them that it had been a wise thing I had not returned to Egypt overland with a stopover as Herod's guest. Octavian was in league with Herod to have me assassinated, which had prompted the invitation to stay at the Judaic court. The plan had been that my cavalcade was to be attacked by Arab tribesmen, who were to ambush me between the narrow mountain passes leading out of Judaea.

The affairs of state occupied my days, but my nights were empty and lonely, and there was an aching void in my heart with Antony gone. I waited anxiously for the sealed letters that came in intermittently from Antony and Eros by couriers. The winter mists then obscured the sea, all navigation was suspended, and letters came by the overland caravan route and took longer, but letter by letter I was able to follow the progress of the Parthian campaign.

In early summer, about the time I arrived back in Alexandria, Antony had crossed the river Araxes and entered Parthia. He arrived at the city of Phrasspa, the Parthian stronghold, and waited in vain for King Artavasdes of Armenia to join him with his army. Artavasdes, as it turned out, was in league with Octavian to turn against Antony and never appeared. Antony also waited in vain for the legions Octavian had promised him.

All that autumn and into the winter, Antony with his army was besieged beneath the walls of Phrasspa. After months, forced to accept defeat with a bitter heart, Antony raised the siege and began the long march through inhospitable, snow-covered mountain passes.

The retreat took twenty-seven days, during which they beat off eighteen attacks by Parthian guerrilla horsemen and archers. Antony shared in all the distresses of his men and valiantly kept up their morale. At nights he visited the men in their tents, consoling them by a display of sincere compassion. The soldiers loved him for the tender and affectionate manner in which he sympathized with their ills. When the men were dying, he was always there to give them a kiss before death.

When the new year began, Antony and the remnants of his army reached White Village, a small town on the Phoenician coast near Sidon. He had accomplished the most disastrous retreat in history, and his soldiers burst into tears and embraced one another with transports of joy. Antony found a ship and sent it off to Alexandria with a letter to me.

The letter arrived at the palace in the middle of the afternoon when I was in my bedchamber, resting from my labors after my noonday meal. I lay on a divan, reading reports, while Iras sang sweetly to the accompaniment of a harp. I am never to be disturbed during this time unless it is a matter of urgency. Mardian had one of my slave girls bring the scroll in to me, and with a plummeting heart I recognized Antony's seal. With trembling hands, I broke the wax seal, unrolled the scroll, and read Antony's plea that I come to his succor at the village where he was encamped.

"Antony, Antony!" I cried, breaking into sobs. "Oh, my beloved husband, I must go to him at White Village!"

Iras, leaving her harp, ran over to me and I quickly told her the news.

"Oh, my Queen, I beg you not to go," she cried. "His defeat is a sign of the gods that you should abandon him!"

"Antony is my husband and I am the mother of three of his children," I cried with pride and fury. "I could never be so dishonorable as to betray those I love."

"Antony betrayed you!" Iras shot back.

"Once, but never again," I cried. "Our lives and stars are irreversibly joined now, and I am going to him."

I issued orders to prepare the journey, and within a week I sailed out of the harbor in my new galley, the *Antonaid,* and several other ships, loaded with provisions and gold. I took the twins and six-month-old Prince Ptolemy with me, hoping that the children would be balm to Antony's despairing soul.

Antony, who had been a brave example to his men all during the campaign and the long retreat, had collapsed with despair at White Village. He was crazed with grief and drank heavily, and walked along the beach anxiously all day long, scanning the horizon of the sea for sight of my ships.

In early April, the *Antonaid* and six other ships finally reached the shore of the small village. Antony and his soldiers lined the white beach, waving their arms ecstatically. Because of the shallow water, we dropped anchor a great distance from shore. Antony climbed into a small boat which was rowed out to my flagship.

I stood on deck, my heart beating furiously, as Antony climbed on board.

"Oh, Antony, my beloved husband!" I cried, rushing into his arms.

"Cleopatra, I thought you would not come!" Antony cried, clasping me against him in a crushing embrace.

It was a deeply emotional, impassioned moment, as we wept and kissed, and the soldiers watched, waved, and cheered from the shore.

"I have brought food, clothes, and gold," I cried.

"And your love, Cleopatra?" Antony asked piteously, searching my face. "Have your brought me your love?"

A lump formed in my throat, and it was painful for me to speak. "Yes, I have brought my love, Antony. Oh, I don't know how I have lived these last twelve long months without you!"

From over my shoulder, Antony glimpsed the twins standing with their nurses. "My children," he murmured, embracing them, "how big you are now!"

I took Ptolemy from his nurse. "My husband, your new son!" I cried, holding the six-month-old infant out toward Antony.

Antony tenderly took the babe and held him in his arms, gazing down on the little face, as tears fell from his eyes and into his unkempt beard. He turned toward shore and held the baby aloft.

"My new son!" Antony cried exultantly as his soldiers cheered from the beach. "My new prince!"

Antony was impressed by the *Antonaid* and was happy that I had named the ship in his honor. Since the fort at White Village was primitive, I lived aboard the *Antonaid* during my stay there, and Antony spent the nights sharing my bed, once again delighting in comfort after the long harsh year of soldiering.

I found the valiant and glorious army I had reviewed in Antioch a little more than a year before now decimated, demoralized, and tattered. In the following days, boats rowed out to my ships and the provisions were unloaded and carried ashore, and Antony's soldiers were equipped with new clothes and food and all that they lacked. I gave his officers rich gifts, and I paid the soldiers all their back pay, plus a bonus of a hundred and forty sesterces to a man.

Though gathered from all parts of the empire, the majority of the soldiers were blond Macedonians and Thracians, and they looked upon me, with my Macedonian blood, with kinship and loyalty. They lined up in the main rustic hall of the small fort, and I sat beside the table laden with Egyptian gold as my chamberlains handed out the pay. After receiving their money, each soldier knelt at my feet. I wanted to make sure that they realized it was I, Cleopatra, Queen of Egypt and the wife of their general, who paid them.

One clear bright spring afternoon, Antony and I walked along the white sandy beach, holding hands, with the twins running playfully around us. A deep azure overspread the sky, seagulls circled and squawked overhead, and the sea lapped rhythmically on the sand near our feet.

"Oh, my love, these last weeks of waiting for you have been such a misery for me," Antony said sighingly. "I remembered Aristotle saying that hope was the dream of a man awake, and so I hoped and dreamed. Waiting is the most painful of all forms of suffering, for it contains an element of fear, and I was afraid you would not come."

"How could you think that I would ever forsake you, Antony?" I cried.

"I am a defeated general," Antony said despairingly.

"All great generals are entitled to one defeat," I said. "Caesar was defeated at Dyrrhachium."

"The Persian campaign was to have made me the supreme master of the world," Antony muttered.

"It was not a defeat, merely a postponement," I cried, squeezing Antony's hand as we walked along the beach. "You have accomplished the retreat with admirable discipline. A lesser general would have perished in Persia like Crassus. After a rest in Alexandria, you will regroup your army and conquer Persia. After that, you will then defeat Octavian. He is your avowed enemy. From now on, you will receive no help from Octavian or from Rome. I am your natural ally, your wife and the mother of your children. Only I will help you, and I live only to love and to serve you."

Antony was in a distraught state and I did my best to soothe him with sweet words and warm caresses. Our separation had taught us how necessary we were to each other, and we kindled the fire of our passions and realized with uncompromising lucidity the enormous depths of our great love.

Seeing that his men were safe and all their needs were cared for, Antony returned with me to Egypt.

Dawn broke tremulously over the sea that morning in early May, as the beacon of light guided us into the Royal Harbor. We had stood for hours on deck, straining for a glimpse of Egyptian land through the mist, and then suddenly the sun rose, illuminating the marble monuments of Alexandria.

"It has been five long years to the month since I left your glorious city," Antony cried with deep emotion. "I am so happy to again set foot on the sacred soil of Egypt."

Antony had always been a great favorite with the Alexandrians, and they received him with joyous enthusiasm. He once again adopted the dress and manners of a Greek and settled into my palace, basking in my love and devotion and the admiration of my people.

"Cleopatra, my little Greek, you are the only woman who has never bored me after a night," Antony told me.

Antony worshipped me, and I was loved and I loved. I felt my power as a woman, and I comported myself to Antony, both in public and in private, as a loving wife.

Antony exercised royal authority with me, as if he were my King-consort, and we dispensed justice together. I looked forward to the day when he would be Emperor of Rome, and I would sit beside him and administer the Roman empire.

The Roman Senate was kept well informed of the failure of the Parthian campaign, for there had been informers in Antony's ranks. Ammonios wrote me and described all the base intrigues of Octavian and his efforts to undermine Antony's popularity and to turn public opinion against him.

It was obvious that Octavian intended to make himself absolute master of Rome. While Antony had been forced to retreat across Asia, Octavian had won important victories. He had forced Lepidus to retire, depriving him of his legions and African provinces and attaching them to his own, and his general Agrippa had defeated Sextus Pompey at the battle of Naulochus. Pompey had fled with only a few vessels that remained of his enormous fleet, sailing to the island of Lesbos where he fortified a stronghold.

Soon after Antony and I had returned to Alexandria, we received a letter from Pompey, offering to enter into an alliance with us against Octavian. I favored an alliance with Sextus in remembrance of the friendship his father had for my father, and because of the fierce struggles he had long sustained against my mortal enemy, Octavian.

"Sextus still enjoys considerable prestige in the Roman world," I pointed out to Antony, "and we should employ his naval talents and his great name in our service."

Agreeing with me, Antony sent an ambassador off to Lesbos to Pompey to conclude a treaty. When our envoy reached Lesbos, however, he found that Sextus, the last descendent of the great house of Pompey, had been assassinated, his throat cut by an unknown ruffian who was undoubtedly in the pay of the bloodthirsty Octavian, who did not want his enemy to ally himself with us. I was incensed and aggrieved at the news of this base act. Pompey's death was another victory for Octavian and only increased his power.

Against these gains and victories of Octavian's, Antony had only the failure of the Persian campaign.

"I cannot remain under the shadow of my defeat and be eclipsed by Octavian," Antony declared. "Artavasdes of Armenia deprived me of the fruits of a Parthian victory by not joining me with his army as promised. I will conquer Armenia and revenge myself by punishing Artavasdes for his desertion and treachery."

Before summer came, Antony sailed off to war again. He went to White Village and collected his legions, and then marched to Armenia. Entering the country, he pillaged every city he came to, and at last reached Nicopolis where Artavasdes, realizing that resistance would be in vain, went to Antony's camp and gave himself up as prisoner with his queen and two small sons.

The Temple of Anaitis, the Venus of Armenia, whose worship is accompanied by immodest ceremonies and to whom the most beautiful maidens are consecrated, was not spared. The temple housed a statue of the goddess in solid gold, and the covetous soldiers smashed the statue to pieces and divided it among themselves. They then raped the priestesses. Even though these women yield their bodies to all who come as an offering to their goddess, this was rape by foreign invaders and a deplorable outrage, but unfortunately such is war.

Antony concluded a treaty with the King of Media, giving him Armenia, and made arrangements to marry our son Alexander to Princess Jotape, the king's only child, so that in time Alexander, the son of Antony and Cleopatra, would rule over the combined kingdoms of Media and Armenia.

In late autumn, after a six-month campaign, Antony returned to Alexandria, bringing with him Artavasdes of Armenia and his family in chains, and the Armenian treasury as his booty.

"My husband," I cried with pride, "you are the first Roman since Caesar to conquer new territories."

Flushed with triumph, Antony was proud and happy. Statues had been erected of him all over the Orient and he had regained his self-respect, and during his absence I had placed several marble likenesses of him in the public squares of Alexandria.

All throughout the Armenian campaign, Antony had taken care to keep the Senate informed of his victories, but Octavian, in a jealous fit, and not wishing that

Antony's glory be enhanced, did not even announce Antony's conquest of Armenia to the Senate. Artavasdes of Armenia was Octavian's secret ally, and Octavian did not want him dragged through the streets of Rome and ignominiously put to death. Antony's friends in Rome made attempts to pass a decree to allow Antony to celebrate a triumph in Rome, to which he was entitled, but Octavian cleverly foiled these motions.

"If Octavian will not allow me to celebrate my triumph on the banks of the Tiber," Antony cried, "I will duplicate the honor on the banks of the Nile. If I cannot place my trophies on the altar of Jupiter, then I will lay them at the feet of my cherished wife."

I was filled with ecstasy at this decision. It would be an unprecedented event, for no Roman general had ever celebrated a triumph anywhere but in Rome. Octavian, of course, would use this move as propaganda against Antony, citing the action as a piece of insolence and contempt for his country. Antony would be defying Roman tradition, but he felt that there were several Roman customs that had to be broken.

The triumph would be a great honor for both myself and my city, and I planned the spectacle in magnificent detail. It would be celebrated on my thirty-sixth birthday, which would give the day an added significance. I wanted to make the triumph a day of history and the most spectacular pageant ever witnessed in Alexandria, and I wanted to use the event to declare emphatically to Rome my position in the world and my designs for the future.

The sun came up on the dawn of my birthday, casting its rays gently, and it was evident from sunrise that the sun would shine in sweet benediction upon the marching soldiers and the people thronging the streets. This was the sun god's special blessing on me.

My people filled the streets early, anxious to contribute their share to the historic day. They had garlanded their houses and wore their finest jewels and clothes, and the public buildings were festooned with flags and the streets hung with colorful ribbons.

Under the glowing sun the triumphal procession started out from the palace in midmorning and wound itself along all the grand boulevards. The parade was led by two thousand cavalry in sparkling armor. The prancing horses were followed by a company of legionnaries marching in martial splendor; their shields, instead of being engraved with the Roman S.P.Q.R., were emblazoned in gold with the letters C and A. They were followed by dozens of chariots laden with gold, silver, statues, and the spoils of Armenia, and the pavements shook as the wheels rolled along. Thousands of Armenian captives followed on foot, linked by silver chains.

Antony followed the captives in a golden chariot drawn by four foaming chargers, striking an imposing figure in robes of purple and a golden laurel crown on his head. He waved the baton of victory at the cheering, adoring crowds as he passed them. Ever the lover of pageantry, adulation, and pomp, his face was glowing ecstatically.

Behind Antony came the royal family of Armenia, King Artavasdes, his queen and two small sons, linked with chains of gold in honor of their former rank. Egyptian troops and my Macedonian Household Guards brought up the rear of the procession.

At high noon, just as Antony entered the farthest end of the Canopic Way, passing the Sema on his way back to the palace, I led my children out to the square in front of the palace. Grouped on the steps were royal functionaries and priests, and curules, the ivory chairs, were reserved for the highest dignitaries. As I descended the stairs with my children, my people gave out with roaring cheers.

A thousand trumpets rang out as I climbed onto the platform of silver which was hung with sumptuous silk of gold in the center of the square, and took my seat on my throne of gold. I was dressed in the resplendent raiment of Isis and wore the double crown on my head.

Caesarion sat on a throne at my right. He was tall for his thirteen years, and he wore the sacred cobra on

627

his forehead, the blue false beard, and the dress of the old pharaohs with all the fastidiousness and pride which would have made his father happy.

I sat there, regarding my firstborn with emotion, realizing that this day, and indeed my entire life, had been lived for him. I had plotted, fought, and schemed for his sake since his birth, and all my dreams of destiny were concentrated in his being.

I awaited my triumphant husband, hero and lover, and at last the chariots filled with the spoils of victory rolled into the square and were laid at my feet. Antony alighted from his chariot and led Artavasdes and his family to the platform to pay me homage.

The crowd fell silent, and the rattling of a thousand sistra and the blowing of trumpets ceased. A great silence reigned as Artavasdes and his family stood before me, holding themselves with erect dignity, not meeting my eyes. I had kept them in honorable confinement and they were not demoralized and their royal spirit was intact.

"Hail, Cleopatra," Artavasdes said in a detached tone.

I sat there, immobile as a statue of Isis, watching Artavasdes through heavy-lidded eyes, waiting for a sign of homage.

Antony, becoming enraged, took a step toward him. "Address Queen Cleopatra by her title and kneel at her feet!"

Artavasdes merely stood there and stared at me out of veiled eyes with a stony look of indifference.

"Kneel, barbarian!" Antony screamed furiously, drawing his sword from its scabbard and raising it over Artavasdes.

The onlookers, astonished and angered at the slight paid me, erupted with shouts of "Kill!" and "Strike!"

"On your knees, Artavasdes, or I'll cut off your head!" Antony screamed stridently, the veins enlarging on his temples.

"Peace, Antony!" I cried out. He shot me a look and

I nodded calmly. It was impossible for me not to admire the boldness of Artavasdes.

Mardian, standing behind me, leaned anxiously over my shoulder. "Great Queen, Artavasdes must be slain," he cried eagerly. "He refuses to prostrate himself before you, the Queen of Kings!"

I reflected a moment, recalling that Artavasdes was a writer of historical tragedies and orations in Greek, works of little merit, I was told, but I still recoiled at the thought of executing a fellow monarch and one who courted, even if in vain, the Muse Melpomene.

"Artavasdes and his family are to be spared," I announced. "Have them returned to their chambers."

"Royal Isis, Artavasdes must suffer for the insult he has paid you before your people!" Mardian screeched. "In Rome, after walking in a triumph, vanquished kings are killed according to the custom of the Republic. Do you not remember King Vercingetorix of the Gauls?"

I remembered only too well that day in Rome and how I had intensely disapproved of Caesar's lack of mercy.

"This is not Rome, but Alexandria," I cried, "and Royal Egypt has her own customs, my Lord Mardian."

Antony, losing his anger, nodded understandingly at me. He turned and gave the order to a centurion, and Artavasdes and his family were led away, still without even a nod at me, by a cordon of soldiers. At first my people shouted their disappointment, but then they accepted my magnanimous gesture and cried their approval.

Trumpeteers blasted, and Antony raised his hands toward the crowds. The trumpets and the people fell silent.

"Beloved Alexandrians!" Antony cried in his rich, powerful voice. "I am your living god, Antony Osiris, and I lay the spoils of my Armenian conquest at the feet of your divine goddess-Queen!"

A deafening roar erupted for the longest time, and then Antony silenced the crowd with his outstretched arms. "By my power as absolute master and emperor of the east and Triumvir of Rome," he declared, "I pronounce Cleopatra, Queen of Egypt, to be Queen of Kings!"

My people responded with shouts of joy at this honor being paid me.

Antony pointed his right arm toward Caesarion. "I proclaim your Pharaoh Ptolemy Caesar to be the sole heir of his divine father, Julius Caesar, and I elevate him to the rank of King of Kings!"

Tears filled my eyes as prolonged ovations rang out.

Antony then proclaimed seven-year-old Prince Alexander Helios as the Presumptive King of Armenia and Media, and Princess Cleopatra Selene as the future Queen of Cyrene, Libya, and Cyprus. Two-year-old Prince Ptolemy Philadelphus was declared to be King of Phoenicia, Syria, and Cilicia. These three children by Antony wore the appropriate costumes from the countries over which they would one day rule. Alexander was clad in the dress of the Medes and wore on his head the tiara and the turban with the upright peak. Little Cleopatra wore the long veils of a North African princess, and Ptolemy wore the mantle, slippers, and the Macedonian cap encircled by a diadem which is the habit of the successors of Alexander the Great. Each of the children came and saluted me in turn.

In solemn procession, as trumpets blared, we left our thrones and returned to the palace. Each of the children was escorted by guards chosen from their prospective kingdoms, whose duty it was to spend their last drop of blood protecting them. Cleopatra was borne aloft in a carrying chair by a cordon of ebony-skinned Libyan soldiers, Alexander was flanked by guards in Armenian dress, and Ptolemy, the smallest king in the world, was carried by Syrian soldiers.

As we disappeared inside the palace, the applause followed us like the roar of a burst dam. My people were frenzied in their excitement, aware that Alexandria, with her group of future monarchs, was indeed the capital of the world. Antony had elevated my kingdom to an importance Egypt had not known for centuries. No ceremony in my day has ever approached this in royal splendor and significance.

There was a spectacular sunset as the sun dropped into the sea. From the gates of Canopus to the Necropolis, the line of houses began to show lights in the gathering darkness, and rooftops glowed red from the flames of torches. All sorts of festivities began. Oil, wine, and wheat were distributed to the eager crowds. In the square in front of the palace, tables were set up and loaded with meats, fruits, and wines, and a public feast was given to the citizens and soldiers. There were spectacles of every variety to suit all manner of tastes.

Inside the palace the corridors were ablaze with torches and lamps. In the evening I sat down to preside over a magnificent banquet in the Great Hall, at which were present all the nobles and dignitaries of the court and city. Adorned in a golden dress and covered with pearls and jewels, I was the focus of all eyes as I sat at a table on the dais. The feast served was sumptuous, and dancers, acrobats, and mimes provided marvels of entertainment.

At midnight, Antony and I stood on the Balcony of Appearances and received the last cheers from a grateful people crowding the great square.

"Today, my birthday, has been the most glorious day of my life," I cried. "Oh, Antony, I thank you for this day."

"Our next victory celebration will be in Rome," Antony said, leading me to our bedchamber.

My soul exulted within me, my proud heart beat rapidly, and a joyous happiness filled me. Yet, in the deep recesses of my mind, the philosophy of my Greek forebears warned that while victory affords great joys and riches, it may also exact a terrible price and a penalty.

CHAPTER VIII

"CLEOPATRA'S NAME IS A BATTLE CRY for the Romans," Ammonios wrote me as the new year dawned. "Rome growls like a wounded wolf at the triumph in Alexandria, for the people regret the loss of festivities and gifts that Caesar lavished upon them at such events. They say that Antony has given away their kingdoms which belong to them, to your children as though they were toys, and that, as you destroyed Caesar, you are now destroying Antony. They see you as a threat to Roman power. It grieves me sorely, O Queen, to be so blunt, but here in the Eternal City the cry is going up to make war against Egypt."

I pondered the letters from Ammonios and my other friends and agents in Rome, all of whom informed me of the temper of the times.

After the triumph, relations between the two Triumvirs continued to deteriorate. Antony wrote demanding a share of the booty Octavian had won from Sextus Pompey and half the legions formerly held under the deposed Lepidus. Octavian replied by saying he would gladly surrender half the booty and soldiers, if Antony would do likewise with his provinces of Armenia and Egypt.

I was outraged to think that Octavian should insinuate that Antony possessed Egypt as a Roman province.

Octavian openly attacked Antony and me in the Senate.

"Cleopatra is an Oriental sorceress and a witch whose evil influence drives to distraction all men who come near her," Octavian fulminated in his high-pitched, screeching voice. "She keeps Antony drunk and drugged and bewitched by magic potions. He is a luxury-living libertine and a lovesick slave, grovelling at her feet in the manner of her sexless eunuchs. He has completely lost all reason, and we must rescue this once great Roman who is imprisoned in shameful bonds!"

The day was coming when Antony and Octavian would measure their strength, one against the other, and my fate would be decided in the outcome.

A throng of parasites crowded my court, such as always can be seen where power and wealth procure an easy existence. My palace teemed with Roman patricians who had flocked to Alexandria to live on my hospitality. I endeavored to be agreeable to these Roman guests, among which were Capito, Dellius, Canidius, and Ahenobarbus, and I overwhelmed them with gifts. The Society of Inimitable Livers was revived, and every night banquets were held in the palace.

In the afternoons, Antony and I always met in the palace gardens, where we relaxed and played with our children. I would read poetry, while Antony and the children sometimes sat on the sea wall and fished, or Antony romped on the grounds with them. Antony was a good father and a loving husband, and he was well aware that his days of being a family man were short, for soon he would have to go off to war again.

Caesarion had a suite of officers who were attached to his person. He studied diligently under Rhodon, Nicolaus of Damascus, and other learned men from the gymnasium. Each evening I always spent an hour with Caesarion, just the two of us, while Antony took a long bath. When Antony joined me, Caesarion would go off with his friend Andronicus. It was not that Caesarion and Antony were hostile to one another, but they politely stayed out of each other's way.

Andronicus, a young cousin of Charmion's, is Caesarion's constant friend and companion. As a young girl Charmion entered my life and brought me such joy and friendship, and now years later, another child from the house of Kallimachos has become attached to my son in a special way. Andronicus, a year older than Caesarion, is a youth of dark beauty and outgoing disposition, of charming manners and bright spirits. The two boys are rarely out of each other's sight. Together they study, wrestle, swim, and exercise at arms. Their friendship and love is a joy for me to behold.

The previous November Antony had turned fifty, and although he had gained weight and was grizzled at the temples, he was in robust health.

"The world with its kingdoms is mine," he liked to boast, "and the most beautiful woman in the world is my wife!"

Antony was occupied with preparations to get off the ground once again his cherished project, the conquest of Parthia. I suspected, however, that Octavian did not want Antony to acquire more laurels by conquering Parthia, and that he would maneuver Antony into conflict to block his plans.

At the beginning of the summer equinox, some six months after the celebration of the Armenian triumph, Antony was all prepared to sail to Ephesus to join his legions. A few days before his departure a ship arrived from Athens, and a certain Roman, Lord Niger, delivered a letter to Antony from Octavia.

I was instantly alerted to this and made my way to Antony's chamber. I found him reading the letter. He nodded consent for me to read it, too, and the scroll shook in my hands as I did so.

"Dearest Antony, I greet you as a devoted wife. I am happy to write that our two beautiful daughters are in good health. Antonia Minor is the image of her father with her curls and blue eyes. A few days ago I arrived safely in Athens. I have brought clothes and arms and a cavalry of three hundred Praetorian soldiers, a gift from my brother to his brother-in-law to aid you in your war against the Parthians. I await your permission to conduct these men and beasts to Ephesus, where I may be reunited with my husband. Your devoted and dearest wife, Octavia."

The arrow of jealousy struck deep. I felt myself

trembling as I let the scroll fall to the floor. "A very clever stroke," I cried.

Antony met my eyes evasively. "Octavia does not want you to have all the credit for aiding my soldiers."

"It is far more complex than that," I said. "This is a chess game. Antony, what is your next move?"

"I must accept her gifts honorably," Antony cried. "To reject them would create a rupture which I wish to avoid."

"Octavian still owes you twenty thousand men from the Treaty of Tarentum in exchange for all the ships you gave him," I argued hotly, "and now four years later he offers three hundred soldiers and some clothes and a few horses!"

"There are gaps in my legions which these Praetorians can readily fill."

"By all means, write the Lady Octavia and instruct her to have this cargo of men and beasts embarked for Ephesus, and order her to return directly to Rome," I cried fiercely, quivering with rage. I was frantic that there could be a reconciliation between them and that I might lose him again. "Oh, Antony, can't you see that this is just a Roman trick to ensnare you in Octavian's trap once again?"

"You are driving me mad with your jealous despotism!" Antony cried. "This is not the propitious time to get embroiled with Octavian. I must go fight the Parthians, not Octavian."

I took a deep breath. "The very day you ever meet Octavia again," I said in a calm, stern voice, "I shall issue a proclamation decreeing our divorce official, and I will never lay eyes on you again."

Antony gave me a stricken look, for he saw that I was sincere and adamant.

"You cannot have two wives, one in the east and one in the west," I continued. "Octavian is forcing you to declare to the world who is your wife. The choice is yours, my Lord Antony. I and Egypt shall, of course, abide by your wishes."

I turned and with an erect posture walked to the door.

"I shall write Octavia today!" Antony blurted out. The words stopped me and I paused, waiting.

"I shall accept her gifts and order her to return to Rome," Antony continued. "Of course, the die will be cast and this insult will make war between Octavian and me inevitable."

"The hour of reckoning between the two of you has been coming for many a year now," I said, gazing calmly upon Antony. "It will be a duel to the death, and you will be the victor."

"I still hope that before taking up a war with Octavian," Antony said, "I will be able to bring the war with the Parthians to an end by a brilliant conquest, and restore my reputation."

"You will be greater than Caesar and Alexander then, my husband," I cried, lacing my fingers through his curly hair.

"And so it is Antony and Cleopatra all the way," he said.

"Yes, all the way to victory," I cried, kissing his mouth.

I returned to my apartments and informed Iras of Octavia's letter.

"That bitch!" Iras said sneeringly. "Oh, my Queen, when you are in Rome, seated on the throne of the world, Octavia must walk shackled behind your litter when you are borne through the streets."

For a moment I relished the thought of this extravagant fancy. "Yes, Iras, she shall indeed," I cried.

"And Calpurnia must be consigned the duty of emptying your chamber pots!" Iras cried, her eyes glowing.

"Oh, really, Iras, such absurd notions the poppy juice gives you," Charmion said contemptuously.

"I think Iras has some brilliant ideas!" I cried.

Just as Antony promised, he wrote Octavia to return to Rome, which filled me with bitter satisfaction.

One of the last things Antony did before sailing for Ephesus was to make a will, by the terms of which he recognized that I was his wife and his three children

637

by me were legitimate offspring. He bequeathed to me his whole fortune, which he had amassed in Armenia, and ordered that his body should be transported to Alexandria and delivered into the hands "of my beloved wife, Queen Cleopatra."

I read the will as Antony closely watched me.

"This copy is for the Alexandrian archives, my dearest," he said.

I looked at Antony through tear-stained eyes. "I am deeply touched by this testament, Antony, for you identify yourself completely with my interests and it irrevocably links our destinies."

"When I am dead I do not want the Romans to burn me like garbage," he cried. "I want to be buried in your tomb so that I can lie beside you through the coming centuries. It has been a lonely grave for Alexander in the Sema without his beloved Hephaistrian, but I want my beloved Cleopatra, one of the most beautiful women who ever walked the earth, beside me. A copy of my will is being sent to Rome to be entrusted to the Vestal Virgins."

"If Octavian learns of your will," I said, "he will use it to outrage public opinion against you."

"The Vestal Virgins can be trusted to keep the will secret until my death."

"Oh, really, Antony, everyone knows that the Vestal Virgins are a coterie of harlots who would sell out their mothers for a copper denarius. I beg you not to send this will to Rome."

"Before I set out for Parthia my affairs must be in order," Antony said firmly. "I must leave nothing to chance."

It was a sun-splashed day in July when Antony departed. All of Alexandria turned out to bid him farewell as he boarded his flagship.

"I go forth to conquer new kingdoms to lay at your feet!" Antony cried as he kissed me in farewell.

It was Antony's intention to spend several months in Ephesus getting his army organized, and then in the spring he would march across the Euphrates and conquer Parthia. I planned to join him at the end of the year for a few months, bringing him gold and provisions.

A few months after Antony's departure, in early autumn, I received a letter from Ammonios which confirmed my worst fears regarding Antony's will. Ammonios wrote that Octavian went to the Temple of Vesta near the Forum, mounted the sacred steps with an escort of twelve lictors, and demanded Antony's will. The priestesses, clad in snow-white robes, made a show of resistance and indignation. They would rather die, they cried, than betray any confidence placed in them. Octavian insisted that in a case of service to one's country such scruples were ridiculous. After some persuasion, the will was handed over.

The next day Octavian read the will in the Senate to an astonished audience. Everyone disregarded the fact that a will is sacred, and that an outrage had been done to the Vestal Virgins. The will was proof of Antony's disloyalty and was the final weapon Octavian used to turn the Senate against Antony.

"The Sorceress of the Nile is the cause of all of Antony's demented follies," Octavian screamed to the senators. "This incestuous daughter of the depraved drunk, Ptolemy the Piper, dreams of destroying Rome and ruling our Republic with the assistance of her eunuchs and her Ethiopian slave lovers. This mad serpent has forced Antony to give up our richest provinces to her bastard children. But of all Antony's contemptible actions in his affair with this whore, his desire to be buried in Egypt is the most detestable. He is so faithless to Rome that he doesn't even want to be buried here!"

The wrath of the Senate reached a fever point, and the whole body stood and cursed me in a crescendo of fury. A vote was taken and war was declared on Egypt. Faithful to the tradition consecrated by his ancestors, Octavian repaired to the Temple of Bellona, trailed by the senators and a mob of citizens he collected on the way. Amid the acclamations of the stirred-up populace, Octavian threw a gold javelin whose point sank in the pedestal at the feet of the goddess, which placed the army under her divine protection.

"Tomorrow we will destroy Cleopatra herself," Octavian screamed frenziedly, "but today we will destroy her statue in my father's forum!"

The enraged citizens ran to the Julian Forum, and tore down my statue which Caesar had erected during my stay in Rome. This beautiful work of art by Archesilaus was broken to bits by the crazed mob.

The war was directed against the foreign foe, Cleopatra of Egypt, but of Antony there was no mention. Octavian had no desire to ask the people to do battle against one who had been their favorite, while he knew that the project of destroying the Egyptian harlot would be hailed with delight. Stories were spread about my riches, the soldiers were excited with visions of the booty which awaited them, and were all eager to loot my palace.

When Antony received the declaration of war in Ephesus, he realized that the Parthian campaign would have to be postponed. I had suspected all along that Octavian would never allow Antony the chance to add the new gem of the Parthian conquest to his crown.

The two elected Roman consuls, Sosius and Domitius, who were Antony's supporters, were compelled by threats to quit Rome. They went to Ephesus, along with several senators, and joined Antony. An assembly was convened, and war was in turn declared upon Octavian.

All that autumn and winter military preparations went forth for the coming struggle. I gave orders for the cessation of public works that were being carried out in Egypt and deployed all my resources to wage war against Octavian.

At the beginning of the new year, I was prepared to sail to Ephesus with my fleet filled with war provisions.

I ordered Apollodorus to stay behind as the commander of Caesarion's bodyguard. This was the first time since I was ten years old that he would be parted from me, but there was no one I could trust to protect Caesarion more ably. Apollodorus protested, but then concurred, knowing where his duty lay. All my children were being left behind in the palace under the care of their foster parents. I would sorely miss them, and only the gods knew how long I would be gone, but I was determined not to leave Antony's side until my golden goals had been attained.

Caesarion passionately protested being left behind. "I want to go with you, Mother," he pleaded.

"You are only fourteen, my son," I said sternly. "You must stay here and complete your studies."

"Octavian has declared war against you, Mother," Caesarion cried, "but it is against me that this war will be fought, not you or Antony or Egypt, but me!"

"Yes, my Pharaoh," I cried. "In Rome there is an upstart calling himself Caius Octavian Julius Caesar. He has the name and the titles which are rightfully yours. There cannot be two Caesars in the world, just as there cannot be two suns in the sky. When I return to Egypt, you will be the only Caesar walking the earth."

"Then I should be there in the battle with a sword in my hand," Caesarion cried, his young face glowing.

"Your duty is to stay here and be Pharaoh!" I said fervently. "We cannot both be gone from our people."

As soon as the seas were calm in early March, I left Alexandria. My four children and chief councillors came on board my flagship, the *Antonaid,* to bid me an emotional farewell. Caesarion, beside his friend Andronicus, stood tall and straight, but there were tears in his eyes.

"Oh, my golden prince, you are Caesar's flesh and blood," I cried, embracing him. "I leave to pave the way for your future when you will be emperor of the world."

"I will pray to the gods every day to watch over you until you return, Mother!" Caesarion cried.

To the sound of trumpets and cheers from my people, I sailed out of the Great Harbor, standing on deck with Charmion and Iras beside me. The *Antonaid* sailed past Pharos and out into the shimmering blue sea, and

I did not leave the deck until the white marble domes of Alexandria were swallowed up by the horizon.

My fleet, loaded with gold, munitions, and food, sailed by the emerald isles of the Ionian coast, all associated with famous men—Chios the birthplace of Homer, Samos where Pythagoras lived, and Kos where Hippocrates had his school of medicine. At last I sailed into the harbor of the great city of Ephesus and dropped anchor.

Antony rushed on board and we embraced with tenderness.

"There's been an aching emptiness in my heart these eight months since I last saw you," Antony cried.

I was thrilled to be in the city which has always played an important role in Hellenistic history. A cavalcade, led by Antony, took me from the harbor up the main colonnaded boulevard to the old palace. There was a lavish banquet in the great hall that evening, where I met several of Antony's officers and all the local dignitaries.

Antony and I were overjoyed at being together again. The following day he took me to visit the Artemision, and I marvelled at the huge marble temple surrounded by columns, the roof lined with effigies of the gods, and the great statue of the goddess.

"I see why this temple ranks, along with Pharos, as one of the seven wonders of the world," I remarked.

As a sedan bore us away from the temple, I tried not to think that it had been there that my sister Princess Arsinoë had met her tragic end.

The Greek youth, Eros, confided to me that before my arrival, Antony had been deep in his cups, falling into bed in a drunken state each night. Now that I was with him he drank less, but I knew if I left him he would lose himself in a lethargy of loose discipline again.

I was tortured by the canker of jealousy, and it was a source of grating misery that Antony still had a Roman wife.

"According to Roman law you are still married to Octavia," I told Antony, "She is the rope that ties you to Octavian, and that rope must be cut or it will strangle you."

"I will send Octavia a bill of divorcement," Antony decided.

The bill of divorcement was sent off to Octavia. Her brother insisted that she leave Antony's house, and he issued a proclamation saying that Antony ordered her to do so. This was an outrageous lie, since Antony had no objections to Octavia's keeping the townhouse. Octavia played into her brother's hands and made a great show of leaving the house with all her children, and Octavian made sure a crowd witnessed the event. This further excited the people against Antony, since it was looked upon as an act of humiliation to one of their noblest matrons on account of a foreign adventuress who hoped to bring Rome under her yoke.

My reunion with Antony in Ephesus was all sweet harmony for a few weeks, and then I perceived that the camp was rent by a conflict owing to my presence. The four hundred senators gathered in Ephesus, all enemies of Octavian, wanted me to return to Egypt now that I had delivered the war chest. Domitius Ahenobarbus, who addressed me with characteristic rudeness by name rather than my title, kept urging Antony to have me sent away.

There was much talk about regaining the Republic from the Dictator Octavian, which was an absurd notion since Antony and I were committed to establishing the monarchy of Rome over the world. I saw the dangers of my position, and I realized I could not leave Antony's side. Where he went, I would go, and he would plan no undertaking without my consent.

"I am fighting for your sake, dear wife, preparing for our future victory," Antony cried zealously, "but I will be able to accomplish our ends better without your presence. The army cannot be encumbered by a royal entourage. In Egypt you can await peacefully the event of this campaign. Your duty is to manage your kingdom, and I will manage this war."

"Never will I leave your side, Antony!" I cried fiercely. "You will sink to ruin without me and you know it."

"I am the laughingstock of my soldiers!" Antony bellowed desperately. "There are jokes being bandied about at my expense, saying that I am a soldier sold into slavery to a woman, that I stoop to serve her councillors who have no testicles!"

"Your Romans hate me, but they love my gold," I retorted. "I have learned from the past never to trust your inconstant nature again. I would put a dagger into my heart before I would go back to Egypt. If I were to leave you, they would reconcile you with Octavian again. They say you are my besotted slave, but they want to make you instead the slave of Octavian and his sister. I've been used by Caesar and you before, but I'll not be used and thrown aside again. If I return to Egypt, all my gold and ships go with me. It is my wealth which is paying for this war. I hold firm to the resolution that, whatever happens, nothing shall separate us. I shall be at your side when Octavian is defeated, and sail with your conquering army for the throne that awaits us in Rome."

By all the strategic feminine resources, tears and threats, I sought to remain in the camp. All the vassal kings, who were bringing their armies to Antony, threatened that if I were to withdraw, they would withdraw. They were fighting this war under my call, for they saw the war as a revolt against Roman oppression led by Hellenistic monarchs.

At length, by lavish use of gold, I won several of Antony's friends to my side, among them Publius Canidius, who made a stirring speech in my behalf to the four hundred senators.

"Fellow Romans," Canidius cried, "it is not just to remove from the scene of action a great princess who has furnished us with considerable aid. To me, the brilliant and beautiful Queen Cleopatra does not seem less prudent than any of the kings fighting under the banner of our Autocrator, since she has long governed a mighty empire, unaided and alone."

This speech was effective and opposition against me

ceased. I believe Antony was secretly relieved that I would stay, since he relied on my personal warmth and political sagacity.

"No man or woman will ever love you as much as I do, Antony," I told him passionately. "And no creature will ever be as devoted and as trustworthy. Your closest friends, lovers, and allies all could possibly betray you, but I never shall, and you know that in your heart."

"Yes, my love, I know that," Antony said in a melting voice.

As the weeks went by, Antony assembled a great army at Ephesus. There was a gathering of many kings and tetrarchs of allied countries who arrived with their ranks. These eastern rulers, who had long suffered under the Roman bondage, were intent on the overthrow of Rome and the establishment of the supremacy of the east.

On the fields outside Ephesus, Antony and I reviewed our great army.

"Remember, Antony," I pointed out with pride, "you may be the leader of your Roman legions, but I lead the eastern kings and their soldiers who form three quarters of our host."

"I remember it well, for it was I who made you Queen of Kings," Antony cried. "It gives me pleasure to see that you relish your role of a warlike Egeria, my love."

After the final preparations were made, Antony and I felt the time ripe for a celebration in the anticipation of victory. As spring broke, we sailed to the small, beautiful isle of Samos. The first glimpse of this gem of an island took my breath away, with its lush greenery, forests of pine, cypress, olive groves, and vineyards, and white villas dotting the shoreline. Our fleet anchored in the crescent-shaped bay, and Rhoemetacles, Tyrant of Samos, met us with a show of fanfare. Antony and I were installed in a lovely villa, built in the Roman style, which stands at the edge of the sea overlooking the bay.

Samos had never seen such a cortege of kings, crowned with tiaras and clad in exotic, embroidered robes, as those who accompanied us. The members of our entourage spent days and nights in revelry. Antony and I were anxious that our supporters should have no opportunity for remarking any disquieting signs on the political horizon, and we wished the princes of the east to believe that we were perfectly sure of victory.

While the fate of empires and the world hung in the balance, the small island resounded to music. A drama and musical festival was held, and troupes of comedians, musicians, dancers, singers, clowns, and acrobats entertained. Several cities sent oxen for sacrifice, and our allied kings ceremoniously took oaths of allegiance to Antony and myself.

"Divine Queen and Mighty Autocrator," Adallas of Thrace cried one night at a banquet, "what kind of a gesture will you make in your triumph, when your very preparations for war are so splendid?"

"Victory will crown that glorious day with equalled splendor," Antony replied.

"This war will be a turning point in history," King Tarcondemus cried. "The last great war the world will know."

"Nonsense, my dear Tarcondemus," I said scoffingly. "As long as the world exists, there will be wars!"

The Tyrant Rhoemetacles escorted me to the Temple of Diana, and as I admired the statue of the goddess, he offered it to me as a present, but of course I declined. Let it not be said that Cleopatra visited Samos and left with its greatest treasure.

One day Antony and I, with a small party, went to a cove set beween rocky promontories and swam naked in the pellucid water. Swimming in this tiny, private harbor on Samos is one of the loveliest memories that glow in my mind.

A hundred thousand soldiers were under our command, and our legions lay scattered at various garrisons across Asia Minor and Greece. It was decided that we would sail to Athens and from there direct operations for the coming war.

In a sanguine mood, we left Samos the middle of May. It was a glorious experience to sail across the azure, foam-crested Aegean, passing thousands of small isles, that in the words of Homer are "like shields lying on the face of the sea." Above the sea stretched the noble arch of the heavens with its dazzling sparkle of sky.

Dawn was breaking as we sailed into the Bay of Pireaus. The sun had just pushed above the long ridge of mountains, sending a slanting red bar of light across the Attic plain and touching the slopes with livid fire. As Greece loomed before me for the first time, I was wonder-struck by the natural beauty of land and sea and sky.

As we disembarked onto the marble harbor, which was teeming with mariners busily lading and unlading vessels, we were met by a great delegation headed by Antony's cousin, Antoninus, who was Proconsul of Greece, and a host of distinguished Athenian personages.

"We welcome you as a Greek princess to the land of your forefathers," Nicharchus, an Athenian elder, addressed me.

"It has been my dream since childhood to visit Athens, the greatest of Greek cities," I cried, "for Athens has given the world a radiance of wisdom which will never be equalled."

Knowing that these sons of Themistocles respected military pomp, Antony made his entrance into Athens on horseback leading a contingent of marching soldiers. A cortege of litters conveyed me and my suite from the harbor town to Athens. We took the direct road, four miles long, leading between towering ramparts of the Long Walls, two mighty barriers running parallel from the sea to the city proper.

The Athenians knew me by reputation and were eager to see me, and they lined the road and threw flowers on my litter as I passed along.

It was sunset as we entered the city gates, and I saw for the first time the hill of a steep, colossal rock, its shape an irregular oval, a thousand feet long and four hundred feet high, rising from the Attic plain, forming undoubtedly the most famous site the world will ever know, the Acropolis. The vision of ruddy lights of sunset, touching the red crags of the hill, and the pink, gold, and white-tinted marble buildings of the lofty temple was a breathtaking sight.

We were conducted through narrow, crooked and ill-paved streets, and it was dark when we finally reached the ancient palace of the Archons, a somewhat dilapidated dwelling standing close to the foot of the Acropolis.

The very next morning, with Antony, Iras, and Charmion, I went on foot up the hill to the venerated sanctuary of the Acropolis. With a surge of joy I traversed the ancient sacred marble stones, marvelled at the temples, and contemplated the sights with respectful admiration. Although Athens had been damaged by Sulla's troops, the monuments of the Acropolis are undisturbed, for no profane hand has touched the pure glory of the Parthenon; the Poecile still holds her brilliant decorations, fresh as the day they were completed four centuries ago.

"Now you can see for yourself," Antony cried, "that your beloved Alexandria is indeed the daughter of Athens."

Standing on the Acropolis, I looked out over the city in every direction, drinking in the beauty before me.

"I can see why this land, even if it were not the seat of a famous race, would still be known as one of the most beautiful spots in the world," I cried. "I understand why Greece, with its colors and contours, has long formed a glorious model for the sculptor and painter, and one perpetual inspiration for the poet."

With a feeling of joy, I settled down in Athens, the mother city of civilization. I was thirty-seven years old, but using the beauty the gods blessed me with, and exercising all my charm, I had little difficulty in winning friends in a country where Romans are hated. The people escorted my litter through the streets, bearing laurel branches by day, throwing flowers on my path everywhere I went, carrying torches to light my way at night, and singing songs beneath my windows.

Nicharchus, a philosopher and orator, a man of charm and noble character, well advanced in years, was often at my side during those days. We frequently dined together and discoursed on the works of Homer, the wisdom of Plato, and other topics.

"We Greeks are accustomed to foreign rule and no longer hate our conquerors," Nicharchus told me bluntly one evening. "Indeed, we love Antony, who is as handsome as Alcibiades and comparable to Themistocles in his warlike virtues. Since we Greeks count strength and beauty as the highest gifts the gods can bestow, this son of Mars has won all our hearts. As for you, Great Queen, every peddler in the bazaar knows that you are a Greek princess, a flowering sprig from the same royal family tree as Alexander."

"My Greek heart is warmed by your words, my noble Nicharchus," I said, taking an indolent sip of wine. "But did not the Athenians pay every hospitality to the Lady Octavia while she sat at Antony's side when he administered the eastern provinces from this city?"

I gazed calmly on the old man's wrinkled face, seeing he was embarrassed at the turn of the conversation.

"It was only seven years ago, Nicharchus," I ventured softly. "You do remember the Lady Octavia, don't you?"

"The Lady Octavia left little impression on our minds, Divine Majesty!" Nicharchus said with a dismissive jerking of a palsied hand. "She was a cold, matronly lady who lacked charm and grace, and we Athenians, who worship beauty, did not take to her." His old eyes blazed merrily. "Ah, but you have won every Athenian heart from the moment you stepped on the land of the Hellenes."

Touched by these words, I immediately summoned Charmion to bring me a casket of rings.

"As a mark of my affection, select one, my beloved friend," I said, holding out the gold casket.

Nicharchus peered into the casket and after some deliberation took a gold ring with a small ruby.

"No, no, that one is too small and flawed," I cried, selecting a ring with a huge, priceless, flawless ruby. "Here, this one is much nicer, noble friend."

Nicharchus took the ring, his face flushing happily as he murmured his thanks.

The Athenians naturally paid me more honors than they had paid Octavia during her stay in the city. My statue, dressed in the robes of Isis, was set up upon the Acropolis beside Antony's, and coins were minted bearing my profile. As for Antony, he had always been a favorite in Athens, and they included him among their gods and placed his statue in the Temple of Dionysus.

Meanwhile, it was evident from reports that Octavian was in a bad way in Italy since his military preparations were not complete. He lacked money and was compelled to levy a heavy tax, which elicited grave discontent, and insurrections erupted all over the country.

As the summer equinox came, I was impatient to wage battle.

"I do not think we should temporize, Antony," I cried. "Athenagoras says that the stars and signs are propitious for us to strike this year, but next year will not be so favorable. We must forestall Octavian, assemble our armies, invade Italy, and demolish Octavian now."

"A battle lasts but a few hours, my sweet dove," Antony said condescendingly, "but preparation and strategy take months if victory is to be achieved."

"It is stupid to defer our attack and allow Octavian time to repress the mutinies and to complete his preparations," I cried. "We must be aware of the crucial importance of timing. Opportunities cannot be hoarded like gold. Once lost they are irretrievable. If you invade Italy now you will find the people on your side, for there are riots because of the taxation. We must strike now while Octavian is weak."

"I will go to Italy with my triumph sealed after the battle has been won, and it must be an honorable battle," Antony replied. "Let it not be written by the historians that Mark Antony struck down a foe who had no sword in his hand. I will not invade the motherland and have the native soil stained with the blood of my brothers. The question between Antony and Octavian will be decided in Greece, as it was between Caesar and Pompey and between Antony and Brutus. I have been lucky in the land of your forebears, for do not forget that sixteen years ago I commanded Caesar's right flank at Pharsalia to great victory, and then ten years ago I won at Philippi. My lucky star shines over Greece."

I settled down to a long stay in Athens. I provided for the maintenance of the motley crowd that made up our court, giving banquets and entertainments to divert our entourage until the war should come to a head.

As my court was not so sumptuously equipped as at Alexandria, I endeavored to make up for what was lacking in comfort by a gracious manner, but I did not succeed in satisfying all the senators and knights with us, accustomed as they were to every luxury. If Antony had led his adherents straight to battle, they would have endured in silence all the privations of war. I have never been a glutton, and Antony, too, can eat the simplest food, but our officers never ceased complaining that there were no peacock brains or nightingale tongues served and that the wine was bad.

The nightly banquets were a strain for me. I remember one evening in late summer, when the wine, inferior as it might have been, was circulating freely. Adallas of Thrace was sitting with Antony and I at the table on the dais. A handsome Athenian boy served us, and Adallas, an earthy man, eyed him lewdly and made an obscene remark, provoking laughter.

"Adallas," I cried out, "surely you recall that master of tragedy, Sophocles, who shared your tastes. He once went with Pericles on a campaign for the subjugation of Samos. One day Sophocles made a lascivious remark about the beauty of a young Samian, and Pericles chided him, saying that a commander and a writer must always strive to keep not only his hands but also his mind pure."

"Oh, Queen Cleopatra," Adallas cried in his husky, robust voice, "my mind never pays any attention to what my hands do, or any other part of my body for that matter!"

There was a general outburst of laughter, which quickly faded as my guests resumed their disgruntled moods. Looking over the glowering faces before me, I noticed Geminius, a young senator recently arrived from Rome, who I suspected was Octavian's spy. He was at a couch in the back of the hall. I whispered to Antony to ask Geminius what had brought him to Athens, and Antony complied.

"Matters of great importance, my Lord Antony, which require a sober head, and we have both drunk too much tonight," Geminius cried in a harsh voice. "However, one thing I'll say, drunk or sober, that all will be fine if only Cleopatra would return to Egypt!"

Antony's face flushed crimson. "How dare you speak such impudence before my wife!" he sputtered furiously.

"Well done, Geminius," I interceded in my calmest, clearest tone, my voice carrying over the stunned whispers. "You have told us your secret without being put to the rack."

Dellius, who had long exhibited hostility for me, was sitting on a couch near Geminius. "I have kept a sober head myself because I'd rather drink water than foul brew," he replied, "but I daresay that back in Rome old Sarmentus is drinking the best Falernian!"

There were astonished murmurs and titters at this aspersion made to wound me, for everyone in the hall knew that Sarmentus had been one of Caesar's favorite boyfriends in his youth.

The Festival of Adonis was celebrated in early September, and Antony and I presided over the competitions held on the Pnyx. It was with joy that I saw that Greek youths were still faithful to the tradition of keeping a sound mind in a healthy body. I was dazzled by feats of fencing, wrestling and discus and javelin throwing. Surrounded by distinguished Athenians, we awarded prizes of laurel wreaths and gold lockets to the winners.

All that summer and into the autumn our troops were on the march, slowly advancing toward the shores of the Adriatic, congregating at various strategic locations at our chain of fortified stations. We had garrisons on the islands of Leukas and Crete and in Cyrene, and several legions were stationed near the Gulf of Ambracia. Our greatest force was concentrated on the Peloponnesus, at Methone under the command of King Bocchus of Mauretania, and at an encampment outside the city of Patrae.

As time went on, I realized that Octavian's prospects were becoming brighter. He had won to his side the soldiers who had mutinied as well as quelling the disturbances that had broken out in consequence of the tax, for once the people paid, they thought of it no longer. He had eighty thousand soldiers in his camp in Brandisium. By late summer, Agrippa sailed from Sicily with his fleet and dropped anchor before Brandisium, ready to transport the legions across the Ionian sea to Greece.

"We can no longer halt the march of history, Antony," I said one day in early October as we sat at a table studying reports of military maneuvers in Italy.

"Yes," Antony agreed, taking a deep breath. "We must break up our court here in Athens and sail to our garrison at Patrae."

I watched silently as Antony nervously drank from a wine goblet. "Perhaps you should do as many of your supporters suggest," I said calmly, "and go without me."

An expression of fear flickered across his face.

"It is one thing for me to be at your court in Athens, but another to be in your armed camp," I resumed. "Perhaps my presence would be a drawback to your cause, for there is no place for a woman in military operations. I could return to Egypt, for it's been a year since I've been gone from my kingdom. Egypt, my people, Caesarion, our children, they all need me."

653

"I need you!" Antony protested in a strangled voice, a hand stretching across the table toward me.

Smiling tenderly, I took his hand in mine.

"We must stay together and stand together," Antony cried. "To defeat or to victory."

"To victory!" I cried passionately.

I watched as Antony drained his wine goblet, and I realized that he needed me as much as he needed wine.

On a crisp, bright October day, after five months in Athens, we left Piraeus. The harbor was lined with people cheering us in farewell. We sailed around the Peloponnesus, and after a week's voyage arrived. We anchored the *Antonaid* in the Bay of Patrae, and then made our entrance into the city, which has risen to great importance since Rome's destruction of Corinth a century ago.

Several of our legions were encamped on the outskirts of Patrae, and the next day we reviewed our troops. On a field that stretched from the coast to a mountain range, there lay scattered thousands of tents that lodged our soldiers. A pavilion of regal dimensions, consisting of several connecting tents, housed Antony and me and our suite.

I was bedazzled by the beauty of the place. Every evening it was my greatest joy to stand outside my pavilion, which was pitched near the edge of the sea beside a small craggy peninsula and a lovely pebbled beach. I would watch the sunsets, the sun slowly sinking below the horizon, the ravishing rays of Ra flaming and turning the sea and sky the color of blood red.

Across the narrow strip of the Ionian sea, on the southeast coast of Italy, I knew that Octavian waited with his legions. The hour of the decisive battle was near at hand, when a battle for the world would be fought. It seemed I had lived all my life for that day, a day I knew would settle not only my fate, but the fate of the world for centuries to come.

CHAPTER IX

MANY MENACING PORTENTS arose that winter which filled me with acute distress. First of all, there was the great earthquake that shook the whole eastern shores of the Mediterranean from Greece to the coasts of Asia about a month after I arrived in Patrae. I was in my tent in midmorning, lying on a lionskin-covered couch, surrounded by burning braziers to ward off the cold. I was dictating dispatches to be sent back to Egypt, when suddenly the ground began trembling violently, shaking the tent. Iras and Charmion screamed hysterically, but I remained calm with self-possession. After a few minutes, thanks to the gods, the earth mercifully ceased vibrating and all danger passed.

I was soon to learn that other cities were not so lucky as Patrae. Several Phoenician towns were destroyed that November day, and Pisaurum, a colony which Antony had founded with retired soldiers on the Adriatic, was swallowed up into the earth.

"All the world will believe this earthquake to be the wrath of the gods against me!" Antony cried balefully.

Other ominous occurrences, each happening quickly upon the other, followed and soon reached our ears. On the day we sailed from Piraeus, that night a thunderstorm broke over Athens and a violent whirlwind threw down the colossal statue of Antony that stood on the Acropolis. From Italy a rumor came that Antony's statue in Alba was covered with moisture for many days, which reappeared in spite of its being frequently wiped. Then a nest of swallows in the rigging of our flagship, which was berthed in the Bay of Patrae, were

655

attacked by an eagle and driven off. A few days after this, during a torrential storm, lightning struck the Temple of Hercules near the city gates, knocking down the statue of Hercules.

"I am descended from Hercules!" Antony growled despairingly. "This will surely be interpreted by my soldiers as proof that the heavenly powers have turned from me."

"How ridiculous!" I said scoffingly. "Omens can be interpreted many ways and they are frequently misinterpreted by evil-doers with malicious intent. You're still the greatest and most beloved figure in the world. Your very name is a synonym for courage and victory, and there is no doubt that your progress to the summit of mortal ambition will be achieved. I have great confidence in your destiny, and I believe that the gods, as well as your men, will obey your wishes."

A hopeless terror took possession of the camp at these ill omens, and depression spread throughout our ranks. Antony became overwhelmed with despair, worried to the point of frenzy, and drank heavily.

It was at Patrae that the first desertions began. Marcus Silanus, who had followed Antony in all his previous campaigns, absconded.

"I can no longer endure the caprices of Caesar's widow and her insolent usage of me," Silanus wrote Antony in a letter left behind.

It annoyed me to be used as an excuse for this defection, since I had always been agreeable to Silanus.

Winter set in with rain, gusty winds, and severe cold. Each evening, in our pavilion, Antony and I gave a banquet for our officers and vassal kings. The table put forth was even less appetizing than had been given at Athens, and there was much murmuring and discontent. Although the repast was poor, the entertainment was not. I had dancers, acrobats, mimes, and singers performing nightly, but these diversions did not dissipate the dour spirits which prevailed.

I was popular with the vassal kings, but Antony's Roman supporters continued to detest me. Reports came in from Rome of the growing hatred of me, nurtured by ridiculous tales of my vices and cruelties, which Octavian's hack poets fabricated in salacious verses to blacken my name and to stir up the people against me.

All military decisions were made by Antony, but we discussed all operations at length.

"I think we should send three hundred of our best ships from the fleet up the coast and anchor them in the Gulf of Ambracia," Antony said. "The gulf is a natural harbor, an inlet of the sea, and will provide excellent winter quarters for the ships."

"Where exactly is the gulf?" I inquired.

"It's just off the sea on the coast near the town of Actium."

I consulted a map, and with a finger Antony pointed to Actium and the Gulf of Ambracia.

"Very well, Antony," I agreed with a nod.

The ships were sent up to Actium. A strong garrison was placed on the southern entrance of the Ambracian Gulf, and during that winter our legions deployed there were eventually to constitute our greatest force. I was happy about this, since such a force protected my cherished fleet.

All that winter I wondered what course of action Octavian would adopt. It was my tremendous fear that he would send a strong expedition eastward to launch an attack on Egypt and kill Caesarion and my other children. We had a strong fleet around Crete to intercept such a maneuver. It was the widespread belief, however, that when spring came, Octavian would cross over to Greece and the two armies would pitch battle at an agreed location.

In the early days of March, a messenger arrived with the startling tidings that Agrippa, with part of Octavian's fleet, had sailed across the Ionian sea to Greece and had attacked our station at Methone. The garrison had fallen, and King Bocchus of Mauretania and the troops he commanded were massacred.

A few days later, the city state of Sparta came into Octavian's orbit. The Spartan leader, Eurycles, declared himself for Octavian. Needless to say, the loss of a strategic harbor fortress and the defection of one of the leading cities on the Peloponnesus came as a shock.

As April came and the seas calmed with the advent of spring, Octavian crossed the sea and descended in full force upon our garrison on the isle of Corfu, which surrendered without battle. Octavian then sailed to Actium and landed eighty thousand men on the mainland opposite our garrison at Actium.

With a bustle of activity, we broke camp at Patrae, and at the end of April, we sailed on the *Antonaid,* leading northward a hundred ships filled with our attendant kings, princes, generals, and legions.

The sea was placid as we sailed out of the Bay of Patrae, but on the second day of the voyage dark clouds obscured the spring sun, and boisterous winds played havoc with our fleet. Antony, Iras, and Charmion became sick with the relentless rolling of the sea and the perpetual motion of the vessel, but I am a good mariner and rough seas do not affect me. After a week we finally arrived at Actium, miraculously escaping the perils of the stormy passage.

Our flagship, the *Antonaid,* with a sail ripped from a mast, sailed past Actium point, entered the narrow mouth and glided into the shimmering peacock-blue Gulf of Ambracia. Our garrison was stationed on the southern side of the gulf, and Octavian and his army had fortified a position on the northern peninsula of Actium, upon high ground known as the Ladle.

I was overjoyed to see before me the three hundred brassbound warships of my Egyptian fleet, like floating citadels with their high towers, riding at anchor along the gulf's southern shore.

Later in the afternoon we went ashore. Antony, holding my hand, helped me disembark.

"You have stepped on Macedonian soil, the land of your forefathers!" Antony cried jubilantly.

I sank to my knees, and bending over, kissed the Macedonian earth. The soldiers about me, many of them Macedonians, cheered me heartily and my blood raced. I felt that on the terrain of my ancestors, twenty generations of kings, my destiny would be fulfilled and the position I had been denied by Caesar's murder would be mine through Antony's victory.

Accompanied by Iras and Charmion, I climbed the green hill above our camp to the little marble Temple of Apollo where a beautiful golden statue of Apollo stands nearby looking out over the sea. The priests greeted me and took me inside, and I said prayers and made sacrifice.

Antony and I slept on the *Antonaid* a few nights until the royal pavilion was pitched near the temple. Thousands of smaller tents were put up to lodge our legions on the plains that stretched for five miles from the gulf to the foot of the Othrys mountains. The peak of the towering Pindus was still covered with snow. On the opposite side of the Ambracian channel, I could see the tents of Octavian's soldiers. The two armies confronted one another across the blue water.

A few days after our arrival at Actium, I was awakened early in the morning by excited cries from soldiers. My serving girls threw a robe around me and I ran outside the pavilion. I stood on the hill, and with a glance, I could see that during the night, Agrippa had arrived with a fleet of four hundred ships which now lay at anchor on the sea at the mouth of the gulf. My heart stopped, for it was plain that my fleet was bottled up inside the Gulf of Ambracia.

I went to Antony in a highly distraught state. "I thought the gulf would be a refuge for my ships, but instead it has become a prison," I cried.

"It doesn't matter, my love," Antony said with a shrug. "Our armies will move inland to an agreed spot, and the battle will be fought there."

To my consternation, I learned that Agrippa, following his victory at Methone, had sailed to the island of Leukas, where our troops, following the example of Corfu, surrendered without a fight. And now Agrippa had arrived at Actium to blockade my fleet.

My head was spinning at this series of misfortunes.

Methone, Sparta, Corfu, Leukas! Circumstances were no longer in our favor, and it seemed the tide was turning against us. Antony was mortified by these setbacks, and each day left him more despondent.

It had been a severe winter and our ships had deteriorated at their moorings in the gulf. Ships and sailors rot in harbor, as the old Phoenicians used to say. Our crews were not in good shape, for there had been an epidemic which had taken a heavy toll of lives.

I was naturally chagrined at these developments. I could not excuse Antony's poor generalship, for he should have invaded Italy the previous summer, when he would have defeated Octavian with ease. Having failed to do so, he had left our fleet to rot in the gulf. He had frittered the summer away at Athens and the winter at Patrae in drinking bouts and procrastinations and quarrels.

"I assure you, my little Greek love, the situation is not serious," Antony cried, mustering his bravado. "I still outnumber Octavian by twenty thousand men, and in a land battle my soldiers shall triumph."

As the winter had been unusually severe for Greece, so now the spring became unusually warm. It seemed Octavian was not so anxious to pitch battle. Morning after morning, Antony and Octavian drew up their respective armies on either side of the gulf, surveying one another in hostile silence, the soldiers sweating under their armor with the blazing sun.

Antony sent emissaries to Octavian, asking him where he wished the battle to be fought, saying that Octavian could choose the ground. Octavian, however, remained silent and did not even give the courtesy of a reply.

The month of June came, marking five weeks of the stalemate.

"I shall send Octavian an offer that this matter be settled in single combat between the two of us," Antony announced.

"What an irrational proposal, Antony," I said impatiently. "Twenty years older and dead drunk, and you could still cut the cowardly, puny Octavian to pieces, so naturally he will refuse. Let us speak of the real world."

"I've sent him proposals that our armies move inland and meet at Pharsalia and the issue be decided there, but he only ignores my letters," Antony said glumly.

"Yes, Octavian refuses," I said bleakly, bitterly. "I see it all very clearly now. Octavian does not wish to fight a land battle because he knows he would lose, and he does not wish to fight a sea battle, either. We are locked inside the gulf and are short of provisions. We have a hundred thousand mouths to feed and every day it's more difficult to find food. Agrippa's fleet has us cut off from all communications in the Mediterranean, and we're threatened by famine, while Octavian is getting supplies from Italy without delay." I paused for a deep sigh. "No, Octavian wishes to fight no battle at all. He is winning by doing nothing."

There was a lull while Antony avoided my eyes, refilling his goblet with spiced wine.

I stiffened with a stern look. "Last summer you said you did not want to go down in history as the man who vanquished a foe who had no sword. Well, your noble adversary is not as honorable as you. If you had invaded Italy last summer as I begged you to do, we would be emperor and empress of the world today."

"Never doubt that we will have ultimate victory!" Antony bellowed. "I will force Octavian to battle."

"Then you must act!" I rejoined fiercely. "You're sulking in your tent like Achilles at the siege of Troy. Do something!"

The following day, Antony led a detachment of soldiers around the gulf and made an attack on the Ladle, but Octavian's defenses repelled the assault. At this point Antony could have cut off the enemy's water supply, which was obtained from the river Charadrus, but he decided that would not be an honorable thing to do.

"You seem intent on being honorable, even if you must lose this war by being so," I told Antony mockingly.

It was the hottest summer in any living man's memory. I had frozen at Patrae, and I was roasting at Actium. I longed for my beloved Alexandria, where the weather is temperate the year long. I missed the devotion of Caesarion and the buoyant spirits of the twins and little Ptolemy and was fearful that the tidings of our reversals would reach Egypt and arouse the people to insurrection. I could only pray to the gods that Mardian, Apollodorus, and Athenion had a firm grip on Egypt during my absence.

The torrid summer sun shone over Actium, melting the snow on top of Pindus and heating up the marshy flats at the edge of our camp. The warm marshes bred swarms of mosquitoes which tormented the soldiers, and even I, a divine goddess-Queen, was not immune to their sting. An outbreak of marsh fever claimed many lives.

The drowsy days dragged by, and the deadlock was trying on everyone's nerves. Our encampment on the southern promontory of Actium was a hotbed of discontent, crowded with a dozen vassal kings, hundreds of eunuchs and slaves, entertainers and camp followers, a contingent of senators, military commanders, and a hundred thousand soldiers from a score of nations, all herded together and treading on one another's feet. There were arguments over the distribution of food, and squabbling about precedence in being invited to the royal pavilion. Each evening Antony and I presided over a banquet with a hundred guests crowded into our tent, and invariably excitable debates ensued about what measures to adopt.

Whatever suggestions were offered were of no avail, however, since Octavian had no thought of bestirring himself other than to make his defenses more secure. Only a few small engagements, on land and by sea, broke the monotony of those stifling summer months. Octavian's fortified position on the Ladle remained unassailable, and he refused to be provoked into a pitched large-scale land battle.

Profound disharmony pervaded our camp. In Antony's mind there was a confusion of thought and misery. My disdainful attitude toward him only induced in him a greater dependence upon me, a dog-like devotion pitiful to behold. He was often drunk, and even when sober was overwrought and quarrelsome.

Desertions, like an epidemic, became more numerous every day. In order to restore discipline among his troops, Antony was compelled to administer martial law with rigor. The senator, Quintus Postumius, was caught one night with his bags in a boat ready to row himself across the gulf, and he was executed the following morning.

I was especially upset by the betrayal of the Arab Prince Zamblichus, who was caught sending a letter to Octavian by courier pigeon. Zamblichus had been with me during my exile in Syria and had been my friend for seventeen years. He had joined us at Ephesus, and during many a night at Samos, Athens, Patrae, and Actium, he had played chess with me in my pavilion into the dawning hours. I was fiercely fond of Zamblichus, but the evidence against him was irrefutable, and with sorrow and anger I agreed to his decapitation.

The camp was a nest of hate and intrigue. Other executions followed, and terror was widespread throughout our ranks. On the other hand, by all reports, harmony reigned in the encampment across the gulf.

Charmion stood by me with steadfast support and devotion, in her indomitable way, during all those weeks at Actium. Iras, however, with her fragile, high-strung nerves, was like a broken sparrow bereft of spirit. She never went outside, but stayed in her quarters within the pavilion, sipping poppy juice and plucking discordantly on a harp and singing tuneless songs.

Iras had always tended my hair, but this duty was now beyond her. My hair had been prematurely streaked with silver for years, but now under the stress of that Actium summer, I was turning white. Aspasia, one of my ladies, saw to it that my tresses were as golden as ever, thanks to the artful application of dyes. Although I had celebrated my thirty-eighth birthday the winter at Patrae, the graying of my hair was the only visible sign that the years had left a mark on me. I still had the lithe figure of a young girl, and the ravages of time and the struggles which had racked my heart, all the pain and accumulated history of innumerable sadnesses, had not left a wrinkle on my face.

The gloom and the loss of morale among our ranks intensified with each passing, stifling day. I endeavored to revive the spirits of those about me, but in vain. My witticisms, my puns, even my sarcastic barbs, were of no avail, and in spite of all my efforts I failed to restore any serenity to our camp.

I shared all the hardships and tribulations of the war and the dreary, crude life of our beleagured camp with Antony. During the day he was in the field, supervising his soldiers and their exercises with wooden swords and blunt weapons, keeping them in shape for the battle that never came.

Antony had lost his easygoing manner and his sense of humor, and I despaired at the state of his damaged nerves and his excessive drinking. Although a giant, Antony is a child at heart, and more dependent upon me than any of my children. Life with Antony has always been a series of stormy, emotional scenes. During those nights at Actium, after overwrought days, we always retired to our bedchamber in the pavilion, hung with gold tapestries and silk hangings, and we invariably released our tensions in ecstasy. Even during times of our severest antagonisms, there has always been that sharp, physical desire for each other. We love one another passionately, for the tie that binds us, the fleshly bond that habit has made stronger, is of the kind that rarely breaks or stales.

The end of summer came. No rain had fallen for weeks, and we were tormented by heat and mosquitoes. Now autumn was nigh and winter imminent. There was little food left, and once winter set in, it would be impossible to transport supplies over the mountains.

"We cannot go on like this, Antony," I cried. "We must bring matters to a head. I would rather die fighting than ignobly starve and freeze to death."

"You're right, my love," Antony said.

A council of war was called on a humid, hot morning in our pavilion. Antony and I sat together on a raised dais. Our vassal kings and generals reclined on couches before us, and slaves stood about swatting flies and passing wine. Antony opened the session by making a candid exposition of his anxieties, and asked our allies to advise us. A fierce debate commenced with many proposals put forth, with Canidius and most of the Romans favoring a land battle.

"I am a general and not an admiral," Antony said. "I would prefer to fight on land, and Queen Cleopatra is willing to abandon her fleet and retire with our armies into Macedonia. But would Octavian follow us and engage in a land battle, or would he raise anchor and sail his legions to Egypt? We all know what the outcome of that would be!"

"We will never abandon our Queen of Kings to such a possible fate!" King Adallas of Thrace cried fervently.

The vassal monarchs seconded this statement with hearty shouts, but the Roman officers gave only half-hearted murmurs.

"Since Octavian refuses to be lured into a land battle, we have no option but to break the blockade and fight a battle at sea," Antony direfully concluded.

We had a hundred thousand soldiers at the beginning of summer, but lost a fourth because of death and desertions. It was decided that out of our fleet, three hundred vessels would participate in the battle. Twenty-two thousand soldiers would be embarked on these ships, and the remaining forces would remain behind on land. If the sea battle went in our favor, the land force would then make an assault upon the Ladle.

All of Antony's Roman generals were hoping that the blockade could be broken so that I could sail through with my squadron and make my way to Egypt, and at last they would be rid of me. Although I had vowed never to leave Antony's side until we had achieved either defeat or victory, I came to the conclusion that, in the case of an indecisive sea battle, it would be best for our cause if I could return safely to Alexandria.

If there was to be a second battle on land, the Roman soldiers would be more willing to fight under Antony with me no longer being at his side. I could only hope that, in the moment of victory, Antony would not forget me.

With a furor of activity, preparations speedily went forth for the execution of the sea battle. All my private treasure, jewels and plate were carried down to my vessels. When Antony ordered the soldiers and archers to embark on the galleys, many of them were reluctant to obey. This was vividly demonstrated to us one evening as we returned from the Temple of Apollo after sacrificing a ram, when Marcus Atilius, a grizzled old centurion with many scars, accosted us.

"Great General, I have followed you all my life and fought several battles under you," Atilius cried.

"Yes, Marcus, so you have," Antony cried, clasping him affectionately.

"Twenty-five years ago I was beside you at the battle of Pelusium," Atilius said, and then looked at me. "Queen Cleopatra, that was the battle we fought for your father, King Ptolemy, so that he might regain his throne for you to inherit. You were but a little girl at the time. This scar on my left cheek is a souvenir from Pelusium."

"Yes, Marcus, and I thank you," I said warmly.

"Aye, and many battles and scars since!" Atilius cried, looking back to Antony. "Will you distrust these honest scars and rest your hopes on those rotten, wooden ships? Let the Egyptians and Phoenicians skirmish at sea, but give us the solid ground, the land of Macedonia, for it is there that we have learned to conquer or to die."

"We have no choice, my worthy soldier," Antony said, choked with emotion. "Octavian refuses to meet us on land; so pretend that the decks are as the land, and we will carry the day."

On the eve that the battle was scheduled to be fought,

we had an early banquet in our pavilion with our generals. While we were dining, a westerly gale suddenly blew up, and the pavilion swayed uneasily on its poles in the fierce wind. For four days the gale persisted, blowing around Actium, delaying the battle because it prevented our ships from leaving the gulf. It was an agonizing four days with the sound and fury of the wind, the waiting and the mounting tension which frayed everyone's nerves to the breaking point.

Domitius Ahenobarbus took advantage of the delay to desert us. Although old and sick, he rowed himself over in a small boat during the night across the choppy waters of the channel. Antony, although grieved, put a good face on this betrayal, and the next morning good-naturedly sent after the traitor his bags and servants.

Quintus Dellius also profited by the delay to pass over to the enemy camp.

"I can no longer put up with the ill-treatment from Cleopatra," Dellius wrote in a letter left for Antony. "I have it on very good authority that she who is Isis on Earth has designs upon my life because of a passing remark I made about the wine she served."

Although it had been Dellius who had coaxed me to go meet Antony at Tarsus ten years before, we had long since fallen out. I had come to detest him, and his defection did not surprise me.

"Do not doubt, Antony," I said grimly, "that your false friend Dellius, contemptible creature that he is, will not be content with deserting you at the supreme moment of your life, but will be seeking his new master's favor by betraying all our battle plans."

"You have turned all my friends against me!" Antony screamed reproachfully.

"Once this storm lets up, break the blockade and you will be rid of me forever!" I rejoined bitterly.

One of our tempestuous scenes ensued, but as usual it was quickly over with, once our emotions were spent.

In the early evening of September the first, the gale stopped and the weather cleared. The swell subsided

667

and the sea became calm again, and there was not a whisper of wind in the air.

"Tomorrow we will wage battle," Antony announced.

After the pigs and rams were roasted over pits, and the soldiers ate a hearty meal and sat around the campfires, Antony went around to the various groups and made stirring speeches to them.

"I've achieved countless victories on land," he cried. "The sea is a new element for my war spirit, but I trust that Neptune will smile upon me. Do not think I am a victim of the Dionysian wine, for I am at the acme of my powers, whereas Octavian is a physical weakling and a coward who has never fought a battle in his life. Many of you were with me at Philippi when Octavian ran away under cover of sickness, and I led you into battle the next day against Brutus."

On the other side of the gulf, Octavian was making speeches to his soldiers, inflaming them about the harlot of Egypt and all her riches and gold which would belong to them.

The night before the battle, I slept fitfully in Antony's arms.

At dawn I awoke, alone in bed, for Antony had gotten up hours before to see about organizing the day.

The scarlet mantle, the customary signal displayed in Roman camps on the morning of a day of battle, was flapping in the wind from atop our pavilion, and our troops were preparing themselves to fight.

I dressed and ate a little, and then Antony came to take me to attend the morning sacrifice. As we stepped outside the pavilion, priests draped garlands around our necks. In the procession to the sacrificial site, the priest who led the way, holding a golden image of Apollo, stumbled and fell to the ground, throwing the statue into the mud.

The air was punctuated by gasps from the soldiers.

I stood there, feeling a sinking sensation, and I looked at Antony to see panic registering on his face.

"I swear by all the gods the priest was paid by Octavian to stumble!" I hissed under my breath to Antony.

Antony took my arm, and we resumed the procession. During the sacrifice, I stood stiff and silent. The priests gave a good reading, for the liver was not streaked, but I was still full of foreboding, knowing that the soldiers regarded the stumbling of the priest as an unfavorable omen.

After the sacrifice, Antony and I returned to the pavilion and I made him eat a little food.

"What will the day bring?" Antony sighed.

I clutched his hand. "Whatever the fates decree, we will have the invincible strength of being together."

Holding hands, we left the pavilion and walked down to the shore of the gulf. Our three hundred ships, armed and equipped with formidable engines, were already boarded by twenty-two thousand soldiers and archers and were ready to sail. We rowed out in a small boat to the *Antonaid* and climbed aboard, and the harsh grating of the anchor chain was heard being pulled up.

It was midmorning when the signal was given. The galley rowers dipped their oars into the gulf to the measured beat of the gongs, and our ships sailed slowly across the smooth, calm waters to the sea.

Antony decided to have himself rowed in a small boat from one warship to the other so that he might shout encouragement to the men, and before parting we embraced with emotion. For an endless moment we stood without exchanging a word, hearing only the beating of our hearts and the monotonous splashing of the oars in steady rhythm.

"Oh, my husband, my hero, my mighty warrior!" I cried tearfully. "You are as strong as a bull and as bold as a lion. At Troy your forefather Hercules found Hector and killed him. Octavian is your Hector, Antony, and Actium is your Troy!"

Antony kissed me with fervor. "You are a brave woman and a great queen, and no man ever had a more wondrous wife!" he cried.

There was one last kiss, and then he was gone, climbing the ladder over the side of the *Antonaid* to a small boat. I stood waving as the boat sped away, and in the coming hour I heard Antony's cries of exhortation ringing out, as he quickly moved between the ships.

On both sides of the gulf, the land forces were drawn up and silently watched as we sailed along. Our fleet was formed into three separate squadrons, and my squadron, with the *Antonaid* in the center, drew up the rear. The ships were so close that at times the opposing oars clashed.

Octavian and Agrippa, aware of our intentions, thanks to the traitor Dellius, had twice as many men as we had crowded onto four hundred triremes on the sea facing the gulf's entrance, and were anticipating our approach.

I stood on deck as the sun blazed above me. I reflected that many of my soldiers would not see the sun set that day nor ever rise again, and perhaps neither would I. With nervous fingers, I played with the locket that hung from my neck which contained a vial of poison. If the issue of the battle was disastrous for me, and if enemy soldiers boarded my ship, I was determined not to be taken alive.

It was high noon with the sun at its zenith when Antony's ship, leading the way, reached the narrow and difficult passage of the gulf's mouth. Antony called a halt, and our ships stopped so that the rowers could rest and take food and drink.

Silence hung in the still hot air around Actium, and the sun beat down with an unrelenting glare and intensity.

Antony stood in the prow of his ship and surveyed the four hundred enemy vessels that were spread out in three lines in the distance on the sea. An hour passed while neither side made a move, and then Antony impatiently gave the command for our fleet to go forward.

The floating fortresses of my ships hoisted sail and the oars cut swiftly into the water as Antony bravely led his ships out to attack the enemy. The *Antonaid* hung back, resting in the mouth of the gulf with a dozen other ships which carried my court and belongings. Antony had planned this so I would be out of range of the battle.

I stood on deck with a furiously racing heart, watching as the rest of my royal fleet sailed off.

The tranquil summer afternoon was at last rent asunder as the two opposing fleets rushed at each other, maneuvering into position, and the din and clash of battle rang out over the waters.

I soon perceived that the more numerous enemy ships, relying on only three banks of oars and without sails, were easy to maneuver and darted in and out between my cumbersome warships. Antony had blundered in ordering our sails to be hoisted, for the sails became easy targets. Soon after the battle had begun I saw the first sails flaming brightly from catapulted fireballs.

Iras began screaming at the sight of burning ships and ran below deck, but Charmion and several chamberlains remained with me on deck.

Frantic with anxiety, my innards tightening like a clenched fist, I paced the deck, watching the battle enfolding before my very eyes. The fighting was fierce as ships rushed at each other. Arrows and javelins whistled through the air, and projectiles and burning balls of resin were hurled from high wooden towers mounted on decks.

The carnage of battle and the sight and sound of slaughter froze my blood. Swords clashed, and as the steel slashed with deadly accuracy, I saw limbs and heads fall to the deck or into the sea. The screams of the wounded and the dying filled me with horror.

Terror seized my heart when, about an hour into the battle, I saw through the smoke and confusion that several small enemy craft had surrounded Antony's ship. Like a locust, swarms of Octavian's soldiers crowded aboard; but Antony and his men bravely put up a fierce struggle, and against overwhelming odds, slew the enemy to the man.

All afternoon the ships attacked, withdrew, and returned to the charge. I watched the battle with mounting concern, for it was now apparent that we were losing.

"I beg you, Cleopatra," Charmion cried, shuddering and gasping and wringing her hands, "Antony has affected a break in the blockade and that is our signal to retreat!"

"The day is not decided!" I cried stubbornly. "I will not depart the scene of battle until victory or defeat is confirmed."

Anguish engulfed me as I saw my glorious fleet fall into great confusion, when ship after ship blazed with fire. My chamberlains kept count, and by late afternoon more than three score of my quinqueremes were on fire, had been sunk, or were drifting aimlessly, all their men killed, burned, drowned, or captured. I saw soldiers, some afire, attempt to throw off their heavy armor and dive into the sea. Death was indeed reaping an abundant harvest.

My eunuch chamberlains, hovering about me on deck, begged me in a chorus of high-pitched supplications to give the command to sail. I could no longer see Antony and I shuddered at the thought that a chance blow might have killed him. If he were still alive, I knew he would undoubtedly be taken prisoner if he did not kill himself first.

"We will be captured, Cleopatra," Charmion cried, trembling in terror, tugging my arm. "We cannot delay the retreat any longer."

"The day still hangs in the balance!" I cried irrationally, but then, with a suffusion of pain, I knew that the day had been lost.

"Antony!" I moaned as if in a litany. "Antony!"

Suddenly, to the north, I saw several small ships of Octavian's heading toward the *Antonaid,* their steel piked prows and deadly battering rams pointing straight at me, the soldiers on deck brandishing swords and javelins.

My eunuchs were quaking and screaming with fright. Archidemus, the captain of the *Antonaid,* rushed up to me.

"The battle is all but lost, Queen Cleopatra!" Archidemus cried. "The time for flight is now, or we will be overtaken."

A strong breeze from the northwest had sprung up.

"Hoist every stitch of canvas!" I uttered in a choked voice. "Let us make for Egypt!"

The purple sails of the *Antonaid* were hoisted and flared out, catching the gale, and the galley rowers dipped their oars into the sea. I felt the ship beneath me begin to plow at full speed southward toward the opening in the blockade and the rolling seas beyond. A dozen of my royal vessels followed.

"Pray to the gods we are not pursued and captured!" one of my eunuchs cried out in a shrieking voice.

"With a fair wind," Archidemus said hopefully, "we will be in Alexandria within ten days."

I stood on deck for a while longer, my cloak flapping about me, my hair whipping in the wind and the salt brine mixing with the tears on my cheeks. I gave one final look at the frightful scene of battle with the sea stained with blood and bodies floating on the surface.

In a daze I turned away, and supported by Charmion, I stumbled down to my stateroom. The sound of the screams of the dying and the din of battle mercifully receded from my ears. The unspeakable horrors of the day had been too much for my overstrained nerves, and I collapsed in utter despair and exhaustion across my bed, shivering and sobbing uncontrollably.

The ship began to pitch recklessly upon reaching the open, tossing sea. As I lay there, overcome with torment and weariness, I prayed that Antony had not been killed, that by some miracle he could return to his land forces and a second battle be fought and this time he would be victorious. After a time, however, reality penetrated through these mad thoughts, and I knew that the day had been lost and so had Antony, that he had been slain or taken prisoner or had killed himself. He was my husband and lover, and in that hour of distraught delirium, I sobbed heartbrokenly for his fate.

I did not know then that when Antony saw the fleeing *Antonaid,* he left his flagship and jumped into a small trireme, followed by three faithful companions, the Greek boy Eros, and two officers. Antony ordered the rowers to bear down heavily on the oars, and the ship raced across the sea and soon caught up with the *Antonaid*. With his friends, Antony climbed aboard and crossed the bridge in a trance. He went to the prow of the ship and dropped on a bench, burying his head in his arms, as Eros crouched at his feet.

One of my chamberlains came below to my stateroom, and Charmion went to the door and learned the news from him.

"Antony has come on board!" Charmion cried, coming to my bed, all excited. "Antony is alive!"

I sat up, at first incredulous. "Antony, alive?" I saw from her look that this was so, and I fell back across the bed with a deep sigh, thanking the gods that he was safe. "Bring Antony to me," I cried, sobbing with emotion.

Antony refused to come to me, not wanting to face me in defeat. After a few hours of rest, I sipped a little wine to give me strength, and then I climbed up on deck just as we were passing the island of Leukas.

Twilight was falling, and the sunset cast rose-colored waves over the surface of the sea. Even in that moment of distracted sorrow, I was aware of the beauty of the sea. Leaning on the arm of Charmion, the wind blowing sharply against me, I could see Antony at the end of the ship, and my heart swelled painfully at the sight of him. He sat there, worn out from the rigors and horrors of the battle, numb and heartbroken, his head bowed in shame.

"Oh, my Antony!" I whispered. "I must go to him."

I began walking across the swaying deck. Eros, sitting at Antony's feet, saw me and touched Antony in warning. Antony looked up and groaned. He turned his back, not wanting me to see him in his misery and misfortune.

Stopping, I stood there, irresolute. I almost toppled over with the swaying ship, and Charmion steadied me. For a long moment I listened to the moaning wind and the sobbing waves, and it was as if the sea itself was lamenting the day. With a sigh, I turned and staggered back down to my stateroom, took a heavy sleeping potion, and lay abed, longing for sleep to come.

As I lay there, burning and shivering with fever, the draught slowly took effect and I sank into a fitful sleep.

Antony's friends, Aristocrates and Lucilius, were assigned a cabin, but Antony remained on deck for three days and three nights, with Eros, who never left his side. The steadfast Eros, who loves Antony madly and who adores me, later told me of a conversation that transpired between them the first night at sea.

"I am deserted by the world," Antony said morosely. "No one stays faithful to a defeated general."

"Until death I will stand by you!" Eros said. "Oh, I would shed my last drop of blood for you."

"Yes, Eros, I believe you would," Antony said. "It is not your blood I need, however, but a vow."

Eros looked up at Antony with a searching, loving expression. "Yes?" he said eagerly.

"Promise that the moment I ask you to do it," Antony cried, "you will plunge my sword into my heart."

Eros burst into tears, burying his head in Antony's lap and his arms encircling his waist. "Oh, never, never, I could never do that!" he sobbed brokenly. "I am yours, my sword, my body, my life, to do with as you wish, but don't extract such a promise from me!"

"Yes, you must promise, Eros," Antony said, gently stroking the blond curly head that lay in his lap. "If you love me as you say, you will do as I command."

During this time I never left my stateroom, but lay abed, overcome with fever. I sent messages up to Antony, but he refused to read them. Gradually my fever abated and I got out of bed. I was weak and stood unsteadily on my legs, but I felt a sense of liberation and was thankful to be freed from the beleaguered camp.

On the fourth morning at sea, when the steady northwest wind had carried us past the Peloponnesus, Iras went up on deck to see Antony. For years she had felt great hostility for him, but now in his defeat she had only compassion. Eros and she had always shared a deep affinity, both sharing a perennial childlike spirit, and they sat together at Antony's feet and between them coaxed him to rouse himself.

"You must not destroy the life that is so precious to my mistress," Iras said beseechingly.

Antony, haggard and unkempt, stirred from his stupor and was led below deck. Eros and a body slave washed the stench of battle from him and dressed him in a clean tunic. As if he were a sleepwalker, he followed Eros into my stateroom early in the evening.

"My beloved husband!" I said, embracing him tenderly and kissing his freshly shaved cheek.

"Cleopatra," Antony muttered weakly.

There were five of us there, Iras, Charmion, Eros, Antony, and I, and we all sat down to dine. None of us had much of an appetite and merely picked at the food and sipped at the wine, and no one said much. Iras after a while picked up her harp and sang a few sweet songs as night fell over the sea outside.

"Leave us, all of you!" Antony suddenly cried.

Iras, Charmion, and Eros obediently rose and left the chamber.

Antony and I were alone. I cautiously watched him drain a goblet, as if he hoped the wine would give him the courage to speak.

"I abandoned my fleet and all the loyal men who were fighting and dying for me to run after you," Antony said with bitter self-reproach. "When I saw your ship taking you away, I knew I would never see you again, and I couldn't bear that thought. All reason fled, and a power stronger than my will, my love for you, made me abandon my post and chase after you."

"I am happy that you did, Antony, for I could not face life without you," I said softly.

"It was my duty to stay and die with my men!" Antony cried. "I am marked with dishonor forever."

"The day was lost," I explained. "You would have been killed or taken prisoner. Flight was not the most honorable action, but it was sensible. We were outmaneuvered by Octavian and Agrippa for months. To have won the sea battle would have been a miraculous feat, but at least we have extricated ourselves from a hopeless predicament. We would have died at Actium, but we are free now. We have eighty thousand soldiers in Egypt and Asia, and we will return to Alexandria and continue to run our eastern empire and prepare for another round with Octavian. The issue between Antony and Octavian has not been decisively settled and will be concluded on another day."

Antony was so absorbed in his misery that my words did not penetrate.

"I, Antony the hero, have become Antony the coward!" he cried, castigating himself with words. "I am forsaken by the gods. I lost all honor at Actium. I have only myself to blame, for all these years I rarely took your advice and committed one blunder after another."

"You blundered to think Octavian would fight honorably on the field of battle, instead of blockading us and cornering us like rats," I said.

"Life is like ashes in my mouth," Antony muttered despairingly. "I lived for glory, and now I am ruined. I feel like a man robbed and left naked by the roadside. Oh, Cleopatra, how can I live with all my honor gone?"

"Together we will give one another the strength to carry on the struggle," I said.

Antony drank another goblet of wine. I got up and put out the lamps. I stood by a window and looked out over the surging, silver sea.

"Look, Antony, the night is jewelled with stars and wears the moon on her brow like the Hathor of Egypt," I cried.

In the darkness I found Antony's hand and led him to bed. He followed me submissively, and together we lay down beside one another in silence.

The language of silence was sufficient for the moment. Words had no power to express our thoughts. There was no need to speak of our shattered dreams. We lay side by side, and suddenly the swaying of the ship, tossing sharply to one side, threw our bodies together. My arms went around Antony, and he moaned as he embraced me.

Deeper than our despair, we felt the intoxicating joy of being together, and this wiped out all other feelings. We clung to one another, free for the moment from the remorse which had poisoned our lives.

Antony laid his head on my breasts, and my fingers played with his thick curls. I remembered once, years before, that he had told me that a kiss from Cleopatra was worth all the kingdoms of the earth, and I wondered silently if he still cherished the same sentiment.

On the surge of the Mediterranean swell the ship dipped and pitched, propelled by the northwest winds, plowing through the rough autumnal seas, speeding us safely home to Egypt.

CHAPTER X

BANNERS AND GARLANDS WAVED from the masts of the *Antonaid* and the accompanying vessels when we sailed into the Royal Harbor, to delude the people that victory had smiled upon their queen. Truth, as the Greeks of old used to say, always arrives by limping messenger. I was not empress of the world, but I was still Queen, High Priestess, and supreme judge of Egypt, and there was united in me all the authority, divine and temporal, by which all Egyptians are ruled, and I resolved to take firm measures to exercise the absolute power the gods had invested in me.

A few days previously I had put into the port of Paraetonium, a desolate town on the northwestern border of Egypt, where Antony and his friends had gone ashore. Demoralized by defeat, he wanted to spend a few days at this small Greek settlement before returning to the capital. This would give him the chance to check with the garrison at the fort at Paraetonium as well as with the legions encamped not far off in Cyrene, and to make plans for renewing the war.

I was glad for this separation, for we both needed a rest from each other. Antony was crushed, and I was impatient with his eternal lamentations. I was once again defiantly facing the world, my mind brimming with plans for defending myself in Egypt and preserving the heritage of my forefathers. It was not in my nature to collapse like Antony. The sea voyage had revived me, and like King Sisyphus of Corinth, I was once again ready to start rolling the heavy stone up the steep hill.

A flourish of trumpets blasted from the decks of my ships to announce my homecoming as I docked along the harbor beneath my palace that bright September morning. Thousands of Alexandrians crowded the docks, excited by the gay decorations that decked my ships, waving and cheering their welcome.

I sent instructions up to the palace for my children to await me there, but I had Apollodorus and Mardian come down to my flagship.

"Much water has flowed down the Nile since our last meeting," I cried with a warm smile, "and I trust my two kingdoms have fared well under your guardianship."

I was assured that Egypt was secure in peace and prosperity, and for the moment I was evasive about the outcome of Actium.

At high noon I was carried in splendid royal state, sitting in a carved, ornamented golden chair, up the glittering white marble steps to the palace.

My four children, with their tutors and attendants, were waiting for me in the Great Alabaster Hallway. My eyes immediately fell on Caesarion, who was sixteen now, so handsome, slim, and dignified, and the sight of him filled me with deep emotion.

The smaller children came running up to me, and I knelt and embraced them with demonstrative affection, all of us laughing and sobbing happily together.

"Mother!" Caesarion said in a deep voice, a voice that had changed in the eighteen months I had been gone.

I now had to look up to him, and I did so with tears brimming my eyes. He was more than ever the image of his father, a young Caesar indeed. "My son!" I whispered.

"Welcome to Egypt, Mother!" Caesarion cried.

In front of the court, we embraced affectionately.

I was joyously happy to once again be ensconced in my palace after living all those months in a tent. I went to my private apartments, followed by my children and courtiers. After a while I took Caesarion and broke away from the others, and we went alone into my bed-chamber.

"Oh, Caesarion, how I've missed you!" I said, clutching his hands in mine. "You are a man now, and in looks and body you recall, even more than your name, your divine father."

"Yes, so they all tell me!" Caesarion said proudly.

Taking him by the hands, I led him to a divan and we sat down. I described to him the summer months I had just lived through.

"The battle was only a minor skirmish to break the blockade since Octavian cowardly refused to fight on land," I summed up. "The final battle has yet to be fought. We lost a battle, but not the war. All those months, nothing has been gained, but nothing has been lost, either. Actium has deprived us of getting a firm footing in Italy, but Antony and I still rule our eastern empire. And you are Pharaoh of Egypt!"

Caesarion had listened to me expressionlessly. "And my father's inheritance?" he asked in a tight voice.

"Your Roman rights were not secured as yet."

"Soon I will be a man and will fight my own battles!" Caesarion cried resolutely. "Alexander the Great at sixteen led his first soldiers and took the chief town of the rebellious Maedi, and at eighteen led his first command at the battle of Chareonea. I will defeat my adopted stepbrother, Octavian, and show him who is the real son of Caesar!"

"You fill me with such pride, Caesarion!" I cried, clasping his hands. "You are your father's true son, not only in looks and stance, but in spirit and ambition."

Caesarion stood and wandered about the chamber, and at last stopped beside a bust of Antony sitting on a pedestal.

"And so my stepfather is at Paraetonium," he muttered.

"Yes, for a few weeks of rest," I explained.

"Perhaps he will kill himself."

"Antony is broken by misfortune," I said, "but hope

is reviving in him for the future, and I don't believe he will destroy himself."

"He lacks the courage?" Caesarion asked coldly. He began pacing restlessly, his sandals flapping on the marble floor. "I have been studying history, Mother, and I've learned that suicide is an honorable exit from the stage of life after defeat. Did not Cato, Brutus, and Cassius kill themselves? Then there was my great-uncle Ptolemy of Cyprus, and my grandmother Queen Cleopatra, who chose death rather than be removed from the throne and banished. Yes, suicide would be the proper course for Antony to adopt now."

I sat there, saying nothing, full of unease, silently thinking that the day might not be far distant when I, too, would have to turn to death as the reward for all my struggles and life labors.

Caesarion went to the window and gazed out at the sea, and the sun caught his hair, making it look as if it had been dipped in gold. "If Antony does not kill himself," he resumed thoughtfully, "Octavian will surely hunt him down and do it for him. He will not be so full of pride now, but I imagine he will be as full of wine as ever. My stepfather is unbearable when drunk and not much better when sober. Defeat is one thing, Mother, but disgrace another."

"All that you say of your second cousin may be true, Caesarion," I said quietly, "but you must never forget that it was Antony who waged this war for you, and who also avenged the murder of your father and hunted down and destroyed every last one of your father's murderers. You must always respect him for that, my son."

Caesarion came back to me. "Very well, Mother," he said, smiling. "I shall always credit Antony for that."

I took his hands in mine, smiling, and he kissed my cheek as I embraced him urgently.

"In time you will see, Mother," Caesarion whispered intensely in my ear, "that I am worth a hundred Antonys!"

That first night back in Egypt, the sailors from my

ships were in the taverns, telling the truth about Actium, and the news of my defeat spread like wildfire throughout the city. The first symptoms of unrest were not long in manifesting themselves as riots broke out. Apollodorus and his soldiers dispersed the mobs with brutal force and rounded up the ringleaders. As it was important to avoid any disturbances, I had all instigators put to death. Because of these energetic actions, I was able to prevent any more disorders, and peace was restored. I let my people know that their goddess-Queen still controlled her country.

While Antony wandered the beaches at Paraetonium, lost in melancholy gloom, I plunged into frantic activities to safeguard the future. Caesarion was always at my side, sitting in on council sessions, lending me support and taking part in all decisions. While I had been away he had worked closely with Mardian and the regency council, and he had a great grasp of state affairs that belied his tender years.

One morning in late September, a ship arrived bringing Canidius, who told me that after Antony and I had left the scene of battle at Actium, Octavian destroyed our remaining galleys. Canidius, in charge of our land forces, had ordered his men to march into Macedonia the following morning, but the soldiers refused. Canidius knew that Octavian would forgive the soldiers to a man, but would kill him, so he took a swift horse and sped down the coast. When he came to the port of Taenarus, he embarked on a ship, and a strong gusty wind drove him straight to Egypt.

A few days later, in early October, Antony arrived in a small ship. He entered my apartments, and as I embraced him, I saw by the look of doom on his face that he had disheartening news to tell me. He called for wine, and lying on a couch, he told me between gulps of wine of his recent happenings.

I listened with a gathering fear, as Antony described how he had sent envoys across the desert to his general Scarpus who commanded the legions stationed in Cyreneica. The news of the Actium defeat had preceded these messengers, and Scarpus had decided to cast his lot with Octavian. He put to death Antony's envoys and massacred his soldiers who had sympathy for Antony's cause.

"The defection of Scarpus and the loss of my legions in Cyreneica deeply afflicted me, and I resolved to kill myself, but I was hindered by Eros," Antony explained mournfully.

"How stands our garrison at Paraetonium?" I asked.

"For the moment they remain loyal," Antony said. "Not long ago I was master of half the world, Triumvir of the East, leader of a hundred thousand soldiers, and now I am a fugitive forsaken by all. I had hoped to begin a new race of kings, but will our children ever sit on the thrones I conquered for them?"

"Antony, my husband," I cried, keeping my spirit even with this latest shocking setback, "have you forgotten that you came out of the defeats of Mutina and Phraasta unharmed and more glorious than before? We still have legions in Syria and Egypt, and our vassal kings remain devoted to our cause."

"The gods have abandoned us, and so will all the kinglets, one by one," Antony moaned with self-pity. "The bright star of Antony has set forever, and the world belongs to Octavian, the moneylender's grandson."

I was weary of Antony's grumblings, and I did not have time to commiserate with him since I was too preoccupied with plans. My strong love of life compelled me in the face of all misfortunes to look to the future, and it was obvious that Antony would be of little help to me. He settled into his private apartments next to mine, surrounded by a few companions, and began drinking heavily.

A week later, I decided that it might be a good idea to show ourselves at the theater to let the people see us together and to dispel the current gossip that we were finished with one another. Accordingly I sent for Pisistratus, who has long managed the Theater of Dionysus for me.

"I would like to see a special play performed, Pisistratus," I said.

"Shall we do one of the tragedies of Euripides, O Queen?" he asked.

"In my happy days, Pisistratus, I was partial to tragedies," I explained, "but now in these tragic days I prefer to see comedies. There is enough tragedy here at the palace without getting more at the theater, too!"

"Then shall we do a comedy by Aristophanes, Divine Majesty? What about *Timon of Athens?*"

"An excellent choice, Pisistratus," I cried. "Such a marvelous play will bring Lord Antony out of his black mood."

It was a lovely, cool October evening when we went to the theater to see *Timon of Athens*. The theater was packed, with every place taken. As I made my entrance into the theater, with Caesarion, Antony, and our friends, the audience stood and applauded wildly and kept cheering long after we were seated in our royal enclosure at the side of the stage. The cheers delayed the start of the play. Antony waved to the audience with tears in his eyes. He had always been a great favorite with the Alexandrians, and he was moved to see that, in spite of the reversal of his fortunes, he was still adored in his adopted city.

Under a galaxy of stars, the play was performed superbly by an excellent company of actors, headed by the divinely droll Melesippidas in the title role of Timon, the misanthropic philosopher who hates everyone and repells their approaches with sarcastic barbs.

I was amused by the famous scene in which Timon invites Apamentus to his gloomy house on the edge of the sea so that the two of them, both misanthropes, can celebrate the festival of flacons together. "What a pleasant party, Timon!" Apemantus cries. "It would be," Timon retorts, "if you weren't here."

Caesarion and his friend Andronicus laughed, the audience laughed, and I laughed, but Antony remained silent beside me, deep in melancholy.

"Men of Athens," Timon cries in a later scene, "I

have a little plot of land and on it grows a fig tree, and if any of you wish, you are certainly welcome to hang yourselves on it at my pleasure."

The funniest scene was at the banquet when Timon has a group of guests in, only to suddenly start throwing stones, painted as artichokes, at them.

Funny to everyone, that is, but not to Antony.

As events were to prove, Antony took this comedy seriously.

"I feel a great affinity for Timon," Antony announced when we returned to the palace after the performance. " 'I am sick of this false, vile world,' " he cried, quoting one of Timon's lines. "Henceforth I shall emulate Timon and retire from public affairs and avoid all people."

"You cannot live without people, Antony," I cried.

"That's what you think," Antony declared. "I shall take up residence in that little temple on the Hephaistrium Mole, and I will call the place the Timoneum in memory of Timon, since there is a similarity in our fortunes and philosophies. I shall live on bread and water for the purification of my body, which has been corrupted by meat and wine."

The next day Antony took a few belongings and two aged eunuchs and went off to the Timoneum, refusing to take even Eros with him. It has always been characteristic of Antony to dramatize his life, and I saw this move as a show of theater. I ordered guards to patrol near the temple for his protection.

Canidius, Luculius, and several others of Antony's friends were incensed at this absurd behavior, but their pleadings could not avail Antony to tear himself away from his new residence.

I discussed the matter with my physician, Olympus.

"It is obvious, O Queen," Olympus pronounced gravely, "that Lord Antony is retreating from a world he can no longer understand or control. I think the Timoneum will have a therapeutic effect on him, for the lapping of the sea gently at the side of the marble walls will be soothing to his damaged nerves. After a few weeks he will return to your side, restored in health."

I prayed to the gods that Olympus would be right. I hated Antony, but I loved him even more. I could not live with him, but I could not live without him, and it seemed we were fated to quarrel and reconcile.

While Antony was living at the Timoneum, I plunged into feverish activities to strengthen the defenses of my kingdom. With the help of Athenion and Apollodorus, new soldiers were recruited, and the troops scattered in the provinces were concentrated in Alexandria. The fortresses of Pelusium and Paraetonium were adequately garrisoned to protect Egypt's borders, and I began a shipbuilding program to replace the fleet lost at Actium.

I spent much time consulting with Simonides, the great master builder, who designed my mausoleum. The Sema is overflowing with three centuries of dead Ptolemies, and so five years ago I began constructing my own tomb on the harbor next to the Temple of Isis. It is a structure extraordinary in beauty and magnificence, built of black marble, a last sleeping place worthy of my rank. Under my supervision, I now had Simonides busily put the finishing touches to my tomb.

All my thoughts were not only of death, for life still held out its magic arms to me. I realized that from now on I had to look to the east, and so I sent ambassadors in all directions to assure myself of the loyalty of the client kings on the Levant.

I was anxious to secure the sympathy of the King of the Medes since my son Alexander will one day marry his daughter Jolape and succeed to the crowns of Media and Armenia. The Median monarch had always despised his life-long enemy, Artavasdes of Armenia, who had lain in my prison for three years since he had walked in Antony's triumph. At the time I had refused to execute Artavasdes, but now in a gesture to earn the goodwill of the Medes I had him beheaded. The head was embalmed, and an ambassador took it to Media as a gift to their king.

Reports filtered into Egypt that Octavian left Actium

and sailed to Athens, with a small entourage. The legions at Actium stayed behind, refusing to march since they had received neither booty or pay. Octavian might be victorious but he was penniless.

It was painful for me to contemplate that Athens, the most glorious of Greek cities where I had been received as a Greek princess just a year before, was now acclaiming Octavian. After a few weeks of homage by the Athenians, he sailed to Ephesus and sent one of his officers to Quintus Didius, who commanded Antony's legions in Syria, in an effort to negotiate a settlement. If these legions, forty thousand strong, capitulated, Octavian would immediately be able to march on Egypt. He wanted my head, Antony's head, Caesarion's head, and he wanted my treasury of a thousand talents in gold to pay his armies.

It was about this time that my envoys were arriving at the palaces of the kings of Asia Minor, only to be turned away. The kings and princes were all hastening to Ephesus to render Octavian homage. Antony was no longer Imperator of the east. The Hellenistic kingdoms had made a bid for independence under my banner. They lost, and once again they are being enslaved by Rome.

Everything pointed to disaster. With a certain clarity, I saw that perhaps I was engaged in a lamentable, hopeless struggle. The one ray of hope that came from the east was a message from Didius, who held Antioch and commanded the legions, affirming that he would stand steadfast by Antony.

It was essential that Antony be enticed from his solitary confinement, and that we face the future together. Realizing that his fifty-third birthday was drawing near, I conceived the plan of giving him a lavish banquet to mark the occasion. He had turned away all his friends from the door of the Timoneum, but I knew he would not have the heart to turn away nine-year-old Princess Cleopatra Selene, his favorite child, his pride and joy.

Little Cleopatra went off to the Timoneum, and

Antony permitted her to enter while guards waited at the door. When she found her father on a pallet in a corner of the dank, dark tower, she threw herself at his feet and burst into tears. After an afternoon of entreaties, she accomplished her mission.

"Go tell your mother, my little princess, that I shall return to the palace after nightfall," Antony said.

Antony did not want anyone to see him in his wretched state, and so he waited until midnight. From my balcony window I watched as Apollodorus and a few soldiers led him along the mole back to the palace, and I could see that there would have been little chance of anyone recognizing him, since he looked like the poorest beggar. In his apartments his squalid clothes were removed, his three-week beard shaved, and his dirty hair and body washed. In the morning, dressed in a clean chiton, he came to me.

"My Egyptian Venus, I have returned to be by your side." He smiled wanly. "My days of being a hermit philosopher are over, and I realize how futile it is to try to endure life without you."

Antony had lost weight and his cheeks were sunken, but he looked more handsome than he had in years.

"Oh, my Antony!" I cried, embracing him tenderly.

The children came in and joined us for the morning meal. I had my family around me again and I was happy. As Olympus had predicted, I saw that the retreat in the Timoneum had restored Antony. He was composed and talked lucidly of the future.

"Egypt can still be held and armies can be raised," Antony said. "There's still hope."

"While we have each other, Antony, we have all!" I cried, kissing his cheek. "Our love is as timeless as forever."

Harmony was restored to the royal household, and I showed myself more affectionate and loving to Antony than ever.

The banquet celebrating Antony's birthday on the Ides of November was the most lavish affair held at the palace since the Armenian Triumph three years before.

Antony, dressed in a purple chiton and wearing a golden crown on his head and many rings and jewelled lockets, was again the proudest of human peacocks. Although in private his shoulders slumped under the weight of grief, he entered the hall beside me with a straight-backed, imperial stance, wearing his merry smile and evoking the hearty Antony of yesterdays.

The most delectable foods were served, roast goose, fruits steeped in honey, and wine spiced with myrrh.

"My Lord Antony," Athenagoras asked, "shall we revive the Society of Inimitable Livers?"

"Oh, no," Antony said. "Queen Cleopatra and I are forming a new club, the Society of Those Who Die Together!"

Our revellers laughed at this suggestion, and one and all vowed that they would join up.

Caesarion, sitting on the royal dais, frowned at the increasingly riotous atmosphere of the banquet and soon begged leave and went off with his devoted friend Andronicus.

I gave out gold chains to honor friends, and I told each guest that the gold plate and gem-encrusted goblets they used could be taken home with them. Many guests came to the banquet poor and left rich.

It was dawn when the last guests were helped by slaves into their litters in the courtyard and I helped Antony back to our bedchamber.

"Dearest Antony," I said as we lay abed, "do you remember the banquets we had at Tarsus which inaugurated our love? We shall have banquets like that every night from now on. If these are our last days, we shall go out in laughter and wine."

When my thirty-ninth birthday came some six weeks later, however, I let the occasion pass with little notice as befitting my fallen fortunes.

For two months Octavian had been in Ephesus, and although the vassal kings had sworn fealty to him, the Roman legions in Syria would not. He was obsessed with the desire to attack Egypt, but he had no army. He then received disquieting news from Rome. The citizens, who expected a share of Egypt's spoils, were indignant that I had escaped Actium with my war chest. When taxes were imposed in order to pay the legions, riots broke out. Agrippa sent messages to Octavian saying he could not hold order alone. Although the seas were stormy, Octavian had no choice but to sail back to Italy.

"Perhaps Octavian's ship will sink in the rough winter seas and he'll drown," Iras cried hopefully.

The news of Octavian's return to Italy restored hope to the drooping spirits around the court. I was grateful for this respite, although I knew that Octavian would inevitably be returning to the east the following spring or summer.

Antony roused from his torpor and his spirits revived. His deep laugh was heard once again with frequency around the palace. Our mutual sufferings and the irresistible need of our love drew us together, and we faced the future side by side.

I was pleased also that Antony took an interest in defensive measures and in supervising the swordplay exercises between Caesarion and Andronicus.

"Your son may know his Homer and how to play the flute," Antony said, "but he doesn't have much expertise with the sword."

From an upper palace window, I anxiously watched Caesarion crossing swords with Andronicus in a courtyard as Antony shouted relentless instructions beside them. I had been assiduous in seeing that Caesarion's brain was cultivated, but I had neglected to develop his physical prowess. His physique had always been frail, and he perspired and panted heavily during the swordplay sessions. Antony reminded me that Caesar had been delicate in body but through disciplined exercises he had hardened himself up, and so would his son.

"You must remember that you are half a Julian, Caesarion," Antony said. "So am I, for my mother was your father's cousin. Your father, watching from Mount Olympus, must see that his son is a man who can smite his enemies with a blade."

691

With deep pride I saw my son and his best friend, as the weeks went by, become extremely dexterous in this heroic craft.

In the hope of creating a diversion in the public's minds, I decided to celebrate the coming of age of Caesarion. In a solemn ceremony conducted in the Great Hall, with the whole court looking on, Caesarion had his beautiful blond locks shorn by a barber, the down on his cheeks and chin was shaved off, and he received the toga virilis as trumpets blasted. He struck a gloriously handsome figure as he stood there in the ceremonial toga with its narrow red border.

"My beloved son," I cried, kissing his smooth cheek, "this is one of the greatest days of my life, for you are now a man!"

Antony helped Caesarion buckle on his new suit of gold armor. Caesarion left the palace, and astride a white charger, rode through the streets of the capital, sword in hand, leading a contingent of soldiers. This display showed my people that they had a young prince who would lead them against invaders.

There was a banquet at the palace that evening in which Caesarion sat at the center of the table on the dais, with Andronicus, Antony, and me beside him. I gave out gifts to all who took part in the day's ceremony. Wine was distributed to the populace, and singers and musicians entertained in the public squares. Several days were given up exclusively to games and merrymaking. Even though the people forgot their imminent danger with feasting, anxiety hung like a pall over the gilded rooftops of Alexandria.

The citizens of the capital were demoralized by the dark political horizon. All those who had a stake in the kingdom were aware of the trend of affairs. Commercial relations with foreign powers terminated, to the consternation of Alexandrians whose foreign trade was their chief resource.

Every evening I sat down in the great hall to a sumptuous feast with many guests. The crowd of Roman senators, foreign princes, and adventurers no longer encumbered my court as in earlier days, but I still held sway over an illustrious group of patricians, philosophers, and artists. Every attempt was made to preserve the prestige of my court in the eyes of my people. I meant to show that, if these were to be my last days, they would be spent in the grand and lavish manner for which I am noted.

Antony and I talked together of the possibility of death.

"I hope to die fighting with a sword in my hand," Antony said. "If I see the game is lost, I will plunge the sword into my heart. Suicide is a virtue among the ancients, when life is no longer the distaff from which Clotho spins days of silk and gold, and when one gives it up simply as a useless thing."

"Yes, Antony, but I am not a soldier but a queen, and my death will be more difficult," I said. "Of course, I shall fight to the last, and I come from a long line of survivors, but when all hope is gone, we Ptolemies know how to die well. My life has been a great drama, and my last scene will be a glorious one and most carefully executed."

I gave much thought to the subject of death during these days. I have always been familiar with the method of poisons, and have done away with many conspirators, traitors, and unworthy ministers in this way. It has never concerned me how painful or prolonged death is for an enemy, but for myself I am more particular.

Lord Olympus was brought to my side for a private consultation.

"I have lived thirty-nine years and my body has remained impervious to the ravages of time, my noble physician," I cried. "If by chance I must end my life, how might I accomplish the act painlessly and with no risk of spoiling my beauty and body?"

"As you know, Queen Cleopatra, poisons invariably do their work with painful convulsions," Olympus explained. "With your permission, I should like to mix poisons and experiment on criminals and see if I may come up with a bane that will suit your requirements."

In the palace dungeons, Olympus carried out his experiments. Lethal concoctions were funneled down the throats of condemned men, and Olympus watched carefully, noting the death struggles. The victims writhed as the various poisonous mixtures devoured them, and they twisted and screamed in agony, often dying with tongues hanging out and faces and stomachs bloated.

"Death is always unseemly with vegetable poisons, O Queen," Olympus told me. "Some poisons bring prompt effect but with a cruel seizure, while gentle poisons produce a slow and lingering death. On the other hand, the venom of the kingdom of serpents is more favorable."

I remembered how my beloved childhood nurse, Tamaratet, had died from the venom of an asp which my stepmother the Lady Arsinoë had meant for me. I discussed this with Olympus.

"Oh, certainly, my queen," Olympus said. "The bite of the sacred asp would be a painless death."

It had been thirty years since Tamaratet had died in my arms, and I wanted to again observe carefully such a death. I went down to the dungeons, accompanied by Charmion and Apollodorus, and watched as a conspirator, who had been an agent for Octavian, was put to death. He was tied to a rack dressed only in a loincloth. A snake charmer held the asp to the throat of the criminal, who screamed and strained against the straps that bound him. At last the asp struck and made a slight puncture on the victim's throat.

With a racing heart, holding Charmion's hand, I moved closer. The criminal immediately ceased screaming, his eyelids closed, and the muscles of his body went slack.

Olympus, standing on the other side of the rack, put a hand over the victim's chest. "The heart is beating slowly, Divine Majesty," he explained. "As you can see, the venom has induced a kind of lethargy in the criminal, his senses are sinking into stupefaction without pain, and his face is covered with a gentle sweat. Ah, the heart has stopped beating!"

I stood there, watching the man's face, noting the tranquil expression on the dead features.

"Have asps available for me at all times," I ordered.

"Yes, O Royal Isis!" Olympus replied.

Turning away as the physicians and guards sank to their knees, I marched up the stone staircase that leads out of the dungeons.

"I have found my elixir of death," I whispered to Charmion and Apollodorus. "Octavian will never carry me off alive."

The idea of the asp as an agent of death captured my imagination, for the asp is the divine minister of the sun god which raises its head and adorns my forehead, guarding me from my enemies, and to my people death by an asp has always been a mark of divine blessing.

During that winter, Octavian restored order in Rome. Once again he changed his name, now calling himself Caius Octavian Julius Caesar Augustus. Augustus, the Exalted One!

With the coming of spring, Octavian crossed the calm seas to Rhodes. From there he sent an ambassador on to Ephesus to meet with Quintus Didius. This time there were no negotiations, and all the legions were handed over to Octavian. The defection of Didius placed the whole of Syria and Phoenicia in Octavian's orbit.

Sailing to Ephesus, Octavian assumed control of all the legions in Asia and prepared to lead an attack on Egypt. It seemed only yesterday that Antony and I had reigned in supreme command in Ephesus, rulers of the east, where all the eastern monarchs had flocked around us. These same kings were now on their knees to Octavian.

At the beginning of May, an ambassador arrived in Alexandria from Octavian. The envoy was a young, handsome freedman named Thyrsus. Antony was outraged that Octavian should send a freedman instead of a patrician as envoy, but I realized that this was the least of the slights Octavian planned for us.

I received Thyrsus in the grand colonnaded hall of the throne room, seated on my lion-footed golden throne, beneath the canopy of state and with the sacred symbols in my hands. Iras, Charmion, and Apollodorus stood near me in the places reserved for the favored of the sovereign, and around me stood the chief fan-bearers and chamberlains and priests. Although many of my nobles had already abandoned me, I still had an impressive assemblage, and I wanted Thyrsus to report to his master that I was still mistress of my kingdom.

"My master, Caius Octavian Julius Caesar Augustus, has sent me on this mission, Queen Cleopatra," Thyrsus said in a pleasant voice, "to say he has every hope of making peace with the Queen of the Nile. May I humbly suggest how your Sacred Majesty might be able to save your life and your throne?"

"Royal Egypt is curious," I remarked.

"There are ways in which you might conclude an advantageous peace with my master," Thyrsus said, smiling.

"Get to the point of your mission," I demanded bluntly. "By what action must I undertake to appease your master?"

Thyrsus took a deep breath and looked me boldly in the eye. "You may rest assured, O Queen, that you will find most favorable treatment at the hands of Caesar Augustus, provided you either put the Lord Antony to death or banish him from your realm."

Fury quivered through me, and the crook and the scourge shook in my hands. "Your master must believe his own propaganda, that I am indeed the Egyptian sorceress who is capable of anything!" I cried vehemently. "How little insight he has to think I could commit such an act that is so contrary to my character. Return to the Exalted One and tell him that the Queen of Egypt will never harm her beloved husband nor deliver him into the hands of the enemy. Inform Octavian that if he wants Antony's head, he will have to come and get it, and while he's at it he can have my head also."

During this audience, Antony was waiting out of sight but within earshot, and he became provoked by the insolence of Thyrsus. When the envoy left the palace, Antony had him seized and flogged. He then sent a letter to Octavian by Thyrsus. "I am sorry that I whipped your freedman," he wrote, "but if it will be of any satisfaction to you, you have a freedman of mine in your power, by the name of Hipparchus, and you may flog him in the like manner."

Since Hipparchus had abandoned Antony a month before to go over to Octavian, this was a great joke, and I was delighted by Antony's spirited behavior.

"Octavian wants my head!" Antony cried. "Alive, I am an obstacle to his triumph. He knows that he can never drag behind his chariot through the streets of Rome, on foot and loaded with chains, the bravest general that Rome ever boasted, the friend and cousin of his adopted father, Julius Caesar."

"Yes, you are not a barbarian like Vercingetorix and Artavasdes," I cried. "However, Cleopatra can be dragged through the streets and the people will rejoice. Octavian intends me to be the finest ornament of his triumph celebrating his victory over Egypt, and then I will be strangled afterward like Vercingetorix. If we are to die, Antony, it will be at our pleasure, not Octavian's, and we will choose the time and place."

In the rush and turmoil of these days, Antony, knowing that Octavian was preparing to strike the final blow against us, again lost all mastery of himself. He accused me of entering into secret negotiations with Octavian to save myself with the price of his head. I grew tired of his constant suspicions. At banquets while we dined in front of the court, he made me eat from each plate laid before him. I decided to show him that his fears were absurd and groundless.

I had Olympus prepare a poison in which a chaplet of fresh roses was steeped in the deadly brew. That evening in the great hall I placed the poisoned wreath on Antony's head. As the feast wore on, Antony as usual forced me to sample his food.

At last I took the wreath from Antony's brow. "Let's steep your roses in wine to make the drink more sweet."

"What a clever idea," Antony cried eagerly, dipping the roses into the goblet for some time, and then he lifted the drink to his lips.

"Wait!" I cried out, taking the goblet from his hand as he gazed wonderingly at me. "The cup of Antony, with this special rose taste, should be given as a token to one of his cherished friends." My eyes searched the various couches before us, and finally settled on Antony's Greek steward, Leonidas.

That very afternoon, Apollodorus had discovered that Leonidas was planning to flee the palace during the night, taking with him many treasures.

"Lord Leonidas," I cried with a radiant smile, "come here and drink from the cup of Antony."

"What a pleasure, Queen Cleopatra!" Leonidas cried, leaving his couch and bouncing up to the royal dais. He held the goblet aloft toward us. "I drink pledging the happiness of my beloved master and his glorious wife, Queen Cleopatra!"

Antony, beside me, had fallen silent, perhaps suspecting something, but Leonidas greedily emptied the goblet to the last drop. He then went to place the goblet back on the table.

"Keep the goblet, Lord Leonidas, as a reward for your fidelity," I cried.

"I humbly thank you, O Queen," Leonidas said. He sank to one knee and bowed his head, and returned happily to his couch. He sat, surrounded by friends, in a gay mood for having been singled out by royal favor.

For some time I talked pleasantly to Antony of mundane things, and then suddenly Leonidas leapt to his feet, clutching his stomach.

"I—I am poisoned!" Leonidas screamed, staggering about, shrieking, clutching his stomach, and then stumbling to the floor.

The musicians stopped playing and the guests fell

silent, murmuring in shocked whispers. They all watched Leonidas lying in the center of the hall as he gasped for breath and foamed at the mouth, his body thrashing about in violent convulsions.

"Poisoned!" Leonidas kept croaking. "Mother, help! Zeus, help! In the name of the gods, someone help, help!"

No one went near him.

Antony turned to me, his face scarlet. "What do you mean by this savage joke, Cleopatra?" he demanded.

"It serves a double purpose, dear Antony," I explained placidly, digging a clam out of a shell. "This very night your friend Leonidas was planning to flee to Octavian."

"And the second purpose?" Antony demanded.

I paused to eat the clam and washed it down with wine. "You fear that I would poison you, my lord," I said. "Well, that wreath of roses you stewed in your wine is dewed with deadly bane. If I had a notion to make an end of you, I would not have stayed your hand, and you would be on the floor dying instead of Leonidas. In the future, my husband, trust me. You will meet with many cruel deceptions and treasons from many friends. There is one, however, who will never betray you. Your wife! The woman who gave you three children, who gave you her body and soul." I put a hand on his head, my fingers pulling at his locks. "Oh, Antony, I would sooner slay myself than harm one curl on your beloved head!"

All the guests sat in stunned silence, having lost their appetites. I was the only one who continued to eat and drink with nonchalance. Leonidas lay groaning and praying for pity, as the poison slowly did its lethal work.

"This is almost as entertaining as a group of dancing girls," I remarked blithely. I peered at the corner where the musicians sat, their instruments lying limply on their laps. "Let's have some music to drown out these unpleasant noises."

The musicians obediently picked up their flutes and harps, but the music that issued forth was half-hearted.

It was an hour before Leonidas gave up the spirit. His convulsions ceased, his face stilled in a rictus of torment, his eyes peered from open folds, and although he was dead, a hand still twitched.

"Such a difficult death," I murmured with a sigh. "I thought he would never pass into the next life. Slaves, take the body away, but don't feed it to the crocodiles, since we don't want them poisoned!"

Only Charmion grunted a laugh at this remark. As slaves bore the body away, I poured Antony a goblet of wine and without hesitation he drank from it.

Apollodorus approached us and made obeisance.

"Speak, my beloved First Friend," I said.

"Queen Cleopatra, I found in the chamber of Leonidas his baggage filled with much stolen jewels and treasure."

At this revelation astonished murmurs sounded.

"I should think all will be warned," I cried out imperiously, "that it is not wise to play false with Royal Egypt!"

A hushed silence fell over the hall.

"This banquet is no longer amusing," I said at length. "Good night, my noble husband." I kissed Antony on the cheek as he slouched there. I rose and with Iras and Charmion walked out of the hall, my long robe trailing behind me, and all the guests stood and sank to their knees as I passed by.

"I was the greatest Roman of them all," I heard Antony mumble drunkenly, to no one in particular, as I left the hall. "I was greater than my cousin Caesar."

After that night, Antony trusted me completely.

In the days that followed, I was well informed of Octavian's movements. He sent his general, Cornelius Gallus, with orders to sail to Cyrene and join forces with Scarpus and attack Egypt from the west at Paraetonium, while he himself, with the help of King Herod, marched with his legions through Judaea toward Pelusium. His soldiers were excited by the promise of a share of Egypt's spoils.

"The forts at Paraetonium and Pelusium are well-armed," Antony told me confidently. "They are indeed impregnable. Alexandria is defended with forty thousand soldiers, and your royal fleet, cruising before the harbors, is capable of repelling any assault from the sea. With a show of valor and strength, Cleopatra, Egypt has a fair chance at being defended."

At the beginning of June, a messenger arrived informing us that Paraetonium, the impregnable fortress, had been taken by the combined forces of Scarpus and Gallus. Instead of being disheartened by this news, Antony roused himself and decided to march with a detachment of troops to Paraetonium and recapture the fort.

"Like the phoenix," Antony cried, "I will rise out of the ashes of Actium. Once more I am Antony, and I lead my soldiers to battle!"

"Yes, Antony, you are the bold son of Hercules and Mars!" I cried with pride, kissing him passionately.

Antony rode off, astride his white Arabian charger, leading his troops by forced marches to Paraetonium. I was torn by anxiety in the days that followed, worried about the fate of this expedition.

A week later, Apollodorus came to me with a stricken look. "O Queen, a messenger arrived informing us that Octavian and his army reached Pelusium a week ago," he said in a choked voice. "Our garrison was taken, and the army defending the eastern frontiers was cut to pieces."

Shocked to my soul, I felt a wave of pain shoot through me, but I quickly managed to tap a reserve of spirit to remain calm and to keep my nerve and heart.

All of Alexandria was in turmoil at the news that Pelusium had fallen. Apollodorus reported to me that a rumor was going about that Pelusium had not been taken by storm, but that I had ordered the gates opened since I was in league with Octavian. It was said that I wanted to rid myself of Antony so that I might gain the same amorous ascendency over Octavian that I had previously enjoyed over Caesar and Antony.

"How painful it is to know that, even at this final

hour, I am maligned in my own kingdom," I said bitterly.

"Cleopatra and Octavian?" Iras cried with a twisted face. "I would think two Romans in one lifetime is quite enough! What fictions will the people devise next, my Queen?"

I shrugged. "I remember one of my father's favorite old Macedonian sayings. 'A dog barks, but the wind blows the sound away.' "

A few days later, in late afternoon as the sky above Alexandria was all purple clouds and rivers of dying sunlight, Antony returned to the palace. I stood on a balcony overlooking the palace forecourt as he came through the gates, leading only a hundred or so wretched soldiers out of the five thousand he had taken with him to Paraetonium. I sensed instantly that their crusade had been disastrous.

Antony came to our apartments, and I watched as servants took off his dusty armor. I gave him a goblet of wine, and he sprawled wearily across a divan.

"I suffered a disgraceful defeat," Antony said in a lifeless voice. "I was unable, in spite of superhuman efforts, to take the fort by storm, and all my attacks were repulsed."

I then broke the news about Pelusium. His reaction was extreme in its intensity, and an attack of uncontrollable hysteria seized him. I ordered slaves to bathe and massage him, which somewhat calmed him. We ate some food, and then I took him into my bedchamber.

As we lay together in my great golden bed, I soothed Antony with my caresses and tenderness. His body smelled of sweet-smelling oils, and his mane of dark curly hair, soft from washing, fell across his forehead. My body burned with a sensuous fire, and I ached to enjoy his virility.

"Both Paraetonium and Pelusium have fallen," Antony said, "and armies from both east and west are marching to corner us in Alexandria. The final hour is upon us. Is now the time that I, in the tradition of

702

defeated Romans, should fall upon my sword, my little Greek girl?"

"Not yet, dear Antony," I said calmly, kissing his wine-scented lips. "We are on the precipice of extinction, but we will fix the hour for leaving life and step into the next world together, and we will do it in a grand style worthy of two of the greatest and most glorious creatures who ever walked the earth."

Antony took me with a conqueror's boldness, and in our passionate coupling, we were able to quell, for the moment, all restlessness and fears of tomorrow.

CHAPTER XI

THE ROMAN EAGLES CIRCLES the sky, shrieking and flapping its wings, about to sweep down and sink its ready talons into Egypt and rend her. I have lived my life with my every action designed solely to keep Egypt free from Roman tyranny, and now I have lost. Since childhood I have played a game on the chessboard of world politics, against the greatest generals of my epoch, but now I have been checkmated. For years I held back the Roman tide, but now I am about to be engulfed. I, Cleopatra, will answer to my fellow gods and to history, but never to Octavian. If I cannot live a queen, I will die one.

The road to Alexandria is clear to Octavian now that Pelusium has fallen. I no longer have any illusions about the future, and I realize that the most lamentable end to my struggles is in sight. In my methodical way, I am preparing for the final scenes of my life, for I know that queens are mortal in this world if not the next.

As I prepared for my death, I planned that Caesarion, who is on the threshold of manhood, shall live, and I knew that his life depended upon his leaving Egypt. I had him brought to my apartments in midmorning so that I could break the news to him. In two weeks he would celebrate his seventeenth birthday, but the day would not be marked by a palace banquet.

"My beloved son," I cried, reaching for his hands as we sat on a divan, "it is imperative that you leave Egyptian soil. In your twofold capacity as the son of Caesar and the presumptive pharaoh, you inspire jealousy and hatred in Octavian. If you remain here, you run the risk of being put to death when Octavian arrives with his army."

"Is it not my duty to stay with my people?" Caesarion asked earnestly.

"You will not be able to help your people as a corpse or a prisoner."

"Where will I go, Mother?"

"I think it best that you go with your dear friend Andronicus and Lord Rhodon and a small party, and travel up the Nile to Coptos and from there cross by caravan to the port of Berenice," I suggested. "A royal squadron lies at anchor in Berenice ready to take you to India. There you can wait out events in Egypt. Perhaps I may ride out this storm and conclude some accommodation with Octavian. At any event, you will be safe. If Egypt is lost, you can enter into an alliance with the King of Parthia, who detests the Romans. The day may come when you will lead an army of Parthians and return to liberate Egypt."

"When will I leave?" Caesarion whispered.

"This afternoon," I replied. "To delay would be foolish."

"I shall abide by your wishes, Mother," Caesarion said gravely.

The next hours were painful as the last frantic preparations were made for Caesarion's journey. The irretrievable moments rushed by, and the time of his departure arrived. I stood in the portico of the palace, watching with tears in my eyes as Caesarion made his farewells. He embraced Charmion and Iras, and then his little half-siblings who sobbed heartbrokenly that their big brother was leaving them. Antony hugged Caesarion and gave him a few final words of encouragement, and Charmion tenderly embraced her cousin, Andronicus.

While these farewells were taking place, I took Rhodon aside. "Guard Prince Caesarion with your life," I said solemnly. "Surely you know that beneath his reserve and dignified manner, he is still a timid boy who is subject to fits."

"I vow an oath to the gods and to you, O Queen, that you will never regret this duty with which you have charged me," Rhodon cried ardently, kneeling at my feet and kissing my hand. "Under my care, Prince Caesarion shall fulfill his divine destiny."

"Rise, my Lord Rhodon," I said. "It gives me satisfaction to know that my prince is in your hands."

I had given Rhodon a great bag of gold, and his cloaks were sewn with thousands of rich gems.

Caesarion and I, holding hands, walked down the long flight of marble steps to the courtyard where his friends who were going with him were waiting. A military escort was there to accompany Caesarion and his party across the city to the galley that was anchored on the banks of the Nile.

"I wish you were going with me, Mother," Caesarion said.

"In accordance with my coronation and nuptial oaths," I replied, "I will never abandon my people and my husband."

In the courtyard, Caesarion and I, mother and son, faced one another. We knew the chances of our ever seeing each other again were remote. We held back our emotions with an effort.

From around my neck, I took a gold chain strung to a gold medallion which had a carved cameo of Caesar on one side and my profile on the reverse. I placed the chain around Caesarion's slim neck. "Never forget," I cried, my voice ringing, "that you are Ptolemy Caesar, a Ptolemy and a Caesar, the son of Cleopatra and Caesar!"

Caesarion stared intently into my eyes. "You loved my father best, didn't you, Mother?" he asked in a choked voice.

The question surprised me and I remained mute.

"Didn't you, Mother?" Caesarion insisted.

"Yes, Caesarion," I replied, making my voice sound sincere to disguise the lie, my heart swelling painfully, "I loved your father best."

Caesarion, in a surge of gratitude, embraced me.

At length I pushed him gently away, and took his face between my hands. "Remember that when I was twenty-one I was forced to flee Egypt with Apollodorus," I cried zealously. "I returned victoriously with the help of your father, and you will also return in triumph. Never forget that holy blood runs in your veins. You are Pharaoh, direct descendant of our deity, Amon-Ra, god of the sun who rules the heavens as he rules the earth. It is inevitable that the Romans will enslave Egypt, just as the Persians once did. Alexander liberated Egypt from the Persian yoke, and then his brother Ptolemy founded our dynasty and restored Egypt to greatness. You will return like Alexander and assume the burden of your divine destiny as Pharaoh the celestial son of Amon!"

"I promise, Mother, that I shall fulfill your faith in me," Caesarion cried timorously, his young face shining with intensity.

My heart was aching as I covered my firstborn's face with kisses. "Farewell, my son," I cried, releasing him.

"Farewell, Mother!" Caesarion said tremulously, turning away from me just as tears began to slide from his eyes.

I watched Caesarion mount his horse. We waved at one another and exchanged shaky smiles. He was gloriously handsome in his gold armor and cloak, with his blond hair struck golden by the summer sun. I drank in his young, pure beauty for the last time as he spurred his golden stirrups into the flanks of his horse and galloped off, leading his party out of the courtyard and through the gigantic copper gates.

As my son disappeared down the Canopic Boulevard, tears streamed down my face. Antony came and put his strong arms around me, and falling against him, I began sobbing uncontrollably.

I had just endured one of the most painful moments of my life.

"Come, my sweet love," Antony said, his voice touched with sympathy, and as if I were as light as a child, he swept me up in his great arms and carried me easily back up the flight of marble steps.

Later that afternoon I went to the Temple of Isis, and said fervent prayers for Caesarion's safety.

I recall that great play by Sophocles, *Oedipus at Colonus*, in which Oedipus tells his two daughters, Antigone and Ismene, "You shall never have more love from any man than you have had from me." In this line, Oedipus eloquently expresses the feelings of every father who ever lived. In the same spirit, I know that never will Caesarion have more love from any woman than he has had from his mother.

A few days afterward, I learned that Octavian was still at Pelusium. I decided to send Epaphroditus, the tutor to the twins, to Pelusium in order to find out whether, by offering gifts to this greedy man, I could conclude an honorable peace. I remembered that my father had bought off the Romans with gold for thirty years. Epaphroditus, who was a first cousin to my beloved Iras, took a talent of gold and a golden crown to Octavian. Epaphroditus was authorized to say that I was prepared to abdicate in favor of Caesarion. Within two weeks Epaphroditus returned to say that Octavian willingly accepted my gifts, but his reply to my proposals was categorically negative.

"If Cleopatra lays down her arms and abdicates immediately," Octavian said, "I will consider later what to do with her person."

I realized that my enemy was not a man who allowed himself to be turned from his course by gifts, and that I could never expect favorable treatment or terms at his hands.

The following days were passed in my palace full of wretchedness. Just as on board a ship that is floundering in a storm and all discipline ends, so at the news of the approach of Octavian, order could no longer be maintained in Alexandria. Most of my nobles left the palace, and only my most faithful friends remained—Apollodorus, Mardian, Olympus, and my children's masters. The scholars and artists, who had been so favored by

709

me, abandoned the museum and the library, never so much as dreaming that I, their benefactress, might have need of their counsel at such a crisis. Several nobles and merchants journeyed to meet Octavian on the road, and to assist him in capturing Alexandria and reducing their country to slavery. The capital was crowded with four legions, but many of the officers were deserting, and the soldiers gave themselves up to rapine and pillaging. General confusion reigned, and the disorderly crowds in the streets caused me intense anxiety.

Charmion and Apollodorus were pillars of strength for me during these dreadful days, but Antony and Iras were of no help, broken in spirit as they were. Iras, addicted to poppy juice, roamed my apartments in distraction, her face baleful and her dark eyes set in a hallucinated stare. Antony's reliance on wine had sapped his strength, and the flame of his great spirit had guttered out.

"I know I embarrass you with my cringing fears, my love," Antony said pathetically one evening as we supped. "You are charged with demons and possessed by the gods, and with your mixture of exquisite calm and passionate excess, you can endure all misfortunes with fortitude, but I cannot. I still hunger for life. I am defeated, yet I hope to live. Perhaps I will be able to work out a modus vivendi with Octavian. Lepidus was permitted to retire to his country estate, and so perhaps Octavian will permit me to retire to an Aegean island where I can live privately and write my memoirs."

"Stop dreaming, Antony," I said impatiently. "Octavian allowed Lepidus to live because he was no longer dangerous. As long as you live, you could be plotting a return to power. How can you think of retiring with a few friends, to drink and eat, to exist like an animal, and after being master of half the world, to be master of a rock dropped in the sea? I, Cleopatra, will be a queen and nothing less. One lives only to die, and one rises only to fall. We have fallen, Antony, and we must not think how to live, but how to die. I am preparing for the next world, and if you wish, I shall leave you this one."

"It is only human to hope for the best even against the blackest of odds," Antony said lugubriously.

"Then we must stand and fight!" I cried. "We still have four legions, and Alexandria can easily hold out in a long siege, as Caesar and I proved years ago during the Alexandrian War."

I had Apollodorus supervise the slaves who removed all my precious belongings from the palace to my black marble tomb next to the Temple of Isis. My gold, silver, precious stones of pearls, rubies, and emeralds, and gold-spun dresses and tapestries, were all heaped on beds of flax. A number of torches were also stored in the tomb. This mausoleum would be my last place of refuge, and I had resolved that my treasures and I would perish in flame to escape the hands of Octavian.

Octavian, while he was hastening with his army toward Alexandria, and fearful that I might do something rash, sent a message on ahead, assuring me of his "general and honorable treatment."

From the west, the troops of Scarpus and Gallus marched toward the capital, and Octavian's legions advanced from the east. Soon Alexandria would be surrounded on all sides. When news came that Octavian's army had crossed the Canopic mouth of the Nile, Antony, summoning hidden strengths, roused himself and led a cavalry of two thousand men to attack Octavian's advance guard. With a furious rush, in a brilliant action, he broke their ranks and drove them back.

Flushed with victory, Antony returned to the palace as the embers of sunset were glowing over the monuments of the city. In a transport of excitement, I ran down to meet him at the palace gates.

"My darling," Antony cried rapturously, "once more victory has placed her crown on my head!"

"Has Octavian fallen?" I asked anxiously, flinging my arms around his sweaty neck.

"No, but I beat his cavalry to pieces!"

"My husband," I cried exultantly, "once again you are my magnificent, intrepid hero!"

"I've sent a message to Octavian challenging him to

711

single combat," Antony said. "If he accepts, the world will know who is the best man."

Antony's success that day exhilarated me, and arm in arm we went to our apartments as he boasted proudly. I watched happily as servants took off his armor and washed the grime from his big, fleshy body.

Early that evening a messenger came to the palace informing us that Octavian and his main force were pitching camp at the Hippodrome in Canopus. The messenger brought a letter from Octavian.

"Greetings to Antony from Caesar Augustus," the letter said. "I refuse your offer of single combat. The Lord Antony might think of many other ways to die."

"I will lead my men to Octavian and ferret him out from the ranks," Antony cried. "His soldiers will be exhausted from the long march from Pelusium, so I will attack them tomorrow before they have time to rest. I can still turn the tide of fortune to our favor, my falcon queen."

"I believe you will, dear husband," I said warmly.

When Antony left to consult with his captains, Apollodorus handed me a scroll with Octavian's seal.

"The Imperator Augustus Caesar sends greetings to the Queen of Egypt," I read. "Although I am the victor, I desire only to be friends with the vanquished. The Lord Antony, the degenerate drunk who betrayed Rome, stands between us. I swear by the memory of my father, Julius Caesar, that you will keep Egypt and win the friendship of Rome by sending me Antony's head."

I trembled with rage. "What little judgment Octavian shows, mocking me in this matter," I cried. "Does he think I would ever trust the word of a Roman again? I will die first."

Later in the evening, in a gown blazing with jewels, I walked into the great hall on the arm of Antony to preside over a banquet for our soldiers. There was a joyful mood over the victory that day.

After the main courses, Antony had a soldier who had distinguished himself during the battle, brought to our table. Antony made a speech of praise, and I gave the soldier a golden breastplate with a crest of the Ptolemaic eagle. The musicians played the national songs, dancing girls danced in the Greek fashion, and everyone ate his fill and became merry with wine and music.

"Soldiers and friends," Antony cried, standing up on the table on the royal dais. "Companions whom many a time I have led to victory, hear my words. No longer will we wait for the flood of war, but will plunge into battle against the enemy and will snatch the conqueror's crown or fall to dust."

The soldiers interrupted Antony's speech with thunderous shouts expressing their fidelity and devotion.

"Tomorrow's battle will be a hazardous affair," Antony resumed in his great orator's voice, "but we have faced fiercer perils in the past, and before the day was done, we vanquished armies and counted the spoils of kings by sunset. If we stand together, tomorrow night the head of Octavian will be impaled on the gates of the palace!"

The hall reverberated with the soldiers' shouts.

"Ah, my friends, I love you like my brothers!" Antony cried in a thrilling voice. "Tomorrow at dawn we will spring at Octavian's throat, both by land and sea. Swear that you will stand by me!"

"We swear, Lord Antony!" the soldiers cried frenziedly. "By all the holy gods, we swear to stand steadfast!"

Soldiers crowded around the table, some of them weeping like children, clutching and kissing Antony's hands.

"Once more my star shines bright!" Antony cried, deeply moved by the emotional demonstrations from his men.

Antony and I left the hall to shouts of "Hail, Antony!" and "Hail, Cleopatra!" ringing in our ears.

Alone in our bedchamber, Antony and I dismissed all the servants and helped one another undress. The curtains were left open, and the radiance from the moon

713

and Pharos illuminated the chamber. We lay abed, clinging to one another.

"Oh, Antony," I said sweetly, "do you remember the first time I met you?"

"Yes, you were fourteen and I had just won Egypt back for your father almost single-handedly," Antony said with remembered pride.

"You were my hero then and you still are," I said tenderly. "You are the legendary hero of our age. How Homer would have loved to have written about you!" Antony, overjoyed by my words, held me tightly against his huge, hairy body. "Do you remember our meeting at Tarsus?" I asked.

"Yes, my whole body ached for you, but you made me follow you to Egypt," Antony said wistfully "And then, in this very bed, I took you for the first time."

"Eleven years ago," I said. "You were in the prime of manhood and I was at the peak of womanhood."

"We are still at the prime and the peak!" Antony insisted.

"Since then we have had so many glorious, precious moments," I said stirringly. "We have given each other everything—ecstasy, joy, grief, hate, rancor, jealousy, and it has all made our love complete."

Antony's mouth silenced me with a kiss, and then glorying in his virility, he gave me sensual satisfaction which was as sharp and dazzling as ever. Although as always the pleasures he gave me were of the flesh, my very spirit and soul were shaken.

Like a child, I fell asleep in his great arms.

The dark mantle of night rolled back and the sun of Amon rose in a bright day. We stirred against one another, wanting to hold back the day.

With my own hands, I served Antony the morning meal. I watched him, admiring his tall, large-boned figure filled out with great strength and commanding aspect, as slaves buckled on his armor. With his arm around me, we went down to the courtyard where his soldiers were already astride their horses.

"Farewell, my little Greek wife," Antony cried. "I go

orth to win a soldier's victory or a soldier's death. I
still have as many soldiers as stars in the sky, and I
might yet tip the scales of fate to our side."

"You shall win victory, Antony!" I cried with spirit.
"You will be like that great Athenian, Themistocles,
whose capacity for seizing victory from the jaws of defeat has echoed down through the ages!"

"Farewell, my adoring wife!" Antony cried, kissing
me passionately.

I stood with tears in my eyes, watching Antony ride
off leading his soldiers to battle, with Eros at his side.
Perhaps he was doomed to failure, but I was filled with
love and admiration for this last show of valor.

"Antony is no Themistocles, Cleopatra," Apollodorus said grimly. "He is not Alexander and he is not
Caesar."

"No, he is Antony and the world will remember him
just as well," I said with pride, walking up the marble
steps to the palace. "It is true Antony is weak one day,
but on the next, typical Scorpio that he is, he is heroic
on a grand, Homeric scale. He is one of the most striking figures the world will ever know, and the only man
of true feeling in this corrupt age. Mark my words,
Apollodorus, Antony will have the sympathy and admiration of the world in the ages to come."

"Antony has brought Egypt and you to ruin," Apollodorus said bitterly, "and yet you love him still."

"If he was my undoing, I was his undoing," I cried.
"Together we had a magnificent dream and we lost."

In a sad mood I returned to my private apartments.
When noon came I had my children brought to me so
we could eat together. The ten-year-old twins and
seven-year-old Prince Ptolemy were wise and serious,
being the young royals that they are, and they sensed
they were living through fateful days. They did not
scamper about my chamber in laughter and mischief as
in former days, but sat on their couches, subdued and
withdrawn, deporting themselves with solemn dignity.
Not one of them asked where their father was, as though

715

they all knew. None of us ate much of the food that was set before us.

At last I embraced my children for the last time.

"I will not be seeing you tomorrow, my darling children," I said, forcing a smile. "Obey your foster parents, the ladies Diana and Daphne and the lords Euphronius and Epaphroditus, in all things, and love them as you do your father and me."

The smallest, Prince Ptolemy, so grave and proud, clung desperately to me, his blue eyes sparkling with tears. "Please, Mother," he cried beseechingly, "I don't want to leave you!"

"Ptolemy, you are the child who gave me the least trouble at birth, but you have made up for it since with your mischief!" I chided gently.

"Come, Ptolemy, we must go now," Cleopatra Selene, in her little taskmistress way, cried as she reached for his hand.

"Yes, Ptolemy, go to your lessons," I said, smiling bravely, kissing my beautiful youngest child one last time on his soft cheek.

Ptolemy was choking back tears as he was led away. A painful rush of agony shot through me, but I did not let my sobs break forth until the children had filed through the huge doors and were in the corridor. They all stopped, surrounded by their attendants, and turned around to look back at me. I waved at them, the guards closed the doors, and then I started sobbing, knowing that I would never see them again. Their fates were now in the hands of Octavian. I was reassured, however, to think that Octavian would never dare harm the children of Antony, for the Romans would never forgive him for that.

I glanced at the water clock, seeing that it was one hour into the afternoon.

"Surely the battle is being fought now," I remarked to Apollodorus.

Apollodorus did not respond, but shuffled nervously near the windows overlooking the harbor.

"In all probability Antony will die in the thick of the

716

fight, a sword in hand, which is what he wants," I said
with deep resignation. "Octavian will enter the city
tomorrow or the day after. It is almost time, Apollodorus, for you to take me to my tomb."

Apollodorus came and stood in front of me. "What I
want to do is roll you up in a carpet, fling you over my
shoulder, and dressed as a merchant, walk out of the
palace with you," he cried with emotion.

I smiled affectionately. "There are no Caesars to take
me to, my beloved friend."

Leaving me that morning, Antony led his troops out
of the city and posted them on high ground near the sea
on the road to Canopus. He saw the Egyptian fleet sailing out from the two harbors, as planned, toward the
fleet of Octavian. When the two fleets came together at
high noon, they hailed each other with their oars in a
friendly manner. Then the whole body of ships, forming
a single fleet, began sailing directly to the harbors.

This was a heartbreaking scene for Antony to witness.

The summer sun was at its zenith as Antony led his
perspiring soldiers toward Canopus. Finally, in the distance, he sighted the enemy lines drawn up and waiting.
They paused for a moment, and then Antony gave the
signal to charge. His soldiers, however, instead of raising their swords, sheathed them, and in a body galloped
off toward the enemy with olive branches dangling from
their swords as a sign of peace.

Realizing that he was being deserted by all his men,
Antony, mad with rage, seized a fleeing soldier and
threw him to the ground. He drew his sword and held
it on high, while the deserter, covering his face, awaited
death.

"Rise!" Antony cried, dropping his sword. "Go to
Octavian with your comrades, and good luck. I loved
you once, so why among so many traitors should I
single you out for death?"

The soldier rose and looked sorrowfully upon Antony. Shame overwhelmed him, and with a great cry he
plunged his sword into his own heart and fell dead.

In a stupor, Antony gazed at the dead soldier. In the

distance, he saw his soldiers riding into the ranks of Octavian's legions, and instead of crossing swords, they embraced like long-lost brothers.

"Everyone has deserted and betrayed me!" Antony cried out in anguish.

"I am still here, Antony," Eros cried, standing beside his master and reaching for his hand.

With a sob of gratitude, Antony embraced Eros. The two of them stood alone on the field by the sea, clinging to each other, as all the soldiers in the far distance watched.

In midafternoon, when messengers came and told me that the supreme effort had failed, that my fleet had deserted and my army no longer existed, I took my two favorites, Iras and Charmion, and went to my tomb. At the entrance I kissed Apollodorus, Demetrius, Olympus, and Mardian in farewell. I entered my house of death with my ladies, and we bolted the doors from within.

I breathed a long sigh, at once engulfed by the silence and coolness of the place. My mausoleum is a noble and imposing structure of black marble, a little palace of death with hallways and dozens of marble staircases intricately interconnected and leading to small chambers, enclosures, and sacred altars. I walked up a great flight of stairs to the main chamber and stood gazing at the two huge marble vaults which are designated for the bodies of Antony and Cleopatra, and where we will rest beside one another through the coming ages.

Eternal flames glowed from altars in niches, which gave a soft, subdued light. Three couches had been brought from the palace and were set up beside the vaults, and I lay across one now. Iras, with her white spectral face and dark fevered eyes, sipped a little poppy juice and picked up her harp and began plucking at the strings, making a soft, sweet melody. Charmion, as is her wont, went about the huge main chamber, efficiently checking that we had supplies and all was in order.

As I lay I listened to the rhythmic swell of the sea against the back wall of the tomb, which was in tune with my shallow heartbeat, and the soothing music that

Iras made on her harp. A certain calm possessed me. The tumult and cares of the world receded, and I found myself falling into a tranquil trance, and already I sensed how peaceful death would be.

Not long after I had shut myself up in my tomb, around the fourth hour of the afternoon, Antony galloped into the palace courtyard with Eros. Rushing into the Alabaster Hallway, he was met by Apollodorus.

"Where is the Queen?" Antony demanded.

"In her tomb," Apollodorus cried.

Antony, thinking I was dead, rushed to our bedchamber. He unfastened his armor and took off his shirt of mail. Apollodorus had followed him and Eros, hanging back, watched from behind a pillar near the door.

"Oh, my beloved Eros!" Antony cried. "My honor can still be saved, but only by death. I must follow Cleopatra to the shades. Eros, you have loved me since I found you ten years ago in Athens. You were fourteen then, an orphan, and you have grown to manhood at my side. As my favorite you have found riches and have been ennobled by my wife, and now you must discharge your debt. Remember the promise I extracted from you after Actium? Draw your sword and make an end of me!"

"No, Antony, I cannot!" Eros protested wretchedly. "When I went with you to Parthia, thousands of Parthian arrows and darts missed you. How can you ask me to do what the Parthians could not?"

"Do not quarrel with me, Eros!" Antony snapped hotly. "For ten years you have obeyed my every desire, and this is no time to start a precedent. If you love me, show it by thrusting your sword into my heart and ending my misery."

With tears falling down his face, Eros drew his sword. "Farewell, my beloved Antony!" he cried.

"Oh, Eros, I knew you would do my bidding," Antony said gratefully, sinking to his knees and baring his breast for Eros to strike, closing his eyes and stiffening for the mortal blow.

Holding his sword above Antony as if to strike him, Eros suddenly turned away. "I cannot slay the man I love!" he cried, plunging the sword into his own heart.

Antony watched as Eros fell to the floor, and he gathered the dying young Greek up in his arms. "Eros, my boy!"

Eros looked up at Antony. "This way I escape the sorrow of Antony's death," he whispered faintly.

"How aptly you were named, Eros, my love," Antony said.

Hearing these words, Eros sighed his last breath.

"Nobly done, valiant Eros," Antony murmured. "I must now have the courage to do what you and Cleopatra have done." He kissed the boy's cheek once more, and then let the body slide gently to the floor.

Antony, with resolution, took his Philippian sword and plunged the tip into his bowels, letting out a piercing groan.

At this point Apollodorus rushed to Antony's side.

"Oh, Apollodorus," Antony beseeched, "I have bungled the job, so please make an end of what I have begun."

Kneeling, Apollodorus drew the sword from Antony's innards and placed him on the bed. He stanched the flow of blood. The wound was not so deep as to be immediately mortal. Servants came crowding about to see great Antony die. Antony entreated those around him to put him out of his pain; but no one would take the responsibility, and many fled from his tortured pleas.

Finally Olympus came and told Antony that I was in my tomb, but living still.

"Queen Cleopatra alive?" Antony cried. "Oh, I beg to be taken to her so that I might die in her arms."

Slaves placed Antony on a litter and carried him to the barred entrance of the tomb. I looked down from a high window and saw my husband bleeding to death. I was fearful that soldiers were posted ready to rush the door if I opened it, so I let down from the window a rope and chains which were secured around Antony's stretcher. Iras, Charmion, and I pulled on the ropes with all our strength, and inch by inch we lifted Antony up the wall of the tomb. Down on the ground, Apollodorus, Demetrius, Olympus, and others stood and watched this sad spectacle, and their exhortations encouraged us as we three frail women, straining every muscle and gasping with the violence of the effort, lifted this giant of a man. Twice we nearly lost our grip and Antony was about to fall to earth, but with the help of the gods and superhuman strength born out of love, we at last drew the stretcher to the window. We pulled Antony inside, and the ropes and stretcher were dropped to the ground.

All my deep love for Antony flared within me as the lifeblood flowed from his gaping wound. I became hysterical, and kneeling at his side, I covered him with kisses and wiped his blood with my robe.

"Oh, my lord, my emperor, my husband!" I sobbed convulsively, my hair streaming wildly about me and my tears falling on my face.

"Cleopatra, calm yourself," Antony whispered, a hand touching my cheek. "Wine, wine to give me strength to speak my last words."

Charmion quickly brought a goblet of wine, and I held the rim to Antony's lips as he sipped. I also took a drink and with an effort controlled my hysteria. I knew that he was breathing his last, and I wanted to give him comfort as he entered the door of death.

"Shed no more tears for me, Cleopatra," Antony whispered faintly. "There is no need to weep, for we have had happiness. I am dying in your bosom, and I am content."

"Yes, Antony," I said tremulously, leaning over and kissing him tenderly on the mouth.

"I advise you to seek some way of bringing your own affairs honorably to a safe conclusion," Antony said. "Of all the friends of Octavian, trust only Proculeius. He was a good friend in the old days."

"Proculeius," I muttered, giving him a sip of wine.

"Do not pity me, Cleopatra, but dwell on the blessings of my life," Antony resumed. "I was born noble but impoverished, and I rose by my own efforts to the summit of glory. I leave life in full possession of my faculties, and Antony has slain Antony. I hope it is a fitting end."

"Yes, Antony, and the manner is worthy of your greatness," I said, my hands gently touching his perspiring face.

"Although I did so very much want to die as a soldier in battle," Antony said with a trace of regret.

"You have been a great lover as well as a great soldier, dearest Antony," I said admiringly. "This is a most seemly end for Antony the great lover."

A small smile appeared on Antony's face. "Whatever judgment the world will form of us, Cleopatra, we were indeed a man and a woman who knew how to live and to love."

"Yes, the world will have to credit us with that!" I cried tearfully.

Antony closed his eyes and his breathing became shallow. I clutched his hands tightly as I felt him dying and deserting me. A convulsive shudder, an unmistakable death spasm, passed through his body.

"Oh, my Antony!" I cried out desperately. "Antony!"

With a great effort, Antony opened his eyes. "I die happily, Cleopatra, for I die in your arms. You have given me thousands of kisses. One more, my love, one more kiss to take my breath away."

"Yes, Antony," I said. I leaned down, my mouth searching his lips. "I love you!" I whispered, and then I kissed him. I held my lips against his until the last sighing breath came into my mouth, and then I felt his body go still as his spirit fled.

I lifted my head and gazed upon his face, seeing the stillness of death on his features. "Death has frozen the warmest heart that ever throbbed!" I cried. Then an outcry of mortal anguish broke from my lips. "Antony!" I broke out in a great bitter cry, "Antony!"

A surge of lacerating pains shot through my soul, and I began to tremble with uncontrollable sobs. I fell over, my hands clutching the great body of manly beauty and physical strength which had given me so much pride and joy, which now had turned to lifeless clay.

After some time, Charmion and Iras pulled me away from Antony and covered his body with a silk coverlet. They helped me down the staircase to the main chamber. I lay on my golden couch. Charmion held a goblet of wine to my lips. The wine benumbed me a little, and I lay back, my girls kneeling beside my couch. We were all whimpering in deep pain, our muscles bruised from pulling Antony up on the ropes, and our hands burning like fire from the flesh that had been rubbed away. There was also the pain of my grieving heart, and I kept moaning Antony's name over and over. I lay in a fit of delirium. Antony was dead and it seemed the world stood still.

I did not know it then, but as soon as Antony had stabbed himself, a messenger rode out to Octavian's camp and informed him of this event. Octavian sent Proculeius into the city to find me.

As the sun was setting, there came a pounding at the doors of the tomb. I lay on my couch, barely conscious. Charmion went down to see who it was, and in a state of excitement came up to tell me it was Proculeius. My ladies supported me as I went down to the fortified entrance, and through a grating I had discourse with Proculeius.

"Queen Cleopatra, I come bearing the condolences of my master Caesar Augustus and of the Roman army on the death of your great husband," Proculeius said. "When my master learned the sorrowful news, he was overcome with grief and made a speech to his soldiers expressing his remorse."

I realized that Octavian remembered what a pretense of grief Caesar had made when my brother had presented Pompey's head to him, and so he thought a similar show would now be appropriate. Perhaps his soldiers were fooled, but I was not.

"Lord Proculeius," I said, "my husband said that you were the only Roman I could trust."

723

"Divine Queen, I beg to be admitted so that we can talk together," Proculeius said pleadingly.

"I cannot unless I have assurances from Octavian that my kingdom will be given to my children."

"Be of good courage, Great Queen, and trust Octavian in all things," Proculeius cried. "My master is planning a great funeral for Lord Antony. Rome smiles upon you, and as Octavian's father the Great Caesar protected Egypt, so shall his worthy son."

This conference went on for some time, but I continued to resist these overtures and the doors remained bolted.

During this prolonged parley, soldiers fixed a scaling ladder to the window through which Antony had been pulled. Gallus and a dozen soldiers entered the upper chamber, stepping over the body of Antony, and then made their way down to the hallway where I stood. It was Iras who first saw the soldiers coming down the steps toward us.

"Cleopatra, you are taken prisoner!" she shrieked.

I spun around and saw Gallus and several soldiers rapidly descending the staircase in front of me.

"You are our prisoner, O Queen," Gallus cried, brandishing a sword.

I drew from my girdle a tiny dagger which I always kept on my person, but too late, for a soldier sprang at me. I struggled in a fit of hysteria, screaming, "Death, death, death!" as I was wrestled to the floor and the dagger taken from me.

"Search her whole body to see that there is no poison on her," Gallus commanded harshly. "And her ladies, too!"

There followed one of the most brutalizing and humiliating experiences I have ever endured. Big, burly soldiers overwhelmed me, pinning me down, and their rough hands pulled at my clothes and violated every secret place of my body, and the same cruel, gross indignity was executed on the bodies of Charmion and Iras.

When Gallus was satisfied that our bodies concealed

nothing, he stood over me. "For shame, O Queen," he said, "for why rob my master of so fair an occasion of showing his celebrated clemency?"

I was pulled to my feet, and I was so stupefied by despair and shock that I could barely stand.

"You will be conducted to your palace with your ladies, O Queen," Gallus announced.

I left my tomb with Iras and Charmion, our clothes torn and dishevelled and our hair in disarray. We were marched back to the palace under heavy guard. The marble walks and squares along the Great Harbor were almost deserted, although a few citizens witnessed my shame. A light breeze blew in from the sea. It was about the ninth hour of the evening when the red ball of the sun was falling into the ocean. The last rays of the power and glory of the Lagidae were being extinguished with those of the setting sun. My children and I were now in the hands of the victor, and the Egyptian empire was destroyed.

"The Queen is left in your charge, Proculeius," Gallus said at the doors of my apartments. "You have strict orders, on pain of death, to see that she does not take her life."

A dozen soldiers were posted in the corners of my bedchamber to stand sentry over my every waking and sleeping moment.

I took to my bed with Iras and Charmion. I was still clothed in the torn, bloodstained dress which I had used to stanch Antony's mortal wound. The three of us huddled together, crushed and weary. Iras especially was in a state of crazed despair, and she whimpered in my arms like a wounded little animal. I was alarmed that her wits had deserted her, and I held her close through the long night of fever and torment.

It was the last day of July. Caesarion had left Alexandria three weeks before, I calculated, and surely at that very moment he was mounted on a camel, journeying in a caravan, across the desert from Coptos to Berenice. In a few days he would embark on a ship bound for India and freedom. My one consolation was

725

that Caesarion, though a royal fugitive without a country, was alive and free.

At dawn I heard the thump of marching troops, as Octavian made his triumphal entry into Alexandria at the head of his legions. The citizens threw themselves at his feet along the boulevards and begged for mercy. Heralds announced that Octavian would address them in the great public square in front of the palace at high noon. The citizens awaited him, crowding the huge concourse, and as he made his appearance, they all fell prostrate to the marble ground.

Octavian mounted the tribunal at the side of the philosopher Arius, who had been once my dear friend. Looking out over the vast, crowded square, Octavian bade everyone rise. He spoke in Latin and Arius translated.

"Alexandrians!" Octavian cried. "I acquit you from any blame in this war. Why should you suffer for the sins of Antony and Cleopatra?"

The citizens cheered at this remark.

"Rest assured," Octavian resumed when the cheers died down, "that I will spare your beloved city for the sake of Alexander who built it, for the city's sake since I admire its beauty, and to gratify my dear friend Arius who was born here."

Once again the people erupted with shouts of joy.

"Egypt is now under the protection of Rome," Octavian cried. "I promise that Egypt will flourish with my friendship."

Octavian dismissed the assembly and made his way to the royal palace, taking up residence in the east wing. The first action he took was to dispatch a detachment of soldiers to catch up with Caesarion before he sailed for India.

In the afternoon, Proculeius came to me, saying that Octavian did not wish to deprive the widow of her due and that I could prepare for the obsequies of the dead and I was allowed to spend whatever sums I deemed necessary. I asked that Lord Apollodorus assist me in arranging Antony's funeral, but I was told that Apollodorus and Mardian were under arrest.

I soon discovered that Octavian lied, for I was restricted in the funeral arrangements. Octavian insisted that the body be interred within two days, which did not allow time for embalming. It was obvious that Octavian did not want Antony's body to be preserved, in the manner of Alexander's corpse, for future generations to gaze upon. The children were not allowed to attend their father's funeral, since Octavian did not relish the sight of their publicly grieving for their father. Octavian knew how the Alexandrians loved Antony, and he wanted to keep all public displays of lamentation at a minimum.

Months before at my orders, gold coffins had been made to receive my body and Antony's but these coffins were now confiscated and melted down, along with all my golden plate. Antony was interred in a simple ebony casket. Roman soldiers lined the boulevard from the palace to the tomb, holding back all the citizens and discouraging any show of grief.

Mark Antony, one of the greatest men who ever lived, had a simple funeral. I followed his casket and Iras, Charmion, Olympus, and a few aged eunuchs and ladies of the court came afterward as soldiers, on foot, carried it to the mausoleum.

It was only when the coffin was being lowered into the sarcophagus, and the marble lid placed over it and sealed, that my composure broke. I began wailing in the torment of despair, rent my dress and clawed at my breasts. Then I swooned and had to be carried back to the palace.

Octavian was too busy to attend the funeral. While I was burying my husband, Octavian went down to explore my treasury vaults below the palace. Preceded by slaves bearing torches, he walked through subterranean passages which house works of art, priceless jewels, precious carpets, stores of ingots, piles of coins, stacks of silver, and a hundred thousand talents in bars of gold. Octavian, not known for showing emotion, shouted with glee as he took an inventory of my riches. The fortune he had inherited from Caesar was only a fraction of my treasure which I have nurtured over two decades of prudent management of Egypt. This bounty will pay his soldiers and his debts. Egypt is now his personal property, and he envisions a steady stream of gold and wheat flowing from these lands into Rome in the years to come. It is this wealth which will put the imperial crown of the world on his head.

A day after the funeral, I saw to it that Eros was buried in a corner of the tomb, not far from Antony, an honor that Eros earned with fidelity to the death.

Fever struck me and I abstained from food, hoping to invite death. My buoyant spirit had finally been crushed. Olympus was brought to me, first being searched lest he had a vial of poison to slip me. Olympus knew I was courting death, and he counselled me that in this manner I would soon be delivered from my wretched existence.

Foreseeing my intentions, Octavian sent Proculeius to me with menacing threats against my children to keep me from carrying out my design. Fearful for their lives, I had to permit those about me to give me what medicines and nourishment they pleased.

I became acquainted with the young Cornelius Dolabella, a scion of one of the oldest families of the Roman aristocracy. Dolabella, a staff officer of Octavian's, was assigned to keep watch over me. His father, of the same name, had been consul with Antony at the time of Caesar's murder and one of Antony's friends since childhood.

"When you were about ten years old, I remember your father bringing you to my villa in the Transpontine Gardens," I told Dolabella. "How proud your father would be of his fair son today!"

"Most glorious of queens," Dolabella said, his intense, handsome face radiant as he gazed upon me, "my heart thrills to at last be able to thank you for the aid you gave my father thirteen years ago when he was Proconsul of Syria."

"Your father's defeat at such despicable hands as Cassius' is one of the saddest chapters in Roman history," I cried.

"As head of my noble family, I feel an obligation to Royal Egypt," Dolabella cried, "and if I may be able to repay this debt I would do so with pleasure."

"Perhaps you will be able to help me, my Lord Dolabella," I said. "When your father was cornered by enemy forces, in the honorable fashion of fallen Romans, he slew himself, and his boyhood friend Antony did likewise. I, on the other hand, desire deeply to live. Could you not impress Octavian that I wish only to go to Rome for his triumph? I cannot renounce this life before assuring myself of my children's welfare. These guards in my chamber, day and night, I find unendurable. Only if I have privacy will I be able to regain the spirit and strength which will enable me to journey to Rome."

"I have Octavian's ear and trust, O Queen," Dolabella said earnestly, "and I promise these guards shall be removed."

Dolabella was true to his promise, for the guards were withdrawn and I breathed a sigh of relief. Octavian was convinced that I desired to live, and I had the freedom to make whatever arrangements I wished.

"Oh, Cleopatra, my love," Iras said, "even in your fallen state, your charm and courage are intact and you exercise a potent spell on all those who come near you. Dolabella is beguiled by you and you have him in your power."

Dolabella deeply empathizes with my misfortunes and has promised to communicate to me everything that passes in Octavian's councils.

Rome has now won its greatest prize, the conquest of Egypt. Octavian has been busily consolidating the administration of his new province. Wishing to judge the resources of Alexandria himself, he has visited all the warehouses and factories. Anxious to establish friendly relations, he has devoted attentions to all the nobles and flattered their pride. He has attended the theater, visited the museum and the temples. He has catered to the priests, and they have declared that he is a god.

The Age of Hellenism, inaugurated by Alexander, is ending with me. Alexander's vision of a community of Hellenic culture, encompassing east and west, of one flock living together in one fold, will not become a reality with Antony and Cleopatra. I inspired Antony with the idea of becoming master of a transformed world, but our grand plan failed. Antony paid with his life and so shall I, and a world tyrannized by Rome will lament our passing.

My forefathers, men from Macedonia, took Egypt and made her young and rich again, but the Romans will enslave this land. I have not imposed taxes for fifteen years, relying on the revenues from my royal monopolies to pay for the expenses of my kingdom, but now Octavian has levied harsh taxes on every Egyptian to the poorest farmer. In the years to come he will bleed this ancient land, and Egypt will degenerate into an insignificant Roman province as did once glorious Greece.

Out of the gigantic struggles that I waged, the Roman empire is being born, but not quite in my vision. Octavian will return to Rome and become emperor, the emperor Julius Caesar should have become years ago. I have no wish to live in a world that is enslaved by Octavian and Rome.

In the days since the fall of Egypt, Octavian's soldiers have been occupied with looting my palace and the museum of the city. All the great works of Grecian art have been crated and loaded onto the ships in the harbor. These treasures, which my family has collected and sponsored for three centuries, will adorn the public buildings and villas in Rome.

The statues of Antony, that bring him to life in all his heroic beauty, and which I had set up in the city squares, are being shattered. Undoubtedly my statues will soon meet the same fate.

The Caesareum, the temple on the harbor which I built to honor Caesar and Caesarion, has been changed to the Augusteum, and shall henceforth be consecrated to the worship of the deified god Octavian Caesar Augustus.

Octavian visited Alexander's tomb. He remarked that, now at thirty-three, he is the same age as Alexander had been at death. He had the crystal covering removed from the coffin, and greedy to the point of profanation, handled the body intimately, as if he was not satisfied with merely looking at the earthly form of one who had conceived and carried out such marvelous enterprises. In his eager handling of the body, a piece of the nose broke off.

When Dolabella told me of this visit, I was deeply upset to think that the body of my revered relative, perfectly preserved for two hundred and ninety-three years, should be desecrated by barbarian hands.

One of the reasons Octavian has lingered in Alexandria is that he hesitates to depart until he knows that Caesarion either has sailed away to safety or has been captured. His heart is set on capturing Caesarion, but I have every confidence that my firstborn has gotten away to freedom.

On the third week of my captivity, Dolabella informed me that Octavian would visit me.

"He will come tomorrow at high noon," Dolabella explained.

In anticipation of Octavian's coming, I had busts of Caesar set up around my chamber and his letters to me placed on a table. Iras and Charmion laid out my royal robes to be donned the next morning. I hoped that my regal raiment would give me the confidence to endure the confrontation, and I wanted Octavian to see me dressed as a queen.

I had not seen Octavian since before Caesar's death some fourteen years before. He had been nineteen then, and now he was my conqueror and master of the world. I was in a state of anxiety as I went to bed that night. Sleeping potions were denied me for fear I would take a lethal draught, and in my restless condition I had difficulty sleeping, although I so wanted to be rested and to look my best for Octavian.

An hour before dawn, Octavian arrived at my chamber and entered unannounced. My ladies awoke me from my fitful sleep. Stupefied, I arose from my bed, my hair in disorder, my eyes sunken from lack of sleep, and dressed only in a simple bedgown. My regal dress lay on a nearby divan. Once more I had been out-maneuvered by my cold and wily antagonist.

"Welcome, Great Conqueror!" I said in a trembling voice, sinking to my knees before him, my eyes downcast.

The short, slight figure stood before me, studying me in silence for a long moment. Even in my deplorable condition, I am sure Octavian took note that my native elegance gleamed forth.

"Rise, Cleopatra," Octavian said in his colorless voice.

I was weak, and Iras and Charmion supported me.

"Pray, be seated," Octavian said, looking at me with a remote gaze.

My ladies helped me to a couch. Octavian motioned them to move away, and they retreated into the background.

Octavian moved stealthily around my chamber, gazing at the murals on the panelled walls which depicted scenes from the Trojan war. I observed him, seeing his lank, yellow, thin hair falling over his forehead, his skin as pale as I remembered but now heavily lined. I perceived that no sincere words would come from his narrow, close-lipped mouth.

At length Octavian stood before a bust of Caesar. "How handsome my father was," he remarked, examining the bust with a stubby hand.

I cringed to hear Octavian call his great uncle "father."

Octavian came and took a seat some distance from me. Victor and vanquished confronted one another, each on guard and ready for the swordplay match which was about to ensue.

"I trust your health improves, my lady," Octavian said, smiling thinly, but his eyes were hard as light blue stones and did not smile along with his weak mouth.

"Yes, my lord," I replied, speaking in my crystal-clear Latin so as to not embarrass him in his wretched Greek. "I am completely recovered, although when my beloved husband Lord Antony died I thought I could not go on living."

"And now?" Octavian asked with interest.

"Now I live for my cherished children," I replied staunchly.

"Have no fear for your children," Octavian assured me. "If you put your faith in me and comply with all my requests, no harm shall come to them. Although I am now master of all things, do not look upon me as an enemy. Submit to my kindly rule and all will be well."

"Oh, yes, Great Conqueror," I cried, "I know you are a generous master."

"Do I have your word that you will not destroy yourself and that you will come to Rome?" Octavian asked.

I stared at Octavian like a Medusa, meeting the cold challenge of his Libran eyes. "I give my word on the honor of my children," I said strongly. "You are my sovereign master. Wherever you choose to take me I will follow you submissively."

To demonstrate that from this time on I was his vassal, I took from Charmion a scroll, an inventory of my personal jewelry.

"This is a list of my jewels," I explained. "I have kept some precious ornaments in order to offer them myself to the ladies Livia and Octavia, by whose good offices I hope to find favor with you."

However skilled Octavian might be in the art of deception, he is chiefly accustomed to dealing with men, and he did not understand my subtleties. I could tell by his pale, weak eyes that I was deceiving him totally. He actually flattered himself that I was willing to live as his slave.

"Whatever jewels you have reserved you may dispose

of at your pleasure, my lady," Octavian said, "and you may depend upon my honorable treatment."

Octavian nervously rose, and then his eyes fell upon the table heaped with letters. He wandered over and lifted one of the scrolls and studied the seal.

"Letters your beloved father wrote me, my lord," I cried.

I saw his hands tremble a little and his body stiffened, and then he threw the scroll on the heap, not wishing to deal with this proof of the love Caesar had for me.

"Good day, my lady," Octavian said, and began walking toward the doors.

"Great Caesar Augustus!" I cried in a fervent voice, rising from my couch. "May I see my children?"

My request stopped Octavian at the doors, and he turned to gaze at me with his pale eyes and he almost smiled. "Yes, the first night at sea on the voyage to Rome you shall dine with them."

"And when do we sail, my lord?" I asked.

"Soon," Octavian replied. "And remember, Cleopatra, come to Rome with me and you shall return to Egypt and rule as my vassal. You are a marvel of an administrator, and no Proconsul could manage this kingdom as efficiently as you. In Rome you shall be lodged in my father's old villa. Does that please you?"

"Greatly, my lord," I said. "Cannot Lord Apollodorus be released from captivity to assist me in my preparations for the journey?"

Octavian nodded. "So be it," he said.

"I have one more favor to ask, my lord," I cried. "Before I leave, might I visit my husband's tomb?"

"I grant your request," Octavian said. "Now I must go to attend to affairs of great import."

"Farewell, Great Conqueror!" I cried, sinking to my knees as he left.

Iras ran over to my side. "Oh, Cleopatra, he will let you rule Egypt. You need only to walk in his triumph and you can return to your kingdom!"

"Don't be a fool, Iras," Charmion said sternly. "Cleopatra will be strangled at the end of the triumph, and so shall we."

Iras gave me a desperate look, and then she realized the foolishness of her hopes.

"I shall not be the dupe of Octavian," I said, "but he will be the dupe of Cleopatra!"

Dolabella promised to warn me in advance of the departure, and I made up my mind to end my life the day before.

It was a stifling hot afternoon when I was conveyed in a litter under an armed escort to my tomb, accompanied by Apollodorus, Iras, and Charmion. Inside the mausoleum I approached the purple porphyry sepulcher. Dolabella and more than a hundred soldiers crowded the tomb to witness the sad demonstration at my husband's grave.

"It is not long, my beloved Antony, since with these hands I buried you," I cried out in a ringing voice so that all could hear my words. "Since you left life, my own life has been a misery to me, and my captive body is reserved to adorn Octavian's triumph in Rome."

Iras and Charmion handed me golden urns full of holy Nile water, oil, and wine, the mystic nourishment of the dead, and I emptied the urns over the sepulcher. "While you stay buried here in Egypt, I go to your country with your conqueror," I cried. "I shall gladly follow Octavian's chariot through the same streets where I was once carried in triumph, if by doing so I can return to Egypt to be near your sacred remains. The gods of Egypt have forsaken me, and I put myself into the power of the gods of Rome who I know will treat me with honor and mercy."

I crowned the sepulcher with sacred water lilies, and then I knelt and kissed the tomb. A wave of uncontrollable grief assailed me, and my ladies raised me by my arms, leading me away, and I was carried back to the palace.

The effect of this pathetic farewell was just what I had hoped for. The most skeptical are convinced that I no longer have any inclinations to do away with myself.

The supervision of my apartments has been relaxed even further, with the exits and entrances unguarded. Even the wary and wily Proculeius believes that I am resigned to my fate. Any desire I have is satisfied, and my health has been restored.

In the last days I have been writing the final pages of my memoirs, dictating them to my faithful scribe, Demetrius. His lover Apollodorus has been released from captivity and has been allowed to once again join my service. The goings and comings of Apollodorus are unchecked, and he is in league with Olympus. The asps are ready, reassuring me that at the appointed hour my means of freedom, and the mercy of death, will be mine.

I know that in Rome they will receive news of my death with delight, although they will be angered to be denied a chance to jeer me. I will be carried in the triumph as a waxen effigy only. My three children will undoubtedly be forced to participate in the gaudy procession, but Dolabella assures me that in the end they will be honorably treated as children of Antony, and no doubt Octavia will rear them along with their half-siblings, the two sons Antony had by Fulvia and Antony's two daughters by Octavia. Antony's seven children will grow up together, but I trust my three children will never forget that they come from the womb of Cleopatra.

Faithful to his promise, Dolabella informed me that my departure has been fixed and that I shall sail tomorrow. Cornelius Gallus will stay on as Proconsul of Egypt, and he will rule with a harsh hand.

Today, the last day of August, shall be my last day of life, a day marked on the dial of history. I will avoid by two days the anniversary of my defeat at Actium, and I will have lived, minus four months, for forty years.

I sent one of my chamberlains to Apollodorus with the code word that the time had come. At noon Apollodorus entered my apartments with three small woven baskets of figs, each containing an asp, one each for Iras, Charmion, and myself. Apollodorus has always

736

looked younger than his years, but as he entered my presence I was struck at how he had aged overnight, and his body, always so erect, was bent like an old man's.

"The baskets were not searched, Apollodorus?"

"No, Cleopatra," Apollodorus replied.

I noticed that he was avoiding looking at me and his eyes were red from weeping. "You have been crying, Apollodorus," I said disapprovingly. "I do not want you to shed tears for me, but to rejoice that I will soon be delivered from the slavery of life into the freedom of death."

"Yes, my Queen," Apollodorus said, his head hung low.

"There is a such a symmetry to my life," I said joyously. "I feel that it could have been a tragic play written by one of the old Greek masters. Thirty years ago, Apollodorus, you were a young guardsman of fifteen, and I was a ten-year-old princess, and you slew the asp which my stepmother meant for me, the asp which felled my devoted Tamaratet. It was not in my stars to die so young, but it is in my stars to die now, closing the circle of my life."

Apollodorus stood there, rigid and silent.

"I pray to the gods that Demetrius and you will enjoy a life of rich happiness together for many years to come," I cried. "Do not weep for me, today or ever, but remember the joys of love and friendship we have shared."

"Yes, my Queen," Apollodorus said, struggling with himself.

"Remember that I die happily, Apollodorus," I cried exultantly. "I feel that Octavian will never harm my children by Antony, and I know that my beloved Caesarion has gotten away to safety."

A stifled sob shook Apollodorus, and he turned his back on me. His whole body trembled as he restrained his emotions. As I sat on my couch, watching him, a realization suddenly gripped me.

"Turn around and look at me, Apollodorus," I said.

737

Apollodorus refused to move, and an awful silence followed. I rose and stood behind him.

"Caesarion is safe, is he not, Apollodorus?" I asked. "Caesarion embarked on a ship at Berenice and is sailing now across the seas toward India and freedom, is that not so?"

The dam that held back his emotions broke and Apollodorus fell at my feet, sobbing heartbrokenly. I knew then that Caesarion had not escaped. Across the chamber, Iras began weeping.

"Oh, Cleopatra, my Queen!" Apollodorus cried pathetically.

I looked down at his dark, thick hair which now shows streaks of silver. "You must tell me everything, Apollodorus," I said calmly. "It is your duty not to let me leave life without this knowledge. I have lived through so many tragedies, I will be able to withstand one more. I must have the truth. Caesarion did not escape from Egypt, did he?"

Apollodorus sat up on his knees, still not looking at me, his face transfixed with pain. "No, Cleopatra," he said, his mouth struggling to form the words. "Caesarion arrived at Berenice with his escort, but Rhodon delayed the sailing, not wanting to leave Egypt, and knowing that a detachment of soldiers from Octavian would be on the way. Rhodon tried to convince Caesarion that Octavian would make him King of Egypt, but Caesarion would not be taken in by such a stratagem. Finally, the soldiers arrived and Caesarion was delivered by Rhodon into the hands of the enemy."

"Is Caesarion alive?" I cried. "Is he in the dungeons?"

Apollodorus could only whimper, and I had my answer.

"No, of course not," I whispered. "Caesarion is dead. Octavian wants me alive, but never Caesarion. Caesarion looks too much like his father and would excite the pity of the Romans if he were to walk in the triumph. How was my son killed?"

"The word among the soldiers is that it was by strangulation, my Queen," Apollodorus said. "It is

738

rumored that Andronicus was killed at the same time."

"I pray it was a quick and painless death," I muttered.

The chamber was filled with the sound of Iras sobbing bitterly, and even Charmion, who rarely is moved to tears, was overcome.

"I cannot cry," I said in surprise. "There are no tears left in Cleopatra. My heart is a stone within my breast and incapable of feeling further pain. I must not think of this last, greatest of my misfortunes, or I shall go mad, and I must be lucid for the last hours that are left me on earth."

Charmion brought some wine. Apollodorus and I passed the goblet between us, and the wine composed us somewhat.

"Let us say farewell, not as Queen and subject, but as friend to friend," I said warmly.

I sent Apollodorus off with a kiss and a lingering embrace, and the last look we had of each other, we were smiling.

Summoning my last strength, I am now about to play the final scene, so that I will win the applause of all the audience of the world to come.

I have lived a life filled wtih scenes of elegance and beauty, and my royal pride demands that my last scene will be a glorious spectacle so that Octavian, Agrippa, Proculeius, and all these vulgar Romans will admire not only the courage which has sustained me during the humiliating farce they forced upon me, but my grand exit from the world stage.

My death must be in accord with my dignity as a divine queen. The last moments of my life have been planned in minute detail. Roses will be scattered over the marble floor of my bedchamber, rich incense will burn in the cressets, and the shaded lamps will give off a soft, rich light. I shall bathe in warm, perfumed water. The servants will be admitted with the evening meal, and Iras, Charmion, and I will sit down to our last banquet. After I have eaten, my face will be painted, with kohl giving a touch of mystery to my blue eyes. At

739

last I shall don my coronation robe made of sheaves of gold, which I wore twenty-one years ago.

Iras has begged that she must not be called upon to look upon me in death, and so she will lift the lid of her basket and put her hand inside for the bite of the hungry asp, and then I will hold her to my bosom as she dies in my arms, as did Antony. Charmion, the strong one all these years, must be the strongest now at the end. She has promised me that she will be the last to go, and that she will see to it that I am stretched out across my great bed with its golden canopy and the bedposts supported by golden Sphinxes. I will be royally robed, and the cobra and vulture crown of the Two Lands will adorn my head, and the whip and crook will be in my hands and folded across my chest. Charmion vows that I will be a vision of royal beauty and that my regalia will be properly arranged.

The letter I have written Octavian will be sent off by a chamberlain just before the fatal act.

"Cleopatra to Octavian, Salutations!

"In every life cycle there comes an hour when, rather than endure those troubles that overwhelm us, we put off the body and take flight into oblivion. Caesar, you have conquered. The world and all the spoils of victory are yours, but Cleopatra cannot grace your gaudy triumph. Royal Egypt asks only of Augustus that you suffer me to lie in the tomb beside Antony, and also my noble ladies, Iras of the house of Epaphroditus and Charmion of the house of Kallimachos. Farewell!"

My days of majesty and power are ended. The sun of Ptolemy is set, and my day is done. Dynasties die out, kingdoms rise only to fall, and glory and greatness crumble and scatter like dust. This is the cycle of the world. I am happy to die in my palace, without sacrificing my dignity or pride. I shall be as beautiful in death as in life, and my body will bear no wounds except for a slight prick made by the asp, the sacred cobra which is the messenger of the gods. No child of Caesar and Cleopatra will walk the earth, but there are still three children from the loins of Antony and Cleopatra, whom

I trust the gods will allow to be treated with the consideration due their birth. In time I hope they will attain glorious destinies worthy of their heritage.

The life voyage beset by storms is over, and now I embark on a voyage into death which will be a new cycle and a great adventure. My body will die, but my spirit will live eternally, for dying is a journey of immortality. I do not fear death, for it is the price we must pay for having been born and having lived. My heart is weary and my body longs for eternal rest. There is no sanctuary left for me except in death. I have reached the end of my misfortunes, and I feel sanctified by the gods for my sufferings. Death will be easy, easier than the sorrows of life. Life is but a brief dream, and death will be a rebirth of a more marvelous dream. Soon I will be dust, but my name, interlaced with Caesar's and Antony's, will be inscribed in history, and my life will be a song that will be sung by man as long as the world exists.

I, Cleopatra, born of the gods, and to the gods I return.

FROM
PLUTARCH

Octavian Caesar, breaking the seal of Cleopatra's letter, and finding pathetic prayers and entreaties that she might be buried in the same tomb with Antony, soon guessed what had happened. At first he thought of hastening to her chambers, but sent others to see first. The messenger came at full speed and found the guards aware of nothing, but on opening the doors of her bedchamber they saw Cleopatra stone-dead, lying upon a bed of gold, set out in all her royal ornaments. Iras, one of her women, lay dead at her feet, and Charmion, dying, scarce able to hold up her head, was adjusting the Queen's diadem.

"Was this well done of your lady?" one of the Roman soldiers demanded.

"Extremely well, my lord," Charmion answered, falling down beside the bed, and with her last breaths, she added, "as befitting a queen descended from such a long line of glorious kings."

AUTHOR'S NOTE

CLEOPATRA was buried beside Antony in her tomb in 30 B.C. Octavian ordered that, to ensure quick decay, neither body be embalmed. He did not want their bodies preserved and revered as Alexander's had been. He honored Cleopatra's request that Charmion and Iras be buried in the tomb, and statues of these two favorites were erected on either side of the entrance to honor their fidelity to the death. As for Caesarion, Octavian saw to it that his body was never recovered nor the manner of his death revealed.

When Octavian celebrated his Egyptian triumph a year later, Cleopatra's three children were carried in the procession. Afterward Octavia took them under her wing. Five years later, when Cleopatra Selene was fifteen, she married Juba, the prince of Numidia who had been carried in Caesar's triumph which Cleopatra had witnessed during her Roman stay. Octavian made Juba king of his father's old kingdom of Numidia and adjacent Mauretania (present-day Algeria and Morocco). Cleopatra Selene's two brothers, Ptolemy and Alexander, went with her to North Africa. It was one way of getting Cleopatra's children out of the way. The two boys disappear from history; they evidently thought it prudent to live outside public affairs.

Cleopatra Selene became a queen who would have made her mother proud. When King Juba died in 23 A.D., their son, who had been audaciously named Ptolemy, succeeded. Statues show Ptolemy to be handsome with the type of classical Grecian looks for which his maternal forebears were famed. On a state visit to

Rome in 40 A.D., Ptolemy was murdered by his jealous cousin, Caligula. The North Africans hoped that Ptolemy's sister, Princess Drusilla, would become queen, but Rome declared Numidia and Mauretania provinces again. Drusilla went to Rome and, during the reign of Claudius, she married Antonius Felix, the brother of Pallas, who was the Emperor's secretary. Felix, a Greek freedman, had amassed a fortune. Drusilla went with him to Judaea where he served for several years as Procurator under Nero, and it was there that she probably died. She left no children, and the blood of Cleopatra died out with this granddaughter.

In the course of events, the line of Antony triumphed over that of Octavian. Pythodoris, the granddaughter of Antony and his first wife and cousin, Antonia, became Queen of Pontus. Antony's oldest son by Fulvia, Antyllus, was murdered by Octavian, but the younger son, Jullus, survived. Octavian's only child, Julia, was forced to marry Empress Livia's son, Tiberius. In 2 A.D., Julia and Jullus Antony became lovers and formed a conspiracy to murder Octavian and take the throne. The plot was discovered, Jullus killed himself, and Julia was exiled to the bleak island of Pandateria. In 14 A.D. when Octavian died after being Emperor for 41 years, Tiberius succeeded and had Julia murdered.

Caligula, the great-grandson of Antony and Octavia, smothered his uncle Tiberius and became Emperor in 37 A.D. He was murdered four years later by Praetorian guards, and his uncle Claudius, grandson of Antony and Octavia, was proclaimed Emperor. Claudius's Empress, Messalina, like her great-grandfather Antony, had a strong capacity for sensual pleasure, which proved to be her undoing. His second Empress, his niece Agrippina, poisoned him so that her son Nero could become Emperor. When Nero, great-grandson of Antony, committed suicide in 68 A.D., he ended a glorious saga that had begun 116 years before when Cleopatra was rolled out of a rug at Caesar's feet. The Caesars who came after Nero no longer were of the blood of the Caesars.

All of Cleopatra's statues were destroyed during

Octavian's reign, but a dozen coin portraits survive, showing a perfect Grecian profile, a long, graceful neck, unmistakably the head of a queen of beauty, dignity, and intelligence. Ancient historians describe her as a blonde and blue-eyed Macedonian.

The glory of Egypt passed with Cleopatra, and she became a legend among the Egyptians who lived under the harsh rule of Roman administrators. The country was looted and heavily taxed, and it deteriorated in the manner of all the eastern provinces. In the Roman empire, Greeks and Hellenic easterners were barred from the pinnacle of power. If Antony and Cleopatra had become emperor and empress of the world, there would have been a partnership and balance of east and west. Actium tipped the scales and paved the way for western supremacy, and Occidentalism has ruled supreme to this day. In history, it is generally the Octavians and the Stalins who triumph, not the Antonys and the Trotskys.

Alexandria, the city the Ptolemies built, was activated by the Greek spirit for several centuries. People the world over continued to flock there to study science, medicine, and the arts in the schools founded by the Ptolemies. In the 7th century, the Arabs occupied the city. The Great Library was still functioning, although undoubtedly in disorder. The conquering Caliph Omar ordered all books not agreeing with the Koran to be destroyed. It was a pernicious policy, but the Christians have exercised the same prerogative down to this day. One needs only to reflect on the destruction of Sappho's books by the Christians to observe the prevalence of the practice. The Arabs destroyed the marble buildings and the tombs, and the bodies of Alexander, Cleopatra, and Antony disappeared. Pharos, built in 300 B.C., survived the longest. It was damaged in the earthquakes of 1303 and 1398 and finally collapsed into the sea. The Greeks remained in Alexandria and continued to be a powerful force until the 1950s when they were driven out by the Nasser regime.

Cleopatra has stirred the imagination of creative

artists for two thousand years. Michelangelo sketched her. Since the Renaissance, she has inspired hundreds of plays, operas, biographies, novels, and ballets.

In my research, the list of books consulted would fill pages, but I would like to give a partial listing. Among ancient sources: Arrian, Dio Cassius, Appian, Caesar, Suetonius, Lucan, Strabo, Josephus, and particularly Plutarch. Of modern works, I wish to single out the two biographies by Arthur Weigall, *The Life and Times of Cleopatra* (1924) and *The Life and Times of Mark Antony* (1931), which for scholarship, scope, and style remain unsurpassed on these subjects. Other British biographers of Cleopatra have been Philip Sergeant (1909), Jack Lindsay (1970), Ernle Bradford (1971), and Michael Grant (1972). I must not fail to mention another British writer, Robert Graves, who gave us superb translations of Lucan's *Pharsalia* and Suetonius's *The Twelve Caesars* (1957), as well as two of the greatest historical novels, *I, Claudius* and *Claudius the God* (1934). Germany has produced Cleopatra studies by A. Stahr (1864), H. Stadelmann (1925), Oscar von Wertheimer (1930), Emil Ludwig (1937), and Hans Volkmann (1953). The French have given us biographies by Desiré de Bernath (1907), Gaston Delayen (1934), and *L'Histoire des Lagides* by A. Bouché-Leclercq (1904). From Italy we have had works by Guglielmo Ferrero (1911) and Carlo Maria Franzero (1957).

In the cinema, Cleopatra has been portrayed by Theda Bara (1917), Claudette Colbert (1934), Vivien Leigh (1945), and Elizabeth Taylor (1963). In the 1950s, Kim Stanley played Cleopatra in a live television performance which left a deep impression on this author. Martha Graham did a ballet of Cleopatra in 1961. Of all the plays, Shakespeare's *Antony and Cleopatra* (1606–07) is the most transcendental interpretation of this fabled pair. It has been played on stage by Tallulah Bankhead (1937), Katharine Cornell (1947), Vivien Leigh (1951), Katharine Hepburn (1960), Maggie Smith and Delphine Seyrig (both in

1976). This play was the source of Samuel Barber's opera which opened the Metropolitan at Lincoln Center in 1966, starring Leontyne Price in a production by Franco Zeffirelli.

Almost nothing is known specifically of Cleopatra's first twenty-one years, until she met Caesar. I am the first author to do a fictional portrait which covers the whole spectrum of her life cycle from birth to death, and it was my design to make Book I, covering her unknown period, consistent with what we know of her mature years. This part was based on just a few historical facts. The events in Books II and III, depicting her years with Caesar and Antony, of course, are well documented, although where there are gaps I filled in with fictions. While there are many excellent biographies of Cleopatra, the dozen or so novels on this subject in the last century have been, in my view, travesties of history. My aim was to remain faithful to the ancient annals, and when I had to invent, it was my intention not to contradict known facts. All ancient historians cite the bisexuality of Caesar and Antony, but not of Cleopatra. I am the first writer to dramatize this point; although if one studies carefully the scenes between Cleopatra, Charmion, and Iras, Shakespeare came close. In the context of the culture of the times, my treatment of Cleopatra's sexuality is feasible. One thing is certain, Caesar and Antony were her only male lovers.

A special thanks to four special people: Julian Bach, my literary agent, Fredda Isaacson, my editor, Bernard Shir-Cliff, editor-in-chief, and Howard Kaminsky, president of Warner Books. Because they believed.

                                                            W.B.

New York City
July 1977

THE BEST OF THE BESTSELLERS
FROM WARNER BOOKS!

THE BEST OF THE BESTSELLERS
FROM WARNER BOOKS!